GRIMM'S
Complete Fairy Tales

GRIMM'S
Complete Fairy Tales

Doubleday Direct, Inc.

GARDEN CITY, NEW YORK

ISBN: 1-56865-047-7

Printed in the United States of America

Contents

GRIMM'S
Complete Fairy Tales

The Frog Prince

LONG AGO, when wishes often came true, there lived a King whose daughters were all handsome, but the youngest was so beautiful that the sun himself, who has seen everything, was bemused every time he shone over her because of her beauty. Near the royal castle there was a great dark wood, and in the wood under an old linden tree was a well; and when the day was hot, the King's daughter used to go forth into the wood and sit by the brink of the cool well, and if the time seemed long, she would take out a golden ball, and throw it up and catch it again, and this was her favorite pastime.

Now it happened one day that the golden ball, instead of falling back into the maiden's little hand which had sent it aloft, dropped to the ground near the edge of the well and rolled in. The King's daughter followed it with her eyes as it sank, but the well was deep, so deep that the bottom could not be seen. Then she began to weep, and she wept and wept as if she could never be comforted.

And in the midst of her weeping she heard a voice saying to her, "What ails you, King's daughter? Your tears would melt a heart of stone."

And when she looked to see where the voice came from, there was nothing but a frog stretching his thick ugly head out of the water. "Oh, is it you, old waddler?" said she; "I weep because my golden ball has fallen into the well."

"Never mind, do not weep," answered the frog; "I can help you; but what will you give me if I fetch up your ball again?"

"Whatever you like, dear frog," said she; "any of my clothes, my pearls and jewels, or even the golden crown that I wear."

"Your clothes, your pearls and jewels, and your golden crown are not for me," answered the frog; "but if you would love me, and have me for your companion and play-fellow, and let me sit by you at table, and eat from your plate, and drink from your cup, and sleep in your little bed—if you would promise all this, then would I dive below the water and fetch you your golden ball again."

"Oh yes," she answered; "I will promise it all, whatever you want; if you will only get me my ball again." But she thought to herself, "What nonsense he talks! as if he could do anything but sit in the water and croak with the other frogs, or could possibly be any one's companion."

But the frog, as soon as he heard her promise, drew his head under the water and sank down out of sight, but after a while he came to the surface again with the ball in his mouth, and he threw it on the grass.

The King's daughter was overjoyed to see her pretty plaything again, and she caught it up and ran off with it.

"Stop, stop!" cried the frog; "take me up too; I cannot run as fast as you!"

But it was of no use, for croak, croak after her as he might, she would not listen to him, but made haste home, and very soon forgot all about the poor frog, who had to betake himself to his well again.

The next day, when the King's daughter was sitting at table with the King and all the court, and eating from her golden plate, there came something pitter-patter up the marble stairs, and then there came a knocking at the door, and a voice crying, "Youngest King's daughter, let me in!"

And she got up and ran to see who it could be, but when she opened the door, there was the frog sitting outside. Then she shut the door hastily and went back to her seat, feeling very uneasy.

The King noticed how quickly her heart was beating, and said, "My child, what are you afraid of? Is there a giant standing at the door ready to carry you away?" "Oh no," answered she; "no giant, but a horrid frog." "And what does the frog want?" asked the King.

"O dear father," answered she, "when I was sitting by the well yesterday, and playing with my golden ball, it fell into the water, and while I was crying for the loss of it, the frog came and got it again for me on condition I would let him be my companion, but I never thought that he could leave the water and come after me; but now there he is outside the door, and he wants to come in to me."

And then they all heard him knocking the second time and crying,

> *"Youngest King's daughter,*
> *Open to me!*

By the well water
What promised you me?
Youngest King's daughter
Now open to me!"

"That which thou hast promised must thou perform," said the King; "so go now and let him in."

So she went and opened the door, and the frog hopped in, following at her heels, till she reached her chair. Then he stopped and cried, "Lift me up to sit by you."

But she delayed doing so until the King ordered her. When once the frog was on the chair, he wanted to get on the table, and there he sat and said, "Now push your golden plate a little nearer, so that we may eat together."

And so she did, but everybody might see how unwilling she was, and the frog feasted heartily, but every morsel seemed to stick in her throat.

"I have had enough now," said the frog at last, "and as I am tired, you must carry me to your room, and make ready your silken bed, and we will lie down and go to sleep."

Then the King's daughter began to weep, and was afraid of the cold frog, that nothing would satisfy him but he must sleep in her pretty clean bed. Now the King grew angry with her, saying, "That which thou hast promised in thy time of necessity, must thou now perform."

So she picked up the frog with her finger and thumb, carried him upstairs and put him in a corner, and when she had lain down to sleep, he came creeping up, saying, "I am tired and want sleep as much as you; take me up, or I will tell your father."

Then she felt beside herself with rage, and picking him up, she threw him with all her strength against the wall, crying, "Now will you be quiet, you horrid frog!"

But as he fell, he ceased to be a frog, and became all at once a Prince with beautiful kind eyes. And it came to pass that, with her father's consent, they became bride and bridegroom. And he told her how a wicked witch had bound him by her spells, and how no one but she alone could have released him, and that they two would go together to his father's kingdom. And there came to the door a carriage drawn by eight white horses, with white plumes on their heads, and with golden harness, and behind the carriage was standing faithful Henry, the servant of the young Prince.

Now, faithful Henry had suffered such care and pain when his master was turned into a frog, that he had been obliged to wear three iron bands over his heart, to keep it from breaking with trouble and anxiety. When the carriage started to take the Prince to his kingdom, and faithful Henry had helped them both in, he got up behind, and was full of joy at his master's deliverance. And when they had gone a part of the way, the Prince heard a sound at the back of the carriage, as if something had broken, and he turned round and cried, "Henry, the wheel must be breaking!" but Henry answered,

> *"The wheel does not break,*
> *'Tis the band round my heart*
> *That, to lessen its ache,*
> *When I grieved for your sake,*
> *I bound round my heart."*

Again, and yet once again there was the same sound, and the Prince thought it must be the wheel breaking. But it was the breaking of the other bands from faithful Henry's heart, because he was so relieved and happy.

The Gallant Tailor

ONE SUMMER MORNING a little tailor was sitting on his board near the window, and working cheerfully with all his might, when an old woman came down the street crying, "Good jelly to sell! Good jelly to sell!"

The cry sounded pleasant in the little tailor's ears, so he put his head out of the window, and called out, "Here, my good woman— come here, if you want a customer."

So the poor woman climbed the steps with her heavy basket, and was obliged to unpack and display all her pots to the tailor. He looked at every one of them, and lifting all the lids, applied his nose to each, and said at last, "The jelly seems pretty good; you may weigh me out four half ounces, or I don't mind having a quarter of a pound."

The woman, who had expected to find a good customer, gave him what he asked for, but went off angry and grumbling.

"This jelly is the very thing for me," cried the little tailor; "it will give me strength and cunning"; and he took down the bread from the cupboard, cut a whole round of the loaf, and spread the jelly on it, laid it near him, and went on stitching more gallantly than ever. All the while the scent of the sweet jelly was spreading throughout the room, where there were quantities of flies, who were attracted by it and flew to partake.

"Now then, who asked you to come?" said the tailor, and drove the unbidden guests away. But the flies, not understanding his language, were not to be got rid of like that, and returned in larger numbers than before. Then the tailor, not being able to stand it any longer, took from his chimney-corner a ragged cloth, and saying, "Now, I'll let you have it!" beat it among them unmercifully. When he ceased, and counted the slain, he found seven lying dead before him. "This is indeed somewhat," he said, wondering at his own gallantry; "the whole town shall know this."

So he hastened to cut out a belt, and he stitched it, and put on it in large capitals, "Seven at one blow!" "—The town, did I say!" said the little tailor; "the whole world shall know it!" And his heart quivered with joy, like a lamb's tail.

The tailor fastened the belt round him, and began to think of going out into the world, for his workshop seemed too small for his worship. So he looked about in all the house for something that would be useful to take with him, but he found nothing but an old cheese, which he put in his pocket. Outside the door he noticed that a bird had got caught in the bushes, so he took that and put it in his pocket with the cheese. Then he set out gallantly on his way, and as he was light and active he felt no fatigue.

The way led over a mountain, and when he reached the topmost peak he saw a terrible giant sitting there and looking about him at his ease. The tailor went bravely up to him, called out to him, and said, "Comrade, good day! There you sit looking over the wide world! I am on the way thither to seek my fortune; have you a fancy to go with me?"

The giant looked at the tailor contemptuously, and said, "You little rascal! You miserable fellow!"

"That may be!" answered the little tailor, and undoing his coat he showed the giant his belt; "you can read there whether I am a man or not!"

The giant read: "Seven at one blow!" and thinking it meant men that the tailor had killed, felt at once more respect for the little fellow. But as he wanted to prove him, he took up a stone and squeezed it so hard that water came out of it. "Now you can do that," said the giant—"that is, if you have the strength for it."

"That's not much," said the little tailor, "I call that play," and he put his hand in his pocket and took out the cheese and squeezed it, so that the whey ran out of it. "Well," said he, "what do you think of that?"

The giant did not know what to say to it, for he could not have believed it of the little man. Then the giant took up a stone and threw it so high that it was nearly out of sight. "Now, little fellow, suppose you do that!"

"Well thrown," said the tailor; "but the stone fell back to earth again—I will throw you one that will never come back." So he felt in his pocket, took out the bird, and threw it into the air. And the bird, when it found itself at liberty, took wing, flew off, and returned no more. "What do you think of that, comrade?" asked the tailor.

"There is no doubt that you can throw," said the giant; "but we will see if you can carry."

He led the little tailor to a mighty oak tree which had been felled, and was lying on the ground, and said, "Now, if you are strong enough, help me to carry this tree out of the wood."

"Willingly," answered the little man; "you take the trunk on your shoulders, I will take the branches with all their foliage, that is much the most difficult."

So the giant took the trunk on his shoulders, and the tailor seated himself on a branch, and the giant, who could not see what he was doing, had the whole tree to carry, and the little man on it as well. And the little man was very cheerful and merry, and whistled the tune: *"There were three tailors riding by,"* as if carrying the tree was mere child's play. The giant, when he had struggled on under his heavy load a part of the way, was tired out, and cried, "Look here, I must let go the tree!"

The tailor jumped off quickly, and taking hold of the tree with both arms, as if he were carrying it, said to the giant, "You see you can't carry the tree though you are such a big fellow!"

They went on together a little farther, and presently they came to a cherry tree, and the giant took hold of the topmost branches, where the ripest fruit hung, and pulling them downwards, gave them to the tailor to hold, bidding him eat. But the little tailor was much too weak to hold the tree, and as the giant let go, the tree sprang back, and the tailor was caught up into the air. And when he dropped down again without any damage, the giant said to him, "How is this? Haven't you strength enough to hold such a weak sprig as that?"

"It is not strength that is lacking," answered the little tailor; "how should it be to one who has slain seven at one blow! I just jumped over the tree because the hunters are shooting down there in the bushes. You jump it too, if you can."

The giant made the attempt, and not being able to vault the tree, he remained hanging in the branches, so that once more the little tailor got the better of him. Then said the giant, "As you are such a gallant fellow, suppose you come with me to our den, and stay the night."

The tailor was quite willing, and he followed him. When they reached the den there sat some other giants by the fire, and each had a roasted sheep in his hand, and was eating it. The little tailor looked round and thought, "There is more elbow-room here than in my workshop."

And the giant showed him a bed, and told him he had better lie down upon it and go to sleep. The bed was, however, too big for the tailor, so he did not stay in it, but crept into a corner to sleep. As soon as it was midnight the giant got up, took a great staff of iron and beat the bed through with one stroke, and supposed he had made an end of that grasshopper of a tailor. Very early in the morning the giants went into the wood and forgot all about the little tailor, and when they saw him coming after them alive and merry, they were terribly frightened, and, thinking he was going to kill them, they ran away in all haste.

So the little tailor marched on, always following his nose. And after he had gone a great way he entered the court-yard belonging to a King's palace, and there he felt so overpowered with fatigue that he lay down and fell asleep. In the meanwhile came various people, who looked at him very curiously, and read on his belt, "Seven at one blow!"

"Oh!" said they, "why should this great lord come here in time of peace? What a mighty champion he must be!"

Then they went and told the King about him, and they thought that if war should break out what a worthy and useful man he would be, and that he ought not to be allowed to depart at any price. The King then summoned his council, and sent one of his courtiers to the little tailor to beg him, as soon as he should wake up, to consent to serve in the King's army. So the messenger stood and waited at the sleeper's side until his limbs began to stretch, and his eyes to open, and then he carried his answer back. And the answer was: "That was the reason for which I came. I am ready to enter the King's service."

So he was received into it very honorably, and a separate dwelling set apart for him.

But the rest of the soldiers were very much set against the little tailor, and they wished him a thousand miles away. "What shall be done about it?" they said among themselves; "if we pick a quarrel and fight with him then seven of us will fall at each blow. That will be of no good to us."

So they came to a resolution, and went all together to the King to ask for their discharge. "We never intended," said they, "to serve with a man who kills seven at a blow."

The King felt sorry to lose all his faithful servants because of one man, and he wished that he had never seen him, and would willingly get rid of him if he might. But he did not dare to dismiss the little tailor for fear he should kill all the King's people, and place himself upon the throne. He thought a long while about it, and at last made up his mind what to do. He sent for the little tailor, and told him that as he was so great a warrior he had a proposal to make to him. He told him that in a wood in his dominions dwelt two giants, who did great damage by robbery, murder, and fire, and that no man durst go near them for fear of his life. But that if the tailor should overcome and slay both these giants the King would give him his only daughter in marriage, and half his kingdom as dowry, and that a hundred horsemen should go with him to give him assistance.

"That would be something for a man like me!" thought the little tailor, "a beautiful Princess and half a kingdom are not to be had every day," and he said to the King, "Oh yes, I can soon overcome the giants, and yet have no need of the hundred horsemen; he who can kill seven at one blow has no need to be afraid of two."

So the little tailor set out, and the hundred horsemen followed him. When he came to the border of the wood he said to his escort, "Stay here while I go to attack the giants."

Then he sprang into the wood, and looked about him right and left. After a while he caught sight of the two giants; they were lying down under a tree asleep, and snoring so that all the branches shook. The little tailor, all alive, filled both his pockets with stones and climbed up into the tree, and made his way to an overhanging bough, so that he could seat himself just above the sleepers; and from there he let one stone after another fall on the chest of one of the giants. For a long time the giant was quite unaware of this, but at last he waked up and pushed his comrade, and said, "What are you hitting me for?"

"You are dreaming," said the other, "I am not touching you." And they composed themselves again to sleep, and the tailor let fall a stone on the other giant.

"What can that be?" cried he, "what are you casting at me?" "I am casting nothing at you," answered the first, grumbling.

They disputed about it for a while, but as they were tired, they gave it up at last, and their eyes closed once more. Then the little tailor began his game anew, picked out a heavier stone and threw it down with force upon the first giant's chest.

"This is too much!" cried he, and sprang up like a madman and struck his companion such a blow that the tree shook above them. The other paid him back with ready coin, and they fought with such fury that they tore up trees by their roots to use for weapons against each other, so that at last they both of them lay dead upon the ground. And now the little tailor got down.

"Another piece of luck!" said he, "that the tree I was sitting in did not get torn up too, or else I should have had to jump like a squirrel from one tree to another."

Then he drew his sword and gave each of the giants a few hacks in the breast, and went back to the horsemen and said, "The deed is done, I have made an end of both of them, but it went hard with me; in the struggle they rooted up trees to defend themselves, but it was of no use, they had to do with a man who can kill seven at one blow."

"Then are you not wounded?" asked the horsemen. "Nothing of the sort!" answered the tailor, "I have not turned a hair."

The horsemen still would not believe it, and rode into the wood to see, and there they found the giants wallowing in their blood, and all about them lying the uprooted trees.

The little tailor then claimed the promised boon, but the King repented him of his offer, and he sought again how to rid himself of the hero. "Before you can possess my daughter and the half of my kingdom," said he to the tailor, "you must perform another heroic act. In the wood lives a unicorn who does great damage; you must secure him."

"A unicorn does not strike more terror into me than two giants. Seven at one blow!—that is my way," was the tailor's answer.

So, taking a rope and an axe with him, he went out into the wood, and told those who were ordered to attend him to wait outside. He had not far to seek, the unicorn soon came out and sprang at him, as if he would make an end of him without delay. "Softly, softly," said he "most haste, worst speed," and remained standing until the animal came quite near, then he slipped quietly behind a tree. The unicorn ran with all his might against the tree and stuck his horn so deep into the trunk that he could not get it out again, and so was taken.

"Now I have you," said the tailor, coming out from behind the tree, and, putting the rope round the unicorn's neck, he took the axe, set free the horn, and when all his party were assembled he led forth the animal and brought it to the King.

The King did not yet wish to give him the promised reward, and set him a third task to do. Before the wedding could take place the tailor was to secure a wild boar which had done a great deal of damage in the wood. The huntsmen were to accompany him.

"All right," said the tailor, "this is child's play."

But he did not take the huntsmen into the wood, and they were all the better pleased, for the wild boar had many a time before received them in such a way that they had no fancy to disturb him. When the boar caught sight of the tailor he ran at him with foaming mouth and gleaming tusks to bear him to the ground, but the nimble hero rushed into a chapel which chanced to be near, and jumped quickly out of a window on the other side. The boar ran after him, and when he got inside the door shut after him, and there he was imprisoned, for the creature was too big and unwieldly to jump out of the window too. Then the little tailor called the huntsmen that they might see the prisoner with their own eyes; and then he betook himself to the King, who now, whether he liked it or not, was obliged to fulfill his promise, and give him his daughter and the half of his kingdom. But if he had known that the great warrior was only a little tailor he would have taken it still more to heart. So the wedding was celebrated with great splendor and little joy, and the tailor was made into a King.

One night the young Queen heard her husband talking in his sleep and saying, "Now boy, make me that waistcoat and patch me those breeches, or I will lay my yard measure about your shoulders!"

And so, as she perceived of what low birth her husband was, she went to her father the next morning and told him all, and begged him to set her free from a man who was nothing better than a tailor. The King bade her be comforted, saying, "Tonight leave your bedroom door open, my guard shall stand outside, and when he is asleep they shall come in and bind him and carry him off to a ship, and he shall be sent to the other side of the world."

So the wife felt consoled, but the King's water-bearer, who had been listening all the while, went to the little tailor and disclosed to him the whole plan.

"I shall put a stop to all this," said he.

At night he lay down as usual in bed, and when his wife thought that he was asleep, she got up, opened the door and lay down again. The little tailor, who only made believe he was asleep, began to murmur plainly, "Now, boy, make me that waistcoat and patch me those breeches, or I will lay my yard measure about your shoulders! I have slain seven at one blow, killed two giants, caught a unicorn, and taken a wild boar, and shall I be afraid of those who are standing outside my room door?"

And when they heard the tailor say this, a great fear seized them; they fled away as if they had been wild hares, and none of them would venture to attack him.

And so the little tailor remained a King all of his lifetime.

The Giant and the Tailor

A CERTAIN TAILOR who was great at boasting but poor at doing, took it into his head to go abroad for a while, and look about the world. As soon as he could manage it, he left his workshop, and wandered on his way, over hill and dale, sometimes hither, sometimes thither, but ever on and on. Once when he was out he perceived in the blue distance a steep hill, and behind it a tower reaching to the clouds, which rose up out of a wild dark forest. "Thunder and lightning," cried the tailor, "what is that?" and as he was strongly goaded by curiosity, he went boldly towards it. But what made the tailor open his eyes and mouth when he came near it, was to see that the tower had legs, and leapt in one bound over the steep hill, and was now standing as an all-powerful giant before him.

"What do you want here, you little fly's leg?" cried the giant, with a voice as if it were thundering on every side. The tailor whimpered, "I want just to look about and see if I can earn a bit of bread for myself in this forest." "If that is what you are after," said the giant, "you may have a place with me." "If it must be, why not? What wages shall I receive?" "You shall hear what wages you shall have. Every year three hundred and sixty-five days, and when it is leap-year, one more into the bargain. Does that suit you?" "All right," replied the tailor, and thought, in his own mind, "a man must cut his coat according to his cloth; I will try to get away as fast as I can."

On this the giant said to him, "Go, little ragamuffin, and fetch me a jug of water." "Had I not better bring the well itself at once, and the spring too?" asked the boaster, and went with the pitcher to the water. "What! the well and the spring too," growled the giant in his beard, for he was rather clownish and stupid, and began to be afraid. "That knave is not a fool, he has a wizard in his body. Be on your guard, old Hans, this is no serving-man for you."

When the tailor had brought the water, the giant bade him go into the forest, and cut a couple of blocks of wood and bring them back. "Why not the whole forest at once, with one stroke. The whole forest, young and old, with all that is there, both rough and smooth?" asked the little tailor, and went to cut the wood. "What! the whole forest, young and old, with all that is there, both rough and smooth, and the well and its spring too," growled the credulous giant in his beard, and was still more terrified. "The knave can do much more than bake apples, and has a wizard in his body. Be on your guard, old Hans, this is no serving-man for you!"

When the tailor had brought the wood the giant commanded him to shoot two or three wild boars for supper. "Why not rather a thousand at one shot, and bring them all here?" inquired the ostentatious tailor. "What!" cried the timid giant in great terror. "Let well alone tonight, and lie down to rest."

The giant was so terribly alarmed that he could not close an eye all night long for thinking what would be the best way to get rid of this accursed sorcerer of a servant. Time brings counsel. Next morning the giant and the tailor went to a marsh, round which stood a number of willow trees. Then said the giant, "Hark you, tailor, seat yourself on one of the willow-branches, I long of all things to see if you are big enough to bend it down." All at once the tailor was sitting on it, holding his breath, and making himself so heavy that the bough bent down. When, however, he was compelled to draw breath, it hurried him (for unfortunately he had not put his goose in his pocket) so high into the air that he never was seen again, and this to the great delight of the giant. If the tailor has not fallen down again, he must still be hovering about in the air.

The Little Farmer

THERE WAS a certain village where lived many rich farmers and only one poor one, whom they called the Little Farmer. He had not even a cow, and still less had he money to buy one; and he and his wife greatly wished for such a thing. One day he said to her, "Listen, I have a good idea; it is that your godfather the joiner shall make us a calf of wood and paint it brown, so as to look just like any other; and then in time perhaps it will grow big and become a cow."

This notion pleased the wife, and godfather joiner set to work to saw and plane, and soon turned out a calf complete, with its head down and neck stretched out as if it were grazing.

The next morning, as the cows were driven to pasture, the Little Farmer called out to the drover, "Look here, I have got a little calf to go, but it is still young and must be carried."

"All right!" said the drover, and tucked it under his arm, carried it into the meadows, and stood it in the grass. So the calf stayed where it was put, and seemed to be eating all the time, and the drover thought to himself, "It will soon be able to run alone, if it grazes at that rate!"

In the evening, when the herds had to be driven home, he said to the calf, "If you can stand there eating like that, you can just walk off on your own four legs; I am not going to lug you under my arm again!"

But the Little Farmer was standing by his house-door, and waiting for his calf; and when he saw the cow-herd coming through the village without it, he asked what it meant. The cow-herd answered, "It is still out there eating away, and never attended to the call, and would not come with the rest."

Then the Little Farmer said, "I will tell you what, I must have my beast brought home."

And they went together through the fields in quest of it, but some one had stolen it, and it was gone. And the drover said, "Mostly likely it has run away."

But the Little Farmer said, "Not it!" and brought the cow-herd before the bailiff, who ordered him for his carelessness to give the Little Farmer a cow for the missing calf.

So now the Little Farmer and his wife possessed their long-

wished-for cow; they rejoiced with all their hearts, but unfortunately they had no fodder for it, and could give it nothing to eat, so
that before long they had to kill it. Its flesh they salted down, and
the Little Farmer went to the town to sell the skin and buy a new
calf with what he got for it. On the way he came to a mill, where a
raven was sitting with broken wings, and he took it up out of pity
and wrapped it in the skin. The weather was very stormy, and it
blew and rained, so he turned into the mill and asked for shelter.

The miller's wife was alone in the house, and she said to the
Little Farmer, "Well, come in and lie down in the straw," and she
gave him a piece of bread and cheese. So the Little Farmer ate, and
then lay down with his skin near him, and the miller's wife thought
he was sleeping with fatigue. After a while in came another man,
and the miller's wife received him very well, saying, "My husband
is out; we will make good cheer."

The Little Farmer listened to what they said, and when he heard
good cheer spoken of, he grew angry to think he had been put off
with bread and cheese. For the miller's wife presently brought out
roast meat, salad, cakes, and wine.

Now as the pair were sitting down to their feast, there came a
knock at the door. "Oh dear," cried the woman, "it is my husband!"
In a twinkling she popped the roast meat into the oven, the wine
under the pillow, the salad in the bed, the cakes under the bed, and
the man in the linen-closet. Then she opened the door to her
husband, saying, "Thank goodness, you are here! What weather it
is, as if the world were coming to an end!"

When the miller saw the Little Farmer lying in the straw, he
said, "What fellow have you got there?" "Oh!" said the wife, "the
poor chap came in the midst of the wind and rain and asked for
shelter, and I gave him some bread and cheese and spread some
straw for him."

The husband answered, "Oh well, I have no objection, only get
me something to eat at once." But the wife said, "There is nothing
but bread and cheese."

"Anything will do for me," answered the miller, "bread and
cheese for ever!" and catching sight of the Little Farmer, he cried,
"Come along, and keep me company!" The Little Farmer did not
wait to be asked twice, but sat down and ate.

After a while the miller noticed the skin lying on the ground
with the raven wrapped up in it, and he said, "What have you got
there?" The Little Farmer answered, "A fortune-teller." And the
miller asked, "Can he tell my fortune?" "Why not?" answered the

Little Farmer. "He will tell four things, and the fifth he keeps to himself." Now the miller became very curious, and said, "Ask him to say something."

And the Little Farmer pinched the raven, so that it croaked, "Crr, crr." "What does he say?" asked the miller. And the Little Farmer answered, "First he says that there is wine under the pillow."

"That would be jolly!" cried the miller, and he went to look, and found the wine, and then asked, "What next?"

So the Little Farmer made the raven croak again, and then said, "He says, secondly, that there is roast meat in the oven."

"That would be jolly!" cried the miller, and he went and looked, and found the roast meat. The Little Farmer made the fortune-teller speak again, and then said, "He says, thirdly, that there is salad in the bed."

"That would be jolly!" cried the miller, and went and looked and found the salad. Once more the Little Farmer pinched the raven, so that he croaked, and said, "He says, fourthly and lastly, that there are cakes under the bed."

"That would be jolly!" cried the miller, and he went and looked, and found the cakes.

And now the two sat down to table, and the miller's wife felt very uncomfortable, and she went to bed and took all the keys with her. The miller was eager to know what the fifth thing could be, but the Little Farmer said, "Suppose we eat the four things in peace first, for the fifth thing is a great deal worse."

So they sat and ate, and while they ate, they bargained together as to how much the miller would give for knowing the fifth thing; and at last they agreed upon three hundred dollars. Then the Little Farmer pinched the raven, so that he croaked aloud. And the miller asked what he said, and the Little Farmer answered, "He says that there is a demon in the linen-closet."

"Then," said the miller, "that demon must come out of the linen-closet," and he unbarred the house-door, while the Little Farmer got the key of the linen-closet from the miller's wife, and opened it. Then the man rushed forth, and out of the house, and the miller said, "I saw the black rogue with my own eyes; so that is a good riddance."

And the Little Farmer took himself off by daybreak next morning with the three hundred dollars.

And after this the Little Farmer by degrees got on in the world, and built himself a good house, and the other farmers said, "Surely the Little Farmer has been where it rains gold pieces, and has brought home money by the bushel."

And he was summoned before the bailiff to say whence his riches came. And all he said was, "I sold my calf's skin for three hundred dollars."

When the other farmers heard this they wished to share such good luck, and ran home, killed all their cows, skinned them in order to sell them also for the same high price as the Little Farmer. And the bailiff said, "I must be beforehand with them." So he sent his servant into the town to the skin-buyer, and he only gave her three dollars for the skin, and that was faring better than the others, for when they came, they did not get as much as that, for the skin-buyer said, "What am I to do with all these skins?"

Now the other farmers were very angry with the Little Farmer for misleading them, and they vowed vengeance against him, and went to complain of his deceit to the bailiff. The poor Little Farmer was with one voice sentenced to death, and to be put into a cask with holes in it, and rolled into the water. So he was led to execution, and a priest was fetched to say a mass for him, and the rest of the people had to stand at a distance. As soon as the Little Farmer caught sight of the priest he knew him for the man who was hid in the linen-closet at the miller's. And he said to him, "As I let you out of the cupboard, you must let me out of the cask."

At that moment a shepherd passed with a flock of sheep, and the Little Farmer knowing him to have a great wish to become bailiff himself, called out with all his might, "No, I will not, and if all the world asked me, I would not!"

The shepherd, hearing him, came up and asked what it was he would not do. The Little Farmer answered, "They want to make me bailiff, if I sit in this cask, but I will not do it!"

The shepherd said, "If that is all there is to do in order to become bailiff I will sit in the cask and welcome." And the Little Farmer answered, "Yes, that is all, just you get into the cask, and you will become bailiff." So the shepherd agreed, and got in, and the Little Farmer fastened on the top; then he collected the herd of sheep and drove them away.

The priest went back to the parish-assembly, and told them the mass had been said. Then they came and began to roll the cask into the water, and as it went the shepherd inside called out, "I consent to be bailiff!"

They thought that it was the Little Farmer who spoke, and they answered, "All right; but first you must go down below and look about you a little," and they rolled the cask into the water.

Upon that the farmers went home, and when they reached the village, there they met the Little Farmer driving a flock of sheep, and looking quite calm and contented. The farmers were astonished and cried, "Little Farmer, whence come you? How did you get out of the water?"

"Oh, easily," answered he, "I sank and sank until I came to the bottom; then I broke through the cask and came out of it, and there were beautiful meadows and plenty of sheep feeding, so I brought away this flock with me."

Then said the farmers, "Are there any left?" "Oh yes," answered the Little Farmer, "more than you can possibly need."

Then the farmers agreed that they would go and fetch some sheep also, each man a flock for himself; and the bailiff said, "Me first." And they all went together, and in the blue sky there were little fleecy clouds like lambskins, and they were reflected in the water; and the farmers cried out, "There are the sheep down there at the bottom."

When the bailiff heard that he pressed forward and said, "I will go first and look about me, and if things look well, I will call to you." And he jumped plump into the water, and they all thought that the noise he made meant "Come," so the whole company jumped in one after the other.

So perished all the proprietors of the village, and the Little Farmer, as sole heir, became a rich man.

The Golden Key

IN THE winter time, when deep snow lay on the ground, a poor boy was forced to go out on a sledge to fetch wood. When he had gathered it together, and packed it, he wished, as he was so frozen with cold, not to go home at once, but to light a fire and warm himself a little. So he scraped away the snow, and as he was thus clearing the ground, he found a tiny, gold key. Hereupon he thought that where the key was, the lock must be also, and dug in the ground and found an iron chest. "If the key does but fit it!" thought he; "no doubt there are precious things in that little box."

He searched, but no keyhole was there. At last he discovered one, but so small that it was hardly visible. He tried it, and the key fitted it exactly. Then he turned it once round, and now we must wait until he has quite unlocked it and opened the lid, and then we shall learn what wonderful things were lying in that box.

Sharing Joy and Sorrow

THERE WAS once a tailor, who was a quarrelsome fellow, and his wife, who was good, industrious, and pious, never could please him. Whatever she did, he was not satisfied, but grumbled and scolded, and knocked her about and beat her. As the authorities at last heard of it, they had him summoned and put in prison in order to make him better. He was kept for a while on bread and water, and then set free again. He was forced, however, to promise not to beat his wife any more, but to live with her in peace, and share joy and sorrow with her, as married people ought to do.

All went on well for a time, but then he fell into his old ways, and was surly and quarrelsome. And because he dared not beat her, he would seize her by the hair and tear it out. The woman escaped from him, and sprang out into the yard, but he ran after her with his yard-measure and scissors, and chased her about, and threw the yard-measure and scissors at her, and whatever else came in his way. When he hit her he laughed, and when he missed her, he stormed and swore. This went on so long that the neighbors came to the wife's assistance.

The tailor was again summoned before the magistrates, and reminded of his promise. "Dear gentlemen," said he, "I have kept my word; I have not beaten her, but have shared joy and sorrow with her." "How can that be," said the judge, "when she continually brings such heavy complaints against you?" "I have not beaten her, but just because she looked so strange I wanted to comb her hair with my hand; she, however, got away from me, and left me quite spitefully. Then I hurried after her, and in order to bring her back to her duty, I threw at her as a well-meant admonition whatever came readily to hand. I have shared joy and sorrow with her also, for whenever I hit her I was full of joy, and she of sorrow; and if I missed her, then she was joyful, and I sorry." The judges were not satisfied with this answer, but gave him the reward he deserved.

The Nail

A MERCHANT had done good business at the fair; he had sold his wares, and lined his money-bags with gold and silver. Then he wanted to travel homewards, and be in his own house before nightfall. So he packed his trunk with the money on his horse, and rode away.

At noon he rested in a town, and when he wanted to go farther the stable-boy brought out his horse and said, "A nail is wanting, sir, in the shoe of its left hind foot." "Let it be wanting," answered the merchant; "the shoe will certainly stay on for six miles I have still to go. I am in a hurry."

In the afternoon, when he once more alighted and had his horse fed, the stable-boy went into the room to him and said, "Sir, a shoe is missing from your horse's left hind foot. Shall I take him to the blacksmith?" "Let it still be wanting," answered the man; "the horse can very well hold out for the couple of miles which remain. I am in haste."

He rode forth, but before long the horse began to limp. It had not limped long before it began to stumble, and it had not stumbled long before it fell down and broke its leg. The merchant was forced to leave the horse where it was, and unbuckle the trunk, take it on his back, and go home on foot. And there he did not arrive until quite late at night. "And that unlucky nail," said he to himself, "has caused all this disaster."

Make haste slowly.

Tom Thumb

THERE WAS once a poor countryman who used to sit in the chimney-corner all evening and poke the fire, while his wife sat at her spinning-wheel.

And he used to say, "How dull it is without any children about us; our house is so quiet, and other people's houses so noisy and merry!"

"Yes," answered his wife, and sighed, "if we could only have one, and that one ever so little, no bigger than my thumb, how happy I should be! It would, indeed, be having our heart's desire."

Now, it happened that after a while the woman had a child who was perfect in all his limbs, but no bigger than a thumb. Then the parents said, "He is just what we wished for, and we love him very much," and they named him according to his stature, "Tom Thumb." And though they gave him plenty of nourishment, he grew no bigger, but remained exactly the same size as when he was first born; and he had very good faculties, and was very quick and prudent, so that all he did prospered.

One day his father made ready to go into the forest to cut wood, and he said, as if to himself, "Now, I wish there was some one to bring the cart to me." "O father," cried Tom Thumb, "if I can bring the cart, let me alone for that, and in proper time, too!"

Then the father laughed, and said, "How will you manage that? You are much too little to hold the reins." "That has nothing to do with it, father; while my mother goes on with her spinning I will sit in the horse's ear and tell him where to go." "Well," answered the father, "we will try it for once."

When it was time to set off, the mother went on spinning, after setting Tom Thumb in the horse's ear; and so he drove off, crying, "Gee-up, gee-wo!"

So the horse went on quite as if his master were driving him, and drew the wagon along the right road to the wood.

Now it happened just as they turned a corner, and the little fellow was calling out "Gee-up!" that two strange men passed by.

"Look," said one of them, "how is this? There goes a wagon, and the driver is calling to the horse, and yet he is nowhere to be seen." "It is very strange," said the other; "we will follow the wagon, and see where it belongs."

And the wagon went right through the forest, up to the place where the wood had been hewed. When Tom Thumb caught sight of his father, he cried out, "Look, father, here am I with the wagon; now, take me down."

The father held the horse with his left hand, and with the right he lifted down his little son out of the horse's ear, and Tom Thumb sat down on a stump, quite happy and content. When the two strangers saw him they were struck dumb with wonder. At last one of them, taking the other aside, said to him, "Look here, the little chap would make our fortune if we were to show him in the town for money. Suppose we buy him."

So they went up to the woodcutter, and said, "Sell the little man to us; we will take care he shall come to no harm." "No," answered the father; "he is the apple of my eye, and not for all the money in the world would I sell him."

But Tom Thumb, when he heard what was going on, climbed up by his father's coat tails, and, perching himself on his shoulder, he whispered in his ear, "Father, you might as well let me go. I will soon come back again."

Then the father gave him up to the two men for a large piece of money. They asked him where he would like to sit. "Oh, put me on the brim of your hat," said he. "There I can walk about and view the country, and be in no danger of falling off."

So they did as he wished, and when Tom Thumb had taken leave of his father, they set off all together. And they traveled on until it grew dusk, and the little fellow asked to be set down a little while for a change, and after some difficulty they consented. So the man took him down from his hat, and set him in a field by the roadside, and he ran away directly, and, after creeping about among the furrows, he slipped suddenly into a mouse-hole, just what he was looking for.

"Good evening, my masters, you can go home without me!" cried he to them, laughing. They ran up and felt about with their sticks in the mouse-hole, but in vain. Tom Thumb crept farther and farther in, and as it was growing dark, they had to make the best of their way home, full of vexation, and with empty purses.

When Tom Thumb found they were gone, he crept out of his hiding-place underground. "It is dangerous work groping about these holes in the darkness," said he; "I might easily break my neck."

But by good fortune he came upon an empty snail shell. "That's all right," said he. "Now I can get safely through the night"; and he settled himself down in it.

Before he had time to get to sleep, he heard two men pass by, and one was saying to the other, "How can we manage to get hold of the rich parson's gold and silver?" "I can tell you how," cried Tom Thumb. "How is this?" said one of the thieves, quite frightened, "I hear some one speak!"

So they stood still and listened, and Tom Thumb spoke again: "Take me with you; I will show you how to do it!" "Where are you, then?" asked they. "Look about on the ground and notice where the voice comes from," answered he.

At last they found him, and lifted him up. "You little elf," said they, "how can you help us?" "Look here," answered he, "I can easily creep between the iron bars of the parson's room and hand out to you whatever you would like to have." "Very well," said they, "we will try what you can do."

So when they came to the parsonage-house, Tom Thumb crept into the room, but cried out with all his might, "Will you have all that is here?" So the thieves were terrified, and said, "Do speak more softly, lest any one should be awaked."

But Tom Thumb made as if he did not hear them, and cried out again, "What would you like? Will you have all that is here?" so that the cook, who was sleeping in a room hard by, heard it, and raised herself in bed and listened. The thieves, however, in their fear of being discovered, had run back part of the way, but they took courage again, thinking that it was only a jest of the little fellow's. So they came back and whispered to him to be serious, and to hand them out something.

Then Tom Thumb called out once more as loud as he could, "Oh yes, I will give it all to you, only put out your hands."

Then the listening maid heard him distinctly that time, and jumped out of bed, and burst open the door. The thieves ran off as if the wild huntsman were behind them; but the maid, as she could see nothing, went to fetch a light. And when she came back with one, Tom Thumb had taken himself off, without being seen by her, into the barn; and the maid, when she had looked in every hole and corner and found nothing, went back to bed at last, and thought that she must have been dreaming with her eyes and ears open.

So Tom Thumb crept among the hay, and found a comfortable nook to sleep in, where he intended to remain until it was day, and then to go home to his father and mother. But other things were to befall him; indeed, there is nothing but trouble and worry in this world!

The maid got up at dawn of day to feed the cows. The first place she went to was the barn, where she took up an armful of hay, and it happened to be the very heap in which Tom Thumb lay asleep. And he was so fast asleep, that he was aware of nothing, and never waked until he was in the mouth of the cow, who had taken him up with the hay.

"Oh dear," cried he, "how is it that I have got into a mill!" but he soon found out where he was, and he had to be very careful not to get between the cow's teeth, and at last he had to descend into the cow's stomach. "The windows were forgotten when this little room was built," said he, "and the sunshine cannot get in; there is no light to be had."

His quarters were in every way unpleasant to him, and, what was the worst, new hay was constantly coming in, and the space was being filled up. At last he cried out in his extremity, as loud as he could, "No more hay for me! No more hay for me!" The maid was then milking the cow, and as she heard a voice, but could see no one, and as it was the same voice that she had heard in the night, she was so frightened that she fell off her stool, and spilt the milk. Then she ran in great haste to her master, crying, "Oh, master dear, the cow spoke!"

"You must be crazy," answered her master, and he went himself to the cow-house to see what was the matter. No sooner had he put his foot inside the door, than Tom Thumb cried out again, "No more hay for me! No more hay for me!"

Then the parson himself was frightened, supposing that a bad spirit had entered into the cow, and he ordered her to be put to death. So she was killed, but the stomach, where Tom Thumb was lying, was thrown upon a dunghill. Tom Thumb had great trouble to work his way out of it, and he had just made a space big enough for his head to go through, when a new misfortune happened. A hungry wolf ran up and swallowed the whole stomach at one gulp.

But Tom Thumb did not lose courage. "Perhaps," thought he, "the wolf will listen to reason," and he cried out from the inside of the wolf, "My dear wolf, I can tell you where to get a splendid meal!" "Where is it to be had?" asked the wolf. "In such and such a house, and you must creep into it through the drain, and there you will find cakes and bacon and broth, as much as you can eat," and he described to him his father's house.

The wolf needed not to be told twice. He squeezed himself

through the drain in the night, and feasted in the store-room to his heart's content. When at last he was satisfied, he wanted to go away again, but he had become so big, that to creep the same way back was impossible. This Tom Thumb had reckoned upon, and began to make a terrible din inside the wolf, crying and calling as loud as he could.

"Will you be quiet?" said the wolf; "you will wake the folks up!" "Look here," cried the little man, "you are very well satisfied, and now I will do something for my own enjoyment," and began again to make all the noise he could.

At last the father and mother were awakened, and they ran to the room-door and peeped through the chink, and when they saw a wolf in occupation, they ran and fetched weapons—the man an axe, and the wife a scythe. "Stay behind," said the man, as they entered the room; "when I have given him a blow, and it does not seem to have killed him, then you must cut at him with your scythe."

Then Tom Thumb heard his father's voice, and cried, "Dear father, I am here in the wolf's inside."

Then the father called out full of joy, "Thank heaven that we have found our dear child!" and told his wife to keep the scythe out of the way, lest Tom Thumb should be hurt with it. Then he drew near and struck the wolf such a blow on the head that he fell down dead; and then he fetched a knife and a pair of scissors, slit up the wolf's body, and let out the little fellow.

"Oh, what anxiety we have felt about you!" said the father. "Yes, father, I have seen a good deal of the world, and I am very glad to breathe fresh air again."

"And where have you been all this time?" asked his father. "Oh, I have been in a mouse-hole and a snail's shell, in a cow's stomach and a wolf's inside; now I think I will stay at home."

"And we will not part with you for all the kingdoms of the world," cried the parents, as they kissed and hugged their dear little Tom Thumb. And they gave him something to eat and drink, and a new suit of clothes, as his old ones were soiled with travel.

Tom Thumb's Travels

THERE WAS once a tailor who had a son no higher than a thumb, so he was called Tom Thumb. Notwithstanding his small size, he had plenty of spirit, and one day he said to his father, "Father, go out into the world I must and will."

"Very well, my son," said the old man, and taking a long darning needle, he put a knob of sealing-wax on the end, saying, "Here is a sword to take with you on your journey."

Now the little tailor wanted to have one more meal first, and so he trotted into the kitchen to see what sort of farewell feast his mother had cooked for him. It was all ready, and the dish was standing on the hearth. Then said he, "Mother, what is the fare today?"

"You can see for yourself," said the mother. Then Tom Thumb ran to the hearth and peeped into the dish, but as he stretched his neck too far over it, the steam caught him and carried him up the chimney. For a time he floated about with the steam in the air, but at last he sank down to the ground. Then the little tailor found himself out in the wide world, and he wandered about, and finally engaged himself to a master tailor, but the food was not good enough for him.

"Mistress," said Tom Thumb, "if you do not give us better victuals, I shall go out early in the morning and write with a piece of chalk on the house-door, 'Plenty of potatoes to eat, and but little meat; so good-bye, Mr. Potato.'"

"What are you after, grasshopper?" said the mistress, and growing angry she seized a piece of rag to beat him off; but he crept underneath her thimble, and then peeped at her, and put his tongue out at her. She took up the thimble, and would have seized him, but he hopped among the rags, and as the mistress turned them over to find him, he stepped into a crack in the table. "He-hee! Mistress!" cried he, sticking out his head, and when she was just going to grasp him, he jumped into the table-drawer. But in the end she caught him, and drove him out of the house.

So he wandered on until he came to a great wood; and there he met a gang of robbers that were going to rob the King's treasury. When they saw the little tailor, they thought to themselves, "Such a little fellow might easily creep through a key-hole, and serve instead of a pick-lock." "Holloa!" cried one, "you giant Goliath, will you come with us to the treasure-chamber? You can slip in, and then throw us out the money."

Tom Thumb considered a little, but at last he consented and went with them to the treasure-chamber. Then he looked all over the door above and below, but there was no crack to be seen; at last he found one broad enough to let him pass, and he was getting through, when one of the sentinels that stood before the door saw him, and said to the other, "See what an ugly spider is crawling there! I will put an end to him." "Let the poor creature alone," said the other, "it has done you no harm."

So Tom Thumb got safely through the crack into the treasure-chamber, and he opened the window beneath which the thieves were standing, and he threw them out one dollar after another. Just as he had well settled to the work, he heard the King coming to take a look at his treasure, and so Tom Thumb had to creep away. The King presently remarked that many good dollars were wanting, but could not imagine how they could have been stolen, as the locks and bolts were in good order, and everything seemed secure. And he went away, saying to the two sentinels, "Keep good guard; there is some one after the money."

When Tom Thumb had set to work anew, they heard the chink, chink of the money, and hastily rushed in to catch the thief. But the little tailor, as he heard them coming, was too quick for them, and, hiding in a corner, he covered himself up with a dollar, so that nothing of him was to be seen, and then he mocked the sentinels, crying, "Here I am!" They ran about, and when they came near him, he was soon in another corner under a dollar, crying, "Here I am!" Then the sentinels ran towards him, and in a moment he was in a third corner, crying, "Here I am!" In this way he made fools of them, and dodged them so long about the treasure-chamber, that they got tired and went away. Then he set to work, and threw the dollars out of the window, one after the other, till they were all gone; and when it came to the last, as he flung it with all his might, he jumped nimbly on it, and flew with it out of the window.

The robbers gave him great praise, saying, "You are a most valiant hero; will you be our captain?"

But Tom Thumb thanked them, and said he would like to see the world first. Then they divided the spoil; but the little tailor's share was only one farthing, which was all he was able to carry.

Then binding his sword to his side, he bid the robbers good day, and started on his way. He applied to several master tailors, but they would not have anything to do with him; and at last he hired himself as indoor servant at an inn. The maid-servants took a great dislike to him, for he used to see everything they did without being seen by them, and he told the master and mistress about what they took from the plates, and what they carried away out of the cellar. And they said, "Wait a little, we will pay you out," and took counsel together to play him some mischievous trick.

Once when one of the maids was mowing the grass in the garden she saw Tom Thumb jumping about and creeping among the cabbages, and she mowed him with the grass, tied all together in a bundle, and threw it to the cows. Among the cows was a big black one, who swallowed him down, without doing him any harm. But he did not like his lodging, it was so dark, and there was no candle to be had. When the cow was being milked, he cried out,

> *"Strip, strap, strull,*
> *Will the pail soon be full?"*

But he was not understood because of the noise of the milk.

Presently the landlord came into the stable and said, "Tomorrow this cow is to be slaughtered."

At that Tom Thumb felt very terrified; and with his shrillest voice he cried, "Let me out first; I am sitting inside here!"

The master heard him quite plainly, but could not tell where the voice came from. "Where are you?" asked he. "Inside the black one," answered Tom Thumb, but the master, not understanding the meaning of it all, went away.

The next morning the cow was slaughtered. Happily, in all the cutting and slashing he escaped all harm, and he slipped among the sausage-meat. When the butcher came near to set to work, he cried with all his might, "Don't cut so deep, don't cut so deep, I am underneath!" But for the sound of the butcher's knife his voice was not heard.

Now, poor Tom Thumb was in great straits, and he had to jump nimbly out of the way of the knife, and finally he came through with a whole skin. But he could not get quite away, and he had to let himself remain with the lumps of fat to be put in a black pudding. His quarters were rather narrow, and he had to be hung up in the chimney in the smoke, and to remain there a very long while. At last, when winter came, he was taken down, for the black pudding was to be set before a guest. And when the landlady cut the black pudding in slices, he had to great care not to lift up his head too much, or it might be shaved off at the neck. At last he saw his opportunity, took courage, and jumped out.

But as things had gone so badly with him in that house, Tom Thumb did not mean to stay there, but betook himself again to his wanderings. His freedom, however, did not last long. In the open fields there came a fox who snapped him up without thinking.

"Oh, Mr. Fox," cried Tom Thumb, "here I am sticking in your throat; let me out again." "Very well," answered the fox. "It is true you are no better than nothing; promise me the hens in your father's yard, then I will let you go." "With all my heart," answered Tom Thumb, "you shall have them all, I promise you."

Then the fox let him go, and he ran home. When the father saw his dear little son again, he gave the fox willingly all the hens that he had.

"And look, besides, what a fine piece of money I've got for you!" said Tom Thumb, and handed over the farthing which he had earned in his wanderings.

But how, you ask, could they let the fox devour all the poor chicks? Why, you silly child, you know that your father would rather have you than the hens in his yard!

The Young Giant

A LONG TIME ago a countryman had a son who was as big as a thumb, and did not become any bigger, and during several years did not grow one hair's breadth. Once when the father was going out to plough, the little one said, "Father, I will go out with thee." "Thou wouldst go out with me?" said the father. "Stay here, thou wilt be of no use out there, besides thou mightst get lost!" Then Thumbling began to cry, and for the sake of peace his father put him in his pocket, and took him with him.

When he was outside in the field, he took him out again, and set him in a freshly-cut furrow.

While he was there, a great giant came over the hill. "Dost thou see that great monster?" said the father, for he wanted to frighten the little fellow to make him good. "He is coming to fetch thee." The giant, however, had scarcely taken two steps with his long legs before he was in the furrow. He took up little Thumbling carefully with two fingers, examined him, and without saying one word went away with him. His father stood by, but could not utter a sound for terror, and he thought nothing else but that his child was lost, and that as long as he lived he should never set eyes on him again.

The giant, however, carried him home, suckled him, and Thumbling grew and became tall and strong after the manner of giants. When two years had passed, the old giant took him into the forest, wanted to try him, and said, "Pull up a stick for thyself." Then the boy was already so strong that he tore up a young tree out of the earth by the roots. But the giant thought, "We must do better than that," took him back again, and suckled him two years longer.

When he tried him, his strength had increased so much that he could tear an old tree out of the ground. That was still not enough for the giant; he again suckled him for two years, and when he then went with him into the forest and said, "Now, just tear up a proper stick for me," the boy tore up the strongest oak tree from the earth, so that it split, and that was a mere trifle to him. "Now that will do," said the giant, "thou art perfect," and took him back to the field from whence he had brought him. His father was there following the plough. The young giant went up to him, and said, "Does my father see what a fine man his son has grown into?"

The farmer was alarmed, and said, "No, thou art not my son; I don't want thee—leave me!" "Truly I am your son; allow me to do your work, I can plough as well as you, nay better." "No, no, thou art not my son, and thou canst not plough—go away!" However, as he was afraid of this great man, he left hold of the plough, stepped back and stood at one side of the piece of land. Then the youth took the plough, and just pressed it with one hand, but his grasp was so strong that the plough went deep into the earth. The farmer could not bear to see that, and called to him, "If thou art determined to plough, thou must not press so hard on it, that makes bad work." The youth, however, unharnessed the horses, and drew the plough himself, saying, "Just go home, father, and bid my mother make ready a large dish of food, and in the meantime I will go over the field." Then the farmer went home, and ordered his wife to prepare the food; but the youth ploughed the field, which was two acres large, quite alone, and then he harnessed himself to the harrow, and harrowed the whole of the land, using two harrows at once. When he had done it, he went into the forest, and pulled up two oak trees, laid them across his shoulders, and hung one harrow on them behind and one before, and also one horse behind and one before, and carried all as if it had been a bundle of straw, to his parents' house.

When he entered the yard, his mother did not recognize him, and asked, "Who is that horrible tall man?" The farmer said, "That is our son." She said, "No, that cannot be our son, we never had such a tall one, ours was a little thing." She called to him, "Go away, we do not want thee!" The youth was silent, but led his horses to the stable, gave them oats and hay, and all that they wanted. When he had done this, he went into the parlor, sat down on the bench and said, "Mother, now I should like something to eat, will it soon be ready?" Then she said, "Yes," and brought in two immense dishes full of food, which would have been enough to satisfy herself and her husband for a week. The youth, however, ate the whole of it himself, and asked if she had nothing more to set before him. "No," she replied, "that is all we have." "But that was only a taste, I must have more."

She did not dare to oppose him, and went and put a huge caldron full of food on the fire, and when it was ready, carried it in. "At length come a few crumbs," said he, and ate all there was, but it was still not sufficient to appease his hunger. Then said he, "Father, I see well that with thee I shall never have food enough; if thou will get me an iron staff which is strong, and which I cannot break against my knees, I will go out into the world."

The farmer was glad, put his two horses in his cart, and fetched from the smith a staff so large and thick that the two horses could only just bring it away. The youth laid it across his knees, and snap! he broke it in two in the middle like a beanstick, and threw it away.

The father then harnessed four horses, and brought a bar which was so long and thick, that the four horses could only just drag it. The son snapped this also in twain against his knees, threw it away, and said, "Father, this can be of no use to me, thou must harness more horses, and bring a stronger staff." So the father harnessed eight horses, and brought one which was so long and thick, that the eight horses could only just carry it. When the son took it in his hand, he broke a bit from the top of it also, and said, "Father, I see that thou wilt not be able to procure me any such staff as I want, I will remain no longer with thee."

So he went away, and gave out that he was a smith's apprentice. He arrived at a village, wherein lived a smith who was a greedy fellow, who never did a kindness to any one, but wanted everything for himself. The youth went into the smithy to him, and asked if he needed a journeyman. "Yes," said the smith, and looked at him, and thought, "That is a strong fellow who will strike out well, and earn his bread." So he asked, "How much wages dost thou want?" "I don't want any at all," he replied, "only every fortnight, when the other journeymen are paid, I will give thee two blows, and thou must bear them." The miser was heartily satisfied, and thought he would thus save much money.

Next morning, the strange journeyman was to begin to work, but when the master brought the glowing bar, and the youth struck his first blow, the iron flew asunder, and the anvil sank so deep into the earth, that there was no bringing it out again. Then the miser grew angry, and said, "Oh, but I can't make any use of thee, thou strikest far too powerfully; what wilt thou have for the one blow?"

Then said he, "I will only give thee quite a small blow, that's all." And he raised his foot, and gave him such a kick that he flew away over four loads of hay. Then he sought out the thickest iron bar in the smithy for himself, took it as a stick in his hand, and went onwards.

When he had walked for some time, he came to a small farm, and asked the bailiff if he did not require a head-servant. "Yes," said the bailiff, "I can make use of one; you look a strong fellow who can do something, how much a year do you want as wages?" He again replied that he wanted no wages at all, but that every year he would give him three blows, which he must bear. Then the bailiff was satisfied, for he, too, was a covetous fellow. Next morning all the servants were to go into the wood, and the others were already up, but the head-servant was still in bed. Then one of them called to him, "Get up, it is time; we are going into the wood, and thou must go with us."

"Ah," said he quite roughly and surlily, "you may just go, then; I shall be back again before any of you."

Then the others went to the bailiff, and told him that the head-man was still lying in bed, and would not go into the wood with them. The bailiff said they were to awake him again, and tell him to harness the horses. The head-man, however, said as before, "Just go there, I shall be back again before any of you." And then he stayed in bed two hours longer. At length he arose from the feathers, but first he got himself two bushels of peas from the loft, made himself some broth with them, ate it at his leisure, and when that was done, went and harnessed the horses, and drove into the wood.

Not far from the wood was a ravine through which he had to pass, so he first drove the horses on, and then stopped them, and went behind the cart, took trees and brushwood, and made a great barricade, so that no horse could get through. When he was entering the wood, the others were just driving out of it with their loaded carts to go home; then said he to them, "Drive on, I will still get home before you do." He did not drive far into the wood, but at once tore two of the very largest trees of all out of the earth, threw them on his cart, and turned round. When he came to the barricade, the others were still standing there, not able to get through. "Don't you see," said he, "that if you had stayed with me, you would have got home just as quickly, and would have had another hour's sleep?"

He now wanted to drive on, but his horses could not work their way through, so he unharnessed them, laid them at the top of the cart, took the shafts in his own hands, and drew it over, and he did this just as easily as if it had been laden with feathers. When he was over, he said to the others, "There, you see, I have got over quicker than you," and drove on, and the others had to stay where they were. In the yard, however, he took a tree in his hand, showed it to the bailiff, and said, "Isn't that a fine bundle of wood?" Then said the bailiff to his wife, "The servant is a good one, if he does sleep long, he is still home before the others."

So he served the bailiff a year, and when that was over, and the other servants were getting their wages, he said it was time for him to have his too. The bailiff, however, was afraid of the blows which he was to receive, and earnestly entreated him to excuse him from having them; for rather than that, he himself would be head-servant, and the youth should be bailiff. "No," said he, "I will not be a bailiff, I am head-servant, and will remain so, but I will administer that which we agreed on." The bailiff was willing to give him whatsoever he demanded, but it was of no use, the head-servant said no to everything.

Then the bailiff did not know what to do, and begged for a fortnight's delay, for he wanted to find some way to escape. The head-servant consented to this delay. The bailiff summoned all his clerks together, and they were to think the matter over, and give him advice. The clerks pondered for a long time, but at last they said that no one was sure of his life with the head-servant, for he could kill a man as easily as a midge, and that the bailiff ought to make him get into the well and clean it, and when he was down below, they would roll up one of the mill-stones which was lying there, and throw it on his head; and then he would never return to daylight.

The advice pleased the bailiff, and the head-servant was quite willing to go down the well. When he was standing down below at the bottom, they rolled down the largest mill-stone and thought they had broken his skull, but he cried, "Chase away those hens from the well, they are scratching in the sand up there, and throwing the grains into my eyes, so that I can't see." So the bailiff cried, "Sh-sh"—and pretended to frighten the hens away.

When the head-servant had finished his work, he climbed up and said, "Just look what a beautiful necktie I have on," and behold it was the mill-stone which he was wearing round his neck. The head-servant now wanted to take his reward, but the bailiff again begged for a fortnight's delay. The clerks met together and advised him to send the head-servant to the haunted mill to grind corn by night, for from thence as yet no man had ever returned in the morning alive. The proposal pleased the bailiff, he called the head-servant that very evening, and ordered him to take eight bushels of corn to the mill, and grind it that night, for it was wanted.

So the head-servant went to the loft, and put two bushels in his right pocket, and two in his left, and took four in a wallet, half on his back, and half on his breast, and thus laden went to the haunted mill. The miller told him that he could grind there very well by day, but not by night, for the mill was haunted, and that up to the present time whosoever had gone into it at night had been found in the morning, lying dead inside. He said, "I will manage it, just you go away to bed." Then he went into the mill, and poured out the corn.

About eleven o'clock he went into the miller's room, and sat down on the bench. When he had sat there a while, a door suddenly opened, and a large table came in, and on the table, wine and roasted meats placed themselves, and much good food besides, but everything came of itself, for no one was there to carry it. After this the chairs pushed themselves up, but no people came, until all at once he beheld fingers, which handled knives and forks, and laid food on the plates, but with this exception he saw nothing. As he was hungry, and saw the food, he, too, placed himself at the table, ate with those who were eating, and enjoyed it.

When he had had enough, and the others also had quite emptied their dishes, he distinctly heard all the candles being suddenly snuffed out, and as it was now pitch dark, he felt something like a box on the ear. Then he said, "If anything of that kind comes again, I shall strike out in return." And when he had received a second box on the ear, he, too, struck out. And so it continued the whole night, he took nothing without returning it, but repaid everything with interest, and did not lay about him in vain.

At daybreak, however, everything ceased. When the miller had got up, he wanted to look after him, and wondered if he were still alive. Then the youth said, "I have eaten my fill, have received some boxes on the ear, but I have given some in return." The miller rejoiced, and said that the mill was now released from the spell, and wanted to give him much money as a reward. But he said, "Money, I will not have, I have enough of it." So he took his meal on his back, went home, and told the bailiff that he had done what he had been told to do, and would now have the reward agreed on.

When the bailiff heard that, he was seriously alarmed and quite beside himself; he walked backwards and forwards in the room, and drops of perspiration ran down from his forehead. Then he opened the window to get some fresh air, but before he was aware the head-servant had given him such a kick that he flew through the window out into the air, and so far away that no one ever saw him again. Then said the head-servant to the bailiff's wife, "If he does not come back, thou must take the other blow." She cried, "No, no, I cannot bear it," and opened the other window, because drops of perspiration were running down her forehead. Then he gave her such a kick that she, too, flew out, and as she was lighter she went much higher than her husband. Her husband cried, "Do come to me," but she replied, "Come thou to me, I cannot come to thee."

They hovered about there in the air, and could not get to each other, and whether they are still hovering about or not, I do not know, but the young giant took up his iron bar, and went on his way.

Sweet Porridge

THERE WAS a poor but good little girl who lived alone with her mother, and they no longer had anything to eat. So the child went into the forest, and there an aged woman met her who was aware of her sorrow, and presented her with a little pot, which when she said, "Cook, little pot, cook," would cook good, sweet porridge; and when she said, "Stop, little pot," it ceased to cook. The girl took the pot home to her mother, and now they were freed from their poverty and hunger, and ate sweet porridge as often as they chose.

Once on a time when the girl had gone out, her mother said, "Cook, little pot, cook." And it did cook and she ate till she was satisfied, and then she wanted the pot to stop cooking, but did not know the word. So it went on cooking and the porridge rose over the edge, and still it cooked on until the kitchen and whole house were full, and then the next house, and then the whole street, just as if it wanted to satisfy the hunger of the whole world; and there was the greatest distress, but no one knew how to stop it.

At last when only one single house remained, the child came home and just said, "Stop, little pot," and it stopped and gave up cooking, and whosoever wished to return to the town had to eat his way back.

The Elves

i

THERE WAS once a shoemaker, who, through no fault of his own, became so poor that at last he had nothing left but just enough leather to make one pair of shoes. He cut out the shoes at night, so as to set to work upon them next morning; and as he had a good conscience, he laid himself quietly down in his bed, committed himself to heaven, and fell asleep.

In the morning, after he had said his prayers, and was going to get to work, he found the pair of shoes made and finished, and standing on his table. He was very much astonished, and could not tell what to think, and he took the shoes in his hand to examine them more closely; and they were so well made that every stitch was in its right place, just as if they had come from the hand of a master-workman.

Soon after, a purchaser entered, and as the shoes fitted him very well, he gave more than the usual price for them, so that the shoemaker had enough money to buy leather for two more pairs of shoes. He cut them out at night, and intended to set to work the next morning with fresh spirit; but that was not to be, for when he got up they were already finished, and even a customer was not lacking, who gave him so much money that he was able to buy leather enough for four new pairs. Early next morning he found the four pairs also finished, and so it always happened; whatever he cut out in the evening was worked up by the morning, so that he was soon in the way of making a good living, and in the end became very well-to-do.

One night, not long before Christmas, when the shoemaker had finished cutting out, and before he went to bed, he said to his wife, "How would it be if we were to sit up tonight and see who it is that does us this service?"

His wife agreed, and set a light to burn. Then they both hid in a corner of the room behind some coats that were hanging up, and then they began to watch. As soon as it was midnight they saw come in two neatly-formed naked little men, who seated themselves before the shoemaker's table, and took up the work that was already prepared, and began to stitch, to pierce, and to hammer so cleverly and quickly with their little fingers that the shoemaker's eyes could scarcely follow them, so full of wonder was he. And they never left off until everything was finished and was standing ready on the table, and then they jumped up and ran off.

The next morning the shoemaker's wife said to her husband, "Those little men have made us rich, and we ought to show ourselves grateful. With all their running about, and having nothing to cover them, they must be very cold. I'll tell you what; I will make little shirts, coats, waistcoats, and breeches for them, and knit each of them a pair of stockings, and you shall make each of them a pair of shoes."

The husband consented willingly, and at night, when everything was finished, they laid the gifts together on the table, instead of the cut-out work, and placed themselves so that they could observe how the little men would behave. When midnight came, they rushed in, ready to set to work, but when they found, instead of the pieces of prepared leather, the neat little garments put ready for them, they stood a moment in surprise, and then they showed the greatest delight. With the greatest swiftness they took up the pretty garments and slipped them on, singing,

> *"What spruce and dandy boys are we!*
> *No longer cobblers we will be."*

Then they hopped and danced about, jumping over the chairs and tables, and at last they danced out at the door.

From that time they were never seen again; but it always went well with the shoemaker as long as he lived, and whatever he took in hand prospered.

ii

THERE WAS once a poor servant maid, who was very cleanly and industrious; she swept down the house every day, and put the sweepings on a great heap by the door. One morning, before she began her work, she found a letter, and as she could not read, she laid her broom in the corner, and took the letter to her master and mistress, to see what it was about; and it was an invitation from the elves, who wished the maid to come and stand godmother to one of their children. The maid did not know what to do; and as she was told that no one ought to refuse the elves anything, she made up her mind to go.

So there came three little elves, who conducted her into the middle of a high mountain, where the little people lived. Here everything was of a very small size, but more fine and elegant than can be told. The mother of the child lay in a bed made of ebony, studded with pearls; the counterpane was embroidered with gold, the cradle was of ivory, and the bathing-tub of gold. So the maid stood godmother, and was then for going home, but the elves begged her to stay at least three more days with them; and so she consented, and spent the time in mirth and jollity, and the elves seemed very fond of her. At last, when she was ready to go away, they filled her pockets full of gold, and led her back again out of the mountain.

When she got back to the house, she was going to begin working again, and took her broom in her hand—it was still standing in the corner where she had left it—and began to sweep. Then came up some strangers and asked her who she was, and what she was doing. And she found that instead of three days, she had been seven years with the elves in the mountain, and that during that time her master and mistress had died.

iii

THE elves once took a child away from its mother, and left in its place a changeling with a big head and staring eyes, who did nothing but eat and drink. The mother in her trouble went to her neighbors and asked their advice. The neighbors told her to take the changeling into the kitchen and put it near the hearth, and then to make up the fire, and boil water in two egg-shells; that would make the changeling laugh, and if he laughed, it would be all over with him. So the woman did as her neighbors advised. And when she set the egg-shells of water on the fire, the changeling said,

> *"Though old I be*
> *As forest tree,*
> *Cooking in an egg-shell never did I see!"*

and began to laugh. And directly there came in a crowd of elves bringing in the right child; and they laid it near the hearth, and carried the changeling away with them.

Fair Katrinelje and Pif-Paf-Poltrie

GOOD-DAY, Father Hollenthe." "Many thanks, Pif-Paf-Poltrie." "May I be allowed to have your daughter?" "Oh, yes, if Mother Malcho (Milch-cow), Brother High-and-Mighty, Sister Käsetraut, and fair Katrinelje are willing, you can have her." "Where is Mother Malcho, then?" "She is in the cow-house, milking the cow."

"Good-day, Mother Malcho." "Many thanks, Pif-paf-poltrie." "May I be allowed to have your daughter?" "Oh, yes, if Father Hollenthe, Brother High-and-Mighty, Sister Käsetraut, and fair Katrinelje are willing, you can have her." "Where is Brother High-and-Mighty, then?" "He is in the room chopping some wood."

"Good-day, Brother High-and-Mighty." "Many thanks, Pif-paf-poltrie." "May I be allowed to have your sister?" "Oh, yes, if Father Hollenthe, Mother Malcho, Sister Käsetraut, and fair Katrinelje are willing, you can have her." "Where is Sister Käsetraut, then?" "She is in the garden cutting cabbages."

"Good-day, Sister Käsetraut." "Many thanks, Pif-paf-poltrie." "May I be allowed to have your sister?" "Oh, yes, if Father Hollenthe, Mother Malcho, Brother High-and-Mighty, and fair Katrinelje are willing, you may have her." "Where is fair Katrinelje, then?" "She is in the room counting out her farthings."

"Good-day, fair Katrinelje." "Many thanks, Pif-paf-poltrie."

"Wilt thou be my bride?" "Oh, yes, if Father Hollenthe, Mother Malcho, Brother High-and-Mighty, and Sister Käsetraut are willing, I am ready."

"Fair Katrinelje, how much dowry hast thou?" "Fourteen farthings in ready money, three and a half groschen owing to me, half a pound of dried apples, a handful of fried bread, and a handful of spices.

> *And many other things are mine,*
> *Have I not a dowry fine?*

Pif-paf-poltrie, what is thy trade? Art thou a tailor?" "Something better." "A shoemaker?" "Something better." "A husbandman?" "Something better." "A joiner?" "Something better." "A smith?" "Something better." "A miller?" "Something better." "Perhaps a broom-maker?" "Yes, that's what I am, is it not a fine trade?"

The Old Beggar-Woman

THERE WAS once an old woman, but thou hast surely seen an old woman go a-begging before now? This woman begged likewise, and when she got anything she said, "May God reward you." The beggar-woman came to a door, and there by the fire a friendly rogue of a boy was standing warming himself. The boy said kindly to the poor old woman as she was standing shivering thus by the door, "Come, old mother, and warm yourself." She came in, but stood too near the fire, so that her old rags began to burn, and she was not aware of it. The boy stood and saw that, but he ought to have put the flames out. And if he could not find any water, then should he have wept all the water in his body out of his eyes, and that would have supplied two fine streams with which to extinguish them.

The Jew Among Thorns

THERE WAS once a rich man who had a servant who served him diligently and honestly. Every morning the servant was the first out of bed, and the last to go to rest at night; and, whenever there was a difficult job to be done, which nobody cared to undertake, he was always the first to set himself to it. Moreover, he never complained, but was contented with everything, and always merry.

When a year was ended, his master gave him no wages, for he said to himself, "That is the cleverest way; for I shall save something, and he will not go away, but stay quietly in my service." The servant said nothing, but did his work the second year as he had done it the first; and when at the end of this, likewise, he received no wages, he made himself happy, and still stayed on.

When the third year also was past, the master considered, put his hand in his pocket, but pulled nothing out. Then at last the servant said, "Master, for three years I have served you honestly; be so good as to give me what I ought to have, for I wish to leave, and look about me a little more in the world."

"Yes, my good fellow," answered the old miser; "you have served me industriously, and therefore you shall be cheerfully rewarded"; and he put his hand into his pocket, but counted out only three farthings, saying, "There, you have a farthing for each year; that is large and liberal pay, such as you would have received from few masters."

The honest servant, who understood little about money, put his fortune into his pocket, and thought, "Ah! now that I have my purse full, why need I trouble and plague myself any longer with hard work!" So on he went, up the hill and down dale; and sang and jumped to his heart's content. Now it came to pass that as he was going by a thicket a little man stepped out, and called to him, "Whither away, merry brother? I see you do not carry many cares." "Why should I be sad?" answered the servant; "I have enough; three years' wages are jingling in my pocket."

"How much is your treasure?" the dwarf asked him. "How much? Three farthings sterling, all told."

"Look here," said the dwarf, "I am a poor needy man, give me your three farthings; I can work no longer, but you are young, and can easily earn your bread."

And as the servant had a good heart, and felt pity for the old man, he gave him the three farthings, saying, "Take them in the name of Heaven, I shall not be any the worse for it."

Then the little man said, "As I see you have a good heart I grant you three wishes, one for each farthing, they shall all be fulfilled."

"Aha?" said the servant, "you are one of those who can work wonders! Well, then, if it is to be so, I wish, first, for a gun, which shall hit everything that I aim at; secondly, for a fiddle, which when I play on it, shall compel all who hear it to dance; thirdly, that if I ask a favor of any one he shall not be able to refuse it."

"All that shall you have," said the dwarf; and put his hand into the bush; and only think, there lay a fiddle and gun, all ready, just as if they had been ordered. These he gave to the servant, and then said to him, "Whatever you may ask at any time, no man in the world shall be able to deny you."

"Heart alive! What more can one desire?" said the servant to himself, and went merrily onwards. Soon afterwards he met a Jew with a long goat's-beard, who was standing listening to the song of a bird which was sitting up at the top of a tree. "Good heavens," he was exclaiming, "that such a small creature should have such a fearfully loud voice! If it were but mine! If only some one would sprinkle some salt upon its tail!"

"If that is all," said the servant, "the bird shall soon be down here"; and taking aim he pulled the trigger, and down fell the bird into the thorn-bushes. "Go, you rogue," he said to the Jew, "and fetch the bird out for yourself!"

"Oh!" said the Jew, "leave out the rogue, my master, and I will do it at once. I will get the bird out for myself, as you really have hit it." Then he lay down on the ground, and began to crawl into the thicket.

When he was fast among the thorns, the good servant's humor so tempted him that he took up his fiddle and began to play. In a moment the Jew's legs began to move, and to jump into the air, and the more the servant fiddled the better went the dance. But the thorns tore his shabby coat for him, combed his beard, and pricked and plucked him all over the body. "Oh dear," cried the Jew, "what do I want with your fiddling? Leave the fiddle alone, master; I do not want to dance."

But the servant did not listen to him, and thought, "You have fleeced people often enough, now the thorn-bushes shall do the same to you"; and he began to play over again, so that the Jew had to jump higher than ever, and scraps of his coat were left hanging on the thorns. "Oh, woe's me!" cried the Jew; "I will give the gentleman whatsoever he asks if only he leaves off fiddling—a purse full of gold." "If you are so liberal," said the servant, "I will stop my music; but this I must say to your credit, that you dance to it so well that it is quite an art"; and having taken the purse he went his way.

The Jew stood still and watched the servant quietly until he was far off and out of sight, and then he screamed out with all his might, "You miserable musician, you beer-house fiddler! Wait till I catch you alone, I will hunt you till the soles of your shoes fall off! You ragamuffin! Just put five farthings in your mouth, and then you may be worth three halfpence!" and went on abusing him as fast as he could speak.

As soon as he had refreshed himself a little in this way, and got his breath again, he ran into the town to the justice. "My lord judge," he said, "I have come to make a complaint; see how a rascal has robbed and ill-treated me on the public highway! A stone on the ground might pity me; my clothes all torn, my body pricked and scratched, my little all gone with my purse—good ducats, each piece better than the last; for God's sake let the man be thrown into prison!"

"Was it a soldier," said the judge, "who cut you thus with his sabre?" "Nothing of the sort!" said the Jew; "it was no sword that he had, but a gun hanging at his back, and a fiddle at his neck; the wretch may easily be known."

So the judge sent his people out after the man, and they found the good servant, who had been going quite slowly along, and they found, too, the purse with the money upon him. As soon as he was taken before the judge he said, "I did not touch the Jew, nor take his money; he gave it to me of his own free will, that I might leave off fiddling because he could not bear my music." "Heaven defend us!" cried the Jew, "his lies are as thick as flies upon the wall."

But the judge also did not believe his tale, and said, "This is a bad defense, no Jew would do that." And because he had committed robbery on the public highway, he sentenced the good servant to be hanged. As he was being led away the Jew again screamed after him, "You vagabond! You dog of a fiddler! now you are going to receive your well-earned reward!"

The servant walked quietly with the hangman up the ladder, but upon the last step he turned round and said to the judge, "Grant me just one request before I die." "Yes, if you do not ask your life," said the judge. "I do not ask for life," answered the servant, "but as a last favor let me play once more upon my fiddle."

The Jew raised a great cry of "Murder! murder! for goodness' sake do not allow it! Do not allow it!" But the judge said, "Why should I not let him have this short pleasure? It has been granted to him, and he shall have it." However, he could not have refused on account of the gift which had been bestowed on the servant.

Then the Jew cried, "Oh! woe's me! tie me, tie me fast!" while the good servant took his fiddle from his neck, and made ready. As he gave the first scrape, they all began to quiver and shake, the judge, his clerk, and the hangman and his men, and the cord fell out of the hand of the one who was going to tie the Jew fast. At the second scrape all raised their legs, and the hangman let go his hold of the good servant, and made himself ready to dance. At the third scrape they all leaped up and began to dance; the judge and the Jew being the best at jumping. Soon all who had gathered in the market-place out of curiosity were dancing with them; old and young, fat and lean, one with another. The dogs, likewise, which had run there got up on their hind legs and capered about; and the longer he played, the higher sprang the dancers, so that they knocked against each other's heads, and began to shriek terribly.

At length the judge cried, quite out of breath, "I will give you your life if you will only stop fiddling." The good servant thereupon had compassion, took his fiddle and hung it round his neck again, and stepped down the ladder. Then he went up to the Jew, who was lying upon the ground panting for breath, and said, "You rascal, now confess, whence you got the money, or I will take my fiddle and begin to play again." "I stole it, I stole it!" cried he; "but you have honestly earned it." So the judge had the Jew taken to the gallows and hanged as a thief.

King Thrushbeard

A KING had a daughter who was beautiful beyond measure, but so proud and overbearing that none of her suitors were good enough for her; she not only refused one after the other, but made a laughing-stock of them.

Once the King appointed a great feast, and bade all the marriageable men to it from far and near. And they were all put in rows, according to their rank and station: first came the Kings, then the Princes, the dukes, the earls, the barons, and lastly the noblemen. The Princess was led in front of the rows, but she had a mocking epithet for each. One was too fat, "What a tub!" said she; another too tall, "Long and lean is ill to be seen," said she; a third too short, "Fat and short, not fit to court," said she. A fourth was too pale—"A regular death's-head"; a fifth too red-faced—"A gamecock," she called him. The sixth was not well-made enough— "Green wood ill dried!" cried she. So every one had something against him, and she made especially merry over a good King who was very tall, and whose chin had grown a little peaked. "Only look," cried she, laughing, "he has a chin like a thrush's beak."

And from that time they called him King Thrushbeard. But the old King, when he saw that his daughter mocked every one, and scorned all the assembled suitors, swore in his anger that she should have the first beggar that came to the door for a husband.

A few days afterwards came a traveling ballad-singer, and sang under the window in hopes of a small alms. When the King heard of it, he said that he must come in. And so the ballad-singer entered in his dirty tattered garments, and sang before the King and his daughter; when he had done, he asked for a small reward. But the King said, "Your song has so well pleased me, that I will give you my daughter to wife."

The Princess was horrified; but the King said, "I took an oath to give you to the first beggar that came, and so it must be done."

There was no remedy. The priest was fetched, and she had to be married to the ballad-singer out of hand. When all was done, the King said, "Now, as you are a beggar-wife, you can stay no longer in my castle, so off with you and your husband."

The beggar-man led her away, and she was obliged to go forth with him on foot. On the way they came to a great wood, and she asked,

"Oh, whose is this forest, so thick and so fine?"

He answered,

"It is King Thrushbeard's, and might have been thine."

And she cried,

"Oh, I was a silly young thing, I'm afeared,
Would I had taken that good King
Thrushbeard!"

Then they passed through a meadow, and she asked,

"Oh, whose is this meadow, so green and so fine?"

He answered,

"It is King Thrushbeard's, and might have been thine."

And she cried,

"I was a silly young thing, I'm afeared,
Would I had taken that good King
Thrushbeard!"

Then they passed through a great town, and she asked,

"Whose is this city, so great and so fine?"

He answered,

"Oh, it is King Thrushbeard's, and might have been thine."

And she cried,

"I was a silly young thing, I'm afeared,
Would I had taken that good King
Thrushbeard!"

Then said the beggar-man, "It does not please me to hear you always wishing for another husband; am I not good enough for you?"

At last they came to a very small house, and she said,

"Oh dear me! what poor little house do I see?
And whose, I would know, may the wretched hole be?"

The man answered, "That is my house and yours, where we must live together."

She had to stoop before she could go in at the door.

"Where are the servants?" asked the King's daughter.

"What servants?" answered the beggar-man, "what you want to have done you must do yourself. Make a fire quickly, and put on water, and cook me some food; I am very tired."

But the King's daughter understood nothing about fire-making and cooking, and the beggar-man had to lend a hand himself in order to manage it at all. And when they had eaten their poor fare, they went to bed; but the man called up his wife very early in the morning, in order to clean the house.

For a few days they lived in this indifferent manner, until they came to the end of their store. "Wife," said the man, "this will not do, stopping here and earning nothing; you must make baskets."

So he went out and cut willows, and brought them home; and she began to weave them, but the hard twigs wounded her tender hands. "I see this will not do," said the man, "you had better try spinning."

So she sat her down and tried to spin, but the harsh thread cut her soft fingers, so that the blood flowed. "Look now!" said the man, "you are no good at any sort of work; I made a bad bargain when I took you. I must see what I can do to make a trade of pots and earthen vessels; you can sit in the market and offer them for sale."

"Oh dear!" thought she, "suppose while I am selling in the market people belonging to my father's kingdom should see me, how they would mock at me!" But there was no help for it; she had to submit, or else die of hunger.

The first day all went well; the people bought her wares eagerly, because she was so beautiful, and gave her whatever she asked, and some of them gave her the money and left the pots after all behind them. And they lived on these earnings as long as they lasted; and then the man bought a number of new pots. So she seated herself in a corner of the market, and stood the wares before her for sale. All at once a drunken horse-soldier came plunging by, and rode straight into the midst of her pots, breaking them into a thousand pieces. She could do nothing for weeping. "Oh dear, what will become of me," cried she; "what will my husband say?" and she hastened home and told him her misfortune.

"Who ever heard of such a thing as sitting in the corner of the market with earthenware pots!" said the man; "now leave off crying; I see you are not fit for any regular work. I have been asking at your father's castle if they want a kitchen-maid, and they say they don't mind taking you; at any rate you will get your victuals free."

And the King's daughter became a kitchen-maid, to be at the cook's beck and call, and to do the hardest work. In each of her pockets she fastened a little pot, and brought home in them whatever was left, and upon that she and her husband were fed. It happened one day, when the wedding of the eldest Prince was celebrated, the poor woman went upstairs, and stood by the parlor door to see what was going on. And when the place was lighted up, and the company arrived, each person handsomer than the one before, and all was brilliancy and splendor, she thought on her own fate with a sad heart, and bewailed her former pride and haughtiness which had brought her so low, and plunged her in so great poverty. And as the rich and delicate dishes smelling so good were carried to and fro every now and then, the servants would throw her a few fragments, which she put in her pockets, intending to take home. And then the Prince himself passed in, clothed in silk and velvet, with a gold chain round his neck. And when he saw the beautiful woman standing in the doorway, he seized her hand and urged her to dance with him, but she refused, all trembling, for she saw it was King Thrushbeard, who had come to court her, whom she had turned away with mocking. It was of no use her resisting, he drew her into the room; and all at once the band to which her pockets were fastened broke, and the pots fell out, and the soup ran about, and the fragments were scattered all round. And when the people saw that, there was great laughter and mocking, and she felt so ashamed, that she wished herself a thousand fathoms underground.

She rushed to the door to fly from the place, when a man caught her just on the steps, and when she looked at him, it was King Thrushbeard again. He said to her in a kind tone, "Do not be afraid, I and the beggar-man with whom you lived in the wretched little hut are one. For love of you I disguised myself, and it was I who broke your pots in the guise of a horse-soldier. I did all that to bring down your proud heart, and to punish your haughtiness, which caused you to mock at me."

Then she wept bitterly, and said, "I have done great wrong, and am not worthy to be your wife."

But he said, "Take courage, the evil days are gone over; now let us keep our wedding-day."

Then came the ladies-in-waiting and put on her splendid clothing; and her father came, and the whole court, and wished her joy on her marriage with King Thrushbeard; and then the merrymaking began in good earnest. I cannot help wishing that you and I could have been there too.

Clever Gretel

THERE WAS once a cook called Gretel, who wore shoes with red heels, and when she went out in them she gave herself great airs, and thought herself very fine indeed. When she came home again, she would take a drink of wine to refresh herself, and as that gave her an appetite, she would take some of the best of whatever she was cooking, until she had had enough—"for," said she, "a cook must know how things taste."

It happened that one day her master came to her and said, "Gretel, I expect a guest this evening; you must make ready a pair of fowls." "I will see to it," answered Gretel.

So she killed the fowls, cleaned them, and plucked them, and put them on the spit, and then, as evening drew near, placed them before the fire to roast. And they began to be brown, and were nearly done, but the guest had not come.

"If he does not make haste," cried Gretel to her master, "I must take them away from the fire; it's a pity and a shame not to eat them now, just when they are done to a turn." And the master said he would run himself and fetch the guest. As soon as he had turned his back, Gretel took the fowls from before the fire.

"Standing so long before the fire," said she, "makes one hot and thirsty—and who knows when they will come! In the meanwhile I will go to the cellar and have a drink." So down she ran, took up a mug, and saying, "Here's to me!" took a good draught. "One good drink deserves another," she said "and it should not be cut short"; so she took another hearty draught. Then she went and put the fowls down to the fire again, and, basting them with butter, she turned the spit briskly round. And now they began to smell so good that Gretel saying, "I must find out whether they really are all right," licked her fingers, and then cried, "Well, I never! the fowls are good; it's a sin and a shame that no one is here to eat them!"

So she ran to the window to see if her master and his guest were coming, but as she could see nobody she went back to her fowls. "Why, one of the wings is burning!" she cried presently, "I had better eat it and get it out of the way." So she cut it off and ate it up, and it tasted good, and then she thought, "I had better cut off the other too, in case the master should miss anything." And when both wings had been disposed of she went and looked for the master, but still he did not come.

"Who knows," said she, "whether they are coming or not? they may have put up at an inn." And after a pause she said again, "Come, I may as well make myself happy, and first I will make sure of a good drink and then of a good meal, and when all is done I shall be easy; the gifts of the gods are not to be despised." So first she ran down into the cellar and had a famous drink, and ate up one of the fowls with great relish. And when that was done, and still the master did not come, Gretel eyed the other fowl, saying, "What one is the other must be, the two belong to each other, it is only fair that they should be both treated alike; perhaps when I have had another drink, I shall be able to manage it." So she took another hearty drink, and then the second fowl went the way of the first.

Just as she was in the middle of it the master came back. "Make haste, Gretel," cried he, "the guest is coming directly!" "Very well, master," she answered, "it will soon be ready." The master went to see that the table was properly laid, and, taking the great carving knife with which he meant to carve the fowls, he sharpened it upon the step. Presently came the guest, knocking very genteelly and softly at the front door. Gretel ran and looked to see who it was, and when she caught sight of the guest she put her finger on her lip saying, "Hush! make the best haste you can out of this, for if my master catches you, it will be bad for you; he asked you to come to supper, but he really means to cut off your ears! Just listen how he is sharpening his knife!"

The guest, hearing the noise of the sharpening, made off as fast as he could go. And Gretel ran screaming to her master. "A pretty guest you have asked to the house!" cried she. "How so, Gretel? what do you mean?" asked he. "What indeed!" said she; "why, he has gone and run away with my pair of fowls that I had just dished up."

"That's pretty sort of conduct!" said the master, feeling very sorry about the fowls; "he might at least have left me one, that I might have had something to eat." And he called out to him to stop, but the guest made as if he did not hear him; then he ran after him, the knife still in his hand, crying out, "Only one! only one!" meaning that the guest should let him have one of the fowls and not take both; but the guest thought he meant to have only one of his ears, and he ran so much the faster that he might get home with both of them safe.

Fitcher's Bird

THERE WAS once a wizard who used to take the form of a poor man. He went to houses and begged, and caught pretty girls. No one knew whither he carried them, for they were never seen more. One day he appeared before the door of a man who had three pretty daughters. He looked like a poor weak beggar, and carried a basket on his back, as if he meant to collect charitable gifts in it. He begged for a little food, and when the eldest daughter came out and was just reaching him a piece of bread, he did but touch her, and she was forced to jump into his basket. Thereupon he hurried away with long strides, and carried her away into a dark forest to his house, which stood in the midst of it.

Everything in the house was magnificent; he gave her whatsoever she could possibly desire, and said, "My darling, thou wilt certainly be happy with me, for thou hast everything thy heart can wish for." This lasted a few days, and then he said, "I must journey forth, and leave thee alone for a short time; there are the keys of the house; thou mayst go everywhere and look at everything except into one room, which this little key here opens, and there I forbid thee to go on pain of death." He likewise gave her an egg and said, "Preserve the egg carefully for me, and carry it continually about with thee, for a great misfortune would arise from the loss of it."

She took the keys and the egg, and promised to obey him in everything. When he was gone, she went all round the house from the bottom to the top, and examined everything. The rooms shone with silver and gold, and she thought she had never seen such great splendor.

At length she came to the forbidden door; she wished to pass it by, but curiosity let her have no rest. She examined the key, it looked just like any other; she put it in the keyhole and turned it a little, and the door sprang open. But what did she see when she went in? A great bloody basin stood in the middle of the room, and therein lay human beings, dead and hewn to pieces, and hard by was a block of wood, and a gleaming axe lay upon it. She was so terribly alarmed that the egg which she held in her hand fell into the basin. She got it out and washed the blood off, but in vain, it appeared again in a moment. She washed and scrubbed, but she could not get it out.

It was not long before the man came back from his journey, and the first things which he asked for were the key and the egg. She gave them to him, but she trembled as she did so, and he saw at once by the red spots that she had been in the bloody chamber. "Since thou hast gone into the room against my will," said he, "thou shalt go back into it against thine own. Thy life is ended." He threw her down, dragged her thither by her hair, cut her head off on the block, and hewed her in pieces so that her blood ran on the ground. Then he threw her into the basin with the rest.

"Now I will fetch myself the second," said the wizard, and again he went to the house in the shape of a poor man, and begged. Then the second daughter brought him a piece of bread; he caught her like the first, by simply touching her, and carried her away. She did not fare better than her sister. She allowed herself to be led away by her curiosity, opened the door of the bloody chamber, looked in, and had to atone for it with her life on the wizard's return.

Then he went and brought the third sister. But she was clever and crafty. When he had given her the keys and the egg, and had left her, she first put the egg away with great care, and then she examined the house, and at last went into the forbidden room. Alas, what did she behold! Both her sisters lay there in the basin, cruelly murdered, and cut in pieces. She began to gather their limbs together and put them in order, head, body, arms and legs. And when nothing further was lacking, the limbs began to move and unite themselves together, and both the maidens opened their eyes and were once more alive. Then they rejoiced and kissed and caressed each other.

On his arrival, the man at once demanded the keys and the egg, and as he could perceive no trace of any blood on it, he said, "Thou hast stood the test, thou shalt be my bride." He now had no longer any power over her, and was forced to do whatsoever she desired. "Oh, very well," said she, "thou shalt first take a basketful of gold to my father and mother, and carry it thyself on thy back; in the meantime I will prepare for the wedding."

Then she ran to her sisters, whom she had hidden in a little chamber and said, "The moment has come when I can save you. The wretch shall himself carry you home again, but as soon as you are at home send help to me." She put both of them in a basket and covered them quite over with gold, so that nothing of them was to be seen, then she called in the wizard and said to him, "Now carry the basket away, but I shall look through my little window and watch to see if thou stoppest on the way to stand or to rest."

The wizard raised the basket on his back and went away with it, but it weighed him down so heavily that the perspiration streamed from his face. Then he sat down and wanted to rest awhile, but immediately one of the girls in the basket cried, "I am looking through my little window, and I see that thou art resting. Wilt thou go on at once?" He thought his bride was calling that to him; and got up on his legs again. Once more he was going to sit down, but instantly she cried, "I am looking through my little window, and I see that thou art resting. Wilt thou go on directly?"

Whenever he stood still, she cried this, and then he was forced to go onwards, until at last, groaning and out of breath, he took the basket with the gold and the two maidens into their parents' house. At home, however, the bride prepared the marriage-feast, and sent invitations to the friends of the wizard. Then she took a skull with grinning teeth, put some ornaments on it and a wreath of flowers, carried it upstairs to the garret-window, and let it look out from thence. When all was ready, she got into a barrel of honey, and then cut the feather-bed open and rolled herself in it, until she looked like a wondrous bird, and no one could recognize her. Then she went out of the house, and on her way she met some of the wedding-guests, who asked,

> "O, Fitcher's bird, how com'st thou here?"
>
> "I come from Fitcher's house quite near."
>
> "And what may the young bride be doing?"
>
> "From cellar to garret she's swept all clean,
> And now from the window she's peeping, I ween."

At last she met the bridegroom, who was coming slowly back. He, like the others, asked,

> "O, Fitcher's bird, how com'st thou here?"
>
> "I come from Fitcher's house quite near."
>
> "And what may the young bride be doing?"
>
> "From cellar to garret she's swept all clean,
> And now from the window she's peeping, I ween."

The bridegroom looked up, saw the decked-out skull, thought it was his bride, and nodded to her, greeting her kindly. But when he and his guests had all gone into the house, the brothers and kinsmen of the bride, who had been sent to rescue her, arrived. They locked all the doors of the house, that no one might escape, set fire to it, and the wizard and all his crew were burned.

The Robber Bridegroom

THERE WAS once a miller who had a beautiful daughter, and when she was grown up he became anxious that she should be well married and taken care of; so he thought, "If a decent sort of man comes and asks her in marriage, I will give her to him."

Soon after a suitor came forward who seemed very well-to-do, and as the miller knew nothing to his disadvantage, he promised him his daughter. But the girl did not seem to love him as a bride should love her bridegroom; she had no confidence in him; as often as she saw him or thought about him, she felt a chill at her heart.

One day he said to her, "You are to be my bride, and yet you have never been to see me." The girl answered, "I do not know where your house is." Then he said, "My house is a long way in the wood."

She began to make excuses, and said she could not find the way to it; but the bridegroom said, "You must come and pay me a visit next Sunday; I have already invited company, and I will strew ashes on the path through the wood, so that you will be sure to find it."

When Sunday came, and the girl set out on her way, she felt very uneasy without knowing exactly why; and she filled both pockets full of peas and lentils. There were ashes strewn on the path through the wood, but nevertheless, at each step she cast to the right and left a few peas on the ground. So she went on the whole day until she came to the middle of the wood, where it was darkest, and there stood a lonely house, not pleasant in her eyes, for it was dismal and unhomelike. She walked in, but there was no one there, and the greatest stillness reigned. Suddenly she heard a voice cry,

> *"Turn back, turn back, thou pretty bride,*
> *Within this house thou must not bide,*
> *For here do evil things betide."*

The girl glanced round, and perceived that the voice came from a bird who was hanging in a cage by the wall. And again it cried,

"Turn back, turn back, thou pretty bride,
Within this house thou must not bide,"
For here do evil things betide."

Then the pretty bride went on from one room into another through the whole house, but it was quite empty, and no soul to be found in it. At last she reached the cellar, and there sat a very old woman nodding her head.

"Can you tell me," said the bride, "if my bridegroom lives here?"

"Oh, poor child," answered the old woman, "do you know what has happened to you? You are in a place of cutthroats. You thought you were a bride, and soon to be married, but death will be your spouse. Look here, I have a great kettle of water to set on, and when once they have you in their power they will cut you in pieces without mercy, cook you, and eat you, for they are cannibals. Unless I have pity on you, and save you, all is over with you!"

Then the old woman hid her behind a great cask, where she could not be seen. "Be as still as a mouse," said she; "do not move or go away, or else you are lost. At night, when the robbers are asleep, we will escape. I have been waiting a long time for an opportunity."

No sooner was it settled than the wicked gang entered the house. They brought another young woman with them, dragging her along, and they were drunk, and would not listen to her cries and groans. They gave her wine to drink, three glasses full, one of white wine, one of red, and one of yellow, and then they cut her in pieces; the poor bride all the while shaking and trembling when she saw what a fate the robbers had intended for her.

One of them noticed on the little finger of their victim a golden ring, and as he could not draw it off easily, he took an axe and chopped it off, but the finger jumped away, and fell behind the cask on the bride's lap. The robber took up a light to look for it, but he could not find it. Then said one of the others, "Have you looked behind the great cask?" But the old woman cried, "Come to supper, and leave off looking till tomorrow; the finger cannot run away.

Then the robbers said the old woman was right, and they left off searching, and sat down to eat, and the old woman dropped some sleeping stuff into their wine, so that before long they stretched themselves on the cellar floor, sleeping and snoring.

When the bride heard that, she came from behind the cask, and had to make her way among the sleepers lying all about on the ground, and she felt very much afraid lest she might awaken any of them. But by good luck she passed through, and the old woman with her, and they opened the door, and they made haste to leave that house of murderers. The wind had carried away the ashes from the path, but the peas and lentils had budded and sprung up, and the moonshine upon them showed the way. And they went on through the night, till in the morning they reached the mill. Then the girl related to her father all that had happened to her.

When the wedding-day came, the friends and neighbors assembled, the miller having invited them, and the bridegroom also appeared. When they were all seated at table, each one had to tell a story. But the bride sat still, and said nothing, till at last the bridegroom said to her, "Now, sweetheart, do you know no story? Tell us something."

She answered, "I will tell you my dream. I was going alone through a wood, and I came at last to a house in which there was no living soul, but by the wall was a bird in a cage, who cried,

> *'Turn back, turn back, thou pretty bride,*
> *Within this house thou must not bide,*
> *For here do evil things betide.'*

"And then again it said it. Sweetheart, the dream is not ended. Then I went through all the rooms, and they were all empty, and it was so lonely and wretched. At last I went down into the cellar, and there sat an old old woman, nodding her head. I asked her if my bridegroom lived in that house, and she answered, 'Ah, poor child, you have come into a place of cutthroats; your bridegroom does live here, but he will kill you and cut you in pieces, and then cook and eat you.' Sweetheart, the dream is not ended. But the old woman hid me behind a great cask, and no sooner had she done so than the robbers came home, dragging with them a young woman, and they gave her to drink wine thrice, white, red, and yellow. Sweetheart, the dream is not yet ended. And then they killed her, and cut her in pieces. Sweetheart, my dream is not yet ended. And one of the robbers saw a gold ring on the finger of the young woman, and as it was difficult to get off, he took an axe and chopped off the finger, which jumped upwards, and then fell behind the great cask on my lap. And here is the finger with the ring!"

At these words she drew it forth, and showed it to the company. The robber, who during the story had grown deadly white, sprang up, and would have escaped, but the folks held him fast, and delivered him up to justice. And he and his whole gang were, for their evil deeds, condemned and executed.

Old Hildebrand

ONCE UPON a time lived a peasant and his wife, and the parson of the village had a fancy for the wife, and had wished for a long while to spend a whole day happily with her, and the peasant woman, too, was quite willing. One day, therefore, he said to the woman, "Listen, my dear friend, I have now thought of a way by which we can for once spend a whole day happily together. I'll tell you what: on Wednesday, you must take to your bed, and tell your husband you are ill, and if you only complain and act being ill properly, and go on doing it until Sunday when I have to preach, I will then say in my sermon that whosoever has at home a sick child, a sick husband, a sick wife, a sick father, a sick mother, a sick sister, brother or whosoever else it may be, and makes a pilgrimage to the Göckerli hill in Italy, where you can get a peck of laurel-leaves for a kreuzer, the sick child, the sick husband, the sick wife, the sick father, or sick mother, the sick sister, or whosoever else it may be, will be restored to health immediately."

"I will manage it," said the woman directly. Now therefore, on the Wednesday, the peasant woman took to her bed, and complained and lamented as agreed on, and her husband did everything for her that he could think of, but nothing did her any good, and when Sunday came the woman said, "I feel as ill as if I were going to die at once, but there is one thing I should like to do before my end—I should like to hear the parson's sermon that he is going to preach today." On that the peasant said, "Ah, my child, do not do it—you might make yourself worse if you were to get up. Look, I will go to the sermon, and will attend to it very carefully, and will tell you everything the parson says."

"Well," said the woman, "go, then, and pay great attention, and repeat to me all that you hear." So the peasant went to the sermon, and the parson began to preach and said, if any one had at home a sick child, a sick husband, a sick wife, a sick father, a sick mother, a sick sister, brother or any one else, and would make a pilgrimage to the Göckerli hill in Italy, where a peck of laurel-leaves costs a kreuzer, the sick child, sick husband, sick wife, sick father, sick mother, sick sister, brother, or whosoever else it might be, would be restored to health instantly; and whosoever wished to undertake the journey was to go to him after the service was over, and he would give him the sack for the laurel-leaves and the kreuzer.

No one was more rejoiced than the peasant, and after the service was over, he went at once to the parson, who gave him the bag for the laurel-leaves and the kreuzer. After that he went home, and even at the house door he cried, "Hurrah! dear wife, it is now almost the same thing as if you were well! The parson has preached today that whosoever had at home a sick child, a sick husband, a sick wife, a sick father, a sick mother, a sick sister, brother or whoever it might be, and would make a pilgrimage to the Göckerli hill in Italy, where a peck of laurel-leaves costs a kreuzer, the sick child, sick husband, sick wife, sick father, sick mother, sick sister, brother or whosoever else it was, would be cured immediately; and now I have already got the bag and the kreuzer from the parson, and will at once begin my journey so that you may get well the faster," and thereupon he went away. He was, however, hardly gone before the woman got up, and the parson was there directly.

But now we will leave these two for a while, and follow the peasant, who walked on quickly without stopping, in order to get the sooner to the Göckerli hill; and on his way he met his gossip. His gossip was an egg-merchant, and was just coming from the market, where he had sold his eggs. "May you be blessed," said the gossip, "where are you off to so fast?"

"To all eternity, my friend," said the peasant, "my wife is ill, and I have been today to hear the parson's sermon, and he preached that if any one had in his house a sick child, a sick husband, a sick wife, a sick father, a sick mother, a sick sister, brother or any one else, and made a pilgrimage to the Göckerli hill in Italy, where a peck of laurel-leaves costs a kreuzer; the sick child, the sick husband, the sick wife, the sick father, the sick mother, the sick sister, brother, or whosoever else it was, would be cured immediately; and so I have got the bag for the laurel-leaves and the kreuzer from the parson, and now I am beginning my pilgrimage." "But listen, gossip," said the egg-merchant to the peasant, "are you, then, stupid enough to believe such a thing as that? Don't you know what it means? The parson wants to spend a whole day alone with your wife in peace, so he has given you this job to do to get you out of the way."

"My word!" said the peasant. "How I'd like to know if that's true!"

"Come, then," said the gossip, "I'll tell you what to do. Get into my egg-basket and I will carry you home, and then you will see for yourself." So that was settled, and the gossip put the peasant into his egg-basket, and carried him home.

When they got to the house, hurrah! but all was going merrily there! The woman had already had nearly everything killed that was in the farmyard, and had made pancakes; and the parson was there, and had brought his fiddle with him. The gossip knocked at the door, and the woman asked who was there. "It is I, gossip," said the egg-merchant, "give me shelter this night; I have not sold my eggs at the market, so now I have to carry them home again, and they are so heavy that I shall never be able to do it, for it is dark already."

"Indeed, my friend," said the woman, "you come at a very inconvenient time for me, but as you are here it can't be helped; come in, and take a seat there on the bench by the stove." Then she placed the gossip and the basket which he carried on his back on the bench by the stove. The parson, however, and the woman were as merry as possible. At length the parson said, "Listen, my dear friend, you can sing beautifully; sing something to me." "Oh," said the woman, "I cannot sing now, in my young days indeed I could sing well enough, but that's all over now." "Come," said the parson once more, "do sing some little song."

Then the woman sang,

> "*I've sent my husband away from me*
> *To the Göckerli hill in Italy.*"

Thereupon the parson sang,

> "*I wish 'twas a year before he came back,*
> *I'd never ask him for the laurel-leaf sack.*
> *Hallelujah.*"

Then the gossip, who was in the background, began to sing (but I ought to tell you the peasant was called Hildebrand), so the gossip sang,

> "*What art thou doing, my Hildebrand dear,*
> *There on the bench by the stove so near?*
> *Hallelujah.*"

Then the peasant sang from his basket,

> "*All singing I ever shall hate from this day,*

"And here in this basket no longer I'll stay.
                              Hallelujah."

And he got out of the basket and drove the parson out of the house.

The Singing Bone

A CERTAIN COUNTRY was greatly troubled by a wild boar that attacked workers in the fields, killed men, and tore them to pieces with its terrible tusks. The King of the country had offered rich rewards to any one who would rid the land of this terror. But the beast was so huge and ferocious that no man could even be persuaded to enter the forest where the animal made its home.

At last the King made a proclamation that he would give his only daughter in marriage to any man who would bring the wild boar to him, dead or alive.

There lived two brothers in that country, the sons of a poor man, who gave notice of their readiness to enter on this perilous undertaking. The elder, who was clever and crafty, was influenced by pride; the younger, who was innocent and simple, offered himself from kindness of heart.

Thereupon the King advised that, as the best and safest way would be to take opposite directions in the wood, the elder was to go in the evening and the younger in the morning.

The younger had not gone far when a little fairy stepped up to him. He held in his hand a black spear, and said, "I will give you this spear because your heart is innocent and good. With this you can go out and discover the wild boar, and he shall not be able to harm you."

He thanked the little man, took the spear, placed it on his shoulder, and without delay went further into the forest. It was not long before he espied the animal coming toward him, and fiercely making ready to spring. But the youth stood still and held the spear firmly in front of him. In wild rage the fierce beast ran violently toward him, and was met by the spear, on the point of which he threw himself, and, as it pierced his heart, he fell dead.

Then the youngster took the dead monster on his shoulder and went to find his brother. As he approached the other side of the wood, where stood a large hall, he heard music, and found a number of people dancing, drinking wine, and making merry. His elder brother was among them, for he thought the wild boar would not run far away, and he wished to get up his courage for the evening by cheerful company and wine.

When he caught sight of his younger brother coming out of the forest laden with his booty, the most restless jealousy and malice rose in his heart. But he disguised his bitter feelings and spoke kindly to his brother, and said, "Come in and stay with us, dear brother, and rest awhile, and get up your strength by a cup of wine."

So the youth, not suspecting anything wrong, carried the dead boar into his brother's house, and told him of the little man he had met in the wood, who had given him the spear, and how he had killed the wild animal.

The elder brother persuaded him to stay and rest till the evening, and then they went out together in the twilight and walked by the river till it became quite dark. A little bridge lay across the river, over which they had to pass, and the elder brother let the young one go before him. When they arrived at the middle of the stream the wicked man gave his younger brother a blow from behind, and he fell down dead instantly.

But fearing he might not be quite dead, he threw the body over the bridge into the river, and through the clear waters saw it sink into the sand. After this wicked deed he ran home quickly, took the dead wild boar on his shoulders, and carried it to the King, with the pretense that he had killed the animal, and that therefore he could claim the Princess as his wife, according to the King's promise.

But these dark deeds are not often concealed, for something happens to bring them to light. Not many years after, a herdsman, passing over the bridge with his flock, saw beneath him in the sand a little bone as white as snow, and thought that it would make a very nice mouthpiece for his horn.

As soon as the flock passed over the bridge, he waded into the middle of the stream—for the water was very shallow—took up the bone, and carried it home to make a mouthpiece for his horn.

But the first time he blew the horn after the bone was in it, it filled the herdsman with wonder and amazement; for it began to sing of itself, and these were the words it sang.

> *"Ah! dear shepherd, you are blowing your horn*
> *With one of my bones, which night and morn*

Lie still unburied, beneath the wave
Where I was thrown in a sandy grave.
I killed the wild boar, and my brother slew me,
And gained the Princess by pretending 'twas he."

"What a wonderful horn," said the shepherd, "that can sing of itself! I must certainly take it to my lord, the King."

As soon as the horn was brought before the King and blown by the shepherd, it at once began to sing the same song and the same words.

The King was at first surprised, but his suspicion being aroused, he ordered that the sand under the bridge should be examined immediately, and then the entire skeleton of the murdered man was discovered, and the whole wicked deed came to light.

The wicked brother could not deny the deed. He was therefore ordered to be tied in a sack and drowned, while the remains of his murdered brother were carefully carried to the churchyard, and laid to rest in a beautiful grave.

Maid Maleen

THERE WAS once a King who had a son who asked in marriage the daughter of a mighty King; she was called Maid Maleen, and was very beautiful. As her father wished to give her to another, the Prince was rejected; but as they both loved each other with all their hearts, they would not give each other up, and Maid Maleen said to her father, "I can and will take no other for my husband."

Then the King flew into a passion, and ordered a dark tower to be built, into which no ray of sunlight or moonlight should enter. When it was finished, he said, "Therein shalt thou be imprisoned for seven years, and then I will come and see if thy perverse spirit is broken." Meat and drink for the seven years were carried into the tower, and then she and her waiting-woman were led into it and walled up, and thus cut off from the sky and from the earth. There they sat in the darkness, and knew not when day or night began. The King's son often went round and round the tower, and called their names, but no sound from without pierced through the thick walls. What else could they do but lament and complain?

Meanwhile the time passed, and by the diminution of the food and drink they knew that the seven years were coming to an end. They thought the moment of their deliverance was come; but no stroke of the hammer was heard, no stone fell out of the wall, and it seemed to Maid Maleen that her father had forgotten her. As they only had food for a short time longer, and saw a miserable death awaiting them, Maid Maleen said, "We must try our last chance, and see if we can break through the wall." She took the breadknife, and picked and bored at the mortar of a stone, and when she was tired, the waiting-maid took her turn. With great labor they succeeded in getting out one stone, and then a second, and third, and when three days were over the first ray of light fell on their darkness, and at last the opening was so large that they could look out.

The sky was blue, and a fresh breeze played on their faces; but how melancholy everything looked all around! Her father's castle lay in ruins, the town and the villages were, so far as could be seen, destroyed by fire, the fields far and wide laid to waste, and no human being was visible. When the opening in the wall was large enough for them to slip through, the waiting-maid sprang down first, and then Maid Maleen followed. But where were they to go? The enemy had ravaged the whole kingdom, driven away the King, and slain all the inhabitants. They wandered forth to seek another country, but nowhere did they find a shelter, or a human being to give them a mouthful of bread, and their need was so great that they were forced to appease their hunger with nettles. When, after long journeying, they came into another country, they tried to get work everywhere; but wherever they knocked they were turned away, and no one would have pity on them. At last they arrived in a large city and went to the royal palace. There also they were ordered to go away, but at last the cook said that they might stay in the kitchen and be scullions.

The son of the King in whose kingdom they were, was, however, the very man who had been betrothed to Maid Maleen. His father had chosen another bride for him, whose face was as ugly as her heart was wicked. The wedding was fixed, and the maiden had already arrived; because of her great ugliness, however, she shut herself in her room, and allowed no one to see her, and Maid Maleen had to take her her meals from the kitchen. When the day came for the bride and the bridegroom to go to church, she was ashamed of her ugliness, and afraid that if she showed herself in the streets, she would be mocked and laughed at by the people.

Then said she to Maid Maleen, "A great piece of luck has befallen thee. I have sprained my foot, and cannot well walk through the streets; thou shalt put on my wedding-clothes and take my place; a greater honor than that thou canst not have!" Maid Maleen, however, refused it, and said, "I wish for no honor which is not suitable for me." It was in vain, too, that the bride offered her gold. At last she said angrily, "If thou dost not obey me, it shall cost thee thy life. I have but to speak the word, and thy head will lie at thy feet." Then she was forced to obey, and put on the bride's magnificent clothes and all her jewels. When she entered the royal hall, every one was amazed at her great beauty, and the King said to his son, "This is the bride whom I have chosen for thee, and whom thou must lead to church." The bridegroom was astonished, and thought, "She is like my Maid Maleen, and I should believe that it was she herself, but she has long been shut up in the tower, or dead." He took her by the hand and led her to church. On the way was a nettle-plant, and she said,

> *"Oh, nettle-plant,*
> *Little nettle-plant,*
> *What dost thou here alone?*
> *I have known the time*
> *When I ate thee unboiled,*
> *When I ate thee unroasted."*

"What art thou saying?" asked the King's son. "Nothing," she replied, "I was only thinking of Maid Maleen." He was surprised that she knew about her, but kept silence. When they came to the foot-plank into the churchyard, she said,

> *"Foot-bridge, do not break,*
> *I am not the true bride."*

"What art thou saying there?" asked the King's son. "Nothing," she replied, "I was only thinking of Maid Maleen." "Dost thou know Maid Maleen?" "No," she answered, "how should I know her; I have only heard of her." When they came to the church-door, she said once more,

> *"Church-door, break not,*
> *I am not the true bride."*

"What art thou saying there?" asked he. "Ah," she answered, "I was only thinking of Maid Maleen." Then he took out a precious chain, put it round her neck, and fastened the clasp. Thereupon they entered the church, and the priest joined their hands together before the alter, and married them. He led her home, but she did not speak a single word the whole way. When they got back to the royal palace, she hurried into the bride's chamber, put off the magnificent clothes and the jewels, dressed herself in her gray gown, and kept nothing but the jewel on her neck, which she had received from the bridegroom.

When the night came, and the bride was to be led into the Prince's apartment, she let her veil fall over her face, that he might not observe the deception. As soon as every one had gone away, he said to her, "What didst thou say to the nettle-plant which was growing by the wayside?" "To which nettle-plant?" asked she; "I don't talk to nettle-plants." "If thou didst not do it, then thou art not the true bride," said he. So she bethought herself, and said,

> *"I must go out unto my maid,*
> *Who keeps my thoughts for me."*

She went out and sought Maid Maleen. "Girl, what hast thou been saying to the nettle?" "I said nothing but,

> *'Oh, nettle-plant,*
> *Little nettle-plant,*
> *What dost thou here alone?*
> *I have known the time*
> *When I ate thee unboiled,*
> *When I ate thee unroasted.'"*

The bride ran back into the chamber, and said, "I know now what I said to the nettle," and she repeated the words which she had just heard. "But what didst thou say to the foot-bridge when we went over it?" asked the King's son. "To the foot-bridge?" she answered; "I don't talk to foot-bridges." "Then thou art not the true bride." She again said,

> *"I must go out unto my maid,*
> *Who keeps my thoughts for me,"*

and ran out and found Maid Maleen, "Girl, what didst thou say to the foot-bridge?" "I said nothing but,

> *'Foot-bridge, do not break,*
> *I am not the true bride.'"*

"That costs thee thy life!" cried the bride, but she hurried into the room, and said, "I know now what I said to the foot-bridge," and she repeated the words. "But what didst thou say to the church-door?" "To the church-door?" she replied; "I don't talk to church-doors." "Then thou art not the true bride."

She went out and found Maid Maleen, and said, "Girl, what didst thou say to the church-door?" "I said nothing but,

*'Church-door, break not,
I am not the true bride.'* "

"That will break thy neck for thee!" cried the bride, and flew into a terrible passion, but she hastened back into the room, and said, "I know now what I said to the church-door," and she repeated the words. "But where hast thou the jewel which I gave thee at the church-door?" "What jewel?" she answered; "thou didst not give me any jewel." "I myself put it round thy neck, and I myself fastened it; if thou dost not know that, thou art not the true bride." He drew the veil from her face, and when he saw her immeasurable ugliness, he sprang back terrified, and said, "How comest thou here? Who art thou?" "I am thy betrothed bride, but because I feared lest the people should mock me when they saw me out of doors, I commanded the scullery-maid to dress herself in my clothes, and to go to church instead of me." "Where is the girl?" said he; "I want to see her, go and bring her here." She went out and told the servants that the scullery-maid was an impostor, and that they must take her out into the court-yard and strike off her head. The servants laid hold of Maid Maleen and wanted to drag her out, but she screamed so loudly for help, that the King's son heard her voice, hurried out of his chamber and ordered them to set the maiden free instantly.

Lights were brought, and then he saw on her neck the gold chain which he had given her at the church-door. "Thou art the true bride," said he, "who went with me to church; come with me now to my room." When they were both alone, he said, "On the way to the church thou didst name Maid Maleen, who was my betrothed bride; if I could believe it possible, I should think she was standing before me—thou art like her in every respect." She answered, "I am Maid Maleen, who for thy sake was imprisoned seven years in the darkness, who suffered hunger and thirst, and has lived so long in want and poverty. Today, however, the sun is shining on me once more. I was married to thee in the church, and I am thy lawful wife." Then they kissed each other, and were happy all the days of their lives. The false bride was rewarded for what she had done by having her head cut off.

The tower in which Maid Maleen had been imprisoned remained standing for a long time, and when the children passed by it they sang,

"Kling, klang, gloria.
Who sits within this tower?
A King's daughter, she sits within,
A sight of her I cannot win,
The wall it will not break,
The stone cannot be pierced.
Little Hans, with your coat so gay,
Follow me, follow me, fast as you may."

The Goose-Girl

THERE WAS once upon a time an old Queen whose husband had been dead for many years, and she had a beautiful daughter. When the Princess grew up she was betrothed to a Prince who lived at a great distance. When the time came for her to be married, and she had to journey forth into the distant kingdom, the aged Queen packed up for her many costly vessels of silver and gold, and trinkets also of gold and silver, and cups and jewels; in short, everything which appertained to a royal dowry, for she loved her child with all her heart. She likewise sent her maid in waiting, who was to ride with her, and hand her over to the bridegroom, and each had a horse for the journey, but the horse of the King's daughter was called Falada, and could speak. So when the hour of parting had come, the aged mother went into her bed-room, took a small knife and cut her finger with it until it bled, then she held a white handkerchief to it into which she let three drops of blood fall, gave it to her daughter and said, "Dear child, preserve this carefully; it will be of service to you on your way."

So they took a sorrowful leave of each other; the Princess put the piece of cloth in her bosom, mounted her horse, and then went away to her bridegroom. After she had ridden for a while she felt a burning thirst, and said to her waiting-maid, "Dismount, and take my cup which you have brought for me, and get me some water from the stream, for I should like to drink." "If you are thirsty," said the waiting-maid, "get off your horse yourself, and lie down and drink out of the water, I don't choose to be your servant." So in her great thirst the Princess alighted, bent down over the water in the stream and drank, and was not allowed to drink out of the golden cup. Then she said, "Ah, Heaven!" And the three drops of blood answered, "If your mother knew this, her heart would break." But the King's daughter was humble, said nothing, and mounted her horse again.

She rode some miles further, but the day was warm, the sun scorched her, and she was thirsty once more, and when they came to a stream of water, she again cried to her waiting-maid, "Dismount, and give me some water in my golden cup," for she had long ago forgotten the girl's ill words. But the waiting-maid said still more haughtily, "If you wish to drink, drink as you can, I don't choose to be your maid." Then in her great thirst the King's daughter alighted, bent over the flowing stream, wept and said, "Ah, Heaven!" And the drops of blood again replied, "If your mother knew this, her heart would break." And as she was thus drinking and leaning right over the stream, the handkerchief with the three drops of blood fell out of her bosom, and floated away with the water without her observing it, so great was her trouble.

The waiting-maid, however, had seen it, and she rejoiced to think that she had now power over the bride, for since the Princess had lost the drops of blood, she had become weak and powerless. So now when she wanted to mount her horse again, the one that was called Falada, the waiting-maid said, "Falada is more suitable for me, and my nag will do for you," and the Princess had to be content with that. Then the waiting-maid, with many hard words, bade the Princess exchange her royal apparel for her own shabby clothes; and at length she was compelled to swear by the clear sky above her, that she would not say one word of this to any one at the royal court, and if she had not taken this oath she would have been killed on the spot. But Falada saw all this, and observed it well.

The waiting-maid now mounted Falada, and the true bride the bad horse, and thus they traveled onwards, until at length they entered the royal palace. There were great rejoicings over her arrival, and the Prince sprang forward to meet her, lifted the waiting-maid from her horse, and thought she was his consort. She was conducted upstairs, but the real Princess was left standing below. Then the old King looked out of the window and saw her standing in the courtyard, and how dainty and delicate and beautiful she was, and instantly went to the royal apartment, and asked the bride about the girl she had with her who was standing down below in the courtyard, and who she was. "I picked her up on my way for a companion; give the girl something to work at, that she may not stand idle."

But the old King had no work for her, and knew of none, so he said, "I have a little boy who tends the geese, she may help him." The boy was called Conrad, and the true bride had to help him tend the geese. Soon afterwards the false bride said to the young King, "Dearest husband, I beg you to do me a favor." He answered, "I will do so most willingly." "Then send for the knacker, and have the head of the horse on which I rode here cut off, for it vexed me on the way." In reality, she was afraid that the horse might tell how she had behaved to the King's daughter. Then she succeeded in making the King promise that it should be done, and the faithful Falada was to die.

This came to the ears of the real Princess, and she secretly promised to pay the knacker a piece of gold if he would perform a small service for her. There was a great dark-looking gateway in the town, through which morning and evening she had to pass with the geese; would he be so good as to nail up Falada's head on it, so that she might see him again, more than once. The knacker's man promised to do that, and cut off the head, and nailed it fast beneath the dark gateway.

Early in the morning, when she and Conrad drove out their flock beneath this gateway, she said in passing,

> *"Alas, Falada, hanging there!"*

Then the head answered,

> *"Alas, young Queen, how ill you fare!*
> *If this your tender mother knew,*
> *Her heart would surely break in two."*

Then they went still further out of the town, and drove their geese into the country. And when they had come to the meadow, she sat down and unbound her hair which was like pure gold, and Conrad saw it and delighted in its brightness, and wanted to pluck out a few hairs. Then she said,

> *"Blow, blow, thou gentle wind, I say,*
> *Blow Conrad's little hat away,*
> *And make him chase it here and there,*
> *Until I have braided all my hair,*
> *And bound it up again."*

And there came such a violent wind that it blew Conrad's hat far away across country, and he was forced to run after it. When he came back she had finished combing her hair and was putting it up again, and he could not get any of it. Then Conrad was angry, and would not speak to her, and thus they watched the geese until the evening, and then they went home.

Next day when they were driving the geese out through the dark gateway, the maiden said,

> *"Alas, Falada, hanging there!"*

Falada answered,

> *"Alas, young Queen, how ill you fare!*
> *If this your tender mother knew,*
> *Her heart would surely break in two."*

And she sat down again in the field and began to comb out her hair, and Conrad ran and tried to clutch it, so she said in haste,

> *"Blow, blow, thou gentle wind, I say,*
> *Blow Conrad's little hat away,*
> *And make him chase it here and there,*
> *Until I have braided all my hair,*
> *And bound it up again."*

Then the wind blew, and blew his little hat off his head and far away, and Conrad was forced to run after it, and when he came back, her hair had been put up a long time, and he could get none of it, and so they looked after their geese till evening came.

But in the evening after they had got home, Conrad went to the old King, and said, "I won't tend the geese with that girl any longer!" "Why not?" inquired the aged King. "Oh, because she vexes me the whole day long." Then the aged King commanded him to relate what it was that she did to him. And Conrad said, "In the morning when we pass beneath the dark gateway with the flock, there is a sorry horse's head on the wall, and she says to it,

> *'Alas, Falada, hanging there!'*

"And the head replies,

> *'Alas, young Queen, how ill you fare!*
> *If this your tender mother knew,*
> *Her heart would surely break in two.'"*

And Conrad went on to relate what happened on the goose pasture, and how when there he had to chase his hat.

The aged King commanded him to drive his flock out again next day, and as soon as morning came, he placed himself behind the dark gateway, and heard how the maiden spoke to the head of Falada, and then he too went into the country, and hid himself in the thicket in the meadow. There he soon saw with his own eyes the goose-girl and the goose-boy bringing their flock, and how after a while she sat down and unplaited her hair, which shone with radiance. And soon she said,

> *"Blow, blow, thou gentle wind, I say,*
> *Blow Conrad's little hat away,*
> *And make him chase it here and there,*
> *Until I have braided all my hair,*
> *And bound it up again."*

Then came a blast of wind and carried off Conrad's hat, so that he had to run far away, while the maiden quietly went on combing and plaiting her hair, all of which the King observed. Then, quite unseen, he went away, and when the goose-girl came home in the evening, he called her aside, and asked why she did all these things. "I may not tell you that, and I dare not lament my sorrows to any human being, for I have sworn not to do so by the heaven which is above me; if I had not done that, I should have lost my life." He urged her and left her no peace, but he could draw nothing from her. Then said he, "If you will not tell me anything, tell your sorrows to the iron-stove there," and he went away.

Then she crept into the iron-stove, and began to weep and lament, and emptied her whole heart, and said, "Here am I deserted by the whole world, and yet I am a King's daughter, and a false waiting-maid has by force brought me to such a pass that I have been compelled to put off my royal apparel, and she has taken my place with my bridegroom, and I have to perform menial service as a goose-girl. If my mother did but know that, her heart would break."

The aged King, however, was standing outside by the pipe of the stove, and was listening to what she said, and heard it. Then he came back again, and bade her come out of the stove. And royal garments were placed on her, and it was marvelous how beautiful she was! The aged King summoned his son, and revealed to him that he had got the false bride who was only a waiting-maid, but that the true one was standing there, as the sometime goose-girl. The young King rejoiced with all his heart when he saw her beauty and youth, and a great feast was made ready to which all the people and all good friends were invited.

At the head of the table sat the bridegroom with the King's daughter at one side of him, and the waiting-maid on the other, but the waiting-maid was blinded, and did not recognize the Princess in her dazzling array. When they had eaten and drunk, and were merry, the aged King asked the waiting-maid as a riddle, what a person deserved who had behaved in such and such a way to her master, and at the same time related the whole story, and asked what sentence such an one merited.

Then the false bride said, "She deserves no better fate than to be stripped entirely naked, and put in a barrel which is studded inside with pointed nails, and two white horses should be harnessed to it, which will drag her along through one street after another, till she is dead." "It is you," said the aged King, "and you have pronounced your own sentence, and thus shall it be done unto you." When the sentence had been carried out, the young King married his true bride, and both of them reigned over their kingdom in peace and happiness.

The Skilful Huntsman

THERE ONCE was a young fellow who had learnt the trade of locksmith, and told his father he would now go out into the world and seek his fortune. "Very well," said his father, "I am quite content with that," and gave him some money for his journey. So he traveled about and looked for work. After a time he resolved not to follow the trade of locksmith any more, for he no longer liked it, but he took a fancy for hunting. Then there met him in his rambles a huntsman dressed in green, who asked whence he came and whither he was going. The youth said he was a locksmith's apprentice, but that the trade no longer pleased him, and he had a liking for huntsmanship—would he teach it to him? "Oh, yes," said the huntsman, "if thou wilt go with me."

The young fellow went with him, bound himself to him for some years, and learnt the art of hunting. After this he wished to try his luck elsewhere, and the huntsman gave him nothing in the way of payment but an air-gun, which had, however, this property, that it hit its mark without fail whenever he shot with it. Then he set out and found himself in a very large forest, which he could not get to the end of in one day. When evening came he seated himself in a high tree in order to escape from the wild beasts.

Towards midnight, it seemed to him as if a tiny little light glimmered in the distance. He looked down through the branches towards it, and kept well in his mind where it was. But in the first place, he took off his hat and threw it down in the direction of the light, so that he might go to the hat as a mark when he had descended. Then he got down and went to his hat, put it on again and went straight forwards. The farther he went, the larger the light grew, and when he got close to it he saw that it was an enormous fire, and that three giants were sitting by it, who had an ox on the spit, and were roasting it. Presently one of them said, "I must just taste if the meat will soon be fit to eat," and pulled a piece off, and was about to put it in his mouth when the huntsman shot it out of his hand. "Well, really," said the giant, "if the wind has not blown the bit out of my hand!" and helped himself to another. But when he was just about to bite into it, the huntsman again shot it away from him. On this the giant gave the one who was sitting next him a box on the ear, and cried angrily, "Why art thou snatching my piece away from me?" "I have not snatched it away," said the other, "a sharpshooter must have shot it away from thee." The giant took another piece, but could not, however, keep it in his hand, for the huntsman shot it out. Then the giant said, "That must be a good shot to shoot the bit out of one's very mouth, such an one would be useful to us." And he cried aloud, "Come here, thou sharpshooter, seat thyself at the fire beside us and eat thy fill, we will not hurt thee; but if thou wilt not come, and we have to bring thee by force, thou art a lost man!"

At this invitation the youth went up to them and told them he was a skilled huntsman, and that whatever he aimed at with his gun, he was certain to hit. Then they said if he would go with them he should be well treated, and they told him that outside the forest there was a great lake, behind which stood a tower, and in the tower was imprisoned a lovely Princess, whom they wished very much to carry off. "Yes," said he, "I will soon get her for you." Then they added, "But there is still something else; there is a tiny little dog, which begins to bark directly any one goes near, and as soon as it barks every one in the royal palace wakens up, and for this reason we cannot get there; canst thou undertake to shoot it dead?" "Yes," said he, "that will be a little bit of fun for me." After this he got into a boat and rowed over the lake, and as soon as he landed, the little dog came running out, and was about to bark, but the huntsman took his air-gun and shot it dead. When the giants saw that, they rejoiced, and thought they already had the King's daughter safe, but the huntsman wished first to see how matters stood, and told them that they must stay outside until he called them. Then he went into the castle, and all was perfectly quiet within, and every one was asleep.

When he opened the door of the first room, a sword was hanging on the wall which was made of pure silver, and there was a golden star on it, and the name of the King, and on a table near it lay a sealed letter which he broke open, and inside it was written that whosoever had the sword could kill everything which opposed him. So he took the sword from the wall, hung it at his side and went onwards; then he entered the room where the King's daughter was lying sleeping, and she was so beautiful that he stood still and, holding his breath, looked at her. He thought to himself, "How can I give an innocent maiden into the power of the wild giants, who have evil in their minds?" He looked about further, and under the bed stood a pair of slippers; on the right one was her father's name with a star, and on the left her own name with a star. She wore also a great neck-kerchief of silk embroidered with gold, and on the right side was her father's name, and on the left her own, all in golden letters. Then the huntsman took a pair of scissors and cut the right corner off, and put it in his knapsack, and then he also took the right slipper with the King's name, and thrust that in.

The maiden still lay sleeping, and she was quite sewn into her night-dress, and he cut a morsel from this also, and thrust it in with the rest, but he did all without touching her. Then he went forth and left her lying asleep undisturbed, and when he came to the gate again, the giants were still standing outside waiting for him, and expecting that he was bringing the Princess. But he cried to them that they were to come in, for the maiden was already in their power, that he could not open the gate to them, but there was a hole through which they must creep. Then the first approached, and the huntsman wound the giant's hair round his hand, pulled the head in, and cut it off at one stroke with his sword, and then drew the rest of him in. He called to the second and cut his head off likewise, and then he killed the third also, and he was well pleased that he had freed the beautiful maiden from her enemies, and he cut out their tongues and put them in his knapsack. Then thought he, "I will go home to my father and let him see what I have already done, and afterwards I will travel about the world; the luck which God is pleased to grant me will easily find me."

When the King in the castle awoke, he saw the three giants lying there dead. So he went into the sleeping-room of his daughter, awoke her, and asked who could have killed the giants. Then said she, "Dear father, I know not, I have been asleep." But when she arose and would have put on her slippers, the right one was gone, and when she looked at her neck-kerchief it was cut, and the right corner was missing, and when she looked at her night-dress a piece was cut out of it. The King summoned his whole court together, soldiers and every one else who was there, and asked who had set his daughter at liberty, and killed the giants.

Now it happened that he had a captain, who was one-eyed and a hideous man, and he said that he had done it. Then the old King said that as he had accomplished this, he should marry his daughter. But the maiden said, "Rather than marry him, dear father, I will go away into the world as far as my legs can carry me." The King said that if she would not marry him she should take off her royal garments and wear peasant's clothing, and go forth, and that she should go to a potter, and begin a trade in earthen vessels. So she put off her royal apparel, and went to a potter and borrowed crockery enough for a stall, and she promised him also that if she had sold it by the evening, she would pay for it. Then the King said she was to seat herself in a corner with it and sell it, and he arranged with some peasants to drive over it with their carts, so that everything should be broken into a thousand pieces. When therefore the King's daughter had placed her stall in the street, by came the carts, and broke all she had into tiny fragments. She began to weep and said, "Alas, how shall I ever pay for the pots now?" The King had, however, wished by this to force her to marry the captain; but instead of that, she again went to the potter, and asked him if he would lend to her once more. He said, "No," she must first pay for the things she had already had.

Then she went to her father and cried and lamented, and said she would go forth into the world. Then said he, "I will have a little hut built for thee in the forest outside, and in it thou shalt stay all thy life long and cook for every one, but thou shalt take no money for it." When the hut was ready, a sign was hung on the door whereon was written, "Today given, tomorrow sold." There she remained a long time, and it was rumored about the world that a maiden was there who cooked without asking for payment, and that this was set forth on a sign outside her door. The huntsman heard it likewise, and thought to himself, "That would suit thee. Thou art poor, and hast no money." So he took his air-gun and his knapsack, wherein all the things which he had formerly carried away with him from the castle as tokens of his truthfulness were still lying, and went into the forest, and found the hut with the sign, "Today given, tomorrow sold."

He had put on the sword with which he had cut off the heads of the three giants, and thus entered the hut, and ordered something to eat to be given to him. He was charmed with the beautiful maiden, who was indeed as lovely as any picture. She asked him whence he came and whither he was going, and he said, "I am roaming about the world." Then she asked him where he had got the sword, for that truly her father's name was on it. He asked her if she were the King's daughter. "Yes," answered she. "With this sword," said he, "did I cut off the heads of three giants." And he took their tongues out of his knapsack in proof. Then he also showed her the slipper, and the corner of the neck-kerchief, and the bit of the night-dress. Hereupon she was overjoyed, and said that he was the one who had delivered her.

They went together to the old King, and fetched him to the hut, and she led him into her room, and told him that the huntsman was the man who had really set her free from the giants. And when the aged King saw all the proofs of this, he could no longer doubt, and said that he was very glad he knew how everything had happened, and that the huntsman should have her to wife, on which the maiden was glad at heart. Then she dressed the huntsman as if he were a foreign lord, and the King ordered a feast to be prepared. When they went to table, the captain sat on the left side of the King's daughter, but the huntsman was on the right, and the captain thought he was a foreign lord who had come on a visit.

When they had eaten and drunk, the old King said to the captain that he would set before him something which he must guess. "Supposing any one said that he had killed the three giants and he were asked where the giants' tongues were, and he were forced to go and look, and there were none in their heads, how could that happen?" The captain said, "Then they cannot have had any." "Not so," said the King. "Every animal has a tongue," and then he likewise asked what any one would deserve who made such an answer. The captain replied, "He ought to be torn in pieces." Then the King said he had pronounced his own sentence, and the captain was put in prison and then torn in four pieces; but the King's daughter was married to the huntsman. After this he brought his father and mother, and they lived with their son in happiness, and after the death of the old King he received the kingdom.

The Princess in Disguise

A KING once had a wife with golden hair who was so beautiful that none on earth could be found equal to her. It happened that she fell ill, and as soon as she knew she must die, she sent for the King and said to him, "After my death I know you will marry another wife; but you must promise me that, however beautiful she may be, if she is not as beautiful as I am and has not golden hair like mine you will not marry her."

The King had no sooner given his promise than she closed her eyes and died.

For a long time he refused to be comforted, and thought it was impossible he could ever take another wife. At length his counselors came to him, and said, "A King should not remain unmarried; we ought to have a Queen."

So he at last consented, and then messengers were sent far and wide to find a bride whose beauty should equal that of the dead Queen. But none was to be found in the whole world; for even when equally beautiful they had not golden hair. So the messengers returned without obtaining what they sought.

Now, the King had a daughter who was quite as beautiful as her dead mother, and had also golden hair. She had all this while been growing up, and very soon the King noticed how exactly she resembled her dead mother. So he sent for his counselors, and said to them, "I will marry my daughter; she is the image of my dead wife, and no other bride can be found to enable me to keep my promise to her."

When the counselors heard this, they were dreadfully shocked, and said, "It is forbidden for a father to marry his daughter; nothing but evil could spring from such a sin, and the kingdom will be ruined."

When the King's daughter heard of her father's proposition she was greatly alarmed, the more so as she saw how resolved he was to carry out his intention. She hoped, however, to be able to save him and herself from such ruin and disgrace, so she said to him, "Before I consent to your wish I shall require three things—a dress as golden as the sun, another as silvery as the moon, and a third as glittering as the stars; and besides this, I shall require a mantle made of a thousand skins of rough fur sewn together, and every animal in the kingdom must give a piece of his skin toward it."

"Ah!" she thought, "I have asked for impossibilities, and I hope I shall be able to make my father give up his wicked intentions."

The King, however, was not to be diverted from his purpose. All the most skilful young women in the kingdom were employed to weave the three dresses, one to be as golden as the sun, another as silvery as the moon, and the third as glittering as the stars. He sent hunters into the forest to kill the wild animals and bring home their skins, of which the mantle was to be made; and at last when all was finished he brought them and laid them before her, and then said, "Tomorrow our marriage shall take place."

Then the King's daughter saw that there was no hope of changing her father's heart, so she determined to run away from the castle.

In the night, when every one slept, she rose and took from her jewel-case a gold ring, a gold spinning-wheel, and a golden hook. The three dresses of the sun, moon, and stars she folded in so small a parcel that they were placed in a walnut-shell; then she put on the fur mantle, stained her face and hands black with walnut-juice, and committing herself to the care of Heaven, she left her home.

After traveling the whole night she came at last to a large forest, and feeling very tired she crept into a hollow tree and went to sleep. The sun rose, but she still slept on, and did not awake till nearly noon.

It happened on this very day that the King to whom the wood belonged was hunting in the forest, and when his hounds came to the tree they sniffed about, and ran round and round the tree barking loudly. The King called to his hunters, and said, "Just go and see what wild animal the dogs are barking at."

They obeyed, and quickly returning told the King that in the hollow tree was a most beautiful creature, such as they had never seen before, that the skin was covered with a thousand different sorts of fur, and that it was fast asleep.

"Then," said the King, "go and see if you can capture it alive. Then bind it on the wagon and bring it home."

While the hunters were binding the maiden she awoke, and full of terror cried out to them, "I am only a poor child, forsaken by my father and mother; take pity on me, and take me with you!" "Well," they replied, "you may be useful to the cook, little Roughskin. Come with us; you can at least sweep up the ashes."

So they seated her on the wagon and took her home to the King's castle. They showed her a little stable under the steps, where no daylight ever came, and said, "Roughskin, here you can live and sleep." So the King's daughter was sent into the kitchen to fetch the wood, draw the water, stir the fire, pluck the fowls, look after the vegetables, sweep the ashes, and do all the hard work.

Poor Roughskin, as they called her, lived for a long time most miserably, and the beautiful King's daughter knew not when it would end or how. It happened, however, after a time that a festival was to take place in the castle, so she said to the cook, "May I go out for a little while to see the company arrive? I will stand outside the door." "Yes, you may go," he replied, "but in half an hour I shall want you to sweep up the ashes and put the kitchen in order."

Then she took her little oil-lamp, went into the stable, threw off the fur coat, washed the nut-stains from her face and hands, so that her full beauty appeared before the day. After this she opened the nutshell and took out the dress that was golden as the sun, and put it on. As soon as she was quite dressed she went out and presented herself at the entrance of the castle as a visitor. No one recognized her as Roughskin; they thought she was a King's daughter, and sent and told the King of her arrival. He went to receive her, offered her his hand, and while they danced together he thought in his heart, "My eyes have never seen any maiden before so beautiful as this."

As soon as the dance was over she bowed to the King, and before he could look round she had vanished, no one knew where. The sentinel at the castle gate was called and questioned, but he had not seen any one pass.

But she had run to her stable, quickly removed her dress, stained her face and hands, put on her fur coat, and was again Roughskin. When she entered the kitchen and began to do her work and sweep up the ashes, the cook said, "Leave that alone till tomorrow; I want you to cook some soup for the King. I will also taste a little when it is ready. But do not let one of your hairs fall in, or you will get nothing to eat in future from me."

Then the cook went out, and Roughskin made the King's soup as nicely as she could, and cut bread for it, and when it was ready she fetched from her little stable her gold ring and laid it in the dish in which the soup was prepared.

After the King had left the ball-room he called for the soup, and while eating it thought he had never tasted better soup in his life. But when the dish was nearly empty he saw to his surprise a gold ring lying at the bottom, and could not imagine how it came there. Then he ordered the cook to come to him, and he was in a terrible fright when he heard the order. "You must certainly have let a hair fall into the soup; if you have, I shall thrash you!" he said.

As soon as he appeared the King said, "Who cooked this soup?" "I cooked it," he replied. "That is not true," said the King. "This soup is made quite differently and much better than you ever made it."

Then the cook was obliged to confess that Roughskin had made the soup. "Go and send her to me," said the King.

As soon as she appeared the King said to her, "Who art thou, maiden?" She replied, "I am a poor child, without father or mother." He asked again, "Why are you in my castle?" "Because I am trying to earn my bread by helping the cook," she replied. "How came this ring in the soup?" he said again. "I know nothing about the ring!" she replied.

When the King found he could learn nothing from Roughskin, he sent her away. A little time after this there was another festival, and Roughskin had again permission from the cook to go and see the visitors. "But," he added, "come back in half an hour and cook for the King the soup that he is so fond of."

She promised to return, and ran quickly into her little stable, washed off the stains, and took out of the nutshell her dress, silvery as the moon, and put it on. Then she appeared at the castle like a King's daughter, and the King came to receive her with great pleasure; he was so glad to see her again, and while the dancing continued the King kept her as his partner. When the ball ended she disappeared so quickly that the King could not imagine what had become of her. But she had rushed down to her stable, made herself again the rough little creature that was called Roughskin, and went into the kitchen to cook the soup.

While the cook was upstairs she fetched the golden spinning-wheel and dropped it into the soup as soon as it was ready. The King again ate it with great relish; it was as good as before, and when he sent for the cook and asked who made it, he was obliged to own that it was Roughskin. She was also ordered to appear before the King, but he could get nothing out of her, excepting that she was a poor child, and knew nothing of the golden spinning-wheel.

At the King's third festival everything happened as before. But the cook said, "I will let you go and see the dancing-room this time, Roughskin; but I believe you are a witch, for although the soup is good, and the King says it is better than I can make it, there is always something dropped into it which I cannot understand." Roughskin did not stop to listen; she ran quickly to her little stable, washed off the nut-stains, and this time dressed herself in the dress that glittered like the stars. When the King came as before to receive her in the hall, he thought he had never seen such a beautiful woman in his life. While they were dancing he contrived, without being noticed by the maiden, to slip a gold ring on her finger, and he had given orders that the dancing should continue longer than usual. When it ended, he wanted to hold her hand still, but she pulled it away, and sprang so quickly among the people that she vanished from his eyes.

She ran out of breath to her stable under the steps, for she knew that she had remained longer away than half an hour, and there was not time to take off her dress, so she threw on her fur cloak over it, and in her haste she did not make her face black enough, nor hide her golden hair properly; her hands also remained white. However, when she entered the kitchen, the cook was still away, so she prepared the King's soup, and dropped into it the golden hook.

The King, when he found another trinket in his soup, sent immediately for Roughskin, and as she entered the room he saw the ring on her white finger which he had placed there. Instantly he seized her hand and held her fast, but in her struggles to get free the fur mantle opened and the star-glittering dress was plainly seen. The King caught the mantle and tore it off, and as he did so her golden hair fell over her shoulders, and she stood before him in her full splendor, and felt that she could no longer conceal who she was. Then she wiped the soot and stains from her face, and was beautiful to the eyes of the King as any woman upon earth.

"You shall be my dear bride," said the King, "and we will never be parted again, although I know not who you are."

Then she told him her past history, and all that had happened to her, and he found that she was, as he thought, a King's daughter. Soon after the marriage was celebrated, and they lived happily till their death.

Cinderella

THERE WAS once a rich man whose wife lay sick, and when she felt her end drawing near she called to her only daughter to come near her bed, and said,

"Dear child, be good and pious, and God will always take care of you, and I will look down upon you from heaven, and will be with you."

And then she closed her eyes and died. The maiden went every day to her mother's grave and wept, and was always pious and good. When the winter came the snow covered the grave with a white covering, and when the sun came in the early spring and melted it away, the man took to himself another wife.

The new wife brought two daughters home with her, and they were beautiful and fair in appearance, but at heart were black and ugly. And then began very evil times for the poor step-daughter.

"Is the stupid creature to sit in the same room with us?" said they; "those who eat food must earn it. She is nothing but a kitchen-maid!"

They took away her pretty dresses, and put on her an old gray kirtle, and gave her wooden shoes to wear.

"Just look now at the proud princess, how she is decked out!" cried they laughing, and then they sent her into the kitchen. There she was obliged to do heavy work from morning to night, get up early in the morning, draw water, make the fires, cook, and wash. Besides that, the sisters did their utmost to torment her—mocking her, and strewing peas and lentils among the ashes, and setting her to pick them up. In the evenings, when she was quite tired out with her hard day's work, she had no bed to lie on, but was obliged to rest on the hearth among the cinders. And because she always looked dusty and dirty, as if she had slept in the cinders, they named her Cinderella.

It happened one day that the father went to the fair, and he asked his two step-daughters what he should bring back for them. "Fine clothes!" said one. "Pearls and jewels!" said the other. "But what will you have, Cinderella?" said he. "The first twig, father, that strikes against your hat on the way home; that is what I should like you to bring me."

So he bought for the two step-daughters fine clothes, pearls, and jewels, and on his way back, as he rode through a green lane, a hazel twig struck against his hat; and he broke it off and carried it home with him. And when he reached home he gave to the step-daughters what they had wished for, and to Cinderella he gave the hazel twig. She thanked him, and went to her mother's grave, and planted this twig there, weeping so bitterly that the tears fell upon it and watered it, and it flourished and became a fine tree. Cinderella went to see it three times a day, and wept and prayed, and each time a white bird rose up from the tree, and if she uttered any wish the bird brought her whatever she had wished for.

Now it came to pass that the King ordained a festival that should last for three days, and to which all the beautiful young women of that country were bidden, so that the King's son might choose a bride from among them. When the two step-daughters heard that they too were bidden to appear, they felt very pleased, and they called Cinderella and said, "Comb our hair, brush our shoes, and make our buckles fast, we are going to the wedding feast at the King's castle."

When she heard this, Cinderella could not help crying, for she too would have liked to go to the dance, and she begged her step-mother to allow her. "What! You Cinderella!" said she, "in all your dust and dirt, you want to go to the festival! you that have no dress and no shoes! you want to dance!"

But as she persisted in asking, at last the step-mother said, "I have strewed a dishful of lentils in the ashes, and if you can pick them all up again in two hours you may go with us."

Then the maiden went to the back-door that led into the garden, and called out,

> *"O gentle doves, O turtle-doves,*
> *And all the birds that be,*
> *The lentils that in ashes lie*
> *Come and pick up for me!*
> *The good must be put in the dish,*
> *The bad you may eat if you wish."*

Then there came to the kitchen-window two white doves, and after them some turtle-doves, and at last a crowd of all the birds under heaven, chirping and fluttering, and they alighted among the ashes; and the doves nodded with their heads, and began to pick, peck, pick, peck, and then all the others began to pick, peck, pick, peck, and put all the good grains into the dish. Before an hour was over all was done, and they flew away.

Then the maiden brought the dish to her step-mother, feeling joyful, and thinking that now she should go to the feast; but the step-mother said, "No, Cinderella, you have no proper clothes, and you do not know how to dance, and you would be laughed at!" And when Cinderella cried for disappointment, she added, "If you can pick two dishes full of lentils out of the ashes, nice and clean, you shall go with us," thinking to herself, "for that is not possible." When she had strewed two dishes full of lentils among the ashes the maiden went through the back-door into the garden, and cried,

> *"O gentle doves, O turtle-doves,*
> *And all the birds that be,*
> *The lentils that in ashes lie*
> *Come and pick up for me!*
> *The good must be put in the dish,*
> *The bad you may eat if you wish."*

So there came to the kitchen-window two white doves, and then some turtle-doves, and at last a crowd of all the other birds under heaven, chirping and fluttering, and they alighted among the ashes, and the doves nodded with their heads and began to pick, peck, pick, peck, and then all the others began to pick, peck, pick, peck, and put all the good grains into the dish. And before half-an-hour was over it was all done, and they flew away. Then the maiden took the dishes to the step-mother, feeling joyful, and thinking that now she should go with them to the feast; but she said, "All this is of no good to you; you cannot come with us, for you have no proper clothes, and cannot dance; you would put us to shame." Then she turned her back on poor Cinderella and made haste to set out with her two proud daughters.

And as there was no one left in the house, Cinderella went to her mother's grave, under the hazel bush, and cried,

> *"Little tree, little tree, shake over me,*
> *That silver and gold may come down and cover me."*

Then the bird threw down a dress of gold and silver, and a pair of slippers embroidered with silk and silver. And in all haste she put on the dress and went to the festival. But her step-mother and sisters did not know her, and thought she must be a foreign Princess, she looked so beautiful in her golden dress. Of Cinderella they never thought at all, and supposed that she was sitting at home, and picking the lentils out of the ashes. The King's son came to meet her, and took her by the hand and danced with her, and he refused to stand up with any one else, so that he might not be obliged to let go her hand; and when any one came to claim it he answered, "She is my partner."

And when the evening came she wanted to go home, but the Prince said he would go with her to take care of her, for he wanted to see where the beautiful maiden lived. But she escaped him, and jumped up into the pigeon-house. Then the Prince waited until the father came, and told him the strange maiden had jumped into the pigeon-house. The father thought to himself, "It surely cannot be Cinderella," and called for axes and hatchets, and had the pigeon-house cut down, but there was no one in it. And when they entered the house there sat Cinderella in her dirty clothes among the cinders, and a little oil-lamp burnt dimly in the chimney; for Cinderella had been very quick, and had jumped out of the pigeon-house again, and had run to the hazel bush; and there she had taken off her beautiful dress and had laid it on the grave, and the bird had carried it away again, and then she had put on her little gray kirtle again, and had sat down in the kitchen among the cinders.

The next day, when the festival began anew, and the parents and step-sisters had gone to it, Cinderella went to the hazel bush and cried,

> *"Little tree, little tree, shake over me,*
> *That silver and gold may come down and cover me."*

Then the bird cast down a still more splendid dress than on the day before. And when she appeared in it among the guests every one was astonished at her beauty. The Prince had been waiting until she came, and he took her hand and danced with her alone. And when any one else came to invite her he said, "She is my partner."

And when the evening came she wanted to go home, and the Prince followed her, for he wanted to see to what house she belonged; but she broke away from him, and ran into the garden at the back of the house. There stood a fine large tree, bearing splendid pears; she leapt as lightly as a squirrel among the branches, and the Prince did not know what had become of her. So he waited until the father came, and then he told him that the strange maiden had rushed from him, and that he thought she had gone up into the pear tree. The father thought to himself, "It surely cannot be Cinderella," and called for an axe, and felled the tree, but there was no one in it. And when they went into the kitchen there sat Cinderella among the cinders, as usual, for she had got down the other side of the tree, and had taken back her beautiful clothes to the bird on the hazel bush, and had put on her old gray kirtle again.

On the third day, when the parents and the step-children had set off, Cinderella went again to her mother's grave, and said to the tree,

> *"Little tree, little tree, shake over me,*
> *That silver and gold may come down and cover me."*

Then the bird cast down a dress, the like of which had never been seen for splendor and brilliancy, and slippers that were of gold.

And when she appeared in this dress at the feast nobody knew what to say for wonderment. The Prince danced with her alone, and if any one else asked her he answered, "She is my partner."

And when it was evening Cinderella wanted to go home, and the Prince was about to go with her, when she ran past him so quickly that he could not follow her. But he had laid a plan, and had caused all the steps to be spread with pitch, so that as she rushed down them the left shoe of the maiden remained sticking in it. The Prince picked it up, and saw that it was of gold, and very small and slender. The next morning he went to the father and told him that none should be his bride save the one whose foot the golden shoe should fit.

Then the two sisters were very glad, because they had pretty feet. The eldest went to her room to try on the shoe, and her mother stood by. But she could not get her great toe into it, for the shoe was too small; then her mother handed her a knife, and said, "Cut the toe off, for when you are Queen you will never have to go on foot." So the girl cut her toe off, squeezed her foot into the shoe, concealed the pain, and went down to the Prince. Then he took her with him on his horse as his bride, and rode off. They had to pass by the grave, and there sat the two pigeons on the hazel bush, and cried,

> *"There they go, there they go!*
> *There is blood on her shoe;*
> *The shoe is too small,*
> *—Not the right bride at all!"*

Then the Prince looked at her shoe, and saw the blood flowing. And he turned his horse round and took the false bride home again, saying she was not the right one, and that the other sister must try on the shoe. So she went into her room to do so, and got her toes comfortably in, but her heel was too large. Then her mother handed her the knife, saying, "Cut a piece off your heel; when you are Queen you will never have to go on foot."

So the girl cut a piece off her heel, and thrust her foot into the shoe, concealed the pain, and went down to the Prince, who took his bride before him on his horse and rode off. When they passed by the hazel bush the two pigeons sat there and cried,

> *"There they go, there they go!*
> *There is blood on her shoe;*
> *The shoe is too small,*
> *—Not the right bride at all!"*

Then the Prince looked at her foot, and saw how the blood was flowing from the shoe, and staining the white stocking. And he turned his horse round and brought the false bride home again. "This is not the right one," said he, "have you no other daughter?"

"No," said the man, "only my dead wife left behind her a little stunted Cinderella; it is impossible that she can be the bride." But the King's son ordered her to be sent for, but the mother said, "Oh no! she is much too dirty, I could not let her be seen." But he would have her fetched, and so Cinderella had to appear.

First she washed her face and hands quite clean, and went in and curtseyed to the Prince, who held out to her the golden shoe. Then she sat down on a stool, drew her foot out of the heavy wooden shoe, and slipped it into the golden one, which fitted it perfectly. And when she stood up, and the Prince looked in her face, he knew again the beautiful maiden that had danced with him, and he cried, "This is the right bride!"

The step-mother and the two sisters were thunderstruck, and grew pale with anger; but he put Cinderella before him on his horse and rode off. And as they passed the hazel bush, the two white pigeons cried,

> *"There they go, there they go!*
> *No blood on her shoe;*
> *The shoe's not too small,*
> *The right bride is she after all."*

And when they had thus cried, they came flying after and perched on Cinderella's shoulders, one on the right, the other on the left, and so remained.

And when her wedding with the Prince was appointed to be held the false sisters came, hoping to curry favor, and to take part in the festivities. So as the bridal procession went to the church, the eldest walked on the right side and the younger on the left, and the pigeons picked out an eye of each of them. And as they returned the elder was on the left side and the younger one on the right, and the pigeons picked out the other eye of each of them. And so they were condemned to go blind for the rest of their days because of their wickedness and falsehood.

Simeli Mountain

THERE WERE once two brothers, the one rich, the other poor. The rich one, however, gave nothing to the poor one, and he gained a scanty living by trading in corn, and often did so badly that he had no bread for his wife and children. Once when he was wheeling a barrow through the forest he saw, on one side of him, a great, bare, naked-looking mountain, and as he had never seen it before, he stood still and stared at it with amazement.

While he was thus standing he saw twelve great, wild men coming towards him, and as he believed they were robbers he pushed his barrow into the thicket, climbed up a tree, and waited to see what would happen. The twelve men, however, went to the mountain and cried, "Semsi mountain, Semsi mountain, open"; and immediately the barren mountain opened down the middle, and the twelve went into it, and as soon as they were within, it shut. After a short time, however, it opened again, and the men came forth carrying heavy sacks on their shoulders, and when they were all once more in the daylight they said, "Semsi mountain, Semsi mountain, shut thyself"; then the mountain closed together, and there was no longer any entrance to be seen to it, and the twelve went away.

When they were quite out of sight the poor man got down from the tree, and was curious to know what really was secretly hidden in the mountain. So he went up to it and said, "Semsi mountain,

Semsi mountain, open"; and the mountain opened to him also. Then he went inside, and the whole mountain was a cavern full of silver and gold, and behind lay great piles of pearls and sparkling jewels, heaped up like corn. The poor man hardly knew what to do, and whether he might take any of these treasures for himself or not; but at last he filled his pockets with gold, but he left the pearls and precious stones where they were. When he came out again he also said, "Semsi mountain, Semsi mountain, shut thyself"; and the mountain closed itself, and he went home with his barrow.

And now he had no more cause for anxiety, but could buy bread for his wife and children with his gold, and wine into the bargain. He lived joyously and uprightly, gave help to the poor, and did good to every one. When, however, the money came to an end he went to his brother, borrowed a measure that held a bushel, and brought himself some more, but did not touch any of the most valuable things. When for the third time he wanted to fetch something, he again borrowed the measure of his brother. The rich man had, however, long been envious of his brother's possessions, and of the handsome way of living which he had set on foot, and could not understand from whence the riches came, and what his brother wanted with the measure. Then he thought of a cunning trick, and covered the bottom of the measure with pitch, and when he got the measure back a piece of money was sticking in it.

He went at once to his brother and asked him, "What hast thou been measuring in the bushel measure?" "Corn and barley," said the other. Then he showed him the piece of money, and threatened that if he did not tell the truth he would accuse him before a court of justice. The poor man then told him everything, just as it had happened. The rich man, however, ordered his carriage to be made ready, and drove away, resolved to use the opportunity better than his brother had done, and to bring back with him quite different treasures.

When he came to the mountain he cried, "Semsi mountain, Semsi mountain, open." The mountain opened, and he went inside it. There lay the treasures all before him, and for a long time he did not know which to clutch at first. At length he loaded himself with as many precious stones as he could carry. He wished to carry his burden outside, but, as his heart and soul were entirely full of the treasures, he had forgotten the name of the mountain, and cried, "Simeli mountain, Simeli mountain, open." That, however, was not the right name, and the mountain never stirred, but remained shut. Then he was alarmed, but the longer he thought about it the more his thoughts confused themselves, and his treasures were no more of any use to him.

In the evening the mountain opened, and the twelve robbers came in, and when they saw him they laughed, and cried out, "Bird, have we caught thee at last! Didst thou think we had never noticed that thou hadst been in here twice? We could not catch thee then; this third time thou shalt not get out again!" Then he cried, "It was not I, it was my brother," but let him beg for his life and say what he would, they cut his head off.

The Glass Coffin

LET NO ONE ever say that a poor tailor cannot do great things and win high honors; all that is needed is that he should go to the right smithy, and what is of most consequence, that he should have good luck. A civil, adroit tailor's apprentice once went out traveling, and came into a great forest, and, as he did not know the way, he lost himself. Night fell, and nothing was left for him to do, but to seek a bed in this painful solitude. He might certainly have found a good bed on the soft moss, but the fear of wild beasts let him have no rest there, and at last he was forced to make up his mind to spend the night in a tree. He sought out a high oak, climbed up to the top of it, and thanked God that he had his goose with him, for otherwise the wind which blew over the top of the tree would have carried him away.

After he had spent some hours in the darkness, not without fear and trembling, he saw at a very short distance the glimmer of a light, and as he thought that a human habitation might be there, where he would be better off than on the branches of a tree, he got carefully down and went towards the light. It guided him to a small hut that was woven together of reeds and rushes. He knocked boldly, the door opened, and by the light which came forth he saw a little hoary old man who wore a coat made of bits of colored stuff sewn together.

"Who are you, and what do you want?" asked the man in a grumbling voice. "I am a poor tailor," he answered, "whom night has surprised here in the wilderness, and I earnestly beg you to take me into your hut until morning." "Go your way," replied the old man in a surly voice, "I will have nothing to do with rascals. Seek shelter elsewhere." After these words he was about to slip into his hut again, but the tailor held him so tightly by the corner of his coat, and pleaded so piteously, that the old man, who was not so ill-natured as he wished to appear, was at last softened, and took him into the hut with him where he gave him something to eat, and then pointed out to him a very good bed in a corner.

The weary tailor needed no rocking; but slept sweetly till morning, but even then would not have thought of getting up, if he had not been aroused by a great noise. A violent sound of screaming and roaring forced its way through the thin walls of the hut. The tailor, full of unwonted courage, jumped up, put his clothes on in haste, and hurried out. Then close by the hut, he saw a great black bull and a beautiful stag, which were just preparing for a violent struggle. They rushed at each other with such extreme rage that the ground shook with their trampling, and the air resounded with their cries. For a long time it was uncertain which of the two would gain the victory; at length the stag thrust his horns into his adversary's body, whereupon the bull fell to the earth with a terrific roar, and was thoroughly despatched by a few strokes from the stag.

The tailor, who had watched the fight with astonishment, was still standing there motionless, when the stag in full career bounded up to him, and before he could escape, caught him up on his great horns. He had not much time to collect his thoughts, for it went in a swift race over stock and stone, mountain and valley, wood and meadow. He held with both hands to the tops of the horns, and resigned himself to his fate. It seemed to him, however, just as if he were flying away. At length the stag stopped in front of a wall of rock, and gently let the tailor down. The tailor, more dead than alive, required a longer time than that to come to himself. When he had in some degree recovered, the stag, which had remained standing by him, pushed its horns with such force against a door which was in the rock, that it sprang open. Flames of fire shot forth, after which followed a great smoke, which hid the stag from his sight.

The tailor did not know what to do, or whither to turn, in order to get out of this desert and back to human beings again. While he was standing thus undecided, a voice sounded out of the rock, which cried to him, "Enter without fear, no evil shall befall thee." He certainly hesitated, but driven by a mysterious force, he obeyed the voice and went through the iron-door into a large spacious hall, whose ceiling, walls and floor were made of shining polished square stones, on each of which were cut letters which were unknown to him. He looked at everything full of admiration, and was on the point of going out again, when he once more heard the voice which said to him, "Step on the stone which lies in the middle of the hall, and great good fortune awaits thee."

His courage had already grown so great that he obeyed the order. The stone began to give way under his feet, and sank slowly down into the depths. When it was once more firm, and the tailor looked round, he found himself in a hall which in size resembled the former. Here, however, there was more to look at and to admire. Hollow places were cut in the walls, in which stood vases of transparent glass which were filled with colored spirit or with a bluish vapor. On the floor of the hall two great glass chests stood opposite to each other, which at once excited his curiosity. When he went to one of them he saw inside it a handsome structure like a castle surrounded by farm-buildings, stables and barns, and a quantity of other good things. Everything was small, but exceedingly carefully and delicately made, and seemed to be cut out by a dexterous hand with the greatest exactitude.

He might not have turned away his eyes from the consideration of this rarity for some time, if the voice had not once more made itself heard. It ordered him to turn round and look at the glass chest which was standing opposite. How his admiration increased when he saw therein a maiden of the greatest beauty! She lay as if asleep, and was wrapped in her long fair hair as in a precious mantle. Her eyes were closely shut, but the brightness of her complexion and a ribbon which her breathing moved to and fro, left no doubt that she was alive.

The tailor was looking at the beauty with beating heart, when she suddenly opened her eyes, and started up at the sight of him in joyful terror. "Just Heaven!" cried she, "my deliverance is at hand! Quick, quick, help me out of my prison; if you push back the bolt of this glass coffin, then I shall be free." The tailor obeyed without delay, and she immediately raised up the glass lid, came out and hastened into the corner of the hall, where she covered herself with a large cloak. Then she seated herself on a stone, ordered the young man to come to her, and after she had imprinted a friendly kiss on his lips, she said, "My long-desired deliverer, kind Heaven has guided you to me, and put an end to my sorrows. On the self-same day when they end, shall your happiness begin. You are the husband chosen for me by Heaven, and you shall pass your life in unbroken joy, loved by me, and rich to overflowing in every earthly possession. Seat yourself and listen to the story of my life:

"I am the daughter of a rich count. My parents died when I was still in my tender youth, and recommended me in their last will to my elder brother, by whom I was brought up. We loved each other so tenderly, and were so alike in our way of thinking and our inclinations, that we both embraced the resolution never to marry, but to stay together to the end of our lives. In our house there was no lack of company; neighbors and friends visited us often, and we showed the greatest hospitality to every one. So it came to pass one evening that a stranger came riding to our castle, and, under pretext of not being able to get on to the next place, begged for shelter for the night. We granted his request with ready courtesy, and he entertained us in the most agreeable manner during supper by conversation intermingled with stories. My brother liked the stranger so much that he begged him to spend a couple of days with us, to which, after some hesitation, he consented. We did not rise from table until late in the night, the stranger was shown to a room, and I hastened, as I was tired, to lay my limbs in my soft bed.

"Hardly had I slept for a short time, when the sound of faint and delightful music awoke me. As I could not conceive from whence it came, I wanted to summon my waiting-maid who slept in the next room, but to my astonishment I found that speech was taken away from me by an unknown force. I felt as if a mountain were weighing down my breast, and was unable to make the very slightest sound. In the meantime, by the light of my night-lamp, I saw the stranger enter my room through two doors which were fast bolted. He came to me and said, that by magic arts which were at his command, he had caused the lovely music to sound in order to awaken me, and that he now forced his way through all fastenings with the intention of offering me his hand and heart. My repugnance to his magic arts was, however, so great that I vouchsafed him no answer. He remained for a time standing without moving, apparently with the idea of waiting for a favorable decision, but as I continued to keep silence, he angrily declared he would revenge himself and find means to punish my pride, and left the room. I passed the night in the greatest disquietude, and only fell asleep towards morning. When I awoke, I hurried to my brother, but did not find him in his room, and the attendants told me that he had ridden forth with the stranger to the chase by daybreak.

"I at once suspected nothing good. I dressed myself quickly, ordered my palfrey to be saddled, and accompanied only by one servant, rode full gallop to the forest. The servant fell with his horse, and could not follow me, for the horse had broken its foot. I pursued my way without halting, and in a few minutes I saw the stranger coming towards me with a beautiful stag which he led by a cord. I asked him where he had left my brother, and how he had come by this stag, out of whose great eyes I saw tears flowing. Instead of answering me, he began to laugh loudly. I fell into a great rage at this, pulled out a pistol and discharged it at the monster; but the ball rebounded from his breast and went into my horse's head. I fell to the ground, and the stranger muttered some words which deprived me of consciousness.

"When I came to my senses again I found myself in this underground cave in a glass coffin. The magician appeared once again, and said he had changed my brother into a stag, my castle with all that belonged to it, diminished in size by his arts, he had shut up in the other glass chest, and my people, who were all turned into smoke, he had confined in glass bottles. He told me that if I would now comply with his wish, it was an easy thing for him to put everything back in its former state, as he had nothing to do but open the vessels, and everything would return once more to its natural form. I answered him as little as I had done the first time. He vanished and left me in my prison, in which a deep sleep came on me. Among the visions which passed before my eyes, that was the most comforting in which a young man came and set me free, and when I opened my eyes today I saw you, and beheld my dream fulfilled. Help me to accomplish the other things which happened in those visions. The first is that we lift the glass chest in which my castle is enclosed, on to that broad stone."

As soon as the stone was laden, it began to rise up on high with the maiden and the young man, and mounted through the opening of the ceiling into the upper hall, from whence they then could easily reach the open air. Here the maiden opened the lid, and it was marvelous to behold how the castle, the houses, and the farm buildings which were enclosed, stretched themselves out and grew to their natural size with the greatest rapidity. After this, the maiden and the tailor returned to the cave beneath the earth, and had the vessels which were filled with smoke carried up by the stone. The maiden had scarcely opened the bottles when the blue smoke rushed out and changed itself into living men, in whom she recognized her servants and her people. Her joy was still more increased when her brother, who had killed the magician in the form of a bull, came out of the forest towards them in his human form. And on the self-same day the maiden, in accordance with her promise, gave her hand at the alter to the lucky tailor.

Rapunzel

THERE ONCE lived a man and his wife who had long wished for a child, but in vain. Now there was at the back of their house a little window which overlooked a beautiful garden full of the finest vegetables and flowers; but there was a high wall all round it, and no one ventured into it, for it belonged to a witch of great might, and of whom all the world was afraid. One day when the wife was standing at the window, and looking into the garden, she saw a bed filled with the finest rampion; and it looked so fresh and green that she began to wish for some; and at length she longed for it greatly. This went on for days, and as she knew she could not get the rampion, she pined away, and grew pale and miserable.

Then the man was uneasy, and asked, "What is the matter, dear wife?" "Oh," answered she, "I shall die unless I can have some of that rampion to eat that grows in the garden at the back of our house." The man, who loved her very much, thought to himself, "Rather than lose my wife I will get some rampion, cost what it will."

So in the twilight he climbed over the wall into the witch's garden, plucked hastily a handful of rampion and brought it to his wife. She made a salad of it at once, and ate of it to her heart's content. But she liked it so much, and it tasted so good, that the next day she longed for it thrice as much as she had done before; if she was to have any rest the man must climb over the wall once more. So he went in the twilight again; and as he was climbing back, he saw, all at once, the witch standing before him, and was terribly frightened, as she cried, with angry eyes, "How dare you climb over into my garden like a thief, and steal my rampion! It shall be the worse for you!"

"Oh," answered he, "be merciful rather than just; I have only done it through necessity; for my wife saw your rampion out of the window, and became possessed with so great a longing that she would have died if she could not have had some to eat."

Then the witch said, "If it is all as you say, you may have as much rampion as you like, on one condition—the child that will come into the world must be given to me. It shall go well with the child, and I will care for it like a mother."

In his distress of mind the man promised everything; and when the time came when the child was born the witch appeared, and, giving the child the name of Rapunzel (which is the same as rampion), she took it away with her.

Rapunzel was the most beautiful child in the world. When she was twelve years old the witch shut her up in a tower in the midst of a wood, and it had neither steps nor door, only a small window above. When the witch wished to be let in, she would stand below and would cry, "Rapunzel, Rapunzel! Let down your hair!"

Rapunzel had beautiful long hair that shone like gold. When she heard the voice of the witch she would undo the fastening of the upper window, unbind the plaits of her hair, and let it down twenty ells below, and the witch would climb up by it.

After they had lived thus a few years it happened that as the King's son was riding through the wood, he came to the tower; and as he drew near he heard a voice singing so sweetly that he stood still and listened. It was Rapunzel in her loneliness trying to pass away the time with sweet songs. The King's son wished to go in to her, and sought to find a door in the tower, but there was none. So he rode home, but the song had entered into his heart, and every day he went into the wood and listened to it.

Once, as he was standing there under a tree, he saw the witch come up, and listened while she called out, "Oh Rapunzel, Rapunzel! Let down your hair."

Then he saw how Rapunzel let down her long tresses, and how the witch climbed up by them and went in to her, and he said to himself, "Since that is the ladder, I will climb it, and seek my fortune." And the next day, as soon as it began to grow dusk, he went to the tower and cried, "Oh Rapunzel, Rapunzel! Let down your hair." And she let down her hair, and the King's son climbed up by it.

Rapunzel was greatly terrified when she saw that a man had come in to her, for she had never seen one before; but the King's son began speaking so kindly to her, and told her how her singing had entered into his heart, so that he could have no peace until he had seen her himself. Then Rapunzel forgot her terror, and when he asked her to take him for her husband, and she saw that he was young and beautiful, she thought to herself, "I certainly like him much better than old mother Gothel," and she put her hand into his hand, saying, "I would willingly go with you, but I do not know how I shall get out. When you come, bring each time a silken rope, and I will make a ladder, and when it is quite ready I will get down by it out of the tower, and you shall take me away on your horse."

They agreed that he should come to her every evening, as the old woman came in the day-time. So the witch knew nothing of all this until once Rapunzel said to her unwittingly, "Mother Gothel, how is it that you climb up here so slowly, and the King's son is with me in a moment?"

"O wicked child," cried the witch, "what is this I hear! I thought I had hidden you from all the world, and you have betrayed me!"

In her anger she seized Rapunzel by her beautiful hair, struck her several times with her left hand, and then grasping a pair of shears in her right—snip, snap—the beautiful locks lay on the ground. And she was so hard-hearted that she took Rapunzel and put her in a waste and desert place, where she lived in great woe and misery.

The same day on which she took Rapunzel away she went back to the tower in the evening and made fast the severed locks of hair to the window-hasp, and the King's son came and cried, "Rapunzel, Rapunzel! Let down your hair."

Then she let the hair down, and the King's son climbed up, but instead of his dearest Rapunzel he found the witch looking at him with wicked, glittering eyes.

"Aha!" cried she, mocking him, "you came for your darling, but the sweet bird sits no longer in the nest, and sings no more; the cat has got her, and will scratch out your eyes as well! Rapunzel is lost to you; you will see her no more."

The King's son was beside himself with grief, and in his agony he sprang from the tower; he escaped with life, but the thorns on which he fell put out his eyes. Then he wandered blind through the wood, eating nothing but roots and berries, and doing nothing but lament and weep for the loss of his dearest wife.

So he wandered several years in misery until at last he came to the desert place where Rapunzel lived with her twin-children that she had borne, a boy and a girl. At first he heard a voice that he thought he knew, and when he reached the place from which it seemed to come Rapunzel knew him, and fell on his neck and wept. And when her tears touched his eyes they became clear again, and he could see with them as well as ever.

Then he took her to his kingdom, where he was received with great joy, and there they lived long and happily.

The Sleeping Beauty

IN TIMES PAST there lived a King and Queen, who said to each other every day of their lives, "Would that we had a child!" and yet they had none. But it happened once that when the Queen was bathing, there came a frog out of the water, and he squatted on the ground, and said to her, "Thy wish shall be fulfilled; before a year has gone by, thou shalt bring a daughter into the world."

And as the frog foretold, so it happened; and the Queen bore a daughter so beautiful that the King could not contain himself for joy, and he ordained a great feast. Not only did he bid to it his relations, friends, and acquaintances, but also the wise women, that they might be kind and favorable to the child. There were thirteen of them in his kingdom, but as he had only provided twelve golden plates for them to eat from, one of them had to be left out.

However, the feast was celebrated with all splendor; and as it drew to an end, the wise women stood forward to present to the child their wonderful gifts: one bestowed virtue, one beauty, a third riches, and so on, whatever there is in the world to wish for. And when eleven of them had said their say, in came the uninvited thirteenth, burning to revenge herself, and without greeting or respect, she cried with a loud voice, "In the fifteenth year of her age the Princess shall prick herself with a spindle and shall fall down dead." And without speaking one more word she turned away and left the hall.

Every one was terrified at her saying, when the twelfth came forward, for she had not yet bestowed her gift, and though she could not do away with the evil prophecy, yet she could soften it, so she said, "The Princess shall not die, but fall into a deep sleep for a hundred years."

Now the King, being desirous of saving his child even from this misfortune, gave commandment that all the spindles in his kingdom should be burnt up.

The maiden grew up, adorned with all the gifts of the wise women; and she was so lovely, modest, sweet, and kind and clever, that no one who saw her could help loving her.

It happened one day, she being already fifteen years old, that the King and Queen rode abroad; and the maiden was left behind alone in the castle. She wandered about into all the nooks and corners, and into all the chambers and parlors, as the fancy took her, till at last she came to an old tower. She climbed the narrow winding stair which led to a little door, with a rusty key sticking out of the lock; she turned the key, and the door opened, and there in the little room sat an old woman with a spindle, diligently spinning her flax.

"Good day, mother," said the Princess, "what are you doing?" "I am spinning," answered the old woman, nodding her head. "What thing is that that twists round so briskly?" asked the maiden, and taking the spindle into her hand she began to spin; but no sooner had she touched it than the evil prophecy was fulfilled, and she pricked her finger with it. In that very moment she fell back upon the bed that stood there, and lay in a deep sleep, and this sleep fell upon the whole castle. The King and Queen, who had returned and were in the great hall, fell fast asleep, and with them the whole court. The horses in their stalls, the dogs in the yard, the pigeons on the roof, the flies on the wall, the very fire that flickered on the hearth, became still, and slept like the rest; and the meat on the spit ceased roasting, and the cook, who was going to pull the scullion's hair for some mistake he had made, let him go, and went to sleep. And the wind ceased, and not a leaf fell from the trees about the castle.

Then round about that place there grew a hedge of thorns thicker every year, until at last the whole castle was hidden from view, and nothing of it could be seen but the vane on the roof. And a rumor went abroad in all that country of the beautiful sleeping Rosamond, for so was the Princess called; and from time to time many Kings' sons came and tried to force their way through the hedge; but it was impossible for them to do so, for the thorns held fast together like strong hands, and the young men were caught by them, and not being able to get free, there died a lamentable death.

Many a long year afterwards there came a King's son into that country, and heard an old man tell how there should be a castle standing behind the hedge of thorns, and that there a beautiful enchanted Princess named Rosamond had slept for a hundred years, and with her the King and Queen, and the whole court. The old man had been told by his grandfather that many Kings' sons had sought to pass the thorn-hedge, but had been caught and pierced by the thorns, and had died a miserable death. Then said the young man, "Nevertheless, I do not fear to try; I shall win through and see the lovely Rosamond." The good old man tried to dissuade him, but he would not listen to his words.

For now the hundred years were at an end, and the day had come when Rosamond should be awakened. When the Prince drew near the hedge of thorns, it was changed into a hedge of beautiful large flowers, which parted and bent aside to let him pass, and then closed behind him in a thick hedge. When he reached the castle-yard, he saw the horses and brindled hunting-dogs lying asleep, and on the roof the pigeons were sitting with their heads under their wings. And when he came indoors, the flies on the wall were asleep, the cook in the kitchen had his hand uplifted to strike the scullion, and the kitchenmaid had the black fowl on her lap ready to pluck. Then he mounted higher, and saw in the hall the whole court lying asleep, and above them, on their thrones, slept the King and the Queen. And still he went farther, and all was so quiet that he could hear his own breathing; and at last he came to the tower, and went up the winding stair, and opened the door of the little room where Rosamond lay.

And when he saw her looking so lovely in her sleep, he could not turn away his eyes; and presently he stooped and kissed her, and she awaked, and opened her eyes, and looked very kindly on him. And she rose, and they went forth together, the King and the Queen and whole court waked up, and gazed on each other with great eyes of wonderment. And the horses in the yard got up and shook themselves, the hounds sprang up and wagged their tails, the pigeons on the roof drew their heads from under their wings, looked round, and flew into the field, the flies on the wall crept on a little farther, the kitchen fire leapt up and blazed, and cooked the meat, the joint on the spit began to roast, the cook gave the scullion such a box on the ear that he roared out, and the maid went on plucking the fowl.

Then the wedding of the Prince and Rosamond was held with all splendor, and they lived very happily together until their lives' end.

Old Rinkrank

THERE WAS once upon a time a King who had a daughter, and he caused a glass-mountain to be made, and said that whosoever could cross to the other side of it without falling should have his daughter to wife. Then there was one who loved the King's daughter, and he asked the King if he might have her. "Yes," said the King; "if you can cross the mountain without falling, you shall have her." And the Princess said she would go over it with him, and would hold him if he were about to fall.

So they set out together to go over it, and when they were halfway up the Princess slipped and fell, and the glass-mountain opened and shut her up inside it, and her betrothed could not see where she had gone, for the mountain closed immediately. Then he wept and lamented much, and the King was miserable too, and had the mountain broken open where she had been lost, and thought he would be able to get her out again, but they could not find the place into which she had fallen.

Meantime the King's daughter had fallen quite deep down into the earth into a great cave. An old fellow with a very long gray beard came to meet her, and told her that if she would be his servant and do everything he bade her, she might live; if not, he would kill her. So she did all he bade her. In the mornings he took his ladder out of his pocket, and set it up against the mountain and climbed to the top by its help, and then he drew up the ladder after him. The Princess had to cook his dinner, make his bed, and do all his work, and when he came home again he always brought with him a heap of gold and silver. When she had lived with him for many years, and had grown quite old, he called her Mother Mansrot, and she had to call him Old Rinkrank. Then once when he was out, and she had made his bed and washed his dishes, she shut the doors and windows all fast, and there was one little window through which the light shone in, and this she left open.

When Old Rinkrank came home, he knocked at his door, and cried, "Mother Mansrot, open the door for me." "No," said she, "Old Rinkrank, I will not open the door for you." Then he said,

"Here stand I, poor Rinkrank,
On my seventeen long shanks,

> *On my weary, worn-out foot,*
> *Wash my dishes, Mother Mansrot."*

"I have washed your dishes already," said she. Then again he said,

> *"Here stand I, poor Rinkrank,*
> *On my seventeen long shanks,*
> *On my weary, worn-out foot,*
> *Make me my bed, Mother Mansrot."*

"I have made your bed already," said she. Then again he said,

> *"Here stand I, poor Rinkrank,*
> *On my seventeen long shanks,*
> *On my weary, worn-out foot,*
> *Open the door, Mother Mansrot."*

Then he ran all round his house, and saw that the little window was open, and thought, "I will look in and see what she can be about, and why she will not open the door for me." He tried to peep in, but could not get his head through because of his long beard. So he first put his beard through the open window, but just as he had got it through, Mother Mansrot came by and pulled the window down with a cord which she had tied to it, and his beard was shut fast in it. Then he began to cry most piteously, for it hurt him very much, and to entreat her to release him again. But she said not until he gave her the ladder with which he ascended the mountain. Then, whether he would or not, he had to tell her where the ladder was. And she fastened a very long ribbon to the window, and then she set up the ladder, and ascended the mountain, and when she was at the top of it she opened the window.

She went to her father, and told him all that had happened to her. The King rejoiced greatly, and her betrothed was still there, and they went and dug up the mountain, and found Old Rinkrank inside it with all his gold and silver. Then the King had Old Rinkrank put to death, and took all his gold and silver. The Princess married her betrothed, and lived right happily in great luxury and joy.

Hansel and Gretel

NEAR a great forest there lived a poor woodcutter and his wife and his two children; the boy's name was Hansel and the girl's Gretel. They had very little to bite or to sup, and once, when there was great dearth in the land, the man could not even gain the daily bread.

As he lay in bed one night thinking of this, and turning and tossing, he sighed heavily, and said to his wife, "What will become of us? We cannot even feed our children; there is nothing left for ourselves."

"I will tell you what, husband," answered the wife; "we will take the children early in the morning into the forest, where it is thickest; we will make them a fire, and we will give each of them a piece of bread, then we will go to our work and leave them alone; they will never find the way home again, and we shall be quit of them."

"No, wife," said the man, "I cannot do that; I cannot find in my heart to take my children into the forest and to leave them there alone; the wild animals would soon come and devour them."

"O you fool," said she, "then we will all four starve; you had better get the coffins ready"—and she left him no peace until he consented.

"But I really pity the poor children," said the man.

The two children had not been able to sleep for hunger, and had heard what their step-mother had said to their father. Gretel wept bitterly, and said to Hansel, "It is all over with us." "Do be quiet, Gretel," said Hansel, "and do not fret. I will manage something."

And when the parents had gone to sleep he got up, put on his little coat, opened the back door, and slipped out. The moon was shining brightly, and the white flints that lay in front of the house glistened like pieces of silver. Hansel stooped and filled the little pocket of his coat as full as it would hold. Then he went back again, and said to Gretel, "Be easy, dear little sister, and go to sleep quietly; God will not forsake us," and laid himself down again in his bed.

When the day was breaking, and before the sun had risen, the wife came and awakened the two children, saying, "Get up, you lazy bones; we are going into the forest to cut wood."

Then she gave each of them a piece of bread, and said, "That is for dinner, and you must not eat it before then, for you will get no more."

Gretel carried the bread under her apron, for Hansel had his pockets full of the flints. Then they set off all together on their way to the forest. When they had gone a little way Hansel stood still and looked back towards the house, and this he did again and again, till his father said to him, "Hansel, what are you looking at? Take care not to forget your legs."

"O father," said Hansel, "I am looking at my little white kitten, who is sitting up on the roof to bid me good-bye."

"You young fool," said the woman, "that is not your kitten, but the sunshine on the chimney pot."

Of course Hansel had not been looking at his kitten, but had been taking every now and then a flint from his pocket and dropping it on the road.

When they reached the middle of the forest the father told the children to collect wood to make a fire to keep them warm; and Hansel and Gretel gathered brushwood enough for a little mountain; and it was set on fire, and when the flame was burning quite high the wife said, "Now lie down by the fire and rest yourselves, you children, and we will go and cut wood; and when we are ready we will come and fetch you."

So Hansel and Gretel sat by the fire, and at noon they each ate their pieces of bread. They thought their father was in the wood all the time, as they seemed to hear the strokes of the axe, but really it was only a dry branch hanging to a withered tree that the wind moved to and fro. So when they had stayed there a long time their eyelids closed with weariness, and they fell fast asleep.

When at last they woke it was night, and Gretel began to cry, and said, "How shall we ever get out of this wood?" But Hansel comforted her, saying, "Wait a little while longer, until the moon rises, and then we can easily find the way home."

And when the full moon got up Hansel took his little sister by the hand, and followed the way where the flint stones shone like silver, and showed them the road. They walked on the whole night through, and at the break of day they came to their father's house. They knocked at the door, and when the wife opened it and saw it was Hansel and Gretel she said, "You naughty children, why did you sleep so long in the wood? We thought you were never coming home again!" But the father was glad, for it had gone to his heart to leave them both in the woods alone.

Not very long after that there was again great scarcity in those parts, and the children heard their mother say at night in bed to their father, "Everything is finished up; we have only half a loaf, and after that the tale comes to an end. The children must be off; we will take them farther into the wood this time, so that they shall not be able to find the way back again; there is no other way to manage."

The man felt sad at heart, and he thought, "It would be better to share one's last morsel with one's children." But the wife would listen to nothing that he said, but scolded and reproached him. He who says A must say B too, and when a man has given in once he has to do it a second time.

But the children were not asleep, and had heard all the talk. When the parents had gone to sleep Hansel got up to go out and get more flint stones, as he did before, but the wife had locked the door, and Hansel could not get out; but he comforted his little sister, and said, "Don't cry, Gretel, and go to sleep quietly, and God will help us."

Early the next morning the wife came and pulled the children out of bed. She gave them each a little piece of bread—less than before; and on the way to the wood Hansel crumbled the bread in his pocket, and often stopped to throw a crumb on the ground.

"Hansel, what are you stopping behind and staring for?" said the father.

"I am looking at my little pigeon sitting on the roof, to say good-bye to me," answered Hansel.

"You fool," said the wife, "that is no pigeon, but the morning sun shining on the chimney pots."

Hansel went on as before, and strewed bread crumbs all along the road.

The woman led the children far into the wood, where they had never been before in all their lives. And again there was a large fire made, and the mother said, "Sit still there, you children, and when you are tired you can go to sleep; we are going into the forest to cut wood, and in the evening, when we are ready to go home we will come and fetch you."

So when noon came Gretel shared her bread with Hansel, who had strewed his along the road. Then they went to sleep, and the evening passed, and no one came for the poor children. When they awoke it was dark night, and Hansel comforted his little sister, and said, "Wait a little, Gretel, until the moon gets up, then we shall be able to see the way home by the crumbs of bread that I have scattered along it."

So when the moon rose they got up, but they could find no crumbs of bread, for the birds of the woods and of the fields had come and picked them up. Hansel thought they might find the way all the same, but they could not. They went on all that night, and the next day from the morning until the evening, but they could not find the way out of the wood, and they were very hungry, for they had nothing to eat but the few berries they could pick up. And when they were so tired that they could no longer drag themselves along, they lay down under a tree and fell asleep.

It was now the third morning since they had left their father's house. They were always trying to get back to it, but instead of that they only found themselves farther in the wood, and if help had not soon come they would have starved. About noon they saw a pretty snow-white bird sitting on a bough, and singing so sweetly that they stopped to listen. And when he had finished the bird spread his wings and flew before them, and they followed after him until they came to a little house, and the bird perched on the roof, and when they came nearer they saw that the house was built of bread, and roofed with cakes, and the window was of transparent sugar.

"We will have some of this," said Hansel, "and make a fine meal. I will eat a piece of the roof, Gretel, and you can have some of the window—that will taste sweet."

So Hansel reached up and broke off a bit of the roof, just to see how it tasted, and Gretel stood by the window and gnawed at it. Then they heard a thin voice call out from inside,

> *"Nibble, nibble, like a mouse,*
> *Who is nibbling at my house?"*

And the children answered,

> *"Never mind,*
> *It is the wind."*

And they went on eating, never disturbing themselves. Hansel, who found that the roof tasted very nice, took down a great piece of it, and Gretel pulled out a large round window-pane, and sat her down and began upon it. Then the door opened, and an aged woman came out, leaning upon a crutch. Hansel and Gretel felt very frightened, and let fall what they had in their hands. The old woman, however, nodded her head, and said, "Ah, my dear children, how come you here? You must come indoors and stay with me, you will be no trouble."

So she took them each by the hand, and led them into her little house. And there they found a good meal laid out, of milk and pancakes, with sugar, apples, and nuts. After that she showed them two little white beds, and Hansel and Gretel laid themselves down on them, and thought they were in heaven.

The old woman, although her behavior was so kind, was a wicked witch, who lay in wait for children, and had built the little house on purpose to entice them. When they were once inside she used to kill them, cook them, and eat them, and then it was a feast-day with her. The witch's eyes were red, and she could not see very far, but she had a keen scent, like the beasts, and knew very well when human creatures were near. When she knew that Hansel and Gretel were coming, she gave a spiteful laugh, and said triumphantly, "I have them, and they shall not escape me!"

Early in the morning, before the children were awake, she got up to look at them, and as they lay sleeping so peacefully with round rosy cheeks, she said to herself, "What a fine feast I shall have!"

Then she grasped Hansel with her withered hand, and led him into a little stable, and shut him up behind a grating; and call and scream as he might, it was no good. Then she went back to Gretel and shook her, crying, "Get up, lazy bones; fetch water, and cook something nice for your brother; he is outside in the stable, and must be fattened up. And when he is fat enough I will eat him."

Gretel began to weep bitterly, but it was no use, she had to do what the wicked witch bade her.

And so the best kind of victuals was cooked for poor Hansel, while Gretel got nothing but crab-shells. Each morning the old woman visited the little stable, and cried, "Hansel, stretch out your finger, that I may tell if you will soon be fat enough."

Hansel, however, used to hold out a little bone, and the old woman, who had weak eyes, could not see what it was, and supposing it to be Hansel's finger, wondered very much that it was not getting fatter. When four weeks had passed and Hansel seemed to remain so thin, she lost patience and could wait no longer.

"Now then, Gretel," cried she to the little girl; "be quick and draw water; be Hansel fat or be he lean, tomorrow I must kill and cook him."

Oh what a grief for the poor little sister to have to fetch water, and how the tears flowed down over her cheeks! "Dear God, pray help us!" cried she; "if we had been devoured by wild beasts in the wood at least we should have died together."

"Spare me your lamentations," said the old woman; "they are of no avail."

Early next morning Gretel had to get up, make the fire, and fill the kettle. "First we will do the baking," said the old woman; "I have heated the oven already, and kneaded the dough."

She pushed poor Gretel towards the oven, out of which the flames were already shining. "Creep in," said the witch, "and see if it is properly hot, so that the bread may be baked."

And Gretel once in, she meant to shut the door upon her and let her be baked, and then she would have eaten her. But Gretel perceived her intention, and said, "I don't know how to do it; how shall I get in?"

"Stupid goose," said the old woman, "the opening is big enough, do you see? I could get in myself!" and she stooped down and put her head in the oven's mouth. Then Gretel gave her a push, so that she went in farther, and she shut the iron door upon her, and put up the bar. Oh how frightfully she howled! But Gretel ran away, and left the wicked witch to burn miserably. Gretel went straight to Hansel, opened the stable-door, and cried, "Hansel, we are free! the old witch is dead!"

Then out flew Hansel like a bird from its cage as soon as the door is opened. How rejoiced they both were! How they fell each on the other's neck and danced about, and kissed each other! And as they had nothing more to fear they went over all the old witch's house, and in every corner there stood chests of pearls and precious stones.

"This is something better than flint stones," said Hansel, as he filled his pockets; and Gretel, thinking she also would like to carry something home with her, filled her apron full.

"Now, away we go," said Hansel—"if we only can get out of the witch's wood."

When they had journeyed a few hours they came to a great piece of water. "We can never get across this," said Hansel, "I see no stepping-stones and no bridge." "And there is no boat either," said Gretel; "but here comes a white duck; if I ask her she will help us over." So she cried,

> *"Duck, duck, here we stand,*
> *Hansel and Gretel, on the land,*
> *Stepping-stones and bridge we lack,*
> *Carry us over on your nice white back."*

And the duck came accordingly, and Hansel got upon her and told his sister to come too. "No," answered Gretel, "that would be too hard upon the duck; we can go separately, one after the other."

And that was how it was managed, and after that they went on happily, until they came to the wood, and the way grew more and more familiar, till at last they saw in the distance their father's house. Then they ran till they came up to it, rushed in at the door, and fell on their father's neck. The man had not had a quiet hour since he left his children in the wood; but the wife was dead. And when Gretel opened her apron the pearls and precious stones were scattered all over the room, and Hansel took one handful after another out of his pocket. Then was all care at an end, and they lived in great joy together.

> *Sing every one,*
> *My story is done.*
> *And look! round the house*
> *There runs a little mouse.*
> *He that can catch her before she scampers in*
> *May make himself a fur-cap out of her skin.*

The Straw, the Coal, and the Bean

THERE LIVED in a certain village a poor old woman who had collected a mess of beans, and was going to cook them. So she made a fire on her hearth, and, in order to make it burn better, she put in a handful of straw. When the beans began to bubble in the pot, one of them fell out and lay, never noticed, near a straw which was already there; soon a red-hot coal jumped out of the fire and joined the pair.

The straw began first, and said, "Dear friends, how do you come here?" The coal answered, "I jumped out of the fire by great good luck, or I should certainly have met with my death. I should have been burned to ashes." The bean said, "I too have come out of it with a whole skin, but if the old woman had kept me in the pot I should have been cooked into a soft mass like my comrades."

"Nor should I have met with a better fate," said the straw; "the old woman has turned my brothers into fire and smoke, sixty of them she took up at once and deprived of life. Very luckily I managed to slip through her fingers."

"What had we better do now?" said the coal. "I think," answered the bean, "that as we have been so lucky as to escape with our lives, we will join in good fellowship together, and, lest any more bad fortune should happen to us here, we will go abroad into foreign lands."

The proposal pleased the two others, and forthwith they started on their travels. Soon they came to a little brook, and as there was no stepping-stone, and no bridge, they could not tell how they were to get to the other side. The straw was struck with a good idea, and said, "I will lay myself across, so that you can go over me as if I were a bridge!"

So the straw stretched himself from one bank to the other, and the coal, who was of an ardent nature, quickly trotted up to go over the new-made bridge. When, however, she reached the middle, and heard the water rushing past beneath her, she was struck with terror, and stopped, and could get no farther. So the straw began to get burnt, broke in two pieces, and fell in the brook; and the coal slipped down, hissing as she touched the water, and gave up the ghost.

The bean, who had prudently remained behind on the bank, could not help laughing at the sight, and not being able to contain herself, went on laughing so excessively that she burst. And now would she certainly have been undone for ever, if a tailor on his travels had not by good luck stopped to rest himself by the brook. As he had a compassionate heart, he took out needle and thread and stitched her together again. The bean thanked him in the most elegant manner, but as he had sewn her up with black stitches, all beans since then have a black seam.

The Death of the Hen

ONCE on a time the cock and the hen went to the nut mountain, and they agreed beforehand that whichever of them should find a nut was to divide it with the other. Now the hen found a great big nut, but said nothing about it, and was going to eat it all alone, but the kernel was such a fat one that she could not swallow it down, and it stuck in her throat, so that she was afraid she should choke.

"Cock!" cried she, "run as fast as you can and fetch me some water, or I shall choke!"

So the cock ran as fast as he could to the brook, and said, "Brook, give me some water, the hen is up yonder choking with a big nut stuck in her throat." But the brook answered, "First run to the bride and ask her for some red silk."

So the cock ran to the bride and said, "Bride, give me some red silk; the brook wants me to give him some red silk; I want him to give me some water, for the hen lies yonder choking with a big nut stuck in her throat."

But the bride answered, "First go and fetch me my garland that hangs on a willow." And the cock ran to the willow and pulled the garland from the bough and brought it to the bride, and the bride gave him red silk, and he brought it to the brook, and the brook gave him water. So then the cock brought the water to the hen, but alas, it was too late; the hen had choked in the meanwhile, and lay there dead. And the cock was so grieved that he cried aloud, and all the beasts came and lamented for the hen; and six mice built a little wagon on which to carry the poor hen to her grave, and when it was ready they harnessed themselves to it, and the cock drove.

On the way they met the fox. "Halloa, cock," cried he, "where are you off to?" "To bury my hen," answered the cock. "Can I come too?" said the fox. "Yes, if you follow behind," said the cock.

So the fox followed behind and he was soon joined by the wolf, the bear, the stag, the lion, and all the beasts in the wood. And the procession went on till they came to a brook.

"How shall we get over?" said the cock. Now in the brook there was a straw, and he said, "I will lay myself across, so that you may pass over on me." But when the six mice had got upon this bridge, the straw slipped and fell into the water and they all tumbled in and were drowned. So they were as badly off as ever, when a coal came up and said he would lay himself across and they might pass over him; but no sooner had he touched the water than he hissed, went out, and was dead. A stone, seeing this, was touched with pity, and, wishing to help the cock, he laid himself across the stream. And the cock drew the wagon with the dead hen in it safely to the other side, and then began to draw the others who followed behind across too, but it was too much for him, the wagon turned over, and all tumbled into the water one on the top of another, and were drowned.

So the cock was left all alone with the dead hen, and he dug a grave and laid her in it, and he raised a mound above her, and sat himself down and lamented so sore that at last he died. And so they were all dead together.

The Rabbit's Bride

THERE WAS once a woman who lived with her daughter in a beautiful cabbage-garden; and there came a rabbit and ate up all the cabbages. At last said the woman to her daughter, "Go into the garden, and drive out the rabbit."

"Shoo! shoo!" said the maiden; "don't eat up all our cabbages, little rabbit!" "Come, maiden," said the rabbit, "sit on my tail and go with me to my rabbit-hutch." But the maiden would not.

Another day, back came the rabbit, and ate away at the cabbages, until the woman said to her daughter, "Go into the garden, and drive away the rabbit."

"Shoo! shoo!" said the maiden; "don't eat up all our cabbages, little rabbit!" "Come, maiden," said the rabbit, "sit on my tail and go with me to my rabbit-hutch." But the maiden would not.

Again, a third time back came the rabbit, and ate away at the cabbages, until the woman said to her daughter, "Go into the garden, and drive away the rabbit."

"Shoo! shoo!" said the maiden; "don't eat up all our cabbages, little rabbit!" "Come, maiden," said the rabbit, "sit on my tail and go with me to my rabbit-hutch." And then the girl seated herself on the rabbit's tail, and the rabbit took her to his hutch.

"Now," said he, "set to work and cook some bran and cabbage; I am going to bid the wedding guests." And soon they were all collected. Would you like to know who they were? Well, I can only tell you what was told to me. All the hares came, and the crow who was to be the parson to marry them, and the fox for the clerk, and the alter was under the rainbow. But the maiden was sad, because she was so lonely.

"Get up! get up!" said the rabbit, "the wedding folk are all merry." But the bride wept and said nothing, and the rabbit went away, but very soon came back again. "Get up! get up!" said he, "the wedding folk are waiting." But the bride said nothing, and the rabbit went away.

Then she made a figure of straw, and dressed it in her own clothes, and gave it a red mouth, and set it to watch the kettle of bran, and then she went home to her mother. Back again came the rabbit, saying, "Get up! get up!" and he went up and hit the straw figure on the head, so that it tumbled down.

And the rabbit thought that he had killed his bride, and he went away and was very sad.

The Hare and the Hedgehog

THIS STORY, my dear young folks, seems to be false, but it really is true, for my grandfather, when relating it always used to say, "It must be true, my son, or else no one could tell it to you." The story is as follows.

One Sunday morning about harvest time, just as the buckwheat was in bloom, the sun was shining brightly in heaven, the east wind was blowing warmly over the stubble-fields, the larks were singing in the air, the bees buzzing among the buckwheat, the people were all going in their Sunday clothes to church, and all creatures were happy, and the hedgehog was happy too.

The hedgehog, however, was standing by his door with his arms akimbo, enjoying the morning breezes, and slowly trilling a little song to himself, which was neither better nor worse than the songs which hedgehogs are in the habit of singing on a blessed Sunday morning. While he was thus singing half aloud to himself, it suddenly occurred to him that while his wife was washing and drying the children, he might very well take a walk into the field, and see how his turnips were going on. The turnips were, in fact, close beside his house, and he and his family were accustomed to eat them, for which reason he looked upon them as his own. No sooner said than done. The hedgehog shut the house-door behind him, and took the path to the field. He had not gone very far from home, and was just turning round the sloe-bush which stands there outside the field, to go up into the turnip-field, when he observed the hare, who had gone out on business of the same kind, namely, to visit his cabbages.

When the hedgehog caught sight of the hare, he bade him a friendly good morning. But the hare, who was in his own way a distinguished gentleman, and frightfully haughty, did not return the hedgehog's greeting, but said to him, assuming at the same time a very contemptuous manner, "How do you happen to be running about here in the field so early in the morning?" "I am taking a walk," said the hedgehog. "A walk!" said the hare, with a smile. "It seems to me that you might use your legs for a better purpose." This answer made the hedgehog furiously angry, for he can bear anything but an attack on his legs, just because they are crooked by nature.

So now the hedgehog said to the hare, "You seem to imagine that you can do more with your legs than I with mine." "That is just what I do think," said the hare. "That can be put to the test," said the hedgehog. "I wager that if we run a race, I will outstrip you." "That is ridiculous! You with your short legs!" said the hare. "But for my part I am willing, if you have such a monstrous fancy for it. What shall we wager?" "A golden louis-d'or and a bottle of brandy," said the hedgehog. "Done," said the hare. "Shake hands on it, and then it may as well come off at once." "Nay," said the hedgehog, "there is no such great hurry! I am still fasting, I will go home first, and have a little breakfast. In half an hour I will be back again at this place."

Hereupon the hedgehog departed, for the hare was quite satisfied with this. On his way the hedgehog thought to himself, "The hare relies on his long legs, but I will contrive to get the better of him. He may be a great man, but he is a very silly fellow, and he shall pay for what he has said." So when the hedgehog reached home, he said to his wife, "Wife, dress yourself quickly, you must go out to the field with me." "What is going on, then?" said his wife. "I have made a wager with the hare, for a gold louis-d'or and a bottle of brandy. I am to run a race with him, and you must be present." "Good heavens, husband," the wife now cried, "are you out of your mind? Have you completely lost your wits? What can make you want to run a race with the hare?" "Hold your tongue, woman," said the hedgehog, "that is my affair. Don't begin to discuss things which are matters for men. Be off, dress, and come with me." What could the hedgehog's wife do? She was forced to obey him, whether she liked it or not.

So when they had set out on their way together, the hedgehog said to his wife, "Now pay attention to what I am going to say. Look you, I will make the long field our race-course. The hare shall run in one furrow, and I in another, and we will begin to run from the top. Now all that you have to do is to place yourself here below in the furrow, and when the hare arrives at the end of the furrow on the other side of you, you must cry out to him, 'I am here already!' "

Then they reached the field, and the hedgehog showed his wife her place, and then walked up the field. When he reached the top, the hare was already there. "Shall we start?" said the hare. "Certainly," said the hedgehog. "Then both at once." So saying, each placed himself in his own furrow. The hare counted, "Once, twice, thrice, and away!" and went off like a whirlwind down the field. The hedgehog, however, only ran about three paces, and then he stooped down in the furrow, and stayed quietly where he was.

When the hare therefore arrived in full career at the lower end of the field, the hedgehog's wife met him with the cry, "I am here already!" The hare was shocked and wondered not a little. He thought it was the hedgehog himself who was calling to him, for the hedgehog's wife looked just like her husband. The hare, however, thought to himself, "That has not been done fairly," and cried, "It must be run again, let us have it again." Once more he went off like the wind in a storm, so that he seemed to fly. But the hedgehog's wife stayed quietly in her place. So when the hare reached the top of the field, the hedgehog himself cried out to him, "I am here already." The hare, however, quite beside himself with anger, cried, "It must be run again, we must have it again." "All right," answered the hedgehog, "for my part we'll run as often as you choose." So the hare ran seventy-three times more, and the hedgehog always held out against him, and every time the hare reached either the top or the bottom, either the hedgehog or his wife said, "I am here already."

At the seventy-fourth time, however, the hare could no longer reach the end. In the middle of the field he fell to the ground, the blood streamed out of his mouth, and he lay dead on the spot. But the hedgehog took the louis-d'or which he had won and the bottle of brandy, called his wife out of the furrow, and both went home together in great delight, and if they are not dead, they are living there still.

This is how it happened that the hedgehog made the hare run races with him on the Buxtehude heath till he died, and since that time no hare has ever had any fancy for running races with a Buxtehude hedgehog.

The moral of this story, however, is, firstly, that no one, however great he may be, should permit himself to jest at any one beneath him, even if he be only a hedgehog. And, secondly, it teaches, that when a man marries, he should take a wife in his own position, who looks just as he himself looks. So whosoever is a hedgehog let him see to it that his wife is a hedgehog also, and so forth.

The Dog and the Sparrow

THERE WAS once a sheep-dog whose master behaved ill to him and did not give him enough to eat, and when for hunger he could bear it no longer, he left his service very sadly. In the street he was met by a sparrow, who said, "Dog, my brother, why are you so sad?"

And the dog answered, "I am hungry and have nothing to eat."

Then said the sparrow, "Dear brother, come with me into the town; I will give you plenty."

Then they went together into the town, and soon they came to a butcher's stall, and the sparrow said to the dog, "Stay here while I reach you down a piece of meat," and he perched on the stall, looked round to see that no one noticed him, and packed, pulled, and dragged so long at a piece that lay near the edge of the board that at last it slid to the ground. The dog picked it up, ran with it into a corner, and ate it up. Then said the sparrow, "Now come with me to another stall, and I will get you another piece, so that your hunger may be satisfied."

When the dog had devoured a second piece the sparrow asked, "Dog, my brother, are you satisfied now?" "Yes, as to meat, I am," answered he, "but I have had no bread."

Then said the sparrow, "That also shall you have; come with me." And he led him to a baker's stall and pecked at a few little rolls until they fell to the ground, and as the dog still wanted more, they went to another stall farther on and got more bread.

When that was done the sparrow said, "Dog, my brother, are you satisfied yet?" "Yes," answered he, "and now we will walk a little outside the town."

And they went together along the high road. It was warm weather, and when they had gone a little way the dog said, "I am tired, and would like to go to sleep." "Well, do so," said the sparrow; "in the meanwhile I will sit near on a bough."

The dog laid himself in the road and fell fast asleep, and as he lay there a wagoner came up with a wagon and three horses, laden with two casks of wine. The sparrow, seeing that he was not going to turn aside but kept in the beaten track, just where the dog lay, cried out, "Wagoner, take care, or you shall suffer for it!"

But the wagoner, muttering, "What harm can you do to me?" cracked his whip and drove his wagon over the dog, and he was crushed to death by the wheels. Then the sparrow cried, "You have killed the dog my brother and it shall cost you horses and cart!" "Oh! horses and cart!" said the wagoner, "what harm can you do me, I should like to know?" and drove on.

The sparrow crept under the covering of the wagon and pecked at the bung-hole of one of the the casks until the cork came out, and all the wine ran out without the wagoner noticing. After a while, looking round, he saw that something dripped from the wagon, and on examining the casks he found that one of them was empty, and he cried out, "I am a ruined man!"

"Not ruined enough yet!" said the sparrow, and flying to one of the horses he perched on his head and pecked at his eyes. When the wagoner saw that he took out his axe to hit the sparrow, who at that moment flew aloft, and the wagoner, missing him, struck the horse on the head, so that he fell down dead. "Oh, I am a ruined man!" cried he.

"Not ruined enough yet!" said the sparrow, and as the wagoner drove on with the two horses that were left, the sparrow crept again under the wagon-covering and pecked the cork out of the second cask, so that all the wine leaked out. When the wagoner became aware of it, he cried out again, "Oh! I am a ruined man!"

But the sparrow answered, "Not ruined enough yet!" and perched on the second horse's head and began pecking at his eyes. Back ran the wagoner and raised his axe to strike, but the sparrow flying aloft, the stroke fell on the horse, so that he was killed. "Oh! I am a ruined man!" cried the wagoner.

"Not ruined enough yet!" said the sparrow, and perching on the third horse began pecking at his eyes. The wagoner struck out in his anger at the sparrow without taking aim, and missing him, he laid his third horse dead. "Oh! I am a ruined man!" he cried.

"Not ruined enough yet!" answered the sparrow, flying off; "I will see to that at home."

So the wagoner had to leave his wagon standing, and went home full of rage. "Oh!" said he to his wife, "what ill-luck I have had! The wine is spilt, and the horses are all three dead."

"Oh husband!" answered she, "such a terrible bird has come to this house; he has brought with him all the birds of the air, and there they are in the midst of our wheat, devouring it." And he looked and there were thousands upon thousands of birds sitting on the ground, having eaten up all the wheat, and the sparrow in the midst, and the wagoner cried, "Oh! I am a ruined man!"

"Not ruined enough yet!" answered the sparrow. "Wagoner, it shall cost you your life!" and he flew away.

Now the wagoner, having lost everything he possessed, went indoors and sat down, angry and miserable, behind the stove. The sparrow was perched outside on the window-sill, and cried, "Wagoner, it shall cost you your life!"

Then the wagoner seized his axe and threw it at the sparrow, but it broke the window sash in two and did not touch the sparrow, who now hopped inside, perched on the stove, and cried, "Wagoner, it shall cost you your life!" and he, mad and blind with rage, beat in the stove, and as the sparrow flew from one spot to another, hacked everything in pieces—furniture, looking-glasses, benches, table, and the very walls of his house—and yet did not touch the sparrow.

At last he caught and held him in his hand.

"Now," said his wife, "shall I not kill him?" "No!" cried he, "that were too easy a death; I will swallow him," and as the bird was fluttering in the man's mouth, it stretched out its head, saying, "Wagoner, it shall cost you your life!"

Then the wagoner reached the axe to his wife saying, "Wife, strike me this bird dead."

The wife struck, but missed her aim, and the blow fell on the wagoner's head, and he dropped down dead.

But the sparrow flew over the hills and away.

Old Sultan

THERE WAS once a peasant who owned a faithful dog called Sultan, now grown so old that he had lost all his teeth, and could lay hold of nothing. One day the man was standing at the door of his house with his wife, and he said, "I shall kill old Sultan tomorrow; he is of no good any longer."

His wife felt sorry for the poor dog, and answered, "He has

served us for so many years, and has kept with us so faithfully; he deserves food and shelter in his old age."

"Dear me, you do not seem to understand the matter," said the husband; "he has never a tooth, and no thief would mind him in the least, so I do not see why he should not be made away with. If he has served us well, we have given him plenty of good food."

The poor dog, who was lying stretched out in the sun not far off, heard all they said, and was very sad to think that the next day would be his last. He bethought him of his great friend the wolf, and slipped out in the evening to the wood to see him, and related to him the fate that was awaiting him.

"Listen to me, old fellow," said the wolf; "be of good courage, I will help you in your need. I have thought of a way. Early tomorrow morning your master is going hay-making with his wife, and they will take their child with them, so that no one will be left at home. They will be sure to lay the child in the shade behind the hedge while they are at work; you must lie by its side, just as if you were watching it. Then I will come out of the wood and steal away the child and you must rush after me, as if to save it from me. Then I must let it fall, and you must bring it back again to its parents, who will think that you have saved it, and will be much too grateful to do you any harm. On the contrary, you will be received into full favor, and they will never let you want for anything again."

The dog was pleased with the plan, which was carried out accordingly. When the father saw the wolf running away with his child he cried out, and when old Sultan brought it back again, he was much pleased with him, and patted him, saying, "Not a hair of him shall be touched; he shall have food and shelter as long as he lives." And he said to his wife, "Go home directly and make some good stew for old Sultan, something that does not need biting; and get the pillow from my bed for him to lie on."

From that time old Sultan was made so comfortable that he had nothing left to wish for.

Before long the wolf paid him a visit, to congratulate him that all had gone so well. "But, old fellow," said he, "you must wink at my making off by chance with a fat sheep of your master's; perhaps one will escape some fine day." "Don't reckon on that," answered the dog; "I cannot consent to it; I must remain true to my master."

But the wolf, not supposing it was said in earnest, came sneaking in the night to carry off the sheep. But the master, who had been warned by the faithful Sultan of the wolf's intention, was waiting for him, and gave him a fine hiding with the threshing-flail. So the wolf had to make his escape, calling out to the dog, "You shall pay for this, you traitor!"

The next morning the wolf sent the wild boar to call out the dog, and to appoint a meeting in the wood to receive satisfaction from him. Old Sultan could find no second but a cat with three legs, and as they set off together, the poor thing went limping along, holding her tail up in the air. The wolf and his second were already on the spot. When they saw the antagonists coming, and caught sight of the elevated tail of the cat, they thought it was a saber they were bringing with them. And as the poor thing came limping on three legs, they supposed it was lifting a big stone to throw at them. This frightened them very much; the wild boar crept among the leaves, and the wolf clambered up into a tree. And when the dog and cat came up, they were surprised not to see any one there. However, the wild boar was not perfectly hidden in the leaves, and the tips of his ears peeped out. And when the cat caught sight of one, she thought it was a mouse, and sprang upon it, seizing it with her teeth. Out leaped the wild boar with a dreadful cry, and ran away shouting, "There is the culprit in the tree!"

And the dog and the cat, looking up, caught sight of the wolf, who came down, quite ashamed of his timidity, and made peace with the dog once more.

Mr. Korbes

A COCK and a hen once wanted to go on a journey together. So the cock built a beautiful carriage with four red wheels, and he harnessed four little mice to it. And the cock and the hen got into it, and were driven off. Very soon they met a cat, who asked where they were going. The cock answered,

> *"On Mr.Korbes a call to pay,*
> *And that is where we go today!"*

"Take me with you," said the cat.

The cock answered, "Very well, only you must sit well back, and then you will not fall forward.

> *"And pray take care*
> *Of my red wheels there;*

And wheels be steady,
And mice be ready
On Mr. Korbes a call to pay,
For that is where we go today!"

Then there came up a mill-stone, then an egg, then a duck, then a pin, and lastly a needle, who all got up on the carriage, and were driven along. But when they came to Mr. Korbes's house he was not at home. So the mice drew the carriage into the barn, the cock and the hen flew up and perched on a beam, the cat sat by the fireside, the duck settled on the water; but the egg wrapped itself in the towel, the pin stuck itself in the chair cushion, the needle jumped into the bed among the pillows, and the mill-stone laid itself by the door.

Then Mr. Korbes came home, and went to the hearth to make a fire, but the cat threw ashes in his eyes. Then he ran quickly into the kitchen to wash himself, but the duck splashed water in his face. Then he was going to wipe it with the towel, but the egg broke in it, and stuck his eyelids together. In order to get a little peace he sat down in his chair, but the pin ran into him, and, starting up, in his vexation he threw himself on the bed, but as his head fell on the pillow, in went the needle, so that he called out with the pain, and madly rushed out. But when he reached the housedoor the mill-stone jumped up and struck him dead.

What a bad man Mr. Korbes must have been!

The Vagabonds

THE COCK said to the hen, "It is nutting time; let us go together to the mountains and have a good feast for once, before the squirrels come and carry all away." "Yes," answered the hen, "come along; we will have a jolly time together."

Then they set off together to the mountains, and as it was a fine day they stayed there till the evening. Now whether it was that they had eaten so much, or because of their pride and haughtiness, I do not know, but they would not go home on foot; so the cock set to work to make a little carriage out of nutshells. When it was ready, the hen seated herself in it, and said to the cock, "Now you can harness yourself to it."

"That's all very fine," said the cock, "I would sooner go home on foot than do such a thing, and I never agreed to it. I don't mind being coachman, and sitting on the box; but as to drawing it myself, it's quite out of the question."

As they were wrangling, a duck came quacking, "You thieving vagabonds, who told you you might go to my mountain? Look out, or it will be the worse for you!" And she flew at the cock with bill wide open. But the cock was not backward, and he gave the duck a good dig in the body, and hacked at her with his spurs so valiantly that she begged for mercy, and willingly allowed herself to be harnessed to the carriage. Then the cock seated himself on the box and was coachman; so off they went at a great pace, the cock crying out "Run, duck, as fast as you can!"

When they had gone a part of the way they met two foot-passengers—a pin and a needle. They cried "Stop! stop!" and said that it would soon be blindman's holiday; that they could not go a step farther; that the ways were very muddy; might they just get in for a little? They had been standing at the door of the tailors' house of call and had been delayed because of beer.

The cock, seeing they were slender folks that would not take up a great deal of room, let them both step in, only they must promise not to tread on his toes nor on the hen's.

Late in the evening they came to an inn, and there they found that they could not go any farther that night, as the duck's paces were not good—she waddled so much from side to side—so they turned in. The landlord at first made some difficulty; his house was full already, and he thought they had no very distinguished appearance. At last, however, when they had made many fine speeches, and had promised him the egg that the hen had laid on the way, and that he should keep the duck, who laid one every day, he agreed to let them stay the night; and so they had a very gay time.

Early in the morning, when it was beginning to grow light, and everybody was still asleep, the cock waked up the hen, fetched the egg, and made a hole in it, and they ate it up between them, and put the eggshell on the hearth. Then they went up to the needle, who was still sleeping, picked him up by his head, and stuck him in the landlord's chair-cushion, and, having also placed the pin in his towel, off they flew over the hills and far away. The duck, who had chosen to sleep in the open air, and had remained in the yard, heard the rustling of their wings, and, waking up, looked about till she found a brook, down which she swam a good deal faster than she had drawn the carriage.

A few hours later the landlord woke, and, leaving his feather-bed, began washing himself; but when he took the towel to dry himself he drew the pin all across his face, and made a red streak from ear to ear. Then he went into the kitchen to light his pipe, but when he stooped towards the hearth to take up a coal the eggshell flew in his eyes.

"Everything goes wrong this morning," said he, and let himself drop, full of vexation, into his grandfather's chair; but up he jumped in a moment, crying, "Oh dear!" for the needle had gone into him.

Now he became angry, and had his suspicions of the guests who had arrived so late the evening before; and when he looked round for them they were nowhere to be seen.

Then he swore that he would never more harbor such vagabonds, that consumed so much, paid nothing, and played such nasty tricks into the bargain.

The Owl

TWO OR THREE hundred years ago, when people were far from being so crafty and cunning as they are nowadays, an extraordinary event took place in a little town. By some mischance one of the great owls, called horned owls, had come from the neighboring woods into the barn of one of the townsfolk in the night-time, and when day broke did not dare to venture forth again from her retreat, for fear of the other birds, which raised a terrible outcry whenever she appeared.

In the morning when the manservant went into the barn to fetch some straw, he was so mightily alarmed at the sight of the owl sitting there in a corner, that he ran away and announced to his master that a monster, the like of which he had never set eyes on in his life, and which could devour a man without the slightest difficulty, was sitting in the barn, rolling its eyes about in its head.

"I know you already," said the master, "you have courage enough to chase a blackbird about the fields, but when you see a dead hen lying, you have to get a stick before you go near it. I must go and see for myself what kind of a monster it is," added the master, and went quite boldly into the granary and looked round him. When, however, he saw the strange grim creature with his own eyes, he was no less terrified than the servant had been. With two bounds he sprang out, ran to his neighbors, and begged them imploringly to lend him assistance against an unknown and dangerous beast, or else the whole town might be in danger if it were to break loose out of the barn, where it was shut up.

A great noise and clamor arose in all the streets, the townsmen came armed with spears, hay-forks, scythes, and axes, as if they were going out against an enemy; finally, the senators appeared with the burgomaster at their head. When they had drawn up in the market-place, they marched to the barn, and surrounded it on all sides. Thereupon one of the most courageous of them stepped forth and entered with his spear lowered, but came running out immediately afterwards with a shriek, and as pale as death, and could not utter a single word. Yet two others ventured in, but they fared no better.

At last one stepped forth, a great strong man who was famous for his warlike deeds, and said, "You will not drive away the monster by merely looking at him; we must be in earnest here, but I see that you have all turned into women, and not one of you dares to encounter the animal." He ordered them to give him some armor, had a sword and spear brought, and armed himself. All praised his courage, though many feared for his life. The two barn-doors were opened, and they saw the owl, which in the meantime had perched herself on the middle of a great cross-beam. He had a ladder brought, and when he raised it, and made ready to climb up, they all cried out to him that he was to bear himself bravely, and commended him to St.George, who slew the dragon. When he had just got to the top, and the owl perceived that he had designs on her, and was also bewildered by the crowd and the shouting, and knew not how to escape, she rolled her eyes, ruffled her feather, flapped her wings, snapped her beak, and cried, "Tuwhit, tuwhoo," in a harsh voice. "Strike home! strike home!" screamed the crowd outside to the valiant hero. "Any one who was standing where I am standing," answered he, "would not cry 'strike home!'" He certainly did plant his foot one rung higher on the ladder, but then he began to tremble, and half-fainting, went back again.

And now there was no one left who dared to put himself in such danger. "The monster," said they, "has poisoned and mortally wounded the very strongest man among us, by snapping at him and just breathing on him! Are we, too, to risk our lives?" They took counsel as to what they ought to do to prevent the whole town being destroyed. For a long time everything seemed to be of no use, but at length the burgomaster found an expedient. "My opinion," said he, "is that we ought, out of the common purse, to pay for this barn, and whatsoever corn, straw, or hay it contains, and thus indemnify the owner, and then burn down the whole building, and the terrible beast with it. Thus no one will have to endanger his life. This is no time for thinking of expense, and niggardliness would be ill applied." All agreed with him. So they set fire to the barn at all four corners, and with it the owl was miserably burnt. Let any one who will not believe it, go thither and inquire for himself.

The Bremen Town Musicians

THERE WAS once an ass whose master had made him carry sacks to the mill for many a long year, but whose strength began at last to fail, so that each day as it came, found him less capable of work. Then his master began to think of turning him out, but the ass, guessing that something was in the wind that boded him no good, ran away, taking the road to Bremen; for there he thought he might get an engagement as town musician.

When he had gone a little way he found a hound lying by the side of the road panting, as if he had run a long way. "Now, Holdfast, what are you so out of breath about?" said the ass.

"Oh dear!" said the dog, "now I am old, I get weaker every day, and can do no good in the hunt, so, as my master was going to have me killed, I have made my escape; but now how am I to gain a living?"

"I will tell you what," said the ass, "I am going to Bremen to become town musician. You may as well go with me, and take up music too. I can play the lute, and you can beat the drum." And the dog consented, and they walked on together.

It was not for long before they came to a cat sitting in the road, looking as dismal as three wet days. "Now then, what is the matter with you, old shaver?" said the ass.

"I should like to know who would be cheerful when his neck is in danger?" answered the cat. "Now that I am old my teeth are getting blunt, and I would rather sit by the oven and purr than run about after mice, and my mistress wanted to drown me, so I took myself off; but good advice is scarce, and I do not know what is to become of me."

"Go with us to Bremen," said the ass, "and become town musician. You understand serenading." The cat thought well of the idea, and went with them accordingly.

After that the three travelers passed by a yard, and a cock was perched on the gate crowing with all his might. "Your cries are enough to pierce bone and marrow," said the ass; "what is the matter?"

"I have foretold good weather for Lady-day, so that all the shirts may be washed and dried; and now on Sunday morning company is coming, and the mistress has told the cook that I must be made into soup, and this evening my neck is to be wrung, so that I am crowing with all my might while I can."

"You had much better go with us, Chanticleer," said the ass. "We are going to Bremen. At any rate that will be better than dying. You have a powerful voice, and when we are all performing together it will have a very good effect." So the cook consented, and they went on all four together.

But Bremen was too far off to be reached in one day, and towards evening they came to a wood, where they determined to pass the night. The ass and the dog lay down under a large tree; the cat got up among the branches; and the cock flew up to the top, as that was the safest place for him. Before he went to sleep he looked all round him to the four points of the compass, and perceived in the distance a little light shining, and he called out to his companions that there must be a house not far off, as he could see a light, so the ass said, "We had better get up and go there, for these are uncomfortable quarters." The dog began to fancy a few bones, not quite bare, would do him good. And they all set off in the direction of the light, and it grew larger and brighter, until at last it led them to a robber's house, all lighted up. The ass, being the biggest, went up to the window, and looked in.

"Well, what do you see?" asked the dog. "What do I see?" answered the ass; "here is a table set out with splendid eatables and drinkables, and robbers sitting at it and making themselves very comfortable." "That would just suit us," said the cock. "Yes, indeed, I wish we were there," said the ass.

Then they consulted together how it should be managed so as to get the robbers out of the house, and at last they hit on a plan. The ass was to place his fore-feet on the window-sill, the dog was to get on the ass's back, the cat on the top of the dog, and lastly, the cock was to fly up and perch on the cat's head. When that was done, at a given signal they all began to perform their music. The ass brayed, the dog barked, the cat mewed, and the cock crowed; then they burst through into the room, breaking all the panes of glass. The robbers fled at the dreadful sound; they thought it was some goblin, and fled to the wood in the utmost terror. Then the four companions sat down to table, made free with the remains of the meal, and feasted as if they had been hungry for a month. And when they had finished they put out the lights, and each sought out a sleeping-place to suit his nature and habits. The ass laid himself down outside on the dunghill, the dog behind the door, the cat on the hearth by the warm ashes, and the cock settled himself in the cockloft; and as they were all tired with their long journey they soon fell fast asleep.

When midnight drew near, and the robbers from afar saw that no light was burning, and that everything appeared quiet, their captain said to them that he thought that they had run away without reason, telling one of them to go and reconnoitre. So one of them went, and found everything quite quiet. He went into the kitchen to strike a light, and taking the glowing fiery eyes of the cat for burning coals, he held a match to them in order to kindle it. But the cat, not seeing the joke, flew into his face, spitting and scratching. Then he cried out in terror, and ran to get out at the back door, but the dog, who was lying there, ran at him and bit his leg; and as he was rushing through the yard by the dunghill the ass struck out and gave him a great kick with his hindfoot; and the cock, who had been wakened with the noise, and felt quite brisk, cried out, "Cock-a-doodle-doo!"

Then the robber got back as well as he could to his captain, and said, "Oh dear! in that house there is a gruesome witch, and I felt her breath and her long nails in my face; and by the door there stands a man who stabbed me in the leg with a knife; and in the yard there lies a black specter, who beat me with his wooden club; and above, upon the roof, there sits the justice, who cried, 'Bring that rogue here!' And so I ran away from the place as fast as I could."

From that time forward the robbers never ventured to that

house, and the four Bremen town musicians found themselves so well off where they were, that there they stayed. And the person who last related this tale is still living, as you see.

The Wonderful Musician

A WONDERFUL MUSICIAN was walking through a forest, thinking of nothing in particular. When he had nothing more left to think about, he said to himself, "I shall grow tired of being in this wood, so I will bring out a good companion."

He took the fiddle that hung at his back and fiddled so that the wood echoed. Before long a wolf came through the thicket and trotted up to him.

"Oh, here comes a wolf! I had no particular wish for such company," said the musician. But the wolf drew nearer, and said to him, "Ho, you musician, how finely you play! I must learn how to play too." "That is easily done," answered the musician; "you have only to do exactly as I tell you." "Oh musician," said the wolf, "I will obey you, as a scholar does his master."

The musician told him to come with him. As they went a part of the way together they came to an old oak tree, which was hollow within and cleft through the middle. "Look here," said the musician, "if you want to learn how to fiddle, you must put your forefeet in this cleft."

The wolf obeyed, but the musician took up a stone and quickly wedged both his paws with one stroke, so fast, that the wolf was a prisoner, and there obliged to stop. "Stay there until I come back again," said the musician, and went his way.

After a while he said again to himself, "I shall grow weary here in this wood; I will bring out another companion"; and he took his fiddle and fiddled away in the wood. Before long a fox came slinking through the trees.

"Oh, here comes a fox!" said the musician; "I had no particular wish for such company."

The fox came up to him and said, "Oh my dear musician, how finely you play! I must learn how to play too." "That is easily done," said the musician; "you have only to do exactly as I tell you." "Oh musician," answered the fox, "I will obey you, as a scholar his master."

"Follow me," said the musician; and as they went a part of the way together they came to a footpath with a high hedge on each side. Then the musician stopped, and taking hold of a hazel-branch bent it down to the earth, and put his foot on the end of it; then he bent down a branch from the other side, and said, "Come on, little fox, if you wish to learn something, reach me your left fore-foot."

The fox obeyed, and the musician bound the foot to the left-hand branch. "Now, little fox," said he, "reach me the right one"; then he bound it to the right-hand branch. And when he had seen that the knots were fast enough he let go, and the branches flew back and caught up the fox, shaking and struggling, in the air. "Wait there until I come back again," said the musician, and went his way.

By and by he said to himself, "I shall grow weary in this wood; I will bring out another companion." So he took his fiddle, and the sound echoed through the wood. Then a hare sprang out before him. "Oh, here comes a hare!" said he; "that's not what I want."

"Ah, my dear musician," said the hare, "how finely you play! I should like to learn how to play too." "That is soon done," said the musician, "only you must do whatever I tell you."

"Oh musician," answered the hare, "I will obey you, as a scholar his master."

So they went a part of the way together, until they came to a clear place in the wood where there stood an aspen tree. The musician tied a long string round the neck of the hare, and knotted the other end of it to the tree.

"Now then, courage, little hare! Run twenty times round the tree!" cried the musician, and the hare obeyed. As he ran round the twentieth time the string had wound twenty times round the tree trunk and the hare was imprisoned, and pull and tug as he would he only cut his tender neck with the string. "Wait there until I come back again," said the musician, and walked on.

The wolf meanwhile had struggled, and pulled, and bitten at the stone, and worked away so long, that at last he made his paws free and got himself out of the cleft. Full of anger and fury he hastened after the musician to tear him to pieces.

When the fox saw him run by he began groaning, and cried out with all his might, "Brother wolf, come and help me! The musician has betrayed me." The wolf then pulled the branches down, bit the knots in two, and set the fox free, and he went with him to take vengeance on the musician. They found the imprisoned hare, and set him likewise free, and then they all went on together to seek their enemy.

The musician had once more played his fiddle, and this time he had been more fortunate. The sound had reached the ears of a poor wood-cutter, who immediately, and in spite of himself, left his work, and, with his axe under his arm, came to listen to the music.

"At last here comes the right sort of companion," said the musician; "it was a man I wanted, and not wild animals." And then he began to play so sweetly that the poor man stood as if enchanted, and his heart was filled with joy. And as he was standing there up came the wolf, the fox, and the hare, and he could easily see that they meant mischief. Then he raised his shining axe, and stood in front of the musician, as if to say, "Whoever means harm to him had better take care of himself, for he will have to deal with me!"

Then the animals were frightened, and ran back into the wood, and the musician, when he had played once more to the man to show his gratitude, went on his way.

The Mouse, the Bird, and the Sausage

ONCE on a time, a mouse and a bird and a sausage lived and kept house together in perfect peace among themselves, and in great prosperity. It was the bird's business to fly to the forest every day and bring back wood; the mouse had to draw the water, make the fire, and set the table; and the sausage had to do the cooking. Nobody is content in this world; much will have more! One day the bird met another bird on the way, and told him of his excellent condition in life. But the other bird called him a poor simpleton to do so much work, while the two others led easy lives at home.

When the mouse had made up her fire and drawn water, she went to rest in her little room until it was time to lay the cloth. The sausage stayed by the saucepans, looked to it that the victuals were well cooked, and just before dinner-time he stirred the broth or the stew three or four times well round himself, so as to enrich and season and flavor it. Then the bird used to come home and lay down his load, and they sat down to table, and after a good meal they would go to bed and sleep their fill till the next morning. It really was a most satisfactory life.

But the bird came to the resolution next day never again to fetch wood. He had, he said, been their slave long enough; now they must change about and make a new arrangement. So in spite of all the mouse and the sausage could say, the bird was determined to have his own way. So they drew lots to settle it, and it fell so that the sausage was to fetch wood, the mouse was to cook, and the bird was to draw water.

Now see what happened. The sausage went away after wood, the bird made up the fire, and the mouse put on the pot, and they waited until the sausage should come home, bringing the wood for the next day. But the sausage was absent so long, that they thought something must have happened to him, and the bird went part of the way to see if he could see anything of him. Not far off he met with a dog on the road, who, looking upon the sausage as lawful prey, had picked him up, and made an end of him. The bird then lodged a complaint against the dog as an open and flagrant robber, but it was all no good, as the dog declared that he had found forged letters upon the sausage, so that he deserved to lose his life.

The bird then very sadly took up the wood and carried it home himself, and related to the mouse all he had seen and heard. They were both very troubled, but determined to look on the bright side of things, and still to remain together. And so the bird laid the cloth, and the mouse prepared the food, and finally got into the pot, as the sausage used to do, to stir and flavor the broth; but then she had to part with fur and skin, and lastly with life!

And when the bird came to dish up the dinner, there was no cook to be seen; and he turned over the heap of wood, and looked and looked, but the cook never appeared again. By accident the wood caught fire, and the bird hastened to fetch water to put it out, but he let fall the bucket in the well, and himself after it, and as he could not get out again, he was obliged to be drowned.

The Crumbs on the Table

A COUNTRYMAN one day said to his little puppies, "Come into the parlor and enjoy yourselves, and pick up the bread-crumbs on the table; your mistress has gone out to pay some visits." Then the little dogs said, "No, no, we will not go. If the mistress gets to know it, she will beat us." The countryman said, "She will know nothing about it. Do come; after all, she never gives you anything good." Then the little dogs again said, "Nay, nay, we must let it alone, we must not go." But the countryman let them have no peace until at last they went, and got on the table, and ate up the bread-crumbs with all their might. But at that very moment the mistress came, and seized the stick in great haste, and beat them and treated them very badly. And when they were outside the house, the little dogs said to the countryman, "Do, do, do, do, do you see what happened?" Then the countryman laughed and said, "Didn't, didn't, didn't you expect it?" So they just had to run away.

The Cat and the Mouse in Partnership

A CAT having made acquaintance with a mouse, pretended such great love for her, that the mouse agreed that they should live and keep house together.

"We must make provision for the winter," said the cat, "or we shall suffer hunger, and you, little mouse, must not stir out, or you will be caught in a trap."

So they took counsel together and bought a little pot of fat. And then they could not tell where to put it for safety, but after long consideration the cat said there could not be a better place than the church, for nobody would steal there; and they would put it under the altar and not touch it until they were really in want. So this was done, and the little pot placed in safety.

But before long the cat was seized with a great wish to taste it. "Listen to me, little mouse," said he; "I have been asked by my cousin to stand god-father to a little son she has brought into the world; he is white with brown spots; and they want to have the christening today; so let me go to it, and you stay at home and keep house."

"Oh yes, certainly," answered the mouse, "pray go, by all means; and when you are feasting on all the good things, think of me. I should so like a drop of the sweet red wine."

But there was not a word of truth in all this; the cat had no cousin, and had not been asked to stand god-father. He went to the church, straight up to the little pot, and licked the fat off the top. Then he took a walk over the roofs of the town, saw his acquaintances, stretched himself in the sun, and licked his whiskers as often as he thought of the little pot of fat, and then when it was evening he went home.

"Here you are at last," said the mouse; "I expect you have had a merry time." "Oh, pretty well," answered the cat. "And what name did you give the child?" asked the mouse. "Top-off," answered the cat, drily. "Top-off!" cried the mouse, "that is a singular and wonderful name! Is it common in your family?" "What does it matter?" said the cat; "it's not any worse than Crumb-picker, like your god-child."

A little time after this the cat was again seized with a longing. "Again I must ask you," said he to the mouse, "to do me a favor, and keep house alone for a day. I have been asked a second time to stand god-father; and as the little one has a white ring round its neck, I cannot well refuse."

So the kind little mouse consented, and the cat crept along by the town wall until he reached the church, and going straight to the little pot of fat, devoured half of it. "Nothing tastes so well as what one keeps to oneself," said he, feeling quite content with his day's work.

When he reached home, the mouse asked what name had been given to the child. "Half-gone," answered the cat. "Half-gone!" cried the mouse, "I never heard such a name in my life! I'll bet it's not to be found in the calendar."

Soon after that the cat's mouth began to water again for the fat. "Good things always come in threes," said he to the mouse; "again I have been asked to stand god-father. The little one is quite black with white feet, and not any white hair on its body; such a thing does not happen every day, so you will let me go, won't you?"

"Top-off, Half-gone," murmured the mouse, "they are such curious names, I cannot but wonder at them!" "That's because you are always sitting at home," said the cat, "in your little gray frock and hairy tail, never seeing the world, and fancying all sorts of things."

So the little mouse cleaned up the house and set it all in order. Meanwhile the greedy cat went and made an end of the little pot of fat. "Now all is finished, one's mind will be easy," said he, and came home in the evening, quite sleek and comfortable.

The mouse asked at once what name had been given to the third child. "It won't please you any better than the others," answered the cat. "It is called All-gone." "All-gone!" cried the mouse. "What an unheard-of name! I never met with anything like it! All-gone! Whatever can it mean?" And shaking her head, she curled herself round and went to sleep. After that the cat was not again asked to stand god-father.

When the winter had come and there was nothing more to be had out of doors, the mouse began to think of their store. "Come, cat," said she, "we will fetch our pot of fat; how good it will taste, to be sure!" "Of course it will," said the cat, "just as good as if you stuck your tongue out of the window!"

So they set out, and when they reached the place, they found the pot, but it was standing empty.

"Oh, now I know what it all meant," cried the mouse; "now I see what sort of a partner you have been! Instead of standing god-father you have devoured it all up; first Top-off, then Half-gone, then"—

"Will you hold your tongue!" screamed the cat, "another word, and I devour you too!"

And the poor little mouse, having "All-gone" on her tongue, out it came, and the cat leaped upon her and made an end of her. And that is the way of the world.

The Spider and the Flea

A SPIDER and a Flea dwelt together in one house, and brewed their beer in an egg-shell. One day, when the Spider was stirring it up, she fell in and scalded herself. Thereupon the Flea began to scream. And then the Door asked, "Why are you screaming, Flea?" "Because little Spider has scalded herself in the beer-tub," replied she.

Thereupon the Door began to creak as if it were in pain; and a Broom, which stood in the corner, asked, "What are you creaking for, Door?" "May I not creak?" it replied,

> *"The little Spider's scalded herself,*
> *And the Flea weeps."*

So the Broom began to sweep industriously, and presently a little Cart came by, and asked the reason. "May I not sweep?" replied the Broom,

> *"The little Spider's scalded herself,*
> *And the Flea weeps;*
> *The little Door creaks with the pain."*

Thereupon the little Cart said, "So will I run," and began to run very fast past a heap of Ashes, which cried out, "Why do you run, little Cart?" "Because," replied the Cart,

> *"The little Spider's scalded herself,*
> *And the Flea weeps;*
> *The little Door creaks with the pain,*
> *And the Broom sweeps."*

"Then," said the Ashes, "I will burn furiously." Now, next the Ashes there grew a Tree, which asked, "Little heap, why do you burn?" "Because," was the reply,

> *"The little Spider's scalded herself,*
> *And the Flea weeps;*
> *The little Door creaks with the pain,*
> *And the Broom sweeps;*
> *The little Cart runs on so fast."*

Thereupon the Tree cried, "I will shake myself!" and went on shaking till all its leaves fell off.

A little girl passing by with a water-pitcher saw it shaking, and asked, "Why do you shake yourself, little Tree?" "Why may I not?" said the Tree,

> *"The little Spider's scalded herself,*
> *And the Flea weeps;*
> *The little Door creaks with the pain,*
> *And the Broom sweeps;*
> *The little Cart runs on so fast,*
> *And the Ashes burn."*

Then the Maiden said, "If so, I will break my pitcher"; and she threw it down and broke it.

At this the Streamlet, from which she drew the water, asked, "Why do you break your pitcher, my little Girl?" "Why may I not?" she replied; for

*"The little Spider's scalded herself,
And the Flea weeps;
The little Door creaks with the pain,
And the Broom sweeps;
The little Cart runs on so fast,
And the Ashes burn;
The little Tree shakes down its leaves—
Now it is my turn!"*

"Ah, then," said the Streamlet, "now must I begin to flow." And it flowed and flowed along, in a great stream, which kept getting bigger and bigger, until at last it swallowed up the little Girl, the little Tree, the Ashes, the Cart, the Broom, the Door, the Flea and, last of all, the Spider, all together.

The Wolf and the Seven Little Kids

THERE WAS once on a time an old goat who had seven little kids, and loved them with all the love of a mother for her children. One day she wanted to go into the forest and fetch some food. So she called all seven to her and said, "Dear children, I have to go into the forest; be on your guard against the wolf; if he comes in, he will devour you all—skin, hair, and all. The wretch often disguises himself, but you will know him at once by his rough voice and his black feet."

The kids said, "Dear mother, we will take good care of ourselves; you may go away without any anxiety." Then the old one bleated, and went on her way with an easy mind.

It was not long before some one knocked at the house-door and cried, "Open the door, dear children; your mother is here, and has brought something back with her for each of you."

But the little kids knew that it was the wolf, by the rough voice. "We will not open the door," cried they, "you are not our mother. She has a soft, pleasant voice, but your voice is rough; you are the wolf!" The wolf went away to a shopkeeper and bought himself a great lump of chalk, ate this and made his voice soft with it.

Then he came back, knocked at the door of the house, and cried, "Open the door, dear children, your mother is here and has brought something back with her for each of you."

But the wolf had laid his black paws against the window, and the children saw them and cried, "We will not open the door, our mother has not black feet like you: you are the wolf!" Then the wolf ran to a baker and said, "I have hurt my feet; rub some dough over them for me." And when the baker had rubbed his feet over, he ran to the miller and said, "Strew some white meal over my feet for me." The miller thought to himself, "The wolf wants to deceive some one," and refused; but the wolf said, "If you will not do it, I will devour you." Then the miller was afraid, and made his paws white for him.

Now the wretch went for the third time to the house-door, knocked at it and said, "Open the door for me, children, your dear little mother has come home, and has brought every one of you something back from the forest with her." The little kids cried, "First show us your paws that we may know if you are our dear little mother." Then he put his paws in through the window, and when the kids saw that they were white, they believed that all he said was true, and opened the door. But who should come in but the wolf!

They were terrified and wanted to hide themselves. One sprang under the table, the second into the bed, the third into the stove, the fourth into the kitchen, the fifth into the cupboard, the sixth under the washing-bowl, and the seventh into the clock-case. But the wolf found them all, and used no great ceremony; one after the other he swallowed them down his throat. The youngest in the clock-case was the only one he did not find.

When the wolf had satisfied his appetite he took himself off, laid himself down under a tree in the green meadow outside, and began to sleep.

Soon afterwards the old goat came home again from the forest. Ah! what a sight she saw there! The house-door stood wide open. The table, chairs, and benches were thrown down, the washing-bowl lay broken to pieces, and the quilts and pillows were pulled off the bed. She sought her children, but they were nowhere to be found. She called them one after another by name, but no one answered. At last, when she came to the youngest, a soft voice cried, "Dear mother, I am in the clock-case." She took the kid out, and it told her that the wolf had come and had eaten all the others. Then you may imagine how she wept over her poor children.

At length in her grief she went out, and the youngest kid ran with her. When they came to the meadow, there lay the wolf by the tree and snored so loud that the branches shook. She looked at him on every side and saw that something was moving and struggling in his gorged body. "Ah, heavens," said she, "is it possible that my poor children whom he has swallowed down for his supper, can be still alive?"

Then the kid had to run home and fetch scissors, and a needle and thread, and the goat cut open the monster's stomach, and hardly had she made one cut, than one little kid thrust its head out, and when she had cut farther, all six sprang out one after another, and were all still alive, and had suffered no injury whatever, for in his greediness the monster had swallowed them down whole. What rejoicing there was! Then they embraced their dear mother, and jumped like a tailor at his wedding.

The mother, however, said, "Now go and look for some big stones, and we will fill the wicked beast's stomach with them while he is still asleep." Then the seven kids dragged the stones thither with all speed, and put as many of them into his stomach as they could get in; and the mother sewed him up again in the greatest haste, so that he was not aware of anything and never once stirred.

When the wolf at length had had his sleep out, he got on his legs, and as the stones in his stomach made him very thirsty, he wanted to go to a well to drink. But when he began to walk and to move about, the stones in his stomach knocked against each other and rattled. Then cried he,

> *"What rumbles and tumbles*
> *Against my poor bones?*
> *I thought 'twas six kids,*
> *But it's naught but big stones."*

And when he got to the well and stooped over the water and was just about to drink, the heavy stones made him fall in and there was no help, but he had to drown miserably. When the seven kids saw that, they came running to the spot and cried aloud, "The wolf is dead! The wolf is dead!" and danced for joy round about the well with their mother.

The Wolf and the Fox

A WOLF and a fox once lived together. The fox, who was the weaker of the two, had to do all the hard work, which made him anxious to leave his companion.

One day, passing through a wood, the wolf said, "Red-fox, get me something to eat, or I shall eat you."

The fox answered, "I know a place where there are a couple of nice young lambs; if you like, we will go and fetch one."

This pleased the wolf, so they went. The fox stole one, brought it to the wolf, and then ran away, leaving his comrade to devour it. This done, the wolf was not content, but wishing for the other, went himself to fetch it; and being very awkward, the old sheep saw him, and began to cry and bleat so horribly that the farmer's people came running to see what was the matter. Of course they found the wolf there, and beat him so unmercifully, that, howling and limping, he returned to the fox. "You had already shown me how, so I went to fetch the other lamb," said he, "but the farmer's people discovered me, and have nearly killed me."

"Why are you such a glutton?" replied the fox.

The next day they went again into the fields. "Red-fox," said the wolf, "get me something quickly to eat, or I shall eat you!"

"Well," replied the fox, "I know a farm, where the woman is baking pancakes this evening; let us go and fetch some." They went accordingly, and the fox, slipping round the house, peeped and sniffed so long, that he found out at last where the dish stood, then quietly abstracting six pancakes, he carried them to the wolf.

"Here is something for you to eat," said he, and then went away. The wolf had swallowed the six pancakes in a very short space of time, and said, "I should very much like some more." But going to help himself, he pulled the dish down from the shelf; it broke into a thousand pieces, and the noise, in addition, brought out the farmer's wife to discover what was the matter. Upon seeing the wolf, she raised such an alarm, that all the people came with sticks or any weapon they could snatch. The consequence was that the wolf barely escaped with his life; he was beaten so severely that he could scarcely hobble to the wood where the fox was.

"Pretty mischief you have led me into," said the wolf, when he saw him, "the peasants have caught, and nearly flayed me."

"Why, then, are you such a glutton?" replied the fox.

Upon a third occasion, being out together, and the wolf only able with difficulty to limp about, he nevertheless said again, "Red-fox, get me something to eat, or I shall eat you!"

"Well," said the fox, "I know a man who has been butchering, and has all the meat salted down in a tub in his cellar. We will go and fetch it."

"That will do," said the wolf, "but I must go with you, and you can help me to get off, if anything should happen."

The fox then showed him all the by-ways, and at last they came to the cellar, where they found meat in abundance, which the wolf instantly greedily attacked, saying at the same time to himself, "Here, there is no occasion to hurry." The fox also showed no hesitation, only, while eating, he looked sharply about him, and ran occasionally to the hole by which they had entered in order to try if he was still small enough to get out by the same way he had come in.

"Friend fox," said the wolf, "pray tell me why you are so fidgety, and why you run about in such an odd manner." "I am looking out, lest any one should come," replied the cunning creature. "Come, are you not eating too much?"

"I am not going away," said the wolf, "until the tub is empty; that would be foolish!"

In the meantime, the farmer, who had heard the fox running about, came into the cellar to see what was stirring, and upon the first sight of him, the fox with one leap was through the hole and on his way to the wood. But when the wolf attempted to follow, he had so increased his size by his greediness, that he could not succeed, and stuck in the hole, which enabled the farmer to kill him with his cudgel. The fox, however, reached the wood in safety, and rejoiced to be freed from the old glutton.

The Wolf and the Man

A FOX was one day talking to a Wolf about the strength of man. "No animals," he said, "could withstand Man, and they were obliged to use cunning to hold their own against him."

The Wolf answered, "If ever I happen to see a Man, I should attack him all the same."

"Well, I can help you to that," said the Fox. "Come to me early tomorrow, and I will show you one!"

The Wolf was early astir, and the Fox took him out to a road in the forest, traversed daily by a Huntsman.

First came an old discharged soldier. "Is that a Man?" asked the Wolf. "No," answered the Fox. "He has been a Man."

After that a little boy appeared on his way to school. "Is that a Man?" "No; he is going to be a Man."

At last the Huntsman made his appearance, his gun on his back, and his hunting-knife at his side. The Fox said to the Wolf, "Look! There comes a Man. You may attack him, but I will make off to my hole!"

The Wolf set on the Man, who said to himself when he saw him, "What a pity my gun isn't loaded with ball," and fired a charge of shot in the Wolf's face. The Wolf made a wry face, but he was not to be so easily frightened, and attacked him again. Then the Huntsman gave him the second charge. The Wolf swallowed the pain, and rushed at the Huntsman. But the Man drew his bright hunting-knife, and hit out right and left with it, so that, streaming with blood, the Wolf ran back to the Fox.

"Well, brother Wolf," said the Fox, "and how did you get on with the Man?"

"Alas!" said the Wolf. "I never thought the strength of man would be what it is. First, he took a stick from his shoulder, and blew into it, and something flew into my face, which tickled frightfully. Then he blew into it again, and it flew into my eyes and nose like lightning and hail. Then he drew a shining rib out of his body, and struck at me with it till I was more dead than alive."

"Now, you see," said the Fox, "what a braggart you are. You throw your hatchet so far that you can't get it back again."

Gossip Wolf and the Fox

THE SHE-WOLF brought forth a young one, and invited the fox to be godfather. "After all, he is a near relative of ours," said she, "he has a good understanding, and much talent; he can instruct my little son, and help him forward in the world." The fox, too, appeared quite honest, and said, "Worthy Mrs. Gossip, I thank you for the honor which you are doing me; I will, however, conduct myself in such a way that you shall be repaid for it."

He enjoyed himself at the feast, and made merry. Afterwards he said, "Dear Mrs. Gossip, it is our duty to take care of the child, it must have good food that it may be strong. I know a sheep-fold from which we might fetch a nice morsel."

The wolf was pleased, and she went out with the fox to the farmyard. He pointed out the fold from afar, and said, "You will be able to creep in there without being seen, and in the meantime I will look about on the other side to see if I can pick up a chicken." He, however, did not go there, but sat down at the entrance to the forest, stretched his legs and rested.

The she-wolf crept into the stable. A dog was lying there, and it made such a noise that the peasants came running out, caught Gossip Wolf, and poured a strong burning mixture, which had been prepared for washing, over her skin. At last she escaped, and dragged herself outside.

There lay the fox, who pretended to be full of complaints, and said, "Ah, dear Mistress Gossip, how ill I have fared, the peasants have fallen on me, and have broken every limb I have; if you do not want me to lie where I am and perish, you must carry me away." The she-wolf herself was only able to go away slowly, but she was in such concern about the fox that she took him on her back, and slowly carried him perfectly safe and sound to her house.

Then the fox cried to her, "Farewell, dear Mistress Gossip, may the roasting you have had do you good," laughed heartily at her, and bounded off.

Little Red Riding Hood

THERE WAS once a sweet little maid, much beloved by everybody, but most of all by her grandmother, who never knew how to make enough of her. Once she sent her a little riding hood of red velvet, and as it was very becoming to her, and she never wore anything else, people called her Little Red Riding Hood.

One day her mother said to her, "Come, Little Red Riding Hood, here are some cakes and a flask of wine for you to take to grandmother; she is weak and ill, and they will do her good. Make haste and start before it grows hot, and walk properly and nicely, and don't run, or you might fall and break the flask of wine, and there would be none left for grandmother. And when you go into her room, don't forget to say good morning, instead of staring about you." "I will be sure to take care," said Little Red Riding Hood to her mother, and gave her hand upon it.

Now the grandmother lived away in the wood, half an hour's walk from the village; and when Little Red Riding Hood had reached the wood, she met the wolf; but as she did not know what a bad sort of animal he was, she did not feel frightened.

"Good day, Little Red Riding Hood," said he. "Thank you kindly, wolf," answered she. "Where are you going so early, Little Red Riding Hood?" "To my grandmother's." "What are you carrying under your apron?" "Cakes and wine; we baked yesterday; and my grandmother is very weak and ill, so they will do her good, and strengthen her."

"Where does your grandmother live, Little Red Riding Hood?" "A quarter of an hour's walk from here; her house stands beneath the three oak trees, and you may know it by the hazel bushes," said Little Red Riding Hood.

The wolf thought to himself, "That tender young thing would be a delicious morsel, and would taste better than the old one; I must manage somehow to get both of them."

Then he walked by Little Red Riding Hood a little while, and said, "Little Red Riding Hood, just look at the pretty flowers that are growing all round you; and I don't think you are listening to the song of the birds; you are posting along just as if you were going to school, and it is so delightful out here in the wood."

Little Red Riding Hood glanced round her, and when she saw the sunbeams darting here and there through the trees, and lovely flowers everywhere, she thought to herself, "If I were to take a fresh nosegay to my grandmother she would be very pleased, and it is so early in the day that I shall reach her in plenty of time"; and so she ran about in the wood, looking for flowers. And as she picked one she saw a still prettier one a little farther off, and so she went farther and farther into the wood.

But the wolf went straight to the grandmother's house and knocked at the door. "Who is there?" cried the grandmother. "Little Red Riding Hood," he answered, "and I have brought you some cake and wine. Please open the door." "Lift the latch," cried the grandmother; "I am too feeble to get up."

So the wolf lifted the latch, and the door flew open, and he fell on the grandmother and ate her up without saying one word. Then he drew on her clothes, put on her cap, lay down in her bed, and drew the curtains.

Little Red Riding Hood was all this time running about among the flowers, and when she had gathered as many as she could hold, she remembered her grandmother, and set off to go to her. She was surprised to find the door standing open, and when she came inside she felt very strange, and thought to herself, "Oh dear, how uncomfortable I feel, and I was so glad this morning to go to my grandmother!"

And when she said, "Good morning," there was no answer. Then she went up to the bed and drew back the curtains; there lay the grandmother with her cap pulled over her eyes, so that she looked very odd.

"O grandmother, what large ears you have!" "The better to hear with."

"O grandmother, what great eyes you have!" "The better to see with."

"O grandmother, what large hands you have!" "The better to take hold of you with."

"But, grandmother, what a terrible large mouth you have!" "The better to devour you!" And no sooner had the wolf said it than he made one bound from the bed, and swallowed up poor Little Red Riding Hood.

Then the wolf, having satisfied his hunger, lay down again in the bed, went to sleep, and began to snore loudly. The huntsman heard him as he was passing by the house, and thought, "How the old woman snores—I had better see if there is anything the matter with her."

Then he went into the room, and walked up to the bed, and saw the wolf lying there. "At last I find you, you old sinner!" said he; "I have been looking for you a long time."

And he made up his mind that the wolf had swallowed the grandmother whole, and that she might yet be saved. So he did not fire, but took a pair of shears and began to slit up the wolf's body. When he made a few snips Little Red Riding Hood appeared, and after a few more snips she jumped out and cried, "Oh dear, how frightened I have been! It is so dark inside the wolf." And then out came the old grandmother, still living and breathing. But Little Red Riding Hood went and quickly fetched some large stones, with which she filled the wolf's body, so that when he waked up, and was going to rush away, the stones were so heavy that he sank down and fell dead.

They were all three very pleased. The huntsman took off the wolf's skin, and carried it home. The grandmother ate the cakes, and drank the wine, and held up her head again, and Little Red Riding Hood said to herself that she would never more stray about in the wood alone, but would mind what her mother told her.

It must also be related how a few days afterwards, when Little Red Riding Hood was again taking cakes to her grandmother, another wolf spoke to her, and wanted to tempt her to leave the path; but she was on her guard, and went straight on her way, and told her grandmother how that the wolf had met her, and wished her good day, but had looked so wicked about the eyes that she thought if it had not been on the high road he would have devoured her.

"Come," said the grandmother, "we will shut the door, so that he may not get in."

Soon after came the wolf knocking at the door, and calling out, "Open the door, grandmother, I am Little Red Riding Hood, bringing you cakes." But they remained still, and did not open the door. After that the wolf slunk by the house, and got at last upon the roof to wait until Little Red Riding Hood should return home in the evening; then he meant to spring down upon her, and devour her in the darkness. But the grandmother discovered his plot. Now there stood before the house a great stone trough, and the grandmother said to the child, "Little Red Riding Hood, I was boiling sausages yesterday, so take the bucket, and carry away the water they were boiled in, and pour it into the trough."

And Little Red Riding Hood did so until the great trough was quite full. When the smell of the sausages reached the nose of the wolf he snuffed it up, and looked round, and stretched out his neck so far that he lost his balance and began to slip, and he slipped down off the roof straight into the great trough, and was drowned. Then Little Red Riding Hood went cheerfully home, and came to no harm.

How Mrs. Fox Married Again

i

THERE WAS once an old fox with nine tails, who wished to put his wife's affection to proof. He pretended to be dead, and stretched himself under the bench quite stiff, and never moved a joint; on which Mrs. Fox retired to her room and locked herself in, while her maid, the cat, stayed by the kitchen fire and attended to the cooking.

When it became known that the old fox was dead, some suitors prepared to come forward, and presently the maid heard some one knocking at the house door; she went and opened it, and there was a young fox, who said,

> *"What is she doing, Miss Cat?*
> *Is she sleeping, or waking, or what is she at?"*

And the cat answered,

> *"I am not asleep, I am quite wide awake;*
> *Perhaps you would know what I'm going to make;*
> *I'm melting some butter, and warming some beer,*
> *Will it please you sit down, and partake of my cheer?"*

"Thank you, miss," said the fox. "What is Mrs. Fox doing?" The maid answered,

> *"She is sitting upstairs in her grief,*
> *And her eyes with her weeping are sore;*
> *From her sorrow she gets no relief,*
> *Now poor old Mr. Fox is no more!"*

"But just tell her, miss, that a young fox has come to woo her." "Very well, young master," answered the cat.

> *Up went the cat, pit-a-pat, pit-a-pat.*
> *She knocks at the door, rat-a-tat, rat-a-tat!*
> *"Mrs. Fox, are you there?"*
> *"Yes, yes, pussy dear!"*
> *"There's a suitor below,*
> *Shall I tell him to go?"*

"But what is he like?" asked Mrs. Fox. "Has he nine beautiful tails, like dear Mr. Fox?" "Oh no," answered the cat; "he has only one." "Then I won't have him," said Mrs. Fox. So the cat went down-stairs, and sent the suitor away.

Soon there was another knock at the door. It was another fox come to woo. He had two tails, but he met with no better success than the first. Then there arrived more foxes, one after another, each with one more tail than the last, but they were all dismissed, until there came one with nine tails like old Mr. Fox. When the widow heard that she cried, full of joy, to the cat,

> *"Now, open door and window wide,*
> *And turn old Mr. Fox outside."*

But before they could do so, up jumped old Mr. Fox from under the bench, and cudgeled the whole pack, driving them, with Mrs. Fox, out of the house.

ii

WHEN old Mr. Fox died there came a wolf to woo, and he knocked at the door, and the cat opened to him; and he made her a bow, and said,

> *"Good day, Miss Cat, so brisk and gay,*
> *How is it that alone you stay?*
> *And what is it you cook today?"*

The cat answered,

> *"Bread so white, and milk so sweet,*
> *Will it please you sit and eat?"*

"Thank you very much, Miss Cat," answered the wolf; "but is Mrs. Fox at home?"

Then the cat said,

> *"She is sitting upstairs in her grief,*
> *And her eyes with her weeping are sore;*
> *From her sorrow she gets no relief,*
> *Now poor old Mr. Fox is no more!"*

The wolf answered,

> *"Won't she take another spouse,*
> *To protect her and her house?"*
> *Up went the cat, pit-a-pat, pit-a-pat.*
> *She knocks at the door, rat-a-tat, rat-a-tat!*
> *"Mrs. Fox, are you there?"*
> *"Yes, yes, pussy dear!"*
> *"There's a suitor below,*
> *Shall I tell him to go?"*

But Mrs. Fox asked, "Has the gentleman red breeches and a sharp nose?" "No," answered the cat. "Then I won't have him," said Mrs. Fox.

After the wolf was sent away, there came a dog, a stag, a hare, a bear, a lion, and several other wild animals. But they all of them lacked the good endowments possessed by the late Mr. Fox, so that the cat had to send them all away.

At last came a young fox. And Mrs. Fox inquired whether he had

red breeches and a sharp nose. "Yes, he has," said the cat. "Then I
will have him," said Mrs. Fox, and bade the cat make ready the
wedding-feast.

> *"Now, cat, sweep the parlors and bustle about,*
> *And open the window, turn Mr. Fox out;*
> *Then, if you've a fancy for anything nice,*
> *Just manage to catch for yourself a few mice,*
> *You may eat them alone,*
> *I do not want one."*

So she was married to young Master Fox with much dancing and
rejoicing, and for anything I have heard to the contrary, they may
be dancing still.

The Fox and the Geese

THE FOX once came to a meadow in which was a flock of fine fat
geese, on which he smiled and said, "I come at the nick of time, you
are sitting together quite beautifully, so that I can eat you up one
after the other." The geese cackled with terror, sprang up, and
began to wail and beg piteously for their lives. But the fox would
listen to nothing, and said, "There is no mercy to be had! You must
die."

At length one of them took heart and said, "If we poor geese are
to yield up our vigorous young lives, show us the only possible favor
and allow us one more prayer, that we may not die in our sins, and
then we will place ourselves in a row, so that you can always pick
yourself out the fattest." "Yes," said the fox, "that is reasonable, and
a pious request. Pray away, I will wait till you are done." Then the
first began a good long prayer, forever saying, "Ga! Ga!" and as she
would make no end, the second did not wait until her turn came,
but began also, "Ga! Ga!" The third and fourth followed her, and
soon they were all cackling together.

When they have done praying, the story shall be continued
further, but at present they are still praying, and they show no sign
of stopping.

The Fox and the Horse

A PEASANT had a faithful horse which had grown old and could do no more work, so his master would no longer give him anything to eat and said, "I can certainly make no more use of you, but still I mean well by you; if you prove yourself still strong enough to bring me a lion here, I will maintain you, but now take yourself away out of my stable," and with that he chased him into the open country. The horse was sad, and went to the forest to seek a little protection there from the weather.

There a fox met him and said, "Why do you hang your head so, and go about all alone?" "Alas," replied the horse, "avarice and fidelity do not dwell together in one house. My master has forgotten what services I have performed for him for so many years, and because I can no longer plough well, he will give me no more food, and has driven me out." "Without giving you a chance?" asked the fox. "The chance was a bad one. He said, if I were still strong enough to bring him a lion, he would keep me, but he well knows that I cannot do that." The fox said, "I will help you. Just lay yourself down, stretch yourself out, as if you were dead, and do not stir." The horse did as the fox desired, and the fox went to the lion, who had his den not far off, and said, "A dead horse is lying outside there, just come with me, you can have a rich meal." The lion went with him, and when they were both standing by the horse the fox said, "After all it is not very comfortable for you here—I tell you what—I will fasten it to you by the tail, and then you can drag it into your cave, and devour it in peace."

This advice pleased the lion. He lay down, and in order that the fox might tie the horse fast to him, he kept quite quiet. But the fox tied the lion's legs together with the horse's tail, and twisted and fastened all so well and so strongly that no strength could break it. When he had finished his work, he tapped the horse on the shoulder and said, "Pull, white horse, pull." Then up sprang the horse at once, and drew the lion away with him. The lion began to roar so that all the birds in the forest flew out in terror, but the horse let him roar, and drew him and dragged him over the country to his master's door.

When the master saw the lion, he was of a better mind, and said to the horse, "You shall stay with me and fare well," and he gave him plenty to eat until he died.

The Fox and the Cat

IT HAPPENED that the cat met the fox in a forest, and as she thought to herself, "He is clever and full of experience, and much esteemed in the world," she spoke to him in a friendly way. "Good day, dear Mr. Fox, how are you? How is all with you? How are you getting through this dear season?"

The fox, full of all kinds of arrogance, looked at the cat from head to foot, and for a long time did not know whether he would give any answer or not. At last he said, "Oh, thou wretched beard-cleaner, thou piebald fool, thou hungry mousehunter, what canst thou be thinking of? Dost thou venture to ask how I am getting on? What has thou learnt? How many arts dost thou understand?"

"I understand but one," replied the cat, modestly. "What art is that?" asked the fox. "When the hounds are following me, I can spring into a tree and save myself." "Is that all?" said the fox. "I am master of a hundred arts, and have into the bargain a sackful of cunning. Thou makest me sorry for thee; come with me, I will teach thee how people get away from the hounds."

Just then came a hunter with four dogs. The cat sprang nimbly up a tree, and sat down at the top of it, where the branches and foliage quite concealed her. "Open your sack, Mr. Fox, open your sack," cried the cat to him, but the dogs had already seized him, and were holding him fast. "Ah, Mr. Fox," cried the cat. "You with your hundred arts are left in the lurch! Had you been able to climb like me, you would not have lost your life."

The Sole

THE FISHES had for a long time been discontented because no order prevailed in their kingdom. None of them turned aside for the others, but all swam to the right or the left as they fancied, or darted between those who wanted to stay together, or got into their way; and a strong one gave a weak one a blow with its tail, which drove it away, or else swallowed it up without more ado. "How delightful it would be," said they, "if we had a King who enforced law and justice among us!" And they met together to choose for their ruler the one who could cleave through the water most quickly and give help to the weak ones.

They placed themselves in rank and file by the shore, and the pike gave the signal with his tail, on which they all started. Like an arrow, the pike darted away, and with him the herring, the gudgeon, the perch, the carp, and all the rest of them. Even the sole swam with them, and hoped to reach the winning-place. All at once, the cry was heard, "The herring is first. The herring is first!" "Who is first?" screamed angrily the flat envious sole, who had been left far behind, "who is first?" "The herring! The herring," was the answer. "The naked herring?" cried the jealous creature, "the naked herring?"

Since that time the sole's mouth has been at one side for a punishment.

The Willow-Wren

IN DAYS gone by every sound had its meaning and application. When the smith's hammer resounded, it cried, "Strike away! Strike away." When the carpenter's plane grated, it said, "Here goes! Here goes." If the mill wheel began to clack, it said, "Help, Lord God! Help, Lord God!" And if the miller was a cheat and happened to leave the mill, it spoke High German, and first asked slowly, "Who is there? Who is there?" and then answered quickly, "The miller! The miller!" and at last quite in a hurry, "He steals bravely! He steals bravely! Three pecks in a bushel."

At this time the birds also had their own language which every one understood; now it only sounds like chirping, screeching, and whistling, and to some, like music without words. It came into the birds' minds, however, that they would no longer be without a ruler, and would choose one of themselves to be their King. One alone among them, the green plover, was opposed to this. He had lived free and would die free, and anxiously flying hither and thither, he cried, "Where shall I go? Where shall I go?" He retired into a solitary and unfrequented marsh, and showed himself no more among his fellows.

The birds now wished to discuss the matter, and on a fine May morning they all gathered together from the woods and fields: eagles and chaffinches, owls and crows, larks and sparrows—how can I name them all? Even the cuckoo came, and the hoopoe, his clerk, who is so called because he is always heard a few days before him; and a very small bird, which as yet had no name, mingled with the band. The hen, which by some accident had heard nothing of the whole matter, was astonished at the great assemblage. "What, what, what is going to be done?" she cackled; but the cock calmed his beloved hen, and said, "Only rich people," and told her what they had on hand. It was decided, however, that the one who could fly the highest should be King. A tree-frog which was sitting among the bushes, when he heard that, cried a warning, "No, no, no! no!" because he thought that many tears would be shed because of this; but the crow said, "Caw, caw," and that all would pass off peaceably.

It was now determined that on this fine morning they should at once begin to ascend, so that hereafter no one should be able to say, "I could easily have flown much higher, but the evening came on, and I could do no more." On a given signal, therefore, the whole troop rose up in the air. The dust ascended from the land, and there was tremendous fluttering and whirring and beating of wings, and it looked as if a black cloud was rising up. The little birds were, however, soon left behind. They could go no farther, and fell back to the ground. The larger birds held out longer, but none could equal the eagle, who mounted so high that he could have picked the eyes out of the sun. When he saw that the others could not get up to him, he thought, "Why should I fly still higher? I am the King." And he began to let himself down again. The birds beneath him at once cried, "You must be our King; no one has flown so high." "Except me," screamed the little fellow without a name, who had crept into the breast-feathers of the eagle. And as he was not at all tired, he rose up and mounted so high that he reached heaven itself. When, however, he had gone as far as this, he folded his wings together, and called down with clear and penetrating voice, "I am King! I am King."

"You, our King!" cried the birds angrily. "You have compassed it by trick and cunning!" So they made another condition. He should be King who could go down lowest in the ground. How the goose did flap about with its broad breast when it was once more on the land! How quickly the cock scratched a hole! The duck came off the worst of all, for she leapt into a ditch, but sprained her legs, and waddled away to a neighboring pond, crying, "Cheating, cheating!" The little bird without a name, however, sought out a mouse-hole, slipped down into it, and cried out of it with his small voice, "I am King! I am King!"

"You our King!" cried the birds still more angrily. "Do you think your cunning shall prevail?" They determined to keep him a prisoner in the hole and starve him out. The owl was placed as sentinel in front of it, and was not to let the rascal out if she had any value for her life. When evening was come all the birds were feeling very tired after exerting their wings so much, so they went to bed with their wives and children. The owl alone remained standing by the mouse-hole, gazing steadfastly into it with her great eyes. In the meantime she, too, had grown tired and thought to herself, "You might certainly shut one eye, you will still watch with the other, and the little miscreant shall not come out of his hole." So she shut one eye, and with the other looked straight at the mouse-hole. The little fellow put his head out and peeped, and wanted to slip away, but the owl came forward immediately, and he drew his head back again. Then the owl opened the one eye again, and shut the other, intending to shut them in turn all through the night.

But when she next shut the one eye, she forgot to open the other, and as soon as both her eyes were shut she fell asleep. The little fellow soon observed that, and slipped away.

From that day forth, the owl has never dared to show herself by daylight, for if she does the other birds chase her and pluck her feathers out. She only flies out by night, but hates and pursues mice because they make such ugly holes. The little bird, too, is very unwilling to let himself be seen, because he is afraid it will cost him his life if he is caught. He steals about in the hedges, and when he is quite safe, he sometimes cries, "I am King," and for this reason, the other birds call him in mockery, "King of the hedges."

No one, however, was so happy as the lark at not having to obey the little King. As soon as the sun appears, she ascends high in the air and cries, "Ah, how beautiful that is! Beautiful that is! Beautiful, beautiful! Ah, how beautiful that is!"

The Willow-Wren and the Bear

ONE SUMMER DAY the bear and the wolf were walking in the forest, and the bear heard a bird singing so beautifully that he said, "Brother wolf, what bird is it that sings so well?" "That is the King of the birds," said the wolf, "before whom we must bow down." It was, however, in reality the willow-wren. "If that's the case," said the bear, "I should very much like to see his royal palace; come, take me thither." "That is not done quite as you seem to think," said the wolf; "you must wait until the Queen comes." Soon afterwards, the Queen arrived with some food in her beak, and the lord King came too, and they began to feed their young ones. The bear would have liked to go at once, but the wolf held him back by the sleeve, and said, "No, you must wait until the lord and lady Queen have gone away again." So they observed the hole in which was the nest, and trotted away.

The bear, however, could not rest until he had seen the royal palace, and when a short time had passed, again went to it. The King and Queen had just flown out, so he peeped in and saw five or six young ones lying in it. "Is that the royal palace?" cried the bear; "it is a wretched palace, and you are not King's children, you are disreputable children!" When the young wrens heard that, they were frightfully angry, and screamed, "No, that we are not! Our parents are honest people! Bear, you will have to pay for that!"

The bear and the wolf grew uneasy, and turned back and went into their holes. The young willow-wrens, however, continued to cry and scream, and when their parents again brought food they said, "We will not so much as touch one fly's leg, no, not if we were dying of hunger, until you have settled whether we are respectable children or not; the bear has been here and has insulted us!" Then the old King said, "Be easy, he shall be punished," and he at once flew with the Queen to the bear's cave, and called in, "Old Growler, why have you insulted my children? You shall suffer for it —we will punish you by a bloody war."

Thus war was announced to the bear, and all four-footed animals were summoned to take part in it—oxen, asses, cows, deer, and every other animal the earth contained. And the willow-wren summoned everything which flew in the air; not only birds, large and small, but midges, and hornets, bees and flies had to come.

When the time came for the war to begin, the willow-wren sent out spies to discover who was the enemy's commander-in-chief. The gnat, who was the most crafty, flew into the forest where the enemy was assembled, and hid herself beneath a leaf of the tree where the watchword was to be given. There stood the bear, and he called the fox before him and said, "Fox, you are the most cunning of all animals, you shall be general and lead us." "Good," said the fox, "but what signal shall we agree upon?" No one knew that, so the fox said, "I have a fine long bushy tail, which almost looks like a plume of red feathers. When I lift my tail up quite high, all is going well, and you must charge; but if I let it hang down, run away as fast as you can." When the gnat had heard that, she flew away again, and revealed everything, with the greatest minuteness, to the willow-wren.

When day broke, and the battle was to begin, all the four-footed animals came running up with such a noise that the earth trembled. The willow-wren also came flying through the air with his army with such a humming, and whirring, and swarming, that every one was uneasy and afraid; and on both sides they advanced against each other. But the willow-wren sent down the hornet, with orders to get beneath the fox's tail, and sting it with all his might. When the fox felt the first sting, he started so that he drew up one leg, with the pain, but he bore it, and still kept his tail high in the air; at the second sting, he was forced to put it down for a moment; at the third, he could hold out no longer, and screamed out and put his tail between his legs. When the animals saw that, they thought all was lost, and began to fly, each into his hole, and the birds had won the battle.

Then the King and Queen flew home to their children and cried, "Children, rejoice, eat and drink to your heart's content, we have won the battle!" But the young wrens said, "We will not eat yet, the bear must come to the nest, and beg for pardon and say that we are honorable children, before we will do that." Then the willow-wren flew to the bear's hole and cried, "Growler, you are to come to the nest to my children, and beg their pardon, or else every rib of your body shall be broken." So the bear crept thither in the greatest fear, and begged their pardon. And now at last the young wrens were satisfied, and sat down together and ate and drank, and made merry till quite late into the night.

The Little Folks' Presents

A TAILOR and a goldsmith were traveling together, and one evening when the sun had sunk behind the mountains, they heard the sound of distant music, which became more and more distinct. It sounded strange, but so pleasant that they forgot all their weariness and stepped quickly onwards. The moon had already arisen when they reached a hill on which they saw a crowd of little men and women, who had taken each other's hands, and were whirling round in the dance with the greatest pleasure and delight.

They sang to it most charmingly, and that was the music which the travelers had heard. In the midst of them sat an old man who was rather taller than the rest. He wore a parti-colored coat, and his iron-gray beard hung down over his breast. The two remained standing full of astonishment, and watched the dance. The old man made a sign that they should enter, and the little folks willingly opened their circle. The goldsmith, who had a hump, and like all hunchbacks was brave enough, stepped in; the tailor felt a little afraid at first, and held back, but when he saw how merrily all was going, he plucked up his courage, and followed. The circle closed again directly, and the little folks went on singing and dancing with the wildest leaps.

The old man, however, took a large knife which hung to his girdle, whetted it, and when it was sufficiently sharpened, he looked round at the strangers. They were terrified, but they had not much time for reflection, for the old man seized the goldsmith and with the greatest speed, shaved the hair of his head clean off, and then the same thing happened to the tailor. But their fear left them when, after he had finished his work, the old man clapped them both on the shoulder in a friendly manner, as much as to say, they had behaved well to let all that be done to them willingly, and without any struggle. He pointed with his finger to a heap of coals which lay at one side, and signified to the travelers by his gestures that they were to fill their pockets with them. Both of them obeyed, although they did not know of what use the coals would be to them, and then they went on their way to seek a shelter for the night. When they had got into the valley, the clock of the neighboring monastery struck twelve, and the song ceased. In a moment all had vanished, and the hill lay in solitude in the moonlight.

The two travelers found an inn, and covered themselves up on their straw-beds with their coats, but in their weariness forgot to take the coals out of them before doing so. A heavy weight on their limbs awakened them earlier than usual. They felt in the pockets, and could not believe their eyes when they saw that they were not filled with coals, but with pure gold; happily, too, the hair of their heads and beards was there again as thick as ever.

They had now become rich folks, but the goldsmith, who, in accordance with his greedy disposition, had filled his pockets better, was as rich again as the tailor. A greedy man, even if he has much, still wishes to have more, so the goldsmith proposed to the tailor that they should wait another day, and go out again in the evening in order to bring back still greater treasures from the old man on the hill. The tailor refused, and said, "I have enough and am content; now I shall be a master, and marry my dear object (for so he called his sweetheart), and I am a happy man." But he stayed another day to please him.

In the evening the goldsmith hung a couple of bags over his shoulders that he might be able to stow away a great deal, and took the road to the hill. He found, as on the night before, the little folks at their singing and dancing, and the old man again shaved him clean, and signed to him to take some coal away with him. He was not slow about sticking as much into his bags as would go, went back quite delighted, and covered himself over with his coat. "Even if the gold does weigh heavily," said he, "I will gladly bear that," and at last he fell asleep with the sweet anticipation of waking in the morning an enormously rich man.

When he opened his eyes, he got up in haste to examine his pockets, but how amazed he was when he drew nothing out of them but black coals, and that howsoever often he put his hands in them! "The gold I got the night before is still there before me," thought he, and went and brought it out, but how shocked he was when he saw that it likewise had again turned into coal! He smote his forehead with his dusty black hand, and then he felt that his whole head was bald and smooth, as was also the place where his beard should have been. But his misfortunes were not yet over; he now remarked for the first time that in addition to the hump on his back, a second, just as large, had grown in front of his breast. Then he recognized the punishment of his greediness, and began to weep aloud. The good tailor, who was wakened by this, comforted the unhappy fellow as well as he could, and said, "You have been my comrade in my traveling time; you shall stay with me and share my wealth." He kept his word, but the poor goldsmith was obliged to carry the two humps as long as he lived, and to cover his bald head with a cap.

The Elf

THERE WAS once upon a time a rich King who had three daughters, who daily went to walk in the palace garden. The King was a great lover of all kinds of fine trees, but there was one for which he had such an affection that if anyone gathered an apple from it he wished him a hundred fathoms under ground. And when harvest time came, the apples on this tree were all as red as blood. The three daughters went every day beneath the tree, and looked to see if the wind had not blown down an apple, but they never by any chance found one, and the tree was so loaded with them that it was almost breaking, and the branches hung down to the ground.

The King's youngest child had a great desire for an apple, and said to her sisters, "Our father loves us far too much to wish us underground, it is my belief that he would only do that to people who were strangers." And while she was speaking, the child plucked off quite a large apple, and ran to her sisters, saying, "Just taste, my dear little sisters, for never in my life have I tasted anything so delightful." Then the two other sisters also ate some of the apple, whereupon all three sank deep down into the earth, where they could hear no cock crow.

When mid-day came, the King wished to call them to come to dinner, but they were nowhere to be found. He sought them everywhere in the palace and garden, but could not find them. Then he was much troubled, and made known to the whole land that whosoever brought his daughters back again should have one of them to wife. Hereupon so many young men went about the country in search, that there was no counting them, for every one loved the three children because they were so kind to all, and so fair of face. Three young huntsmen also went out, and when they had traveled about for eight days, they arrived at a great castle, in which were beautiful apartments, and in one room a table was laid on which were delicate dishes which were still so warm that they were smoking, but in the whole of the castle no human being was either to be seen or heard.

They waited there for half a day, and the food still remained warm and smoking, and at length they were so hungry that they sat down and ate, and agreed with each other that they would stay and live in that castle, and that one of them, who should be chosen by casting lots, should remain in the house, and the two others seek the King's daughters. They cast lots, and the lot fell on the eldest; so next day the two younger went out to seek, and the eldest had to stay at home.

At mid-day came a small, small mannikin and begged for a piece of bread; then the huntsman took the bread which he had found there, and cut a round off the loaf and was about to give it to him, but while he was giving it to the mannikin, the latter let it fall, and asked the huntsman to be so good as to give him that piece again. The huntsman was about to do so and stopped, on which the mannikin took a stick, seized him by the hair, and gave him a good beating.

Next day, the second stayed at home, and he fared no better. When the two others returned in the evening, the eldest said, "Well, how have you got on?" "Oh, very badly," said he, and then they lamented their misfortune together, but they said nothing about it to the youngest, for they did not like him at all, and always called him Stupid Hans, because he did not exactly belong to the forest.

On the third day, the youngest stayed at home, and again the little mannikin came and begged for a piece of bread. When the youth gave it to him, the elf let it fall as before, and asked him to be so good as to give him that piece again. Then said Hans to the little mannikin, "What! canst thou not pick up that piece thyself? If thou wilt not take as much trouble as that for thy daily bread, thou dost not deserve to have it." Then the mannikin grew very angry and said he was to do it, but the huntsman would not, and took my dear mannikin, and gave him a thorough beating. Then the mannikin screamed terribly, and cried, "Stop, stop, and let me go, and I will tell thee where the King's daughters are."

When Hans heard that, he left off beating him and the mannikin told him that he was an earth-mannikin, and that there were more than a thousand like him, and that if he would go with him he would show him where the King's daughters were. Then he showed him a deep well, but there was no water in it. And the elf said that he knew well that the companions Hans had with him did not intend to deal honorably with him, therefore if he wished to deliver the King's children, he must do it alone. The two other brothers would also be very glad to recover the King's daughters, but they did not want to have any trouble or danger. Hans was therefore to take a large basket, and he must seat himself in it with his hanger and a bell, and be let down. Below were three rooms, and in each of them was a Princess, with a many-headed dragon, whose heads she was to comb and trim, but he must cut them off. And having said all this, the elf vanished.

When it was evening the two brothers came and asked how he had got on, and he said, "pretty well so far," and that he had seen no one except at mid-day when a little mannikin had come who had begged for a piece of bread, that he had given some to him, but that the mannikin had let it fall and had asked him to pick it up again; but as he did not choose to do that, the elf had begun to lose his temper, and that he had done what he ought not, and had given the elf a beating, on which he had told him where the King's daughters were. Then the two were so angry at this that they grew green and yellow.

Next morning they went to the well together, and drew lots who should first seat himself in the basket, and again the lot fell on the eldest, and he was to seat himself in it, and take the bell with him. Then he said, "If I ring, you must draw me up again immediately." When he had gone down for a short distance, he rang, and they at once drew him up again. Then the second seated himself in the basket, but he did just the same as the first, and then it was the turn of the youngest, but he let himself be lowered quite to the bottom. When he had got out of the basket, he took his hanger, and went and stood outside the first door and listened, and heard the dragon snoring quite loudly. He opened the door slowly, and one of the Princesses was sitting there, and had nine dragon's heads lying upon her lap, and was combing them. Then he took his hanger and hewed at them, and the nine fell off. The Princess sprang up, threw her arms round his neck, embraced and kissed him repeatedly, and took her stomacher, which was made of red gold, and hung it round his neck. Then he went to the second Princess, who had a dragon with five heads to comb, and delivered her also, and to the youngest, who had a dragon with four heads, he went likewise. And they all rejoiced, and embraced him and kissed him without stopping.

Then he rang very loud, so that those above heard him, and he placed the Princesses one after the other in the basket, and had them all drawn up, but when it came to his own turn he remembered the words of the elf, who had told him that his comrades did not mean well by him. So he took a great stone which was lying there, and placed it in the basket, and when it was about half way up, his false brothers above cut the rope, so that the basket with the stone fell to the ground, and they thought that he was dead, and ran away with the three Princesses, making them promise to tell their father that it was they who had delivered them, and then they went to the King, and each demanded a Princess in marriage.

In the meantime the youngest huntsman was wandering about the three chambers in great trouble, fully expecting to have to end his days there, when he saw, hanging on the wall, a flute; then said he, "Why do you hang there, no one can be merry here?" He looked at the dragon's head likewise and said, "You cannot help me now." He walked backwards and forwards for such a long time that he made the surface of the ground quite smooth. At last other thoughts came to his mind, and he took the flute from the wall, and played a few notes on it, and suddenly a number of elves appeared, and with every note that he sounded one more came.

He played until the room was entirely filled. They all asked what he desired, so he said he wished to get above ground back to daylight, on which they seized him by every hair that grew on his head, and thus they flew with him on to the earth again. When he was above ground, he at once went to the King's palace just as the wedding of one Princess was about to be celebrated, and he went to the room where the King and his three daughters were. When the Princesses saw him they fainted. Hereupon the King was angry, and ordered him to be put in prison at once, because he thought he must have done some injury to the children. When the Princesses came to themselves, however, they entreated the King to set him free again. The King asked why, and they said that they were not allowed to tell that, but their father said that they were to tell it to the stove. And he went out, listened at the door, and heard everything. Then he caused the two brothers to be hanged on the gallows, and to the third he gave his youngest daughter, and on that occasion I wore a pair of glass shoes, and I struck them against a stone, and they said, "Klink," and were broken.

The Foundling Bird

A FORESTER went out shooting one day. He had not gone far into the wood when he heard, as he thought, the cry of a child. He turned his steps instantly toward the sound, and at length came to a high tree, on one of the branches of which sat a little child.

A mother, some short time before, had seated herself under the tree with the child in her lap, and fallen asleep. A bird of prey, seeing the child, seized it in its beak and carried it away; but hearing the sound of the sportman's gun, the bird let the child fall, its clothes caught in the branches of a high tree, and there it hung, crying, till the forester came by.

The mother, on awaking and missing her child, rushed away in great agony to find it, so that the poor little thing would have been left alone in the world to die had not the sportsman made his appearance.

"Poor little creature!" he said to himself as he climbed up the tree and brought the child down, "I will take it home with me, and it shall be brought up with my own little Lena."

He kept his word, and the little foundling grew up with the forester's little daughter, till they loved each other so dearly that they were always unhappy when separated, even for a short time. The forester had named the child Birdie, because she had been carried away by the bird; and Lena and Birdie were for several years happy little children together.

But the forester had an old cook, who was not fond of children, and she wanted to get rid of Birdie, who she thought was an intruder.

One evening Lena saw the woman take two buckets to the well, and carry them backward and forward more than twenty times. "What are you going to do with all that water?" asked the child. "If you will promise not to say a word, I will tell you," replied the woman. "I will never tell any one," she said. "Oh, very well, then look here. Tomorrow morning, early, I mean to put all this water into a kettle on the fire, and when it boils I shall throw Birdie in and cook her for dinner."

Away went poor Lena, in great distress, to find Birdie. "If you will never forsake me, I will never forsake you," said Lena. "Then," said Birdie, "I will never, never leave you, Lena." "Well, then," she replied, "I am going away and you must go with me, for old cook says she will get up early tomorrow morning, and boil a lot of water to cook you in, while my father is out hunting. If you stay with me, I can save you. So you must never leave me." "No, never, never!" said Birdie.

So the children lay awake till dawn, and then they got up and ran away so quickly that by the time the wicked old witch got up to prepare the water, they were far out of her reach.

She lit her fire, and as soon as the water boiled went into the sleeping-room to fetch poor little Birdie and throw her in. But when she came to the bed and found it empty, she was very much frightened to find both the children gone, and said to herself, "What will the forester say when he comes home if the children are not here? I must go downstairs as fast as I can and send some one to catch them." Down she went, and sent three of the farm servants to run after the children and bring them back.

The children, who were sitting among the trees in the wood, saw them coming from a distance.

"I will never forsake you, Birdie!" said Lena quickly. "Will you forsake me?" "Never, never!" was the reply. "Then," cried Lena, "you shall be turned into a rose bush, and I will be one of the roses!"

The three servants came up to the place where the old witch had told them to look; but nothing was to be seen but a rose tree and a rose. "There are no children here," they said.

So they went back and told the cook that they had found only roses and bushes, but not a sign of the children.

The old woman scolded them well when they told her this, and said, "You stupid fools! you should have cut off the stem of the rose bush, and plucked one of the roses, and brought them home with you as quickly as possible. You must just go again a second time."

Lena saw them coming, and she changed herself and Birdie so quickly that when the three servants arrived at the spot to which the old woman had sent them they found only a little church with a steeple—Birdie was the church and Lena the steeple.

Then the men said one to another: "What was the use of our coming here? We may as well go home."

But how the old woman did scold! "You fools!" she said, "you should have brought the church and the steeple here. However, I will go myself this time!"

So the wicked old woman started off to find the children, taking the three servants with her.

When they saw the three servants coming in the distance, and the old woman waddling behind, Lena said, "Birdie, we will never forsake each other." "No, no! never, never!" replied the little foundling. "Then you shall be changed into a pond, and I will be a duck swimming upon it."

The old woman drew near, and as soon as she saw the pond she laid herself down by it, and, leaning over, intended to drink it all up. But the duck was too quick for her. She seized the head of the old woman with her beak, and drew it under the water, and held it there till the old witch was drowned.

Then the two children resumed their proper shape, and went home with the three servants, all of them happy and delighted to think that they had got rid of such a wicked old woman. The forester was full of joy in his home with the children near the wood; and if they are not dead they all live there still.

The Water of Life

A KING was very ill, and no one believed that he would come out of it with his life. He had three sons who were much distressed about it, and went down into the palace-garden and wept. There they met an old man who inquired as to the cause of their grief. They told him that their father was so ill that he would most certainly die, for nothing seemed to cure him. Then the old man said, "I know of one more remedy, and that is the water of life; if he drinks of it he will become well again; but it is hard to find." The eldest said, "I will manage to find it," and went to the sick King, and begged to be allowed to go forth in search of the water of life, for that alone could save him. "No," said the King, "the danger of it is too great. I would rather die." But he begged so long that the King consented. The Prince thought in his heart, "If I bring the water, then I shall be best beloved of my father, and shall inherit the kingdom."

So he set out, and when he had ridden forth a little distance, a dwarf stood there in the road who called to him and said, "Whither away so fast?" "Silly shrimp," said the Prince, very haughtily, "it is nothing to you," and rode on. But the little dwarf had grown angry, and had wished an evil wish. Soon after this the Prince entered a ravine, and the further he rode the closer the mountains drew together, and at last the road became so narrow that he could not advance a step further; it was impossible either to turn his horse or to dismount from the saddle, and he was shut in there as if in prison. The sick King waited long for him, but he came not.

Then the second son said, "Father, let me go forth to seek the water," and thought to himself, "If my brother is dead, then the kingdom will fall to me." At first the King would not allow him to go either, but at last he yielded, so the Prince set out on the same road that his brother had taken, and he too met the dwarf, who stopped him to ask whither he was going in such haste. "Little shrimp," said the Prince, "that is nothing to you," and rode on without giving him another look. But the dwarf bewitched him, and he, like the other, got into a ravine, and could neither go forwards nor backwards. So fare haughty people.

As the second son also remained away, the youngest begged to be allowed to go forth to fetch the water, and at last the King was obliged to let him go. When he met the dwarf and the latter asked him whither he was going in such haste, he stopped, gave him an explanation, and said, "I am seeking the water of life, for my father is sick unto death." "Dost thou know, then, where that is to be found?" "No," said the Prince. Then said the dwarf: "As thou hast borne thyself politely and not haughtily like thy false brothers, I will give thee the information and tell thee how thou mayst obtain the water of life. It springs from a fountain in the court-yard of an enchanted castle, but thou wilt not be able to make thy way to it, if I do not give thee an iron wand and two small loaves of bread. Strike thrice with the wand on the iron door of the castle, and it will spring open. Inside lie two lions with gaping jaws, but if thou throwest a loaf to each of them, they will be quieted; then hasten to fetch some of the water of life before the clock strikes twelve, else the door will shut again, and thou wilt be imprisoned."

The Prince thanked him, took the wand and the bread, and set out on his way. When he arrived, everything was as the dwarf had said. The door sprang open at the third stroke of the wand, and when he had appeased the lions with the bread, he entered into the castle, and came in a large and splendid hall, wherein sat some enchanted Princes whose rings he drew off their fingers. A sword and a loaf of bread were lying there, which he carried away. After this, he entered a chamber in which was a beautiful maiden who rejoiced when she saw him, kissed him, and told him that he had delivered her, and should have the whole of her kingdom, and that if he would return in a year their wedding should be celebrated;

likewise she told him where the spring of the water of life was, and that he was to hasten and draw some of it before the clock struck twelve. Then he went onwards, and at last entered a room where there was a beautiful newly-made bed, and as he was very weary, he felt inclined to rest a little. So he lay down and fell asleep.

When he awoke, it was striking a quarter to twelve. He sprang up in a fright, ran to the spring, drew some water in a cup which stood near, and hastened away. But just as he was passing through the iron door, the clock struck twelve, and the door fell to with such violence that it carried away a piece of his heel. He, however, rejoicing at having obtained the water of life, went homewards, and again passed the dwarf. When the latter saw the sword and the loaf, he said, "With these thou hast won great wealth; with the sword thou canst slay whole armies, and the bread will never come to an end."

But the Prince would not go home to his father without his brothers, and said, "Dear dwarf, canst thou not tell me where my two brothers are? They went out before I did in search of the water of life, and have not returned." "They are imprisoned between two mountains," said the dwarf. "I have condemned them to stay there, because they were so haughty." Then the Prince begged until the dwarf released them; he warned him, however, and said, "Beware of them, for they have bad hearts."

When his brothers came, he rejoiced, and told them how things had gone with him, that he had found the water of life, and had brought a cupful away with him, and had delivered a beautiful Princess, who was willing to wait a year for him, and then their wedding was to be celebrated, and he would obtain a great kingdom.

After that they rode on together, and chanced upon a land where war and famine reigned, and the King already thought he must perish, for the scarcity was so great. Then the Prince went to him and gave him the loaf, wherewith he fed and satisfied the whole of his kingdom, and then the Prince gave him the sword also, wherewith he slew the hosts of his enemies, and could now live in rest and peace. The Prince then took back his loaf and his sword, and the three brothers rode on.

After this they entered two more countries where war and famine reigned, and each time the Prince gave his loaf and his sword to the Kings, and had now delivered three kingdoms, and after that they went on board a ship and sailed over the sea. During the passage, the two eldest conversed apart and said, "The youngest has found the water of life and not we; for that our father will give him the kingdom—the kingdom which belongs to us, and he will rob us of all our fortune." They began to seek revenge, and plotted with each other to destroy him. They waited until once when they found him fast asleep, then they poured the water of life out of the cup, and took it for themselves, but into the cup they poured salt seawater. Now therefore, when they arrived at home, the youngest took his cup to the sick King in order that he might drink out of it, and be cured. But scarcely had he drunk a very little of the salt seawater than he became still worse than before. And as he was lamenting over this, the two eldest brothers came, and accused the youngest of having intended to poison him, and said that they had brought him the true water of life, and handed it to him. He had scarcely tasted it, when he felt his sickness departing, and became strong and healthy as in the days of his youth.

After that they both went to the youngest, mocked him, and said, "You certainly found the water of life, but you have had the pain, and we the gain. You should have been sharper, and should have kept your eyes open. We took it from you while you were asleep at sea, and when a year is over, one of us will go and fetch the beautiful Princess. But beware that you do not disclose aught of this to our father; indeed he does not trust you, and if you say a single word, you shall lose your life into the bargain, but if you keep silent, you shall have it as a gift."

The old King was angry with his youngest son, and thought he had plotted against his life. So he summoned the court together, and had sentence pronounced upon his son that he should be secretly shot. And once when the Prince was riding forth to the chase, suspecting no evil, the King's huntsman had to go with him, and when they were quite alone in the forest, the huntsman looked so sorrowful that the Prince said to him, "Dear huntsman, what ails you?" The huntsman said, "I cannot tell you, and yet I ought." Then the Prince said, "Say openly what it is, I will pardon you." "Alas!" said the huntsman, "I am to shoot you dead, the King has ordered me to do it." Then the Prince was shocked, and said, "Dear huntsman, let me live; there, I give you my royal garments; give me your common ones in their stead." The huntsman said, "I will willingly do that, indeed I should not have been able to shoot you." Then they exchanged clothes, and the huntsman returned home; the Prince, however, went further into the forest.

After a time three wagons of gold and precious stones came to the King for his youngest son, which were sent by the three Kings who had slain their enemies with the Prince's sword, and maintained their people with his bread, and who wished to show their gratitude for it. The old King then thought, "Can my son have been innocent?" and said to his people, "Would that he were still alive; how it grieves me that I have suffered him to be killed!" "He still lives," said the huntsman, "I could not find it in my heart to carry out your command," and told the King how it had happened. Then a great weight fell from the King's heart, and he had it proclaimed in every country that his son might return and be taken into favor again.

The Princess, however, had a road made up to her palace which was quite bright and golden, and told her people that whosoever came riding straight along it to her, would be the right wooer and was to be admitted, and whoever rode by the side of it, was not the right one, and was not to be admitted. As the time was now close at hand, the eldest son thought he would hasten to go to the King's daughter, and give himself out as her deliverer, and thus win her for his bride, and the kingdom to boot. Therefore he rode forth, and when he arrived in front of the palace, and saw the splendid golden road, he thought it would be a sin and a shame if he were to ride over that, and turned aside, and rode on the right side of it. When he came to the door, the servants told him that he was not the right man, and was to go away again.

Soon after this the second Prince set out, and when he came to the golden road, and his horse had put one foot on it, he thought it would be a sin and a shame to tread a piece of it off, and he turned aside and rode on the left side of it, and when he reached the door, the attendants told him he was not the right one, and was to go away again.

When at last the year had entirely expired, the third son likewise wished to ride out of the forest to his beloved, with her to forget his sorrows. So he set out and thought of her so incessantly, and wished to be with her so much, that he never noticed the golden road at all. So his horse rode onwards up the middle of it, and when he came to the door, it was opened and the Princess received him with joy, and said he was her deliverer, and lord of the kingdom, and their wedding was celebrated with great rejoicing.

When it was over she told him that his father invited him to come to him, and had forgiven him. So he rode thither, and told him everything; how his brothers had betrayed him, and how he had nevertheless kept silence. The old King wished to punish them, but they had put to sea, and never came back as long as they lived.

The Water Sprite

A LITTLE brother and sister were one day playing together by the side of a well, and not being careful, they both fell in. Under the water they found a fairy, who said to them, "Now I have caught you, I intend you to work for me." So she carried them both away.

When they arrived at her home she set the maiden to spin hard, tangled flax, and gave her a cask full of holes to fill with water; and she sent the boy to the wood with a blunt axe, and told him to cut wood for the fire.

The children became at last so impatient with this treatment that they waited till one Sunday, when the fairy was at church, and ran away. But the church was close by, and as they were flying away like two birds she espied them, and went after them with great strides.

The children saw her coming in the distance, and the maiden threw behind her a great brush, which instantly became a mountain covered with prickly points, over which the fairy had the greatest trouble to climb. But the children saw that she had managed to get over and was coming near.

The boy then threw a comb behind him, which became a mountain of combs, with hundred of teeth sticking up; but the fairy knew how to hold fast on this, and soon clambered over it.

The maiden next threw a looking-glass behind, which became a mountain also, and was so slippery that it was impossible to get over it.

Then thought the fairy, "I will go home and fetch my axe and break the looking-glass."

But when she came back and had broken the looking-glass, the children had been for a long time too far away for her to overtake them, so she was obliged to sink back into the well.

The Table, the Ass, and the Stick

THERE WAS once a tailor who had three sons and one goat. And the goat, as she nourished them all with her milk, was obliged to have good food, and so she was led every day down to the willows by the water-side; and this business the sons did in turn. One day the eldest took the goat to the churchyard, where the best sprouts are, that she might eat her fill and gambol about.

In the evening, when it was time to go home, he said, "Well, goat, have you had enough?" The goat answered,

> *"I am so full,*
> *I cannot pull*
> *Another blade of grass—ba! baa!"*

"Then come home," said the youth, and fastened a string to her, led her to her stall, and fastened her up.

"Now," said the old tailor, "has the goat had her proper food?" "Oh," answered the son, "she is so full, she no more can pull." But the father, wishing to see for himself, went out to the stall, stroked his dear goat, and said, "My dear goat, are you full?" And the goat answered,

> *"How can I be full?*
> *There was nothing to pull,*
> *Though I looked all about me—ba! baa!"*

"What is this that I hear?" cried the tailor, and he ran and called out to the youth, "O you liar, to say that the goat was full, and she has been hungry all the time!" And in his wrath he took up his yard-measure and drove his son out of the house with many blows.

The next day came the turn of the second son, and he found a fine place in the garden hedge, where there were good green sprouts, and the goat ate them all up. In the evening, when he came to lead her home, he said, "Well, goat, have you had enough?" And the goat answered,

> *"I am so full*
> *I cannot pull*
> *Another blade of grass—ba! baa!"*

"Then come home," said the youth, and led her home, and tied her up.

"Now," said the old tailor, "has the goat had her proper food?" "Oh," answered the son, "she is so full, she no more can pull."

The tailor, not feeling satisfied, went out to the stall, and said, "My dear goat, are you really full?" And the goat answered,

> *"How can I be full?*
> *There was nothing to pull,*
> *Though I looked all about me—ba! baa!"*

"The good-for-nothing rascal," cried the tailor, "to let the dear creature go fasting!" and, running back, he chased the youth with his yard-wand out of the house.

Then came the turn of the third son, who, meaning to make all sure, found some shrubs with the finest sprouts possible, and left the goat to devour them. In the evening, when he came to lead her home, he said, "Well, goat, are you full?" And the goat answered,

> *"I am so full,*
> *I cannot pull*
> *Another blade of grass—ba! baa!"*

"Then come home," said the youth, and he took her to her stall, and fastened her up.

"Now," said the old tailor, "has the goat had her proper food?" "Oh," answered the son, "she is so full, she no more can pull."

But the tailor, not trusting his word, went to the goat and said, "My dear goat, are you really full?" The malicious animal answered,

> *"How can I be full?*
> *There was nothing to pull,*
> *Though I looked all about me—ba! baa!"*

"Oh, the wretches!" cried the tailor; "the one as good-for-nothing and careless as the other. I will no longer have such fools about me"; and rushing back, in his wrath he laid about him with his yard-wand, and belabored his son's back so unmercifully that he ran away out of the house.

So the old tailor was left alone with the goat. The next day he went out to the stall, and let out the goat, saying, "Come, my dear creature, I will take you myself to the willows."

So he led her by the string, and brought her to the green hedges and pastures where there was plenty of food to her taste, and saying to her, "Now, for once, you can eat to your heart's content," he left her there till the evening. Then he returned, and said, "Well, goat, are you full?" She answered,

> *"I am so full,*
> *I cannot pull*
> *Another blade of grass—ba! baa!"*

"Then come home," said the tailor, and leading her to her stall, he fastened her up.

Before he left her he turned once more, saying, "Now then, for once you are full." But the goat actually cried,

> *"How can I be full?*
> *There was nothing to pull,*
> *Though I looked all about me—ba! baa!"*

When the tailor heard that he marveled, and saw at once that his three sons had been sent away without reason. "Wait a minute," cried he, "you ungrateful creature! It is not enough merely to drive you away—I will teach you to show your face again among honorable tailors."

So in haste he went and fetched his razor, and seizing the goat he shaved her head as smooth as the palm of his hand. And as the yard-measure was too honorable a weapon, he took the whip and fetched her such a crack that with many a jump and spring she ran away.

The tailor felt very sad as he sat alone in his house, and would willingly have had his sons back again, but no one knew where they had gone.

The eldest son, when he was driven from home, apprenticed himself to a joiner, and he applied himself diligently to his trade, and when the time came for him to travel, his master gave him a little table, nothing much to look at, and made of common wood; but it had one great quality. When any one set it down and said, "Table, be covered!" all at once the good little table had a clean cloth on it, and a plate, and knife, and fork, and dishes with roast and boiled meat, and a large glass of red wine sparkling so as to cheer the heart. The young apprentice thought he was set up for life, and he went merrily out into the world, and never cared whether an inn were good or bad, or whether he could get anything to eat there or not. When he was hungry, it did not matter where he was, whether in the fields, in the woods, or in a meadow, he set down his table and said, "Be covered!" and there he was provided with everything that heart could wish. At last it occurred to him that he would go back to his father, whose wrath might by this time have subsided, and perhaps because of the wonderful table he might receive him again gladly.

It happened that one evening during his journey home he came to an inn that was quite full of guests, who bade him welcome, and asked him to sit down with them and eat, as otherwise he would have found some difficulty in getting anything. "No," answered the young joiner, "I could not think of depriving you; you had much better be my guests."

Then they laughed, and thought he must be joking. But he brought his little wooden table, and put it in the middle of the room, and said, "Table, be covered!" Immediately it was set out with food much better than the landlord had been able to provide, and the good smell of it greeted the noses of the guests very agreeably. "Fall to, good friends," said the joiner; and the guests, when they saw how it was, needed no second asking, but taking up knife and fork fell to valiantly. And what seemed most wonderful was that when a dish was empty immediately a full one stood in its place. All the while the landlord stood in a corner, and watched all that went on. He could not tell what to say about it; but he thought "such cooking as that would make my inn prosper."

The joiner and his fellowship kept it up very merrily until late at night. At last they went to sleep, and the young joiner, going to bed, left his wishing-table standing against the wall. The landlord, however, could not sleep for thinking of the table, and he remembered that there was in his lumber room an old table very like it, so he fetched it, and taking away the joiner's table, he left the other in its place. The next morning the joiner paid his reckoning, took up the table, not dreaming that he was carrying off the wrong one, and went on his way. About noon he reached home, and his father received him with great joy.

"Now, my dear son, what have you learned?" said he to him. "I have learned to be a joiner, father," he answered.

"That is a good trade," returned the father; "but what have you brought back with you from your travels?" "The best thing I've got, father, is this little table," said he.

The tailor looked at it on all sides, and said, "You have certainly produced no masterpiece. It is a rubbishing old table."

"But it is a very wonderful one," answered the son. "When I set it down, and tell it to be covered, at once the finest meats are standing on it, and wine so good that it cheers the heart. Let us invite all the friends and neighbors, that they may feast and enjoy themselves, for the table will provide enough for all."

When the company was all assembled, he put his table in the middle of the room, and commanded it, "Table, be covered!"

But the table never stirred, and remained just as empty as any other table that does not understand talking. When the poor joiner saw that the table remained unfurnished, he felt ashamed to stand there like a fool. The company laughed at him freely, and were obliged to return unfilled and uncheered to their houses. The father gathered his pieces together and returned to his tailoring, and the son went to work under another master.

The second son had bound himself apprentice to a miller. And when his time was up, his master said to him, "As you have behaved yourself so well, I will give you an ass of a remarkable kind: he will draw no cart, and carry no sack." "What is the good of him then?" asked the young apprentice. "He spews forth gold," answered the miller. "If you put a cloth before him and say, 'Bricklebrit,' out come gold pieces from back and front."

"That is a capital thing," said the apprentice, and thanking his master, he went out into the world. Whenever he wanted gold he had only to say "Bricklebrit" to his ass, and there was a shower of gold pieces, and so he had no cares as he traveled about. Wherever he came he lived on the best, and the dearer the better, as his purse was always full. And when he had been looking about him about the world a long time, he thought he would go and find out his father, who would perhaps forget his anger and receive him kindly because of his gold ass.

And it happened that he came to lodge in the same inn where his brother's table had been exchanged. He was leading his ass in his hand, and the landlord was for taking the ass from him to tie it up, but the young apprentice said, "Don't trouble yourself, old fellow, I will take him into the stable myself and tie him up, and then I shall know where to find him."

The landlord thought this was very strange, and he never supposed that a man who was accustomed to look after his ass himself could have much to spend; but when the stranger, feeling in his pocket, took out two gold pieces and told him to get him something good for supper, the landlord stared, and ran and fetched the best that could be got. After supper the guest called the reckoning, and the landlord, wanting to get all the profit he could, said that it would amount to two gold pieces more. The apprentice felt in his pocket, but his gold had come to an end.

"Wait a moment, landlord," said he, "I will go and fetch some money," and he went out of the room, carrying the tablecloth with him. The landlord could not tell what to make of it, and, curious to know his proceedings, slipped after him, and as the guest shut the stable-door, he peeped in through a knothole. Then he saw how the stranger spread the cloth before the ass, saying, "Bricklebrit," and directly the ass let gold pieces fall from back and front, so that it rained down money upon the ground.

"Dear me," said the landlord, "that is an easy way of getting ducats; a purse of money like that is no bad thing."

After that the guest paid his reckoning and went to bed; but the landlord slipped down to the stable in the middle of the night, led the gold ass away, and tied up another ass in his place. The next morning early the apprentice set forth with his ass, never doubting that it was the right one. By noon he came to his father's house, who was rejoiced to see him again, and received him gladly.

"What trade have you taken up, my son?" asked the father. "I am a miller, dear father," answered he.

"What have you brought home from your travels?" continued the father. "Nothing but an ass," answered the son.

"We have plenty of asses here," said the father. "You had much better have brought me a nice goat!" "Yes," answered the son, "but this is no common ass. When I say, 'Bricklebrit,' the good creature spits out a whole clothful of gold pieces. Let me call all the neighbors together. I will make rich people of them all."

"That will be fine!" said the tailor. "Then I need labor no more at my needle"; and he rushed out himself and called the neighbors together. As soon as they were all assembled, the miller called out to them to make room, and brought in the ass, and spread his cloth before him.

"Now, pay attention," said he, and cried, "Bricklebrit!" but no gold pieces came, and that showed that the animal was not more scientific than any other ass.

So the poor miller made a long face when he saw that he had been taken in, and begged pardon of the neighbors, who all went home as poor as they had come. And there was nothing for it but that the old man must take to his needle again, and that the young one should take service with a miller.

The third brother had bound himself apprentice to a turner; and as turning is a very ingenious handicraft, it took him a long time to learn it. His brothers told him in a letter how badly things had gone with them, and how on the last night of their travels the landlord deprived them of their treasures. When the young turner had learnt his trade, and was ready to travel, his master, to reward him for his good conduct, gave him a sack, and told him that there was a stick inside it.

"I can hang up the sack, and it may be very useful to me," said the young man. "But what is the good of the stick?"

"I will tell you," answered the master. "If any one does you any harm, and you say, 'Stick, out of the sack!' the stick will jump out upon them, and will belabor them so soundly that they shall not be able to move or to leave the place for a week, and it will not stop until you say, 'Stick, into the sack!' "

The apprentice thanked him, and took up the sack and started on his travels, and when any one attacked him he would say, "Stick, out of the sack!" and directly out jumped the stick, and dealt a shower of blows on the coat or jerkin, and the back beneath, which quickly ended the affair. One evening the young turner reached the inn where his two brothers had been taken in. He laid his knapsack on the table, and began to describe all the wonderful things he had seen in the world.

"Yes," said he, "you may talk of your self-spreading table, gold-supplying ass, and so forth; very good things, I do not deny, but they are nothing in comparison with the treasure that I have acquired and carry with me in that sack!"

Then the landlord opened his ears. "What in the world can it be?" thought he. "Very likely the sack is full of precious stones; and I have a perfect right to it, for all good things come in threes."

When bedtime came the guest stretched himself on a bench, and put his sack under his head for a pillow, and the landlord, when he thought the young man was sound asleep, came, and, stooping down, pulled gently at the sack, so as to remove it cautiously, and put another in its place. The turner had only been waiting for this to happen, and just as the landlord was giving a last courageous pull, he cried, "Stick, out of the sack!" Out flew the stick directly, and laid to heartily on the landlord's back; and in vain he begged for mercy; the louder he cried the harder the stick beat time on his back, until he fell exhausted to the ground.

Then the turner said, "If you do not give me the table and the ass directly, this game shall begin all over again."

"Oh dear, no!" cried the landlord, quite collapsed; "I will gladly give it all back again if you will only make this terrible goblin go back into the sack."

Then said the young man, "I will be generous instead of just, but beware!" Then he cried, "Stick, into the sack!" and left him in peace.

The next morning the turner set out with the table and the ass on his way home to his father. The tailor was very glad indeed to see him again, and asked him what he had learned abroad. "My dear father," answered he, "I am become a turner."

"A very ingenious handicraft," said the father. "And what have you brought with you from your travels?" "A very valuable thing, dear father," answered the son. "A stick in a sack!"

"What!" cried the father. "A stick! The thing is not worth so much trouble when you can cut one from any tree."

"But it is not a common stick, dear father," said the young man. "When I say, 'Stick, out of the bag!' out jumps the stick upon any one who means harm to me, and makes him dance again, and does not leave off till he is beaten to the earth, and asks pardon. Just look here, with this stick I have recovered the table and the ass which the thieving landlord had taken from my two brothers. Now, let them both be sent for, and bid all the neighbors too, and they shall eat and drink to their hearts' content, and I will fill their pockets with gold."

The old tailor could not quite believe in such a thing, but he called his sons and all the neighbors together. Then the turner brought in the ass, opened a cloth before him, and said to his brother, "Now, my dear brother, speak to him." And the miller said, "Bricklebrit!" and immediately the cloth was covered with gold pieces, until they had all got more than they could carry away. (I tell you this because it is a pity you were not there.) Then the turner set down the table, and said, "Now, my dear brother, speak to it." And the joiner said, "Table, be covered!" and directly it was covered, and set forth plentifully with the richest dishes. Then they held a feast such as had never taken place in the tailor's house before, and the whole company remained through the night, merry and content.

The tailor after that locked up in a cupboard his needle and thread, his yard-measure and goose, and lived ever after with his three sons in great joy and splendor.

But what became of the goat, the unlucky cause of the tailor's sons being driven out? I will tell you. She felt so ashamed of her bald head that she ran into a fox's hole and hid herself. When the fox came home he caught sight of two great eyes staring at him out of the darkness, and was very frightened and ran away. A bear met him, and seeing that he looked very disturbed, asked him, "What is the matter, brother fox, that you should look like that?"

"Oh dear," answered the fox, "a grisly beast is sitting in my hole, and he stared at me with fiery eyes!"

"We will soon drive him out," said the bear; and went to the hole and looked in, but when he caught sight of the fiery eyes he likewise felt great terror seize him, and not wishing to have anything to do with so grisly a beast, he made off. He was soon met by a bee, who remarked that he had not a very courageous air, and said to him, "Bear, you have a very depressed countenance, what has become of your high spirit?"

"You may well ask," answered the bear. "In the fox's hole there sits a grisly beast with fiery eyes, and we cannot drive him out."

The bee answered, "I know you despise me, bear. I am a poor feeble little creature, but I think I can help you."

So she flew into the fox's hole, and settling on the goat's smooth-shaven head, stung her so severely that she jumped up, crying, "Ba-baa!" and ran out like mad into the world. And to this hour no one knows where she ran to.

One-Eye, Two-Eyes, and Three-Eyes

THERE WAS once a woman who had three daughters, the eldest of whom was called One-eye, because she had only one eye in the middle of her forehead, and the second, Two-eyes, because she had two eyes like other folks, and the youngest, Three-eyes, because she had three eyes; and her third eye was also in the center of her forehead. However, as Two-eyes saw just as other human beings did, her sisters and her mother could not endure her. They said to her, "Thou, with thy two eyes, art no better than the common people; thou dost not belong to us!" They pushed her about, and threw old clothes to her, and gave her nothing to eat but what they left, and did everything that they could to make her unhappy. It came to pass that Two-eyes had to go out into the fields and tend the goat, but she was still quite hungry, because her sisters had given her so little to eat. So she sat down on a ridge and began to weep, and so bitterly that two streams ran down from her eyes.

And once when she looked up in her grief, a woman was standing beside her, who said, "Why art thou weeping, little Two-eyes?" Two-eyes answered, "Have I not reason to weep, when I have two eyes like other people, and my sisters and mother hate me for it, and push me from one corner to another, throw old clothes at me, and give me nothing to eat but the scraps they leave? Today they have given me so little that I am still quite hungry." Then the wise woman said, "Wipe away thy tears, Two-eyes, and I will tell thee something to stop thee ever suffering from hunger again. Just say to thy goat,

> *'Bleat, my little goat, bleat,*
> *Cover the table with something to eat',*

and then a clean well-spread little table will stand before thee, with the most delicious food upon it of which thou mayst eat as much as thou art inclined for, and when thou hast had enough, and hast no more need of the little table, just say,

> *'Bleat, bleat, my little goat, I pray,*
> *And take the table quite away',*

and then it will vanish again from thy sight." Hereupon the wise woman departed.

But Two-eyes thought, "I must instantly make a trial, and see if what she said is true, for I am far too hungry," and she said,

> *"Bleat, my little goat, bleat,*
> *Cover the table with something to eat,"*

and scarcely had she spoken the words than a little table, covered with a white cloth, was standing there, and on it was a plate with a knife and fork, and a silver spoon; and the most delicious food was there also, warm and smoking as if it had just come out of the kitchen. Then Two-eyes said the shortest prayer she knew, "Lord God, be with us always, Amen," and helped herself to some food, and enjoyed it. And when she was satisfied, she said, as the wise woman had taught her,

> *"Bleat, bleat, my little goat, I pray,*
> *And take the table quite away,"*

and immediately the little table and everything on it was gone again. "That is a delightful way of keeping house!" thought Two-eyes, and was quite glad and happy.

In the evening, when she went home with her goat, she found a small earthenware dish with some food, which her sisters had set ready for her, but she did not touch it. Next day she again went out with her goat, and left the few bits of broken bread which had been handed to her, lying untouched. The first and second time that she did this, her sisters did not remark it at all, but as it happened every time, they did observe it, and said, "There is something wrong about Two-eyes, she always leaves her food untasted, and she used to eat up everything that was given her; she must have discovered other ways of getting food." In order that they might learn the truth, they resolved to send One-eye with Two-eyes when she went to drive her goat to the pasture, to observe what Two-eyes did when she was there, and whether any one brought her anything to eat and drink. So when Two-eyes set out the next time, One-eye went to her and said, "I will go with you to the pasture, and see that the goat is well taken care of, and driven where there is food."

But Two-eyes knew what was in One-eye's mind, and drove the goat into high grass and said, "Come, One-eye, we will sit down, and I will sing something to you." One-eye sat down and was tired with the unaccustomed walk and the heat of the sun, and Two-eyes sang constantly,

> *"One eye, wakest thou?*
> *One eye, sleepest thou?"*

until One-eye shut her one eye, and fell asleep, and as soon as Two-eyes saw that One-eye was fast asleep, and could discover nothing, she said,

> *"Bleat, my little goat, bleat,*
> *Cover the table with something to eat,"*

and seated herself at her table, and ate and drank until she was satisfied, and then she again cried,

> *"Bleat, bleat, my little goat, I pray,*
> *And take the table quite away,"*

and in an instant all was gone.

Two-eyes now awakened One-eye, and said, "One-eye, you want to take care of the goat, and go to sleep while you are doing it, and in the meantime the goat might run all over the world. Come, let us go home again." So they went home, and again Two-eyes let her little dish stand untouched, and One-eye could not tell her mother why she would not eat it, and to excuse herself said, "I fell asleep when I was out."

Next day the mother said to Three-eyes, "This time you shall go and observe if Two-eyes eats anything when she is out, and if any one fetches her food and drink, for she must eat and drink in secret." So Three-eyes went to Two-eyes, and said, "I will go with you and see if the goat is taken proper care of, and driven where there is food."

But Two-eyes knew what was in Three-eyes' mind, and drove the goat into high grass and said, "We will sit down, and I will sing something to you, Three-eyes." Three-eyes sat down and was tired with the walk and with the heat of the sun, and Two-eyes began the same song as before, and sang,

> *"Three eyes, are you waking?"*

but then, instead of singing,

> *"Three eyes, are you sleeping?"*

as she ought to have done, she thoughtlessly sang,

> *"Two eyes, are you sleeping?"*

and sang all the time,

> *"Three eyes, are you waking?*
> *Two eyes, are you sleeping?"*

Then two of the eyes which Three-eyes had, shut and fell asleep, but the third, as it had not been named in the song, did not sleep. It is true that Three-eyes shut it, but only in her cunning, to pretend it was asleep too, but it blinked, and could see everything very well. And when Two-eyes thought that Three-eyes was fast asleep, she used her little charm:

> *"Bleat, my little goat, bleat,*
> *Cover the table with something to eat,"*

and ate and drank as much as her heart desired, and then ordered the table to go away again:

> *"Bleat, bleat, my little goat, I pray,*
> *And take the table quite away,"*

and Three-eyes had seen everything.

Then Two-eyes came to her, waked her and said, "Have you been asleep, Three-eyes? You are a good care-taker! Come, we will go home." And when they got home, Two-eyes again did not eat, and Three-eyes said to the mother, "Now, I know why that high-minded thing there does not eat. When she is out, she says to the goat,

> 'Bleat, my little goat, bleat,
> Cover the table with something to eat,'

and then a little table appears before her covered with the best of food, much better than any we have here, and when she has eaten all she wants, she says,

> 'Bleat, bleat, my little goat, I pray,
> And take the table quite away.'

and all disappears. I watched everything closely. She put two of my eyes to sleep by using a certain form of words, but luckily the one in my forehead kept awake."

Then the envious mother cried, "Dost thou want to fare better than we do? The desire shall pass away," and she fetched a butcher's knife, and thrust it into the heart of the goat, which fell down dead.

When Two-eyes saw that, she went out full of trouble, seated herself on the ridge of grass at the edge of the field, and wept bitter tears. Suddenly the wise woman once more stood by her side, and said, "Two-eyes, why art thou weeping?" "Have I not reason to weep?" she answered. "The goat which covered the table for me every day when I spoke your charm, has been killed by my mother, and now I shall again have to bear hunger and want." The wise woman said, "Two-eyes, I will give thee a piece of good advice; ask thy sisters to give thee the entrails of the slaughtered goat, and bury them in the ground in front of the house, and thy fortune will be made." Then she vanished, and Two-eyes went home and said to her sisters, "Dear sisters, do give me some part of my goat; I don't wish for what is good, but give me the entrails." Then they laughed and said, "If that's all you want, you can have it." So Two-eyes took the entrails and buried them quietly in the evening, in front of the house-door, as the wise woman had counseled her to do.

Next morning, when they all awoke, and went to the house-door, there stood a strangely magnificent tree with leaves of silver, and fruit of gold hanging among them, so that in all the wide world there was nothing more beautiful or precious. They did not know how the tree could have come there during the night, but Two-eyes saw that it had grown up out of the entrails of the goat, for it was standing on the exact spot where she had buried them.

Then the mother said to One-eye, "Climb up, my child, and gather some of the fruit of the tree for us." One-eye climbed up, but when she was about to get hold of one of the golden apples, the branch escaped from her hands, and that happened each time, so that she could not pluck a single apple, let her do what she might. Then said the mother, "Three-eyes, do you climb up; you with your three eyes can look about you better than One-eye." One-eye slipped down, and Three-eyes climbed up. Three-eyes was not more skilful, and might search as she liked, but the golden apples always escaped her. At length the mother grew impatient, and climbed up herself, but could get hold of the fruit no better than One-eye and Three-eyes, for she always clutched empty air.

Then said Two-eyes, "I will just go up, perhaps I may succeed better." The sisters cried, "You indeed, with your two eyes, what can you do?" But Two-eyes climbed up, and the golden apples did not get out of her way, but came into her hand of their own accord, so that she could pluck them one after the other, and she brought a whole apronful down with her. The mother took them away from her, and instead of treating poor Two-eyes any better for this, she and One-eye and Three-eyes were only envious, because Two-eyes alone had been able to get the fruit, and they treated her still more cruelly.

It so happened that once when they were all standing together by the tree, a young knight came up. "Quick, Two-eyes," cried the two sisters, "creep under this, and don't disgrace us!" and with all speed they turned an empty barrel which was standing close by the tree over poor Two-eyes, and they pushed the golden apples which she had been gathering under it too. When the knight came nearer he was a handsome lord, who stopped and admired the magnificent gold and silver tree, and said to the two sisters, "To whom does this fine tree belong? Any one who would bestow one branch of it on me might in return for it ask whatsoever he desired." Then One-eye and Three-eyes replied that the tree belonged to them, and that they would give him a branch. They both took great trouble, but they were not able to do it, for the branches and fruit both moved away from them every time.

Then said the knight, "It is very strange that the tree should belong to you, and that you should still not be able to break a piece off." They again asserted that the tree was their property. While they were saying so, Two-eyes rolled out a couple of golden apples from under the barrel to the feet of the knight, for she was vexed with One-eye and Three-eyes, for not speaking the truth. When the knight saw the apples he was astonished, and asked where they came from. One-eye and Three-eyes answered that they had another sister, who was not allowed to show herself, for she had only two eyes like any common person. The knight, however, desired to see her, and cried, "Two-eyes, come forth."

Then Two-eyes, quite comforted, came from beneath the barrel, and the knight was surprised at her great beauty, and said, "Thou, Two-eyes, canst certainly break off a branch from the tree for me." "Yes," replied Two-eyes, "that I certainly shall be able to do, for the tree belongs to me." And she climbed up, and with the greatest ease broke off a branch with beautiful silver leaves and golden fruit, and gave it to the knight. Then said the knight, "Two-eyes, what shall I give thee for it?" "Alas!" answered Two-eyes, "I suffer from hunger and thirst, grief and want, from early morning till late night; if you would take me with you, and deliver me from these things, I should be happy." So the knight lifted Two-eyes on to his horse, and took her home with him to his father's castle, and there he gave her beautiful clothes, and meat and drink to her heart's content, and as he loved her so much he married her, and the wedding was solemnized with great rejoicing.

When Two-eyes was thus carried away by the handsome knight, her two sisters grudged her good fortune in downright earnest. "The wonderful tree, however, still remains with us," thought they, "and even if we can gather no fruit from it, still every one will stand still and look at it, and come to us and admire it. Who knows what good things may be in store for us?" But next morning, the tree had vanished, and all their hopes were at an end. And when Two-eyes looked out of the window of her own little room, to her great delight it was standing in front of it, and so it had followed her.

Two-eyes lived a long time in happiness. Once two poor women came to her in her castle, and begged for alms. She looked in their faces, and recognized her sisters, One-eye and Three-eyes, who had fallen into such poverty that they had to wander about and beg their bread from door to door. Two-eyes, however, made them welcome, and was kind to them, and took care of them, so that they both with all their hearts repented the evil that they had done their sister in their youth.

The Knapsack, the Hat, and the Horn

ONCE THERE WERE three brothers, and they grew poorer and poorer, until at last their need was so great that they had nothing left to bite or to break. Then they said, "This will not do; we had better go out into the world and seek our fortune."

So they set out, and went some distance through many green fields, but they met with no good fortune. One day they came to a great wood, in the midst of which was a hill, and when they came near to it, they saw that it was all of silver. Then said the eldest, "Now here is good fortune enough for me, and I desire no better." And he took of the silver as much as he could carry, turned round, and went back home. But the other two said, "We must have something better than mere silver," and they would not touch it, but went on farther.

After they had gone on a few days longer, they came to a hill that was all of gold. The second brother stood still and considered, and was uncertain. "What shall I do?" said he; "shall I take of the gold enough to last me my life, or shall I go farther?" At last, coming to a conclusion, he filled his pockets as full as they would hold, bid good-bye to his brother, and went home. But the third brother said to himself, "Silver and gold do not tempt me; I will not gainsay fortune, who has better things in store for me."

So he went on, and when he had journeyed for three days, he came to a wood still greater than the former ones, so that there was no end to it; and in it he found nothing to eat or to drink, so that he was nearly starving. He got up into a high tree, so as to see how far the wood reached, but as far as his eyes could see, there was nothing but the tops of the trees. And as he got down from the tree, hunger pressed him sore, and he thought, "Oh that for once I could have a good meal!"

And when he reached the ground he saw to his surprise a table beneath the tree richly spread with food, and that smoked before him.

"This time at least," said he, "I have my wish," and without stopping to ask who had brought the meal there, and who had cooked it, he came close to the table and ate with relish, until his hunger was appeased. When he had finished, he thought, "It would be a pity to leave such a good table-cloth behind in the wood," so he folded it up neatly and pocketed it.

Then he walked on, and in the evening, when hunger again seized him, he thought he would put the table-cloth to the proof, and he brought it out and said, "Now I desire that thou shouldst be spread with a good meal," and no sooner were the words out of his mouth, than there stood on it as many dishes of delicious food as there was room for.

"Now that I see," said he, "what sort of a cook thou art, I hold thee dearer than the mountains of silver and of gold," for he perceived that it was a wishing-cloth. Still he was not satisfied to settle down at home with only a wishing-cloth, so he determined to wander farther through the world and seek his fortune.

One evening, in a lonely wood, he came upon a begrimed charcoal-burner at his furnace, who had put some potatoes to roast for his supper. "Good evening, my black fellow," said he, "how do you get on in this lonely spot?" "One day is like another," answered the charcoal-burner; "every evening I have potatoes; have you a mind to be my guest?" "Many thanks," answered the traveler, "I will not deprive you; you did not expect a guest; but if you do not object, you shall be the one to be invited."

"How can that be managed?" said the charcoal-burner; "I see that you have nothing with you, and if you were to walk two hours in any direction, you would meet with no one to give you anything." "For all that," answered he, "there shall be a feast so good, that you have never tasted the like."

Then he took out the table-cloth from his knapsack, and spreading it on the ground, said, "Cloth, be covered," and immediately there appeared boiled and roast meat, quite hot, as if it had just come from the kitchen. The charcoal-burner stared, but did not stay to be asked twice, and fell to, filling his black mouth with ever bigger and bigger pieces.

When they had finished eating, the charcoal-burner smiled, and said, "Look here, I approve of your table-cloth; it would not be a bad thing for me to have here in the wood, where the cooking is not first-rate. I will strike a bargain with you. There hangs a soldier's knapsack in the corner, which looks old and unsightly, but it has wonderful qualities; as I have no further occasion for it, I will give it to you in exchange for the table-cloth."

"First, I must know what these wonderful qualities are," returned the other.

"I will tell you," answered the charcoal-burner; "if you strike it with your hand, there will appear a corporal and six men with swords and muskets, and whatever you wish to have done, that will they do."

"Well, for my part," said the other, "I am quite willing to make the exchange." And he gave the table-cloth to the charcoal-burner, took down the knapsack from its hook, slung it over his shoulder, and took his leave. Before he had gone far he began to want to make a trial of his wonderful knapsack, so he struck it a blow. At once seven soldiers appeared before him, and the corporal said, "What does my lord and master please to want?"

"March in haste to the charcoal-burner and demand my wishing-cloth back," said the man. They wheeled round to the left, and were not long before they had accomplished his desire, and taken away, without wasting many words, the wishing-cloth from the charcoal-burner. Having dismissed them, he wandered on, expecting still more wonderful luck.

About sunset he fell in with another charcoal-burner, who was getting his supper ready at the fire. "Will you join me?" said this black fellow; "potatoes and salt, without butter; sit down to it with me." "No," answered he, "this time you shall be my guest." And he spread out his table-cloth, and it was directly covered with the most delicious victuals. So they ate and drank together and were merry.

After the meal was over the charcoal-burner said, "Over there, on the bench, lies an old worn-out hat, which has wonderful properties: if you put it on and draw it well over your head it is as if a dozen field-pieces went off, one after the other, shooting everything down, so that no one can stand against them. This hat is of no use to me, and I will give it to you in exchange for the table-cloth."

"All right," answered the other, taking the hat and carrying it off, and leaving the table-cloth behind him. Before he had gone far he struck upon the knapsack, and summoned his soldiers to fetch back the table-cloth again. "First one thing, and then another," thought he, "just as if my luck were never to end."

And so it seemed, for at the end of another day's journey he came up to another charcoal-burner, who was roasting his potatoes just like the others. He invited him to eat with him off his wishing-cloth, to which the charcoal-burner took such a fancy, that he gave him for it a horn, which had different properties still from the hat. If a man blew on it, down fell all walls and fortresses, and finally towns and villages in heaps. So the man gave the table-cloth in exchange for it to the charcoal-burner, afterwards sending his men to fetch it back, so that at last he had in his possession knapsack, hat, and horn, all at one time. "Now," said he, "I am a made man, and it is time to go home again and see how my brothers are faring."

When he reached home he found that his brothers had built themselves a fine house with their silver and gold, and lived in clover. He went to see them, but because he wore a half-worn-out coat, a shabby hat, and the old knapsack on his back, they would not recognize him as their brother. They mocked him and said, "It is of no use your giving yourself out to be our brother; he who scorned silver and gold, seeking for better fortune, will return in great splendor, as a mighty King, not as a beggar-man." And they drove him from their door.

Then he flew into a great rage, and struck upon his knapsack until a hundred and fifty men stood before him, rank and file. He ordered them to surround his brothers' house, and that two of them should take hazel-rods, and should beat the brothers until they knew who he was. And there arose a terrible noise; the people ran together and wished to rescue the brothers in their extremity, but they could do nothing against the soldiers. It happened at last that the King of the country heard of it, and he was indignant, and sent a captain with his troops to drive the disturber of the peace out of the town. But the man with his knapsack soon assembled a greater company, who beat back the captain and his people, sending them off with bleeding noses.

Then the King said, "This vagabond fellow must be put down," and he sent the next day a larger company against him, but they could do nothing, for he assembled more men than ever, and in order to bring them more quickly, he pulled his hat twice lower over his brows; then the heavy guns came into play, and the King's people were beaten and put to flight. "Now," said he, "I shall not make peace until the King gives me his daughter to wife, and lets me rule the whole kingdom in his name."

This he caused to be told to the King, who said to his daughter, "This is a hard nut to crack; there is no choice but for me to do as he asks; if I wish to have peace and keep the crown on my head, I must give in to him."

So the wedding took place, but the King's daughter was angry that the bridegroom should be a common man, who wore a shabby hat, and carried an old knapsack. She wished very much to get rid of him, and thought day and night how to manage it. Then it struck her that perhaps all his wonder-working power lay in the knapsack, and she pretended to be very fond of him, and when she had brought him into a good humor she said, "Pray lay aside that ugly knapsack; it misbecomes you so much that I feel ashamed of you."

"My dear child," answered he, "this knapsack is my greatest treasure; so long as I keep it I need not fear anything in the whole world," and then he showed her with what wonderful qualities it was endowed. Then she fell on his neck as if she would have kissed him, but, by a clever trick, she slipped the knapsack over his shoulder and ran away with it.

As soon as she was alone she struck upon it and summoned the soldiers, and bade them seize her husband and bring him to the King's palace. They obeyed, and the false woman had many more to follow behind, so as to be ready to drive him out of the country. He would have been quite done for if he had not still kept the hat. As soon as he could get his hands free he pulled it twice forward on his head; and then the cannon began to thunder and beat all down, till at last the King's daughter had to come and to beg pardon. And as she so movingly prayed and promised to behave better, he raised her up and made peace with her. Then she grew very kind to him, and seemed to love him very much, and he grew so deluded, that one day he confided to her that even if he were deprived of his knapsack nothing could be done against him as long as he should keep the old hat. And when she knew the secret she waited until he had gone to sleep; then she carried off the hat, and had him driven out into the streets. Still the horn remained to him, and in great wrath he blew a great blast upon it, and down came walls and fortresses, towns and villages, and buried the King and his daughter among their ruins. If he had not set down the horn when he did, and if he had blown a little longer, all the houses would have tumbled down, and there would not have been left one stone upon another.

After this no one dared to withstand him, and he made himself King over the whole country.

Sweetheart Roland

THERE WAS once a woman who was a witch, and she had two daughters, one ugly and wicked, one pretty and good. She loved the wicked one because she was her own child, but she hated the good one because she was a step-daughter. One day the step-daughter put on a pretty apron, which the other daughter liked so much that she became envious, and said to her mother that she must and should have the apron.

"Be content, my child," said the old woman, "thou shalt have it. Thy step-sister has long deserved death, and tonight, while she is asleep, I shall come and cut off her head. Take care to lie at the farthest side of the bed, and push her to the outside."

And it would have been all over with the poor girl, if she had not been standing in a corner near and heard it all. She did not dare to go outside the door the whole day long, and when bed-time came the other one got into bed first, so as to lie on the farthest side; but when she had gone to sleep, the step-daughter pushed her towards the outside, and took the inside place next the wall. In the night the old woman came sneaking; in her right hand she held an axe, and with her left she felt for the one who was lying outside, and then she heaved up the axe with both hands, and hewed the head off her only daughter.

When she had gone away, the other girl got up and went to her sweetheart's, who was called Roland, and knocked at his door. When he came to her, she said, "Listen, dear Roland, we must flee away in all haste; my step-mother meant to put me to death, but she has killed her only child instead. When the day breaks, and she sees what she has done, we are lost."

"But I advise you," said Roland, "to bring away her magic wand with you; otherwise we cannot escape her when she comes after to overtake us." So the maiden fetched the magic wand, and she took up the head of her step-sister and let drop three drops of blood on the ground—one by the bed, one in the kitchen, and one on the steps. Then she hastened back to her sweetheart.

When the old witch got up in the morning, she called out to her daughter, to give her the apron, but no daughter came. Then she cried out, "Where art thou?" "Here, at the steps, sweeping!" answered one of the drops of blood.

The old woman went out, but she saw nobody at the steps, and cried again, "Where art thou?" "Here in the kitchen warming myself," cried the second drop of blood.

So she went into the kitchen and found no one. Then she cried again, "Where art thou?" "Oh, here in bed fast asleep!" cried the third drop of blood.

Then the mother went into the room, and up to the bed, and there lay her only child, whose head she had cut off herself. The witch fell into a great fury, rushed to the window, for from it she could see far and wide, and she caught sight of her step-daughter, hastening away with her dear Roland.

"It will be no good to you," cried she, "if you get ever so far away, you cannot escape me." Then she put on her boots, which took her an hour's walk at every stride, and it was not long before she had overtaken them. But the maiden, when she saw the old woman striding up, changed, by means of the magic wand, her dear Roland into a lake, and herself into a duck swimming upon it. The witch stood on the bank and threw in crumbs of bread, and took great pains to decoy the duck towards her, but the duck would not be decoyed, and the old woman was obliged to go back in the evening disappointed.

Then the maiden and her dear Roland took again their natural shapes, and traveled on the whole night through until daybreak. Then the maiden changed herself into a beautiful flower, standing in the middle of a hedge of thorns, and her dear Roland into a fiddle-player. It was not long before the witch came striding up, and she said to the musician, "Dear musician, will you be so kind as to reach that pretty flower for me?" "Oh yes," said he, "I will strike up a tune to it."

Then as she crept quickly up to the hedge to break off the flower, for she knew well who it was, he began to play, and whether she liked it or not, she was obliged to dance, for there was magic in the tune. The faster he played the higher she had to jump, and the thorns tore her clothes, and scratched and wounded her, and he did not cease playing until she was spent, and lay dead.

So now they were saved, and Roland said, "I will go to my father and prepare for the wedding." "And I will stay here," said the maiden, "and wait for you, and so that no one should know me, I will change myself into a red milestone." So away went Roland, and the maiden in the likeness of a stone waited in the field for her beloved.

But when Roland went home he fell into the snares of another maiden, who wrought so, that he forgot his first love. And the poor girl waited a long time, but at last, seeing that he did not come, she was filled with despair, and changed herself into a flower, thinking "Perhaps some one in passing will put his foot upon me and crush me."

But it happened that a shepherd, tending his flock, saw the flower, and as it was so beautiful, he gathered it, took it home with him, and put it in his chest. From that time everything went won-

derfully well in the shepherd's house. When he got up in the
morning, all the work was already done; the room was swept, the
tables and benches rubbed, fire kindled on the hearth, and water
ready drawn; and when he came home in the middle of the day,
the table was laid, and a good meal spread upon it. He could not
understand how it was done, for he never saw anybody in his
house, and it was too little for anybody to hide in. The good serving
pleased him well; but in the end he became uneasy, and went to a
wise woman to take counsel of her. The wise woman said, "There is
magic in it: get up early some morning, and if you hear something
moving in the room, be it what it may, throw a white cloth over it,
and the charm will be broken."

The shepherd did as she told him, and the next morning at
daybreak he saw the chest open, and the flower came out. Then he
jumped up quickly and threw a white cloth over it. So the spell was
broken, and a lovely maiden stood before him; and she told him
that she had been the flower, and had until now cared for his
household matters. She told him all that had happened to her, and
she pleased him so much that he asked her to marry him, but she
answered "No," because she still remained true to her dear Roland, though he had forsaken her; but she promised not to leave
the shepherd, but to go on taking care of his house.

Now the time came when Roland's wedding was to be held; and
there was an old custom in that country that all the girls should be
present, and should sing in honor of the bride and bridegroom. The
faithful maiden, when she knew this, was so sorrowful that she felt
as if her heart would break; and she would not go, until the others
came and fetched her.

And when her turn came to sing she slipped behind, so that she
stood alone, and so began to sing; and as soon as her song reached
Roland's ear he sprang up and cried, "I know that voice! That is the
right bride, and no other will I have." And everything that he had
forgotten, and that had been swept out of his mind, came suddenly
home to him in his heart. And the faithful maiden was married to
her dear Roland; her sorrow came to an end and her joy began.

The Devil's Three Gold Hairs

ONCE THERE WAS a very poor woman who was delighted when her son was born with a caul enveloping his head. This was supposed to bring good fortune, and it was predicted that he would marry the King's daughter when he became nineteen. Soon after, a King came to the village, but no one knew that it was the King. When he asked for news, they told him that a few days before a child had been born in the village, with a caul, and it was prophesied that he would be very lucky. Indeed, it had been said that in his nineteenth year he would have the King's daughter for his wife.

The King, who had a wicked heart, was very angry when he heard this; but he went to the parents in a most friendly manner, and said to them kindly, "Good people, give up your child to me. I will take the greatest care of him."

At first they refused; but when the stranger offered them a large amount of gold, and then mentioned that if their child was born to be lucky everything must turn out for the best with him, they willingly at last gave him up.

The King placed the child in a box and rode away with it for a long distance, till he came to deep water, into which he threw the box containing the child, saying to himself as he rode away, "From this unwelcome suitor have I saved my daughter."

But the box did not sink; it swam like a boat on the water, and so high above it that not a drop got inside. It sailed on to a spot about two miles from the chief town of the King's dominions, where there were a mill and a weir, which stopped it, and on which it rested.

The miller's man, who happened to be standing near the bank, fortunately noticed it, and thinking it would most likely contain something valuable, drew it on shore with a hook; but when he opened it, there lay a beautiful baby, who was quite awake and lively.

He carried it in to the miller and his wife, and as they had no children they were quite delighted, and said Heaven had sent the little boy as a gift to them. They brought him up carefully, and he grew to manhood clever and virtuous.

It happened one day that the King was overtaken by a thunderstorm while passing near the mill, and stopped to ask for shelter.

Noticing the youth, he asked the miller if that tall young man was his son.

"No," he replied; "he is a foundling. Nineteen years ago a box was seen sailing on the mill stream by one of our men, and when it was caught in the weir he drew it out of the water and found the child in it."

Then the King knew that this must be the child of fortune, and therefore the one which he had thrown into the water. He hid his vexation, however, and presently said kindly, "I want to send a letter to the Queen, my wife; if that young man will take it to her I will give him two gold-pieces for his trouble."

"We are at the King's service," replied the miller, and called to the young man to prepare for his errand. Then the King wrote a letter to the Queen, containing these words: "As soon as the boy who brings this letter arrives, let him be killed, and I shall expect to find him dead and buried when I come back."

The youth was soon on his way with this letter. He lost himself, however, in a large forest. But when darkness came on he saw in the distance a glimmering light, which he walked to, and found a small house. He entered and saw an old woman sitting by the fire, quite alone. She appeared frightened when she saw him, and said; "Where do you come from, and what do you want?"

"I am come from the mill," he replied, "and I am carrying a letter to the wife of the King, and, as I have lost my way, I should like very much to stay here during the night."

"You poor young man," she replied, "you are in a den of robbers, and when they come home they may kill you."

"They may come when they like," said the youth; "I am not afraid; but I am so tired that I cannot go a step further." Then he stretched himself on a bench and fell fast asleep.

Soon after the robbers came home, and asked angrily what that youth was lying there for.

"Ah," said the old woman, "he is an innocent child who has lost himself in the wood, and I took him in out of compassion. He is carrying a letter to the Queen, which the King has sent."

Then the robbers went softly to the sleeping youth, took the letter from his pocket, and read in it that as soon as the bearer arrived at the palace he was to lose his life. Then pity arose in the hard-hearted robbers, and their chief tore up the letter and wrote another, in which it was stated that as soon as the boy arrived he should be married to the King's daughter. Then they left him to lie and rest on the bench till the next morning, and when he awoke they gave him the letter and showed him the road he was to take.

As soon as he reached the palace and sent in the letter, the Queen read it, and she acted in exact accordance with what was written—ordered a grand marriage feast, and had the Princess married at once to the fortunate youth. He was very handsome and amiable, so that the King's daughter soon learned to love him very much, and was quite happy with him.

Not long after, when the King returned home to his castle, he found the prophecy respecting the child of fortune fulfilled, and that he was married to a King's daughter. "How has this happened?" said he. "I have in my letter given very different orders!"

Then the Queen gave him the letter, and said: "You may see for yourself what is stated there."

The King read the letter and saw very clearly that it was not the one he had written. He asked the youth what he had done with the letter he had entrusted to him, and where he had brought the other from. "I know not," he replied, "unless it was changed during the night while I slept in the forest."

Full of wrath, the King said, "You shall not get off so easily, for whoever marries my daughter must first bring me three golden hairs from the head of the demon of the Black Forest. If you bring them to me before long, then shall you keep my daughter as a wife, but not otherwise."

Then said the child of fortune, "I will fetch these golden hairs very quickly; I am not the least afraid of the demon." Thereupon he said farewell, and started on his travels. His way led him to a large city, and as he stood at the gate and asked admission, a watchman said to him, "What trade do you follow, and how much do you know?" "I know everything," he replied.

"Then you can do us a favor," answered the watchman, "if you can tell why our master's fountain, from which wine used to flow, is dried up, and never gives us even water now." "I will tell you when I come back," he said; "only wait till then."

He traveled on still further, and came by and by to another town, where the watchman also asked him what trade he followed, and what he knew. "I know everything," he answered.

"Then," said the watchman, "you can do us a favor, and tell us why a tree in our town, which once bore golden apples, now only produces leaves." "Wait till I return," he replied, "and I will tell you."

On he went again, and came to a broad river, over which he

must pass in a ferryboat, and the ferryman asked him the same question about his trade and his knowledge. He gave the same reply, that he knew everything.

"Then," said the man, "you can do me a favor, and tell me how it is that I am obliged to go backward and forward in my ferryboat every day, without a change of any kind." "Wait till I come back," he replied, "then you shall know all about it."

As soon as he reached the other side of the water he found the entrance to the Black Forest, in which was the demon's cove. It was very dark and gloomy, and the demon was not at home; but his old mother was sitting in a large arm-chair, and she looked up and said, "What do you want? You don't look wicked enough to be one of us."

"I just want three golden hairs from the demon's head," he replied; "otherwise my wife will be taken away from me."

"That is asking a great deal," she replied; "for if the demon comes home and finds you here, he will have no mercy on you. However, if you will trust me, I will try to help you."

Then she turned him into an ant, and said: "Creep into the folds of my gown; there you will be safe."

"Yes," he replied, "that is all very good; but I have three things besides that I want to know. First, why a well, from which formerly wine used to flow, should be dry now, so that not even water can be got from it. Secondly, why a tree that once bore golden apples should now produce nothing but leaves. And, thirdly, why a ferryman is obliged to row forward and back every day, without ever leaving off."

"These are difficult questions," said the old woman; "but keep still and quiet, and when the demon comes in, pay great attention to what he says, while I pull the golden hairs out of his head."

Late in the evening the demon came home, and as soon as he entered he declared that the air was not clear. "I smell the flesh of man," he said, "and I am sure that there is some one here." So he peeped into all the corners, and searched everywhere, but could find nothing.

Then his old mother scolded him well, and said, "Just as I have been sweeping, and dusting, and putting everything in order, then you come home and give me all the work to do over again. You have always the smell of something in your nose. Do sit down and eat your supper."

The demon did as she told him, and when he had eaten and drunk enough, he complained of being tired. So his mother made him lie down so that she could place his head in her lap; and he was soon so comfortable that he fell fast asleep and snored.

Then the old woman lifted up a golden hair, twitched it out, and laid it by her side. "Oh!" screamed the demon, waking up; "what was that for?" "I have had a bad dream," answered she, "and it made me catch hold of your hair."

"What did you dream about?" asked the demon. "Oh, I dreamed of a well in a market-place from which wine once used to flow, but now it is dried up, and they can't even get water from it. Whose fault is that?" "Ah, they ought to know that there sits a toad under a stone in the well, and if he were dead wine would again flow."

Then the old woman combed his hair again, till he slept and snored so loud that the windows rattled, and she pulled out the second hair. "What are you about now?" asked the demon in a rage. "Oh, don't be angry," said the woman; "I have had another dream."

"What was this dream about?" he asked. "Why, I dreamed that in a certain country there grows a fruit tree which used to bear golden apples, but now it produces nothing but leaves. What is the cause of this?" "Why, don't they know," answered the demon, "that there is a mouse gnawing at the root? Were it dead the tree would again bear golden apples; and if it gnaws much longer the tree will wither and dry up. Bother your dreams; if you disturb me again, just as I am comfortably asleep, you will have a box on the ear."

Then the old woman spoke kindly to him, and smoothed and combed his hair again, till he slept and snored. Then she seized the third golden hair and pulled it out.

The demon, on this, sprang to his feet, roared out in a greater rage than ever, and would have done some mischief in the house, but she managed to appease him this time also, and said: "How can I help my bad dreams?" "And whatever did you dream?" he asked, with some curiosity. "Well, I dreamed about a ferryman, who complains that he is obliged to take people across the river, and is never free." "Oh, the stupid fellow!" replied the wizard, "he can very easily ask any person who wants to be ferried over to take the oar in his hand, and he will be free at once."

Then the demon laid his head down once more; and as the old mother had pulled out the three golden hairs, and got answers to all the three questions, she let the old fellow rest and sleep in peace till the morning dawned.

As soon as he had gone out next day, the old woman took the ant from the folds of her dress and restored the lucky youth to his former shape. "Here are the three golden hairs for which you wished," said she; "and did you hear all the answers to your three questions?" "Yes," he replied, "every word, and I will not forget them." "Well, then, I have helped you out of your difficulties, and now get home as fast as you can."

After thanking the old woman for her kindness, he turned his steps homeward, full of joy that everything had succeeded so well.

When he arrived at the ferry the man asked for the promised answer. "Ferry me over first," he replied, "and then I will tell you."

So when they reached the opposite shore he gave the ferryman the demon's advice, that the next person who came and wished to be ferried over should have the oar placed in his hand, and from that moment he would have to take the ferryman's place.

Then the youth journeyed on till he came to the town where the unfruitful tree grew, and where the watchman was waiting for his answer. To him the young man repeated what he had heard, and said, "Kill the mouse that is gnawing at the root; then will your tree again bear golden apples."

The watchman thanked him, and gave him in return for his information two asses laden with gold, which were led after him. He very soon arrived at the city which contained the dried-up fountain. The sentinel came forward to receive his answer. Said the youth, "Under a stone in the fountain sits a toad; it must be searched for and killed; then will wine again flow from it." To show how thankful he was for this advice, the sentinel also ordered two asses laden with gold to be sent after him.

At length the child of fortune reached home with his riches, and his wife was overjoyed at seeing him again, and hearing how well he had succeeded in his undertaking. He placed before the King the three golden hairs he had brought from the head of the black demon; and when the King saw these and the four asses laden with gold he was quite satisfied, and said, "Now that you have performed all the required conditions, I am quite ready to sanction your marriage with my daughter; but, my dear son-in-law, tell me how you obtained all this gold. It is indeed a very valuable treasure; where did you find it?" "I crossed the river in a ferryboat, and on the opposite shore I found the gold lying in the sand."

"Can I find some if I go?" asked the King eagerly. "Yes, as much as you please," replied he. "There is a ferryman there who will row you over, and you can fill a sack in no time."

The greedy old King set out on his journey in all haste, and when he came near the river he beckoned to the ferryman to row him over the ferry.

The man told him to step in, and just as they reached the opposite shore he placed the rudder-oar in the King's hand, and sprang out of the boat; and so the King became a ferryman as a punishment for his sins.

I wonder if he still goes on ferrying people over the river! It is very likely, for no one has ever been persuaded to touch the oar since he took it.

The Griffin

THERE WAS once upon a time a King, but where he reigned and what he was called, I do not know. He had no son, but an only daughter who had always been ill, and no doctor had been able to cure her. Then it was foretold to the King that his daughter should eat herself well with an apple. So he ordered it to be proclaimed throughout the whole of his kingdom, that whosoever brought his daughter an apple with which she could eat herself well, should have her to wife, and be King. This became known to a peasant who had three sons, and he said to the eldest, "Go out into the garden and take a basketful of those beautiful apples with the red cheeks and carry them to the court; perhaps the King's daughter will be able to eat herself well with them, and then thou wilt marry her and be King." The lad did so, and set out.

When he had gone a short way he met a little iron man who asked him what he had there in the basket, to which replied Uele, for so was he named, "Frogs' legs." On this the little man said, "Well, so shall it be, and remain," and went away. At length Uele arrived at the palace, and made it known that he had brought apples which would cure the King's daughter if she ate them. This delighted the King hugely, and he caused Uele to be brought before him; but, alas! when he opened the basket, instead of having apples in it he had frogs' legs which were still kicking about. On this the King grew angry, and had him driven out of the house. When he got home he told his father how it had fared with him. Then the father sent the next son, who was called Seame, but all went with him just as it had gone with Uele. He also met the little iron man, who asked what he had there in the basket. Seame said, "Hogs' bristles," and the iron man said, "Well, so shall it be, and remain."

When Seame got to the King's palace and said he brought apples with which the King's daughter might eat herself well, they did not want to let him go in, and said that one fellow had already been there, and had treated them as if they were fools. Seame, however, maintained that he certainly had the apples, and that they ought to let him go in. At length they believed him, and led him to the King. But when he uncovered the basket, he had but hogs' bristles. This enraged the King terribly, so he caused Seame to be whipped out of the house. When he got home he related all that had befallen him.

Then the youngest boy, whose name was Hans, but who was already called Stupid Hans, came and asked his father if he might go with some apples. "Oh!" said the father, "you would be just the right fellow for such a thing! If the clever ones can't manage it, what can you do?" The boy, however, did not believe him, and said, "Indeed, father, I wish to go." "Just get away, you stupid fellow, you must wait till you are wiser," said the father to that, and turned his back. Hans, however, pulled at the back of his smock-frock and said, "Indeed, father, I wish to go." "Well, then, so far as I am concerned you may go, but you will soon come home again!" replied the old man in a spiteful voice. The boy, however, was tremendously delighted and jumped for joy. "Well, act like a fool! you grow more stupid every day!" said the father again. Hans, however, did not care about that, and did not let it spoil his pleasure, but as it was then night, he thought he might as well wait until the morrow, for he could not get to court that day.

All night long he could not sleep in his bed, and if he did doze for a moment, he dreamt of beautiful maidens, of palaces, of gold, and of silver, and all kinds of things of that sort. Early in the morning, he went forth on his way, and directly afterwards the little shabby-looking man in his iron clothes, came to him and asked what he was carrying in the basket. Hans gave him the answer that he was carrying apples with which the King's daughter was to eat herself well. "Then," said the little man, "so shall they be, and remain." But at the court they would none of them let Hans go in, for they said two had already been there who had told them that they were bringing apples, and one of them had frogs' legs, and the other hogs' bristles. Hans, however, resolutely maintained that he most certainly had no frogs' legs, but some of the most beautiful apples in the whole kingdom. As he spoke so pleasantly, the door-keeper thought he could not be telling a lie, and asked him to go in, and he was right, for when Hans uncovered his basket in the King's presence, golden-yellow apples came tumbling out. The King was delighted, and caused some of them to be taken to his daughter, and then waited in anxious expectation until news should be brought to him of the effect they had. But before much time had passed by, news was brought to him: but who do you think it was who came? it was his daughter herself! As soon as she had eaten of those apples, she was cured, and sprang out of her bed.

The joy the King felt cannot be described! But now he did not want to give his daughter in marriage to Hans, and said he must first make him a boat which would go quicker on dry land than on water. Hans agreed to the conditions, and went home, and related how it had fared with him.

Then the father sent Uele into the forest to make a boat of that kind. He worked diligently, and whistled all the time. At mid-day, when the sun was at the highest, came the little iron man and asked what he was making. Uele gave him for answer, "Wooden bowls for the kitchen." The iron man said, "So it shall be, and remain." By evening Uele thought he had now made the boat, but when he wanted to get into it, he had nothing but wooden bowls. The next day Seame went into the forest, but everything went with him just as it had done with Uele. On the third day Stupid Hans went. He worked away most industriously, so that the whole forest resounded with the heavy strokes, and all the while he sang and whistled right merrily. At mid-day, when it was the hottest, the little man came again, and asked what he was making. "A boat which will go quicker on dry land than on the water," replied Hans, "and when I have finished it, I am to have the King's daughter for my wife." "Well," said the little man, "such shall it be, and remain." In the evening, when the sun had turned into gold, Hans finished his boat, and all that was wanted for it. He got into it and rowed to the palace. The boat went as swiftly as the wind.

The King saw it from afar, but would not give his daughter to Hans yet, and said he must first take a hundred hares out to pasture from early morning until late evening, and if one of them got away, he should not have his daughter. Hans was contented with this, and the next day went with his flock to the pasture, and took great care that none of them ran away.

Before many hours had passed came a servant from the palace, and told Hans that he must give her a hare instantly, for some visitors had come unexpectedly. Hans, however, was very well aware what that meant, and said he would not give her one; the King might set some hare soup before his guests next day. The maid, however, would not believe in his refusal, and at last she began to get angry with him. Then Hans said that if the King's daughter came herself, he would give her a hare. The maid told this in the palace, and the daughter did go herself.

In the meantime, however, the little man came again to Hans, and asked him what he was doing there. He said he had to watch over a hundred hares and see that none of them ran away, and then he might marry the King's daughter and be King. "Good," said the little man, "there is a whistle for you, and if one of them runs away, just whistle with it, and then it will come back again." When the King's daughter came, Hans gave her a hare into her apron; but when she had gone about a hundred steps with it, he whistled, and the hare jumped out of the apron, and before she could turn round was back to the flock again. When the evening came the hare-herd whistled once more, and looked to see if all were there, and then drove them to the palace. The King wondered how Hans had been able to take a hundred hares to graze without losing any of them; he would, however, not give him his daughter yet, and said he must now bring him a feather from the Griffin's tail.

Hans set out at once, and walked straight forwards. In the evening he came to a castle, and there he asked for a night's lodging, for at that time there were no inns. The lord of the castle promised him that with much pleasure, and asked where he was going. Hans answered, "To the Griffin." "Oh! to the Griffin! They tell me he knows everything, and I have lost the key of an iron money-chest; so you might be so good as to ask him where it is." "Yes, indeed," said Hans, "I will soon do that." Early the next morning he went onwards, and on his way arrived at another castle in which he again stayed the night. When the people who lived there learnt that he was going to the Griffin, they said they had in the house a daughter who was ill, and that they had already tried every means to cure her, but none of them had done her any good, and he might be so kind as to ask the Griffin what would make their daughter healthy again. Hans said he would willingly do that, and went onwards. Then he came to a lake, and instead of a ferryboat, a tall, tall man was there who had to carry everybody across. The man asked Hans whither he was journeying. "To the Griffin," said Hans. "Then when you get to him," said the man, "just ask him why I am forced to carry everybody over the lake?" "Yes, indeed, most certainly I'll do that," said Hans. Then the man took him up on his shoulders, and carried him across.

At length Hans arrived at the Griffin's house, but the wife only was at home, and not the Griffin himself. Then the woman asked him what he wanted. Thereupon he told her everything: that he had to get a feather out of the Griffin's tail; and that there was a castle where they had lost the key of their money-chest, and he was to ask the Griffin where it was; that in another castle the daughter was ill, and he was to learn what would cure her; and then not far from thence there was a lake and a man beside it, who was forced to carry people across it, and he was very anxious to learn why the man was obliged to do it.

Then said the woman, "But look here, my good friend, no Christian can speak to the Griffin. He devours them all. But if you like, you can lie down under his bed, and in the night, when he is quite fast asleep, you can reach out and pull a feather out of his tail; and as for those things which you are to learn, I will ask about them myself." Hans was quite satisfied with this, and got under the bed. In the evening, the Griffin came home, and as soon as he entered the room said, "Wife, I smell a Christian." "Yes," said the woman, "one was here today, but he went away again." Then the Griffin said no more.

In the middle of the night when the Griffin was snoring loudly, Hans reached out and plucked a feather from his tail. The Griffin woke up instantly, and said, "Wife, I smell a Christian, and it seems to me that somebody was pulling at my tail." His wife said, "You have certainly been dreaming, and I told you before that a Christian was here today, but that he went away again. He told me all kinds of things—that in one castle they had lost the key of their money-chest, and could find it nowhere." "Oh! the fools!" said the Griffin; "the key lies in the wood-house under a log of wood behind the door." "And then he said that in another castle the daughter was ill, and they knew no remedy that would cure her." "Oh! the fools!" said the Griffin; "under the cellar-steps a toad has made its nest of her hair, and if she got her hair back she would be well." "And then he also said that there was a place where there was a lake and a man beside it who was forced to carry everybody across." "Oh, the fool!" said the Griffin; "if he only put one man down in the middle, he would never have to carry another across."

Early the next morning the Griffin got up and went out. Then Hans came forth from under the bed, and he had a beautiful feather, and had heard what the Griffin had said about the key, and the daughter, and the ferry-man. The Griffin's wife repeated it all once more to him that he might not forget it, and then he went home again.

First he came to the man by the lake, who asked him what the Griffin had said, but Hans replied that he must first carry him across, and then he would tell him. So the man carried him across, and when he was over Hans told him that all he had to do was to set one person down in the middle of the lake, and then he would never have to carry over any more. The man was hugely delighted, and told Hans that out of gratitude he would take him once more across, and back again. But Hans said no, he would save him the trouble, he was quite satisfied already, and pursued his way. Then he came to the castle where the daughter was ill; he took her on his shoulders, for she could not walk, and carried her down the cellar-steps and pulled out the toad's nest from beneath the lowest step and gave it into her hand, and she sprang off his shoulder and up the steps before him, and was quite cured. Then were the father and mother beyond measure rejoiced, and they gave Hans gifts of gold and of silver, and whatsoever else he wished for, that they gave him. And when he got to the other castle he went at once into the wood-house, and found the key under the log of wood behind the door, and took it to the lord of the castle. He also was not a little pleased, and gave Hans as a reward much of the gold that was in the chest, and all kinds of things besides, such as cows, and sheep, and goats.

When Hans arrived before the King, with all these things—with the money, and the gold, and the silver and the cows, sheep and goats, the King asked him how he had come by them. Then Hans told him that the Griffin gave every one whatsoever he wanted. So the King thought he himself could make such things useful, and set out on his way to the Griffin; but when he got to the lake, it happened that he was the very first who arrived there after Hans, and the man put him down in the middle of it and went away, and the King was drowned. Hans, however, married the daughter, and became King.

The Sea-Hare

THERE WAS once upon a time a Princess, who, high under the battlements in her castle, had an apartment with twelve windows, which looked out in every possible direction, and when she climbed up to it and looked around her, she could inspect her whole kingdom. When she looked out of the first, her sight was more keen than that of any other human being; from the second she could see still better, from the third more distinctly still, and so it went on, until the twelfth, from which she saw everything above the earth and under the earth, and nothing at all could be kept secret from her. Moreover, as she was haughty, and would be subject to no one, but wished to keep the dominion for herself alone, she caused it to be proclaimed that no one should ever be her husband who could not conceal himself from her so effectually, that it should be quite impossible for her to find him. He who tried this, however, and was discovered by her, was to have his head struck off, and stuck on a post. Ninety-seven posts with the heads of dead men were already standing before the castle, and no one had come forward for a long time. The Princess was delighted, and thought to herself, "Now I shall be free as long as I live."

Then three brothers appeared before her, and announced to her that they were desirous of trying their luck. The eldest believed he would be quite safe if he crept into a limepit, but she saw him from the first window, made him come out, and had his head cut off. The second crept into the cellar of the palace, but she perceived him also from the first window, and his fate was sealed. His head was placed on the nine and ninetieth post. Then the youngest came to her and entreated her to give him a day for consideration, and also to be so gracious as to overlook it if she should happen to discover him twice, but if he failed the third time, he would look on his life as over. As he was so handsome, and begged so earnestly, she said, "Yes, I will grant thee that, but thou wilt not succeed."

Next day he meditated for a long time how he should hide himself, but all in vain. Then he seized his gun and went out hunting. He saw a raven, took a good aim at him, and was just going to fire, when the bird cried, "Don't shoot; I will make it worth thy while not to kill me." He put his gun down, went on, and came to a lake where he surprised a large fish which had come up from the depths below to the surface of the water. When he had aimed at it, the fish cried, "Don't shoot, and I will make it worth thy while." He allowed it to dive down again, went onwards, and met a fox which was lame. He fired and missed it, and the fox cried, "You had much better come here and draw the thorn out of my foot for me." He did this; but then he wanted to kill the fox and skin it. The fox said, "Stop, and I will make it worth thy while." The youth let him go, and then as it was evening, returned home.

Next day he was to hide himself; but howsoever much he puzzled his brains over it, he did not know where. He went into the forest to the raven and said, "I let thee live on, so now tell me where I am to hide myself, so that the King's daughter shall not see me." The raven hung his head and thought it over for a long time. At length he croaked, "I have it." He fetched an egg out of his nest, cut it into two parts, and shut the youth inside it; then made it whole again, and seated himself on it. When the King's daughter went to the first window she could not discover him, nor could she from the others, and she began to be uneasy, but from the eleventh she saw him. She ordered the raven to be shot, and the egg to be brought and broken, and the youth was forced to come out. She said, "For once thou art excused, but if thou dost not do better than this, thou art lost!"

Next day he went to the lake, called the fish to him and said, "I suffered thee to live, now tell me where to hide myself so that the King's daughter may not see me." The fish thought for a while, and at last cried, "I have it! I will shut thee up in my stomach." He swallowed him, and went down to the bottom of the lake. The King's daughter looked through her windows, and even from the eleventh did not see him, and was alarmed; but at length from the twelfth she saw him. She ordered the fish to be caught and killed, and then the youth appeared. Every one can imagine what a state of mind he was in. She said, "Twice thou art forgiven, but be sure that thy head will be set on the hundredth post."

On the last day, he went with a heavy heart into the country, and met the fox. "Thou knowest how to find all kinds of hiding-places," said he; "I let thee live, now advise me where I shall hide myself so that the King's daughter shall not discover me." "That's a hard task," answered the fox, looking very thoughtful. At length he cried, "I have it!" and went with him to a spring, dipped himself in it, and came out as a stall-keeper in the market, and dealer in animals. The youth had to dip himself in the water also, and was changed into a small sea-hare. The merchant went into the town, and showed the pretty little animal, and many persons gathered together to see it.

At length the King's daughter came likewise, and as she liked it very much, she bought it, and gave the merchant a good deal of money for it. Before he gave it over to her, he said to it, "When the King's daughter goes to the window, creep quickly under the braids of her hair."

And now the time arrived when she was to search for him. She went to one window after another in turn, from the first to the eleventh, and did not see him. When she did not see him from the twelfth either, she was full of anxiety and anger, and shut it down with such violence that the glass in every window shivered into a thousand pieces, and the whole castle shook.

She went back and felt the sea-hare beneath the braids of her hair. Then she seized it, and threw it on the ground exclaiming, "Away with thee, get out of my sight!" It ran to the merchant, and both of them hurried to the spring, wherein they plunged, and received back their true forms. The youth thanked the fox, and said, "The raven and the fish are idiots compared with thee; thou knowest the right tune to play, there is no denying that!"

The youth went straight to the palace. The Princess was already expecting him, and accommodated herself to her destiny. The wedding was solemnized, and now he was King, and lord of all the kingdom. He never told her where he had concealed himself for the third time, and who had helped him, so she believed that he had done everything by his own skill, and she had a great respect for him, for she thought to herself, "He is able to do more than I."

The Maiden Without Hands

A MILLER who had gradually become very poor, had nothing left but his mill and a large apple tree behind it. One day when he went into the forest to gather wood, an old man, whom he had never seen before, came toward him, and said, "Why do you take the trouble to cut down wood? I will give you great riches if you will promise to let me have what stands behind your mill."

"That can be no other than my apple tree," thought the miller.

"I possess nothing else." So he said to the old man, "Yes, I will let you have it."

Then the stranger smiled maliciously, and said, "In three years I will come again to claim what belongs to me," and after saying this he departed.

As soon as the miller returned home, his wife came toward him and said: "Miller, from whence have all these riches come so suddenly to our house? All at once every drawer and chest has become full of gold. No one brought it here, and I know not where it came from."

"Oh," replied her husband, "I know all about it. A strange man whom I met in the wood promised me great treasures if I would make over to him what stood behind the mill. I knew I had nothing there but a large apple tree, so I gave him my promise."

"Oh, husband!" said the wife in alarm, "that must have been the wizard. He did not mean the apple tree, but our daughter, who was behind the mill sweeping out the court."

The miller's daughter was a modest and beautiful maiden, and lived in innocence and obedience to her parents for three years, until the day came on which the wicked wizard was to claim her. She knew he was coming, and after washing till she was pure and clean as snow, she drew a circle of white chalk and stood within it.

The wizard made his appearance very early, but he did not dare to venture over the white circle, therefore he could not get near her. In great anger he said to the miller, "Take away every drop of water, that she may not wash, otherwise I shall have no power over her!"

The frightened miller did as he desired, but on the next morning, when the wizard came again, her hands were as pure and clean as ever, for she had wept over them. On this account the wizard was still unable to approach her; so he flew into a rage, and said, "Chop her hands off, otherwise I cannot touch her."

Then the miller was terrified, and exclaimed, "How can I cut off the hands of my own child?"

Then the wicked wizard threatened him, and said, "If you will not do as I desire you, then I can claim you instead of your daughter, and carry you off."

The father listened in agony, and in his fright promised to obey. He went to his daughter, and said to her, "Oh, my child, unless I cut off your two hands the wizard will take me away with him, and in my anguish I have promised. Help me in my trouble, and forgive me for the wicked deed I have promised to do." "Dear father," she replied, "do with me what you will: I am your child."

Thereupon she placed her two hands on the table before him, and he cut them off. The wizard came next day for the third time, but the poor girl had wept so bitterly over the stumps of her arms that they were as clean and white as ever. Then he was obliged to give way, for he had lost all right to the maiden.

As soon as the wizard had departed the miller said, "My child, I have obtained so much good through your conduct that for your whole lifetime I shall hold you most precious and dear." "But I cannot stay here, father," she replied; "I am not safe; let me go away with people who will give me the sympathy I need so much." "I fear such people are very seldom to be found in the world," said her father. However, he let her to. So she tied up her maimed arms and went forth on her way at sunrise.

For a whole day she traveled without food, and as night came on found herself near one of the royal gardens. By the light of the moon she could see many trees laden with beautiful fruit, but she could not reach them, because the place was surrounded by a moat full of water. She had been without a morsel to eat the whole day, and her hunger was so great that she could not help crying out, "Oh, if I were only able to get some of that delicious fruit! I shall die unless I can obtain something to eat very soon."

Then she knelt down and prayed for help, and while she prayed a guardian fairy appeared and made a channel in the water so that she was able to pass through on dry ground.

When she entered the garden the fairy was with her, although she did not know it, so she walked to a tree full of beautiful pears, not knowing that they had been counted.

Being unable to pluck any without hands, she went quite close to the tree and ate one with her mouth as it hung. One, and no more, just to stay her hunger. The gardener, who saw her with the fairy standing near her, thought it was a spirit, and was too frightened to move or speak.

After having satisfied her hunger the maiden went and laid herself down among the shrubs and slept in peace. On the following morning the King, to whom the garden belonged, came out to look at his fruit trees, and when he reached the pear tree and counted the pears, he found one missing. At first he thought it had fallen, but it was not under the tree, so he went to the gardener and asked what had become of it.

Then said the gardener, "There was a ghost in the garden last

night who had no hands, and ate a pear off the tree with its mouth."
"How could the ghost get across the water?" asked the King; "and
what became of it after eating the pear?"

To this the gardener replied, "Some one came first in snow-white
robes from heaven, who made a channel and stopped the flow of
the water so that the ghost walked through on dry ground. It must
have been an angel," continued the gardener; "and therefore I was
afraid to ask questions or to call out. As soon as the specter had
eaten one pear it went away."

Then said the King, "Conceal from every one what you have told
me, and I will watch myself tonight."

As soon as it was dark the King came into the garden and
brought a priest with him to address the ghost, and they both
seated themselves under a tree, with the gardener standing near
them, and waited in silence. About midnight the maiden crept out
from the bushes and went to the pear tree, and the three watchers
saw her eat a pear from the tree without picking it, while an angel
stood near in white garments.

Then the priest went toward her, and said, "Art thou come from
Heaven or earth? Art thou a spirit or a human being?"

Then the maiden answered, "Ah, me! I am no ghost, only a poor
creature forsaken by every one but God."

Then said the King, "You may be forsaken by all the world, but if
you will let me be your friend, I will never forsake you."

So the maiden was taken to the King's castle, and she was so
beautiful and modest that the King learned to love her with all his
heart. He had silver hands made for her, and very soon after they
were married with great pomp.

About a year after, the King had to go to battle, and he placed his
young wife under the care of his mother, who promised to be very
kind to her, and to write to him.

Not long after this the Queen had a little son born, and the King's
mother wrote a letter to him immediately, so that he might have
the earliest intelligence, and sent it by a messenger.

The messenger, however, after traveling a long way, became
tired and sat down to rest by a brook, where he soon fell fast asleep.
Then came the wizard, who was always trying to injure the good
Queen, took away the letter from the sleeping messenger, and
replaced it by another, in which it was stated that the little child
was a changeling.

Knowing nothing of the change, the messenger carried this letter to the King, who, when he read it, was terribly distressed and

troubled. However, he wrote in reply to say that the Queen was to have every attention and care till his return.

The wicked wizard again watched for the messenger, and while he slept exchanged the King's kind letter for another, in which was written to the King's mother an order to kill both the Queen and her child.

The old mother was quite terrified when she read this letter, for she could not believe the King meant her to do anything so dreadful. She wrote again to the King, but there was no answer, for the wicked wizard always interrupted the messengers, and sent false letters. The last was worse than all, for it stated that instead of killing the mother and her child, they were to cut out the tongue of the changeling and put out the mother's eyes.

But the King's mother was too good to attend to these dreadful orders, so she said to the Queen, while her eyes streamed with tears, "I cannot kill you both, as the King desires me to do; but I must not let you remain here any longer. Go, now, out into the world with your child, and do not come here again." Then she bound the boy on his mother's back, and the poor woman departed, weeping as she went.

After walking some time she reached a dense forest, and knew not which road to take. So she knelt down and prayed for help. As she rose from her knees she saw a light shining from the window of a little cottage, on which was hung a small sign-board, with these words: "Every one who dwells here is safe." Out of the cottage stepped a maiden dressed in snowy garments, and said, "Welcome, Queen wife," and led her in. Then she unfastened the baby from his mother's back, and hushed him in her arms till he slept so peacefully that she laid him on a bed in another room, and came back to his mother.

The poor woman looked at her earnestly, and said, "How did you know I was a Queen?" The white maiden replied: "I am a good fairy sent to take care of you and your child."

So she remained in that cottage many years, and was very happy, and so pious and good that her hands, which had been cut off, were allowed to grow again, and the little boy became her great comfort.

Not long after she had been sent away from the castle the King returned, and immediately asked to see his wife and child.

Then his old mother began to weep, and said, "You wicked man, how can you ask me for your wife and child when you wrote me such dreadful letters, and told me to kill two such innocent be-ings?"

The King, in distress, asked her what she meant; and she showed him the letters she had received, which were changed by the dreadful wizard. Then the King began to weep so bitterly for his wife and child that the old woman pitied him, and said, "Do not be so unhappy; they still live; I could not kill them. But your wife and child are gone into the wide world, never to come back for fear of your anger."

Then said the King, "I will go to the ends of the earth to find them, and I will neither eat nor drink till I find my dear wife, even if I should die of hunger."

Thereupon the King started on his expedition, traveling over rocks and valleys, over mountains and highways, for seven long years. But he found her not, and he thought she was starved to death, and that he should never see her again.

He neither ate nor drank during the whole time of earthly food, but Heaven sent him help. At last he arrived at a large forest and found the little cottage with the sign-board, and the words upon it: "Every one who dwells here is safe."

While he stood reading the words the maiden in white raiment came out, took him by the hand, and led him into the cottage, saying, "My lord the King is welcome; but why is he here?" Then he replied, "I have been for seven years traveling about the world hoping to find my wife and child, but I have not yet succeeded. Can you help me?" "Sit down," said the angel, "and take some-thing to eat and drink first."

The King was so tired that he gladly obeyed, for he really wanted rest. Then he laid himself down and slept, and the maiden in the white raiment covered his face.

Then she went into an inner chamber where the Queen sat with her little son, whom she had named "Pain-bringer," and said to her, "Go out together into the other chamber; your husband is come."

The poor Queen went out, but still sorrowfully, for she remem-bered the cruel letters his mother had received, and knew not that he still loved her. Just as she entered the room the covering fell off his face, and she told her little son to replace it.

The boy went forward and laid the cloth gently over the face of the strange man. But the King heard the voice in his slumber, and moved his head so that the covering again fell off.

"My child," said the Queen, "cover the face of thy father."

He looked at her in surprise, and said, "How can I cover my father's face, dear mother? I have no father in this world. You have taught me to pray to 'Our Father, which art in heaven,' and I thought my father was God. This strange man is not my father; I don't know him."

When the King heard this he started up and asked who they were. Then said the Queen, "I am your wife, and this is your son."

The King looked at her with surprise. "Your face and your voice are the same," he said; "but my wife had silver hands, and yours are natural." "My hands have mercifully been allowed to grow again," she replied; and, as he still doubted, the maiden in white entered the room, carrying the silver hands, which she showed to the King.

Then he saw at once that this was indeed his dear lost wife and his own little son; and he embraced them, full of joy, exclaiming, "Now has a heavy stone fallen from my heart!"

The maiden prepared a dinner for them, of which they all partook together; and, after a kind farewell, the King started with his wife and child to return home to the castle, where his mother and all the household received them with great joy.

A second marriage-feast was prepared, and the happiness of their latter days made amends for all they had suffered through the wicked demon who had caused them so much pain and trouble.

The Pink

THERE WAS once a Queen, who had not been blessed with children. As she walked in her garden, she prayed every morning that a son or a daughter might be given to her. One day an Angel came and said to her, "Be content; you shall have a son, and he shall be endowed with the power of wishing, so that whatsoever he wishes for shall be granted to him." She hurried to the King, and told him the joyful news; and when the time came a son was born to them, and they were filled with delight.

Every morning the Queen used to take her little son into the gardens, where the wild animals were kept, to wash him in a clear, sparkling fountain. It happened one day, when the child was a little older, that as she sat with him on her lap she fell asleep.

The old cook, who knew that the child had the power of wishing, came by and stole the infant. He also killed a chicken and dropped some of its blood on the Queen's garments. He took the child away to a secret place, where he placed it out to be nursed. Then he ran back to the King, and accused the Queen of having allowed her child to be carried off by a wild animal.

When the King saw the blood on the Queen's garments he believed the story, and was overwhelmed with anger. He caused a high tower to be built, into which neither the sun nor the moon could penetrate. Then he ordered his wife to be shut up in it, and the door walled up. She was to stay there for seven years, without eating or drinking, so as gradually to pine away. But two Angels from heaven, in the shape of white doves, came to her, bringing food twice a day till the seven years were ended.

But the cook thought, "If the child really has the power of wishing, and I stay here, I might easily fall into disgrace." So he left the palace, and went to the boy, who was old enough to talk now, and said to him, "Wish for a beautiful castle, with a garden, and everything belonging to it." Hardly had the words passed the boy's lips than all that he had asked for was there. After a time the cook said, "It is not good for you to be so much alone; wish for a beautiful maiden to be your companion."

The Prince uttered the wish, and immediately a maiden stood before them, more beautiful than any painter could paint. So they grew very fond of each other, and played together, while the cook went out hunting like any grand gentleman. But the idea came to him one day that the Prince might wish to go to his father some time, and he would thereby be placed in a very awkward position. So he took the maiden aside, and said to her, "Tonight, when the boy is asleep, go and drive this knife into his heart. Then bring me his heart and his tongue. If you fail to do it, you will lose your own life."

Then he went away; but when the next day came, the maiden had not yet obeyed his command, and she said, "Why should I shed his innocent blood, when he has never done any harm to a creature in his life?"

The cook again said, "If you do not obey me, you will lose your own life."

When he had gone away, she ordered a young hind to be brought and killed; then she cut out its heart and its tongue, and put them on a dish. When she saw the old man coming she said to the boy, "Get into bed, and cover yourself right over."

The old scoundrel came in and said, "Where are the tongue and the heart of the boy?"

The maiden gave him the dish; but the Prince threw off the coverings, and said, "You old sinner, why did you want to kill me? Now bear your sentence. You shall be turned into a black poodle, with a gold chain round your neck, and you shall be made to eat live coals, so that flames of fire may come out of your mouth."

As he said the words, the old man was changed into a black poodle, with a gold chain round his neck; and the scullions brought out live coals, which he had to eat till the flames poured out of his mouth.

The Prince stayed on at the castle for a time, thinking of his mother, and wondering if she was still alive. At last he said to the maiden, "I am going into my own country. If you like you can go with me; I will take you."

She answered, "Alas! it is so far off, and what should I do in a strange country where I know no one?"

As she did not wish to go, and yet they could not bear to be parted, he changed her into a beautiful pink, which he took with him.

Then he set out on his journey, and the poodle was made to run alongside till the Prince reached his own country.

Arrived there, he went straight to the tower where his mother was imprisoned, and as the tower was so high he wished for a ladder to reach the top. Then he climbed up, looked in, and cried, "Dearest mother, lady Queen, are you still alive?"

She, thinking it was the Angels who brought her food come back, said, "I have just eaten; I do not want anything more."

Then he said, "I am your own dear son whom the wild animals were supposed to have devoured; but I am still alive, and I shall soon come and rescue you."

Then he got down and went to his father. He had himself announced as a strange huntsman, anxious to take service with the King, who said, "Yes; if you are skilled in game preserving, and can procure plenty of venison, I will engage you. But there has never before been any game in the whole district."

The huntsman promised to procure as much game as the King could possibly require for the royal table.

Then he called the whole hunt together, and ordered them all into the forest with him. He caused a great circle to be enclosed, with only one outlet; then he took his place in the middle, and began to wish as hard as he could. Immediately over two hundred head of game came running into the enclosure. These the huntsmen had to shoot, and then they were piled on to sixty country wagons, and driven home to the King. So for once he was able to load his board with game, after having had none for many years.

The King was much pleased, and commanded his whole court to a banquet on the following day. When they were all assembled, he said to the huntsman, "You shall sit by me as you are so clever."

He answered, "My Lord and King, may it please your Majesty, I am only a poor huntsman!"

The King, however, insisted, and said, "I command you to sit by me."

As he sat there, his thoughts wandered to his dear mother, and he wished one of the courtiers would speak of her. Hardly had he wished it than the Lord High Marshal said, "Your Majesty, we are all rejoicing here, how fares it with Her Majesty the Queen? Is she still alive in the tower, or has she perished?"

But the King answered, "She allowed my beloved son to be devoured by wild animals, and I do not wish to hear anything about her."

Then the huntsman stood up and said, "Gracious father, she is still alive, and I am her son. He was not devoured by wild animals; he was taken away by the scoundrel of a cook. He stole me while my mother was asleep, and sprinkled her garments with the blood of a chicken." Then he brought up the black poodle with the golden chain, and said, "This is the villain."

He ordered some live coals to be brought, which he made the dog eat in the sight of all the people till the flames poured out of his mouth. Then he asked the King if he would like to see the cook in his true shape, and wished him back, and there he stood in his white apron, with his knife at his side. The King was furious when he saw him, and ordered him to be thrown into the deepest dungeon.

Then the huntsman said further, "My father, would you like to see the maiden who so tenderly saved my life when she was ordered to kill me, although by so doing she might have lost her own life?"

The King answered, "Yes, I will gladly see her."

Then his son said, "Gracious father, I will show her to you first in the guise of a beautiful flower."

He put his hand into his pocket, and brought out the pink. It was a finer one than the King had ever seen before. Then his son said, "Now, I will show her to you in her true form."

In a moment after his wish was uttered, she stood before them in all her beauty, which was greater than any artist could paint.

The King sent ladies and gentlemen-in-waiting to the tower to bring the Queen back to his royal table. But when they reached the tower they found that she would no longer eat or drink, and she said, "The merciful God, who has preserved my life so long, will soon release me now."

Three days after she died. At her burial the two white doves which had brought her food during her captivity, followed and hovered over her grave.

The old King caused the wicked cook to be torn into four quarters; but his own heart was filled with grief and remorse, and he died soon after.

His son married the beautiful maiden he had brought home with him as a flower, and, for all I know, they may be living still.

Mother Hulda

A WIDOW had two daughters; one was pretty and industrious, the other was ugly and lazy. And as the ugly one was her own daughter, she loved her much the best, and the pretty one was made to do all the work, and to be the drudge of the house. Every day the poor girl had to sit by a well on the high road and spin until her fingers bled. Now it happened once that as the spindle was bloody, she dipped it into the well to wash it; but it slipped out of her hand and fell in. Then she began to cry, and ran to her step-mother, and told her of her misfortune; and her step-mother scolded her without mercy, and said in her rage, "As you have let the spindle fall in, you must go and fetch it out again!"

Then the girl went back again to the well, not knowing what to do, and in the despair of her heart she jumped down into the well the same way the spindle had gone. After that she knew nothing; and when she came to herself she was in a beautiful meadow, and the sun was shining on the flowers that grew round her. And she walked on through the meadow until she came to a baker's oven that was full of bread; and the bread called out to her, "Oh, take me out, take me out, or I shall burn; I am baked enough already!"

Then she drew near, and with the baker's peel she took out all the loaves one after the other. And she went farther on till she came to a tree weighed down with apples, and it called out to her, "Oh, shake me, shake me, we apples are all of us ripe!" Then she shook the tree until the apples fell like rain, and she shook until there were no more to fall; and when she had gathered them together in a heap, she went on farther.

At last she came to a little house, and an old woman was peeping out of it, but she had such great teeth that the girl was terrified and about to run away, only the old woman called her back. "What are you afraid of, my dear child? Come and live with me, and if you do the house-work well and orderly, things shall go well with you. You must take great pains to make my bed well, and shake it up thoroughly, so that the feathers fly about, and then in the world it snows, for I am Mother Hulda."*

As the old woman spoke so kindly, the girl took courage, consented, and went to her work. She did everything to the old woman's satisfaction, and shook the bed with such a will that the feathers flew about like snow-flakes; and so she led a good life, had never a cross word, but boiled and roast meat every day. When she had lived a long time with Mother Hulda, she began to feel sad, not knowing herself what ailed her; at last she began to think she must be home-sick; and although she was a thousand times better off than at home where she was, yet she had a great longing to go home. At last she said to her mistress, "I am home-sick, and although I am very well off here, I cannot stay any longer; I must go back to my own home."

Mother Hulda answered, "It pleases me well that you should wish to go home, and, as you have served me faithfully, I will undertake to send you there!"

She took her by the hand and led her to a large door standing open, and as she was passing through it there fell upon her a heavy shower of gold, and the gold hung all about her, so that she was covered with it.

"All this is yours, because you have been so industrious," said Mother Hulda; and, besides that, she returned to her her spindle, the very same that she had dropped in the well. And then the door was shut again, and the girl found herself back again in the world, not far from her mother's house; and as she passed through the yard the cock stood on the top of the well and cried,

* In Hesse, when it snows, they still say, "Mother Hulda is making her bed."

> *"Cock-a-doodle doo!*
> *Our golden girl has come home too!"*

Then she went in to her mother, and as she had returned covered with gold she was well received.

So the girl related all her history, and what had happened to her, and when the mother heard how she came to have such great riches she began to wish that her ugly and idle daughter might have the same good fortune. So she sent her to sit by the well and spin; and in order to make her spindle bloody she put her hand into the thorn hedge. Then she threw the spindle into the well, and jumped in herself. She found herself, like her sister, in the beautiful meadow, and followed the same path, and when she came to the baker's oven, the bread cried out, "Oh, take me out, take me out, or I shall burn; I am quite done already!"

But the lazy-bones answered, "I have no desire to black my hands," and went on farther. Soon she came to the apple tree, who called out, "Oh, shake me, shake me, we apples are all of us ripe!" But she answered, "That is all very fine, suppose one of you should fall on my head," and went on farther.

When she came to Mother Hulda's house she did not feel afraid, as she knew beforehand of her great teeth, and entered into her service at once. The first day she put her hand well to the work, and was industrious, and did everything Mother Hulda bade her, because of the gold she expected; but the second day she began to be idle, and the third day still more so, so that she would not get up in the morning. Neither did she make Mother Hulda's bed as it ought to have been made, and did not shake it for the feathers to fly about. So that Mother Hulda soon grew tired of her, and gave her warning, at which the lazy thing was well pleased, and thought that now the shower of gold was coming; so Mother Hulda led her to the door, and as she stood in the doorway, instead of the shower of gold a great kettle full of pitch was emptied over her.

"That is the reward for your service," said Mother Hulda, and shut the door. So the lazy girl came home all covered with pitch, and the cock on the top of the well seeing her, cried,

> *"Cock-a-doodle doo!*
> *Our dirty girl has come home too!"*

And the pitch remained sticking to her fast, and never, as long as she lived, could it be got off.

The True Bride

THERE WAS once on a time a girl who was young and beautiful, but she had lost her mother when she was quite a child, and her step-mother did all she could to make the girl's life wretched. Whenever this woman gave her anything to do, she worked at it indefatigably, and did everything that lay in her power. Still she could not touch the heart of the wicked woman by that; she was never satisfied; it was never enough. The harder the girl worked, the more work was put upon her, and all that the woman thought of was how to weigh her down with still heavier burdens, and make her life still more miserable.

One day she said to her, "Here are twelve pounds of feathers which you must pick, and if they are not done this evening, you may expect a good beating. Do you imagine you can idle away the whole day?" The poor girl sat down to the work, but tears ran down her cheeks as she did so, for she saw plainly enough that it was quite impossible to finish the work in one day. Whenever she had a little heap of feathers lying before her, and she sighed or smote her hands together in her anguish, they flew away, and she had to pick them out again, and begin her work anew. Then she put her elbows on the table, laid her face in her two hands, and cried, "Is there no one, then, on God's earth to have pity on me?"

Then she heard a low voice which said, "Be comforted, my child, I have come to help you." The maiden looked up, and an old woman was by her side. She took the girl kindly by the hand, and said, "Only tell me what is troubling you." As she spoke so kindly, the girl told her of her miserable life, and how one burden after another was laid upon her, and she never could get to the end of the work which was given to her. "If I have not done these feathers by this evening, my step-mother will beat me; she has threatened she will, and I know she keeps her word." Her tears began to flow again, but the good old woman said, "Do not be afraid, my child; rest a while, and in the meantime I will look to your work." The girl lay down on her bed, and soon fell asleep.

The old woman seated herself at the table with the feathers, and how they did fly off the quills, which she scarcely touched with her withered hands! The twelve pounds were soon finished, and when the girl awoke, great snow-white heaps were lying, piled up, and everything in the room was neatly cleared away, but the old woman had vanished. The maiden thanked God, and sat still till evening came, when the step-mother came in and marveled to see the work completed. "Just look, you awkward creature," said she, "what can be done when people are industrious; and why could you not set about something else? There you sit with your hands crossed." When she went out she said, "The creature is worth more than her salt. I must give her some work that is still harder."

Next morning she called the girl, and said, "There is a spoon for you. With that you must empty out for me the great pond which is beside the garden, and if it is not done by night, you know what will happen." The girl took the spoon, and saw that it was full of holes; but even if it had not been, she never could have emptied the pond with it. She set to work at once, knelt down by the water, into which her tears were falling, and began to empty it. But the good old woman appeared again, and when she learnt the cause of her grief, she said, "Be of good cheer, my child. Go into the thicket and lie down and sleep; I will soon do your work."

As soon as the old woman was alone, she barely touched the pond, and a vapor rose up on high from the water, and mingled itself with the clouds. Gradually the pond was emptied, and when the maiden awoke before sunset and came thither, she saw nothing but the fishes which were struggling in the mud. She went to her step-mother, and showed her that the work was done. "It ought to have been done long before this," said she, and grew white with anger, but she meditated something new.

On the third morning she said to the girl, "You must build me a castle on the plain there, and it must be ready by the evening." The maiden was dismayed, and said, "How can I complete such a great work?" "I will endure no opposition," screamed the step-mother. "If you can empty a pond with a spoon that is full of holes, you can build a castle too. I will take possession of it this very day, and if anything is wanting, even if it be the most trifling thing in the kitchen or cellar, you know what lies before you!" She drove the girl out, and when she entered the valley, the rocks were there, piled up one above the other, and all her strength would not have enabled her even to move the very smallest of them. She sat down and wept, and still she hoped the old woman would help her. The old woman was not long in coming; she comforted her and said, "Lie down there in the shade and sleep, and I will soon build the castle for you. If it would be a pleasure to you, you can live in it yourself."

When the maiden had gone away, the old woman touched the gray rocks. They began to rise, and immediately moved together as if giants had built the walls; and on these the building arose, and it seemed as if countless hands were working invisibly, and placing one stone upon another. There was a dull heavy noise from the ground; pillars arose of their own accord on high, and placed themselves in order near each other. The tiles laid themselves in order on the roof, and when noon-day came, the great weather-cock was already turning itself on the summit of the tower, like a golden figure of the Virgin with fluttering garments. The inside of the castle was being finished while evening was drawing near. How the old woman managed it, I know not; but the walls of the room were hung with silk and velvet; embroidered chairs were there, and richly ornamented arm-chairs by marble tables; crystal chandeliers hung down from the ceilings and mirrored themselves in the smooth pavement; green parrots were there in gilt cages, and so were strange birds which sang most beautifully; and there was on all sides as much magnificence as if a King were going to live there.

The sun was just setting when the girl awoke, and the brightness of a thousand lights flashed in her face. She hurried to the castle, and entered by the open door. The steps were spread with red cloth, and the golden balustrade beset with flowering trees. When she saw the splendor of the apartment, she stood as if turned to stone. Who knows how long she might have stood there if she had not remembered the step-mother. "Alas!" she said to herself, "if she could but be satisfied at last, and would give up making my life a misery to me." The girl went and told her that the castle was ready. "I will move into it at once," said she, and rose from her seat.

When they entered the castle, she was forced to hold her hand before her eyes, the brilliancy of everything was so dazzling. "You see," said she to the girl, "how easy it has been for you to do this; I ought to have given you something harder." She went through all the rooms, and examined every corner to see if anything was wanting or defective; but she could discover nothing. "Now we will go down below," said she, looking at the girl with malicious eyes. "The kitchen and the cellar still have to be examined, and if you have forgotten anything you shall not escape punishment." But the fire was burning on the hearth, and the meat was cooking in the pans, the tongs and shovel were leaning against the wall, and the shining brazen utensils all arranged in sight. Nothing was wanting, not even a coal-box and water-pail. "Which is the way to the cellar?" she cried. "If that is not abundantly filled, it shall go ill with you." She herself raised up the trap-door and descended; but she had hardly made two steps before the heavy trap-door which was only laid back, fell down. The girl heard a scream, lifted up the door very quickly to go to her aid, but she had fallen down, and the girl found her lying lifeless at the bottom.

And now the magnificent castle belonged to the girl alone. She at first did not know how to reconcile herself to her good fortune. Beautiful dresses were hanging in the wardrobes, the chests were filled with gold or silver, or with pearls and jewels, and she never felt a desire that she was not able to gratify. And soon the fame of the beauty and riches of the maiden went over all the world. Wooers presented themselves daily, but none pleased her. At length the son of the King came and he knew how to touch her heart, and she betrothed herself to him. In the garden of the castle was a lime tree, under which they were one day sitting together, when he said to her, "I will go home and obtain my father's consent to our marriage. I entreat you to wait for me here under this lime tree; I shall be back with you in a few hours." The maiden kissed him on his left cheek, and said, "Keep true to me, and never let any one else kiss you on this cheek. I will wait here under the lime tree until you return."

The maid stayed beneath the lime tree until sunset, but he did not return. She sat there three days from morning till evening, waiting for him, but in vain. As he still was not there by the fourth day, she said, "Some accident has assuredly befallen him. I will go out and seek him, and will not come back until I have found him." She packed up three of her most beautiful dresses, one embroidered with bright stars, the second with silver moons, the third with golden suns, tied up a handful of jewels in her handkerchief, and set out. She inquired everywhere for her betrothed, but no one had seen him; no one knew anything about him. Far and wide did she wander through the world, but she found him not. At last she hired herself to a farmer as a cow-herd, and buried her dresses and jewels beneath a stone.

And now she lived as a herdswoman, guarded her herd, and was very sad and full of longing for her beloved one. She had a little calf which she taught to know her, and fed it out of her own hand, and when she said,

> *"Little calf, little calf, kneel by my side,*
> *And do not forget thy shepherd-maid,*

> *As the Prince forgot his betrothed bride,*
> *Who waited for him 'neath the lime tree's shade."*

the little calf knelt down, and she stroked it.

And when she had lived for a couple of years alone and full of grief, a report was spread over all the land that the King's daughter was about to celebrate her marriage. The road to the town passed through the village where the maiden was living, and it came to pass that once when the maiden was driving out her herd, her bridegroom traveled by. He was sitting proudly on his horse, and never looked round, but when she saw him she recognized her beloved, and it was just as if a sharp knife had pierced her heart. "Alas!" said she, "I believed him true to me, but he has forgotten me."

Next day he again came along the road. When he was near her she said to the little calf,

> *"Little calf, little calf, kneel by my side,*
> *And do not forget thy shepherd-maid,*
> *As the Prince forgot his betrothed bride,*
> *Who waited for him 'neath the lime tree's shade."*

When he was aware of the voice, he looked down and reined in his horse. He looked into the herd's face, and then put his hands before his eyes as if he were trying to remember something, but he soon rode onwards and was out of sight. "Alas!" said she, "he no longer knows me," and her grief was ever greater.

Soon after this a great festival three days long was to be held at the King's court, and the whole country was invited to it.

"Now will I try my last chance," thought the maiden, and when evening came she went to the stone under which she had buried her treasures. She took out the dress with the golden suns, put it on, and adorned herself with the jewels. She let down her hair, which she had concealed under a handkerchief, and it fell down in long curls about her, and thus she went into the town, and in the darkness was observed by no one. When she entered the brightly lighted hall, every one started back in amazement, but no one knew who she was. The King's son went to meet her, but he did not recognize her. He led her out to dance, and was so enchanted with her beauty, that he thought no more of the other bride. When the feast was over, she vanished in the crowd, and hastened before daybreak to the village, where she once more put on her herd's dress.

Next evening she took out the dress with the silver moons, and put a half-moon made of precious stones in her hair. When she appeared at the festival, all eyes were turned upon her, but the King's son hastened to meet her, and filled with love for her, danced with her alone, and no longer so much as glanced at any one else. Before she went away she was forced to promise him to come again to the festival on the last evening.

When she appeared for the third time, she wore the stardress which sparkled at every step she took, and her hair-ribbon and girdle were starred with jewels. The Prince had already been waiting for her for a long time, and forced his way up to her. "Do but tell who you are," said he, "I feel just as if I had already known you a long time." "Do you not know what I did when you left me?" Then she stepped up to him, and kissed him on his left cheek, and in a moment it was as if scales fell from his eyes, and he recognized the true bride. "Come," said he to her, "here I stay no longer," gave her his hand, and led her down to the carriage.

The horses hurried away to the magic castle as if the wind had been harnessed to the carriage. The illuminated windows already shone in the distance. When they drove past the lime tree, countless glow-worms were swarming about it. It shook its branches, and sent forth their fragrance. On the steps flowers were blooming, and the rooms echoed with the song of strange birds, but in the hall the entire court was assembled, and the priest was waiting to marry the bridegroom to the true bride.

The Three Little Birds

ABOUT a thousand or more years ago, there were in this country nothing but small Kings, and one of them, who lived on the Keuterberg, was very fond of hunting. Once on a time when he was riding forth from his castle with his huntsmen, three girls were watching their cows upon the mountain, and when they saw the King with all his followers, the eldest girl pointed to him, and called to the two other girls, "Hilloa! hilloa! If I do not get that one, I will have none." Then the second girl answered from the other side of the hill, and pointed to the one who was on the King's right hand, "Hilloa! hilloa! If I do not get that one, I will have none." And then the youngest pointed to the one who was on the left hand, and cried, "Hilloa! hilloa! If I do not get him I will have no one." These, however, were the two ministers.

The King heard all this, and when he had come back from the chase, he caused the three girls to be brought to him, and asked them what they had said yesterday on the mountain. They would not tell him that, so the King asked the eldest if she really would take him for her husband. Then she said "Yes," and the two ministers married the two sisters, for they were all three fair and beautiful of face, especially the Queen, who had hair like flax.

The two sisters had no children, and once when the King was obliged to go from home he invited them to come to the Queen in order to cheer her, for she was about to bear a child. She had a little boy who brought a bright red star into the world with him. The two sisters said to each other that they would throw the beautiful boy into the water. When they had thrown him in the river, a little bird flew up into the air, which sang,

> *"To thy death art thou sped,*
> *Until God's word be said.*
> *In the white lily bloom,*
> *Brave boy, is thy tomb."*

When the two heard that, they were frightened to death, and ran away in great haste. When the King came home they told him that the Queen had been delivered of a dog. Then the King said, "What God does, is well done!" But a fisherman who dwelt near the water fished the little boy out again while he was still alive, and as his wife had no children they reared him.

When a year had gone by, the King again went away, and the Queen had another little boy, whom the false sisters likewise took and threw into the water. Then up flew a little bird again and sang,

> *"To thy death art thou sped,*
> *Until God's word be said.*
> *In the white lily bloom,*
> *Brave boy, is thy tomb."*

And when the King came back, they told him that the Queen had once more given birth to a dog, and he again said, "What God does, is well done." The fisherman, however, fished this one also out of the water, and reared him.

Then the King again journeyed forth, and the Queen had a little girl, whom also the false sisters threw into the water. Then again a little bird flew up on high and sang,

> *"To thy death art thou sped,*
> *Until God's word he said.*
> *In the white lily bloom,*
> *Bonny girl, is thy tomb."*

When the King came home they told him that the Queen had been delivered of a cat. Then the King grew angry, and ordered his wife to be cast into prison, and therein was she shut up for many long years.

In the meantime the children had grown up. Then the eldest once went out with some other boys to fish, but the other boys would not have him with them, and said, "Go thy way, foundling."

Hereupon he was much troubled, and asked the old fisherman if that was true. The fisherman told him that once when he was fishing he had drawn him out of the water. So the boy said he would go forth and seek his father. The fisherman, however, entreated him to stay, but he would not let himself be hindered, and at last the fisherman consented. Then the boy went on his way and walked for many days together, and at last he came to a great piece of water by the side of which stood an old woman fishing.

"Good day, mother," said the boy. "Many thanks," said she. "You will fish long enough before you catch anything." "And you will seek long enough before you find your father. How will you get over the water?" said the woman. "God knows."

Then the old woman took him up on her back and carried him through it, and he sought for a long time, but could not find his father.

When a year had gone by, the second boy set out to seek his brother. He came to the water, and all fared with him just as with his brother. And now there was no one at home but the daughter, and she mourned for the brothers so much that at last she also begged the fisherman to let her set forth, for she wished to go in search of her brothers. Then she likewise came to the great piece of water, and she said to the old woman, "Good day, mother." "Many thanks," replied the old woman. "May God help you with your fishing," said the maiden.

When the old woman heard that, she became quite friendly, and carried her over the water, gave her a wand, and said to her, "Go, my daughter, ever onwards by this road, and when you come to a great black dog, you must pass it silently and boldly, without either laughing or looking at it. Then you will come to a great high castle, on the threshold of which you must let the wand fall, and go straight through the castle and out again on the other side. There you will see an old fountain out of which a large tree has grown, whereon hangs a bird in a cage which you must take down. Take likewise a glass of water out of the fountain, and with these two things go back by the same way. Pick up the wand again from the threshold and take it with you, and when you again pass by the dog strike him in the face with it, but be sure that you hit him, and then just come back here to me."

The maiden found everything exactly as the old woman had said, and on her way back she found her two brothers who had sought each other over half the world. They went together to the place where the black dog was lying on the road; she struck it in the face, and it turned into a handsome Prince who went with them to the river. There the old woman was still standing. She rejoiced much to see them again, and carried them all over the water, and then she too went away, for now she was freed. The others, however, went to the old fisherman, and all were glad that they had found each other again, and they hung the bird on the wall.

But the second son could not settle at home, and took his crossbow and went a-hunting. When he was tired he took his flute, and made music. The King, however, was hunting too, and heard that and went thither, and when he met the youth, he said, "Who has given you leave to hunt here?" "Oh, no one." "To whom do you belong, then?" "I am the fisherman's son." "But he has no children." "If you will not believe, come with me."

That the King did and questioned the fisherman, who told everything to him, and the little bird on the wall began to sing,

> *"The mother sits alone*
> *There in the prison small,*
> *O King of royal blood,*
> *These are thy children all.*
> *The sisters twain so false,*
> *They wrought the children woe,*
> *There in the waters deep*
> *Where the fishermen come and go."*

Then they were all terrified, and the King took the bird, the fisherman and the three children back with him to the castle, and ordered the prison to be opened and brought his wife out again. She had, however, grown quite ill and weak. Then the daughter gave her some of the water of the fountain to drink, and she became strong and healthy. But the two false sisters were burnt, and the daughter married the prince.

The Three Snake-Leaves

THERE WAS once a man who was so poor that he could hardly earn enough to keep himself and his son from starving. One day the boy said to him, "Dear father, I see you going about every day looking so sad and tired that I am determined to go out into the world and try to earn my own living."

So his father gave him his blessing and took leave of him with many tears. Just at this time a great King was going to war with the King of another country, and the youth took service under him and marched to the battle-field as a soldier. In the first conflict with the enemy he was in great danger and had a wonderful escape, for his comrades fell on each side of him. Their commander also was wounded, and several were inclined to take flight and run from the field. But the youth stepped forth to raise their courage, and cried, "No, no, we will never allow our fatherland to sink to the ground!" Then they took courage and followed their young leader, who led them forward, attacked and quickly vanquished the enemy. When the King heard to whom he owed this great victory, he sent for the youth, raised him to a position of great honor, gave him great treasures, and made him first in the kingdom next to himself.

Now the King had a daughter who was very beautiful, but she was also very whimsical. She had made a vow that she would take no man for a husband who did not promise that if she should die he would allow himself to be buried alive with her in the grave. "If he loves me," she said, "he will not wish to outlive me." In return for this she would also promise to be buried in the grave with her spouse should he die first.

This strange vow had hitherto frightened away all wooers, but the young soldier was so struck with the beauty of the Princess that he disregarded the vow, although her father warned him and said, "Do you know what a terrible promise you will have to make?" "Yes," replied the young man, "I must be buried with her in the grave if I outlive her. But my love for her is so strong, that I disregard that danger." Then the King gave his consent, and the marriage was celebrated with great pomp.

After they had lived together for some time in great happiness and contentment, the young queen was seized with a terrible illness from which her physicians were unable to restore her. As she lay dead, the young husband remembered what he had promised and the thought of lying in the grave alive filled him with horror, but there was no escape. The King placed a watch at every outlet from the castle, so that it was not possible to avoid his fate. When the day of the funeral arrived and the body had been carried down and placed in the royal vault, he was taken there also, and the door firmly fastened with locks and bolts. Near to the coffin stood a table upon which were four lights, four loaves of bread, and four bottles of wine, and he knew that when these provisions came to an end, he must starve. So he seated himself, feeling full of grief and sorrow, but with a determination to take only a small piece of bread and the least drop of wine, to make them last.

One day when death seemed nearer than ever, he saw from a corner of the vault just opposite to where he sat, a white snake creep out and approach the body. He rose in horror, thinking it was about to gnaw it, and drawing his sword, exclaimed, as with two blows he cut the snake into three pieces, "As long as I live you shall not touch that."

After a while a second snake crept out of the corner, but as soon as he saw the other lying dead in three pieces, he went back and quickly returned with three green leaves in his mouth. Then he took the three separate portions of the snake, placed them together and laid a leaf on each wound, and no sooner were they joined, than the snake raised himself as lively as ever, and went away hastily with his companion.

The leaves remained lying on the ground, and as he looked at them, the thoughts of the poor unfortunate man were full of the wonderful properties they possessed, and it suddenly occurred to him that a leaf which could restore a dead snake to life, might be useful to human beings. He stooped and picked up the leaves, then advancing softly towards the body, he laid one on the mouth of the dead, and the others on both the eyes. In a moment he saw the effect of what he had done. The blood began to circulate in the veins and blushed softly in the pale face and lips of his dead wife. She drew a deep breath, opened her closed eyes and exclaimed faintly, "Where am I?"

"You are with me, dear wife," answered her husband; and then he told her all that had happened, and how he had wakened her to life.

After taking a little of the wine and bread she became stronger, and was able to rise from the bier and walk to the door of the vault with her husband. Here they knocked and called loudly for a long time, till at last the watchman heard them and word was sent to the King. He came himself very quickly and ordered the door of the vault to be opened. How astonished and joyful he was to find them both alive and uninjured, and to know that his anxiety was over! The whole matter had been a great trouble to him.

The three leaves, the young Prince took with him, and gave them to a servant to take care of, saying, "Preserve them carefully for me, and see that they are safe every day; who knows what help they may be to us in any future trouble?"

A great change appeared in the wife of the young Prince after this event—it was as if with her return to life, all her love for her husband had vanished from her heart.

Not long after, he wished to take a voyage across the sea to see his old father, and she accompanied him. While they were on board ship, she forgot all the true and great love he had shown for her in trying to restore her to life when she was dead, and made friends with the captain, who was as wicked as herself.

One day when the young Prince lay asleep on deck, she called the skipper to her and told him to take her husband by the feet, while she raised his head, and before he was awake enough to save himself, these two wicked people threw him overboard into the sea. As soon as this shameful deed was accomplished, she said to the skipper, "Now let us sail home again and say that the Prince has died on the voyage. I will praise and extol you so greatly to my father, that I know he will readily give his consent to our marriage, and leave the crown to you after his death."

But the faithful servant to whom the Prince had entrusted the wonderful leaves saw all that his master's wife had done. Unnoticed, he lowered one of the boats from the ship's side, got on board and very soon discovered the body of the Prince. Dragging it hastily into the boat, he rowed away and soon left the traitors far behind. As soon as he felt safely out of sight, he produced the precious leaves which he always carried about with him, laid one on each eye and one on the mouth of the dead man, who very quickly showed signs of life, and was at last sufficiently restored to help in rowing the boat. They both rowed with all their strength day and night, and their little bark flew so swiftly over the waves, that they arrived at the King's palace long before his daughter and the captain.

The King wondered greatly when he saw his son-in-law and the servant enter, and asked them what had happened. But when he heard of his daughter's wickedness, he said, "I can scarcely believe she would act so basely. However, the truth will soon be brought to light. For the present, I advise you both to hide yourselves in a private chamber, and make yourselves quite at home till the ship returns."

The master and servant took the King's advice, and a few days afterwards the large ship made its appearance, and the King's guilty daughter appeared before her father with a sorrowful countenance.

"Why have you come back alone?" he asked. "Where is your husband?"

"Ah! dear father," she replied, "I come home to you in great sorrow, for, during the voyage, my husband was taken suddenly ill and died, and if the good captain had not stood by me and conducted me home, I cannot tell what evil might have happened to me. He stood by my husband's deathbed, and he can tell you all that occurred."

"Oh!" said the King, "I can restore your dead husband to life again, so do not grieve any longer." He threw open the door of the private room as he spoke, and told his son and the servant to come out.

When the wife saw her husband she was thunderstruck, and sank on her knees imploring mercy.

"I can show you no mercy," said the King. "Your husband was not only ready to be buried and die with you, but he used the means which restored you to life, and you have murdered him while he slept, and shall receive the reward you so truly merit."

Then was she with her accomplice placed in a boat full of holes, and driven out to sea, where they were soon overwhelmed in the waves and drowned.

The White Snake

A LONG TIME ago there lived a King whose wisdom was noised abroad in all the country. Nothing remained long unknown to him, and it was as if the knowledge of hidden things was brought to him in the air. However, he had one curious custom. Every day at dinner, after the table had been cleared and every one gone away, a trusty servant had to bring in one other dish. But it was covered up, and the servant himself did not know what was in it, and no one else knew, for the King waited until he was quite alone before he uncovered the dish.

This had gone on a long time, but at last there came a day when the servant could restrain his curiosity no longer, but as he was carrying the dish away he took it into his own room. As soon as he had fastened the door securely, he lifted the cover, and there he saw a white snake lying on the dish. After seeing it he could not resist the desire to taste it, and so he cut off a small piece and put it in his mouth. As soon as it touched his tongue he heard outside his window a strange chorus of delicate voices. He went and listened, and found that it was the sparrows talking together, and telling each other all they had seen in the fields and woods. The virtue of the snake had given him power to understand the speech of animals.

Now it happened one day that the Queen lost her most splendid ring, and suspicion fell upon the trusty servant, who had the general superintendence, and he was accused of stealing it. The King summoned him to his presence, and after many reproaches told him that if by the next day he was not able to name the thief he should be considered guilty, and punished. It was in vain that he protested his innocence; he could get no better sentence. In his uneasiness and anxiety he went out into the courtyard, and began to consider what he could do in so great a necessity. There sat the ducks by the running water and rested themselves, and plumed themselves with their flat bills, and held a comfortable chat. The servant stayed where he was and listened to them. They told how they had waddled about all yesterday morning and found good food; and then one of them said pitifully, "Something lies very heavy in my craw—it is the ring that was lying under the Queen's window; I swallowed it down in too great a hurry."

Then the servant seized her by the neck, took her into the kitchen, and said to the cook, "Kill this one, she is quite ready for cooking." "Yes," said the cook, weighing it in her hand; "there will be no trouble of fattening this one—it has been ready ever so long."

She then slit up its neck, and when it was opened the Queen's ring was found in its craw. The servant could now clearly prove his innocence, and in order to make up for the injustice he had suffered the King permitted him to ask some favor for himself, and also promised him the place of greatest honor in the royal household.

But the servant refused it, and only asked for a horse and money for traveling, for he had a fancy to see the world, and look about him a little. So his request was granted, and he set out on his way; and one day he came to a pool of water, by which he saw three fishes who had got entangled in the rushes, and were panting for water. Although fishes are usually considered dumb creatures, he understood very well their lament that they were to perish so miserably; and as he had a compassionate heart he dismounted from his horse, and put the three fishes back again into the water. They quivered all over with joy, stretched out their heads, and called out to him, "We will remember and reward you, because you have delivered us."

He rode on, and after a while he heard a small voice come up from the sand underneath his horse's feet. He listened, and understood how an ant-king was complaining, "If only these men would keep off, with their great awkward beasts! Here comes this stupid horse treading down my people with his hard hoofs!"

The man then turned his horse to the side-path, and the ant-king called out to him, "We will remember and reward you!"

The path led him through a wood, and there he saw a father-raven and mother-raven standing by their nest and throwing their young ones out.

"Off with you! young gallows-birds!" cried they; "we cannot stuff you any more; you are big enough to fend for yourselves!" The poor young ravens lay on the ground, fluttering, and beating the air with their pinions, and crying, "We are poor helpless things, we cannot fend for ourselves, we cannot even fly! We can only die of hunger!"

Then the kind young man dismounted, killed his horse with his dagger, and left it to the young ravens for food. They came hopping up, feasted away at it, and cried, "We will remember, and reward you!"

So now he had to use his own legs, and when he had gone a long way he came to a great town. There was much noise and thronging in the streets, and there came a man on a horse, who proclaimed, "The King's daughter seeks a husband, but he who wishes to marry her must perform a difficult task, and if he cannot carry it through successfully, he must lose his life."

Many had already tried, but had lost their lives in vain. The young man, when he saw the King's daughter, was so dazzled by her great beauty, that he forgot all danger, went to the King and offered himself as a wooer.

Then he was led to the sea-side, and a gold ring was thrown into the water before his eyes. Then the King told him that he must fetch the ring up again from the bottom of the sea, saying, "If you come back without it, you shall be put under the waves again and again until you are drowned."

Every one pitied the handsome young man, but they went, and left him alone by the sea. As he was standing on the shore and thinking of what he should do, there came three fishes swimming by, none other than those he had set free. The middle one had a mussel in his mouth, and he laid it on the strand at the young man's feet; and when he took it up and opened it there was the gold ring inside! Full of joy he carried it to the King, and expected the promised reward; but the King's daughter, proud of her high birth, despised him, and set him another task to perform. She went out into the garden, and strewed about over the grass ten sacks full of millet seed. "By the time the sun rises in the morning you must have picked up all these," she said, "and not a grain must be wanting."

The young man sat down in the garden and considered how it was possible to do this task, but he could contrive nothing, and stayed there, feeling very sorrowful, and expecting to be led to death at break of day. But when the first beams of the sun fell on the garden he saw that the ten sacks were all filled, standing one by the other, and not even a grain was missing. The ant-king had arrived in the night with his thousands of ants, and the grateful creatures had picked up all the millet seed, and filled the sacks with great industry. The King's daughter came herself into the garden and saw with astonishment that the young man had performed all that had been given him to do. But she could not let her proud heart melt, but said, "Although he has completed the two tasks, he shall not be my bridegroom unless he brings me an apple from the tree of life."

The young man did not know where the tree of life was to be found, but he set out and went on and on, as long as his legs could carry him, but he had no hope of finding it. When he had gone through three kingdoms he came one evening to a wood, and seated himself under a tree to go to sleep; but he heard a rustling in the boughs, and a golden apple fell into his hand. Immediately three ravens flew towards him, perched on his knee, and said, "We are the three young ravens that you delivered from starving; when we grew big, and heard that you were seeking the golden apple, we flew over the sea to the end of the earth, where the tree of life stands, and we fetched the apple."

Full of joy the young man set off on his way home, and brought the golden apple to the King's beautiful daughter, who was without any further excuse.

So they divided the apple of life, and ate it together; and their hearts were filled with love, and they lived in undisturbed happiness to a great age.

The Three Spinners

THERE WAS once a girl who was lazy and would not spin, and her mother could not persuade her to it, do what she would. At last the mother became angry and out of patience, and gave her a good beating, so that she cried out loudly. At that moment the Queen was going by; as she heard the crying, she stopped; and, going into the house, she asked the mother why she was beating her daughter, so that every one outside in the street could hear her cries.

The woman was ashamed to tell of her daughter's laziness, so she said, "I cannot stop her from spinning; she is forever at it, and I am poor and cannot furnish her with flax enough."

Then the Queen answered, "I like nothing better than the sound of the spinning-wheel, and always feel happy when I hear its humming; let me take your daughter with me to the castle—I have plenty of flax, she shall spin there to her heart's content."

The mother was only too glad of the offer, and the Queen took the girl with her. When they reached the castle the Queen showed her three rooms which were filled with the finest flax as full as they could hold.

"Now you can spin me this flax," said she, "and when you can show it me all done you shall have my eldest son for bridegroom; you may be poor, but I make nothing of that—your industry is dowry enough."

The girl was inwardly terrified, for she could not have spun the flax, even if she were to live to be a hundred years old, and were to sit spinning every day of her life from morning to evening. And when she found herself alone she began to weep, and sat so for three days without putting her hand to it. On the third day the

Queen came, and when she saw that nothing had been done of the spinning she was much surprised; but the girl excused herself by saying that she had not been able to begin because of the distress she was in at leaving her home and her mother. The excuse contented the Queen, who said, however, as she went away, "Tomorrow you must begin to work."

When the girl found herself alone again she could not tell how to help herself or what to do, and in her perplexity she went and gazed out of the window. There she saw three women passing by, and the first of them had a broad flat foot, the second had a big under-lip that hung down over her chin, and the third had a remarkably broad thumb. They all of them stopped in front of the window, and called out to know what it was that the girl wanted. She told them all her need, and they promised her their help, and said, "Then will you invite us to your wedding, and not be ashamed of us, and call us your cousins, and let us sit at your table? If you will promise this, we will finish off your flax-spinning in a very short time." "With all my heart," answered the girl; "only come in now, and begin at once."

Then these same women came in, and she cleared a space in the first room for them to sit and carry on their spinning. The first one drew out the thread and moved the treadle that turned the wheel; the second moistened the thread; the third twisted it, and rapped with her finger on the table; and as often as she rapped a heap of yarn fell to the ground, and it was most beautifully spun. But the girl hid the three spinsters out of the Queen's sight, and only showed her, as often as she came, the heaps of well-spun yarn; and there was no end to the praises she received. When the first room was empty they went on to the second, and then to the third, so that at last all was finished. Then the three women took their leave, saying to the girl, "Do not forget what you have promised, and it will be all the better for you."

So when the girl took the Queen and showed her the empty rooms, and the great heaps of yarn, the wedding was at once arranged, and the bridegroom rejoiced that he should have so clever and diligent a wife, and praised her exceedingly.

"I have three cousins," said the girl, "and as they have shown me a great deal of kindness, I would not wish to forget them in my good fortune; may I be allowed to invite them to the wedding, and to ask them to sit at the table with us?"

The Queen and the bridegroom said at once, "There is no reason against it."

So when the feast began, in came the three spinsters in strange guise, and the bride said, "Dear cousins, you are welcome."

"Oh," said the bridegroom, "how come you to have such dreadfully ugly relations?"

And then he went up to the first spinster and said, "How is it that you have such a broad flat foot?" "With treading," answered she, "with treading."

Then he went up to the second and said, "How is it that you have such a great hanging lip?" "With licking," answered she, "with licking."

Then he asked the third, "How is it that you have such a broad thumb?" "With twisting thread," answered she, "with twisting thread."

Then the bridegroom said that from that time forward his beautiful bride should never touch a spinning-wheel.

And so she escaped that tiresome flax-spinning.

Rumpelstiltskin

THERE WAS once a miller who was poor, but he had one beautiful daughter. It happened one day that he came to speak with the King, and, to give himself consequence, he told him that he had a daughter who could spin gold out of straw. The King said to the miller, "That is an art that pleases me well; if your daughter is as clever as you say, bring her to my castle tomorrow, that I may put her to the proof."

When the girl was brought to him, he led her into a room that was quite full of straw, and gave her a wheel and spindle, and said, "Now set to work, and if by the early morning you have not spun this straw to gold you shall die." And he shut the door himself, and left her there alone.

And so the poor miller's daughter was left there sitting, and could not think what to do for her life: she had no notion how to set to work to spin gold from straw, and her distress grew so great that she began to weep. Then all at once the door opened, and in came a little man, who said, "Good evening, miller's daughter; why are you crying?" "Oh!" answered the girl, "I have got to spin gold out of straw, and I don't understand the business."

Then the little man said, "What will you give me if I spin it for you?" "My necklace," said the girl.

The little man took the necklace, seated himself before the wheel, and whirr, whirr, whirr! three times round and the bobbin was full; then he took up another, and whirr, whirr, whirr! three times round, and that was full; and so he went on till the morning, when all the straw had been spun, and all the bobbins were full of gold. At sunrise came the King, and when he saw the gold he was astonished and very much rejoiced, for he was very avaricious. He had the miller's daughter taken into another room filled with straw, much bigger than the last, and told her that as she valued her life she must spin it all in one night.

The girl did not know what to do, so she began to cry, and then the door opened, and the little man appeared and said, "What will you give me if I spin all this straw into gold?" "The ring from my finger," answered the girl.

So the little man took the ring, and began again to send the wheel whirring round, and by the next morning all the straw was spun into glistening gold. The King was rejoiced beyond measure at the sight, but as he could never have enough of gold, he had the miller's daughter taken into a still larger room full of straw, and said, "This, too, must be spun in one night, and if you accomplish it you shall be my wife." For he thought, "Although she is but a miller's daughter, I am not likely to find any one richer in the whole world."

As soon as the girl was left alone, the little man appeared for the third time and said, "What will you give me if I spin the straw for you this time?" "I have nothing left to give," answered the girl. "Then you must promise me the first child you have after you are Queen," said the little man.

"But who knows whether that will happen?" thought the girl; but as she did not know what else to do in her necessity, she promised the little man what he desired, upon which he began to spin, until all the straw was gold. And when in the morning the King came and found all done according to his wish, he caused the wedding to be held at once, and the miller's pretty daughter became a Queen.

In a year's time she brought a fine child into the world, and thought no more of the little man; but one day he came suddenly into her room, and said, "Now give me what you promised me."

The Queen was terrified greatly, and offered the little man all the riches of the kingdom if he would only leave the child; but the little man said, "No, I would rather have something living than all the treasures of the world."

Then the Queen began to lament and to weep, so that the little man had pity upon her. "I will give you three days," said he, "and if at the end of that time you cannot tell my name, you must give up the child to me."

Then the Queen spent the whole night in thinking over all the names that she had ever heard, and sent a messenger through the land to ask far and wide for all the names that could be found. And when the little man came next day, beginning with Caspar, Melchior, Balthazar, she repeated all she knew, and went through the whole list, but after each the little man said, "That is not my name."

The second day the Queen sent to inquire of all the neighbors what the servants were called, and told the little man all the most unusual and singular names, saying, "Perhaps you are Roast-ribs, or Sheepshanks, or Spindleshanks?" But he answered nothing but "That is not my name."

The third day the messenger came back again, and said, "I have not been able to find one single new name; but as I passed through the woods I came to a high hill, and near it was a little house, and before the house burned a fire, and round the fire danced a comical little man, and he hopped on one leg and cried,

> *"Today do I bake, tomorrow I brew,*
> *The day after that the Queen's child comes in;*
> *And oh! I am glad that nobody knew*
> *That the name I am called is Rumpelstiltskin!"*

You cannot think how pleased the Queen was to hear that name, and soon afterwards, when the little man walked in and said, "Now, Mrs. Queen, what is my name?" she said at first, "Are you called Jack?" "No," answered he. "Are you called Harry?" she asked again. "No," answered he. And then she said, "Then perhaps your name is Rumpelstiltskin!"

"The devil told you that! the devil told you that!" cried the little man, and in his anger he stamped with his right foot so hard that it went into the ground above his knee; then he seized his left foot with both his hands in such a fury that he split in two, and there was an end of him.

The Queen Bee

Two King's sons who sought adventures fell into a wild, reckless way of living, and gave up all thoughts of going home again. Their third and youngest brother, who was called Witling, and had remained behind, started off to seek them; and when at last he found them, they jeered at his simplicity in thinking that he could make his way in the world, while they who were so much cleverer were unsuccessful. But they all three went on together until they came to an ant-hill, which the two eldest brothers wished to stir up, that they might see the little ants hurry about in their fright and carrying off their eggs, but Witling said, "Leave the little creatures alone, I will not suffer them to be disturbed."

And they went on farther until they came to a lake, where a number of ducks were swimming about. The two eldest brothers wanted to catch a couple and cook them, but Witling would not allow it, and said, "Leave the creatures alone, I will not suffer them to be killed."

And then they came to a bee's-nest in a tree, and there was so much honey in it that it overflowed and ran down the trunk. The two eldest brothers then wanted to make a fire beneath the tree, that the bees might be stifled by the smoke, and then they could get at the honey. But Witling prevented them, saying, "Leave the little creatures alone, I will not suffer them to be stifled."

At last the three brothers came to a castle where there were in the stables many horses standing, all of stone, and the brothers went through all the rooms until they came to a door at the end secured with three locks, and in the middle of the door a small opening through which they could look into the room. And they saw a little gray-haired man sitting at a table. They called out to him once, twice, and he did not hear, but at the third time he got up, undid the locks, and came out. Without speaking a word he led them to a table loaded with all sorts of good things, and when they had eaten and drunk he showed to each his bed-chamber. The next morning the little gray man came to the eldest brother, and beckoning him, brought him to a table of stone, on which were written three things directing by what means the castle could be delivered from its enchantment. The first thing was, that in the wood under the moss lay the pearls belonging to the Princess—a thousand in number—and they were to be sought for and collected, and if he who should undertake the task had not finished it by sunset—if but one pearl were missing—he must be turned to stone. So the eldest brother went out, and searched all day, but at the end of it he had only found one hundred; just as was said on the table of stone came to pass and he was turned into stone. The second brother undertook the adventure next day, but it fared with him no better than with the first; he found two hundred pearls, and was turned into stone.

And so at last it was Witling's turn, and he began to search in the moss; but it was a very tedious business to find the pearls, and he grew so out of heart that he sat down on a stone and began to weep. As he was sitting thus, up came the ant-king with five thousand ants, whose lives had been saved through Witling's pity, and it was not very long before the little insects had collected all the pearls and put them in a heap.

Now the second thing ordered by the table of stone was to get the key of the Princess's sleeping-chamber out of the lake. And when Witling came to the lake, the ducks whose lives he had saved came swimming, and dived below, and brought up the key from the bottom.

The third thing that had to be done was the most difficult, and that was to choose out the youngest and loveliest of the three Princesses, as they lay sleeping. All bore a perfect resemblance each to the other, and only differed in this, that before they went to sleep each one had eaten a different sweetmeat—the eldest a piece of sugar, the second a little syrup, and the third a spoonful of honey. Now the Queen-bee of those bees that Witling had protected from the fire came at this moment, and trying the lips of all three, settled on those of the one that had eaten honey, and so it was that the King's son knew which to choose. Then the spell was broken; every one awoke from stony sleep, and took his right form again.

And Witling married the youngest and loveliest Princess, and became King after her father's death. But his two brothers had to put up with the two other sisters.

The Golden Goose

THERE WAS a man who had three sons, the youngest of whom was called the Simpleton, and was despised, laughed at, and neglected, on every occasion. It happened one day that the eldest son wished to go into the forest to cut wood, and before he went his mother gave him a delicious pancake and a flask of wine, that he might not suffer from hunger or thirst. When he came into the forest a little old gray man met him, who wished him good day, and said, "Give me a bit of cake out of your pocket, and let me have a drink of your wine; I am so hungry and thirsty."

But the prudent youth answered, "Give you my cake and my wine? I haven't got any; be off with you." And leaving the little man standing there, he went off.

Then he began to fell a tree, but he had not been at it long before he made a wrong stroke, and the hatchet hit him in the arm, so that he was obliged to go home and get it bound up. That was what came of the little gray man.

Afterwards the second son went into the wood, and the mother gave to him, as to the eldest, a pancake and a flask of wine. The little old gray man met him also, and begged for a little bit of cake and a drink of wine. But the second son spoke out plainly, saying, "What I give you I lose myself, so be off with you." And leaving the little man standing there, he went off.

The punishment followed. As he was chopping away at the tree, he hit himself in the leg so severely that he had to be carried home.

Then said the Simpleton, "Father, let me go for once into the forest to cut wood"; and the father answered, "Your brothers have hurt themselves by so doing; give it up, you understand nothing about it."

But the Simpleton went on begging so long, that the father said at last, "Well, be off with you; you will only learn by experience."

The mother gave him a cake (it was only made with water, and baked in the ashes), and with it a flask of sour beer. When he came into the forest the little old gray man met him, and greeted him, saying, "Give me a bit of your cake, and a drink from your flask; I am so hungry and thirsty."

And the Simpleton answered, "I have only a flour and water cake and sour beer; but if that is good enough for you, let us sit down together and eat." Then they sat down, and as the Simpleton took out his flour and water cake it became a rich pancake, and his sour beer became good wine. Then they ate and drank, and afterwards the little man said, "As you have such a kind heart, and shared what you have so willingly, I will bestow good luck upon you. Yonder stands an old tree; cut it down, and at its roots you will find something," and thereupon the little man took his departure.

The Simpleton went there, and hewed away at the tree, and when it fell he saw, sitting among the roots, a goose with feathers of pure gold. He lifted it out and took it with him to an inn where he intended to stay the night.

The landlord had three daughters who, when they saw the goose, were curious to know what wonderful kind of bird it was, and ended by longing for one of its golden feathers. The eldest thought, "I will wait for a good opportunity, and then I will pull out one of its feathers for myself"; and so, when the Simpleton was gone out, she seized the goose by its wing—but there her finger and hand had to stay, held fast. Soon after came the second sister with the same idea of plucking out one of the golden feathers for herself; but scarcely had she touched her sister than she also was obliged to stay, held fast. Lastly came the third with the same intentions; but the others screamed out, "Stay away! for heaven's sake stay away!" But she did not see why she should stay away, and thought, "If they do so, why should not I?" and went towards them. But when she reached her sisters there she stopped, hanging on with them. And so they had to stay, all night.

The next morning the Simpleton took the goose under his arm and went away, unmindful of the three girls that hung on to it. The three had to run after him, left and right, wherever his legs carried him. In the midst of the fields they met the parson, who, when he saw the procession, said, "Shame on you, girls, running after a young fellow through the fields like this," and forthwith he seized hold of the youngest by the hand to drag her away, but hardly had he touched her when he too was obliged to run after them himself.

Not long after the sexton came that way, and seeing the respected parson following at the heels of the three girls, he called out, "Ho, your reverence, whither away so quickly? You forget that we have another christening today"; and he seized hold of him by his gown; but no sooner had he touched him than he was obliged to follow on too. As the five tramped on, one after another, two peasants with their hoes came up from the fields, and the parson cried out to them, and begged them to come and set him and the sexton free, but no sooner had they touched the sexton than they had to follow on too; and now there were seven following the Simpleton and the goose.

By and by they came to a town where a King reigned, who had an only daughter who was so serious that no one could make her laugh; therefore the King had given out that whoever should make her laugh should have her in marriage. The Simpleton, when he heard this, went with his goose and his hangers-on into the presence of the King's daughter, and as soon as she saw the seven people following always one after the other, she burst out laughing, and seemed as if she could never stop. And so the Simpleton earned a right to her as his bride; but the King did not like him for a son-in-law and made all kinds of objections, and said he must first bring a man who could drink up a whole cellar of wine.

The Simpleton thought that the little gray man would be able to help him, and went out into the forest, and there, on the very spot where he felled the tree, he saw a man sitting with a very sad countenance. The Simpleton asked him what was the matter, and he answered, "I have a great thirst, which I cannot quench: cold water does not agree with me; I have indeed drunk up a whole cask of wine, but what good is a drop like that?"

Then said the Simpleton, "I can help you; only come with me, and you shall have enough."

He took him straight to the King's cellar, and the man sat himself down before the big vats, and drank, and drank, and before a day was over he had drunk up the whole cellar-full. The Simpleton again asked for his bride, but the King was annoyed that a wretched fellow, called the Simpleton by everybody, should carry off his daughter, and so he made new conditions. He was to produce a man who could eat up a mountain of bread. The Simpleton did not hesitate long, but ran quickly off to the forest, and there in the same place sat a man who had fastened a strap round his body, making a very piteous face, and saying, "I have eaten a whole bakehouse full of rolls, but what is the use of that when one is so hungry as I am? My stomach feels quite empty, and I am obliged to strap myself together, that I may not die of hunger."

The Simpleton was quite glad of this, and said, "Get up quickly, and come along with me, and you shall have enough to eat."

He led him straight to the King's courtyard, where all the meal in the kingdom had been collected and baked into a mountain of bread. The man out of the forest settled himself down before it and hastened to eat, and in one day the whole mountain had disappeared.

Then the Simpleton asked for his bride the third time. The King, however, found one more excuse, and said he must have a ship that should be able to sail on land or on water. "So soon," said he, "as you come sailing along with it, you shall have my daughter for your wife."

The Simpleton went straight to the forest, and there sat the little old gray man with whom he had shared his cake, and he said, "I have eaten for you, and I have drunk for you, I will also give you the ship; and all because you were kind to me at the first."

Then he gave him the ship that could sail on land and on water, and when the King saw it he knew that he could no longer withhold his daughter. The marriage took place immediately, and at the death of the King the Simpleton possessed the kingdom, and lived long and happily with his wife.

The Three Feathers

THERE WAS once a King who had three sons. Two of them were considered wise and prudent; but the youngest, who said very little, appeared to others so silly that they gave him the name of Simple. When the King became old and weak, and began to think that his end was near, he knew not to which of his sons to leave his kingdom.

So he sent for them, and said, "I have made a determination that whichever of you brings me the finest carpet shall be King after my death."

They immediately prepared to start on their expedition, and that there might be no dispute between them, they took three feathers. As they left the castle each blew a feather into the air, and said, "We will travel in whatever direction these feathers take." One flew to the east, and the other to the west; but the third soon fell on the earth, and remained there. Then the two eldest brothers turned one to the right, and the other to the left, and they laughed at Simple because where his feather fell he was obliged to remain.

Simple sat down after his brothers were gone, feeling very sad; but presently, looking round, he noticed near where his feather lay a kind of trap-door. He rose quickly, went toward it, and lifted it up. To his surprise he saw a flight of steps, down which he descended, and reached another door; hearing voices within he knocked hastily. The voices were singing,

> *"Little frogs, crooked legs,*
> *Where do you hide?*
> *Go and see quickly*
> *Who is outside."*

At this the door opened of itself, and the youth saw a large fat frog seated with a number of little frogs round her.

On seeing him the large frog asked what he wanted. "I have a great wish for the finest and most beautiful carpet that can be got," he replied. Then the old frog called again to her little ones,

> *"Little frogs, crooked legs,*
> *Run here and there;*
> *Bring me the large bag*
> *That hangs over there."*

The young frogs fetched the bag, and when it was opened the old frog took from it a carpet so fine and so beautifully worked that nothing on earth could equal it. This she gave to the young man, who thanked her and went away up the steps.

Meanwhile, his elder brothers, quite believing that their foolish brother would not be able to get any carpet at all, said one to another, "We need not take the trouble to go further and seek for anything very wonderful; ours is sure to be the best." And as the first person they met was a shepherd, wearing a shepherd's plaid, they bought the large plaid cloth and carried it home to the King.

At the same time the younger brother returned with his beautiful carpet, and when the King saw it he was astonished, and said, "If justice is done, then the kingdom belongs to my youngest son."

But the two elder brothers gave the King no peace; they said it was impossible for Simple to become King, for his understanding failed in everything, and they begged their father to make another condition.

At last he said, "Whoever finds the most beautiful ring and brings it to me shall have the kingdom."

Away went the brothers a second time, and blew three feathers into the air to direct their ways. The feathers of the elder two flew east and west, but that of the youngest fell, as before, near the trap-door and there rested. He at once descended the steps, and told the great frog that he wanted a most beautiful ring. She sent for her large bag and drew from it a ring which sparkled with precious stones, and was so beautiful that no goldsmith on earth could make one like it.

The elder brothers had again laughed at Simple when his feather fell so soon to the ground, and forgetting his former success with the carpet, scorned the idea that he could ever find a gold ring. So they gave themselves no trouble, but merely took a plated ring from the harness of a carriage horse, and brought it to their father.

But when the King saw Simple's splendid ring he said at once, "The kingdom belongs to my youngest son."

His brothers, however, were not yet inclined to submit to the decision; they begged their father to make a third condition, and at last he promised to give the kingdom to the son who brought home the most beautiful woman to be his wife.

They all were again guided by blowing the feathers, and the two elder took the roads pointed out to them. But Simple, without hesitation, went at once to the frog, and said, "This time I am to take home the most beautiful woman."

"Hey-day!" said the frog. "I have not one by me at present, but you shall have one soon." So she gave him a carrot which had been hollowed out, and to which six mice were harnessed.

Simple took it quite sorrowfully, and said, "What am I to do with this?" "Seat one of my little frogs in it," she said.

The youth, on this, caught one up at a venture, and seated it in the carrot. No sooner had he done so than it became a most beautiful young lady; the carrot was turned into a gilded coach; and the mice were changed to prancing horses.

He kissed the maiden, seated himself in the carriage with her, drove away to the castle, and led her to the King.

Meanwhile his brothers had proved more silly than he; not forgetting the beautiful carpet and the ring, they still thought it was impossible for Simple to find a beautiful woman also. They therefore took no more trouble than before, and merely chose the handsomest peasant maidens they could find to bring to their father.

When the King saw the beautiful maiden his youngest son had brought he said, "The kingdom must now belong to my youngest son after my death."

But the elder brothers deafened the King's ears with their cries, "We cannot consent to let our stupid brother be King. Give us one more trial. Let a ring be hung in the hall, and let each woman spring through it." For they thought the peasant maidens would easily manage to do this, because they were strong, and that the delicate lady would, no doubt, kill herself. To this trial the old King consented.

The peasant maidens jumped first; but they were so heavy and awkward that they fell, and one broke her arm and the other her leg. But the beautiful lady whom Simple had brought home sprang as lightly as a deer through the ring, and thus put an end to all opposition.

The youngest brother married the beautiful maiden, and after his father's death ruled the kingdom for many years with wisdom and equity.

The Hut in the Forest

A POOR WOOD-CUTTER lived with his wife and three daughters in a little hut on the edge of a lonely forest. One morning as he was about to go to his work, he said to his wife, "Let my dinner be brought into the forest to me by my eldest daughter, or I shall never get my work done, and in order that she may not miss her way," he added, "I will take a bag of millet with me and strew the seeds on the path." When, therefore, the sun was just above the center of the forest, the girl set out on her way with a bowl of soup, but the field-sparrows, and wood-sparrows, larks and finches, blackbirds and siskins had picked up the millet long before, and the girl could not find the track. Then, trusting to chance, she went on and on until the sun sank and night began to fall. The trees rustled in the darkness, the owls hooted, and she began to be afraid. Then in the distance she perceived a light which glimmered between the trees. "There ought to be some people living there who can take me in for the night," thought she, and went up to the light.

It was not long before she came to a house the windows of which were all lighted up. She knocked, and a rough voice from the inside cried, "Come in." The girl stepped into the dark entrance, and knocked at the door of the room. "Just come in," cried the voice, and when she opened the door, an old gray-haired man was sitting at the table, supporting his face with both hands, and his white beard fell down over the table almost as far as the ground. By the stove lay three animals, a hen, a cock, and a brindled cow. The girl told her story to the old man, and begged for shelter for the night. The man said,

> *"Pretty little hen,*
> *Pretty little cock,*
> *And pretty brindled cow,*
> *What say ye to that?"*

"Duks," answered the animals, and that must have meant, "We are willing," for the old man said, "Here you shall have shelter and food; go to the fire, and cook us our supper." The girl found in the kitchen abundance of everything, and cooked a good supper, but had no thought of the animals. She carried the full dishes to the table, seated herself by the gray-haired man, ate and satisfied her hunger. When she had had enough, she said, "But now I am tired, where is there a bed in which I can lie down, and sleep?" The animals replied,

> *"Thou hast eaten with him,*
> *Thou hast drunk with him,*
> *Thou hast had no thought for us,*
> *So find out for thyself where thou canst pass the night."*

Then said the old man, "Just go upstairs, and you will find a room with two beds, shake them up, and put white linen on them, and then I, too, will come and lie down to sleep." The girl went up, and when she had shaken the beds and put clean sheets on, she lay down in one of them without waiting any longer for the old man. After some time, however, the gray-haired man came, took his candle, looked at the girl and shook his head. When he saw that she had fallen into a sound sleep, he opened a trap-door, and let her down into the cellar.

Late at night the wood-cutter came home, and reproached his wife for leaving him to hunger all day. "It is not my fault," she replied, "the girl went out with your dinner, and must have lost herself, but she is sure to come back tomorrow." The wood-cutter, however, arose before dawn to go into the forest, and requested that the second daughter should take him his dinner that day. "I will take a bag with lentils," said he; "the seeds are larger than millet, the girl will see them better, and can't lose her way." At dinner-time, therefore, the girl took out the food, but the lentils had disappeared. The birds of the forest had picked them up as they had done the day before, and had left none. The girl wandered about in the forest until night, and then she, too, reached the house of the old man, was told to go in, and begged for food and a bed. The man with the white beard again asked the animals,

> *"Pretty little hen,*
> *Pretty little cock,*
> *And pretty brindled cow,*
> *What say ye to that?"*

The animals again replied "Duks," and everything happened just as it had happened the day before. The girl cooked a good meal, ate and drank with the old man, and did not concern herself about the animals, and when she inquired about her bed they answered,

> *"Thou hast eaten with him,*
> *Thou hast drunk with him,*
> *Thou hast had no thought for us,*
> *So find out for thyself where thou canst pass the night."*

When she was asleep the old man came, looked at her, shook his head, and let her down into the cellar.

On the third morning the wood-cutter said to his wife, "Send our youngest child out with my dinner today, she has always been good and obedient, and will stay in the right path, and not run about after every wild bumble-bee, as her sisters did." The mother did not want to do it, and said, "Am I to lose my dearest child, as well?"

"Have no fear," he replied, "the girl will not go astray; she is too prudent and sensible; besides I will take some peas with me, and strew them about. They are still larger than lentils, and will show her the way." But when the girl went out with her basket on her arm, the wood-pigeons had already got all the peas in their crops, and she did not know which way she was to turn. She was full of sorrow and never ceased to think how hungry her father would be, and how her good mother would grieve, if she did not go home. At length when it grew dark, she saw the light and came to the house in the forest. She begged quite prettily to be allowed to spend the night there, and the man with the white beard once more asked his animals,

> *"Pretty little hen,*
> *Pretty little cock,*
> *And pretty brindled cow,*
> *What say ye to that?"*

"Duks," said they. Then the girl went to the stove where the animals were lying, and petted the cock and hen, and stroked their smooth feathers with her hand, and caressed the brindled cow between her horns, and when, in obedience to the old man's orders, she had made ready some good soup, and the bowl was placed upon the table, she said, "Am I to eat as much as I want, and the good animals to have nothing? Outside is food in plenty, I will look after them first." So she went and brought some barley and strewed it for the cock and hen, and a whole armful of sweet-smelling hay for the cow. "I hope you will like it, dear animals," said she, "and you shall have a refreshing draught in case you are thirsty." Then she fetched in a bucketful of water, and the cock and hen jumped on to the edge of it and dipped their beaks in, and then held up their heads as the birds do when they drink, and the brindled cow also took a hearty draught. When the animals were fed, the girl seated herself at the table by the old man, and ate what he had left.

It was not long before the cock and the hen began to thrust their heads beneath their wings, and the eyes of the cow likewise began to blink. Then said the girl, "Ought we not to go to bed?

> *"Pretty little hen,*
> *Pretty little cock,*
> *And beautiful brindled cow,*
> *What say ye to that?"*

The animals answered "Duks,

> *"Thou hast eaten with us,*
> *Thou hast drunk with us,*
> *Thou hast had kind thought for all of us,*
> *We wish thee good-night."*

Then the maiden went upstairs, shook the feather-beds, and laid clean sheets on them, and when she had done it the old man came and lay down on one of the beds, and his white beard reached down to his feet. The girl lay down on the other, said her prayers, and fell asleep.

She slept quietly till midnight, and then there was such a noise in the house that she awoke. There was a sound of cracking and splitting in every corner, and the doors sprang open, and beat against the walls. The beams groaned as if they were being torn out of their joints, it seemed as if the staircase were falling down, and at length there was a crash as if the entire roof had fallen in. As, however, all grew quiet once more, and the girl was not hurt, she stayed quietly lying where she was, and fell asleep again. But when she woke up in the morning with the brilliancy of the sunshine, what did her eyes behold? She was lying in a vast hall, and everything around her shone with royal splendor; on the walls, golden flowers grew up on a ground of green silk, the bed was of ivory, and the canopy of red velvet, and on a chair close by, was a pair of shoes embroidered with pearls.

The girl believed that she was in a dream, but three richly clad attendants came in, and asked what orders she would like to give. "If you will go," she replied, "I will get up at once and make ready some soup for the old man, and then I will feed the pretty little hen, and the cock, and the beautiful brindled cow." She thought the old man was up already, and looked round at his bed; he, however, was not lying in it, but a stranger. And while she was looking at him, and becoming aware that he was young and handsome, he awoke, sat up in bed, and said, "I am a King's son, and was bewitched by a wicked witch, and made to live in this forest, as an old gray-haired man; no one was allowed to be with me but my three attendants in the form of a cock, a hen, and a brindled cow. The spell was not to be broken until a girl came to us whose heart was so good that she showed herself full of love, not only towards mankind, but towards animals—and that thou hast done, and by thee at midnight we were set free, and the old hut in the forest was changed back again into my royal palace." And when they had arisen, the King's son ordered the three attendants to set out and fetch the father and mother of the girl to the marriage feast.

"But where are my two sisters?" inquired the maiden. "I have locked them in the cellar, and tomorrow they shall be led into the forest, and shall live as servants to a charcoal-burner, until they have grown kinder, and do not leave poor animals to suffer hunger."

Donkey Cabbages

THERE WAS once a young huntsman who went into the forest to lie in wait. He had a fresh and joyous heart, and as he was going thither, whistling upon a leaf, an ugly old crone came up, who spoke to him and said, "Good-day, dear huntsman, truly you are merry and contented, but I am suffering from hunger and thirst, do give me an alms." The huntsman had compassion on the poor old creature, felt in his pocket, and gave her what he could afford. He was then about to go further, but the old woman stopped him and said, "Listen, dear huntsman, to what I tell you; I will make you a present in return for your kindness. Go on your way now, but in a little while you will come to a tree, whereon nine birds are sitting which have a cloak in their claws, and are plucking at it; take your gun and shoot into the midst of them, they will let the cloak fall down to you, but one of the birds will be hurt, and will drop down dead. Carry away the cloak, it is a wishing-cloak; when you throw it over your shoulders, you only have to wish to be in a certain place, and you will be there in the twinkling of an eye. Take out the heart of the dead bird and swallow it whole, and every morning early, when you get up, you will find a gold piece under your pillow."

The huntsman thanked the wise woman, and thought to himself, "Those are fine things that she has promised me, if all does but come true." And verily when he had walked about a hundred paces, he heard in the branches above him such a screaming and twittering that he looked up and saw there a crowd of birds who were tearing a piece of cloth about with their beaks and claws, and tugging and fighting as if each wanted to have it all to himself. "Well," said the huntsman, "this is wonderful; it has really come to pass just as the old wife foretold!" and he took the gun from his shoulder, aimed and fired right into the midst of them, so that the feathers flew about. The birds instantly took to flight with loud outcries, but one dropped down dead, and the cloak fell at the same time. Then the huntsman did as the old woman directed him, cut open the bird, sought the heart, swallowed it down, and took the cloak home with him.

Next morning, when he awoke, the promise occurred to him, and he wished to see if it also had been fulfilled. When he lifted up the pillow, the gold piece shone in his eyes, and next day he found another, and so it went on, every time he got up. He gathered together a heap of gold, but at last he thought, "Of what use is all my gold to me if I stay at home? I will go forth and see the world."

He then took leave of his parents, buckled on his huntsman's pouch and gun, and went out into the world. It came to pass, that one day he traveled through a dense forest, and when he came to the end of it, in the plain before him stood a fine castle. An old woman was standing with a wonderfully beautiful maiden, looking out of one of the windows. The old woman, however, was a witch and said to the maiden, "There comes one out of the forest, who has a wonderful treasure in his body, we must filch it from him, my dear daughter, it is more suitable for us than for him. He has a bird's heart about him, by means of which a gold piece lies every morning under his pillow." She told her what she was to do to get it, and what part she had to play, and finally threatened her, and said with angry eyes, "And if you do not attend to what I say, it will be the worse for you." Now when the huntsman came nearer he descried the maiden, and said to himself, "I have traveled about for such a long time, I will take a rest for once, and enter that beautiful castle. I have certainly money enough." Nevertheless, the real reason was that he had caught sight of the pretty girl.

He entered the house, and was well received and courteously entertained. Before long he was so much in love with the young witch that he no longer thought of anything else, and only saw things as she saw them, and did what she desired. The old woman then said, "Now we must have the bird's heart, he will never miss it." She prepared a drink, and when it was ready, poured it into a cup and gave it to the maiden, who was to present it to the huntsman. She did so, saying, "Now, my dearest, drink to me." So he took the cup, and when he had swallowed the draught, he brought up the heart of the bird. The girl had to take it away secretly and swallow it herself, for the old woman would have it so. Thenceforward he found no more gold under his pillow, but it lay instead under that of the maiden, from whence the old woman fetched it away every morning; but he was so much in love and so befooled, that he thought of nothing else but of passing his time with the girl.

Then the old witch said, "We have the bird's heart, but we must also take the wishing-cloak away from him." The girl answered, "We will leave him that, he has lost his wealth." The old woman was angry and said, "Such a mantle is a wonderful thing, and is seldom to be found in this world. I must and will have it!" She gave the girl several blows, and said that if she did not obey, it should fare ill with her. So she did the old woman's bidding, placed herself at the window and looked on the distant country, as if she were very sorrowful. The huntsman asked, "Why dost thou stand there so sorrowfully?" "Ah, my beloved," was her answer, "over yonder lies the Garnet Mountain, where the precious stones grow. I long for them so much that when I think of them, I feel quite sad, but who can get them? Only the birds; they fly and can reach them, but a man, never." "Have you nothing else to complain of?" said the huntsman. "I will soon remove that burden from your heart."

With that he drew her under his mantle, wished himself on the Garnet Mountain, and in the twinkling of an eye they were sitting on it together. Precious stones were glistening on every side so that it was a joy to see them, and together they gathered the finest and costliest of them. Now, the old woman had, through her sorceries, contrived that the eyes of the huntsman should become heavy. He said to the maiden, "We will sit down and rest awhile, I am so tired that I can no longer stand on my feet." Then they sat down, and he laid his head in her lap, and fell asleep. When he was asleep, she unfastened the mantle from his shoulders, and wrapped herself in it, picked up the garnets and stones, and wished herself back at home with them.

But when the huntsman had had his sleep out and awoke, and perceived that his sweetheart had betrayed him, and left him alone on the wild mountain, he said, "Oh, what treachery there is in the world!" and sat down there in care and sorrow, not knowing what to do. But the mountain belonged to some wild and monstrous giants who dwelt thereon and lived their lives there, and he had not sat long before he saw three of them coming towards him, so he lay down as if he were sunk in a deep sleep. Then the giants came up, and the first kicked him with his foot and said, "What sort of an earth-worm is lying curled up here?" The second said, "Step upon him and kill him." But the third said, "That would indeed be worth your while; just let him live, he cannot remain here; and when he climbs higher, towards the summit of the mountain, the clouds will lay hold of him and bear him away." So saying they passed by. But the huntsman had paid heed to their words, and as soon as they were gone, he rose and climbed up to the summit of the mountain, and when he had sat there a while, a cloud floated towards him, caught him up, carried him away, and traveled about for a long time in the heavens. Then it sank lower, and let itself down on a great cabbage-garden, girt round by walls, so that he came softly to the ground on cabbages and vegetables.

Then the huntsman looked about him and said, "If I only had something to eat! I am so hungry, and my hunger will increase in course of time; but I see here neither apples nor pears, nor any other sort of fruit, everywhere nothing but cabbages." At length he thought, "At a pinch I can eat some of the leaves, they do not taste particularly good, but they will refresh me." With that he picked himself out a fine head of cabbage, and ate it, but scarcely had he swallowed a couple of mouthfuls than he felt very strange and quite different.

Four legs grew on him, a large head and two thick ears, and he saw with horror that he was changed into an ass. Still as his hunger increased every minute, and as the juicy leaves were suitable to his present nature, he went on eating with great zest. At last he arrived at a different kind of cabbage, but as soon as he had swallowed it, he again felt a change, and reassumed his former human shape.

Then the huntsman lay down and slept off his fatigue. When he awoke next morning, he broke off one head of the bad cabbages and another of the good ones, and thought to himself, "This shall help me to get my own again and to punish treachery." Then he took the cabbages with him, climbed over the wall, and went forth to seek for the castle of his sweetheart. After wandering about for a couple of days he was lucky enough to find it again. He dyed his face brown, so that his own mother would not have known him; and begged for shelter. "I am so tired," said he, "that I can go no further." The witch asked, "Who are you, countryman, and what is your business?" "I am a King's messenger, and was sent out to seek the most delicious salad which grows beneath the sun. I have even been so fortunate as to find it, and am carrying it about with me; but the heat of the sun is so intense that the delicate cabbage threatens to wither, and I do not know if I can carry it any further."

When the old woman heard of the exquisite salad, she was greedy, and said, "Dear countryman, let me just taste this wonderful salad." "Why not?" answered he, "I have brought two heads with me, and will give you one of them," and he opened his pouch and handed her the bad cabbage. The witch suspected nothing amiss, and her mouth watered so for this new dish that she herself went into the kitchen and dressed it. When it was prepared she could not wait until it was set on the table, but took a couple of leaves at once, and put them in her mouth, but hardly had she swallowed them than she was deprived of her human shape, and she ran out into the courtyard in the form of an ass.

Presently the maid-servant entered the kitchen, saw the salad standing there ready prepared, and was about to carry it up; but on the way, according to habit, she was seized by the desire to taste, and she ate a couple of leaves. Instantly the magic power showed itself, and she likewise became an ass and ran out to the old woman, and the dish of salad fell to the ground. Meantime, the messenger sat beside the beautiful girl, and as no one came with the salad and she also was longing for it, she said, "I don't know what has become of the salad." The huntsman thought, "The salad must have already taken effect," and said, "I will go to the kitchen and inquire about it." As he went down he saw the two asses running about in the courtyard; the salad, however, was lying on the ground. "All right," said he, "the two have taken their portion," and he picked up the other leaves, laid them on the dish, and carried them to the maiden. "I bring you the delicate food myself," said he, "in order that you may not have to wait longer." Then she ate of it, and was, like the others, immediately deprived of her human form, and ran out into the courtyard in the shape of an ass.

After the huntsman had washed his face, so that the transformed ones could recognize him, he went down into the courtyard, and said, "Now you shall receive the wages of your treachery," and bound them together, all three with one rope, and drove them along until he came to a mill. He knocked at the window, the miller put out his head, and asked what he wanted. "I have three unmanageable beasts," answered he, "which I don't want to keep any longer. Will you take them in, and give them food and stable room, and manage them as I tell you, and then I will pay you what you ask." The miller said, "Why not? but how am I to manage them?" The huntsman then said that he was to give three beatings and one meal daily to the old donkey, and that was the witch; one beating and three meals to the younger one, which was the servant-girl; and to the youngest, which was the maiden, no beatings and three meals, for he could not bring himself to have the maiden beaten. After that he went back into the castle, and found therein everything he needed.

After a couple of days, the miller came and said he must inform him that the old ass which had received three beatings and only one meal daily was dead; "the two others," he continued, "are certainly not dead, and are fed three times daily, but they are so sad that they cannot last much longer." The huntsman was moved to pity, put away his anger, and told the miller to drive them back again to him. And when they came, he gave them some of the good salad, so that they became human again. The beautiful girl fell on her knees before him, and said, "Ah, my beloved, forgive me for the evil I have done you; my mother drove me to it; it was done against my will, for I love you dearly. Your wishing-cloak hangs in a cupboard, and as for the bird's-heart I will take a vomiting potion." But he thought otherwise, and said, "Keep it; it is all the same, for I will take you for my true wife." So the wedding was celebrated, and they lived happily together until their death.

Snow-White and Rose-Red

THERE WAS once a poor widow who lived in a lonely cottage. In front of the cottage was a garden wherein stood two rose trees, one of which bore white and the other red roses. She had two children who were like the two rose trees, and one was called Snow-white, and the other Rose-red. They were as good and happy, as busy and cheerful as ever two children in the world were, only Snow-white was more quiet and gentle than Rose-red. Rose-red liked better to run about in the meadows and fields seeking flowers and catching butterflies; but Snow-white sat at home with her mother, and helped her with her house-work, or read to her when there was nothing to do.

The two children were so fond of each other that they always held each other by the hand when they went out together, and when Snow-white said, "We will not leave each other," Rose-red answered, "Never so long as we live," and their mother would add, "What one has she must share with the other."

They often ran about the forest alone and gathered red berries, and no beasts did them any harm, but came close to them trustfully. The little hare would eat a cabbage-leaf out of their hands, the roe grazed by their side, the stag leapt merrily by them, and the birds sat still upon the boughs, and sang whatever they knew.

No mishap overtook them; if they had stayed too late in the forest, and night came on, they laid themselves down near one another upon the moss, and slept until morning came, and their mother knew this and had no distress on their account.

Once when they had spent the night in the wood and the dawn had roused them, they saw a beautiful child in a shining white dress sitting near their bed. He got up and looked quite kindly at them, but said nothing and went away into the forest. And when they looked round they found that they had been sleeping quite close to a precipice, and would certainly have fallen into it in the darkness if they had gone only a few paces further. And their mother told them that it must have been the angel who watches over good children.

Snow-white and Rose-red kept their mother's little cottage so neat that it was a pleasure to look inside it. In the summer Rose-red took care of the house, and every morning laid a wreath of flowers by her mother's bed before she awoke, in which was a rose from each tree. In the winter Snow-white lit the fire and hung the kettle on the hob. The kettle was of copper and shone like gold, so brightly was it polished. In the evening, when the snowflakes fell, the mother said, "Go, Snow-white, and bolt the door," and then they sat round the hearth, and the mother took her spectacles and read aloud out of a large book, and the two girls listened as they sat and spun. And close by them lay a lamb upon the floor, and behind them upon a perch sat a white dove with its head hidden beneath its wings.

One evening, as they were thus sitting comfortably together, some one knocked at the door as if he wished to be let in. The mother said, "Quick, Rose-red, open the door, it must be a traveler who is seeking shelter." Rose-red went and pushed back the bolt, thinking that it was a poor man, but it was not; it was a bear that stretched his broad, black head within the door.

Rose-red screamed and sprang back, the lamb bleated, the dove fluttered, and Snow-white hid herself behind her mother's bed. But the bear began to speak and said, "Do not be afraid, I will do you no harm! I am half-frozen, and only want to warm myself a little beside you."

"Poor bear," said the mother, "lie down by the fire, only take care that you do not burn your coat." Then she cried, "Snow-white, Rose-red, come out, the bear will do you no harm, he means well." So they both came out, and by-and-by the lamb and dove came nearer, and were not afraid of him. The bear said, "Here, children, knock the snow out of my coat a little"; so they brought the broom and swept the bear's hide clean; and he stretched himself by the fire and growled contentedly and comfortably. It was not long before they grew quite at home, and played tricks with their clumsy guest. They tugged his hair with their hands, put their feet upon his back and rolled him about, or they took a hazel-switch and beat him, and when he growled they laughed. But the bear took it all in good part, only when they were too rough he called out, "Leave me alive, children,

> *"Snowy-white, Rosy-red,*
> *Will you beat your lover dead?"*

When it was bed-time, and the others went to bed, the mother said to the bear, "You can lie there by the hearth, and then you will be safe from the cold and the bad weather." As soon as day dawned the two children let him out, and he trotted across the snow into the forest.

Henceforth the bear came every evening at the same time, laid himself down by the hearth, and let the children amuse themselves with him as much as they liked; and they got so used to him that the doors were never fastened until their black friend had arrived.

When spring had come and all outside was green, the bear said one morning to Snow-white, "Now I must go away, and cannot come back for the whole summer." "Where are you going, then, dear bear?" asked Snow-white. "I must go into the forest and guard my treasures from the wicked dwarfs. In the winter, when the earth is frozen hard, they are obliged to stay below and cannot work their way through; but now, when the sun has thawed and warmed the earth, they break through it, and come out to pry and steal; and what once gets into their hands, and in their caves, does not easily see daylight again."

Snow-white was quite sorry for his going away, and as she unbolted the door for him, and the bear was hurrying out, he caught against the bolt and a piece of his hairy coat was torn off, and it seemed to Snow-white as if she had seen gold shining through it, but she was not sure about it. The bear ran away quickly, and was soon out of sight behind the trees.

A short time afterwards the mother sent her children into the forest to get fire-wood. There they found a big tree which lay felled on the ground, and close by the trunk something was jumping backwards and forwards in the grass, but they could not make out what it was. When they came nearer they saw a dwarf with an old withered face and a snow-white beard a yard long. The end of the beard was caught in a crevice of the tree, and the little fellow was jumping backwards and forwards like a dog tied to a rope, and did not know what to do.

He glared at the girls with his fiery red eyes and cried, "Why do you stand there? Can you not come here and help me?" "What are you about there, little man?" asked Rose-red. "You stupid, prying goose!" answered the dwarf; "I was going to split the tree to get a little wood for cooking. The little bit of food that one of us wants gets burnt up directly with thick logs; we do not swallow so much as you coarse, greedy folk. I had just driven the wedge safely in, and everything was going as I wished; but the wretched wood was too smooth and suddenly sprang asunder, and the tree closed so quickly that I could not pull out my beautiful white beard; so now it is tight in and I cannot get away, and the silly, sleek, milk-faced things laugh! Ugh! how odious you are!"

The children tried very hard, but they could not pull the beard out, it was caught too fast. "I will run and fetch some one," said Rose-red. "You senseless goose!" snarled the dwarf; "why should you fetch some one? You are already two too many for me; can you not think of something better?" "Don't be impatient," said Snow-white, "I will help you," and she pulled her scissors out of her pocket, and cut off the end of the beard.

As soon as the dwarf felt himself free he laid hold of a bag which lay amongst the roots of the tree, and which was full of gold, and lifted it up, grumbling to himself, "Uncouth people, to cut off a piece of my fine beard. Bad luck to you!" and then he swung the bag upon his back, and went off without even once looking at the children.

Some time after that Snow-white and Rose-red went to catch a dish of fish. As they came near the brook they saw something like a large grasshopper jumping towards the water, as if it were going to leap in. They ran to it and found it was the dwarf. "Where are you going?" said Rose-red; "you surely don't want to go into the water?" "I am not such a fool!" cried the dwarf; "don't you see that the accursed fish wants to pull me in?" The little man had been sitting there fishing, and unluckily the wind had twisted his beard with the fishing-line; just then a big fish bit, and the feeble creature had not strength to pull it out; the fish kept the upper hand and pulled the dwarf towards him. He held on to all the reeds and rushes, but it was of little good, he was forced to follow the movements of the fish, and was in urgent danger of being dragged into the water.

The girls came just in time; they held him fast and tried to free his beard from the line, but all in vain, beard and line were entangled fast together. Nothing was left but to bring out the scissors and cut the beard, whereby a small part of it was lost. When the dwarf saw that he screamed out, "Is that civil, you toadstool, to disfigure one's face? Was it not enough to clip off the end of my beard? Now you have cut off the best part of it. I cannot let myself be seen by my people. I wish you had been made to run the soles off your shoes!" Then he took out a sack of pearls which lay in the rushes, and without saying a word more he dragged it away and disappeared behind a stone.

It happened that soon afterwards the mother sent the two children to the town to buy needles and thread, and laces and ribbons. The road led them across a heath upon which huge pieces of rock lay strewn here and there. Now they noticed a large bird hovering in the air, flying slowly round and round above them; it sank lower and lower, and at last settled near a rock not far off. Directly afterwards they heard a loud, piteous cry. They ran up and saw with horror that the eagle had seized their old acquaintance the dwarf, and was going to carry him off.

The children, full of pity, at once took tight hold of the little man, and pulled against the eagle so long that at last he let his booty go. As soon as the dwarf had recovered from his first fright he cried with his shrill voice, "Could you not have done it more carefully! You dragged at my brown coat so that it is all torn and full of holes, you helpless clumsy creatures!" Then he took up a sack full of precious stones, and slipped away again under the rock into his hole. The girls, who by this time were used to his thanklessness, went on their way and did their business in the town.

As they crossed the heath again on their way home they surprised the dwarf, who had emptied out his bag of precious stones in a clean spot, and had not thought that any one would come there so late. The evening sun shone upon the brilliant stones; they glittered and sparkled with all colors so beautifully that the children stood still and looked at them. "Why do you stand gaping there?" cried the dwarf, and his ashen-gray face became copper-red with rage. He was going on with his bad words when a loud growling was heard, and a black bear came trotting towards them out of the forest. The dwarf sprang up in a fright, but he could not get to his cave, for the bear was already close. Then in the dread of his heart he cried, "Dear Mr. Bear, spare me, I will give you all my treasures; look, the beautiful jewels lying there! Grant me my life; what do you want with such a slender little fellow as I? you would not feel me between your teeth. Come, take these two wicked girls, they are tender morsels for you, fat as young quails; for mercy's sake eat them!" The bear took no heed of his words, but gave the wicked creature a single blow with his paw, and he did not move again.

The girls had run away, but the bear called to them, "Snow-white and Rose-red, do not be afraid; wait, I will come with you." Then they knew his voice and waited, and when he came up to them suddenly his bearskin fell off, and he stood there a handsome man, clothed all in gold. "I am a King's son," he said, "and I was bewitched by that wicked dwarf, who had stolen my treasures; I have had to run about the forest as a savage bear until I was freed by his death. Now he has got his well-deserved punishment."

Snow-white was married to him, and Rose-red to his brother, and they divided between them the great treasure which the dwarf had gathered together in his cave. The old mother lived peacefully and happily with her children for many years. She took the two rose trees with her, and they stood before her window, and every year bore the most beautiful roses, white and red.

The Poor Miller's Boy and the Cat

THERE ONCE lived an old miller who had neither wife nor child, and three apprentices served under him. As they had been with him several years, one day he said to them, "I am old, and want to sit in the chimney-corner; go out, and whichsoever of you brings me the best horse home, to him will I give the mill, and in return for it he shall take care of me till my death." The third of the boys was, however, the drudge, who was looked on as foolish by the others; they begrudged the mill to him, and afterwards he would not have it. Then all three went out together, and when they came to the village, the two said to stupid Hans, "Thou mayst just as well stay here; as long as thou livest thou wilt never get a horse."

Hans, however, went with them, and when it was night they came to a cave in which they lay down to sleep. The two sharp ones waited until Hans had fallen asleep, then they got up, and went away leaving him where he was. And they thought they had done a very clever thing, but it was certain to turn out ill for them. When the sun arose, and Hans woke up, he was lying in a deep cavern. He looked around on every side and exclaimed, "Oh, heavens, where am I?" Then he got up and clambered out of the cave, went into the forest, and thought, "Here I am quite alone and deserted, how shall I obtain a horse now?"

While he was thus walking full of thought, he met a small tabby-cat which said quite kindly, "Hans, where are you going?" "Alas, you cannot help me." "I well know your desire," said the cat. "You wish to have a beautiful horse. Come with me, and be my faithful servant for seven years long, and then I will give you one more beautiful than any you have ever seen in your whole life." "Well, this is a wonderful cat!" thought Hans, "but I am determined to see if she is telling the truth."

So she took him with her into her enchanted castle, where there were nothing but cats who were her servants. They leapt nimbly upstairs and downstairs, and were merry and happy. In the evening when they sat down to dinner, three of them had to make music. One played the bassoon, the other the fiddle, and the third put the trumpet to his lips, and blew out his cheeks as much as he possibly could. When they had dined, the table was carried away, and the cat said, "Now, Hans, come and dance with me." "No," said he, "I won't dance with a pussy-cat. I have never done that yet." "Then take him to bed," said she to the cats. So one of them lighted him to his bed-room, one pulled his shoes off, one his stockings, and at last one of them blew out the candle.

Next morning they returned and helped him out of bed, one put his stockings on for him, one tied his garters, one brought his shoes, one washed him, and one dried his face with her tail. "That feels very soft!" said Hans. He, however, had to serve the cat, and chop some wood every day, and to do that he had an axe of silver, and the wedge and saw were of silver and the mallet of copper. So he chopped the wood small; stayed there in the house and had good meat and drink, but never saw any one but the tabby-cat and her servants.

Once she said to him, "Go and mow my meadow, and dry the grass," and gave him a scythe of silver, and a whetstone of gold, but bade him deliver them up again carefully. So Hans went thither, and did what he was bidden, and when he had finished the work, he carried the scythe, whetstone, and hay to the house, and asked if it was not yet time for her to give him his reward. "No," said the cat, "you must first do something more for me of the same kind. There is timber of silver, carpenter's axe, square, and everything that is needful, all of silver; with these build me a small house." Then Hans built the small house, and said that he had now done everything, and still he had no horse. Nevertheless, the seven years had gone by with him as if they were six months.

The cat asked him if he would like to see her horses? "Yes," said Hans. Then she opened the door of the small house, and when she had opened it, there stood twelve horses—such horses, so bright and shining, that his heart rejoiced at the sight of them. She gave him to eat and to drink, and said, "Go home, I will not give you your horse away with you; but in three days' time I will follow you and bring it." So Hans set out, and she showed him the way to the mill. She had, however, never once given him a new coat, and he had been obliged to keep on his dirty old smock-frock, which he had brought with him, and which during the seven years had everywhere become too small for him.

When he reached home, the two other apprentices were there again as well, and each of them certainly had brought a horse with him, but one of them was a blind one, and the other lame. They asked Hans where his horse was. "It will follow me in three days' time." Then they laughed and said, "Indeed, stupid Hans, where wilt thou get a horse? It will be a fine one!" Hans went into the parlor, but the miller said he should not sit down to table, for he was so ragged and torn, that they would all be ashamed of him if any one came in. So they gave him a mouthful of food outside, and at night, when they went to rest, the two others would not let him have a bed, and at last he was forced to creep into the goose-house, and lie down on a little hard straw. In the morning when he awoke, the three days had passed, and a coach came with six horses and they shone so bright that it was delightful to see them! And a servant brought a seventh as well, which was for the poor miller's boy.

A magnificent Princess alighted from the coach and went into the mill, and this princess was the little tabby-cat whom poor Hans had served for seven years. She asked the miller where the miller's boy and drudge was? Then the miller said, "We cannot have him here in the mill, for he is so ragged; he is lying in the goose-house." Then the King's daughter said that they were to bring him immediately. So they brought him out, and he had to hold his little smock-frock together to cover himself. The servants unpacked splendid garments, and washed him and dressed him, and when that was done, no King could have looked more handsome. Then the maiden desired to see the horses which the other apprentices had brought home with them, and one of them was blind and the other lame.

So she ordered the servant to bring the seventh horse, and when the miller saw it, he said that such a horse as that had never yet entered his yard. "And that is for the third miller's-boy," said she. "Then he must have the mill," said the miller, but the King's daughter said that the horse was there, and that he was to keep his mill as well, and took her faithful Hans and set him in the coach, and drove away with him.

They first drove to the little house which he had built with the silver tools, and behold it was a great castle, and everything inside it was of silver and gold; and then she married him, and he was rich, so rich that he had enough for all the rest of his life. After this, let no one ever say that any one who is silly can never become a person of importance.

The Old Woman in the Wood

A POOR servant-girl was once traveling with the family she served through a great forest, and when they were in the midst of it, robbers came out of the thicket, and murdered all they found. All perished together except the girl, who had jumped out of the carriage in a fright, and hidden herself behind a tree. When the robbers had gone away with their booty, she came out and beheld the great disaster. Then she began to weep bitterly, and said, "What can a poor girl like me do now? I do not know how to get out of the forest, no human being lives in it, so I must certainly starve." She walked about and looked for a road, but could find none. When it was evening she seated herself under a tree, gave herself into God's keeping, and resolved to sit waiting there and not go away, let what might happen.

When, however, she had sat there for a while, a white dove came flying to her with a little golden key in its mouth. It put the little key in her hand, and said, "Do you see that great tree, therein is a little lock, it opens with the tiny key; inside the tree you will find food enough, and suffer no more hunger." Then she went to the tree and opened it, and found milk in a little dish, and white bread to break into it, so that she could eat her fill. When she was satisfied, she said, "It is now the time when the hens at home go to roost; I am so tired I could go to bed too." Then the dove flew to her again, and brought another golden key in its bill, and said, "Open that tree there, and you will find a bed." So she opened it, and found a beautiful white bed, and she prayed God to protect her during the night, and lay down and slept. In the morning the dove came for the third time, and again brought a little key, and said, "Open that tree there, and you will find clothes." And when she opened it, she found garments beset with gold and with jewels, more splendid than those of any King's daughter. So she lived there for some time, and the dove came every day and provided her with all she needed, and it was a quiet good life.

Once, however, the dove came and said, "Will you do something for my sake?" "With all my heart," said the girl. Then said the little dove, "I will guide you to a small house; enter it, and inside it, an old woman will be sitting by the fire and will say, 'Good-day.' But on your life give her no answer, let her do what she will, but pass by her on the right side; further on, there is a door, open it, and you will enter into a room where a quantity of rings of all kinds are lying, among which are some magnificent ones with shining stones. Leave them, however, where they are, and seek out a plain one, which must likewise be among them, and bring it here to me as quickly as you can."

The girl went to the little house, and came to the door. There sat an old woman who stared when she saw her, and said, "Good-day, my child." The girl gave her no answer, and opened the door. "Whither away," cried the old woman, and seized her by the gown, and wanted to hold her fast, saying, "That is my house; no one can go in there if I choose not to allow it." But the girl was silent, got away from her, and went straight into the room.

On the table lay an enormous quantity of rings, which gleamed and glittered before her eyes. She turned them over and looked for the plain one, but could not find it. While she was seeking, she saw the old woman and how she was stealing away, and wanting to get off with a bird-cage which she had in her hand. So she went after her and took the cage out of her hand, and when she raised it up and looked into it, a bird was inside which had the plain ring in its bill. Then she took the ring, and ran quite joyously home with it, and thought the little white dove would come and get the ring, but it did not.

Then she leant against a tree and determined to wait for the dove, and, as she thus stood, it seemed just as if the tree was soft and pliant, and was letting its branches down. And suddenly the branches twined around her, and were two arms, and when she looked round, the tree was a handsome man, who embraced and kissed her heartily, and said, "You have delivered me from the power of the old woman, who is a wicked witch. She had changed me into a tree, and every day for two hours I was a white dove, and so long as she possessed the ring I could not regain my human form." Then his servants and his horses, who had likewise been changed into trees, were freed from the enchantment also, and stood beside him. And he led them forth to his kingdom, for he was a King's son, and they married, and lived happily.

The Lambkin and the Little Fish

THERE WERE once a little brother and a little sister, who loved each other with all their hearts. Their own mother was, however, dead, and they had a step-mother, who was not kind to them, and secretly did everything she could to hurt them. It so happened that the two were playing with other children in a meadow before the house, and there was a pond in the meadow which came up to one side of the house. The children ran about it, and caught each other, and played at counting out.

> *"Eneke Beneke, let me live,*
> *And I to thee my bird will give.*
> *The little bird, for straw shall seek,*
> *The straw I'll give to the cow to eat.*
> *The pretty cow shall give me milk,*
> *The milk I'll to the baker take.*
> *The baker he shall bake a cake,*
> *The cake I'll give unto the cat.*
> *The cat shall catch some mice for that,*
> *The mice I'll hang up in the smoke,*
> *And then you'll see the* snow."

They stood in a circle while they played this, and the one to whom the word snow fell, had to run away and all the others ran after him and caught him. As they were running about so merrily the step-mother watched them from the window, and grew angry. And as she understood arts of witchcraft she bewitched them both, and changed the little brother into a fish, and the little sister into a lamb. Then the fish swam here and there about the pond and was very sad, and the lambkin walked up and down the meadow, and was miserable, and could not eat or touch one blade of grass.

Thus passed a long time, and then strangers came as visitors to the castle. The false step-mother thought, "This is a good opportunity," and called the cook and said to him, "Go and fetch the lamb from the meadow and kill it, we have nothing else for the visitors." Then the cook went away and got the lamb, and took it into the kitchen and tied its feet, and all this it bore patiently. When he had drawn out his knife and was whetting it on the door-step to kill the lamb, he noticed a little fish swimming backwards and forwards in the water in front of the kitchen-sink and looking up at him. This, however, was the brother, for when the fish saw the cook take the lamb away, it followed them and swam along the pond to the house; then the lamb cried down to it,

> *"Ah, brother, in the pond so deep,*
> *How sad is my poor heart!*
> *Even now the cook he whets his knife*
> *To take away my tender life."*

The little fish answered,

> *"Ah, little sister, up on high,*
> *How sad is my poor heart*
> *While in the this pond I lie."*

When the cook heard that the lambkin could speak and said such sad words to the fish down below, he was terrified and thought this could be no common lamb, but must be bewitched by the wicked woman in the house. Then said he, "Be easy, I will not kill thee," and took another sheep and made it ready for the guests, and conveyed the lambkin to a good peasant woman, to whom he related all that he had seen and heard.

The peasant was, however, the very woman who had been foster-mother to the little sister, and she suspected at once who the lamb was, and went with it to a wise woman. Then the wise woman pronounced a blessing over the lambkin and the little fish, by means of which they regained their human forms, and after this she took them both into a little hut in a great forest, where they lived alone, but were contented and happy.

The Juniper Tree

A LONG long time ago, perhaps as much as two thousand years, there was a rich man, and he had a beautiful and pious wife, and they loved each other very much, and they had no children, though they wished greatly for some, and the wife prayed for one day and night. Now, in the courtyard in front of their house stood a juniper tree; and one day in winter the wife was standing beneath it, and paring an apple, and as she pared it she cut her finger, and the blood fell upon the snow.

"Ah," said the woman, sighing deeply, and looking down at the blood, "if only I could have a child as red as blood, and as white as snow!"

And as she said these words, her heart suddenly grew light, and she felt sure she should have her wish. So she went back to the house, and when a month had passed the snow was gone; in two months everything was green; in three months the flowers sprang out of the earth; in four months the trees were in full leaf, and the branches were thickly entwined; the little birds began to sing, so that the woods echoed, and the blossoms fell from the trees; when the fifth month had passed the wife stood under the juniper tree, and it smelt so sweet that her heart leaped within her, and she fell on her knees for joy; and when the sixth month had gone, the fruit was thick and fine, and she remained still; and the seventh month she gathered the berries and ate them eagerly, and was sick and sorrowful; and when the eighth month had passed she called to her husband, and said, weeping, "If I die, bury me under the juniper tree."

Then she was comforted and happy until the ninth month had passed, and then she bore a child as white as snow and as red as blood, and when she saw it her joy was so great that she died.

Her husband buried her under the juniper tree, and he wept sore; time passed, and he became less sad; and after he had grieved a little more he left off, and then he took another wife.

His second wife bore him a daughter, and his first wife's child was a son, as red as blood and as white as snow. Whenever the wife looked at her daughter she felt great love for her, but whenever she looked at the little boy, evil thoughts came into her heart, of how she could get all her husband's money for her daughter, and how the boy stood in the way; and so she took great hatred to him, and drove him from one corner to another, and gave him a buffet here and cuff there, so that the poor child was always in disgrace; when he came back after school hours there was no peace for him.

Once, when the wife went into the room upstairs, her little daughter followed her, and said, "Mother, give me an apple."

"Yes, my child," said the mother, and gave her a fine apple out of the chest, and the chest had a great heavy lid with a strong iron lock.

"Mother," said the little girl, "shall not my brother have one too?"

That was what the mother expected; and she said, "Yes, when he comes back from school."

And when she saw from the window that he was coming, an evil thought crossed her mind, and she snatched the apple, and took it from her little daughter, saying, "You shall not have it before your brother."

Then she threw the apple into the chest, and shut the lid. Then the little boy came in at the door, and she said to him in a kind tone, but with evil looks, "My son, will you have an apple?"

"Mother," said the boy, "how terrible you look! Yes, give me an apple!"

Then she spoke as kindly as before, holding up the cover of the chest, "Come here and take out one for yourself."

And as the boy was stooping over the open chest, crash went the lid down, so that his head flew off among the red apples. But then the woman felt great terror, and wondered how she could escape the blame. And she went to the chest of drawers in her bedroom and took a white handkerchief out of the nearest drawer, and fitting the head to the neck, she bound them with a handkerchief, so that nothing should be seen, and set him on a chair before the door with the apple in his hand.

Then came little Marjory into the kitchen to her mother, who was standing before the fire stirring a pot of hot water.

"Mother," said Marjory, "my brother is sitting before the door and he has an apple in his hand, and looks very pale; I asked him to give me the apple, but he did not answer me; it seems very strange." "Go again to him," said the mother, "and if he will not answer you, give him a box on the ear."

So Marjory went again and said, "Brother, give me the apple."

But as he took no notice, she gave him a box on the ear, and his head fell off, at which she was greatly terrified, and began to cry and scream, and ran to her mother, and said, "Oh mother! I have knocked my brother's head off!" and cried and screamed, and would not cease.

"Oh Marjory!" said her mother, "what have you done? But keep quiet, that no one may see there is anything the matter; it can't be helped now; we will put him out of the way safely."

When the father came home and sat down to table, he said, "Where is my son?" But the mother was filling a great dish full of black broth, and Marjory was crying bitterly, for she could not refrain. Then the father said again, "Where is my son?" "Oh," said the mother, "he is gone into the country to his great-uncle's to stay for a little while." "What should he go for?" said the father, "and without bidding me good-bye, too!" "Oh, he wanted to go so much, and he asked me to let him stay there six weeks; he will be well taken care of." "Dear me," said the father, "I am quite sad about it; it was not right of him to go without bidding me good-bye."

With that he began to eat, saying, "Marjory, what are you crying for? Your brother will come back some time."

After a while he said, "Well, wife, the food is very good; give me some more."

And the more he ate the more he wanted, until he had eaten it all up, and he threw the bones under the table. Then Marjory went to her chest of drawers, and took one of her best handkerchiefs from the bottom drawer, and picked up all the bones from under the table and tied them up in her handkerchief, and went out at the door crying bitterly. She laid them in the green grass under the juniper tree, and immediately her heart grew light again, and she wept no more.

Then the juniper tree began to wave to and fro, and the boughs drew together and then parted, just like a clapping of hands for joy; then a cloud rose from the tree, and in the midst of the cloud there burned a fire, and out of the fire a beautiful bird arose, and, singing most sweetly, soared high into the air; and when he had flown away, the juniper tree remained as it was before, but the handkerchief full of bones was gone. Marjory felt quite glad and lighthearted, just as if her brother were still alive. So she went back merrily into the house and had her dinner.

The bird, when it flew away, perched on the roof of a goldsmith's house, and began to sing,

> *"It was my mother who murdered me;*
> *It was my father who ate of me;*
> *It was my sister Marjory*
> *Who all my bones in pieces found;*
> *Them in a handkerchief she bound,*
> *And laid them under the juniper tree.*
> *Kywitt, kywitt, kywitt, I cry,*
> *Oh what a beautiful bird am I!"*

The goldsmith was sitting in his shop making a golden chain, and when he heard the bird, who was sitting on his roof and singing, he started up to go and look, and as he passed over his threshold he lost one of his slippers; and he went into the middle of the street with a slipper on one foot and only a sock on the other; with his apron on, and the gold chain in one hand and the pincers in the other; and so he stood in the sunshine looking up at the bird.

"Bird," said he, "how beautifully you sing; do sing that piece over again." "No," said the bird, "I do not sing for nothing twice; if you will give me that gold chain I will sing again." "Very well," said the goldsmith, "here is the gold chain; now do as you said."

Down came the bird and took the gold chain in his right claw, perched in front of the goldsmith, and sang,

> *"It was my mother who murdered me;*
> *It was my father who ate of me;*
> *It was my sister Marjory*
> *Who all my bones in pieces found;*
> *Them in a handkerchief she bound,*
> *And laid them under the juniper tree.*
> *Kywitt, kywitt, kywitt, I cry,*
> *Oh what a beautiful bird am I!"*

Then the bird flew to a shoemaker's, and perched on his roof, and sang,

> *"It was my mother who murdered me;*
> *It was my father who ate of me;*
> *It was my sister Marjory*
> *Who all my bones in pieces found;*
> *Them in a handkerchief she bound,*
> *And laid them under the juniper tree.*
> *Kywitt, kywitt, kywitt, I cry,*
> *Oh what a beautiful bird am I!"*

When the shoemaker heard, he ran out of his door in his shirt sleeves and looked up at the roof of his house, holding his hand to shade his eyes from the sun. "Bird," said he, "how beautifully you sing!" Then he called in at his door, "Wife, come out directly; here is a bird singing beautifully. Just listen."

Then he called his daughter, all his children, and acquaintance, both young men and maidens, and they came up the street and gazed on the bird, and saw how beautiful it was with red and green feathers, and round its throat was as it were gold, and its eyes twinkled in its head like stars.

"Bird," said the shoemaker, "do sing that piece over again." "No," said the bird, "I may not sing for nothing twice; you must give me something." "Wife," said the man, "go into the shop; on the top shelf stands a pair of red shoes; bring them here." So the wife went and brought the shoes. "Now bird," said the man, "sing us that piece again."

And the bird came down and took the shoes in his left claw, and flew up again to the roof, and sang,

"It was my mother who murdered me;
It was my father who ate of me;
It was my sister Marjory
Who all my bones in pieces found;
Them in a handkerchief she bound,
And laid them under the juniper tree.
Kywitt, kywitt, kywitt, I cry,
Oh what a beautiful bird am I!"

And when he had finished he flew away, with the chain in his right claw and the shoes in his left claw, and he flew till he reached a mill, and the mill went "clip-clap, clip-clap, clip-clap." And in the mill sat twenty miller's-men hewing a millstone—"hick-hack, hick-hack, hick-hack," while the mill was going "clip-clap, clip-clap, clip-clap." And the bird perched on a linden tree that stood in front of the mill, and sang,

"It was my mother who murdered me"

Here one of the men looked up.

"It was my father who ate of me";

Then two more looked up and listened.

"It was my sister Marjory"

Here four more looked up.

"Who all my bones in pieces found;
Them in a handkerchief she bound,"

Now there were only eight left hewing.

"And laid them under the juniper tree."

Now only five.

"Kywitt, kywitt, kywitt, I cry,"

Now only one.

"Oh what a beautiful bird am I!"

At length the last one left off, and he only heard the end.

"Bird," said he, "how beautifully you sing; let me hear it all. Sing that again!" "No," said the bird, "I may not sing it twice for nothing; if you will give me the millstone I will sing it again." "Indeed," said the man, "if it belonged to me alone you should have it." "All right," said the others, "if he sings again he shall have it."

Then the bird came down, and all the twenty millers heaved up the stone with poles—"yo! heave-ho! yo! heave-ho!" and the bird stuck his head through the hole in the middle, and with the millstone round his neck he flew up to the tree and sang,

"It was my mother who murdered me;
It was my father who ate of me;
It was my sister Marjory
Who all my bones in pieces found;
Them in a handkerchief she bound,
And laid them under the juniper tree.
Kywitt, kywitt, kywitt, I cry,
Oh what a beautiful bird am I!"

And when he had finished, he spread his wings, having in the right claw the chain, and in the left claw the shoes, and round his neck the millstone, and he flew away to his father's house.

In the parlor sat the father, the mother, and Marjory at the table; the father said, "How light-hearted and cheerful I feel." "Nay," said the mother, "I feel very low, just as if a great storm were coming."

But Marjory sat weeping; and the bird came flying, and perched on the roof.

"Oh," said the father, "I feel so joyful, and the sun is shining so bright; it is as if I were going to meet with an old friend." "Nay," said the wife, "I am terrified, my teeth chatter, and there is fire in my veins," and she tore open her dress to get air; and Marjory sat in a corner and wept, with her plate before her, until it was quite full of tears. Then the bird perched on the juniper tree and sang,

"It was my mother who murdered me";

And the mother stopped her ears and hid her eyes, and would neither see nor hear; nevertheless, the noise of a fearful storm was in her ears, and in her eyes a quivering and burning as of lightning.

"It was my father who ate of me";

"Oh, mother!" said the father, "there is a beautiful bird singing so finely, and the sun shines, and everything smells as sweet as cinnamon."

"It was my sister Marjory"

Marjory hid her face in her lap and wept, and the father said, "I must go out to see the bird." "Oh do not go!" said the wife, "I feel as if the house were on fire."

But the man went out and looked at the bird.

> *"Who all my bones in pieces found;*
> *Them in a handkerchief she bound,*
> *And laid them under the juniper tree.*
> *Kywitt, kywitt, kywitt, I cry,*
> *Oh what a beautiful bird am I!"*

With that the bird let fall the gold chain upon his father's neck, and it fitted him exactly. So he went indoors and said, "Look what a beautiful chain the bird has given me!"

Then his wife was so terrified that she fell down on the floor, and her cap came off. Then the bird began to sing,

> *"It was my mother who murdered me";*

"Oh," groaned the mother, "that I were a thousand fathoms under ground, so as not to be obliged to hear it."

> *"It was my father who ate of me";*

Then the woman lay as if she were dead.

> *"It was my sister Marjory"*

"Oh," said Marjory, "I will go out, too, and see if the bird will give me anything." And out she went.

> *"Who all my bones in pieces found;*
> *Them in a handkerchief she bound,"*

Then he threw the shoes down to her.

> *"And laid them under the juniper tree.*
> *Kywitt, kywitt, kywitt, I cry,*
> *Oh what a beautiful bird am I!"*

And poor Marjory all at once felt happy and joyful, and put on her red shoes, and danced and jumped for joy. "Oh dear," said she, "I felt so sad before I went outside, and now my heart is so light! He is a charming bird to have given me a pair of red shoes."

But the mother's hair stood on end, and looked like flame, and she said, "Even if the world is coming to an end, I must go out for a little relief."

Just as she came outside the door, crash went the millstone on her head, and crushed her flat. The father and daughter rushed out, and saw smoke and flames of fire rise up; but when that had gone by, there stood the little brother; and he took his father and Marjory by the hand, and they felt happy and content, and went indoors, and sat at the table and had their dinner.

Jorinda and Joringel

THERE ONCE was an old castle in the midst of a large and thick forest, and in it an old woman who was a witch dwelt all alone. In the daytime she changed herself into a cat or a screech-owl, but in the evening she took her proper shape again as a human being. She could lure wild beasts and birds to her, and then she killed and boiled and roasted them. If any one came within one hundred paces of the castle he was obliged to stand still, and could not stir from the place until she bade him be free. But whenever an innocent maiden came within the circle, she changed her into a bird, and shut her up in a wicker-work cage, and carried the cage into a room in the castle. She had about seven thousand cages of rare birds in the castle.

Now there was a maiden who was called Jorinda, fairer than all other girls. She and a handsome youth named Joringel had promised to marry each other. They were still in the days of betrothal, and their greatest happiness was being together. One day in order that they might be able to talk together in quiet they went for a walk in the forest. "Take care," said Joringel, "that you do not go too near the castle."

It was a beautiful evening; the sun shone brightly between the trunks of the trees into the dark green forest, and the turtle-doves sang mournfully upon the young boughs of the birch trees.

Jorinda wept now and then. She sat down in the sunshine and was sorrowful. Joringel was sorrowful too; they were as sad as if they were about to die. Then they looked around them, and were quite at a loss, for they did not know by which way they should go home. The sun was still half above the mountain and half set.

Joringel looked through the bushes, and saw the old walls of the castle close at hand. He was horror-stricken and filled with deadly fear. Jorinda was singing,

> *"My little bird, with the necklace red,*
> *Sings sorrow, sorrow, sorrow,*

He sings that the dove must soon be dead,
  Sings sorrow, sor—jug, jug, jug."

Joringel looked for Jorinda. She was changed into a nightingale, and sang "jug, jug, jug." A screech-owl with glowing eyes flew three times round about her, and three times cried "to-whoo, to-whoo, to-whoo!"

Joringel could not move: he stood there like a stone, and could neither weep nor speak, nor move hand or foot.

The sun had now set. The owl flew into the thicket, and directly afterwards there came out of it a crooked old woman, yellow and lean, with large red eyes and a hooked nose, the point of which reached to her chin. She muttered to herself, caught the nightingale, and took it away in her hand.

Joringel could neither speak nor move from the spot; the nightingale was gone. At last the woman came back, and said in a hollow voice, "Greet thee, Zachiel. If the moon shines on the cage, Zachiel, let him loose at once." Then Joringel was freed. He fell on his knees before the woman and begged that she would give him back his Jorinda, but she said that he should never have her again, and went away. He called, he wept, he lamented, but all in vain, "Ah, what is to become of me?"

Joringel went away, and at last came to a strange village; there he kept sheep for a long time. He often walked round and round the castle, but not too near to it. At last he dreamt one night that he found a blood-red flower, in the middle of which was a beautiful large pearl; that he picked the flower and went with it to the castle, and that everything he touched with the flower was freed from enchantment; he also dreamt that by means of it he recovered his Jorinda.

In the morning, when he awoke, he began to seek over hill and dale if he could find such a flower. He sought until the ninth day, and then, early in the morning, he found the blood-red flower. In the middle of it there was a large dew-drop, as big as the finest pearl.

Day and night he journeyed with this flower to the castle. When he was within a hundred paces of it he was not held fast, but walked on to the door. Joringel was full of joy; he touched the door with the flower, and it sprang open. He walked in through the courtyard, and listened for the sound of the birds. At last he heard it. He went on and found the room from whence it came, and there the witch was feeding the birds in the seven thousand cages.

When she saw Joringel she was angry, very angry, and scolded and spat poison and gall at him, but she could not come within two paces of him. He did not take any notice of her, but went and looked at the cages with the birds, but there were many hundred nightingales; how was he to find his Jorinda again?

Just then he saw the old woman quietly take away a cage with a bird in it, and go towards the door.

Swiftly he sprang towards her, touched the cage with the flower, and also the old woman. She could now no longer bewitch any one; and Jorinda was standing there, clasping him round the neck, and she was as beautiful as ever!

The Goose-Girl at the Well

THERE WAS ONCE upon a time a very old woman, who lived with her flock of geese in a waste place among the mountains, and there had a little house. The waste was surrounded by a large forest, and every morning the old woman took her crutch and hobbled into it. There, however, the dame was quite active, more so than any one would have thought, considering her age, and collected grass for her geese, picked all the wild fruit she could reach, and carried everything home on her back. Any one would have thought that the heavy load would have weighed her to the ground, but she always brought it safely home. If any one met her, she greeted him quite courteously. "Good day, dear countryman, it is a fine day. Ah! you wonder that I should drag grass about, but every one must take his burden on his back." Nevertheless, people did not like to meet her if they could help it, and took by preference a roundabout way, and when a father with his boys passed her, he whispered to them, "Beware of the old woman. She has claws beneath her gloves; she is a witch."

One morning a handsome young man was going through the forest. The sun shone bright, the birds sang, a cool breeze crept through the leaves, and he was full of joy and gladness. He had as yet met no one, when he suddenly perceived the old witch kneeling on the ground cutting grass with a sickle. She had already thrust a whole load into her cloth, and near it stood two baskets, which were filled with wild apples and pears. "But, good little mother," said he, "how can you carry all that away?" "I must carry it, dear sir," answered she, "rich folk's children have no need to do such things, but with the peasant folk the saying goes, 'Don't look behind you, you will only see how crooked your back is!' "

"Will you help me?" she said, as he remained standing by her. "You have still a straight back and young legs, it would be a trifle to you. Besides, my house is not so very far from here, it stands there on the heath behind the hill. How soon you would bound up thither!" The young man took compassion on the old woman. "My father is certainly no peasant," replied he, "but a rich count; nevertheless, that you may see that it is not only peasants who can carry things, I will take your bundle." "If you will try it," said she, "I shall be very glad. You will certainly have to walk for an hour, but what will that signify to you; only you must carry the apples and pears as well."

It now seemed to the young man just a little serious, when he heard of an hour's walk, but the old woman would not let him off, packed the bundle on his back; and hung the two baskets on his arm. "See, it is quite light," said she. "No, it is not light," answered the count, and pulled a rueful face. "Verily, the bundle weighs as heavily as if it were full of cobblestones, and the apples and pears are as heavy as lead! I can scarcely breathe." He had a mind to put everything down again, but the old woman would not allow it. "Just look," said she mockingly, "the young gentleman will not carry what I, an old woman, have so often dragged along. You are ready with fine words, but when it comes to be earnest, you want to take to your heels. Why are you standing loitering there?" she continued. "Step out. No one will take the bundle off again."

As long as he walked on level ground, it was still bearable, but when they came to the hill and had to climb, and the stones rolled down under his feet as if they were alive, it was beyond his strength. The drops of perspiration stood on his forehead, and ran, hot and cold, down his back. "Dame," said he, "I can go no farther. I want to rest a little." "Not here," answered the old woman, "when we have arrived at our journey's end, you can rest; but now you must go forward. Who knows what good it may do you?" "Old woman, you are becoming shameless!" said the count, and tried to throw off the bundle, but he labored in vain; it stuck as fast to his back as if it grew there. He turned and twisted, but he could not get rid of it. The old woman laughed at this, and sprang about quite delighted on her crutch. "Don't get angry, dear sir," said she, "you are growing as red in the face as a turkey-cock! Carry your bundle patiently. I will give you a good present when we get home."

What could he do? He was obliged to submit to his fate, and crawl along patiently behind the old woman. She seemed to grow more and more nimble, and his burden still heavier. All at once she made a spring, jumped on to the bundle and seated herself on the top of it; and however withered she might be, she was yet heavier than the stoutest country lass. The youth's knees trembled, but when he did not go on, the old woman hit him about the legs with a switch and with stinging-nettles. Groaning continually, he climbed the mountain, and at length reached the old woman's house, when he was just about to drop. When the geese perceived the old woman, they flapped their wings, stretched out their necks, ran to meet her, cackling all the while. Behind the flock walked, stick in hand, an old wench, strong and big, but ugly as night. "Good mother," said she to the old woman, "has anything happened to you, you have stayed away so long?" "By no means, my dear daughter," answered she, "I have met with nothing bad. On the contrary, only with this kind gentleman, who has carried my burden for me; only think, he even took me on his back when I was tired. The way, too, has not seemed long to us; we have been merry, and have been cracking jokes with each other all the time."

At last the old woman slid down, took the bundle off the young man's back, and the baskets from his arm, looked at him quite kindly, and said, "Now seat yourself on the bench before the door, and rest. You have fairly earned your wages, and they shall not be wanting." Then she said to the goose-girl, "Go into the house, my dear daughter, it is not becoming for you to be alone with a young gentleman; one must not pour oil on to the fire, he might fall in love with you." The count knew not whether to laugh or to cry. "Such a sweetheart as that," thought he, "could not touch my heart, even if she were thirty years younger."

In the meantime the old woman stroked and fondled her geese as if they were children, and then went into the house with her daughter. The youth lay down on the bench, under a wild apple tree. The air was warm and mild; on all sides stretched a green meadow, which was set with cowslips, wild thyme, and a thousand other flowers; through the midst of it rippled a clear brook on which the sun sparkled, and the white geese went walking backwards and forwards, or paddled in the water. "It is quite delightful here," said he, "but I am so tired that I cannot keep my eyes open; I will sleep a little. If only a gust of wind does not come and blow my legs off my body, for they are as rotten as tinder."

When he had slept a little while, the old woman came and shook him till he awoke. "Sit up," said she, "you cannot stay here; I have certainly treated you hardly, still it has not cost you your life. Of money and land you have no need; here is something else for you." Thereupon she thrust a little book into his hand, which was cut out of a single emerald. "Take great care of it," said she, "it will bring you good fortune." The count sprang up, and as he felt that he was quite fresh, and had recovered his vigor, he thanked the old woman for her present, and set off without even once looking back at the "beautiful" daughter. When he was already some way off, he still heard in the distance the noisy cry of the geese.

For three days the count had to wander in the wilderness before he could find his way out. He then reached a large town, and as no one knew him, he was led into the royal palace, where the King and Queen were sitting on their throne. The count fell on one knee, drew the emerald book out of his pocket, and laid it at the Queen's feet. She bade him rise and hand her the little book. Hardly, however, had she opened it, and looked therein, than she fell as if dead to the ground. The count was seized by the King's servants, and was being led to prison, when the Queen opened her eyes, and ordered them to release him, and every one was to go out, as she wished to speak with him in private.

When the Queen was alone, she began to weep bitterly, and said, "Of what use to me are the splendors and honors with which I am surrounded; every morning I awake in pain and sorrow. I had three daughters, the youngest of whom was so beautiful that the whole world looked on her as a wonder. She was as white as snow, as rosy as apple-blossom, and her hair as radiant as sunbeams. When she cried, not tears fell from her eyes, but pearls and jewels only. When she was fifteen years old, the King summoned all three sisters to come before his throne. You should have seen how all the people gazed when the youngest entered, it was just as if the sun were rising!

"Then the King spoke, 'My daughters, I know not when my last day may arrive; I will today decide what each shall receive at my death. You all love me, but the one of you who loves me best, shall fare the best. ' Each of them said she loved him best. 'Can you not express to me, ' said the King, 'how much you do love me, and thus I shall see what you mean?' The eldest spoke. 'I love my father as dearly as the sweetest sugar.' The second, 'I love my father as dearly as my prettiest dress.' But the youngest was silent. Then her father said, 'And you, my dearest child, how much do you love me?' 'I do not know, and can compare my love with nothing.' But her father insisted that she should name something. So she said at last, 'The best food does not please me without salt, therefore I love my father like salt.'

"When the King heard that, he fell into a passion, and said, 'If you love me like salt, your love shall also be repaid you with salt.' Then he divided the kingdom between the two elder, but caused a sack of salt to be bound on the back of the youngest, and two servants had to lead her forth into the wild forest. We all begged and prayed for her," said the Queen, "but the King's anger was not to be appeased. How she cried when she had to leave us! The whole road was strewn with the pearls which flowed from her eyes. The King soon afterwards repented of his great severity, and had the whole forest searched for the poor child, but no one could find her. When I think that the wild beasts have devoured her, I know not how to contain myself for sorrow; many a time I console myself with the hope that she is still alive, and may have hidden herself in a cave, or has found shelter with compassionate people. But picture to yourself, when I opened your little emerald book, a pearl lay therein, of exactly the same kind as those which used to fall from my daughter's eyes; and then you can also imagine how the sight of it stirred my heart. You must tell me how you came by that pearl."

The count told her that he had received it from the old woman in the forest, who had appeared very strange to him, and must be a witch, but he had neither seen nor heard anything of the Queen's child. The King and Queen resolved to seek out the old woman. They thought that there where the pearl had been, they would obtain news of their daughter.

The old woman was sitting in that lonely place at her spinning-wheel, spinning. It was already dusk, and a log which was burning on the hearth gave a scanty light. All at once there was a noise outside, the geese were coming home from the pasture, and uttering their hoarse cries. Soon afterwards the daughter also entered. But the old woman scarcely thanked her, and only shook her head a little. The daughter sat down beside her, took her spinning-wheel, and twisted the threads as nimbly as a young girl. Thus they both sat for two hours, and exchanged never a word. At last something rustled at the window, and two fiery eyes peered in. It was an old night-owl, which cried, "Uhu!" three times. The old woman looked up just a little, then she said, "Now, my little daughter, it is time for you to go out and do your work." She rose and went out, and where did she go?—over the meadows into the valley. At last she came to a well, with three old oak trees standing beside it; meanwhile the moon had risen large and round over the mountain, and it was so light that one could have found a needle. She removed a skin which covered her face, then bent down to the well, and began to wash herself. When she had finished, she dipped the skin also in the water, and then laid it on the meadow, so that it should bleach in the moonlight, and dry again. But how the maiden was changed! Such a change as that was never seen before! When the gray mask fell off, her golden hair broke forth like sunbeams, and spread about like a mantle over her whole form. Her eyes shone out as brightly as the stars in heaven, and her cheeks bloomed a soft red like apple-blossom.

But the fair maiden was sad. She sat down and wept bitterly. One tear after another forced itself out of her eyes, and rolled through her long hair to the ground. There she sat, and would have remained sitting a long time, if there had not been a rustling and cracking in the boughs of the neighboring tree. She sprang up like a roe which had been overtaken by the shot of the hunter. Just then the moon was obscured by a dark cloud, and in an instant the maiden had slipped on the old skin and vanished, like a light blown out by the wind.

She ran back home, trembling like an aspen-leaf. The old woman was standing on the threshold, and the girl was about to relate what had befallen her, but the old woman laughed kindly, and said, "I already know all." She led her into the room and lighted a new log. She did not, however, sit down to her spinning again, but fetched a broom and began to sweep and scour. "All must be clean and sweet," she said to the girl. "But, mother," said the maiden, "why do you begin work at so late an hour? What do you expect?" "Do you know what time it is?" asked the old woman. "Not yet midnight," answered the maiden, "but already past eleven o'clock." "Do you not remember," continued the old woman, "that it is three years today since you came to me? Your time is up, we can no longer remain together." The girl was terrified, and said, "Alas! dear mother, will you cast me off? Where shall I go? I have no friends, and no home to which I can go. I have always done as you bade me, and you have always been satisfied with me; do not send me away."

The old woman would not tell the maiden what lay before her.

"My stay here is over," she said to her, "but when I depart, house and parlor must be clean; therefore do not hinder me in my work. Have no care for yourself; you shall find a roof to shelter you, and the wages which I will give shall also content you." "But tell me what is about to happen," the maiden continued to entreat. "I tell you again, do not hinder me in my work. Do not say a word more, go to your chamber, take the skin off your face, and put on the silken gown which you had on when you came to me, and then wait in your chamber until I call you."

But I must once more tell of the King and Queen, who had journeyed forth with the count in order to seek out the old woman in the wilderness. The count had strayed away from them in the wood by night, and had to walk onwards alone. Next day it seemed to him that he was on the right track. He still went forward, until darkness came on, then he climbed a tree, intending to pass the night there, for he feared that he might lose his way. When the moon illumined the surrounding country he perceived a figure coming down the mountain. She had no stick in her hand, but yet he could see that it was the goose-girl, whom he had seen before in the house of the old woman. "Oho," cried he, "there she comes, and if I once get hold of one of the witches, the other shall not escape me!" But how astonished he was, when she went to the well, took off the skin and washed herself, when her golden hair fell down all about her, and she was more beautiful than any one whom he had ever seen in the whole world. He hardly dared to breathe, but stretched his head as far forward through the leaves as he dared, and stared at her. Either he bent over too far, or whatever the cause might be, the bough suddenly cracked, and that very moment the maiden slipped into the skin, sprang away like a roe, and as the moon was suddenly covered, disappeared from his eyes.

Hardly had she disappeared, before the count descended from the tree, and hastened after her with nimble steps. He had not been gone long before he saw, in the twilight, two figures coming over the meadow. It was the King and Queen, who had perceived from a distance the light shining in the old woman's little house, and were going to it. The count told them what wonderful things he had seen by the well, and they did not doubt that it had been their lost daughter. They walked onwards full of joy, and soon came to the little house. The geese were sitting all round it, and had thrust their heads under their wings and were sleeping, and not one of them moved. The King and Queen looked in at the window, the old woman was sitting there quietly spinning, nodding her head and never looking round. The room was perfectly clean, as if the little mist men, who carry no dust on their feet, lived there. Their daughter, however, they did not see. They gazed at all this for a long time; at last they took heart, and knocked softly at the window.

The old woman appeared to have been expecting them; she rose, and called out quite kindly, "Come in—I know you already." When they had entered the room, the old woman said, "You might have spared yourself the long walk, if you had not three years ago unjustly driven away your child, who is so good and lovable. No harm has come to her; for three years she has had to tend the geese; with them she has learnt no evil, but has preserved her purity of heart. You, however, have been sufficiently punished by the misery in which you have lived." Then she went to the chamber and called, "Come out, my little daughter." Thereupon the door opened, and the Princess stepped out in her silken garments, with her golden hair and her shining eyes, and it was as if an angel from heaven had entered.

She went up to her father and mother, fell on their necks and kissed them, there was no help for it, they all had to weep for joy. The young count stood near them, and when she perceived him she became as red in the face as a moss-rose, she herself did not know why.

The King said, "My dear child, I have given away my kingdom. What shall I give you?" "She needs nothing," said the old woman. "I give her the tears that she has wept on your account; they are precious pearls, finer than those that are found in the sea, and worth more than your whole kingdom, and I give her my little house as payment for her services." When the old woman had said that, she disappeared from their sight. The walls rattled a little, and when the King and Queen looked round, the little house had changed into a splendid palace, a royal table had been spread, and the servants were running hither and thither.

The story goes still further, but my grandmother, who related it to me, had partly lost her memory, and had forgotten the rest. I shall always believe that the beautiful Princess married the count, and that they remained together in the palace, and lived there in all happiness so long as God willed it. Whether the snow-white geese, which were kept near the little hut, were verily young maidens (no one need take offense) whom the old woman had taken under her protection, and whether they now received their human forms again, and stayed as handmaids to the young Queen,

I do not exactly know, but I suspect it. This much is certain, that the old woman was no witch, as people thought, but a wise woman, who meant well. Very likely it was she who, at the Princess's birth, gave her the gift of weeping pearls instead of tears. That does not happen nowadays, or else the poor would soon become rich.

The Three Little Men in the Wood

THERE WAS ONCE a man, whose wife was dead, and a woman, whose husband was dead; the man had a daughter, and so had the woman. The girls were well acquainted with each other, and used to play together in the woman's house. One day the woman said to the man's daughter,

"Listen to me, tell your father that I will marry him, and then you shall have milk to wash in every morning and wine to drink, and my daughter shall have water to wash in and water to drink."

The girl went home and told her father what the woman had said. The man said, "What shall I do! Marriage is a joy, and also a torment."

At last, as he could come to no conclusion, he took off his boot, and said to his daughter, "Take this boot, it has a hole in the sole; go up with it into the loft, hang it on the big nail and pour water in it. If it holds water, I will once more take to me a wife; if it lets out the water, so will I not."

The girl did as she was told, but the water held the hole together, and the boot was full up to the top. So she went and told her father how it was. And he went up to see with his own eyes, and as there was no mistake about it, he went to the widow and courted her, and then they had the wedding.

The next morning, when the two girls awoke, there stood by the bedside of the man's daughter milk to wash in and wine to drink, and by the bedside of the woman's daughter there stood water to wash in and water to drink.

On the second morning there stood water to wash in and water to drink for both of them alike. On the third morning there stood water to wash in and water to drink for the man's daughter, and milk to wash in and wine to drink for the woman's daughter; and so it remained ever after. The woman hated her step-daughter, and never knew how to treat her badly enough from one day to another. And she was jealous because her step-daughter was pleasant and pretty, and her real daughter was ugly and hateful.

Once in winter, when it was freezing hard, and snow lay deep on hill and valley, the woman made a frock out of paper, called her step-daughter, and said, "Here, put on this frock, go out into the wood and fetch me a basket of strawberries; I have a great wish for some."

"Oh dear," said the girl, "there are no strawberries to be found in winter; the ground is frozen, and the snow covers everything. And why should I go in the paper frock? It is so cold out of doors that one's breath is frozen; the wind will blow through it, and the thorns will tear it off my back!"

"How dare you contradict me!" cried the step-mother, "be off, and don't let me see you again till you bring me a basket of strawberries." Then she gave her a little piece of hard bread, and said, "That will do for you to eat during the day," and she thought to herself, "She is sure to be frozen or starved to death out of doors, and I shall never set eyes on her again."

So the girl went obediently, put on the paper frock, and started out with the basket. The snow was lying everywhere, far and wide, and there was not a blade of green to be seen. When she entered the wood she saw a little house with three little men peeping out of it. She wished them good-day, and knocked modestly at the door. They called her in, and she came into the room and sat down by the side of the oven to warm herself and eat her breakfast.

The little men said, "Give us some of it." "Willingly," answered she, breaking her little piece of bread in two, and giving them half. They then said, "What are you doing here in the wood this winter time in your little thin frock?" "Oh," answered she, "I have to get a basket of strawberries, and I must not go home without them."

When she had eaten her bread they gave her a broom, and told her to go and sweep the snow away from the back door. When she had gone outside to do it the little men talked among themselves about what they should do for her, as she was so good and pretty, and had shared her bread with them. Then the first one said, "She shall grow prettier every day." Then second said, "Each time she speaks a piece of gold shall fall from her mouth." The third said, "A king shall come and take her for his wife."

In the meanwhile the girl was doing as the little men had told her, and had cleared the snow from the back of the little house, and what do you suppose she found?—fine ripe strawberries, showing dark red against the snow! Then she joyfully filled her little basket full, thanked the little men, shook hands with them all, and ran home in haste to bring her step-mother the thing she longed for. As she went in and said, "Good evening," a piece of gold fell from her mouth at once. Then she related all that had happened to her in the wood, and at each word that she spoke gold pieces fell out of her mouth, so that soon they were scattered all over the room.

"Just look at her pride and conceit!" cried the step-sister, "throwing money about in this way!" but in her heart she was jealous because of it, and wanted to go too into the wood to fetch strawberries. But the mother said, "No, my dear little daughter, it is too cold, you will be frozen to death."

But she left her no peace, so at last the mother gave in, got her a splendid fur coat to put on, and gave her bread and butter and cakes to eat on the way.

The girl went into the wood and walked straight up to the little house. The three little men peeped out again, but she gave them no greeting, and without looking round or taking any notice of them she came stumping into the room, sat herself down by the oven, and began to eat her bread and butter and cakes.

"Give us some of that," cried the little men, but she answered, "I've not enough for myself; how can I give away any?"

Now when she had done with her eating, they said, "Here is a broom, go and sweep all clean by the back door." "Oh, go and do it yourselves," answered she; "I am not your housemaid."

But when she saw that they were not going to give her anything, she went out to the door. Then the three little men said among themselves, "What shall we do to her, because she is so unpleasant, and has such a wicked jealous heart, grudging everybody everything?" The first said, "She shall grow uglier every day." The second said, "Each time she speaks a toad shall jump out of her mouth at every word." The third said, "She shall die a miserable death."

The girl was looking outside for strawberries, but as she found none, she went sulkily home. And directly she opened her mouth to tell her mother what had happened to her in the wood a toad sprang out of her mouth at each word, so that every one who came near her was quite disgusted.

The step-mother became more and more set against the man's daughter, whose beauty increased day by day, and her only thought was how to do her some injury. So at last she took a kettle, set it on the fire, and scalded some yarn in it. When it was ready she hung it over the poor girl's shoulder, and gave her an axe, and she was to go to the frozen river and break a hole in the ice, and there to rinse the yarn. She obeyed, and went and hewed a hole in the ice, and as she was about it there came by a splendid coach, in which the King sat. The coach stood still, and the King said, "My child, who art thou, and what art thou doing there?" She answered, "I am a poor girl, and am rinsing yarn."

Then the King felt pity for her, and as he saw that she was very beautiful, he said, "Will you go with me?" "Oh yes, with all my heart," answered she; and she felt very glad to be out of the way of her mother and sister.

So she stepped into the coach and went off with the King; and when they reached his castle the wedding was celebrated with great splendor, as the little men in the wood had foretold.

At the end of a year the young Queen had a son; and as the step-mother had heard of her great good fortune she came with her daughter to the castle, as if merely to pay the King and Queen a visit. One day, when the King had gone out, and when nobody was about, the bad woman took the Queen by the head, and her daughter took her by the heels, and dragged her out of bed, and threw her out of the window into a stream that flowed beneath it. Then the old woman put her ugly daughter in the bed, and covered her up to her chin. When the King came back, and wanted to talk to his wife a little, the old woman cried, "Stop, stop! she is sleeping nicely; she must be kept quiet today."

The King dreamt of nothing wrong, and came again the next morning; and as he spoke to his wife, and she answered him, there jumped each time out of her mouth a toad instead of the piece of gold as heretofore. Then he asked why that should be, and the old woman said it was because of her great weakness, and that it would pass away.

But in the night, the boy who slept in the kitchen saw how something in the likeness of a duck swam up the gutter, and said,

> "My King, what mak'st thou?
> Sleepest thou, or wak'st thou?"

But there was no answer. Then it said,

> "What cheer my two guests keep they?"

So the kitchen-boy answered,

> "In bed all soundly sleep they."

It asked again,

"And my little baby, how does he?"

And he answered,

"He sleeps in his cradle quietly."

Then the duck took the shape of the Queen, and went to the child, and gave him to drink, smoothed his little bed, covered him up again, and then, in the likeness of a duck, swam back down the gutter. In this way she came two nights, and on the third she said to the kitchen-boy, "Go and tell the King to brandish his sword three times over me on the threshold!"

Then the kitchen-boy ran and told the King, and he came with his sword and brandished it three times over the duck, and at the third time his wife stood before him living, and hearty, and sound, as she had been before.

The King was greatly rejoiced, but he hid the Queen in a chamber until the Sunday came when the child was to be baptized. And after the baptism he said, "What does that person deserve who drags another out of bed and throws him in the water?" And the old woman answered, "No better than to be put into a cask with iron nails in it, and to be rolled in it down the hill into the water."

Then said the King, "You have spoken your own sentence"; and he ordered a cask to be fetched, and the old woman and her daughter were put into it, and the top hammered down, and the cask was rolled down the hill into the river.

The White Bride and the Black Bride

A WOMAN was going about the countryside with her daughter and her step-daughter, when the Lord came towards them in the form of a poor man, and asked, "Which is the way into the village?" "If you want to know," said the mother, "seek it for yourself," and the daughter added, "If you are afraid you will not find it, take a guide with you." But the step-daughter said, "Poor man, I will take you there, come with me."

Then God was angry with the mother and daughter, and turned His back on them, and wished that they should become as black as night and as ugly as sin. To the poor step-daughter, however, God was gracious, and went with her, and when they were near the village, He said a blessing over her, and spake, "Choose three things for thyself, and I will grant them to thee." Then said the maiden, "I should like to be as beautiful and fair as the sun," and instantly she was white and fair as day. "Then I should like to have a purse of money which would never grow empty." The Lord gave her that also, but He said, "Do not forget what is best of all." She said, "For my third wish, I desire, after my death, to inhabit the eternal kingdom of Heaven." That also was granted unto her, and then the Lord left her.

When the step-mother came home with her daughter, and they saw that they were both as black as coal and ugly, but that the step-daughter was white and beautiful, wickedness increased still more in their hearts, and they thought of nothing else but how they could do her an injury. The step-daughter, however, had a brother called Reginer, whom she loved much, and she told him all that had happened. Once on a time Reginer said to her, "Dear sister, I will take thy likeness, that I may continually see thee before mine eyes, for my love for thee is so great that I should like always to look at thee." Then she answered, "But, I pray thee, let no one see the picture." So he painted his sister and hung up the picture in his room; he, however, dwelt in the King's palace, for he was his coachman.

Every day he went and stood before the picture, and thanked God for the happiness of having such a dear sister. Now it happened that the King whom he served had just lost his wife, who had been so beautiful that no one could be found to compare with her, and on this account the King was in deep grief. The attendants about the court, however, remarked that the coachman stood daily before this beautiful picture, and they were jealous of him, so they informed the King. Then the latter ordered the picture to be brought to him, and when he saw that it was like his lost wife in every respect, except that it was still more beautiful, he fell mortally in love with it. He caused the coachman to be brought before him, and asked whom that portrait represented. The coachman said it was his sister, so the King resolved to take no one but her as his wife, and gave him a carriage and horses and splendid garments of cloth of gold, and sent him forth to fetch his chosen bride.

When Reginer came on this errand, his sister was glad, but the black maiden was jealous of her good fortune, and grew angry above all measure, and said to her mother, "Of what use are all your arts to us now when you cannot procure such a piece of luck for me?" "Be quiet," said the old woman, "I will soon divert it to you"—and by her arts of witchcraft, she so troubled the eyes of the coachman that he was half-blind, and she stopped the ears of the white maiden so that she was half-deaf. Then they got into the carriage, first the bride in her noble royal apparel, then the step-mother with her daughter, and Reginer sat on the box to drive. When they had been on the way for some time the coachman cried,

> *"Cover thee well, my sister dear,*
> *That the rain may not wet thee,*
> *That the wind may not load thee with dust,*
> *That thou may'st be fair and beautiful*
> *When thou appearest before the King."*

The bride asked, "What is my dear brother saying?" "Ah," said the old woman, "he says that you ought to take off your golden dress and give it to your sister." Then she took it off, and put it on the black maiden, who gave her in exchange for it a shabby gray gown. They drove onwards, and a short time afterwards, the brother again cried,

> *"Cover thee well, my sister dear,*
> *That the rain may not wet thee,*
> *That the wind may not load thee with dust,*
> *That thou may'st be fair and beautiful*
> *When thou appearest before the King."*

The bride asked, "What is my dear brother saying?" "Ah," said the old woman, "he says that you ought to take off your golden hood and give it to your sister." So she took off the hood and put it on her sister, and sat with her own head uncovered. And they drove on farther. After a while, the brother once more cried,

> *"Cover thee well, my sister dear,*
> *That the rain may not wet thee,*
> *That the wind may not load thee with dust,*
> *That thou may'st be fair and beautiful*
> *When thou appearest before the King."*

The bride asked, "What is my dear brother saying?" "Ah," said the old woman, "he says you must look out of the carriage." They were, however, just on a bridge, which crossed deep water. When the bride stood up and leant forward out of the carriage, they both pushed her out, and she fell into the middle of the water. At the same moment that she sank, a snow-white duck arose out of the mirror-smooth water, and swam down the river. The brother had observed nothing of it, and drove the carriage on until they reached the court. Then he took the black maiden to the King as his sister, and thought she really was so, because his eyes were dim, and he saw the golden garments glittering. When the King saw the boundless ugliness of his intended bride, he was very angry, and ordered the coachman to be thrown into a pit which was full of adders and nests of snakes. The old witch, however, knew so well how to flatter the King and deceive his eyes by her arts, that he kept her and her daughter until she appeared quite endurable to him, and he really married her.

One evening when the black bride was sitting on the King's knee, a white duck came swimming up the gutter to the kitchen, and said to the kitchen-boy, "Boy, light a fire, that I may warm my feathers." The kitchen-boy did it, and lighted a fire on the hearth. Then came the duck and sat down by it, and shook herself and smoothed her feathers to rights with her bill. While she was thus sitting and enjoying herself, she asked, "What is my brother Reginer doing?" The scullery-boy replied, "He is imprisoned in the pit with adders and with snakes." Then she asked, "What is the black witch doing in the house?" The boy answered, "She is loved by the King and happy." "May God have mercy on him," said the duck, and swam forth by the sink.

The next night she came again and put the same questions, and the third night also. Then the kitchen-boy could bear it no longer, and went to the King and discovered all to him. The King, however, wanted to see it for himself, and next evening went thither, and when the duck thrust her head in through the sink, he took his sword and cut through her neck, and suddenly she changed into a most beautiful maiden, exactly like the picture which her brother had made of her. The King was full of joy, and as she stood there quite wet, he caused splendid apparel to be brought and had her clothed in it. Then she told how she had been betrayed by cunning and falsehood, and at last thrown down into the water, and her first request was that her brother should be brought forth from the pit of snakes, and when the King had fulfilled this request, he went into the chamber where the old witch was, and asked, "What does she deserve who does this and that?" and related what had happened. Then was she so blinded that she was aware of nothing and said, "She deserves to be stripped naked, and put into a barrel with nails, and that a horse should be harnessed to the barrel, and the horse sent all over the world." All of which was done to her, and to her black daughter. But the King married the white and beautiful bride, and rewarded her faithful brother, and made him a rich and distinguished man.

Brother and Sister

A BROTHER took his sister's hand and said to her,

"Since our mother died we have had no good days; our stepmother beats us every day, and if we go near her she kicks us away; we have nothing to eat but hard crusts of bread left over; the dog under the table fares better; he gets a good piece every now and then. If our mother only knew, how she would pity us! Come, let us go together out into the wide world!"

So they went, and journeyed the whole day through fields and meadows and stony places, and if it rained the sister said, "The skies and we are weeping together."

In the evening they came to a great wood, and they were so weary with hunger and their long journey, that they climbed up into a high tree and fell asleep.

The next morning, when they awoke, the sun was high in heaven, and shone brightly through the leaves. Then said the brother, "Sister, I am thirsty; if I only knew where to find a brook, that I might go and drink! I almost think that I hear one rushing." So the brother got down and led his sister by the hand, and they went to seek the brook. But their wicked step-mother was a witch, and had known quite well that the two children had run away, and had sneaked after them, as only witches can, and had laid a spell on all the brooks in the forest. So when they found a little stream flowing smoothly over its pebbles, the brother was going to drink of it; but the sister heard how it said in its rushing,

> *"He a tiger will be who drinks of me,*
> *Who drinks of me a tiger will be!"*

Then the sister cried, "Pray, dear brother, do not drink, or you will become a wild beast, and will tear me in pieces."

So the brother refrained from drinking, though his thirst was great, and he said he would wait till he came to the next brook. When they came to a second brook the sister heard it say,

"He a wolf will be who drinks of me,
Who drinks of me a wolf will be!"

Then the sister cried, "Pray, dear brother, do not drink, or you will be turned into a wolf, and will eat me up!"

So the brother refrained from drinking, and said, "I will wait until we come to the next brook, and then I must drink, whatever you say; my thirst is so great."

And when they came to the third brook the sister heard how in its rushing it said,

"He a fawn will be who drinks of me,
Who drinks of me of a fawn will be!"

Then the sister said, "O my brother, I pray drink not, or you will be turned into a fawn, and run away far from me."

But he had already kneeled by the side of the brook and stooped and drunk of the water, and as the first drops passed his lips he became a fawn. And the sister wept over her poor lost brother, and the fawn wept also, and stayed sadly beside her. At last the maiden said, "Be comforted, dear fawn, indeed I will never leave you."

Then she untied her golden girdle and bound it round the fawn's neck, and went and gathered rushes to make a soft cord, which she fastened to him; and then she led him on, and they went deeper into the forest. And when they had gone a long long way, they came at last to a little house, and the maiden looked inside, and as it was empty she thought, "We might as well live here."

And she fetched leaves and moss to make a soft bed for the fawn, and every morning she went out and gathered roots and berries and nuts for herself, and fresh grass for the fawn, who ate out of her hand with joy, frolicking round her. At night, when the sister was tired, and had said her prayers, she laid her head on the fawn's back, which served her for a pillow, and softly fell asleep. And if only the brother could have got back his own shape again, it would have been a charming life. So they lived a long while in the wilderness alone.

Now it happened that the King of that country held a great hunt in the forest. The blowing of the horns, the barking of the dogs, and the lusty shouts of the huntsmen sounded through the wood, and the fawn heard them and was eager to be among them.

"Oh," said he to his sister, "do let me go to the hunt; I cannot stay behind any longer," and begged so long that at last she consented.

"But mind," said she to him, "come back to me at night. I must lock my door against the wild hunters, so, in order that I may know you, you must knock and say, 'Little sister, let me in,' and unless I hear that I shall not unlock the door."

Then the fawn sprang out, and felt glad and merry in the open air. The King and his huntsmen saw the beautiful animal, and began at once to pursue him, but they could not come within reach of him, for when they thought they were certain of him he sprang away over the bushes and disappeared. As soon as it was dark he went back to the little house, knocked at the door, and said, "Little sister, let me in."

Then the door was opened to him, and he went in, and rested the whole night long on his soft bed. The next morning the hunt began anew, and when the fawn heard the hunting-horns and the tally-ho of the huntsmen he could rest no longer, and said, "Little sister, let me out, I must go." The sister opened the door and said, "Now, mind you must come back at night and say the same words."

When the King and his hunters saw the fawn with the golden collar again, they chased him closely, but he was too nimble and swift for them. This lasted the whole day, and at last the hunters surrounded him, and one of them wounded his foot a little, so that he was obliged to limp and to go slowly. Then a hunter slipped after him to the little house, and heard how he called out, "Little sister, let me in," and saw the door open and shut again after him directly. The hunter noticed all this carefully, went to the King, and told him all he had seen and heard. Then said the King, "To-morrow we will hunt again."

But the sister was very terrified when she saw that her fawn was wounded. She washed his foot, laid cooling leaves round it, and said, "Lie down on your bed, dear fawn, and rest, that you may be soon well." The wound was very slight, so that the fawn felt nothing of it the next morning. And when he heard the noise of the hunting outside, he said, "I cannot stay in, I must go after them; I shall not be taken easily again!" The sister began to weep, and said, "I know you will be killed, and I left alone here in the forest, and forsaken of everybody. I cannot let you go!"

"Then I shall die here with longing," answered the fawn; "when I hear the sound of the horn I feel as if I should leap out of my skin."

Then the sister, seeing there was no help for it, unlocked the door with a heavy heart, and the fawn bounded away into the forest, well and merry. When the King saw him, he said to his hunters, "Now, follow him up all day long till the night comes, and see that you do him no hurt."

So as soon as the sun had gone down, the King said to the huntsmen: "Now, come and show me the little house in the wood." And when he got to the door he knocked at it, and cried, "Little sister, let me in!" Then the door opened, and the King went in, and there stood a maiden more beautiful than any he had seen before.

The maiden shrieked out when she saw, instead of the fawn, a man standing there with a gold crown on his head. But the King looked kindly on her, took her by the hand, and said, "Will you go with me to my castle, and be my dear wife?" "Oh yes," answered the maiden, "but the fawn must come too. I could not leave him." And the King said, "He shall remain with you as long as you live, and shall lack nothing." Then the fawn came bounding in, and the sister tied the cord of rushes to him, and led him by her own hand out of the little house.

The King put the beautiful maiden on his horse, and carried her to his castle, where the wedding was held with great pomp; so she became lady Queen, and they lived together happily for a long while; the fawn was well tended and cherished, and he gamboled about the castle garden.

Now the wicked step-mother, whose fault it was that the children were driven out into the world, never dreamed but that the sister had been eaten up by wild beasts in the forest, and that the brother, in the likeness of a fawn, had been slain by the hunters. But when she heard that they were so happy, and that things had gone so well with them, jealousy and envy arose in her heart, and left her no peace, and her chief thought was how to bring misfortune upon them.

Her own daughter, who was as ugly as sin, and had only one eye, complained to her, and said, "I never had the chance of being a Queen." "Never mind," said the old woman, to satisfy her; "when the time comes, I shall be at hand."

After a while the Queen brought a beautiful baby boy into the world, and that day the King was out hunting. The old witch took the shape of the bed-chamber woman, and went into the room where the Queen lay, and said to her, "Come, the bath is ready; it will give you refreshment and new strength. Quick, or it will be cold."

Her daughter was within call, so they carried the sick Queen into the bath-room, and left her there. And in the bath-room they had made a great fire, so as to suffocate the beautiful young Queen.

When that was managed, the old woman took her daughter, put a cap on her, and laid her in the bed in the Queen's place, gave her also the Queen's form and countenance, only she could not restore the lost eye. So, in order that the King might not remark it, she had to lie on the side where there was no eye.

In the evening, when the King came home and heard that a little son was born to him, he rejoiced with all his heart, and was going at once to his dear wife's bedside to see how she did. Then the old woman cried hastily, "For your life, do not draw back the curtains, to let in the light upon her; she must be kept quiet." So the King went away, and never knew that a false Queen was lying in the bed.

Now, when it was midnight, and every one was asleep, the nurse, who was sitting by the cradle in the nursery and watching there alone, saw the door open, and the true Queen come in. She took the child out of the cradle, laid it in her bosom, and fed it. Then she shook out its little pillow, put the child back again, and covered it with the coverlet. She did not forget the fawn either; she went to him where he lay in the corner, and stroked his back tenderly. Then she went in perfect silence out at the door, and the nurse next morning asked the watchmen if any one had entered the castle during the night, but they said they had seen no one. And the Queen came many nights, and never said a word; the nurse saw her always, but she did not dare speak of it to any one.

After some time had gone by in this manner, the Queen seemed to find voice, and said one night,

> *"My child my fawn twice more I come to see,*
> *Twice more I come and then the end must be."*

The nurse said nothing, but as soon as the Queen had disappeared she went to the King and told him all. The King said, "Ah, heaven! what do I hear! I will myself watch by the child tomorrow night."

So at evening he went into the nursery, and at midnight the Queen appeared, and said,

> *"My child my fawn once more I come to see,*
> *Once more I come, and then the end must be."*

And she tended the child, as she was accustomed to do, before she vanished. The King dared not speak to her, but he watched again the following night, and heard her say,

> *"My child my fawn this once I come to see,*
> *This once I come, and now the end must be."*

Then the King could contain himself no longer, but rushed towards her, saying, "You are no other than my dear wife!" Then she answered, "Yes, I am your dear wife," and in that moment, by the grace of heaven, her life returned to her, and she was once more well and strong. Then she told the King the snare that the wicked witch and her daughter had laid for her.

The King had them both brought to judgment, and sentence was passed upon them. The daughter was sent away into the woods, where she was devoured by the wild beasts, and the witch was burned, and ended miserably. As soon as her body was in ashes the spell was removed from the fawn, and he took human shape again. Then the sister and brother lived happily together until the end.

The Gold Children

A LONG time ago there lived in a little cottage a poor fisherman and his wife, who had very little to live upon but the fish the husband caught. One day as he sat by the water throwing his net he saw a fish drawn out which was quite golden. He examined it with wonder; but what was his surprise to hear it say, "Listen, fisherman! if you will throw me again in the water, I will change your little hut into a splendid castle."

The fisherman replied, "What would be the use of a castle to me when I have nothing to eat?"

"On that account," said the gold fish, "I will take care that there shall be a cupboard in the castle in which, when you unlock it, you will find dishes containing everything to eat that heart can wish."

"If it is so," said the man, "then I am quite willing to do as you please."

"There is, however, one condition," continued the fish; "you must not mention to a living creature in the world, be it who it may, the source of your good fortune. If you utter a single word, it will at once be at an end."

The man, upon this, threw the fish back into the water, and went home. But where his little hut had once stood now rose the walls of a large castle.

He stared with astonishment, and then stepped in and saw his wife dressed in costly clothes, and sitting in a handsomely furnished room. She seemed quite contented, and yet she said, "Husband, how has all this happened? I am so pleased!"

"Yes," said the man, "it pleases me also; but I am so hungry; give me something to eat in our fine house!" "Oh dear!" she replied, "I have nothing, and I don't know where any is to be found here." "There will be no trouble on that account," he replied. "Do you see that great cupboard? Just unlock it."

When the cupboard was opened they saw with surprise that it contained every requisite for a beautiful feast—bread, meat, vegetables, cake, wine, and fruit.

"Dear husband," cried the wife, full of joy, "what more can we desire than this?"

Then they sat down, and ate and drank together in great comfort.

After they had finished the wife said, "Husband, where do all these good things and riches come from?" "Ah!" he replied, "do not ask me; I dare not tell you. If I disclose anything all our good fortune will come to an end."

"Very well," she replied, "if I am not to be told I shall not desire to know"; but this was merely pretense, for she gave her husband no peace night or day, and she tormented and worried the poor man so terribly that she exhausted his patience, and he told her at last.

"This good fortune," he said, "all comes from a wonderful gold fish which I caught, and afterward gave it freedom by throwing it back into the water."

No sooner had he uttered these words than the castle with its wonderful cupboard disappeared, and they were again sitting in the fisherman's hut. The husband was now again obliged to follow his trade and go fishing, and as luck would have it he again caught the golden fish.

"Listen!" cried the fish; "if you will again throw me into the water I will once more give you a castle and a cupboard full of good things; but be firm this time, and reveal to no one from whom it comes, or all will be again lost." "I will keep it to myself," answered the fisherman, and threw the fish into the water.

Everything at home now was in its former splendor, and the fisherman's wife joyful over their good fortune; but her curiosity gave her no peace, and two days had scarcely passed before she began to ask how it all happened, and what was the cause.

Her husband kept silence for a long time, but at last she made him so angry that he incautiously revealed the secret. In a moment the castle and all that it contained vanished, and they were again sitting in their little old hut.

"See what you have done!" he said. "We shall have again to starve with hunger." "Oh, well," she replied, "I would rather not have such riches if I am not to know where they come from; it destroys my peace."

The husband again went fishing, and after a time what should he again pull up in his net but the gold fish for the third time.

"Listen!" cried the fish; "I see I am always to fall into your hands; therefore you must take me to your house, and cut me into two pieces. These you must place in the ground, and you will have gold enough to last your life."

The man took the fish home, and did exactly as he had been told.

It happened after a while that from the pieces of the fish placed in the earth two golden lilies sprang up, which were taken great care of.

Not long after the fisherman's wife had two little children, but they were both golden, as well as the two little foals in the stable. The children grew tall and beautiful, and the lilies and the foals grew also.

One day the children said to their father, "We should like to ride out and see the world on our golden steeds. Will you let us?"

But the parents answered sorrowfully, "How shall we be able to endure the thought that you are far away from us and perhaps ill or in danger?" "Oh," they replied, "the two golden lilies will remain, and by them you can always tell how we are going on. If they are fresh, we are in health; if they fade, we are sick; and when they fall, we shall die!"

So the parents let them go, and they rode away for some time till they came to an inn where a number of people were staying. But when they saw the two gold children they began to laugh and make a mockery of them.

As soon as one of them heard the laughter and mocking words he would not go any further, but turned back and went home to his father. The other, however, rode on till he came to a large forest. As he was about to enter the forest some people came by and said, "You had better not ride there, for the wood is full of robbers who will overcome you and rob you, especially when they see that you and your horse are golden, and you will both be killed."

He would not, however, allow himself to be frightened, but said, "I must and will ride through!"

He took bearskins and threw them over himself and his horse, that the gold might not be seen, and rode confidently into the wood. He had not ridden far when he heard a rustling in the bushes, and voices speaking audibly to each other.

"That is one!" said a voice; but the other said, "No; let him alone —he has nothing on but a bearskin, and is, I dare say, as poor and cold as a church mouse. What do we want with him?"

So the gold child rode through the wood, and no harm happened to him.

One day he came to a town in which he saw a maiden who appeared to him so beautiful that he did not think there could be another so beautiful in the world.

And as his love became stronger for her he went to her and said, "I love you with my whole heart! Will you be my wife?"

The maiden was so pleased that she answered willingly, "Yes, I will be your wife, and be true to you as long as I live."

Very soon after they were married, and just as they were enjoying themselves with the guests on the wedding-day, the bride's father returned home. When he found his daughter already married, he was much astonished, and said, "Where is the bridegroom?" He was pointed out to him, and he still wore the bearskin dress. On seeing him he exclaimed in great anger, "My daughter shall never have a bearskin wearer for a husband!" and wanted to murder him.

But the bride interceded for him as much as she could, and said, "He is already my husband, and I shall always love him with my whole heart." And at last her father was appeased. However, he could not help thinking about it all night, and in the morning, when the bridegroom was dressing, he peeped into his room, and saw a noble-looking golden man, and the bearskin lying on the ground. Then he went back to his own room and said to himself, "How fortunate it is that I restrained my anger last night, or I should have committed a great crime!"

The same morning the gold child told his wife that he had dreamed of being in the hunt and catching a beautiful stag, so that he must on that day go out hunting.

She was very uneasy at the thought, and said, "Pray don't go; a misfortune might so easily happen to you." But he replied, "I will and must go!"

As soon as he was ready he rode out into the wood, and had not been there long before he saw just such a stag as the one in his dream. He raised his gun to shoot it, but the stag sprang away, and he followed it over hedges and ditches the whole day without feeling tired. At last, as night came on, it vanished from his eyes.

The the gold child looked round him and saw close by a small house in which sat an old woman, who was a witch; but he did not know it. He knocked at the door, and she came out and asked him what he wanted so late as that in the middle of the wood.

He said, "Have you seen a stag pass this way?" "Yes," she replied; "I know the stag well."

And while she spoke a little dog that had come out of the house with the old woman began to bark furiously. "Be quiet, will you," he cried, "you spiteful cur, or I will shoot you!"

"What! you will kill my dog?" cried the old witch in a rage. "Ah, I'll soon stop that." And in a moment he lay on the ground turned into stone.

His bride waited for his return in vain, and thought, "Something has certainly happened to him, or else why am I so anxious and troubled in my heart?"

On the same evening the brother, who was at home, was standing by the golden lily, when it suddenly fell drooping on its stem. "Ah me!" he exclaimed; "there has some misfortune happened to my brother; I must go to him. Very likely I shall be able to save him."

Then said his father, "No, no; stay here. If I were to lose both of you, what should I do?" But the youth answered, "I must and will go and find my brother."

Then he mounted his golden horse and rode away quickly to the wood where his brother lay turned to stone.

The old witch saw him in the distance, and came out of her house, and tried to mislead him about his brother, and called to him to come in. But he would not go near her, and raising his gun he cried, "If you do not this moment restore my brother to life, I will shoot you dead!"

She saw he was in earnest, yet she moved unwillingly toward a stone that lay near the door, touched it with her finger, and immediately the gold child stood before his brother in his own form. They were both overjoyed to meet again, and kissed and embraced each other. Then they rode together out of the wood, and there they parted—the one to hasten back to his bride, the other home to his parents.

"Ah," said his father, "we knew that your brother had been

released from his trouble, for the golden lily is again erect and in full bloom."

And after this they lived in happiness and contentment for the rest of their days.

The Twin Brothers

THERE WERE once two brothers; one was rich, the other poor. The rich brother was a goldsmith, and had a wicked heart. The poor brother supported himself by making brooms, and was good and honest. He had two children, twin brothers, who resembled each other as closely as one drop of water resembles another. The two boys went sometimes to the house of their rich uncle to get the pieces that were left from the table, for they were often very hungry.

It happened one day that while their father was in the wood, gathering rushes for his brooms, he saw a bird whose plumage shone like gold—he had never seen in his life any bird like it. He picked up a stone and threw it at the bird, hoping to be lucky enough to secure it; but the stone only knocked off a golden feather, and the bird flew away.

The man took the feather and brought it to his brother, who, when he saw it, exclaimed, "That is real gold!" and gave him a great deal of money for it. Another day, as the man climbed up a beech tree, hoping to find the golden bird's nest, the same bird flew over his head, and on searching further he found a nest, and in it lay two golden eggs. He took the eggs home and showed them to his brother, who said again, "They are real gold," and gave him what they were worth. At last the goldsmith said, "You may as well get me the bird, if you can."

So the poor brother went again to the wood, and after a time, seeing the bird perched on a tree, he knocked it down with a stone and brought it to his brother, who gave him a large heap of money for it. "Now," thought he, "I can support myself for the future," and went home to his house full of joy.

The goldsmith, however, who was clever and cunning, knew well the real value of the bird. So he called his wife, and said,

"Roast the gold bird for me, and be careful that no one comes in, as I wish to eat it quite alone."

The bird was, indeed, not a common bird; it had a wonderful power even when dead. For any person who ate the heart and liver would every morning find under his pillow a piece of gold. The goldsmith's wife prepared the bird, stuck it on the spit, and left it to roast.

Now, it happened that while it was roasting, and the mistress absent from the kitchen about other household work, the two children of the broom-binder came in and stood for a few moments watching the spit as it turned round. Presently two little pieces fell from the bird into the dripping-pan underneath. One of them said, "I think we may have those two little pieces; no one will ever miss them, and I am so hungry." So the children each took a piece and ate it up.

In a few moments the goldsmith's wife came in and saw that they had been eating something, and said, "What have you been eating?" "Only two little pieces that fell from the bird," they replied.

"Oh!" exclaimed the wife in a great fright, "they must have been the heart and liver of the bird!" and then, that her husband might not miss them, for she was afraid of his anger, she quickly killed a chicken, took out the heart and liver, and laid them on the golden bird.

As soon as it was ready she carried it in to the goldsmith, who ate it all up, without leaving her a morsel. The next morning, however, when he felt under his pillow, expecting to find the gold-pieces, nothing was there.

The two children, however, who knew nothing of the good fortune which had befallen them, never thought of searching under their pillow. But the next morning, as they got out of bed, something fell on the ground and tinkled, and when they stooped to pick it up, there were two pieces of gold. They carried them at once to their father, who wondered very much, and said, "What can this mean?"

As, however, there were two more pieces the next morning, and again each day, the father went to his brother and told him of the wonderful circumstances. The goldsmith, as he listened, knew well that these gold-pieces must be the result of the children having eaten the heart and liver of the golden bird, and therefore that he had been deceived. He determined to be revenged, and though hard-hearted and jealous, he managed to conceal the real truth from his brother, and said to him, "Your children are in league with the Evil One; do not touch the gold, and on no account allow your children to remain in your house any longer, for the Evil One has power over them, and could bring ruin upon you through them."

The father feared this power, and therefore, sad as it was to him, he led the twins out into the forest and left them there with a heavy heart.

When they found themselves alone the two children ran here and there in the wood to try and discover the way home, but they wandered back always to the same place. At last they met a hunter, who said to them, "Whose children are you?"

"We are a poor broom-binder's children," they replied, "and our father will not keep us any longer in the house because every morning there is a piece of gold found under our pillows."

"Ah," exclaimed the hunter, "that is not bad! Well, if you are honest, and have told me the truth, I will take you home and be a father to you." In fact, the children pleased the good man, and as he had no children of his own, he gladly took them home with him.

While they were with him he taught them to hunt in the forest, and the gold-pieces which they found every morning under their pillows they gave to him; so for the future he had nothing to fear about poverty.

As soon as the twins were grown up their foster-father took them one day into the wood, and said, "Today you are going to make your first trial at shooting, for I want you to be free if you like, and to be hunters for yourselves."

Then they went with him to a suitable point, and waited a long time, but no game appeared. Presently the hunter saw flying over his head a flock of wild geese, in the form of a triangle, so he said, "Aim quickly at each corner and fire." They did so, and their first proof-shot was successful.

Soon after another flock appeared in the form of a figure 2. "Now," he exclaimed, "shoot again at each corner and bring them down!" This proof-shot was also successful, and the hunter directly said, "Now I pronounce you free; you are quite accomplished sportsmen."

Then the two brothers went away into the wood together, to hold counsel with each other, and at last came to an agreement about what they wished to do.

In the evening, when they sat down to supper, one of them said to their foster-father, "We will not remain to supper, or eat one bit, till you have granted us our request." "And what is your request?" he asked. "You have taught us to hunt, and to earn our living," they replied, "and we want to go out in the world and seek our fortune. Will you give us permission to do so?"

The good old man replied joyfully, "You speak like brave hunters; what you desire is my own wish. Go when you will, you will be sure to succeed." Then they ate and drank together joyfully.

When the appointed day came the hunter presented each of them with a new rifle and a dog, and allowed them to take as much as they would from his store of the gold-pieces. He accompanied them for some distance on the way, and before saying farewell he gave them each a white penknife, and said, "If at any time you should get separated from each other, the knife must be placed crossways in a tree, one side of the blade turning east, the other west, pointing out the road which each should take. If one should die the blade will rust on one side; but as long as he lives it will remain bright."

After saying this he wished the brothers farewell, and they started on their way.

After traveling for some time they came to an immense forest, so large that it was impossible to cross it in one day. They stayed there all night, and ate what they had in their game-bags; but for two days they walked on through the forest without finding themselves any nearer the end.

By this time they had nothing left to eat, so one said to the other, "We must shoot something, for this hunger is not to be endured." So he loaded his gun, and looked about him. Presently an old hare came running by; but as he raised his rifle the hare cried,

> *"Dearest hunters, let me live;*
> *I will to you my young ones give."*

Then she sprang up into the bushes, and brought out two young ones, and laid them before the hunters. The little animals were so full of tricks and played about so prettily that the hunters had not the heart to kill them; they kept them, therefore, alive, and the little animals soon learned to follow them about like dogs.

By and by a fox appeared, and they were about to shoot him, but he cried also,

> *"Dearest hunters, let me live,*
> *And I will you my young ones give."*

Then he brought out two little foxes, but the hunters could not kill them, so they gave them to the hares as companions, and the little creatures followed the hunters wherever they went.

Not long after a wolf stepped before them out of the thicket, and one of the brothers instantly leveled his gun at him, but the wolf cried out,

> *"Dear, kind hunters, let me live;*
> *I will to you my young ones give."*

The hunters took the young wolves and treated them as they had done the other animals, and they followed them also.

Presently a bear came by, and they quite intended to kill him, but he also cried out,

> *"Dear, kind hunters, let me live,*
> *And I will you my young ones give."*

The two young bears were placed with the others, of whom there were already eight.

At last who should come by but a lion, shaking his mane. The hunters were not at all alarmed; they only pointed their guns at him. But the lion cried out in the same manner,

> *"Dear, kind hunters, let me live,*
> *And I will you two young ones give."*

So he fetched two of his cubs, and the hunters placed them with the rest. They had now two lions, two bears, two wolves, two foxes, and two hares, who traveled with them and served them. Yet, after all, their hunger was not appeased.

So one of them said to the fox, "Here, you little sneak, who are so clever and sly, go find us something to eat."

Then the fox answered, "Not far from here lies a town where we have many times fetched away chickens. I will show you the way."

So the fox showed them the way to the village, where they bought some provisions for themselves and food for the animals, and went on further.

The fox, however, knew quite well the best spots in that part of the country, and where to find the hen-houses; and he could, above all, direct the hunters which road to take.

After traveling for a time in this way they could find no suitable place for them all to remain together, so one said to the other, "The only thing for us to do is to separate"; and to this the other agreed. Then they divided the animals so that each had one lion, one bear, one wolf, one fox, and one hare. When the time came to say fare-well they promised to live in brotherly love till death, stuck the knives that their foster-father had given them in a tree, and then one turned to the east, and the other to the west.

The youngest, whose steps we will follow first, soon arrived at a large town, in which the houses were all covered with black crape. He went to an inn, and asked the landlord if he could give shelter to his animals. The landlord pointed out a stable for them, and their master led them in and shut the door.

But in the wall of the stable was a hole, and the hare slipped through easily and fetched a cabbage for herself. The fox followed, and came back with a hen; and as soon as he had eaten it he went for the cock also. The wolf, the bear, and the lion, however, were too large to get through the hole. Then the landlord had a cow killed and brought in for them, or they would have starved.

The hunter was just going out to see if his animals were being cared for when he asked the landlord why the houses were so hung with mourning crape. "Because," he replied, "tomorrow morning our King's daughter will die." "Is she seriously ill, then?" asked the hunter. "No," he answered; "she is in excellent health; still, she must die." "What is the cause of this?" said the young man.

Then the landlord explained. "Outside the town," he said, "is a high mountain in which dwells a dragon, who every year demands a young maiden to be given up to him, otherwise he will destroy the whole country. He has already devoured all the young maidens in the town, and there are none remaining but the King's daughter. Not even for her is any favor shown, and tomorrow she must be delivered up to him."

"Why do you not kill the dragon?" exclaimed the young hunter.

"Ah!" replied the landlord, "many young knights have sought to do so, and lost their lives in the attempt. The King has even promised his daughter in marriage to whoever will destroy the dragon, and also that he shall be heir to his throne."

The hunter made no reply to this; but the next morning he rose early, and taking his animals with him climbed up the dragon's mountain.

There stood near the top a little church, and on the altar inside were three full goblets, bearing this inscription: "Whoever drinks of these goblets will be the strongest man upon earth, and will discover the sword which lies buried before the threshold of this door."

The hunter did not drink; he first went out and sought for the sword in the ground, but he could not find the place. Then he returned and drank up the contents of the goblets. How strong it made him feel! And how quickly he found the sword, which, heavy as it was, he could wield easily!

Meanwhile the hour came when the young maiden was to be given up to the dragon, and she came out accompanied by the King, the marshal, and the courtiers.

They saw from the distance the hunter on the mountain, and the Princess, thinking it was the dragon waiting for her, would not go on. At last she remembered that to save the town from being lost, she must make this painful sacrifice, and therefore wished her father farewell. The King and the court returned home full of great sorrow. The King's marshal, however, was to remain, and see from a distance all that took place.

When the King's daughter reached the top of the mountain, she found, instead of the dragon, a handsome young hunter, who spoke to her comforting words, and, telling her he had come to rescue her, led her into the church, and locked her in.

Before long, with a rushing noise and a roar, the seven-headed dragon made his appearance. As soon as he caught sight of the hunter he wondered to himself, and said at last, "What business have you here on this mountain?" "My business is a combat with you!" replied the hunter.

"Many knights and nobles have tried that, and lost their lives," replied the dragon; "with you I shall make short work!"

And he breathed out fire as he spoke from his seven throats.

The flames set fire to the dry grass, and the hunter would have been stifled with heat and smoke had not his faithful animals run forward and stamped out the fire. Then in a rage the dragon drew near, but the hunter was too quick for him; swinging his sword on high, it whizzed through the air and, falling on the dragon, cut off three of his heads.

Then was the monster furious; he raised himself on his hind legs, spat fiery flames on the hunter, and tried to overthrow him. But the young man again swung his sword, and as the dragon approached, he with one blow cut off three more of his heads. The monster, mad with rage, sank on the ground, still trying to get at the hunter; but the young man, exerting his remaining strength, had no difficulty in cutting off his seventh head, and his tail; and then, finding he could resist no more, he called to his animals to come and tear the dragon in pieces.

As soon as the combat was ended the hunter unlocked the church door, and found the King's daughter lying on the ground;

for during the combat all sense and life had left her, from fear and terror.

He raised her up, and as she came to herself and opened her eyes he showed her the dragon torn in pieces, and told her that she was released from all danger.

Oh, how joyful she felt when she saw and heard what he had done! She said, "Now you will be my dear husband, for my father has himself promised me in marriage to whoever should kill the dragon."

Then she took off her coral necklace of five strings, and divided it among the animals as a reward; the lion's share being in addition the gold clasp. Her pocket handkerchief, which bore her name, she presented to the hunter, who went out, and cut the seven tongues out of the dragon's heads, which he wrapped up carefully in the handkerchief.

After all the fighting, and the fire and smoke, the hunter felt so faint and tired that he said to the maiden, "I think a little rest would do us both good after all the fight and the struggles with the dragon that I have had, and your terror and alarm. Shall we sleep for a little while before I take you home safely to your father's house?" "Yes," she replied, "I can sleep peacefully now."

So she laid herself down, and as soon as she slept he said to the lion, "You must lie near and watch that no one comes to harm us." Then he threw himself on the ground, quite worn out, and was soon fast asleep.

The lion laid himself down at a little distance to watch; but he was also tired and overcome with the combat, so he called to the bear, and said, "Lie down near me; I must have a little rest, and if any one comes, wake me up."

Then the bear lay down; but he was also very tired, so he cried to the wolf, "Just lie down by me; I must have a little sleep, and if anything happens, wake me up."

The wolf complied; but as he was also tired, he called to the fox, and said, "Lie down near me; I must have a little sleep, and if anything comes, wake me up."

Then the fox came and laid himself down by the wolf; but he too was tired, and called out to the hare, "Lie down near me; I must sleep a little, and, whatever comes, wake me up."

The hare seated herself near the fox; but the poor little hare was very tired, and although she had no one to ask to watch and call her, she also went fast asleep. And now the King's daughter, the hunter, the bear, the lion, the wolf, the fox, and the hare were all in a deep sleep, while danger was at hand.

The marshal, from the distance, had tried to see what was going on, and being surprised that the dragon had not yet flown away with the King's daughter, and that all was quiet on the mountain, took courage, and ventured to climb up to the top. There he saw the mangled and headless body of the dragon, and at a little distance the King's daughter, the hunter, and all the animals sunk in a deep sleep. He knew in a moment that the stranger hunter had killed the dragon, and being wicked and envious, he drew his sword and cut off the hunter's head. Then he seized the sleeping maiden by the arm, and carried her away from the mountain.

She woke and screamed; but the marshal said, "You are in my power, and therefore you shall say that I have killed the dragon!" "I cannot say so," she replied, "for I saw the hunter kill him, and the animals tear him in pieces."

Then he drew his sword, and threatened to kill her if she did not obey him; so that to save her life she was forced to promise to say all he wished.

Thereupon he took her to the King, who knew not how to contain himself for joy at finding his dear child still alive, and that she had been saved from the monster's power.

Then the marshal said, "I have killed the dragon and freed the King's daughter, therefore I demand her for my wife, according to the King's promise."

"Is this all true?" asked the King of his daughter.

"Ah, yes," she replied, "I suppose it is true; but I shall refuse to allow the marriage to take place for one year and a day. For," thought she, "in that time I may hear something of my dear hunter."

All this while on the dragon's mountain the animals lay sleeping near their dead master. At last a large bumble-bee settled on the hare's nose, but she only whisked it off with her paw, and slept again. The bee came a second time, but the hare again shook him off, and slept as soundly as before. Then came the bumble-bee a third time, and stung the hare in the nose; thereupon she woke. As soon as she was quite aroused she woke the fox; the fox, the wolf; the wolf, the bear; and the bear, the lion.

But when the lion roused himself, and saw that the maiden was gone and his master dead, he gave a terrible roar, and cried, "Whose doing is this?" Bear, why did you not wake me?" Then said the bear to the wolf, "Wolf, why did you not wake me?" "Fox," cried the wolf, "why did you not wake me?" "Hare," said the fox, "and why did you not wake me?"

The poor hare had no one to ask why he did not wake her, and she knew she must bear all the blame. Indeed, they were all ready to tear her to pieces, but she cried, "Don't destroy my life! I will restore our master. I know a mountain on which grows a root that will cure every wound and every disease if it is placed in the person's mouth; but the mountain on which it grows lies two hundred miles from here."

"Then," said the lion, "we will give you twenty-four hours, but not longer, to find this root and bring it to us."

Away sprang the hare very fast, and in twenty-four hours she returned with the root. As soon as they saw her the lion quickly placed the head of the hunter on the neck; and the hare, when she had joined the wounded parts together, put the root into the mouth, and in a few moments the heart began to beat, and life came back to the hunter.

On awaking he was terribly alarmed to find that the maiden had disappeared. "She must have gone away while I slept," he said, "and is lost to me forever!"

These sad thoughts so occupied him that he did not notice anything wrong about his head, but in truth the lion had placed it on in such a hurry that the face was turned the wrong way. He first noticed it when they brought him something to eat, and then he found that his face looked backward. He was so astonished that he could not imagine what had happened, and asked his animals the cause. Then the lion confessed that they had all slept in consequence of being so tired, and that when they at last awoke they found the Princess gone, and himself lying dead, with his head cut off. The lion told him also that the hare had fetched the healing root, but in their haste they had placed the head on the wrong way. This mistake, they said, could be easily rectified. So they took the hunter's head off again, turned it round, placed it on properly, and the hare stuck the parts together with the wonderful root. After this the hunter went away again to travel about the world, feeling very sorrowful, and he left his animals to be taken care of by the people of the town.

It so happened that at the end of a year he came back again to the same town where he had freed the King's daughter and killed the dragon. This time, instead of black crape the houses were hung with scarlet cloth. "What does it mean?" he said to the landlord.

"Last year when I came your houses were all hung with black crape, and now it is scarlet cloth."

"Oh," replied the landlord, "last year we were expecting our King's daughter to be given up to the dragon, but the marshal fought with him and killed him, and tomorrow his marriage with the King's daughter will take place; that is the cause of our town being so gay and bright—it is joy now instead of sorrow."

The next day, when the marriage was to be celebrated, the hunter said, "Landlord, do you believe that I shall eat bread from the King's table here with any one who will join me?"

"I will lay a hundred gold-pieces," replied the landlord, "that you will do nothing of the kind."

The hunter took the bet, and taking out his purse placed the gold-pieces aside for payment if he should lose.

Then he called the hare, and said to her, "Go quickly to the castle, dear Springer, and bring me some of the bread which the King eats."

Now, the hare was such an insignificant little thing that no one ever thought of ordering a conveyance for her, so she was obliged to go on foot. "Oh," thought she, "when I am running through the streets, suppose the cruel hound should see me." Just as she got near the castle she looked behind her, and there truly was a hound ready to seize her. But she gave a start forward, and before the sentinel was aware rushed into the sentry-box. The dog followed, and wanted to bring her out, but the soldier stood in the doorway and would not let him pass, and when the dog tried to get in he struck him with his staff, and sent him away howling.

As soon as the hare saw that the coast was clear she rushed out of the sentry-box and ran to the castle, and finding the door of the room where the Princess was sitting open, she darted in and hid under her chair. Presently the Princess felt something scratching her foot, and thinking it was the dog, she said, "Be quiet, Sultan; go away!" The hare scratched again at her foot, but she still thought it was the dog, and cried, "Will you go away, Sultan?" But the hare did not allow herself to be sent away, so she scratched the foot a third time. Then the Princess looked down and recognized the hare by her necklace. She took the creature at once in her arms, carried her to her own room, and said, "Dear little hare, what do you want?"

The hare replied instantly, "My master, who killed the dragon, is here and he has sent to ask for some bread that the King eats."

Then was the King's daughter full of joy; she sent for the cook, and ordered him to bring her some of the bread which was made for the King. When he brought it the hare cried, "The cook must go with me, or that cruel hound may do me some harm." So the cook carried the bread, and went with the hare to the door of the inn.

As soon as he was gone she stood on her hind legs, took the bread in her fore-paws, and brought it to her master.

"There!" cried the hunter; "here is the bread, landlord, and the hundred gold-pieces are mine."

The landlord was much surprised, but when the hunter declared he would also have some of the roast meat from the King's table, he said: "The bread may be here, but I'll warrant you will get nothing more."

The hunter called the fox, and said to him, "My fox, go and fetch me some of the roast meat such as the King eats."

The red fox knew a better trick than the hare: he went across the fields, and slipped in without being seen by the hound. Then he placed himself under the chair of the King's daughter, and touched her foot. She looked down immediately, and recognizing him by his necklace, took him into her room. "What do you want, dear fox?" she asked.

"My master, who killed the dragon is here," he replied, "and has sent me to ask for some of the roast meat that is cooked for the King."

The cook was sent for again, and the Princess desired him to carry some meat for the fox to the door of the inn. On arriving, the fox took the dish from the cook, and after whisking away the flies that had settled on it, with his tail, brought it to his master.

"See landlord," cried the hunter, "here are bread and meat such as the King eats, and now I will have vegetables." So he called the wolf, and said, "Dear wolf, go and fetch me vegetables such as the King eats."

Away went the wolf straight to the castle, for he had no fear of anything, and as soon as he entered the room he went behind the Princess and pulled her dress, so that she was obliged to look round. She recognized the wolf immediately by the necklace, took him into her chamber, and said, "Dear wolf, what do you want?" He replied, "My master, who killed the dragon, is here, and has sent me to ask for some vegetables such as the King eats. "

The cook was sent for again, and told to take some vegetables also to the inn door; and as soon as they arrived the wolf took the dish from him and carried it to his master.

"Look here, landlord," cried the hunter, "I have now bread, meat, and vegetables; but I will also have some sweetmeats from the King's table." He called the bear, and said, "Dear bear, I know you are fond of sweets. Now go and fetch me some sweetmeats such as the King eats."

The bear trotted off to the castle, and every one ran away when they saw him coming. But when he reached the castle gates, the sentinel held his gun before him and would not let him pass in. But the bear rose on his hind legs, boxed his ears right and left with his fore-paws, and leaving him tumbled all of a heap in his sentry-box, went into the castle. Seeing the King's daughter entering he followed her and gave a slight growl. She looked behind her and, recognizing the bear, called him into her chamber, and said, "Dear bear, what do you want?"

"My master, who killed the dragon, is here," he replied, "and he has sent me to ask for some sweetmeats like those which the King eats."

The Princess sent for the confectioner, and desired him to bake some sweetmeats and take them with the bear to the door of the inn. As soon as they arrived the bear first licked up the sugar drips which had dropped on his fur, then stood upright, took the dish, and carried it to his master.

"See now, landlord," cried the hunter, "I have bread, and meat, and vegetables, and sweetmeats, and I mean to have wine also, such as the King drinks." So he called the lion to him, and said, "Dear lion, you drink till you are quite tipsy sometimes. Now go and fetch me some wine such as the King drinks."

As the lion trotted through the streets all the people ran away from him. The sentinel, when he saw him coming, tried to stop the way; but the lion gave a little roar, and made him run for his life. Then the lion entered the castle, passed through the King's apartment, and knocked at the door of the Princess's room with his tail. The Princess, when she opened it and saw the lion, was at first rather frightened; but presently she observed on his neck the gold necklace clasp, and knew it was the hunter's lion. She called him into her chamber, and said, "Dear lion, what do you want?"

"My master, who killed the dragon," he replied, "is here, and he has sent me to ask for some wine, such as the King drinks."

Then she sent for the King's cup-bearer, and told him to give the lion some of the King's wine.

"I will go with him," said the lion, "and see that he draws the right sort." So the lion went with the cup-bearer to the wine-cellar, and when he saw him about to draw some of the ordinary wine which the King's vassals drank, the lion cried, "Stop! I will taste the wine first." So he drew himself a pint, and swallowed it down at a gulp. "No," he said, "that is not the right sort."

The cup-bearer saw he was found out; however, he went over to another cask that was kept for the King's marshal. "Stop!" cried the lion again, "I will taste the wine first." So he drew another pint and drank it off. "Ah!" he said, "that is better, but still not the right wine."

Then the cup-bearer was angry, and said, "What can a stupid beast like you understand about wine?"

But the lion, with a lash of his tail, knocked him down, and before the man could move himself found his way stealthily into a little private cellar, in which were casks of wine never tasted by any but the King. The lion drew half a pint, and when he had tasted it, he said to himself, "That is wine of the right sort. " So he called the cup-bearer and made him draw six flagons full.

As they came up from the cellar into the open air the lion's head swam a little, and he was almost tipsy; but as the cup-bearer was obliged to carry the wine for him to the door of the inn, it did not much matter. When they arrived, the lion took the handle of the basket in his mouth, and carried the wine to his master.

"Now, Master landlord," said the hunter, "I have bread, meat, vegetables, sweetmeats, and wine, such as the King has, so I will sit down and with my faithful animals enjoy a good meal"; and, in-deed, he felt very happy, for he knew now that the King's daughter still loved him.

After they had finished, the hunter said to the landlord, "Now that I have eaten and drunk of the same provisions as the King, I will go to the King's castle and marry his daughter."

"Well," said the landlord, "how that is to be managed I cannot tell, when she has already a bridegroom to whom she will today be married."

The hunter, without a word, took out the pocket handkerchief which the King's daughter had given him on the dragon's moun-tain, and opening it, showed the landlord the seven tongues of the monster, which he had cut out and wrapped in the handkerchief. "That which I have so carefully preserved will help me," said the hunter.

The landlord looked at the handkerchief and said, "I may be-lieve all the rest, but I would bet my house and farm-yard that you will never marry the King's daughter."

"Very well," said the hunter, "I accept your bet, and if I lose, there are my hundred gold-pieces"; and he laid them on the table.

That same day, when the King and his daughter were seated at table, the King said, "What did all those wild animals want who came to you today, going in and out of my castle?" "I cannot tell you yet," she replied; "but if you will send into the town for the master of these animals, then I will do so."

The King sent, on hearing this, a servant at once to the inn with an invitation to the stranger who owned the animals, and the servant arrived just as the hunter had finished his bet with the landlord.

"See, landlord!" he cried, "the King has sent me an invitation by his servant; but I cannot accept it yet." He turned to the man who waited, and said, "Tell my lord the King that I cannot obey his commands to visit him unless he sends me suitable clothes for a royal palace, and a carriage with six horses, and servants to wait upon me."

The servant returned with the message, and when the King heard it he said to his daughter, "What shall I do?"

"I would send for him as he requests," she replied.

So they sent royal robes, and a carriage and six horses with servants, and when the hunter saw them coming he said to the landlord, "See! they have sent for me as I wished."

He dressed himself in the kingly clothes, took the handkerchief containing the dragon's tongues, and drove away to the castle.

As soon as he arrived the King said to his daughter, "How shall I receive him?" "I should go and meet him," she replied.

So the King went to meet him, and led him into the royal apartment, and all his animals followed. The King pointed him to a seat by his daughter. The marshal sat on her other side as bridegroom, but the visitor knew it not.

Just at this moment the dragon's seven heads were brought into the room to show to the company, and the King said: "These heads belonged to the dragon who was for so many years the terror of this town. The marshal slew the dragon, and saved my daughter's life; therefore I have given her to him in marriage, according to my promise."

At this the hunter rose, and advancing, opened the seven throats of the dragon, and said, "Where are the tongues?"

The marshal turned white with fear, and knew not what to do. At last he said in his terror, "Dragons have no tongues."

"Liars get nothing for their pains," said the hunter; "the dragon's tongues shall prove who was his conqueror!"

He unfolded the handkerchief as he spoke. There lay the seven tongues. He took them up and placed each in the mouth of the dragon's head to which it belonged, and it fitted exactly. Then he took up the pocket handkerchief which was marked with the name of the King's daughter, showed it to the maiden, and asked her if she had not given it to him. "Yes," she replied; "I gave it to you on the day you killed the dragon."

He called his animals to him, took from each the necklace, and from the lion the one with the golden clasp, and asked to whom they belonged.

"They are mine," she replied; "they are a part of my coral necklace which had five strings of beads, which I divided among the animals because they aided you in killing the dragon, and afterward tore him in pieces. I cannot tell how the marshal could have carried me away from you," she continued, "for you told me to lie down and sleep after the fatigue and fright I had endured."

"I slept myself," he replied, "for I was quite worn out with my combat, and as I lay sleeping the marshal came and cut off my head."

"I began to understand now," said the King; "the marshal carried away my daughter, supposing you were dead, and made us believe that he had killed the dragon, till you arrived with the tongues, the handkerchief, and the necklace. But what restored you to life?" asked the King.

Then the hunter related how one of his animals had healed him and restored him to life through the application of a wonderful root, and how he had been wandering about for a whole year, and had only returned to the town that very day, and heard from the landlord of the marshal's deceit.

Then said the King to his daughter, "Is it true that this man killed the dragon?"

"Yes," she answered, "quite true, and I can venture now to expose the wickedness of the marshal; for he carried me away that day against my wish, and forced me with threats to keep silent. I did not know he had tried to kill the real slayer of the dragon, but I hoped he would come back, and on that account I begged to have the marriage put off for a year and a day."

The King, after this, ordered twelve judges to be summoned to try the marshal, and the sentence passed upon him was that he should be torn to pieces by wild oxen. As soon as the marshal was punished the King gave his daughter to the hunter, and appointed him to the high position of stadtholder over the whole kingdom.

The marriage caused great joy, and the hunter, who was now a Prince, sent for his father and foster-father, and overloaded them with treasures.

Neither did he forget the landlord, but sent for him to come to the castle, and said, "See, landlord, I have married the King's daughter, and your house and farm-yard belong to me." "That is quite true," replied the landlord.

"Ah," said the Prince, "but I do not mean to keep them; they are still yours, and I make you a present of the hundred gold-pieces also."

For a time the young Prince and his wife lived most happily together. He still, however, went out hunting, which was his great delight, and his faithful animals remained with him. They lived, however, in a wood close by, from which he could call them at any time; yet the wood was not safe, for he once went in and did not get out again very easily.

Whenever the Prince had a wish to go hunting, he gave the King no rest till he allowed him to do so. On one occasion, while riding with a large number of attendants in the wood, he saw at a distance a snow-white deer, and he said to his people, "Stay here till I come back; I must have that beautiful creature, and so many will frighten her."

Then he rode away through the wood, and only his animals followed him. The attendants drew rein, and waited till evening, but as he did not come they rode home and told the young Princess that her husband had gone into an enchanted forest to hunt a white deer, and had not returned.

This made her very anxious, more especially when the morrow came and he did not return; indeed, he could not, for he kept riding after the beautiful wild animal, but without being able to overtake it. At times, when he fancied she was within reach of his gun, the next moment she was leaping away at a great distance, and at last she vanished altogether.

Not till then did he notice how far he had penetrated into the forest. He raised his horn and blew, but there was no answer, for his attendants could not hear it; and then as night came on he saw plainly that he should not be able to find his way home till the next day, so he alighted from his horse, lit a fire by a tree, and determined to make himself as comfortable as he could for the night.

As he sat under the tree by the fire, with his animals lying near him, he heard, as he thought, a human voice. He looked round, but could see nothing. Presently there was a groan over his head; he looked up and saw an old woman sitting on a branch, who kept grumbling, "Oh, oh, how cold I am! I am freezing!" "If you are cold, come down and warm yourself," he said. "No, no," she replied; "your animals will bite me." "Indeed they will do no such thing. Come down, old mother," he said kindly; "none of them shall hurt you."

He did not know that she was a wicked witch, so when she said, "I will throw you down a little switch from the tree, and if you just touch them on the back with it they cannot hurt me," he did as she told him, and as soon as they were touched by the wand the animals were all turned to stone. Then she jumped down, and touching the Prince on the back with the switch, he also was instantly turned into stone. Thereupon she laughed maliciously, and dragged him and his animals into a grave where several similar stones lay.

When the Princess found that her husband did not return, her anxiety and care increased painfully, and she became at last very unhappy.

Now, it so happened that just at this time the twin brother of the Prince, who since their separation had been wandering in the East, arrived in the country of which his brother's father-in-law was King. He had tried to obtain a situation, but could not succeed, and only his animals were left to him.

One day, as he was wandering from one place to another, it occurred to his mind that he might as well go and look at the knife which they had stuck in the trunk of a tree at the time of their separation. When he came to it there was his brother's side of the knife half-rusted, and the other half still bright.

In great alarm he thought, "My brother must have fallen into some terrible trouble. I will go and find him. I may be able to rescue him, as the half of the knife is still bright."

He set out with his animals on a journey, and while traveling west came to the town in which his brother's wife, the King's daughter, lived. As soon as he reached the gate of the town the watchman advanced toward him and asked if he should go and announce his arrival to the Princess, who had for two days been in great trouble about him, fearing that he had been detained in the forest by enchantment.

The watchman had not the least idea that the young man was any other than the Prince himself, especially as he had the wild animals running behind him. The twin brother saw this, and he said to himself, "Perhaps it will be best for me to allow myself to be taken for my brother; I shall be able more easily to save him." So he followed the sentinel to the castle, where he was received with great joy.

The young Princess had no idea that this was not her husband, and asked him why he had remained away so long.

He replied, "I rode a long distance into the wood, and could not find my way out again." At night he was taken to the royal bed, but he laid a two-edged sword between him and the young Princess; she did not know what that could mean, but did not venture to ask.

In a few days he discovered all about his brother that he wished to know, and was determined to go and seek for him in the enchanted wood. So he said, "I must go to the hunt just once more."

The King and the young Princess said all they could to dissuade him, but to no purpose, and at length he left the castle with a large company of attendants.

When he reached the wood all happened as it had done with his brother. He saw the beautiful white deer, and told his attendants to wait while he went after it, followed only by his animals; but neither could he overtake it; and the white deer led him far down into the forest, where he found he must remain all night.

After he had lighted a fire he heard, as his brother had done, the old woman in the tree, crying out that she was freezing with cold, and he said to her, "If you are cold, old mother, come down and warm yourself!" "No," she cried, "your animals will bite me!" "No, indeed they will not," he said. "I can't trust them!" she cried; "here, I will throw you a little switch, and if you gently strike them across the back, then they will not be able to hurt me."

When the hunter heard that he began to mistrust the old woman, and said, "No; I will not strike my animals; you come down, or I will fetch you." "Do as you like," she said; "you can't hurt me." "If you don't come down," he replied, "I will shoot you." "Shoot away," she said; "your bullet can do me no harm."

He pointed his gun and shot at her; but the witch was proof against a leaden bullet. She gave a shrill laugh, and cried, "It is no use trying to hit me."

The hunter knew, however, what to do; he cut off three silver buttons from his coat, and loaded his gun with them. Against these she knew all her arts were vain; so as he drew the trigger she fell suddenly to the ground with a scream. Then he placed his foot upon her, and said, "Old witch, if you do not at once confess where my brother is, I will take you up and throw you into the fire."

She was in a great fright, begged for pardon, and said, "He is lying with his animals, turned to stone, in a grave."

Then he forced her to go with him, and said, "You old cat, if you don't instantly restore my brother to life, and all the creatures that are with him, over you go into the fire."

She was obliged to take a switch and strike the stones, and immediately the brother, his animals, and many others—traders, mechanics, and shepherds—stood before him, alive and in their own forms.

Thankful for having gained their freedom and their lives, they all hastened home; but the twin brothers, when they saw each other again, were full of joy, and embraced and kissed each other with great affection. They seized the old witch, bound her, and placed her on the fire, and as soon as she was burned the forest became suddenly clear and light, and the King's castle appeared at a very little distance.

After this the twin brothers walked away together toward the castle, and on the road related to each other the events that had happened to them since they parted. At last the youngest told his brother of his marriage to the King's daughter, and that the King had made him lord over the whole land.

"I know all about it," replied the other; "for when I came to the town, they all took me for you and treated me with kingly state; even the young Princess mistook me for her husband, and made me sit by her side."

But as he spoke his brother became so fierce with jealousy and anger that he drew his sword and cut off his brother's head. Then as he saw him lie dead at his feet his anger was quelled in a moment, and he repented bitterly, crying, "Oh, my brother is dead, and it is I who have killed him!" and kneeling by his side he mourned with loud cries and tears.

In a moment the hare appeared and begged to be allowed to fetch the life-giving root, which she knew would cure him. She was not away long, and when she returned, the head was replaced and fastened with the healing power of the plant, and the brother restored to life, while not even a sign of the wound remained to be noticed.

The brothers now walked on most lovingly together, and the one who had married the King's daughter said, "I see that you have kingly clothes, as I have; your animals are the same as mine. Let us enter the castle at two opposite doors, and approach the old King from two sides together."

So they separated; and as the King sat with his daughter in the royal apartment a sentinel approached him from two distant entrances at the same time, and informed him that the Prince, with his animals, had arrived. "That is impossible!" cried the King; "one of you must be wrong; for the gates at which you watch are quite a quarter of a mile apart."

But while the King spoke the two young men entered at opposite ends of the room, and both came forward and stood before the King.

With a bewildered look the King turned to his daughter, and said, "Which is your husband? For they are both so exactly alike I cannot tell."

She was herself very much frightened, and could not speak; at last she thought of the necklace that she had given to the animals, and looking earnestly among them she saw the glitter of the golden clasp on the lion's neck. "See," she cried in a happy voice, "he whom that lion follows is my husband!"

The Prince laughed, and said, "Yes; you are right; and this is my twin brother."

So they sat down happily together and told the King and the young Princess all their adventures.

When the King's daughter and her husband were alone she said to him, "Why have you for the last several nights always laid a two-edged sword in our bed? I thought you had a wish to kill me."

Then the Prince knew how true and honorable his twin brother had been.

Ferdinand the Faithful and Ferdinand the Unfaithful

ONCE UPON a time there lived a man and a woman who, so long as they were rich, had no children; but when they were poor they had a little boy. They could, however, find no godfather for him, so the man said he would just go to another place to see if he could get one there. As he went, a poor man met him, who asked him where he was going. He said he was going to see if he could get a godfather; that he was poor, so no one would stand as godfather for him.

"Oh," said the poor man, "thou art poor, and I am poor; I will be godfather for thee, but I am so ill-off I can give the child nothing. Go home and tell the nurse that she is to come to the church with the child."

When they all got to the church together, the beggar was already there, and he gave the child the name of Ferdinand the Faithful.

When he was going out of the church, the beggar said, "Now go home, I can give thee nothing, and thou likewise ought to give me nothing." But he gave a key to the nurse, and told her when she got home she was to give it to the father, who was to take care of it until the child was fourteen years old, and then he was to go on the heath where there was a castle, which the key would fit, and that all which was therein should belong to him.

Now when the child was seven years old and had grown very big, he once went to play with some other boys, and each of them boasted that he had got more from his godfather than the other; but the child could say nothing, and was vexed, and went home and said to his father, "Did I get nothing at all, then, from my godfather?" "Oh, yes," said the father, "thou hadst a key—if there is a castle standing on the heath, just go to it and open it." Then the boy went thither, but no castle was to be seen, or heard of.

After seven years more, when he was fourteen years old, he again went thither, and there stood the castle. When he had opened it, there was nothing within but a horse—a white one. Then the boy was so full of joy because he had a horse, that he mounted on it and galloped back to his father. "Now I have a white horse, and I will travel," said he. So he set out, and as he was on his way, a pen was lying on the road. At first he thought he would pick it up, but then again he thought to himself, "Thou shouldst leave it lying there; thou wilt easily find a pen where thou art going, if thou hast need of one." As he was thus riding away, a voice called after him, "Ferdinand the Faithful, take it with thee." He looked around, but saw no one; then he went back again and picked it up.

When he had ridden a little way farther, he passed by a lake, and a fish was lying on the bank, gasping and panting for breath, so he said, "Wait, my dear fish, I will help thee to get into the water," and he took hold of it by the tail, and threw it into the lake. Then the fish put its head out of the water and said, "As thou hast helped me out of the mud, I will give thee a flute; when thou art in any need, play on it, and then I will help thee, and if ever thou lettest anything fall in the water, just play and I will reach it out to thee."

Then he rode away, and there came to him a man who asked him where he was going. "Oh, to the next place." Then the man asked what his name was. "Ferdinand the Faithful." "So! then we have almost the same name, I am called Ferdinand the Unfaithful." And they both set out to the inn in the nearest place.

Now it was unfortunate that Ferdinand the Unfaithful knew everything that the other had ever thought and everything he was about to do; he knew it by means of all kinds of wicked arts.

There was, however, in the inn an honest girl, who had a bright face and behaved very prettily. She fell in love with Ferdinand the Faithful because he was a handsome man, and she asked him whither he was going. "Oh, I am just traveling round about," said he. Then she said he ought to stay there, for the King of that country wanted an attendant or an outrider, and he ought to enter his service. He answered he could not very well go to any one like that and offer himself. Then said the maiden, "Oh, but I will soon do that for thee." And so she went straight to the King, and told him that she knew of an excellent servant for him. He was well pleased with that, and had Ferdinand the Faithful brought to him, and wanted to make him his servant. He, however, liked better to be an outrider, for where his horse was, there he also wanted to be, so the King made him an outrider. When Ferdinand the Unfaithful learnt that, he said to the girl, "What! Dost thou help him and not me?" "Oh," said the girl, "I will help thee too." She thought, "I must keep friends with that man, for he is not to be trusted." She went to the King, and offered him as a servant, and the King was willing.

Now when the King met his lords in the morning, he always lamented and said, "Oh, if I had but my love with me." Ferdinand the Unfaithful was, however, always hostile to Ferdinand the Faithful. So once, when the King was complaining thus, he said, "Thou hast the outrider, send him away to get her, and if he does not do it, his head must be struck off." Then the King sent for Ferdinand the Faithful, and told him that there was, in this place or in that place, a girl he loved, and that he was to bring her to him, and if he did not do it he should die.

Ferdinand the Faithful went into the stable to his white horse, and complained and lamented, "Oh, what an unhappy man I am!" Then some one behind him cried, "Ferdinand the Faithful, why weepest thou?" He looked round but saw no one, and went on lamenting; "Oh, my dear little white horse, now must I leave thee; now must I die." Then some one cried once more, "Ferdinand the Faithful, why weepest thou?" Then for the first time he was aware that it was his little white horse who was putting that question. "Dost thou speak, my little white horse; canst thou do that?" And again, he said, "I am to go to this place and to that, and am to bring the bride; canst thou tell me how I am to set about it?" Then answered the little white horse, "Go thou to the King, and say if he will give thee what thou must have, thou wilt get her for him. If he will give thee a ship full of meat, and a ship full of bread, it will succeed. Great giants dwell on the lake, and if thou takest no meat with thee for them, they will tear thee to pieces, and there are the large birds which would pick the eyes out of thy head if thou hadst no bread for them."

Then the King made all the butchers in the land kill, and all the bakers bake, that the ships might be filled. When they were full, the little white horse said to Ferdinand the Faithful, "Now mount me, and go with me into the ship and then when the giants come, say,

> 'Peace, peace, my dear little giants,
> I have had thought of ye,
> Something I have brought for ye.'

"When the birds come, thou shalt again say,

> 'Peace, peace, my dear little birds,
> I have had thought of ye,
> Something I have brought for ye.'

"They will do nothing to thee, and when thou comest to the castle, the giants will help thee. Then go up to the castle, and take a couple of giants with thee. There the Princess lies sleeping; thou must, however, not awaken her, but the giants must lift her up, and carry her in her bed to the ship." And now everything took place as the little white horse had said, and Ferdinand the Faithful gave the giants and the birds what he had brought with him for them, and that made the giants willing, and they carried the Princess in her bed to the King. And when she came to the King, she said she could not live, she must have her writings, they had been left in her castle. Then by the instigation of Ferdinand the Unfaithful, Ferdinand the Faithful was called, and the King told him he must fetch the writings from the castle, or he should die.

Then he went once more into the stable, and bemoaned himself and said, "Oh, my dear little white horse, now I am to go away again, how am I to do it?" Then the little white horse said he was just to load the ships full again. So it happened again as it had happened before, and the giants and the birds were satisfied, and made gentle by the meat. When they came to the castle, the white horse told Ferdinand the Faithful that he must go in, and that on the table in the Princess's bed-room lay the writings. And Ferdinand the Faithful went in, and fetched them. When they were on the lake, he let his pen fall into the water. Then said the white horse, "Now I cannot help thee at all." But he remembered his flute, and began to play on it, and the fish came with the pen in its mouth, and gave it to him. So he took the writings to the castle, where the wedding was celebrated.

The Queen, however, did not love the King because he had no nose, but she would have much liked to love Ferdinand the Faithful. Once, therefore, when all the lords of the court were together, the Queen said she could do feats of magic, that she could cut off any one's head and put it on again, and that one of them ought just to try it. But none of them would be the first, so Ferdinand the Faithful, again at the instigation of Ferdinand the Unfaithful, undertook it and she hewed off his head, and put it on again for him, and it healed together directly, so that it looked as if he had a red thread round his throat.

Then the King said to her, "My child, and where hast thou learnt that?" "Yes," she said, "I understand the art; shall I just try it on thee also?" "Oh, yes," said he. But she cut off his head, and did not put it on again; but pretended that she could not get it on, and that it would not keep fixed. Then the King was buried, but she married Ferdinand the Faithful.

He, however, always rode on his white horse, and once when he was seated on it, it told him that he was to go on to the heath which he knew, and gallop three times round it. And when he had done that, the white horse stood up on its hind legs, and was changed into a King's son.

The Three Black Princesses

EAST INDIA was besieged by an enemy who would not retire until he had received six hundred dollars. Then the townsfolk caused it to be proclaimed by beat of drum that whosoever was able to procure the money should be burgomaster. Now there was a poor fisherman who fished on the lake with his son, and the enemy came and took the son prisoner, and gave the father six hundred dollars for him. So the father went and gave them to the great men of the town, and the enemy departed, and the fisherman became burgomaster. Then it was proclaimed that whosoever did not say, "Mr. Burgomaster," should be put to death on the gallows.

The son got away again from the enemy, and came to a great forest on a high mountain. The mountain opened, and he went into a great enchanted castle, wherein chairs, tables, and benches were all hung with black. Then came three young Princesses who were entirely dressed in black, but had a little white on their faces; they told him he was not to be afraid, they would not hurt him, and that he could deliver them. He said he would gladly do that, if he did but know how. On this, they told him he must for a whole year not speak to them and also not look at them, and what he wanted to have he was just to ask for, and if they dared give him an answer they would do so. When he had been there for a long while he said he should like to go to his father, and they told him he might go. He was to take with him this purse with money, put on this coat, and in a week he must be back there again.

Then he was caught up, and was instantly in East India. He could no longer find his father in the fisherman's hut, and asked the people where the poor fisherman could be, and they told him he must not say that, or he would come to the gallows. Then he went to his father and said, "Fisherman, how hast thou got here?" Then the father said, "Thou must not say that, if the great men of the town knew of that, thou wouldst come to the gallows." He, however, would not stop, and was brought to the gallows.

When he was there, he said, "O, my master, just give me leave to go to the old fisherman's hut." Then he put on his old smock-frock, and came back to the great men, and said, "Do ye not now see? Am I not the son of the poor fisherman? Did I not earn bread for my father and mother in this dress?" Hereupon his father knew him again, and begged his pardon, and took him home with him, and then he related all that had happened to him, and how he had got into a forest on a high mountain, and the mountain had opened and he had gone into an enchanted castle, where all was black, and three young Princesses had come to him who were black except a little white on their faces. And they had told him not to fear, and that he could deliver them. Then his mother said that might very likely not be a good thing to do, and that he ought to take a holy-water vessel with him, and drop some boiling water on their faces.

He went back again, and he was in great fear, and he dropped the water on their faces as they were sleeping, and they all turned half-white. Then all the three Princesses sprang up, and said, "Thou accursed dog, our blood shall cry for vengeance on thee! Now there is no man born in the world, nor will any ever be born who can set us free! We have still three brothers who are bound by seven chains—they shall tear thee to pieces." Then there was a loud shrieking all over the castle, and he sprang out of the window, and broke his leg, and the castle sank into the earth again, the mountain shut to again, and no one knew where the castle had stood.

Snow-White and the Seven Dwarfs

IT WAS the middle of winter, and the snow-flakes were falling like feathers from the sky, and a Queen sat at her window working, and her embroidery-frame was of ebony. And as she worked, gazing at times out on the snow, she pricked her finger, and there fell from it three drops of blood on the snow. And when she saw how bright and red it looked, she said to herself, "Oh that I had a child as white as snow, as red as blood, and as black as the wood of the embroidery frame!"

Not very long after she had a daughter, with a skin as white as snow, lips as red as blood, and hair as black as ebony, and she was named Snow-white. And when she was born the Queen died.

After a year had gone by the King took another wife, a beautiful woman, but proud and overbearing, and she could not bear to be surpassed in beauty by any one. She had a magic looking-glass, and she used to stand before it, and look in it, and say,

> *"Looking-glass upon the wall,*
> *Who is fairest of us all?"*

And the looking-glass would answer,

> *"You are fairest of them all."*

And she was contented, for she knew that the looking-glass spoke the truth.

Now, Snow-white was growing prettier and prettier, and when she was seven years old she was as beautiful as day, far more so than the Queen herself. So one day when the Queen went to her mirror and said,

> *"Looking-glass upon the wall,*
> *Who is fairest of us all?"*

it answered,

> *"Queen, you are full fair, 'tis true,*
> *But Snow-white fairer is than you."*

This gave the Queen a great shock, and she became yellow and green with envy, and from that hour her heart turned against Snow-white, and she hated her. And envy and pride like ill weeds grew in her heart higher every day, until she had no peace day or night. At last she sent for a huntsman, and said, "Take the child out into the woods, so that I may set eyes on her no more. You must put her to death, and bring me her heart for a token."

The huntsman consented, and led her away; but when he drew his cutlass to pierce Snow-white's innocent heart, she began to weep, and to say, "Oh, dear huntsman, do not take my life; I will go away into the wild wood, and never come home again."

And as she was so lovely the huntsman had pity on her, and said, "Away with you then, poor child"; for he thought the wild animals would be sure to devour her, and it was as if a stone had been rolled away from his heart when he did not put her to death. Just at that moment a young wild boar came running by, so he caught and killed it, and taking out its heart, he brought it to the Queen for a token. And it was salted and cooked, and the wicked woman ate it up, thinking that there was an end of Snow-white.

Now, when the poor child found herself quite alone in the wild woods, she felt full of terror, even of the very leaves on the trees, and she did not know what to do for fright. Then she began to run over the sharp stones and through the thorn bushes, and the wild beasts after her, but they did her no harm. She ran as long as her feet would carry her; and when the evening drew near she came to a little house, and she went inside to rest. Everything there was very small, but as pretty and clean as possible. There stood the little table ready laid, and covered with a white cloth, and seven little plates, and seven knives and forks, and drinking-cups. By the wall stood seven little beds, side by side, covered with clean white quilts. Snow-white, being very hungry and thirsty, ate from each plate a little porridge and bread, and drank out of each little cup a drop of wine, so as not to finish up one portion alone. After that she felt so tired that she lay down on one of the beds, but it did not seem to suit her; one was too long, another too short, but at last the seventh was quite right; and so she lay down upon it, committed herself to Heaven, and fell asleep.

When it was quite dark, the masters of the house came home. They were seven dwarfs, whose occupation was to dig underground among the mountains. When they had lighted their seven candles, and it was quite light in the little house, they saw that some one must have been in, as everything was not in the same order in which they left it.

The first said, "Who has been sitting in my little chair?"

The second said, "Who has been eating from my little plate?"

The third said, "Who has been taking from my little loaf?"

The fourth said, "Who has been tasting my porridge?"

The fifth said, "Who has been using my little fork?"

The sixth said, "Who has been cutting with my little knife?"

The seventh said, "Who has been drinking from my little cup?"

Then the first one, looking round, saw a hollow in his bed, and cried, "Who has been lying on my bed?" And the others came running, and cried, "Some one has been on our beds too!"

But when the seventh looked at his bed, he saw little Snow-white lying there asleep. Then he told the others, who came running up, crying out in their astonishment, and holding up their seven little candles to throw a light upon Snow-white.

"O goodness! O gracious!" cried they, "what beautiful child is this?" and were so full of joy to see her that they did not wake her, but let her sleep on. And the seventh dwarf slept with his comrades, an hour at a time with each, until the night had passed.

When it was morning, and Snow-white awoke and saw the seven dwarfs, she was very frightened; but they seemed quite friendly, and asked her what her name was, and she told them; and then they asked how she came to be in their house. And she related to them how her step-mother had wished her to be put to death, and how the huntsman had spared her life, and how she had run the whole day long, until at last she had found their little house.

Then the dwarfs said, "If you will keep our house for us, and cook, and wash, and make the beds, and sew and knit, and keep everything tidy and clean, you may stay with us, and you shall lack nothing."

"With all my heart," said Snow-white; and so she stayed, and kept the house in good order. In the morning the dwarfs went to the mountain to dig for gold; in the evening they came home, and their supper had to be ready for them. All the day long the maiden was left alone, and the good little dwarfs warned her, saying, "Beware of your step-mother, she will soon know you are here. Let no one into the house."

Now the Queen, having eaten Snow-white's heart, as she supposed, felt quite sure that now she was the first and fairest, and so she came to her mirror, and said,

> "Looking-glass upon the wall,
> Who is fairest of us all?"

And the glass answered,

> "Queen, thou art of beauty rare,
> But Snow-white living in the glen
> With the seven little men
> Is a thousand times more fair."

Then she was very angry, for the glass always spoke the truth, and she knew that the huntsman must have deceived her, and that Snow-white must still be living. And she thought and thought how she could manage to make an end of her, for as long as she was not the fairest in the land, envy left her no rest. At last she thought of a plan; she painted her face and dressed herself like an old peddler woman, so that no one would have known her. In this disguise she went across the seven mountains, until she came to the house of the seven little dwarfs, and she knocked at the door and cried, "Fine wares to sell! fine wares to sell!"

Snow-white peeped out of the window and cried, "Good-day, good woman, what have you to sell?"

"Good wares, fine wares," answered she, "laces of all colors"; and she held up a piece that was woven of variegated silk.

"I need not be afraid of letting in this good woman," thought Snow-white, and she unbarred the door and bought the pretty lace.

"What a figure you are, child!" said the old woman, "come and let me lace you properly for once."

Snow-white, suspecting nothing, stood up before her, and let her lace her with the new lace; but the old woman laced so quickly and tightly that it took Snow-white's breath away, and she fell down as dead.

"Now you have done with being the fairest," said the old woman as she hastened away.

Not long after that, towards evening, the seven dwarfs came

home, and were terrified to see their dear Snow-white lying on the
ground, without life or motion; they raised her up, and when they
saw how tightly she was laced they cut the lace in two; then she
began to draw breath, and little by little she returned to life. When
the dwarfs heard what had happened they said, "The old peddler
woman was no other than the wicked Queen; you must beware of
letting any one in when we are not here!"

And when the wicked woman got home she went to her glass
and said,

> *"Looking-glass against the wall,*
> *Who is fairest of us all?"*

And it answered as before,

> *"Queen, thou art of beauty rare,*
> *But Snow-white living in the glen*
> *With the seven little men*
> *Is a thousand times more fair."*

When she heard that she was so struck with surprise that all the
blood left her heart, for she knew that Snow-white must still be
living.

"But now," said she, "I will think of something that will be her
ruin." And by witchcraft she made a poisoned comb. Then she
dressed herself up to look like another different sort of old woman.
So she went across the seven mountains and came to the house of
the seven dwarfs, and knocked at the door and cried, "Good wares
to sell! good wares to sell!"

Snow-white looked out and said, "Go away, I must not let anybody in."

"But you are not forbidden to look," said the old woman, taking
out the poisoned comb and holding it up. It pleased the poor child
so much that she was tempted to open the door; and when the
bargain was made the old woman said, "Now, for once, your hair
shall be properly combed."

Poor Snow-white, thinking no harm, let the old woman do as she
would, but no sooner was the comb put in her hair than the poison
began to work, and the poor girl fell down senseless.

"Now, you paragon of beauty," said the wicked woman, "this is
the end of you," and went off. By good luck it was now near
evening, and the seven little dwarfs came home. When they saw
Snow-white lying on the ground as dead, they thought directly that
it was the step-mother's doing, and looked about, found the

poisoned comb, and no sooner had they drawn it out of her hair than Snow-white came to herself, and related all that had passed. Then they warned her once more to be on her guard, and never again to let any one in at the door.

And the Queen went home and stood before the looking-glass and said,

> *"Looking-glass against the wall,*
> *Who is fairest of us all?"*

And the looking-glass answered as before,

> *"Queen, thou art of beauty rare,*
> *But Snow-white living in the glen*
> *With the seven little men*
> *Is a thousand times more fair."*

When she heard the looking-glass speak thus she trembled and shook with anger. "Snow-white shall die," cried she, "though it should cost me my own life!"

And then she went to a secret lonely chamber, where no one was likely to come, and there she made a poisonous apple. It was beautiful to look upon, being white with red cheeks, so that any one who should see it must long for it, but whoever ate even a little bit of it must die. When the apple was ready she painted her face and clothed herself like a peasant woman, and went across the seven mountains to where the seven dwarfs lived. And when she knocked at the door Snow-white put her head out of the window and said, "I dare not let anybody in; the seven dwarfs told me not to."

"All right," answered the woman; "I can easily get rid of my apples elsewhere. There, I will give you one."

"No," answered Snow-white, "I dare not take anything."

"Are you afraid of poison?" said the woman, "look here, I will cut the apple in two pieces; you shall have the red side, I will have the white one."

For the apple was so cunningly made, that all the poison was in the rosy half of it. Snow-white longed for the beautiful apple, and as she saw the peasant woman eating a piece of it she could no longer refrain, but stretched out her hand and took the poisoned half. But no sooner had she taken a morsel of it into her mouth than she fell to the earth as dead. And the Queen, casting on her a terrible glance, laughed aloud and cried, "As white as snow, as red as blood, as black as ebony! This time the dwarfs will not be able to bring you to life again."

And when she went home and asked the looking-glass,

> *"Looking-glass against the wall,*
> *Who is fairest of us all?"*

at last it answered, "You are the fairest now of all."

Then her envious heart had peace, as much as an envious heart can have.

The dwarfs, when they came home in the evening, found Snow-white lying on the ground, and there came no breath out of her mouth, and she was dead. They lifted her up, sought if anything poisonous was to be found, cut her laces, combed her hair, washed her face with water and wine, but all was of no avail, the poor child was dead, and remained dead. Then they laid her on a bier, and sat all seven of them round it, and wept and lamented three whole days. And then they would have buried her, but that she looked still as if she were living, with her beautiful blooming cheeks.

So they said, "We cannot hide her away in the black ground." And they had made a coffin of clear glass, so as to be looked into from all sides, and they laid her in it, and wrote in golden letters upon it her name, and that she was a King's daughter. Then they set the coffin out upon the mountain, and one of them always remained by it to watch. And the birds came too, and mourned for Snow-white, first an owl, then a raven, and lastly, a dove.

Now, for a long while Snow-white lay in the coffin and never changed, but looked as if she were asleep, for she was still as white as snow, as red as blood, and her hair was as black as ebony.

It happened, however, that one day a King's son rode through the wood and up to the dwarfs' house, which was near it. He saw on the mountain the coffin, and beautiful Snow-white within it, and he read what was written in golden letters upon it. Then he said to the dwarfs, "Let me have the coffin, and I will give you whatever you like to ask for it."

But the dwarfs told him that they could not part with it for all the gold in the world. But he said, "I beseech you to give it me, for I cannot live without looking upon Snow-white; if you consent I will bring you to great honor, and care for you as if you were my brethren."

When he so spoke the good little dwarfs had pity upon him and gave him the coffin, and the King's son called his servants and bid them carry it away on their shoulders. Now it happened that as they were going along they stumbled over a bush, and with the shaking the bit of poisoned apple flew out of her throat. It was not long before she opened her eyes, threw up the cover of the coffin, and sat up, alive and well.

"Oh dear! where am I?" cried she. The King's son answered, full of joy, "You are near me," and, relating all that had happened, he said, "I would rather have you than anything in the world; come with me to my father's castle and you shall be my bride."

And Snow-white was kind, and went with him, and their wedding was held with pomp and great splendor.

But Snow-white's wicked step-mother was also bidden to the feast, and when she had dressed herself in beautiful clothes she went to her looking-glass and said,

> "Looking-glass upon the wall,
> Who is fairest of us all?"

The looking-glass answered,

> "O Queen, although you are of beauty rare,
> The young bride is a thousand times more fair."

Then she railed and cursed, and was beside herself with disappointment and anger. First she thought she would not go to the wedding; but then she felt she should have no peace until she went and saw the bride. And when she saw her she knew her for Snow-white, and could not stir from the place for anger and terror. For they had ready red-hot iron shoes, in which she had to dance until she fell down dead.

The Shoes That Were Danced to Pieces

THERE WAS once upon a time a King who had twelve daughters, each one more beautiful than the other. They all slept together in one chamber, in which their beds stood side by side, and every night when they were in them the King locked the door, and bolted it. But in the morning when he unlocked the door, he saw that their shoes were worn out with dancing, and no one could find out how that had come to pass. Then the King caused it to be proclaimed that whosoever could discover where they danced at night, should choose one of them for his wife and be King after his death; but that whosoever came forward and had not discovered it within three days and nights, should have forfeited his life.

It was not long before a King's son presented himself, and offered to undertake the enterprise. He was well received, and in the evening was led into a room adjoining the Princesses' sleeping-chamber. His bed was placed there, and he was to observe where they went and danced, and in order that they might do nothing secretly or go away to some other place, the door of their room was left open.

But the eyelids of the Prince grew heavy as lead, and he fell asleep, and when he awoke in the morning, all twelve had been to the dance, for their shoes were standing there with holes in the soles. On the second and third nights it fell out just the same, and then his head was struck off without mercy. Many others came after this and undertook the enterprise, but all forfeited their lives.

Now it came to pass that a poor soldier who had a wound, and could serve no longer, found himself on the road to the town where the King lived. There he met an old woman, who asked him where he was going. "I hardly know myself," answered he, and added in jest, "I had half a mind to discover where the Princesses danced their shoes into holes, and thus become King." "That is not so difficult," said the old woman, "you must not drink the wine which will be brought to you at night, and must pretend to be sound asleep."

With that she gave him a little cloak, and said, "If you put on that, you will be invisible, and then you can steal after the twelve." When the soldier had received this good advice, he went into the thing in earnest, took heart, went to the King, and announced himself as a suitor. He was as well received as the others, and royal garments were put upon him. He was conducted that evening at bed-time into the ante-chamber, and as he was about to go to bed, the eldest came and brought him a cup of wine, but he had tied a sponge under his chin, and let the wine run down into it, without drinking a drop. Then he lay down and when he had lain a while, he began to snore, as if in the deepest sleep.

The twelve Princesses heard that, and laughed, and the eldest said, "He, too, might as well have saved his life." With that they got up, opened wardrobes, presses, cupboards, and brought out pretty dresses; dressed themselves before the mirrors, sprang about, and rejoiced at the prospect of the dance. Only the youngest said, "I know not how it is; you are very happy, but I feel very strange; some misfortune is certainly about to befall us." "You are a goose, who is always frightened," said the eldest. "Have you forgotten how many Kings' sons have already come here in vain? I had hardly any need to give the soldier a sleeping-draught; in any case the clown would not have awakened." When they were all ready they looked carefully at the soldier, but he had closed his eyes and did not move or stir, so they felt themselves quite secure. The eldest then went to her bed and tapped it; it immediately sank into the earth, and one after the other they descended through the opening, the eldest going first.

The soldier, who had watched everything, tarried no longer, put on his little cloak, and went down last with the youngest. Half-way down the steps, he just trod a little on her dress; she was terrified at that, and cried out, "What is that? who is pulling at my dress?" "Don't be so silly!" said the eldest, "you have caught it on a nail."

Then they went all the way down, and when they were at the bottom, they were standing in a wonderfully pretty avenue of trees, all the leaves of which were of silver, and shone and glistened. The soldier thought, "I must carry a token away with me," and broke off a twig from one of them, on which the tree cracked with a loud report. The youngest cried out again, "Something is wrong, did you hear the crack?" But the eldest said, "It is a gun fired for joy, because we have got rid of our Prince so quickly." After that they came into an avenue where all the leaves were of gold, and lastly into a third avenue where they were of bright diamonds. He broke off a twig from each, which made such a crack each time that the youngest started back in terror, but the eldest still maintained that they were salutes. They went on and came to a great lake whereon stood twelve little boats, and in every boat sat a handsome Prince, all of whom were waiting for the twelve, and each took one of them with him, but the soldier seated himself by the youngest. Then her Prince said, "I can't tell why the boat is so much heavier today; I shall have to row with all my strength, if I am to get it across." "What should cause that," said the youngest, "but the warm weather? I feel very warm too." On the opposite side of the lake stood a splendid, brightly lit castle, from whence resounded the joyous music of trumpets and kettle-drums. They rowed over there, entered, and each Prince danced with the girl he loved, but the soldier danced with them unseen, and when one of them had a cup of wine in her hand he drank it up, so that the cup was empty when she carried it to her mouth; the youngest was alarmed at this, but the eldest always made her be silent.

They danced there till three o'clock in the morning when all the shoes were danced into holes, and they were forced to leave off. The Princes rowed them back again over the lake, and this time the soldier seated himself by the eldest. On the shore they took leave of their Princes, and promised to return the following night. When they reached the stairs the soldier ran on in front and lay down in his bed, and when the twelve had come up slowly and wearily, he was already snoring so loudly that they could all hear him, and they said, "So far as he is concerned, we are safe." They took off their beautiful dresses, laid them away, put the worn-out shoes under the bed, and lay down. Next morning the soldier was resolved not to speak, but to watch the wonderful goings on, and again went with them.

Everything was done just as it had been done the first time, and each time they danced until their shoes were worn to pieces. But the third time he took a cup away with him as a token. When the hour had arrived for him to give his answer, he took the three twigs and the cup, and went to the King, but the twelve stood behind the door, and listened for what he was going to say. When the King put the question, "Where have my twelve daughters danced their shoes to pieces in the night?" he answered, "In an underground castle with twelve Princes," and related how it had come to pass, and brought out the tokens.

The King then summoned his daughters, and asked them if the soldier had told the truth, and when they saw that they were betrayed, and that falsehood would be of no avail, they were obliged to confess all. Thereupon the King asked which of them he would have to wife. He answered, "I am no longer young, so give me the eldest." Then the wedding was celebrated on the self-same day, and the kingdom was promised him after the King's death. But the Princes were bewitched for as many days as they had danced nights with the twelve.

The Boots of Buffalo Leather

A SOLDIER who is afraid of nothing, troubles himself about nothing. One of this kind had received his discharge, and as he had learnt no trade and could earn nothing, he traveled about and begged alms of kind people. He had an old water-proof on his back, and a pair of riding-boots of buffalo leather which were still left to him.

One day he was walking, he knew not where, straight out into the open country, and at length came to a forest. He did not know where he was, but saw sitting on the trunk of a tree, which had been cut down, a man who was well dressed and wore a green shooting-coat. The soldier shook hands with him, sat down on the grass by his side, and stretched out his legs. "I see you have good boots which are well blacked," said he to the huntsman; "but if you had to travel about as I have, they would not last long. Look at mine, they are of buffalo leather, and have been worn for a long time, but in them I can go through thick and thin." After a while the soldier got up and said, "I can stay no longer, hunger drives me onwards; but, Brother Bright-boots, where does this road lead to?" "I don't know that myself," answered the huntsman, "I have lost my way in the forest." "Then you are in the same plight as I," said the soldier. "Birds of a feather flock together; let us remain together and seek our way." The huntsman smiled a little, and they walked on further and further, until night fell. "We do not get out of the forest," said the soldier, "but there in the distance I see a light shining, which will help us to something to eat."

They found a stone house, knocked at the door, and an old woman opened it. "We are looking for quarters for the night," said the soldier, "and some lining for our stomachs, for mine is as empty as an old knapsack." "You cannot stay here," answered the old woman. "This is a robber's house, and you would do wisely to get away before they come home, or you will be lost." "It won't be so bad as that," answered the soldier, "I have not had a mouthful for two days, and whether I am murdered here or die of hunger in the forest is all the same to me. I shall go in." The huntsman would not follow, but the soldier drew him in with him by the sleeve. "Come, my dear brother, we shall not come to an end so quickly as that!" The old woman had pity on them and said, "Creep in here behind the stove, and if they leave anything, I will give it to you on the sly when they are asleep." Scarcely were they in the corner before twelve robbers came bursting in, seated themselves at the table which was already laid, and vehemently demanded some food. The old woman brought in some great dishes of roast meat, and the robbers enjoyed that thoroughly.

When the smell of the food reached the nostrils of the soldier, he said to the huntsman, "I cannot hold out any longer, I shall seat myself at the table, and eat with them." "You will bring us to destruction," said the huntsman, and held him back by the arm. But the soldier began to cough loudly. When the robbers heard that, they threw away their knives and forks, leapt up, and discovered the two who were behind the stove. "Aha, gentlemen, are you in the corner?" cried they, "what are you doing here? Have you been sent as spies? Wait a while, and you shall learn how to fly on a dry bough." "But do be civil," said the soldier, "I am hungry, give me something to eat, and then you can do what you like with me."

The robbers were astonished, and the captain said, "I see that you have no fear. Well, you shall have some food, but after that you will die." "We shall see," said the soldier, and seated himself at the table, and began to cut away valiantly at the roast meat. "Brother Bright-boots, come and eat," cried he to the huntsman. "You must be as hungry as I am, and cannot have better roast meat at home." But the huntsman would not eat. The robbers looked at the soldier in astonishment, and said, "The rascal uses no ceremony."

After a while he said, "I have had enough food, now get me something good to drink." The captain was in the mood to humor him in this also, and called to the old woman, "Bring a bottle out of the cellar, and mind it be of the best." The soldier drew the cork out with a loud noise, and then went with the bottle to the huntsman and said, "Pay attention, brother, and you shall see something that will surprise you. I am now going to drink the health of the whole clan." Then he brandished the bottle over the heads of the robbers, and cried, "Long life to you all, but with your mouth open and your right hands lifted up," and then he drank a hearty draught. Scarcely were the words said than they all sat motionless as if made of stone, and their mouths were open and their right hands stretched up in the air.

The huntsman said to the soldier, "I see that you are acquainted with tricks of another kind, but now come and let us go home." "Oho, my dear brother, but that would be marching away far too soon; we have conquered the enemy, and must first take the booty. Those men there are sitting fast, and are opening their mouths with astonishment, but they will not be allowed to move until I permit them. Come, eat and drink." The old woman had to bring another bottle of the best wine, and the soldier would not stir until he had eaten enough to last for three days. At last when the day came, he said, "Now it is time to strike our tents, and that our march may be a short one, the old woman shall show us the nearest way to the town."

When they had arrived there, he went to his old comrades, and said, "Out in the forest I have found a nest full of gallows' birds, come with me and we will take it." The soldier led them, and said to the huntsman, "You must go back again with me to see how they shake when we seize them by the feet." He placed the men round about the robbers, and then he took the bottle, drank a mouthful, brandished it above them, and cried, "Live again." Instantly they all regained the power of movement, but were thrown down and bound hand and foot with cords. Then the soldier ordered them to be thrown into a cart as if they had been so many sacks, and said, "Now drive them straight to prison." The huntsman, however, took one of the men aside and gave him another commission besides. "Brother Bright-boots," said the soldier, "we have safely routed the enemy and been well fed, now we will quietly walk behind them as if we were stragglers!"

When they approached the town, the soldier saw a crowd of people pouring through the gate of the town who were raising loud cries of joy, and waving green boughs in the air. Then he saw that the entire body-guard was coming up. "What can this mean?" said he to the huntsman. "Do you not know," he replied, "That the King has for a long time been absent from his kingdom, and that today he is returning, and every one is going to meet him?" "But where is the King?" said the soldier, "I do not see him." "Here he is," answered the huntsman, "I am the King, and have announced my arrival." Then he opened his hunting-coat, and his royal garments were visible.

The soldier was alarmed, and fell on his knees and begged him to forgive him for having in his ignorance treated him as an equal, and spoken to him by such a name. But the King shook hands with him, and said, "You are a brave soldier, and have saved my life. You shall never again be in want, I will take care of you. And if ever you would like to eat a piece of roast meat as good as that in the robber's house, come to the royal kitchen. But if you would drink a health, you must first ask my permission."

The Six Servants

IN DAYS of old there lived an aged Queen who was a sorceress, and her daughter was the most beautiful maiden under the sun. The old woman, however, had no other thought than how to lure mankind to destruction, and when a wooer appeared, she said that whosoever wished to have her daughter, must first perform a task, or die. Many had been dazzled by the daughter's beauty, and had actually risked this, but they never could accomplish what the old woman enjoined them to do, and then no mercy was shown; they had to kneel down, and their heads were struck off.

A certain King's son who had also heard of the maiden's beauty, said to his father, "Let me go there, I want to demand her in marriage." "Never," answered the King; "If you were to go, it would be going to your death." On this the son lay down and was sick unto death, and for seven years he lay there, and no physician could heal him. When the father perceived that all hope was over, with a heavy heart he said to him, "Go thither, and try your luck, for I know no other means of curing you." When the son heard that, he rose from his bed and was well again, and joyfully set out on his way.

It came to pass that as he was riding across a heath, he saw from afar something like a great heap of hay lying on the ground, and when he drew nearer, he could see that it was the stomach of a man, who had laid himself down there, but the stomach looked like a small mountain. When the fat man saw the traveler, he stood up and said, "If you are in need of any one, take me into your service." The Prince answered, "What can I do with such a great big man?" "Oh," said the Stout One, "This is nothing, when I stretch myself out well, I am three thousand times fatter." "If that's the case," said the Prince, "I can make use of you, come with me." So the Stout One followed the Prince, and after a while they found another man who was lying on the ground with his ear laid to the turf. "What are you doing there?" asked the King's son. "I am listening," replied the man. "What are you listening to so attentively?" "I am listening to what is just going on in the world, for nothing escapes my ears; I even hear the grass growing." "Tell me," said the Prince, "what you hear at the court of the old Queen who has the beautiful daughter." Then he answered, "I hear the whizzing of the sword that is striking off a wooer's head." The King's son said, "I can make use of you, come with me."

They went onwards, and then saw a pair of feet lying and part of a pair of legs, but could not see the rest of the body. When they had walked on for a great distance, they came to the body, and at last to the head also. "Why," said the Prince, "what a tall rascal you are!" "Oh," replied the Tall One, "that is nothing at all yet; when I really stretch out my limbs, I am three thousand times as tall, and taller than the highest mountain on earth. I will gladly enter your service, if you will take me." "Come with me," said the Prince, "I can make use of you." They went onwards and found a man sitting by the road who had bound up his eyes. The Prince said to him, "Have you weak eyes, that you cannot look at the light?" "No," replied the man, "but I must not remove the bandage, for whatsoever I look at with my eyes, splits to pieces, my glance is so powerful. If you can use that, I shall be glad to serve you." "Come with me," replied the King's son, "I can make use of you."

They journeyed onwards and found a man who was lying in the hot sunshine, trembling and shivering all over his body, so that not a limb was still. "How can you shiver when the sun is shining so warm?" said the King's son. "Alack," replied the man, "I am of quite a different nature. The hotter it is, the colder I am, and the frost pierces through all my bones; and the colder it is, the hotter I am. In the midst of ice, I cannot endure the heat, nor in the midst of fire, the cold." "You are a strange fellow!" said the Prince, "but if you will enter my service, follow me."

They traveled onwards, and saw a man standing who made a long neck and looked about him, and could see over all the mountains. "What are you looking at so eagerly?" said the King's son. The man replied, "I have such sharp eyes that I can see into every forest and field, and hill and valley, all over the world." The Prince said, "Come with me if you will, for I am still in want of such an one."

Now the King's son and his six servants came to the town where the aged Queen dwelt. He did not tell her who he was, but said, "If you will give me your beautiful daughter, I will perform any task you set me." The sorceress was delighted to get such a handsome youth as this into her net, and said, "I will set you three tasks, and if you are able to perform them all, you shall be husband and master of my daughter." "What is the first to be?" You shall fetch me my ring which I have dropped into the Red Sea." So the King's son went home to his servants and said, "The first task is not easy. A ring is to be got out of the Red Sea. Come find some way of doing it." Then the man with the sharp sight said, "I will see where it is lying," and looked down into the water and said, "It is sticking there, on a pointed stone." The Tall One carried them thither, and said, "I would soon get it out, if I could only see it." "Oh, is that all!" cried the Stout One, and lay down and put his mouth to the water, on which all the waves fell into it just as if it had been a whirlpool, and he drank up the whole sea till it was as dry as a meadow. The Tall One stooped down a little, and brought out the ring with his hand.

Then the King's son rejoiced when he had the ring, and took it to the old Queen. She was astonished, and said, "Yes, it is the right ring. You have safely performed the first task, but now comes the second. Do you see the meadow in front of my palace? Three hundred fat oxen are feeding there, and these must you eat, skin, hair, bones, horns and all; and down below in my cellar lie three hundred casks of wine, and these you must drink up as well, and if one hair of the oxen, or one little drop of the wine is left, your life will be forfeited to me." "May I invite no guests to this repast?" inquired the Prince, "no dinner is good without some company." The old woman laughed maliciously, and replied, "You may invite one for the sake of companionship, but no more."

The King's son went to his servants and said to the Stout One, "You shall be my guest today, and shall eat your fill." Hereupon the Stout One stretched himself out and ate up the three hundred oxen without leaving one single hair, and then he asked if he was to have nothing but his breakfast. He drank the wine straight from the casks without feeling any need of a glass, and he licked the last drop from his finger-nails.

When the meal was over, the Prince went to the old woman, and told her that the second task also was performed. She wondered at this and said, "No one has ever done so much before, but one task still remains," and she thought to herself, "You shall not escape me, and will not keep your head on your shoulders! This night," said she, "I will bring my daughter to you in your chamber, and you shall put your arms around her, but when you are sitting there together, beware of falling asleep. When twelve o'clock is striking, I will come, and if she is then no longer in your arms, you are lost." The Prince thought, "the task is easy, I will most certainly keep my eyes open." Nevertheless he called his servants, told them what the old woman had said, and remarked, "Who knows what treachery may lurk behind this. Foresight is a good thing—keep watch,

and take care that the maiden does not go out of my room again."
When night fell, the old woman came with her daughter, and gave
her into the Prince's arms, and then the Tall One wound himself
round the two in a circle, and the Stout One placed himself by the
door, so that no living creature could enter. There the two sat, and
the maiden spake never word, but the moon shone through the
window on her face, and the Prince could behold her wonderous
beauty. He did nothing but gaze at her, and was filled with love
and happiness, and his eyes never felt weary. This lasted until
eleven o'clock, when the old woman cast such a spell over all of
them that they fell asleep, and at the self-same moment the
maiden was carried away.

Then they all slept soundly until a quarter to twelve, when the
magic lost its power, and all awoke again. "Oh, misery and misfortune!" cried the Prince, "now I am lost!" The faithful servants also
began to lament, but the Listener said, "Be quiet, I want to listen."
Then he listened for an instant and said, "She is on a rock, three
hundred leagues from hence, bewailing her fate. You alone, Tall
One, can help her; if you will stand up, you will be there in a couple
of steps."

"Yes," answered the Tall One, "but the one with the sharp eyes
must go with me, that we may destroy the rock." Then the Tall
One took the one with bandaged eyes on his back, and in the
twinkling of an eye they were on the enchanted rock. The Tall One
immediately took the bandage from the other's eyes, and he did
but look round, and the rock shivered into a thousand pieces. Then
the Tall One took the maiden in his arms, carried her back in a
second, then fetched his companion with the same rapidity, and
before it struck twelve they were all sitting as they had sat before,
quite merrily and happily.

When twelve struck, the aged sorceress came stealing in with a
malicious face, which seemed to say, "Now he is mine!" for she
believed that her daughter was on the rock three hundred leagues
off. But when she saw her in the Prince's arms, she was alarmed,
and said, "Here is one who knows more than I do!" She dared not
make any opposition, and was forced to give him her daughter. But
she whispered in her ear, "It is a disgrace to you to have to obey
common people, and that you are not allowed to choose a husband
to your own liking."

At this the proud heart of the maiden was filled with anger, and
she meditated revenge. Next morning she caused three hundred
great bundles of wood to be got together, and said to the Prince

that though the three tasks were performed, she would still not be his wife until some one was ready to seat himself in the midst of the wood, and bear the fire. She thought that none of his servants would let themselves be burnt for him, and that out of love for her, he himself would place himself upon it, and then she would be free. But the servants said, "Every one of us has done something except the Frosty One, he must set to work," and they put him in the middle of the pile, and set fire to it. Then the fire began to burn, and burnt for three days until all the wood was consumed, and when the flames had burnt out, the Frosty One was standing amid the ashes, trembling like an aspen leaf, and saying, "I never felt such a frost during the whole course of my life; if it had lasted much longer, I should have been benumbed!"

As no other pretext was to be found, the beautiful maiden was now forced to take the unknown youth as a husband. But when they drove away to church, the old woman said, "I cannot endure the disgrace," and sent her warriors after them with orders to cut down all who opposed them, and bring back her daughter. But the Listener had sharpened his ears, and heard the secret discourse of the old woman. "What shall we do?" said he to the Stout One. But he knew what to do, and spat out once or twice behind the carriage some of the sea-water which he had drunk, and a great sea arose in which the warriors were caught and drowned. When the sorceress perceived that, she sent her mailed knights; but the Listener heard the rattling of their armor, and undid the bandage from one eye of Sharp-eyes, who looked for a while rather fixedly at the enemy's troops, on which they all sprang to pieces like glass. Then the youth and the maiden went on their way undisturbed, and when the two had been blessed in church, the six servants took leave, and said to their master, "Your wishes are now satisfied, you need us no longer, we will go our way and seek our fortunes."

Half a league from the palace of the Prince's father was a village near which a swineherd tended his herd, and when they came thither the Prince said to his wife, "Do you know who I really am? I am no Prince, but a herder of swine, and the man who is there with that herd is my father. We two shall have to set to work also, and help him." Then he alighted with her at the inn, and secretly told the innkeepers to take away her royal apparel during the night. So when she awoke in the morning, she had nothing to put on, and the innkeeper's wife gave her an old gown and a pair of worsted stockings, and at the same time seemed to consider it a great present, and said, "If it were not for the sake of your husband I should have given you nothing at all!" Then the Princess believed that he really was a swineherd, and tended the herd with him, and thought to herself, "I have deserved this for my haughtiness and pride." This lasted for a week, and then she could endure it no longer, for she had sores on her feet. And now came a couple of people who asked if she knew who her husband was. "Yes," she answered, "he is a swineherd, and has just gone out with cords and ropes to try to drive a little bargain." But they said, "Just come with us, and we will take you to him," and they took her to the palace, and when she entered the hall, there stood her husband in kingly raiment. But she did not recognize him until he took her in his arms, kissed her, and said, "I suffered much for you, and now you, too, have had to suffer for me."

Then the wedding was celebrated. And he who had told you all this, wishes that he, too, had been present at it.

Six Soldiers of Fortune

THERE WAS once a man who was a Jack-of-all-trades. He had served in the war, and had been brave and bold, but at the end of it he was sent about his business, with three farthings and his discharge.

"I am not going to stand this," said he. "Wait till I find the right man to help me, and the King shall give me all the treasures of his kingdom before he has done with me."

Then, full of wrath, he went into the forest, and he saw one standing there by six trees which he had rooted up as if they had been stalks of corn. And he said to him, "Will you be my man, and come along with me?"

"All right," answered he. "I must just take this bit of wood home to my father and mother." And taking one of the trees, he bound it round the other five, and putting the faggot on his shoulder, he carried it off; then soon coming back, he went along with his leader, who said, "Two such as we can stand against the whole world."

And when they had gone on a little while, they came to a huntsman who was kneeling on one knee and taking careful aim with his rifle.

"Huntsman," said the leader, "what are you aiming at?" "Two miles from here," answered he, "there sits a fly on the bough of an oak tree, I mean to put a bullet into its left eye." "Oh, come along with me," said the leader; "three of us together can stand against the world."

The huntsman was quite willing to go with him, and so they went on till they came to seven windmills, whose sails were going round briskly, and yet there was no wind blowing from any quarter, and not a leaf stirred.

"Well," said the leader, "I cannot think what ails the windmills, turning without wind"; and he went on with his followers about two miles farther, and then they came to a man sitting up in a tree, holding one nostril and blowing with the other.

"Now then," said the leader, "what are you doing up there?" "Two miles from here," answered he, "there are seven windmills; I am blowing, and they are going round." "Oh, go with me," cried the leader, "four of us together can stand against the world."

So the blower got down and went with them, and after a time they came to a man standing on one leg, and the other had been taken off and was lying near him.

"You seem to have got a handy way of resting yourself," said the leader to the man. "I am a runner," answered he, "and in order to keep myself from going too fast I have taken off a leg, for when I run with both, I go faster than a bird can fly." "Oh, go with me," cried the leader, "five of us together may well stand against the world."

So he went with them all together, and it was not long before they met a man with a little hat on, and he wore it just over one ear.

"Manners! manners!" said the leader; "with your hat like that, you look like a jack-fool." "I dare not put it straight," answered the other; "If I did, there would be such a terrible frost that the very birds would be frozen and fall dead from the sky to the ground." "Oh, come with me," said the leader; "we six together may well stand against the world."

So the six went on until they came to a town where the King had caused it to be made known that whoever would run a race with his daughter and win it might become her husband, but that whoever lost must lose his head into the bargain. And the leader came forward and said one of his men should run for him.

"Then," said the King, "his life too must be put in pledge, and if he fails, his head and yours too must fall."

When this was quite settled and agreed upon, the leader called the runner, and strapped his second leg on to him. "Now, look out," said he, "and take care that we win."

It had been agreed that the one who should bring water first from a far distant brook should be accounted winner. Now the King's daughter and the runner each took a pitcher, and they started both at the same time; but in one moment, when the King's daughter had gone but a very little way, the runner was out of sight, for his running was as if the wind rushed by. In a short time he reached the brook, filled his pitcher full of water, and turned back again. About half-way home, however, he was overcome with weariness, and setting down his pitcher, he lay down on the ground to sleep. But in order to awaken soon again by not lying too soft he had taken a horse's skull which lay near and placed it under his head for a pillow. In the meanwhile the King's daughter, who really was a good runner, good enough to beat an ordinary man, had reached the brook, and filled her pitcher, and was hastening with it back again, when she saw the runner lying asleep.

"The day is mine," said she with much joy, and she emptied his pitcher and hastened on. And now all had been lost but for the huntsman who was standing on the castle wall, and with his keen eyes saw all that happened.

"We must not be outdone by the King's daughter," said he, and he loaded his rifle and took so good an aim that he shot the horse's skull from under the runner's head without doing him any harm. And the runner awoke and jumped up, and saw his pitcher standing empty and the King's daughter far on her way home. But, not losing courage, he ran swiftly to the brook, filled it again with water, and for all that, he got home ten minutes before the King's daughter.

"Look you," said he; "this is the first time I have really stretched my legs; before it was not worth the name of running."

The King was vexed, and his daughter yet more so, that she should be beaten by a discharged common soldier; and they took counsel together how they might rid themselves of him and of his companions at the same time.

"I have a plan," said the King; "Do not fear but that we shall be quit of them forever." Then he went out to the men and bade them to feast and be merry and eat and drink; and he led them into a room, which had a floor of iron, and the doors were iron, the windows had iron frames and bolts; in the room was a table set out with costly food. "Now, go in there and make yourselves comfortable," said the King.

And when they had gone in, he had the door locked and bolted. Then he called the cook, and told him to make a big fire underneath the room, so that the iron floor of it should be red hot. And the cook did so, and the six men began to feel the room growing very warm, by reason, as they thought at first, of the good dinner; but as the heat grew greater and greater, and they found the doors and windows fastened, they began to think it was an evil plan of the King's to suffocate them.

"He shall not succeed, however," said the man with the little hat; "I will bring on a frost that shall make the fire feel ashamed of itself, and creep out of the way."

So he set his hat straight on his head, and immediately there came such a frost that all the heat passed away and the food froze in the dishes. After an hour or two had passed, and the King thought they must have all perished in the heat, he caused the door to be opened, and went himself to see how they fared. And when the door flew back, there they were all six quite safe and sound, and they said they were quite ready to come out, so that they might warm themselves, for the great cold of that room had caused the food to freeze in the dishes.

Full of wrath, the King went to the cook and scolded him, and asked why he had not done as he was ordered. "It is hot enough there, you may see for yourself," answered the cook. And the King looked and saw an immense fire burning underneath the room of iron, and he began to think that the six men were not to be got rid of in that way. And he thought of a new plan by which it might be managed, so he sent for the leader and said to him, "If you will give up your right to my daughter, and take gold instead, you may have as much as you like."

"Certainly, my lord King," answered the man; "let me have as much gold as my servant can carry, and I give up all claim to your daughter." And the King agreed that he should come again in a fortnight to fetch the gold. The man then called together all the tailors in the kingdom, and set them to work to make a sack, and it took them a fortnight. And when it was ready, the strong man who had been found rooting up trees took it on his shoulder, and went to the King.

"Who is this immense fellow carrying on his shoulder a bundle of stuff as big as a house?" cried the King, terrified to think how much gold he would carry off. And a ton of gold was dragged in by sixteen strong men, but he put it all into the sack with one hand, saying, "Why don't you bring some more? this hardly covers the bottom!"

So the King bade them fetch by degrees the whole of his treasure, and even then the sack was not half full.

"Bring more!" cried the man; "these few scraps go no way at all!" Then at last seven thousand wagons laden with gold collected through the whole kingdom were driven up; and he threw them in his sack, oxen and all. "I will not look too closely," said he, "but take what I can get, so long as the sack is full." And when all was put in there was still plenty of room. "I must make an end of this," he said; "if it is not full, it is so much the easier to tie up." And he hoisted it on his back, and went off with his comrades.

When the King saw all the wealth of his realm carried off by a single man he was full of wrath, and he bade his cavalry mount and follow after the six men, and take the sack away from the strong man. Two regiments were soon up to them, and called them to consider themselves prisoners, and to deliver up the sack, or be cut in pieces.

"Prisoners, say you?" said the man who could blow, "suppose you first have a little dance together in the air," and holding one nostril, and blowing through the other, he sent the regiments flying head over heels, over the hills and far away. But a sergeant who had nine wounds and was a brave fellow, begged not to be put to so much shame. And the blower let him down easily, so that he came to no harm, and he bade him go to the King and tell him that whatever regiments he liked to send more should be blown away just the same. And the King, when he got the message, said, "Let the fellows be; they have some right on their side." So the six comrades carried home their treasure, divided it among them, and lived contented till they died.

The Two Travelers

A SHOEMAKER and a tailor once met with each other in their travels. The tailor was a handsome little fellow who was always merry and full of enjoyment. He saw the shoemaker coming towards him from the other side, and as he observed by his bag what kind of a trade he plied, he sang a little mocking song to him:

> "*Sew me the seam,*
> *Draw me the thread,*

Spread it over with pitch,
Knock the nail on the head."

The shoemaker, however, could not endure a joke. He pulled a face as if he had drunk vinegar, and made a gesture as if he were about to seize the tailor by the throat. But the little fellow began to laugh, reached him his bottle, and said, "No harm was meant, take a drink, and swallow thy anger down." The shoemaker took a very hearty drink, and the storm on his face began to clear away. He gave the bottle back to the tailor, and said, "I spoke civilly to thee; one speaks well after much drinking, but not after much thirst. Shall we travel together?" "All right," answered the tailor, "if only it suits thee to go into a big town where there is no lack of work." "That is just where I want to go," answered the shoemaker. "In a small nest there is nothing to earn, and in the country, people like to go barefoot." They traveled therefore onwards together, and always set one foot before the other like a weasel in the snow.

Both of them had time enough, but little to bite and to break. When they reached a town they went about and paid their respects to the tradesmen, and because the tailor looked so lively and merry, and had such pretty red cheeks, every one gave him work willingly, and when luck was good the master's daughters gave him a kiss beneath the porch, as well. When he again fell in with the shoemaker, the tailor had always the most in his bundle. The ill-tempered shoemaker made a wry face, and thought, "The greater the rascal the more the luck," but the tailor began to laugh and to sing, and shared all he got with his comrade. If a couple of pence jingled in his pockets, he ordered good cheer, and thumped the table in his joy till the glasses danced, and it was lightly come, lightly go, with him.

When they had traveled for some time, they came to a great forest through which passed the road to the capital. Two footpaths, however, led through it, one of which was a seven days' journey, and the other only two, but neither of the travelers knew which way was the short one. They seated themselves beneath an oak tree, and took counsel together how they should forecast, and for how many days they should provide themselves with bread. The shoemaker said, "One must look before one leaps, I will take with me bread for a week." "What!" said the tailor, "drag bread for seven days on one's back like a beast of burden, and not be able to look about. I shall trust in God, and not trouble myself about anything! The money I have in my pocket is as good in summer as in winter, but in hot weather bread gets dry, and moldy into the bargain; even my coat does not go as far as it might. Besides, why should we not find the right way? Bread for two days, and that's enough." Each, therefore, bought his own bread, and then they tried their luck in the forest.

It was as quiet there as in a church. No wind stirred, no brook murmured, no bird sang, and through the thickly leaved branches no sunbeam forced its way. The shoemaker spoke never a word, the heavy bread weighed down his back until the perspiration streamed down his cross and gloomy face. The tailor, however, was quite merry, he jumped about, whistled on a leaf, or sang a song, and thought to himself, "God in Heaven must be pleased to see me so happy."

This lasted two days, but on the third the forest would not come to an end, and the tailor had eaten up all his bread, so after all his heart sank down a yard deeper. In the meantime he did not lose courage, but relied on God and on his luck. On the third day he lay down in the evening, hungry, under a tree, and rose again next morning hungry still; so also passed the fourth day, and when the shoemaker seated himself on a fallen tree and devoured his dinner, the tailor was only a looker-on. If he begged for a little piece of bread the other laughed mockingly, and said, "Thou hast always been so merry, now thou canst try for once what it is to be sad: the birds which sing too early in the morning are struck by the hawk in the evening," in short he was pitiless. But on the fifth morning the poor tailor could no longer stand up, and was hardly able to utter one word for weakness; his cheeks were white, and his eyes red. Then the shoemaker said to him, "I will give thee a bit of bread today, but in return for it, I will put out thy right eye." The unhappy tailor who still wished to save his life, could not do it in any other way; he wept once more with both eyes, and then held them out, and the shoemaker, who had a heart of stone, put out his right eye with a sharp knife. The tailor remembered what his mother had formerly said to him when he had been eating secretly in the pantry. "Eat what one can, and suffer what one must."

When he had consumed his dearly bought bread, he got on his legs again, forgot his misery and comforted himself with the thought that he could always see enough with one eye. But on the sixth day, hunger made itself felt again, and gnawed him almost to the heart. In the evening he fell down by a tree, and on the seventh morning he could not raise himself up for faintness, and death was close at hand. Then said the shoemaker, "I will show mercy and give thee bread once more, but thou shalt not have it for nothing, I shall put out thy other eye for it."

And now the tailor felt how thoughtless his life had been, prayed to God for forgiveness, and said, "Do what thou wilt, I will bear what I must, but remember that our Lord God does not always look on passively, and that an hour will come when the evil deed which thou hast done to me, and which I have not deserved of thee, will be requited. When times were good with me, I shared what I had with thee. My trade is of that kind that each stitch must always be exactly like the other. If I no longer have my eyes and can sew no more I must go a-begging. At any rate do not leave me here alone when I am blind, or I shall die of hunger." The shoemaker, however, who had driven God out of his heart, took the knife and put out his left eye. Then he gave him a bit of bread to eat, held out a stick to him, and drew him on behind him.

When the sun went down, they got out of the forest, and before them in the open country stood the gallows. Thither the shoemaker guided the blind tailor, and then left him alone and went his way. Weariness, pain, and hunger made the wretched man fall asleep, and he slept the whole night. When day dawned he awoke, but knew not where he lay. Two poor sinners were hanging on the gallows, and a crow sat on the head of each of them. Then one of the men who had been hanged began to speak, and said, "Brother, art thou awake?" "Yes, I am awake," answered the second. "Then I will tell thee something," said the first; "the dew which this night has fallen down over us from the gallows, gives every one who washes himself with it his eyes again. If blind people did but know this how many would regain their sight who do not believe that to be possible."

When the tailor heard that, he took his pocket-handkerchief, pressed it on the grass, and when it was moist with dew, washed the sockets of his eyes with it. Immediately was fulfilled what the man on the gallows had said, and a couple of healthy new eyes filled the sockets. It was not long before the tailor saw the sun rise behind the mountains; in the plain before him lay the great royal city with its magnificent gates and hundred towers, and the golden balls and crosses which were on the spires began to shine. He could distinguish every leaf on the trees, saw the birds which flew past, and the midges which danced in the air. He took a needle out of his pocket, and as he could thread it as well as ever he had done, his heart danced with delight. He threw himself on his knees, thanked God for the mercy he had shown him, and said his morning prayer.

He did not forget also to pray for the poor sinners who were hanging there swinging against each other in the wind like the pendulums of clocks. Then he took his bundle on his back and soon forgot the pain of heart he had endured, and went on his way singing and whistling.

The first thing he met was a brown foal running about the fields at large. He caught it by the mane, and wanted to spring on it and ride into the town. The foal, however, begged to be set free. "I am still too young," it said, "even a light tailor such as thou art would break my back in two—let me go till I have grown strong. A time may perhaps come when I may reward thee for it." "Run off," said the tailor, "I see thou art still a giddy thing." He gave it a touch with a switch over its back, whereupon it kicked up its hind legs for joy, leapt over hedges and ditches, and galloped away, far out into the open country.

But the little tailor had eaten nothing since the day before. "The sun to be sure fills my eyes," said he, "but the bread does not fill my mouth. The first thing that comes across me and is even half eatable will have to suffer for it." In the meantime a stork stepped solemnly over the meadow towards him. "Halt, halt!" cried the tailor, and seized him by the leg; "I don't know if thou art good to eat or not, but my hunger leaves me no great choice. I must cut thy head off, and roast thee." "Don't do that," replied the stork; "I am a sacred bird which brings mankind great profit, and no one does me an injury. Leave me my life, and I may do thee good in some other way." "Well, be off, Cousin Longlegs," said the tailor. The stork rose up, let its long legs hang down, and flew gently away.

"What's to be the end of this?" said the tailor to himself at last, "my hunger grows greater and greater, and my stomach more and more empty. Whatsoever comes in my way now is lost." At this moment he saw a couple of young ducks which were on a pond come swimming towards him. "You come just at the right moment," said he, and laid hold of one of them and was about to wring its neck. On this an old duck which was hidden among the reeds, began to scream loudly, and swam to him with open beak, and begged him urgently to spare her dear children. "Canst thou not imagine," said she, "how thy mother would mourn if any one wanted to carry thee off, and give thee thy finishing stroke?" "Only be quiet," said the good-tempered tailor, "thou shalt keep thy children," and put the prisoner back into the water.

When he turned round, he was standing in front of an old tree which was partly hollow, and saw some wild bees flying in and out of it. "There I shall at once find the reward of my good deed," said the tailor, "the honey will refresh me." But the Queen-bee came out, threatened him and said, "If thou touchest my people, and destroyeth my nest, our stings shall pierce thy skin like ten thousand red-hot needles. But if thou wilt leave us in peace and go thy way, we will do thee a service for it another time."

The little tailor saw that here also nothing was to be done. "Three dishes empty and nothing on the fourth is a bad dinner!" He dragged himself therefore with his starved-out stomach into the town, and as it was just striking twelve, all was ready-cooked for him in the inn, and he was able to sit down at once to dinner. When he was satisfied he said, "Now I will get to work." He went round the town, sought a master, and soon found a good situation. As, however, he had thoroughly learnt his trade, it was not long before he became famous, and every one wanted to have his new coat made by the little tailor, whose importance increased daily. "I can go no further in skill," said he, "and yet things improve every day." At last the King appointed him court-tailor.

But how things do happen in the world! On the very same day his former comrade, the shoemaker, also became court-shoemaker. When the latter caught sight of the tailor, and saw that he had once more two healthy eyes, his conscience troubled him. "Before he takes revenge on me," thought he to himself, "I must dig a pit for him." He, however, who digs a pit for another, falls into it himself. In the evening when work was over and it had grown dusk, he stole to the King and said, "Lord King, the tailor is an arrogant fellow and has boasted that he will get the gold crown back again which was lost in ancient times." "That would please me very much," said the King, and he caused the tailor to be brought before him next morning, and ordered him to get the crown back again, or to leave the town forever. "Oho!" thought the tailor, "a rogue gives more than he has got. If the surly King wants me to do what can be done by no one, I will not wait till morning, but will go out of the town at once, today."

He packed up his bundle, therefore, but when he was without the gate he could not help being sorry to give up his good fortune, and turn his back on the town in which all had gone so well with him. He came to the pond where he had made the acquaintance of the ducks; at that very moment the old one whose young ones he had spared, was sitting there by the shore, pluming herself with her beak. She knew him again instantly, and asked why he was hanging his head so. "Thou wilt not be surprised when thou hearest what has befallen me," replied the tailor, and told her his fate. "If that be all," said the duck, "we can help thee. The crown fell into the water, and lies down below at the bottom; we will soon bring it up again for thee. In the meantime just spread out thy handkerchief on the bank." She dived down with her twelve young ones, and in five minutes she was up again and sat with the crown resting on her wings, and the twelve young ones were swimming round about and had put their beaks under it, and were helping to carry it. They swam to the shore and put the crown on the handkerchief. No one can imagine how magnificent the crown was; when the sun shone on it, it gleamed like a hundred thousand carbuncles. The tailor tied his handkerchief together by the four corners, and carried it to the King, who was full of joy, and put a gold chain round the tailor's neck.

When the shoemaker saw that one stroke had failed, he contrived a second, and went to the King and said, "Lord King, the tailor has become insolent again; he boasts that he will copy in wax the whole of the royal palace, with everything that pertains to it, loose or fast, inside and out." The King sent for the tailor and ordered him to copy in wax the whole of the royal palace, with everything that pertained to it, movable or immovable, within and without, and if he did not succeed in doing this, if so much as one nail on the wall were wanting, he should be imprisoned for his whole life under ground.

The tailor thought, "It gets worse and worse! No one can endure that!" and threw his bundle on his back, and went forth. When he came to the hollow tree, he sat down and hung his head. The bees came flying out, and the Queen-bee asked him if he had a stiff neck, since he held his head so awry. "Alas, no," answered the tailor, "something quite different weighs me down," and he told her what the King had demanded of him. The bees began to buzz and hum among themselves, and the Queen-bee said, "Just go home again, but come back tomorrow at this time, and bring a large sheet with thee, and then all will be well." So he turned back again, but the bees flew to the royal palace and straight through the open windows, crept round about into every corner, and inspected everything most carefully. Then they hurried back and modeled the palace in wax with such rapidity that any one looking on would have thought it was growing before his eyes. By the evening all was ready, and when the tailor came next morning, the whole of the splendid building was there, and not one nail in the wall or tile of the roof was wanting, and it was delicate withal, and white as snow, and smelt sweet as honey. The tailor wrapped it carefully in his cloth and took it to the King, who could not admire it enough, placed it in his largest hall, and in return for it presented the tailor with a large stone house.

The shoemaker, however, did not give up, but went for the third time to the King and said, "Lord King, it has come to the tailor's ears that no water will spring up in the court-yard of the castle, and he has boasted that it shall rise up in the midst of the court-yard to a man's height and be clear as crystal." Then the King ordered the tailor to be brought before him and said, "If a stream of water does not rise in my court-yard by tomorrow as thou hast promised, the executioner shall in that very place make thee shorter by the head."

The poor tailor did not take long to think about it, but hurried out to the gate, and because this time it was a matter of life and death to him, tears rolled down his face. While he was thus going forth full of sorrow, the foal to which he had formerly given its liberty, and which had now become a beautiful chestnut horse, came leaping towards him. "The time has come," it said to the tailor, "when I can repay thee for thy good deed. I know already what is needful to thee, but thou shalt soon have help; get on me, my back can carry two such as thou." The tailor's courage came back to him; he jumped up in one bound, and the horse went full speed into the town, and right up to the court-yard of the castle. It galloped as quick as lightning thrice round it, and at the third time it fell violently down. At the same instant, however, there was a terrific clap of thunder, a fragment of earth in the middle of the court-yard sprang like a cannon-ball into the air, and over the castle, and directly after it a jet of water rose as high as a man on horseback, and the water was as pure as crystal, and the sunbeams began to dance on it. When the King saw that he arose in amazement, and went and embraced the tailor in the sight of all men.

But good fortune did not last long. The King had daughters in plenty, one prettier than the other, but he had no son. So the malicious shoemaker betook himself for the fourth time to the King, and said, "Lord King, the tailor has not given up his arrogance. He has now boasted that if he liked, he could cause a son to be brought to the Lord King through the air." The King commanded the tailor to be summoned, and said, "If thou causest a son to be brought to me within nine days, thou shalt have my eldest daughter to wife." "The reward is indeed great," thought the little tailor; "one would willingly do something for it, but the cherries grow too high for me, if I climb for them, the bough will break beneath me, and I shall fall."

He went home, seated himself cross-legged on his work-table, and thought what was to be done. "It can't be managed," cried he at last, "I will go away; after all I can't live in peace here." He tied up his bundle and hurried away to the gate. When he got to the meadow, he perceived his old friend the stork, who was walking backwards and forwards like a philosopher. Sometimes he stood still, took a frog into close consideration, and at length swallowed it down. The stork came to him and greeted him. "I see," he began, "that thou hast thy pack on thy back. Why art thou leaving the town?" The tailor told him what the King had required of him, and how he could not perform it, and lamented his misfortune. "Don't let thy hair grow gray about that," said the stork, "I will help thee out of thy difficulty. For a long time now, I have carried the children in swaddling-clothes into the town, so for once in a way I can fetch a little Prince out of the well. Go home and be easy. In nine days from this time repair to the royal palace, and there will I come."

The little tailor went home, and at the appointed time was at the castle. It was not long before the stork came flying thither and tapped at the window. The tailor opened it, and Cousin Longlegs came carefully in, and walked with solemn steps over the smooth marble pavement. He had, however, a baby in his beak that was as lovely as an angel, and stretched out its little hands to the Queen. The stork laid it in her lap, and she caressed it and kissed it, and was beside herself with delight. Before the stork flew away, he took his traveling bag off his back and handed it over to the Queen. In it there were little paper parcels with colored sweetmeats, and they were divided among the little Princesses. The eldest, however, had none of them, but got the merry tailor for a husband. "It seems to me," said he, "just as if I had won the highest prize. My mother was right after all, she always said that whoever trusts in God and only has good luck, can never fail."

The shoemaker had to make the shoes in which the little tailor danced at the wedding festival, after which he was commanded to quit the town forever. The road to the forest led him to the gallows. Worn out with anger, rage, and the heat of the day, he threw himself down. When he had closed his eyes and was about to sleep, the two crows flew down from the heads of the men who were hanging there, and pecked his eyes out. In his madness he ran into the forest and must have died there of hunger, for no one has ever either seen him again or heard of him.

The Ear of Corn

IN FORMER TIMES, when God himself still walked the earth, the fruitfulness of the soil was much greater than it is now; then, the ears of corn did not bear fifty or sixty, but four or five hundred-fold. Then the corn grew from the bottom to the very top of the stalk, and according to the length of the stalk was the length of the ear. Men however are so made, that when they are too well off they no longer value the blessings which come from God, but grow indifferent and careless.

One day a woman was passing by a corn-field when her little child, who was running beside her, fell into a puddle, and dirtied her frock. On this the mother tore up a handful of the beautiful ears of corn, and cleaned the frock with them.

When the Lord, who just then came by, saw that, he was angry, and said, "Henceforth shall the stalks of corn bear no more ears; men are no longer worthy of heavenly gifts." The by-standers who heard this, were terrified, and fell on their knees and prayed that he would still leave something on the stalks, even if the people were undeserving of it, for the sake of the innocent birds which would otherwise have to starve. The Lord, who foresaw their suffering, had pity on them, and granted the request. So the ears were left as they now grow.

The Aged Mother

IN A LARGE TOWN there was an old woman who sat in the evening alone in her room thinking how she had lost first her husband, then both her children, then, one by one, all her relations, and at length, that very day, her last friend; and now she was quite alone and desolate. She was very sad at heart, and heaviest of all her losses to her was that of her sons, and in her pain she blamed God for it.

She was still sitting lost in thought, when all at once she heard the bells ringing for early prayer. She was surprised that she had thus in her sorrow watched through the whole night, and lighted her lantern and went to church. It was already lighted up when she arrived, but not as it usually was with wax candles, but with a dim light. It was also crowded already with people, and all the seats were filled; and when the old woman got to her usual place it also was not empty, but the whole bench was entirely full. And when she looked at the people, they were none other than her dead relations who were sitting there in their old-fashioned garments, but with pale faces. They neither spoke nor sang; but a soft humming and whispering was heard all over the church. Then an aunt of hers stood up, stepped forward, and said to the poor old woman, "Look there beside the altar, and you will see your sons." The old woman looked there and saw her two children, one hanging on the gallows, the other bound to the wheel. Then said the aunt, "Behold, so would it have been with them if they had lived, and if the good God had not taken them to Himself when they were innocent children."

The old woman went trembling home, and on her knees thanked God for having dealt with her more kindly than she had been able to understand, and on the third day she lay down and died.

The Hazel Branch

ONE AFTERNOON the Christ-child had laid himself in his cradle-bed and had fallen asleep. Then his mother came to him, looked at him full of gladness, and said, "Hast thou laid thyself down to sleep, my child? Sleep sweetly, and in the meantime I will go into the wood, and fetch thee a handful of strawberries, for I know that thou wilt be pleased with them when thou awakest." In the wood outside, she found a spot with the most beautiful strawberries; but as she was stooping down to gather one, an adder sprang up out of the grass. She was alarmed, left the strawberries where they were, and hastened away. The adder darted after her; but Our Lady, as you can readily understand, knew what it was best to do. She hid herself behind a hazel bush, and stood there until the adder had crept away again. Then she gathered the strawberries, and as she set out on her way home she said, "As the hazel bush has been my protection this time, it shall in future protect others also." Therefore, from the most remote times, a green hazel branch has been the safest protection against adders, snakes, and everything else which creeps on the earth.

The Old Grandfather's Corner

ONCE UPON a time there was a very old man who lived with his son and daughter-in-law. His eyes were dim, his knees tottered under him when he walked, and he was very deaf. As he sat at table his hand shook so that he would often spill the soup over the tablecloth or on his clothes, and sometimes he could not even keep it in his mouth when it got there. His son and daughter were so annoyed to see his conduct at the table that at last they placed a chair for him in a corner behind the screen, and gave him his meals in an earthenware basin quite away from the rest. He would often look sorrowfully at the table with tears in his eyes, but he did not complain.

One day, while he was thinking sadly of the past, the earthenware basin, which he could scarcely hold in his trembling hands, fell to the ground and was broken. The young wife scolded him well for being so careless, but he did not reply, only sighed deeply. Then she brought him a wooden bowl for a penny and gave him his meals in it.

Some days afterward his son and daughter saw their little boy, who was about four years old, sitting on the ground and trying to fasten together some pieces of wood.

"What are you making, my boy?" asked his father.

"I am making a little bowl for papa and mamma to eat their food in when I grow up," he replied.

The husband and wife looked at each other without speaking for some minutes. At last they began to shed tears, and went and brought their old father back to the table, and from that day he always took his meals with them and was never again treated unkindly.

The Ungrateful Son

A MAN and his wife were once sitting by the door of their house, and they had a roasted chicken set before them, and were about to eat it together. Then the man saw that his aged father was coming, and hastily took the chicken and hid it, for he would not permit him to have any of it. The old man came, took a drink, and went away. The son wanted to put the roasted chicken on the table again, but when he took it up, it had become a great toad, which jumped into his face and sat there and never went away again, and if any one wanted to take it off, it looked venomously at him as if it would jump in his face, so that no one would venture to touch it. And the ungrateful son was forced to feed the toad every day, or else it fed itself on his face; and thus he went about the world without knowing rest.

The Bittern and the Hoopoe

"WHERE DO YOU like best to feed your flocks?" said a man to an old cow-herd. "Here, sir, where the grass is neither too rich nor too poor, or else it is no use." "Why not?" asked the man. "Do you hear that melancholy cry from the meadow there?" answered the shepherd, "that is the bittern; he was once a shepherd, and so was the hoopoe also—I will tell you the story.

"The bittern pastured his flocks on rich green meadows where flowers grew in abundance, so his cows became wild and unmanageable. The hoopoe drove his cattle on to high barren hills, where the wind plays with the sand, and his cows became thin, and got no strength. When it was evening, and the shepherds wanted to drive their cows homewards, the bittern could not get his together again; they were too high-spirited, and ran away from him. He called, 'Come, cows, come,' but it was of no use; they took no notice of his calling. The hoopoe, however, could not even get his cows up on their legs, so faint and weak had they become. 'Up, up, up,' screamed he, but it was in vain, they remained lying on the sand.

That is the way when one has no moderation. And to this day, though they have no flocks now to watch, the bittern cries, 'Come, cows, come'; and the hoopoe, 'Up, up, up,' "

The Three Languages

IN SWITZERLAND there lived an old count, who had an only son, a boy who was so stupid he never learned anything. One day the father said, "My son, listen to what I have to say; do all I may, I can knock nothing into your head. Now you shall go away, and an eminent master shall try his hand with you."

So the youth was sent to a foreign city, and remained a whole year with his master, and at the end of that time he returned home. His father asked him at once what he had learned, and he replied, "My father, I have learned what the dogs bark."

"Heavens!" exclaimed the father, "is this all you have learned? I will send you to some other city, to another master." So the youth went away a second time, and after he had remained a year with this master, came home again. His father asked him, as before, what he had learned, and he replied, "I have learned what the birds sing." This answer put the father in a passion, and he exclaimed, "Oh, you prodigal! Has all this precious time passed, and have you learned nothing? Are you not ashamed to come into my presence? Once more, I will send you to a third master; but if you learn nothing this time I will no longer be a father to you."

With this third master the boy remained, as before, a twelve month; and when he came back to his father, he told him that he had learned the language that the frogs croak. At this the father flew into a great rage, and, calling his people together, said, "This youth is no longer my son; I cast him off, and command that you lead him into the forest and take away his life."

The servants led him away into the forest, but they had not the heart to kill him, so they let him go. They cut out, however, the eyes and the tongue of a fawn, and took them for a token to the old count.

The young man wandered along, and after some time came to a castle, where he asked for a night's lodging. The lord of the castle said, "Yes, if you will sleep down below. There is the tower; you may go, but I warn you it is very perilous, for it is full of wild dogs, which bark and howl at every one, and, at certain hours, a man must be thrown to them, whom they devour."

Now, on account of these dogs the whole country round was in terror and sorrow, for no one could prevent their ravages; but the youth, being afraid of nothing, said, "Only let me in to these barking hounds, and give me something to throw to them; they will not harm me."

Since he himself wished it, they gave him some meat for the wild hounds, and let him into the tower. As soon as he entered, the dogs ran about him quite in a friendly way, wagging their tails, and never once barking. They ate, also, the meat he brought, and did not attempt to do him the least injury. The next morning, to the astonishment of every one, he came forth unharmed, and told the lord of the castle, "The hounds have informed me, in their language, why they thus waste and bring destruction upon the land. They have the guardianship of a large treasure beneath the tower, and till that is raised, they have no rest. In what way and manner this is to be done I have also understood from them."

At these words every one began rejoicing, and the lord promised him his daughter in marriage, if he could raise the treasure. This task he happily accomplished, and the wild hounds thereupon disappeared, and the country was freed from that plague. Then the beautiful maiden was married to him, and they lived happily together.

After some time, he one day got into a carriage with his wife and set out on the road to Rome. On their way thither, they passed a swamp, where the frogs sat croaking. The young count listened, and when he heard what they said, he became quite thoughtful and sad, but he did not tell his wife the reason. At last they arrived at Rome, and found the Pope was just dead, and there was a great contention among the cardinals as to who should be his successor. They at length resolved, that he on whom some miraculous sign should be shown should be elected. Just as they had thus resolved, at the same moment the young count stepped into the church, and suddenly two snow-white Doves flew down, one on each of his shoulders, and remained perched there. The clergy recognized in this circumstance the sign they required, and asked him on the spot whether he would be Pope. The young count was undecided, and knew not whether he were worthy; but the Doves whispered to him that he might take the honor, and so he consented. Then he was anointed and consecrated; and so was fulfilled what the frogs had prophesied—and which had so disturbed him—that he should become Pope. Upon his election he had to sing a mass, of which he knew nothing; but the two Doves sitting upon his shoulder told him all that was required.

The Star Money

THERE WAS once on a time a little girl whose father and mother were dead, and she was so poor that she no longer had any little room to live in, or bed to sleep in, and at last she had nothing else but the clothes she was wearing and a little bit of bread in her hand which some charitable soul had given her. She was, however, good and pious. And as she was thus forsaken by all the world, she went forth into the open country, trusting in the good God.

Then a poor man met her, who said, "Ah, give me something to eat, I am so hungry!" She reached him the whole of her piece of bread, and said, "May God bless it to your use," and went onwards. Then came a child who moaned and said, "My head is so cold, give me something to cover it with." So she took off her hood and gave it to him. And when she had walked a little farther, she met another child who had no jacket and was frozen with cold so she gave it her own. A little farther on one begged for a frock, and she gave away that also. At length she got into a forest and it had already become dark, and there came yet another child, and asked for a little shirt, and the good little girl thought to herself, "It is a dark night and no one sees you, you can very well give your little shirt away"; and took it off, and gave away that also.

And as she so stood, and had not one single thing left, suddenly some stars from heaven fell down, and they were nothing else but hard, smooth pieces of money, and although she had just given her little shirt away, she had a new one which was of the very finest linen. Then she gathered together the money, put it into the shirt and was rich all the days of her life.

The Poor Man and the Rich Man

IN ANCIENT TIMES, when the Lord God himself still used to walk about on this earth among men, it once happened that He was tired and overtaken by the darkness before He could reach an inn. Now there stood on the road before Him two houses facing each other; the one large and beautiful, the other small and poor. The large one belonged to a rich man, and the small one to a poor man.

Then the Lord thought, "I shall be no burden to the rich man, I will stay the night with him." When the rich man heard some one knocking at his door, he opened the window and asked the stranger what he wanted. The Lord answered, "I only ask for a night's lodging."

Then the rich man looked at the traveler from head to foot, and as the Lord was wearing common clothes, and did not look like one who had much money in his pocket, he shook his head, and said, "No, I cannot take you in, my rooms are full of herbs and seeds; and if I were to lodge everyone who knocked at my door, I might very soon go begging myself. Go somewhere else for a lodging." And with this he shut down the window and left the Lord standing there.

So the Lord turned his back on the rich man, and went across to the small house and knocked. He had hardly done so when the poor man opened the little door and bade the traveler come in. "Pass the night with me, it is already dark," said he; "you cannot go any further tonight." This pleased the Lord, and He went in. The poor man's wife shook hands with Him, and welcomed Him, and said He was to make Himself at home and put up with what they had; they had not much to offer Him, but what they had they would give Him with all their hearts. Then she put the potatoes on the fire, and while they were boiling, she milked the goat, that they might have a little milk with them. When the cloth was laid, the Lord sat down with the man and his wife, and He enjoyed their coarse food, for there were happy faces at the table.

When they had had supper and it was bed-time, the woman called her husband apart and said, "Hark you, dear husband, let us make up a bed of straw for ourselves tonight, and then the poor traveler can sleep in our bed and have a good rest, for he has been walking the whole day through, and that makes one weary." "With all my heart," he answered. "I will go and offer it to him"; and he went to the stranger and invited him, if he had no objection, to sleep in their bed and rest his limbs properly. But the Lord was unwilling to take their bed from the two old folks; however, they would not be satisfied, until at length He did it and lay down in their bed, while they themselves lay on some straw on the ground.

Next morning they got up before daybreak, and made as good a breakfast as they could for the guest. When the sun shone in through the little window, and the Lord had got up, He again ate with them, and then prepared to set out on His journey.

But as He was standing at the door He turned round and said, "As you are so kind and good, you may wish three things for yourselves and I will grant them." Then the man said, "What else should I wish for but eternal happiness, and that we two, as long as we live, may be healthy and have every day our daily bread; for the third wish, I do not know what to have." And the Lord said to him, "Will you wish for a new house instead of this old one?" "Oh, yes," said the man; "if I can have that, too, I should like it very much." And the Lord fulfilled his wish, and changed their old house into a new one, again gave them His blessing, and went on.

The sun was high when the rich man got up and leaned out of his window and saw, on the opposite side of the way, a new clean-looking house with red tiles and bright windows, where the old hut used to be. He was very much astonished, and called his wife and said to her, "Tell me, what can have happened? Last night there was a miserable little hut standing there, and today there is a beautiful new house. Run over and see how that has come to pass."

So his wife went and asked the poor man, and he said to her, "Yesterday evening a traveler came here and asked for a night's lodging, and this morning when he took leave of us he granted us three wishes—eternal happiness, health during this life and our daily bread as well, and, besides this, a beautiful new house instead of our old hut."

When the rich man's wife heard this, she ran back in haste and told her husband how it had happened. The man said, "I could tear myself to pieces! If I had but known that! The traveler came to our house too, and wanted to sleep here, and I sent him away." "Quick!" said his wife, "get on your horse. You can still catch the man up, and then you must ask to have three wishes granted you."

The rich man followed the good counsel and galloped away on his horse, and soon came up with the Lord. He spoke to Him softly and pleasantly, and begged Him not to take it amiss that he had not let Him in directly; he had been looking for the front-door key, and in the meantime the stranger had gone away; if He returned the same way He must come and stay with him. "Yes," said the Lord; "if I ever come back again, I will do so." Then the rich man asked if he might not wish for three things too, as his neighbor had done. "Yes," said the Lord, he might, but it would not be to his advantage, and he had better not wish for anything; but the rich man thought that he could easily ask for something which would add to his happiness, if only he knew that it would be granted. So the Lord said to him, "Ride home, then, and three wishes which you shall form, shall be fulfilled."

The rich man had now gained what he wanted, so he rode home, and began to consider what he should wish for. As he was thus thinking he let the bridle fall, and the horse began to caper about, so that he was continually disturbed in his meditations, and could not collect his thoughts at all. He patted its neck, and said, "Gently, Lisa," but the horse only began new tricks. Then at last he was angry, and cried quite impatiently, "I wish your neck was broken!"

Directly he had said the words, down the horse fell on the ground, and there it lay dead and never moved again. And thus was his first wish fulfilled. As he was miserly by nature, he did not like to leave the harness lying there, so he cut it off, and put it on his back; and now he had to go on foot. "I have still two wishes left," said he, and comforted himself with that thought.

And now as he was walking slowly through the sand, and the sun was burning hot at noon-day, he grew quite hot-tempered and angry. The saddle hurt his back, and he had not yet any idea what to wish for. "If I were to wish for all the riches and treasures in the world," said he to himself, "I should still think of all kinds of things besides later on; I know that, beforehand. But I will manage so that there is nothing at all left me to wish for afterwards." Then he sighed and said, "Ah, if I were but that Bavarian peasant, who likewise had three wishes granted to him, and knew quite well what to do, and in the first place wished for a great deal of beer, and in the second for as much beer as he was able to drink, and in the third for a barrel of beer into the bargain."

Many a time he thought he had found it, but then it seemed to him to be, after all, too little. Then it came into his mind, what an easy life his wife had, for she stayed at home in a cool room and enjoyed herself. This really did vex him, and before he was aware, he said, "I just wish she was sitting there on this saddle, and could not get off it, instead of my having to drag it along on my back."

And as the last word was spoken, the saddle disappeared from his back, and he saw that his second wish had been fulfilled. Then he really did feel warm.

He began to run and wanted to be quite alone in his own room at home, to think of something really large for his last wish. But when he arrived there and opened the parlor-door, he saw his wife sitting in the middle of the room on the saddle, crying and complaining, and quite unable to get off it. So he said, "Do bear it, and I will wish for all the riches on earth for you, only stay where you are." She, however, called him a fool, and said, "What good will all the riches on earth do me, if I am to sit on this saddle? You have wished me on it, so you must help me off."

So whether he would or not, he was forced to let his third wish be that she should be quit of the saddle, and able to get off it, and immediately the wish was fulfilled. So he got nothing by it but vexation, trouble, abuse, and the loss of his horse; but the poor people lived happily, quietly, and piously until their happy death.

The Stolen Pennies

A FATHER WAS one day sitting at dinner with his wife and his children, and a good friend who had come on a visit was with them. And as they thus sat, and it was striking twelve o'clock, the stranger saw the door open, and a very pale child dressed in snow-white clothes came in. It did not look around, and it did not speak, but went straight into the next room. Soon afterwards it came back, and went out at the door again in the same quiet manner. On the second and on the third day, it came also exactly in the same way. At last the stranger asked the father to whom the beautiful child that went into the next room every day at noon belonged? "I have never seen it," said he, neither did he know to whom it could belong. The next day when it again came, the stranger pointed it out to the father, who however did not see it, and the mother and the children also all saw nothing.

At this the stranger got up, went to the room door, opened it a little, and peeped in. Then he saw the child sitting on the ground, and digging and seeking about industriously among the crevices between the boards of the floor, but when it saw the stranger, it disappeared. He now told what he had seen and described the child exactly, and the mother recognized it, and said, "Ah, it is my dear child who died a month ago."

They took up the boards and found two pennies which the child had once received from its mother that it might give them to a poor man. It, however, had thought, "I can buy myself a biscuit for that," and had kept the pennies, and hidden them in the openings between the boards. Therefore it had had no rest in its grave, and had come every day at noon to seek for these pennies. The parents gave the money at once to a poor man, and after that the child was never seen again.

The Shroud

THERE WAS once a mother who had a little boy seven years old, who was so handsome and loveable that no one could look at him without liking him, and she herself worshipped him above everything in the world. Now it so happened that he suddenly became ill, and God took him to Himself; and for this the mother could not be comforted, and wept both day and night. But soon afterwards, when the child had been buried, it appeared by night in the places where it had sat and played during its life; and if the mother wept, it wept also, and when morning came it disappeared. As, however, the mother would not stop crying, it came one night, in the little white shroud in which it had been laid in its coffin, and with its wreath of flowers round its head, and stood on the bed at her feet, and said, "Oh, mother, do stop crying, or I shall never fall asleep in my coffin, for my shroud will not dry because of all thy tears, which fall upon it." The mother was afraid when she heard that, and wept no more. The next night the child came again, and held a little light in its hand, and said, "Look, mother, my shroud is nearly dry, and I can rest in my grave." Then the mother gave her sorrow into God's keeping, and bore it quietly and patiently, and the child came no more, but slept in its little bed beneath the earth.

The Wilful Child

ONCE UPON a time there was a child who was wilful, and would not do what her mother wished. For this reason God had no pleasure in her, and let her become ill, and no doctor could do her any good, and in a short time she lay on her death-bed. When she had been lowered into her grave, and the earth was spread over her, all at once her arm came out again, and stretched upwards, and when they had put it in and spread fresh earth over it, it was all to no purpose, for the arm always came out again. Then the mother herself was obliged to go to the grave and strike the arm with a rod, and when she had done that, it was drawn in, and then at last the child had rest beneath the ground.

The Rose

THERE WAS once a poor woman who had two children. The youngest had to go every day into the forest to fetch wood. Once when she had gone a long way to seek it, a little child, who was quite strong, came and helped her industriously to pick up the wood and carry it home, and then before a moment had passed the strange child disappeared. The child told her mother this, but at first she would not believe it. At length she brought a rose home, and told her mother that the beautiful child had given her this rose, and had told her that when it was in full bloom, he would return. The mother put the rose in water. One morning her child could not get out of bed. The mother went to the bed and found her dead, but looking very happy. On the same morning, the rose was in full bloom.

The Tailor in Heaven

ONE very fine day it came to pass that the good God wished to enjoy Himself in the heavenly garden, and took all the apostles and saints with Him, so that no one stayed in heaven but Saint Peter. The Lord had commanded him to let no one in during His absence, so Peter stood by the door and kept watch. Before long someone knocked. Peter asked who was there, and what he wanted.

"I am a poor, honest tailor who prays for admission," replied a smooth voice.

"Honest indeed," said Peter, "like the thief on the gallows! You have been light-fingered and have snipped folks' clothes away. You will not get into heaven. The Lord has forbidden me to let any one in while he is out."

"Come, do be merciful," cried the tailor. "Little scraps which fall off the table of their own accord are not stolen, and are not worth speaking about. Look, I am lame, and have blisters on my feet with walking here, I cannot possibly turn back again. Only let me in, and I will do all the rough work. I will carry the children, and wash their clothes, and wash and clean the benches on which they have been playing, and patch all their torn clothes."

Saint Peter let himself be moved by pity, and opened the door of heaven just wide enough for the lame tailor to slip his lean body in. He was forced to sit down in a corner behind the door, and was to stay quietly and peaceably there, in order that the Lord, when He returned, might not observe him and be angry.

The tailor obeyed, but once when Saint Peter went outside the door, he got up, and full of curiosity, went round about into every corner of heaven, and inspected the arrangement of every place. At length he came to a spot where many beautiful and delightful chairs were standing, and in the midst was a seat all of gold which was set with shining jewels; likewise it was much higher than the other chairs, and a footstool of gold was before it. It was, however, the seat on which the Lord sat when He was at home, and from which He could see everything which happened on earth. The tailor stood still, and looked at the seat for a long time, for it pleased him better than all else. At last he could master his curiosity no longer, and climbed up and seated himself in the chair.

Then he saw everything which was happening on earth, and

observed an ugly old woman who was standing washing by the side of a stream, secretly laying two veils on one side for herself. The sight of this made the tailor so angry that he laid hold of the golden footstool, and threw it down to earth through heaven, at the old thief. As, however, he could not bring the stool back again, he slipped quietly out of the chair, seated himself in his place behind the door, and behaved as if he had never stirred from the spot.

When the Lord and Master came back again with His heavenly companions, He did not see the tailor behind the door, but when He seated Himself on His chair the footstool was missing. He asked Saint Peter what had become of the stool, but he did not know. Then He asked if he had let anyone come in.

"I know of no one who has been here," answered Peter, "but a lame tailor, who is still sitting behind the door." Then the Lord had the tailor brought before Him, and asked him if he had taken away the stool, and where he had put it.

"Oh, Lord," answered the tailor joyously, "I threw it in my anger down to earth at an old woman whom I saw stealing two veils at the washing."

"Oh, you knave," said the Lord, "were I to judge as you judge, how do you think you could have escaped so long? I should long ago have had no chairs, benches, seats, nay, not even an oven-fork, but should have thrown everything down at the sinners. Henceforth you can stay no longer in heaven, but must go outside the door again. Then go where you will. No one shall give punishment here, but I alone, the Lord."

Peter was obliged to take the tailor out of heaven again, and as he had torn shoes, and feet covered with blisters, he took a stick in his hand, and went to the Waitabit inn, where the good soldiers sit and make merry.

Poverty and Humility Lead to Heaven

THERE WAS once a King's son who went out into the world, and he was full of thought and sad. He looked at the sky, which was so beautifully pure and blue, then he sighed, and said, "How well must all be with one up there in heaven!" Then he saw a poor gray-haired man who was coming along the road towards him, and he spoke to him, and asked, "How can I get to heaven?" The man answered, "By poverty and humility. Put on my ragged clothes, wander about the world for seven years, and get to know what misery is, take no money, but if thou art hungry ask compassionate hearts for a bit of bread; in this way thou wilt reach heaven."

Then the King's son took off his magnificent coat, and wore in its place the beggar's garment, went out into the wide world, and suffered great misery. He took nothing but a little food, said nothing, but prayed to the Lord to take him into His heaven.

When the seven years were over, he returned to his father's palace, but no one recognized him. He said to the servants, "Go and tell my parents that I have come back again." But the servants did not believe it, and laughed and left him standing there. Then said he, "Go and tell it to my brothers that they may come down, for I should so like to see them again." The servants would not do that either, but at last one of them went, and told it to the King's children, but these did not believe it, and did not trouble themselves about it.

Then he wrote a letter to his mother, and described to her all his misery, but he did not say that he was her son. So, out of pity, the Queen had a place under the stairs assigned to him, and food taken to him daily by two servants. But one of them was ill-natured and said, "Why should the beggar have the good food?" and kept it for himself, or gave it to the dogs, and took the weak, wasted-away beggar nothing but water; the other, however, was honest, and took the beggar what was sent to him. It was little, but he could live on it for a while, and all the time he was quite patient, but he grew continually weaker. As, however, his illness increased, he desired to receive the last sacrament. When the host was being elevated down below, all the bells in the town and neighborhood began to ring. After mass the priest went to the poor man under the stairs, and there he lay dead. In one hand he had a rose, in the other a lily, and beside him was a paper in which was written his history.

When he was buried, a rose grew on one side of his grave, and a lily on the other.

The Flail from Heaven

A COUNTRYMAN was once going out to plough with a pair of oxen. When he got to the field, both the animals' horns began to grow, and went on growing, and when he wanted to go home they were so big that the oxen could not get through the gateway for them. By good luck a butcher came by just then, and he delivered them over to him, and made the bargain in this way, that he should take the butcher a measure of turnip-seed, and then the butcher was to count him out a Brabant thaler for every seed. I call that well sold! The peasant now went home, and carried the measure of turnip-seed to him on his back. On the way, however, he lost one seed out of the bag. The butcher paid him justly as agreed on, and if the peasant had not lost the seed, he would have had one thaler the more.

In the meantime, when he went on his way back, the seed had grown into a tree which reached up to the sky. Then thought the peasant, "As thou hast the chance, thou must just see what the angels are doing up there above, and for once have them before thine eyes." So he climbed up, and saw that the angels above were threshing oats, and he looked on.

While he was thus watching them, he observed that the tree on which he was standing, was beginning to totter; he peeped down, and saw that some one was just going to cut it down. "If I were to fall down from here it would be a bad thing," thought he, and in his necessity he did not know how to save himself better than by taking the chaff of the oats which lay there in heaps, and twisting a rope of it. He likewise snatched a hoe and a flail which were lying about in heaven, and let himself down by the rope. But he came down on the earth exactly in the middle of a deep, deep hole. So it was a real piece of luck that he had brought the hoe, for he hoed himself a flight of steps with it, and mounted up, and took the flail with him as a token of his truth, so that no one could have any doubt of his story.

The Moon

IN DAYS gone by there was a land where the nights were always dark, and the sky spread over it like a black cloth, for there the moon never rose, and no star shone in the obscurity. At the creation of the world, the light at night had been sufficient. For young fellows once went out of this country on a traveling expedition, and arrived in another kingdom, where, in the evening when the sun had disappeared behind the mountains, a shining globe was placed on an oak tree, which shed a soft light far and wide. By means of this, everything could very well be seen and distinguished, even though it was not so brilliant as the sun. The travelers stopped and asked a countryman who was driving past with his cart what kind of a light that was. "That is the moon," answered he; "our mayor bought it for three thalers, and fastened it to the oak tree. He has to pour oil into it daily, and to keep it clean, so that it may always burn clearly. He receives a thaler a week from us for doing it."

When the countryman had driven away, one of them said, "We could make some use of this lamp, we have an oak tree at home, which is just as big as this, and we could hang it on that. What a pleasure it would be not to have to feel about at night in the darkness!" "I'll tell you what we'll do," said the second; "we will fetch a cart and horses and carry away the moon. The people here may buy themselves another." "I'm a good climber," said the third, "I will bring it down." The fourth brought a cart and horses, and the third climbed the tree, bored a hole in the moon, passed a rope through it, and let it down. When the shining ball lay in the cart, they covered it over with a cloth, that no one might observe the theft. They conveyed it safely into their own country, and placed it on a high oak. Old and young rejoiced when the new lamp let its light shine over the whole land, and bed-rooms and sitting-rooms were filled with it. The dwarfs came forth from their caves in the rocks, and the tiny elves in their little red coats danced in rings on the meadows.

The four took care that the moon was provided with oil, cleaned the wick, and received their weekly thaler; but they became old men, and when one of them grew ill, and saw that he was about to die, he appointed that one quarter of the moon, should, as his property, be laid in the grave with him. When he died, the mayor climbed up the tree, and cut off a quarter with the hedge-shears, and this was placed in his coffin. The light of the moon decreased, but still not visibly. When the second died, the second quarter was buried with him, and the light diminished. It grew weaker still after the death of the third, who likewise took his part of it away with him; and when the fourth was borne to his grave, the old state of darkness recommenced, and whenever the people went out at night without their lanterns they knocked their heads together.

When, however, the pieces of the moon had united themselves together again in the world below, where darkness had always prevailed, it came to pass that the dead became restless and awoke from their sleep. They were astonished when they were able to see again; the moonlight was quite sufficient for them, for their eyes had become so weak that they could not have borne the brilliance of the sun. They rose up and were merry, and fell into their former ways of living. Some of them went to the play and to dance, others hastened to the public-houses, where they asked for wine, got drunk, brawled, quarreled, and at last took up cudgels, and belabored each other. The noise became greater and greater, and at last reached even to heaven.

Saint Peter who guards the gate of heaven thought the lower world had broken out in revolt and gathered together the heavenly troops, which are to drive back the Evil One when he and his associates storm the abode of the blessed. As these, however, did not come, he got on his horse and rode through the gate of heaven, down into the world below. There he reduced the dead to subjection, bade them lie down in their graves again, took the moon away with him, and hung it up in heaven.

The Peasant in Heaven

ONCE UPON a time a poor pious peasant died, and arrived before the gate of heaven. At the same time a very rich, rich lord came there who also wanted to get into heaven. Then Saint Peter came with the key, and opened the door, and let the great man in, but apparently did not see the peasant, and shut the door again. And now the peasant outside heard how the great man was received in heaven with all kinds of rejoicing, and how they were making music, and singing within. At length all became quiet again, and Saint Peter came and opened the gate of heaven, and let the peasant in. The peasant, however, expected that they would make music and sing when he went in also, but all remained quite quiet. He was received with great affection, it is true, and the angels came to meet him, but no one sang.

Then the peasant asked Saint Peter how it was that they did not sing for him as they had done when the rich man went in, and said that it seemed to him that there in heaven things were done with just as much partiality as on earth. Then said Saint Peter, "By no means, thou art just as dear to us as any one else, and wilt enjoy every heavenly delight that the rich man enjoys, but poor fellows like thee come to heaven every day, but a rich man like this does not come more than once in a hundred years!"

Eve's Various Children

WHEN Adam and Eve were driven out of Paradise, they were compelled to build a house for themselves on unfruitful ground, and eat their bread in the sweat of their brow. Adam dug up the land, and Eve span. Every year Eve brought a child into the world; but the children were unlike each other, some pretty, and some ugly.

After a considerable time had gone by, God sent an angel to them, to announce that He was coming to inspect their household. Eve, delighted that the Lord should be so gracious, cleaned her house diligently, decked it with flowers, and strewed reeds on the floor. Then she brought in her children, but only the beautiful ones. She washed and bathed them, combed their hair, put clean raiment on them, and cautioned them to conduct themselves decorously and modestly in the presence of the Lord. They were to bow down before Him civilly, hold out their hands, and to answer His questions modestly and sensibly.

The ugly children were, however, not to let themselves be seen. One hid himself beneath the hay, another under the roof, a third in the straw, the fourth in the stove, the fifth in the cellar, the sixth under a tub, the seventh beneath the wine-cask, the eighth under an old fur cloak, the ninth and tenth beneath the cloth out of which she always made their clothes, and the eleventh and twelfth under the leather out of which she cut their shoes. She had scarcely got ready, before there was a knock at the house-door. Adam looked through a chink, and saw that it was the Lord. Adam opened the door respectfully, and the Heavenly Father entered.

There, in a row, stood the pretty children, and bowed before Him, held out their hands, and knelt down. The Lord, however, began to bless them, laid His hands on the first, and said, "Thou shalt be a powerful king"; and to the second, "Thou a prince"; to the third, "Thou a count"; to the fourth, "Thou a knight"; to the fifth, "Thou a nobleman"; to the sixth, "Thou a burgher"; to the seventh, "Thou a merchant"; to the eighth, "Thou a learned man." He bestowed upon them also all His richest blessings.

When Eve saw that the Lord was so mild and gracious, she thought, "I will bring hither my ill-favored children also; it may be that He will bestow His blessing on them likewise." So she ran and brought them out of the hay, the straw, the stove, and wherever else she had concealed them. Then came the whole coarse, dirty, shabby, sooty band. The Lord smiled, looked at them all, and said, "I will bless these also." He laid His hands on the first, and said to him, "Thou shalt be a peasant"; to the second, "Thou a fisherman"; to the third, "Thou a smith"; to the fourth, "Thou a tanner"; to the fifth, "Thou a weaver"; to the sixth, "Thou a shoemaker"; to the seventh, "Thou a tailor"; to the eighth, "Thou a potter"; to the ninth, "Thou a wagoner"; to the tenth, "Thou a sailor"; to the eleventh, "Thou an errand-boy"; to the twelfth, "Thou a scullion all the days of thy life."

When Eve had heard all this she said, "Lord, how unequally Thou dividest Thy gifts! After all they are all of them my children, whom I have brought into the world, Thy favors should be given to all alike." But God answered, "Eve, thou dost not understand. It is right and necessary that the entire world should be supplied from thy children. If they were all Princes and lords, who would grow corn, thresh it, grind and bake it? Who would be blacksmiths, weavers, carpenters, masons, laborers, tailors and seamstresses? Each shall have his own place, so that one shall support the other, and all shall be fed like the limbs of one body." Then Eve answered, "Ah, Lord, forgive me, I was too quick in speaking to Thee. Have Thy divine will with my children."

The Poor Boy in the Grave

THERE WAS once a poor shepherd-boy whose father and mother were dead, and he was placed by the authorities in the house of a rich man, who was to feed him and bring him up. The man and his wife had, however, bad hearts, and were greedy and anxious about their riches, and vexed whenever any one put a morsel of their bread in his mouth. The poor young fellow might do what he liked, he got little to eat, but only so many blows the more.

One day he had to watch a hen and her chickens, but she ran through a quick-set hedge with them, and a hawk darted down instantly, and carried her off through the air. The boy called, "Thief! thief! rascal!" with all the strength of his body. But what good did that do? The hawk did not bring its prey back again. The man heard the noise, and ran to the spot, and as soon as he saw that his hen was gone, he fell in a rage, and gave the boy such a beating that he could not stir for two days. Then he had to take care of the chickens without the hen, but now his difficulty was greater, for one ran here and the other there. He thought he was doing a very wise thing when he tied them all together with a string, because then the hawk would not be able to steal any of them away from him. But he was very much mistaken. After two days, worn out with running about and hunger, he fell asleep. The bird of prey came, and seized one of the chickens, and as the others were tied fast to it, it carried them all off together, perched itself on a tree, and devoured them. The farmer was just coming home, and when he saw the misfortune, he got angry and beat the boy so unmercifully that he was forced to lie in bed for several days.

When he was on his legs again, the farmer said to him, "You are too stupid for me, I cannot make a herdsman of you, you must go as errand-boy." Then he sent him to the judge, to whom he was to carry a basketful of grapes, and he gave him a letter as well. On the way, hunger and thirst tormented the unhappy boy so violently that he ate two of the bunches of grapes. He took the basket to the judge, but when the judge had read the letter, and counted the bunches he said, "Two clusters are wanting." The boy confessed quite honestly that, driven by hunger and thirst, he had devoured the two which were wanting. The judge wrote a letter to the farmer, and asked for the same number of grapes again. These also the boy had to take to him with a letter. As he again was so extremely hungry and thirsty, he could not help it, and again ate two bunches. But first he took the letter out of the basket, put it under a stone and seated himself thereon in order that the letter might not see and betray him. The judge, however, again made him give an explanation about the missing bunches. "Ah," said the boy, "how have you learnt that? The letter could not know about it, for I put it under a stone before I did it." The judge could not help laughing at the boy's simplicity, and sent the man a letter wherein he cautioned him to keep the poor boy better, and not let him want for meat and drink, and also that he was to teach him what was right and what was wrong.

"I will soon show you the difference," said the hard man. "If you must eat, you must work, and if you do anything wrong, you shall be taught by blows."

The next day he set him a hard task. He was to chop two bundles of straw for food for the horses, and then the man threatened: "In five hours I shall be back again, and if the straw is not cut to chaff by that time, I will beat you until you cannot move a limb." The farmer went with his wife, the manservant and the girl, to the yearly fair, and left nothing behind for the boy but a small bit of bread. The boy seated himself on the bench, and began to work with all his might. As he got warm over it he put his little coat off and threw it on the straw. In his terror lest he should not get done in time he kept constantly cutting, and in his haste, without noticing it, he chopped his little coat as well as the straw. He became aware of the misfortune too late; there was no repairing it. "Ah," cried he, "now all is over with me! The wicked man did not threaten me for nothing; if he comes back and sees what I have done, he will kill me. Rather than that I will take my own life."

The boy had once heard the farmer's wife say, "I have a pot with poison in it under my bed." She, however, had only said that to keep away greedy people, for there was honey in it. The boy crept under the bed, brought out the pot, and ate all that was in it. "I do not know," said he, "folks say death is bitter, but it tastes very sweet to me. It is no wonder that the farmer's wife has so often longed for death." He seated himself in a little chair, and was prepared to die. But instead of becoming weaker he felt himself strengthened by the nourishing food. "It cannot have been poison," thought he, "but the farmer once said there was a small bottle of poison for flies in the box in which he keeps his clothes; that, no doubt, will be the true poison, and bring death to me." It was, however, no poison for flies, but Hungarian wine. The boy got out the bottle, and emptied it. "This death tastes sweet too," said he, but shortly after when the wine began to mount into his brain and stupefy him, he thought his end was drawing near. "I feel that I must die," said he, "I will go away to the church-yard, and seek a grave." He staggered out, reached the church-yard, and laid himself in a newly-dug grave. He lost his senses more and more. In the neighborhood was an inn where a wedding was being kept. When he heard the music, he fancied he was already in Paradise, until at length he lost all consciousness. The poor boy never awoke again; the heat of the strong wine and the cold night-dew deprived him of life, and he remained in the grave in which he had laid himself.

When the farmer heard the news of the boy's death he was terrified, and afraid of being brought to justice—indeed, his distress took such a powerful hold of him that he fell fainting to the ground. His wife, who was standing on the hearth with a pan of hot fat, ran to him to help him. But the flames darted against the pan and the whole house caught fire. In a few hours it lay in ashes, and the rest of the years they had to live they passed in poverty and misery, tormented by the pangs of conscience.

Our Lady's Child

CLOSE to a large forest there lived a wood-cutter and his wife. They had an only child, a little girl three years old. They were so poor that they no longer had daily bread, and did not know how to get food for her. One morning the wood-cutter went out sorrowfully to his work in the forest, and while he was cutting wood, suddenly there stood before him a tall and beautiful woman with a crown of shining stars on her head. She said to him, "I am the Virgin Mary, mother of the child Jesus. Thou art poor and needy, bring thy child to me, I will take her with me and be her mother, and care for her." The wood-cutter obeyed, brought his child, and gave her to the Virgin Mary, who took her up to heaven with her. There the child fared well, ate sugar-cakes, and drank sweet milk, and her clothes were of gold, and the little angels played with her.

And when she was fourteen years of age, the Virgin Mary called her one day and said, "Dear child, I am about to make a long journey, so take into thy keeping the keys of the thirteen doors of heaven. Twelve of these thou mayest open, and behold the glory which is within them, but the thirteenth, to which this little key belongs, is forbidden thee. Beware of opening it, or thou wilt bring misery on thyself." The girl promised to be obedient, and when the Virgin Mary was gone, she began to examine the dwellings of the kingdom of heaven. Each day she opened one of them, until she had made the round of the twelve. In each of them sat one of the Apostles in the midst of a great light, and she rejoiced in all the magnificence and splendor, and the little angels who always accompanied her rejoiced with her.

Then the forbidden door alone remained, and she felt a great desire to know what could be hidden behind it, and said to the angels, "I will not quite open it, and I will not go inside it, but I will unlock it so that we can just see a little through the opening." "Oh, no," said the little angels, "that would be a sin. The Virgin Mary has forbidden it, and it might easily cause thy unhappiness." Then she was silent, but the desire in her heart was not stilled, but gnawed there and tormented her, and let her have no rest. And once when the angels had all gone out, she thought, "Now I am quite alone, and I could peep in. If I do it, no one will ever know."

She took the key, put it in the lock, and turned it round. Then the door sprang open, and she saw there the Trinity sitting in fire and splendor. She stayed there awhile, and looked at everything in amazement; then she touched the light a little with her finger, and her finger became quite golden. Immediately a great fear fell on her. She shut the door violently, and ran away. Nor would her terror quit her, let her do what she might, and her heart beat continually and would not be still; the gold, too, stayed on her finger, and would not go away, let her rub it and wash it ever so much.

It was not long before the Virgin Mary came back from her journey. She called the girl before her, and asked to have the keys of heaven back. When the maiden gave her the bunch, the Virgin looked into her eyes and said, "Hast thou not opened the thirteenth door also?" "No," she replied. Then she laid her hand on the girl's heart, and felt how it beat and beat, and saw right well that she had disobeyed her order and had opened the door. Then she said once again, "Art thou certain that thou hast not done it?" "Yes," said the girl, for the second time. Then she perceived the finger which had become golden from touching the fire of heaven, and saw well that the child had sinned, and said for the third time,

"Hast thou not done it?" "No," said the girl for the third time. Then said the Virgin Mary, "Thou hast not obeyed me, and besides that thou hast lied; thou art no longer worthy to be in heaven."

Then the girl fell into a deep sleep, and when she awoke she lay on the earth below, and in the midst of a wilderness. She wanted to cry out, but she could bring forth no sound. She sprang up and wanted to run away, but whithersoever she turned herself, she was continually held back by thick hedges of thorns through which she could not break. In the desert in which she was imprisoned, there stood an old hollow tree, and this had to be her dwelling-place. Into this she crept when night came, and here she slept. Here, too, she found a shelter from storm and rain, but it was a miserable life, and bitterly did she weep when she remembered how happy she had been in heaven, and how the angels had played with her. Roots and wild berries were her only food, and for these she sought as far as she could go.

In the autumn she picked up the fallen nuts and leaves, and carried them into the hole. The nuts were her food in winter, and when snow and ice came, she crept among the leaves like a poor little animal that she might not freeze. Before long her clothes were all torn, and one bit of them after another fell off her. As soon, however, as the sun shone warm again, she went out and sat in front of the tree, and her long hair covered her on all sides like a mantle. Thus she sat year after year, and felt the pain and misery of the world.

One day, when the trees were once more clothed in fresh green, the King of the country was hunting in the forest, and followed a roe, and as it had fled into the thicket which shut in this bit of the forest, he got off his horse, tore the bushes asunder, and cut himself a path with his sword. When he had at last forced his way through, he saw a wonderfully beautiful maiden sitting under the tree; and she sat there and was entirely covered with her golden hair down to her very feet. He stood still and looked at her full of surprise, then he spoke to her and said, "Who art thou? Why art thou sitting here in the wilderness?" But she gave no answer, for she could not open her mouth. The King continued, "Wilt thou go with me to my castle?" Then she just nodded her head a little. The King took her in his arms, carried her to his horse, and rode home with her, and when he reached the royal castle he caused her to be dressed in beautiful garments, and gave her all things in abundance. Although she could not speak, she was still so beautiful and charming that he began to love her with all his heart, and it was not long before he married her.

After a year or so had passed, the Queen brought a son into the world. Thereupon the Virgin Mary appeared to her in the night when she lay in her bed alone, and said, "If thou wilt tell the truth and confess that thou didst unlock the forbidden door, I will open thy mouth and give thee back thy speech, but if thou perseverest in thy sin, and deniest obstinately, I will take thy new-born child away with me." Then the Queen was permitted to answer, but she remained hard, and said, "No, I did not open the forbidden door"; and the Virgin Mary took the new-born child from her arms, and vanished with it. Next morning, when the child was not to be found, it was whispered among the people that the Queen was a man-eater, and had killed her own child. She heard all this and could say nothing to the contrary, but the King would not believe it, for he loved her so much.

When a year had gone by the Queen again bore a son, and in the night the Virgin Mary again came to her, and said, "If thou wilt confess that thou openedst the forbidden door, I will give thee thy child back and untie thy tongue; but if thou continuest in sin and deniest it, I will take away with me this new child also." Then the Queen again said, "No, I did not open the forbidden door"; and the Virgin Mary took the child out of her arms, and away with her to heaven. Next morning, when this child also had disappeared, the people declared quite loudly that the Queen had devoured it, and the King's councillors demanded that she should be brought to justice. The King, however, loved her so dearly that he would not believe it, and commanded the councillors under pain of death not to say any more about it.

The following year the Queen gave birth to a beautiful little daughter, and for the third time the Virgin Mary appeared to her in the night and said, "Follow me." She took the Queen by the hand and led her to heaven, and showed her there her two elder children, who smiled at her, and were playing with the ball of the world. When the Queen rejoiced thereat, the Virgin Mary said, "Is thy heart not yet softened? If thou wilt own that thou openedst the forbidden door, I will give thee back thy two little sons." But for the third time the Queen answered, "No, I did not open the forbidden door." Then the Virgin let her sink down to earth once more, and took from her likewise her third child.

Next morning, when the loss was reported, all the people cried loudly, "The Queen is a man-eater! She must be judged," and the

King was no longer able to restrain his councillors. Thereupon a trial was held, and as she could not answer, and defend herself, she was condemned to be burnt alive. The wood was got together, and when she was fast bound to the stake, and the fire began to burn round about her, the hard ice of pride melted, her heart was moved by repentance, and she thought, "If I could but confess before my death that I opened the door." Then her voice came back to her, and she cried out loudly, "Yes, Mary, I did it." Straightway rain fell from the sky and extinguished the flames of fire, and a light broke forth above her, and the Virgin Mary descended with the two little sons by her side, and the new-born daughter in her arms. She spoke kindly to her, and said, "He who repents his sin and acknowledges it, is forgiven." Then she gave her the three children, untied her tongue, and granted her happiness throughout her life.

Gambling Hansel

ONCE UPON a time there was a man who did nothing but gamble, and for that reason people never called him anything but Gambling Hansel, and as he never ceased to gamble, he played away his house and all that he had.

Now the very day before his creditors were to take his house from him, came the Lord and St. Peter, and asked him to give them shelter for the night. Then Gambling Hansel said, "For my part, you may stay the night, but I cannot give you a bed or anything to eat."

So the Lord said he was just to take them in, and they themselves would buy something to eat, to which Gambling Hansel made no objection. Thereupon St. Peter gave him three groschen, and said he was to go to the baker's and fetch some bread.

So Gambling Hansel went, but when he reached the house where the other gambling vagabonds were gathered together, they, although they had won all that he had, greeted him clamorously, and said, "Hansel, do come in." "Oh," said he, "do you want to win the three groschen, too?" On this they would not let him go. So he went in, and played away the three groschen also.

Meanwhile St. Peter and the Lord were waiting, and as he was so long in coming, they set out to meet him. When Gambling Hansel came, however, he pretended that the money had fallen into the gutter, and kept raking about in it all the while to find it, but our Lord already knew that he had lost it in play. St. Peter again gave him three groschen, and now he did not allow himself to be led away once more, but fetched them the loaf. Our Lord then inquired if he had no wine, and he said, "Alack, sir, the casks are all empty!" But the Lord said he was to go down into the cellar, for the best wine was still there. For a long time he would not believe this, but at length he said, "Well, I will go down, but I know that there is none there." When he turned the tap, however, lo and behold, the best of wine ran out! So he took it to them, and the two passed the night there.

Early next day our Lord told Gambling Hansel that he might beg three favors. The Lord expected that he would ask to go to Heaven; but Gambling Hansel asked for a pack of cards with which he could win everything, for dice with which he would win everything, and for a tree whereon every kind of fruit would grow, and from which no one who had climbed up, could descend until he bade him do so. The Lord gave him all that he had asked, and departed with St. Peter.

And now Gambling Hansel at once set about gambling in real earnest, and before long he had gained half the world. Upon this St. Peter said to the Lord, "Lord, this thing must not go on, he will win, and Thou lose, the whole world. We must send Death to him." When Death appeared, Gambling Hansel had just seated himself at the gaming-table, and Death said, "Hansel, come out a while." But Gambling Hansel said, "Just wait a little until the game is done, and in the meantime get up into that tree out there, and gather a little fruit that we may have something to munch on our way." Thereupon Death climbed up, but when he wanted to come down again, he could not, and Gambling Hansel left him up there for seven years, during which time no one died.

So St. Peter said to the Lord, "Lord, this thing must not go on. People no longer die; we must go ourselves." And they went themselves, and the Lord commanded Hansel to let Death come down. So Hansel went at once to Death and said to him, "Come down," and Death took him directly and put an end to him.

They went away together and came to the next world, and then Gambling Hansel made straight for the door of Heaven, and knocked at it. "Who is there?" "Gambling Hansel." "Ah, we will have nothing to do with him! Begone!" So he went to the door of

Purgatory, and knocked once more. "Who is there?" "Gambling Hansel." "Ah, there is quite enough weeping and wailing here without him. We do not want to gamble, just go away again." Then he went to the door of Hell, and there they let him in.

There was, however, no one at home but old Lucifer and the crooked devils who had just been doing their evil work in the world. And no sooner was Hansel there than he sat down to gamble again. Lucifer, however, had nothing to lose but his misshapen devils, and Gambling Hansel won them from him, as with his cards he could not fail to do.

Now he was off again with his crooked devils, and they went to Hohenfuert and pulled up a hop-hole, and with it went to Heaven and began to thrust the pole against it, and Heaven began to crack. So again St. Peter said, "Lord, this thing cannot go on, we must let him in, or he will throw us down from Heaven." And they let him in. But Gambling Hansel instantly began to play again, and there was such a noise and confusion that there was no hearing what they themselves were saying. Therefore St. Peter once more said, "Lord, this cannot go on, we must throw him down, or he will make all Heaven rebellious." So they went to him at once, and threw him down, and his soul broke into fragments, and went into the gambling vagabonds who are living this very day.

The Old Man Made Young Again

IN THE TIME when our Lord still walked this earth, He and St. Peter stopped one evening at a smith's and received free quarters. Then it came to pass that a poor beggar, badly pressed by age and infirmity, came to this house and begged alms of the smith. St. Peter had compassion on him and said, "Lord and Master, if it please Thee, cure his torments that he may be able to win his own bread." The Lord said kindly, "Smith, lend Me thy forge, and put on some coals for Me, and then I will make this ailing old man young again." The smith was quite willing, and St. Peter blew the bellows, and when the coal fire sparkled up large and high our Lord took the little old man, pushed him in the forge in the midst of the red-hot fire, so that he glowed like a rose-bush, and praised God with a loud voice. After that the Lord went to the quenching tub, put the glowing little man into it so that the water closed over him, and after He had carefully cooled him, gave him His blessing, when behold! the little man sprang nimbly out, looking fresh, straight, healthy, and as if he were but twenty.

The smith, who had watched everything closely and attentively, invited them all to supper. He, however, had an old, half-blind, crooked mother-in-law who went to the youth, and with great earnestness asked if the fire had burnt him much. He answered that he had never felt more comfortable, and that he had sat in the red heat as if he had been in cool dew. The youth's words echoed in the ears of the old woman all night long, and early next morning, when the Lord had gone on His way again and had heartily thanked the smith, the latter thought he might make his old mother-in-law young again likewise, as he had watched everything so carefully, and it lay in the province of his trade. So he called to ask her if she, too, would like to go bounding about like a girl of eighteen. She said, "With all my heart, as the youth has come out of it so well."

So the smith made a great fire, and thrust the old woman into it, and she writhed about this way and that, and uttered terrible cries of murder. "Sit still; why art thou screaming and jumping about so?" cried he, and as he spoke he blew the bellows again until all her rags were burnt. The old woman cried without ceasing, and the smith thought to himself, "I have not quite the right art," and took her out and threw her into the cooling-tub. Then she screamed so loudly that the smith's wife upstairs and her daughter-in-law heard, and they both ran downstairs, and saw the old woman lying in a heap in the quenching-tub, howling and screaming, with her face wrinkled and shriveled and all out of shape. Thereupon the two, who were both with child, were so terrified that that very night two boys were born who were not made like men but apes, and they ran into the woods, and from them sprang the race of apes.

The Lord's Animals and the Devil's

THE Lord God had created all animals, and had chosen the wolf to be his dog, but he had forgotten the goat. Then the Devil made ready and began to create also, and created goats with fine long tails. Now when they went to pasture, they generally remained caught in the hedges by their tails; then the Devil had to go there and disentangle them with a great deal of trouble. This enraged him at last, and he went and bit off the tail of every goat, as may be seen to this day by the stump. Then he let them go to pasture alone.

It came to pass that the Lord God perceived how at one time they gnawed away at a fruitful tree, at another injured the noble vines, or destroyed other tender plants. This distressed Him, so that in His goodness and mercy He summoned His wolves, who soon tore in pieces the goats that went there.

When the Devil observed this, he went before the Lord and said, "Thy creatures have destroyed mine." The Lord answered, "Why didst thou create things to do harm?" The Devil said, "I was compelled to do it: inasmuch as my thoughts run on evil, what I create can have no other nature, and thou must pay me heavy damages." "I will pay thee as soon as the oak leaves fall; come then, thy money will then be ready counted out." When the oak leaves had fallen, the Devil came and demanded what was due to him. But the Lord said, "In the church of Constantinople stands a tall oak tree which still has all its leaves." With raging and curses, the Devil departed, and went to seek the oak, wandered in the wilderness for six months before he found it, and when he returned, all the oaks had in the meantime covered themselves again with green leaves. Then he had to forfeit his indemnity, and in his rage he put out the eyes of all the remaining goats, and put his own in instead.

This is why all goats have devil's eyes, why their tails are bitten off, and why he likes to assume their shape.

Master Pfriem

MASTER PFRIEM* was a short, thin, but lively man, who never rested a moment. His face, of which his turned-up nose was the only prominent feature, was marked with smallpox and pale as death; his hair was gray and shaggy, his eyes small, but they glanced perpetually about on all sides. He saw everything, criticized everything, knew everything best, and was always in the right. When he went into the streets, he moved his arms about as if he were rowing; and once he struck the pail of a girl, who was carrying water, so high in the air that he himself was wetted all over by it. "Stupid thing," cried he to her, while he was shaking himself, "could you not see that I was coming behind you?"

By trade he was a shoemaker, and when he worked he pulled his thread out with such force that he drove his fist into every one who did not keep far enough off. No apprentice stayed more than a month with him, for he had always some fault to find with the very best work. At one time it was that the stitches were not even; at another that one shoe was too long, or one heel higher than the other, or the leather not cut large enough. "Wait," said he to his apprentice, "I will soon show you how we make skins soft," and he brought a strap and gave him a couple of strokes across the back. He called them all sluggards. He himself did not turn much work out of his hands, for he never sat still for a quarter of an hour.

If his wife got up very early in the morning and lighted the fire, he jumped out of bed, and ran bare-footed into the kitchen, crying, "Will you burn my house down for me? That is a fire one could roast an ox by! Does wood cost nothing?" If the servants were standing by their wash-tubs and laughing, and telling each other all they knew, he scolded them, and said, "There stand the geese cackling, and forgetting their work, to gossip! And why fresh soap? Disgraceful extravagance and shameful idleness into the bargain! They want to save their hands, and not rub the things properly!" And out he would run and knock a pail full of soap and water over, so that the whole kitchen was flooded.

Some one was building a new house, so he hurried to the window to look on. "There, they are using that red sand-stone again that never dries!" cried he. "No one will ever be healthy in that house!

* *Pfriem:* a cobbler's awl.

And just look how badly the fellows are laying the stones! Besides, the mortar is good for nothing! It ought to have gravel in it, not sand. I shall live to see that house tumble down on the people who are in it." He sat down, put a couple of stitches in, and then jumped up again, unfastened his leather-apron, and cried, "I will just go out, and appeal to those men's consciences." He stumbled on the carpenters. "What's this?" cried he, "you are not working by the line! Do you expect the beams to be straight?—one wrong will put all wrong." He snatched an axe out of a carpenter's hand and wanted to show him how he ought to cut; but as a cart loaded with clay came by, he threw the axe away, and hastened to the peasant who was walking by the side of it. "You are not in your right mind," said he, "who yokes young horses to a heavily laden cart? The poor beasts will die on the spot." The peasant did not give him an answer, and Pfriem in a rage ran back into his workshop.

When he was setting himself to work again, the apprentice reached him a shoe. "Well, what's that again?" screamed he. "Haven't I told you you ought not to cut shoes so broad? Who would buy a shoe like this, which is hardly anything else but a sole? I insist on my orders being followed exactly." "Master," answered the apprentice, "you may easily be quite right about the shoe being a bad one, but it is the one which you yourself cut out, and yourself set to work at. When you jumped up a while since, you knocked it off the table, and I have only just picked it up. An angel from heaven, however, would never make you believe that."

One night Master Pfriem dreamed he was dead, and on his way to heaven. When he got there, he knocked loudly at the door. "I wonder," said he to himself, "that they have no knocker on the door—one knocks one's knuckles sore." The apostle Peter opened the door, and wanted to see who demanded admission so noisily. "Ah, it's you, Master Pfriem"; said he, "well, I'll let you in, but I warn you that you must give up that habit of yours, and find fault with nothing you see in heaven, or you may fare ill." "You might have spared your warning," answered Pfriem. "I know already what is seemly, and here, God be thanked, everything is perfect, and there is nothing to blame as there is on earth." So he went in, and walked up and down the wide expanses of heaven. He looked around him, to the left and to the right, but sometimes shook his head, or muttered something to himself.

Then he saw two angels who were carrying away a beam. It was the beam which some one had had in his own eye while he was looking for the splinter in the eye of another. They did not, however, carry the beam lengthways, but obliquely. "Did any one ever see such a piece of stupidity?" thought Master Pfriem; but he said nothing, and seemed satisfied with it. "It comes to the same thing after all, whichever way they carry the beam, straight or crooked, if they only get along with it, and truly I do not see them knock against anything."

Soon after this he saw two angels who were drawing water out of a well into a bucket, but at the same time he observed that the bucket was full of holes, and that the water was running out of it on every side. They were watering the earth with rain. "Hang it," he exclaimed; but happily recollected himself, and thought, "Perhaps it is only a pastime. If it is an amusement, then it seems they can do useless things of this kind even here in heaven, where people, as I have already noticed, do nothing but idle about."

He went farther and saw a cart which had stuck fast in a deep hole. "It's no wonder," said he to the man who stood by it; "who would load so unreasonably? What have you there?" "Good wishes," replied the man. "I could not go along the right way with it, but still I have pushed it safely up here, and they won't leave me sticking here." In fact an angel did come and harnessed two horses to it. "That's quite right," thought Pfriem, "but two horses won't get that cart out, it must at least have four to it." Another angel came and brought two more horses; she did not, however, harness them in front of it, but behind.

That was too much for Master Pfriem. "Clumsy creature," he burst out with, "what are you doing there? Has any one ever since the world began seen a cart drawn in that way? But you, in your conceited arrogance, think that you know everything best." He was going to say more, but one of the inhabitants of heaven seized him by the throat and pushed him forth with irresistible strength. Beneath the gateway Master Pfriem turned his head round to take one more look at the cart, and saw that it was being raised into the air by four winged horses.

At this moment Master Pfriem awoke. "Things are certainly arranged in heaven otherwise than they are on earth," said he to himself, "and that excuses much; but who can see horses harnessed both behind and before with patience; to be sure they had wings, but who could know that? It is, besides, great folly to fix a pair of wings to a horse that has four legs to run with already! But I must get up, or else they will make nothing but mistakes for me in my house. It is a lucky thing for me though, that I am not really dead."

The Heavenly Wedding

A POOR PEASANT-BOY one day heard the priest say in church that whosoever desired to enter into the kingdom of heaven must always go straight onward. So he set out, and walked continually straight onward over hill and valley without ever turning aside. At length his way led him into a great town, and into the midst of a church, where just at that time God's service was being performed. Now when he beheld all the magnificence of this, he thought he had reached heaven, sat down, and rejoiced with his whole heart. When the service was over, and the clerk bade him go out, he replied, "No, I will not go out again, I am glad to be in heaven at last." So the clerk went to the priest, and told him that there was a child in the church who would not go out again, because he believed he was in heaven. The priest said, "If he believes that, we will leave him inside." So he went to him, and asked if he had any inclination to work. "Yes," the little fellow replied, "I am accustomed to work, but I will not go out of heaven again."

So he stayed in the church, and when he saw how the people came and knelt and prayed to Our Lady with the blessed child Jesus which was carved in wood, he thought "that is the good God," and said, "Dear God, how thin You are! The people must certainly let You starve; but every day I will give You half my dinner." From this time forth, he every day took half his dinner to the image, and the image began to enjoy the food. When a few weeks had gone by, people remarked that the image was growing larger and stout and strong, and wondered much. The priest also could not understand it, but stayed in the church, and followed the little boy about, and then he saw how he shared his food with the Virgin Mary, and how She accepted it.

After some time the boy became ill, and for eight days could not leave his bed; but as soon as he could get up again, the first thing he did was to take his food to Our Lady. The priest followed him, and heard him say, "Dear God, do not take it amiss that I have not brought You anything for such a long time, for I have been ill and could not get up." Then the image answered him and said, "I have seen thy good-will, and that is enough for me. Next Sunday thou shalt go with me to the wedding." The boy rejoiced at this, and repeated it to the priest, who begged him to go and ask the image if he, too, might be permitted to go. "No," answered the image, "thou alone." The priest wished to prepare him first, and give him the holy communion and the child was willing, and next Sunday, when the host came to him, he fell down and died, and was at the eternal wedding.

God's Food

THERE WERE once upon a time two sisters, one of whom had no children and was rich, and the other had five and was a widow, and so poor that she no longer had food enough to satisfy herself and her children. In her need, therefore, she went to her sister, and said, "My children and I are suffering the greatest hunger; thou art rich, give me a mouthful of bread." The very rich sister was as hard as a stone, and said, "I myself have nothing in the house," and drove away the poor creature with harsh words.

After some time the husband of the rich sister came home, and was just going to cut himself a piece of bread, but when he made the first cut into the loaf, out flowed red blood. When the woman saw that she was terrified and told him what had occurred. He hurried away to help the widow and her children, but when he entered her room, he found her praying. She had her two younger children in her arms, and the three older ones were lying dead. He offered her food, but she answered, "For earthly food have we no longer any desire. God has already satisfied the hunger of three of us, and He will hearken to our supplications likewise." Scarcely had she uttered these words than the two little ones drew their last breath, whereupon her heart broke, and she sank down dead.

St. Joseph in the Forest

THERE WAS once on a time a mother who had three daughters, the eldest of whom was rude and wicked, the second much better, although she had her faults, but the youngest was a pious, good child. The mother was, however, so strange, that it was just the eldest daughter whom she most loved, and she could not bear the youngest. On this account, she often sent the poor girl out into the great forest in order to get rid of her, for she thought she would lose herself and never come back again. But the guardian-angel which every good child has, did not forsake her, but always brought her into the right path again.

Once, however, the guardian-angel behaved as if he were not there, and the child could not find her way out of the forest again. She walked on constantly until evening came, and then she saw a tiny light burning in the distance, ran up to it at once, and came to a little hut. She knocked, the door opened, and she came to a second door, where she knocked again. An old man, who had a snow-white beard and looked venerable, opened it for her; and he was no other than St. Joseph. He said quite kindly, "Come, dear child, seat thyself on my little chair by the fire, and warm thyself; I will fetch thee clear water if thou art thirsty; but here in the forest, I have nothing for thee to eat but a couple of little roots, which thou must first scrape and boil."

St. Joseph gave her the roots. The girl scraped them clean, then she brought a piece of pancake and the bread that her mother had given her to take with her; mixed all together in a pan, and cooked herself a thick soup. When it was ready, St. Joseph said, "I am so hungry; give me some of thy food." The child was quite willing, and gave him more than she kept for herself, but God's blessing was with her, so that she was satisfied. When they had eaten, St. Joseph said, "Now we will go to bed; I have, however, only one bed, lay thyself in it. I will lie on the ground on the straw." "No," answered she, "stay in thy own bed, the straw is soft enough for me." St. Joseph, however, took the child in his arms and carried her into the little bed, and there she said her prayers, and fell asleep.

Next morning when she awoke, she wanted to say good morning to St. Joseph, but she did not see him. Then she got up and looked for him, but could not find him anywhere; at last she perceived, behind the door, a bag with money so heavy that she could just carry it, and on it was written that it was for the child who had slept there that night. On this she took the bag, bounded away with it, and got safely to her mother, and as she gave her mother all the money, she could not help being satisfied with her.

The next day, the second child also took a fancy to go into the forest. Her mother gave her a much larger piece of pancake and bread. It happened with her just as with the first child. In the evening, she came to St. Joseph's little hut, who gave her roots for a thick soup. When it was ready, he likewise said to her, "I am so hungry, give me some of thy food." Then the child said, "Thou mayest have thy share." Afterwards, when St. Joseph offered her his bed and wanted to lie on the straw, she replied, "No, lie down in the bed, there is plenty of room for both of us." St. Joseph took her in his arms and put her in the bed, and laid himself on the straw.

In the morning when the child awoke and looked for St. Joseph, he had vanished, but behind the door she found a little sack of money that was about as long as a hand, and on it was written that it was for the child who had slept there last night. So she took the little bag and ran home with it, and took it to her mother, but she secretly kept two pieces for herself.

The eldest daughter had by this time grown curious, and the next morning also insisted on going out into the forest. Her mother gave her pancakes with her—as many as she wanted, and bread and cheese as well. In the evening she found St. Joseph in his little hut, just as the two others had found him. When the soup was ready and St. Joseph said, "I am so hungry, give me some of the food," the girl answered, "Wait until I am satisfied; then if there is anything left thou shalt have it." She ate, however, nearly the whole of it, and St. Joseph had to scrape the dish. Afterwards, the good old man offered her his bed, and wanted to lie on the straw. She took it without making any opposition, laid herself down in the little bed, and left the hard straw to the white-haired man.

Next morning when she awoke, St. Joseph was not to be found, but she did not trouble herself about that. She looked behind the door for a money-bag. She fancied something was lying on the ground, but as she could not very well distinguish what it was, she stooped down and examined it closely, but it remained hanging to her nose, and when she got up again, she saw, to her horror, that it was a second nose, which was hanging fast to her own. Then she began to scream and howl, but that did no good; she was forced to see it always on her nose, for it stretched out so far. Then she ran out and screamed without stopping till she met St. Joseph, at whose feet she fell and begged until, out of pity, he took the nose off her again, and even gave her two pennies.

When she got home, her mother was standing before the door, and asked, "What hast thou had given to thee?" Then she lied and said, "A great bag of money, but I have lost it on the way." "Lost it!" cried the mother, "oh, but we will soon find it again," and took her by the hand, and wanted to seek it with her. At first she began to cry, and did not wish to go, but at last she went. On the way, however, so many lizards and snakes broke loose on both of them, that they did not know how to save themselves. At last they stung the wicked child to death, and they stung the mother in the foot, because she had not brought her up better.

The Three Green Twigs

THERE WAS once on a time a hermit who lived in a forest at the foot of a mountain, and passed his time in prayer and good works, and every evening he carried, to the glory of God, two pails of water up the mountain. Many a beast drank of it, and many a plant was refreshed by it, for on the heights above a strong wind blew continually, which dried the air and the ground, and the wild birds which dread mankind wheel about there, and with their sharp eyes search for a drink. And because the hermit was so pious, an angel of God, visible to his eyes, went up with him, counter his steps, and when the work was completed, brought him his food, even as the prophet of old was by God's command fed by the raven. When the hermit in his piety had already reached a great age, it happened that he once saw from afar a poor sinner being taken to the gallows. He said carelessly to himself, "There, that one is getting his deserts!"

In the evening, when he was carrying the water up the mountain, the angel who usually accompanied him did not appear, and also brought him no food. Then he was terrified, and searched his heart, and tried to think how he could have sinned, as God was so angry, but he did not discover it. Then he neither ate nor drank, threw himself down on the ground, and prayed day and night. And as he was one day thus bitterly weeping in the forest, he heard a little bird singing beautifully and delightfully, and then he was still more troubled and said, "How joyously thou singest, the Lord is not angry with thee. Ah, if thou couldst but tell me how I can have offended Him, that I might do penance, and then my heart also would be glad again."

Then the bird began to speak and said, "Thou hast done injustice, in that thou hast condemned a poor sinner who was being led to the gallows, and for that the Lord is angry with thee. He alone sits in judgment. However, if thou wilt do penance and repent thy sins, He will forgive thee." Then the angel stood beside him with a dry branch in his hand and said, "Thou shalt carry this dry branch until three green twigs sprout out of it, but at night when thou wilt sleep, thou shalt lay it under thy head. Thou shalt beg thy bread from door to door, and not tarry more than one night in the same house. That is the penance which the Lord lays on thee."

Then the hermit took the piece of wood, and went back into the world, which he had not seen for so long. He ate and drank nothing but what was given him at the doors; many petitions were, however, not listened to, and many doors remained shut to him, so that he often did not get a crumb of bread.

Once when he had gone from door to door from morning till night, and no one had given him anything, and no one would shelter him for the night, he went forth into a forest, and at last found a cave which some one had made, and an old woman was sitting in it. Then said he, "Good woman, keep me with you in your house for this night"; but she said, "No, I dare not, even if I wished. I have three sons who are wicked and wild; if they come home from their robbing expedition, and find you, they will kill us both." The hermit said, "Let me stay, they will do no injury either to you or to me," and the woman was compassionate, and let herself be persuaded. Then the man lay down beneath the stairs, and put the bit of wood under his head. When the old woman saw him do that, she asked the reason of it, on which he told her that he carried the bit of wood about with him for a penance, and used it at night for a pillow, and that he had offended the Lord, because, when he had seen a poor sinner on the way to the gallows, he had said he was getting his deserts. Then the woman began to weep and cried, "If the Lord thus punishes one single word, how will it fare with my sons when they appear before Him in judgment?"

At midnight the robbers came home and blustered and stormed. They made a fire, and when it had lighted up the cave and they saw a man lying under the stairs, they fell in a rage and cried to their mother, "Who is the man? Have we not forbidden any one whatsoever to be taken in?" Then said the mother, "Let him alone, it is a poor sinner who is expiating his crime." The robbers asked, "What has he done?" "Old man," cried they, "tell us thy sins." The old man raised himself and told them how he, by one single word, had so sinned that God was angry with him, and how he was now expiating this crime.

The robbers were so powerfully touched in their hearts by this story, that they were shocked with their life up to this time, reflected, and began with hearty repentance to do penance for it. The hermit, after he had converted the three sinners, lay down to sleep again under the stairs. In the morning, however, they found him dead, and out of the dry wood on which his head lay, three green twigs had grown up on high. Thus the Lord had once more received him into His favor.

Our Lady's Little Glass

ONCE UPON a time a wagoner's cart which was heavily laden with wine had stuck so fast that in spite of all that he could do, he could not get it to move again. Then it chanced that Our Lady just happened to come by that way, and when She perceived the poor man's distress, She said to him, "I am tired and thirsty, give Me a glass of wine, and I will set thy cart free for thee." "Willingly," answered the wagoner, "but I have no glass in which I can give Thee the wine." Then Our Lady plucked a little white flower with red stripes, called field bindweed, which looks very like a glass, and gave it to the wagoner. He filled it with wine, and then Our Lady drank it, and in the self-same instant the cart was set free, and the wagoner could drive onwards. The little flower is still always called Our Lady's Little Glass.

Brother Frolick

FOR A LONG TIME the King of a certain country had been at war. At last it came to an end, and many soldiers were discharged. One of them was a fellow called Brother Frolick because he was such a lighthearted, jolly fellow; and although he only received a small loaf and four kreutzers in gold, he started on a journey through the world with a merry heart.

He had not gone far, when he saw a poor beggar sitting by the roadside begging, but he did not know that it was a saint in disguise. The beggar asked for alms, and Brother Frolick said, "What shall I give you? I am only a poor, discharged soldier, and all they have given me is a loaf of bread and four kreutzers, and when it is all gone, I must beg as well as you. However, I will give you something." Then he divided the loaf into four pieces, and gave one to the beggar, as well as one of his gold pieces.

The beggar thanked him, and went away, but only to a little distance. Again changing his appearance and face, he seated himself by the highway, waited for Brother Frolick to pass, and again begged for alms. The good-natured soldier gave this beggar also a fourth of his bread and a gold piece.

The saint thanked him, and, after walking some distance, a third time seated himself in another form to beg of Brother Frolick. This time, also, he gave him a third piece of the divided loaf and another kreutzer. The beggar thanked him and went away.

The kindhearted fellow had now only a fourth part of the loaf and one gold piece left, so he went to an inn, ate the bread, and paid his kreutzer for a jug of beer. As soon as he had finished, he went out, and traveled on for some distance, and there again was the saint in the form of a discharged soldier like himself. "Good evening, comrade," he said; "could you give me a piece of bread, and a kreutzer to buy something to drink?"

"Where am I to get it?" answered Brother Frolick. "I had my discharge today, and they gave me a loaf of bread and four gold kreutzers. But I met three beggars on the high road, and I gave them each a fourth part of my bread and a kreutzer, and the last kreutzer I have just paid for something to drink with my last piece of bread. Now I am empty, and if you also have nothing, we can go and beg together."

"No," answered the saint, "we need not do that; I understand a little of medicine and surgery, and can soon earn as much as I shall want." "Well," replied Brother Frolick, "I don't understand doctoring at all, so I must go and beg alone." "No; come with me," cried the other; "whatever I earn, you shall have half." "That is good news for me," said Brother Frolick, so they went away together.

After a time, as they passed a peasant's house, they heard great cries and lamentations, so they went in, and found the husband very ill and at the point of death, and the wife weeping and howling with all her might. "Leave off that noise," said the saint; "I will soon cure your husband." Then he took some salve out of his pocket, and healed the man so quickly that he could stand up and was quite well.

The husband and wife joyfully thanked the stranger, and said, "What can we give you in return for this kindness?" But the saint would name nothing, and, worse still, refused all they brought to him; and although Brother Forlick nudged him more than once, he still said, "No; I will take nothing—we do not want it."

At last the grateful people brought a lamb, and said that he must take it whether he would or not. Then Brother Frolick nudged him in the side, and said, "Take it, stupid; you know we do want it."

Then the saint said at last, "Well, I will take the lamb, but I cannot carry it; you must do that, if you want it so much." "Oh, that will be no trouble to me," cried the other, and taking it on his shoulder they went away together.

After a while, they came to a wood, and Brother Frolick, who began to feel tired and hungry, for the lamb was heavy, proposed that they should stop and rest. "See," he said, "this is a beautiful place for us to cook the lamb and eat it."

"It's all the same to me," replied the saint, "but I can have nothing to do with the cooking; you must do that if you have a kettle, and I will go away for a little while till it is ready. You must not, however, eat any till I come back; I will be here quite in time." "Go along," said Brother Frolick, "I understand how to cook, and I will soon have dinner ready."

Then the saint went away, and Brother Frolick slaughtered the lamb, lighted a fire, and threw some of the flesh into the kettle to boil. The meat was quite ready, however, before the saint returned, and Brother Frolick became so impatient, that he took out of the kettle a part of the flesh, in which was the heart. "The heart is the best of all," he said, tasting it, and finding it very good he ate it all.

At last his comrade returned and said: "You may eat all the lamb yourself, I only want the heart, so just give it to me."

Then Brother Frolick took a knife and fork and began searching among the pieces of meat for the heart, which of course, he could not find. Then he said pertly, "It is not there."

"Then where can it be?" said the saint.

"I do not know," said Brother Frolick; "but see," he added, "why, what a couple of fools we are, searching for a lamb's heart; of course there is not one to be found, for a lamb has no heart."

"Ah," said the other, "that is news. Every animal has a heart, why should not a lamb?"

"No, certainly, brother," he said, "a lamb has no heart; reflect a little, and you will be convinced that it really has none."

"Well, certainly, it is quite clear that there is no heart to be found in this one, and as I do not want any other part, you may eat it all yourself."

"I cannot eat it all," replied Brother Frolick, "so what is left I will put into my knapsack."

When this was done, the two started to continue their journey, and Brother Peter, as the saint called himself, caused a large quantity of water to rise on the road just across where they had to pass. Said Brother Peter, "You go first." "No," answered the other, "I would rather see you across," for he thought, "if the water is very deep, I won't go at all."

So Brother Peter stepped over, and the water only came up to his knees. His comrade prepared to follow, but he had not gone far when the water came up to his neck. "Brother, help me," he cried. "Will you confess, then, that you ate the lamb's heart?" he replied. "No," he said, "I did not eat it."

Immediately the water became deeper, and flowed to his mouth. "Help! help me, brother," he cried. "Will you confess now that you have eaten the lamb's heart?" cried Brother Peter. "No," he replied, "I did not eat it."

Now the saint did not intend to drown him, so he allowed the water to subside, and Brother Frolick crossed over safely. They traveled after this till they reached a foreign land, and in the chief city heard that the King's daughter was very ill, and not expected to live.

"Holloa! brother," said the soldier, "that is a good chance for us; if you cure her, we shall never know want again."

But Brother Peter did not hurry himself, and when his comrade begged him to put his best foot foremost, he went slower than ever. Brother Frolick pushed him and dragged him on, but all to no purpose, and at last they heard that the King's daughter was dead. "There now," cried Brother Frolick, "we have lost our chance, all through your sleepy walking."

"Be quiet, now," said Brother Peter; "I can not only cure the sick, but I can restore the dead to life." "If that is the case," replied his comrade, "you may be sure that the King will be ready to give us the half of his kingdom for joy."

They therefore went to the King's castle, and found them all in great grief. But Brother Peter said to the King, "Do not mourn, I can restore the Princess to life."

He and his comrade were at once led to her room, and telling everyone to go out, they were left alone with the dead Princess. Brother Peter immediately stripped the body of the grave-clothes, and laid it in a bath of very hot water, which he had ordered to be brought. Then he uttered a few strange words, which his comrade tried to remember, and turning to the Princess, said, "I command thee to come out of the bath, and stand on thy feet."

Immediately the Princess rose, and was again alive and well. The chamber-women were sent for, and the Princess in her royal clothes was taken to her father, who received her with great joy, and said to the two strangers, "Name your reward; it shall be yours, even to the half of my kingdom." But Brother Peter replied, "No, I will take no reward for what I have done." "Oh, you foolish fellow," thought Brother Frolick to himself. Then he nudged him again in the side: "How can you be so stupid? If you don't want anything, I do."

Brother Peter, however, still refused, but the King, seeing that his comrade was quite willing to accept something, told his treasurer to fill the soldier's knapsack with gold.

They left the city after this, and traveled on till they came to a wood. Then said Brother Peter, "We may as well divide that gold." "With all my heart," replied the good-natured fellow.

Peter took the gold, and divided it into three portions. "What is that for?" asked Brother Frolick. "What have you got in your head now? There are only two of us."

"Oh," he replied, "it is all right. One third is for myself, one third for you, and one third for him who ate the lamb's heart." "Oh, I ate that," cried Brother Frolick, gathering the money up quickly. "I did indeed; can't you believe me?"

"How can it be true?" replied Peter; "a lamb has no heart." "Nonsense, brother," he said, "what are you thinking of? A lamb has a heart as well as other animals. Why should he not have one?"

"Now really this is too good," replied Brother Peter. "However, you may keep all the gold to yourself, but I will go on my way alone in future." "As you please, brother," answered the soldier. "Farewell." Then Peter started on another road, and left Brother Frolick to go off by himself. "It is just as well," thought he, "but still he is a most wonderful man."

The soldier had now quite as much money as he wanted, but he knew not how to spend it properly. He wasted it or gave it away, till as time went on he was again almost penniless. At last he arrived at a city where he heard that the King's daughter had just died. "Hello," thought he, "here is an opportunity; I know how to restore her to life, and they will pay me something worth having this time." So he went to the King and told him that he could restore his daughter to life.

Now the King had heard of the discharged soldier who had lately given new life to a Princess, and he thought Brother Frolick was the man. Still, as he was not quite sure, he asked him first for his opinion, and whether he would venture if the Princess was really dead.

The soldier had no fear, so he ordered the bath to be filled with hot water, and went into the room with the dead Princess alone. Then he stripped her of her clothes, placed her in the bath, and said, as he supposed, the words which Brother Peter had said, but the dead body did not move, although he repeated the words three times. He now began to feel alarmed, and cried out in angry tones, "Stand up, will you, or you will get what you don't expect."

At this moment the saint appeared in his former shape as a discharged soldier, and entered the room through the window. "You foolish man," he cried, "how can you raise the dead to life? I will help you this time, but don't attempt it again."

Thereupon he pronounced the magic words, and immediately the Princess rose and stood on her feet, and was as well and strong as ever. Then the saint went away through the window, the maids were sent for to dress the Princess in her royal robes, and then the soldier led her to her father. He knew, however, that he was not free to ask for a reward, for Peter had forbidden him to take anything, and therefore when the King asked him what he would have, he said he would take nothing, although he wanted it so much through extravagance and folly. Yet the King ordered his knapsack to be filled with gold, and with many thanks he took his departure.

Outside near the castle gate he met the saint, who said to him, "See now, I forbade you to take anything, and yet you have received a knapsack full of gold." "What could I do," he replied, "when they would put it in for me?"

"Then I can only tell you," was the reply, "that if you get into trouble a second time by undertaking what you cannot perform, it will be worse for you." "All right, brother; I don't care, now I have the gold, and I shall not care about putting dead people into a bath again after this."

"Ah," said the saint, "your gold will not last long. However, if you do not after this go into unlawful paths, I will give to your knapsack the power of containing in itself whatever you may wish for. And now farewell, you will see me no more."

"Good-bye," said the soldier, as he turned away. "Well," he thought, "I am glad that he is gone; he is a wonderful fellow, no doubt, but I am better without him for a companion."

To the wonderful power with which he had endowed his knapsack Brother Frolick never gave a thought.

He went on his way with his gold from place to place, and spent and wasted it as he did before, and at last he had nothing left but four kreutzers. With this sum he entered an inn by the roadside, and felt that the money must go, so he spent three kreutzers in wine, and one in bread.

As he sat eating his bread and drinking his wine, the fragrant smell of roast goose reached his nose. Brother Frolick looked round and peeped about, and at last saw that the landlady had two geese roasting in the oven.

Then he suddenly remembered what his old comrade had said, that whatever he wished for he would find in his knapsack. "Aha," he said to himself, "then I must wish for the geese to be there." Then he went out, and before the door he said, "I wish that the two geese roasting in the oven were in my knapsack." When he had said this he took it off, peeped in, and there they both lay. "Aha!" he exclaimed, "this is all right. I am a mighty fellow after all," and going farther into a meadow, sat down to enjoy his good fare.

Just as he had finished eating one goose, two farmhands came by, and when they saw the remaining goose, they stood still and looked at it with hungry eyes. "Well," thought Brother Frolick, "one is enough for me." So he beckoned the workers nearer, and said, "Here, take this goose, and drink my health as you eat it."

They thanked him and went away quickly to the inn, bought some wine and bread, and then unpacked the goose which had been given them, and began to eat it.

The landlady, when she saw it, went to her husband, and said, "Those two are eating goose, just see if one of ours is gone from the oven."

The landlord ran to look, and found the oven empty. "You thieves!" he exclaimed, running out to them, "where did you get roast goose to eat? Tell me instantly, or I will give you a taste of green hazel juice!" "We are not thieves," they cried; "a discharged soldier gave us this goose yonder in the meadow." "You are not going to make me believe that," cried the landlord; "that soldier has been here, and a most respectable fellow he is; I watched him when he left the house and he had nothing with him then. No; you are the thieves, and shall pay for the goose!" But as they could not pay for it, he took a stick and thrashed them out of the house.

Quite ignorant of all this, Brother Frolick went on his way, till he came to a place where stood a beautiful castle, and not far from it, a large but mean-looking inn. The soldier went up to the inn and asked for a night's lodging. But the landlord said, "There is no room here; the house is full of noble guests." "I wonder at that," said Brother Frolick, "why should they come here instead of going to that beautiful castle yonder?"

"Ah, yes," said the landlord, "many have thought as you do; they have gone to spend a night at the castle, but they have never returned alive. None are allowed to remain," said the landlord, "who do not go in on their heads." "I am not likely to walk in on my head," said the soldier; "but now, landlord, let me take something with me to eat and drink, and I'll go."

So the landlord brought him good supper to take with him, and then Brother Frolick set out to go to the castle. On arriving, he first sat down and ate with great relish, and when he began to feel sleepy, laid himself on the ground, for there was no bed, and was soon asleep.

In the night, however, he was wakened by a terrible noise, and when he roused himself he saw nine hideous imps in the room, dancing round a pole, which they held in their hands. "Dance away," he cried, "as long as you will, but don't come near me." The imps, however, disregarded his orders; nearer and nearer they approached as they danced, till one of them trod on his face, with his heavy foot.

"Keep away, you wretches," he cried. But still they came nearer. Then Brother Frolick grew angry. He started up, seized a chair, and struck out right and left. But nine imps against one soldier is rather too much, and if he struck one before him, another behind would pull his hair most unmercifully. "You demons," he cried suddenly, "I'll take care of you; wait a bit—now then, all nine of you into my knapsack." Whisk! and they were all in; quick as lightning he fastened the bag and threw it into a corner.

Then all was quiet, and Brother Frolick laid himself down again and slept till broad daylight, when the arrival of the landlord of the inn and the nobleman to whom the castle belonged, woke him. They were astonished to find him alive and full of spirits, and said to him, "Have you not seen any ghosts during the night, and did they not try to hurt you?"

"Well, not very much," answered Brother Frolick. "I have them all nine quite safe in my knapsack there," and he pointed to the corner. "You can dwell in your castle in peace now," he said to the nobleman. "They will never trouble you again."

The nobleman thanked the soldier and loaded him with presents; he also begged him to remain in his service, and promised to take care of him for the remainder of his life. But the soldier said, "No; I have a roving disposition; I could never rest in one place. I will go and travel farther."

Then Brother Frolick went to a smith's, and laying the knapsack containing the imps on the anvil, asked the smith and his man to strike it with their great hammers, with all their strength. The imps set up a loud screech, and when at last all was quiet, the knapsack was opened. Eight of them were found quite dead, but the ninth, who had laid himself in a fold, was still living. He slipped out when the knapsack was opened and escaped.

Thereupon Brother Frolick traveled a long time about the world, and those who know can tell many a tale about him. But at last he grew old and thought of his end, so he went to a hermit who was known to be a pious man, and said to him, "I am tired of wandering about, and want now to behave in such a manner that I shall enter into the kingdom of Heaven."

The hermit replied, "There are two roads: One is broad and pleasant, and leads to hell; the other is narrow and rough, and leads to Heaven."

"I should be a fool," thought Brother Frolick, "if I were to take the narrow, rough road." So he set out and took the broad and pleasant road, and at length came to a great black door, which was the door of Hell.

Brother Frolick knocked, and the door-keeper peeped out to see who was there. But when he saw Brother Frolick, he was terrified, for he was the very same ninth imp who had been shut up in the knapsack and had escaped from it with a black eye. So he pushed the bolt in again as quickly as he could, ran to the highest demon, and said, "There is a fellow outside with a knapsack, who wants to come in, but as you value your lives don't allow him to enter, or he will wish the whole of Hell into his knapsack. He once gave me a frightful hammering when I was inside it." So they called out to Brother Frolick to go away again, for he should not get in there!

"If they won't have me here," thought he, "I will see if I can find a place for myself in Heaven, for I must stay somewhere." So he turned about and went onwards until he came to the door of Heaven, where he knocked.

St. Peter was sitting hard by as door-keeper. Brother Frolick recognized him at once, and thought, "Here I find an old friend, I shall get on better." But St. Peter said: "I can hardly believe that you want to come into Heaven." "Let me in, brother; I must get in somewhere; if they would have taken me into Hell, I should not have come here." "No," said St. Peter, "you shall not enter." "Then if you will not let me in, take your knapsack back, for I will have nothing at all from you." "Give it here, then," said St. Peter.

Then Brother Frolick gave him the knapsack into Heaven through the bars, and St. Peter took it and hung it up beside his seat. Then said Brother Frolick, "And now I wish myself inside my knapsack," and in a second he was in it, and in Heaven, and St. Peter was forced to let him stay there.

The Bright Sun Brings It to Light

A TAILOR'S APPRENTICE was traveling about the world in search of work, and at one time he could find none, and his poverty was so great that he had not a penny to live on. Presently he met a Jew on the road, and as he thought he would have a great deal of money about him, the tailor thrust God out of his heart, fell on the Jew, and said, "Give me your money, or I will strike you dead." Then said the Jew, "Grant me my life, I have no money but eight pennies." But the tailor said, "Money you have, and it must be produced," and used violence and beat him until he was near death. And when the Jew was dying, the last words he said were, "The bright sun will bring it to light," and thereupon he died.

The tailor's apprentice felt in his pockets and sought for money, but he found nothing but eight pennies, as the Jew had said. Then he took him up and carried him behind a clump of trees, and went onwards to seek work. After he had traveled about a long while, he got work in a town with a master who had a pretty daughter, with whom he fell in love, and he married her, and lived in good and happy wedlock.

After a long time when he and his wife had two children, the wife's father and mother died, and the young people kept house alone. One morning, when the husband was sitting at the table before the window, his wife brought him his coffee, and when he had poured it out into the saucer, and was just going to drink, the sun shone on it and the reflection gleamed hither and thither on the wall above, and made circles on it. Then the tailor looked up and said, "Yes, it would like very much to bring it to light, and cannot!" The woman said, "Oh, dear husband, and what is that, then? What do you mean by that?" He answered, "I must not tell you." But she said, "If you love me, you must tell me," and used her most affectionate words, and said that no one should ever know it, and left him no rest.

Then he told her how years ago, when he was traveling about seeking work and quite worn out and penniless, he had killed a Jew, and that in the last agonies of death, the Jew had spoken the words, "The bright sun will bring it to light." And now, the sun had just wanted to bring it to light, and had gleamed and made circles on the wall, but had not been able to do it. After this, he again charged her particularly never to tell this, or he would lose his life, and she did promise.

When, however, he had sat down to work again, she went to her great friend and confided the story to her, but she was never to repeat it to any human being, but before two days were over, the whole town knew it, and the tailor was brought to trial, and condemned. And thus, after all, the bright sun did bring it to light.

The Sparrow and His Four Children

A SPARROW had four young ones in a swallow's nest. When they were fledged, some naughty boys pulled out the nest, but fortunately all the birds got safely away in the high wind. Then the old bird was grieved that as his sons had all gone out into the world, he had not first warned them of every kind of danger, and given them good instruction how to deal with each. In the autumn a great many sparrows assembled together in a wheatfield, and there the old bird met his four children again, and full of joy took them home with him. "Ah, my dear sons, what pain I have been in about you all through the summer, because you got away in the wind without my teaching; listen to my words, obey your father, and be well on your guard. Little birds have to encounter great dangers!" Then he asked the eldest where he had spent the summer, and how he had supported himself. "I stayed in the gardens, and looked for caterpillars and small worms, until the cherries got ripe." "Ah, my son," said the father, "tit-bits are not bad, but there is great risk about them; on that account take great care of yourself henceforth, and particularly when people are going about the gardens who carry long green poles which are hollow inside and have a little hole at the top." "Yes, father, but what if a little green leaf is stuck over the hole with wax?" said the son. "Where have you seen that?" "In a merchant's garden," said the youngest. "Oh, my son, merchant folks are quick folks," said the father. "If you have been among the children of the world, you have learned worldly shiftiness enough; only see that you use it well, and do not be too confident."

After this he asked the next, "Where have you passed your time?" "At court," said the son. "Sparrows and silly little birds are of no use in that place—there one finds much gold, velvet, silk, armor, harnesses, sparrow-hawks, screech-owls and hen-harriers; keep to the horses' stable where they winnow oats, or thresh, and then fortune may give you your daily grain of corn in peace." "Yes, father," said the son, "but when the stable-boys make traps and fix their gins and snares in the straw, many a one is caught fast." "Where have you seen that?" said the old bird. "At court, among the stable-boys." "Oh, my son, court boys are bad boys! If you have been to court and among the lords, and have left no feathers there, you have learnt a fair amount, and will know very well how to go about the world, but look around, for the wolves devour the wisest dogs."

The father examined the third also: "Where did you seek your fortune?" "I have broken up tubs and ropes on the cartroads and highways, and sometimes met with a grain of corn or barley." "That is indeed dainty fare," said the father, "but take care what you are about and look carefully around, especially when you see any one stooping and about to pick up a stone; there is not much time to stay then." "That is true," said the son, "but what if any one should carry a bit of rock, or ore, ready beforehand in his breast or pocket?" "Where have you seen that?" "Among the mountaineers, dear father; when they go out, they generally take little bits of ore with them." "Mountain folks are working folks, and clever folks. If you have been among mountain lads, you have seen and learnt something, but when you go thither beware, for many a sparrow has been brought to a bad end by a mountain boy."

At length the father came to the youngest son: "You, my dear chirping nestling, were always the silliest and weakest. Stay with me. The world has many rough, wicked birds which have crooked beaks and long claws, and lie in wait for poor little birds and swallow them. Keep with those of your own kind, and pick up little spiders and caterpillars from the trees, or the house, and then you will live long in peace." "My dear father, he who feeds himself without injury to other people fares well, and no sparrow-hawk, eagle, or kite will hurt him if he specially commits himself and his lawful food, evening and morning, faithfully to God, who is the Creator and Preserver of all forest and village birds, who likewise hears the cry and prayer of the young ravens, for no sparrow or wren ever falls to the ground except by his will." "Where have you learnt this?" The son answered, "When the great blast of wind tore me away from you I came to a church, and there during the summer I have picked up the flies and spiders from the windows, and heard this discourse preached. The Father of all sparrows fed me all the summer through, and kept me from all mischance and from ferocious birds."

"In sooth, my dear son, if you take refuge in the churches and help to clear away spiders and buzzing flies, and cry unto God like the young ravens, and commend yourself to the eternal Creator, all will be well with you, even if the whole world were full of wild malicious birds.

> *"He who to God commits his ways,*
> *In silence suffers, waits, and prays,*
> *Preserves his faith and conscience pure,*
> *He is of God's protection sure."*

The Duration of Life

WHEN God had created the world and was about to fix the length of each creature's life, the ass came and asked, "Lord, how long shall I live?" "Thirty years," replied God; "does that content thee?" "Ah, Lord," answered the ass, "that is a long time. Think of my painful existence! To carry heavy burdens from morning to night, to drag sacks of corn to the mill, that others may eat bread, to be cheered and refreshed with nothing but blows and kicks. Relieve me of a portion of this long time." Then God had pity on him and relieved him of eighteen years.

The ass went away comforted, and the dog appeared. "How long wouldst thou like to live?" said God to him. "Thirty years are too many for the ass, but thou wilt be satisfied with that." "Lord," answered the dog, "is that Thy will? Consider how I shall have to run; my feet will never hold out so long, and when I have once lost my voice for barking, and my teeth for biting, what will be left for me to do but run from one corner to another and growl?" God saw that he was right, and released him from twelve years of life.

Then came the monkey. "Thou wilt certainly live thirty years willingly," said the Lord to him. "Thou hast no need to work as the ass and the dog have to do, and wilt always enjoy thyself." "Ah! Lord," he answered, "it may seem as if that were the case, but it is quite different. When it rains porridge I have no spoon. I am always to play merry pranks, and make faces which force people to laugh, and if they give me an apple, and I bite into it, why it is sour! How often sadness hides itself behind mirth! I shall never be able to hold out for thirty years." God was gracious and took off ten.

At last man appeared, joyous, healthy and vigorous, and begged God to appoint his time for him. "Thirty years shalt thou live," said the Lord. "Is that enough for thee?" "What a short time," cried man, "when I have built my house and my fire burns on my own hearth; when I have planted trees which blossom and bear fruit, and am just intending to enjoy my life, I am to die! O Lord, lengthen my time." "I will add to it the ass's eighteen years," said God. "That is not enough," replied the man. "Thou shalt also have the dog's twelve years." "Still too little!" "Well, then," said God, "I will give thee the monkey's ten years also, but more thou shalt not have." The man went away, but was not satisfied.

So man lives seventy years. The first thirty are his human years, which are soon gone; then is he healthy, merry, works with pleasure, and is glad of his life. Then follow the ass's eighteen years, when one burden after another is laid on him; he has to carry the corn which feeds others, and blows and kicks are the reward of his faithful services. Then come the dog's twelve years, when he lies in the corner, and growls and has no longer any teeth to bite with, and when this time is over the monkey's ten years form the end. Then man is weak-headed and foolish, does silly things, and becomes the jest of the children

The Twelve Apostles

THREE HUNDRED YEARS before the birth of the Lord Christ, there lived a mother who had twelve sons, but was so poor and needy that she no longer knew how she was to keep them alive at all. She prayed to God daily that He would grant that all her sons might be on the earth with the Redeemer who was promised. When her necessity became still greater she sent one of them after the other out into the world to seek bread for her.

The eldest was called Peter, and he went out and had already walked a long way, a whole day's journey, when he came into a great forest. He sought for a way out, but could find none, and went farther and farther astray, and at the same time felt such great hunger that he could scarcely stand. At length he became so weak that he was forced to lie down, and he believed death to be at hand. Suddenly there stood beside him a small boy who shone with brightness, and was as beautiful and kind as an angel. The child smote his little hands together, until Peter was forced to look up and saw him. Then the child said, "Why art thou sitting there in such trouble?" "Alas!" answered Peter, "I am going about the world seeking bread. That I may yet see the dear Saviour who is promised, that is my greatest desire." The child said, "Come with me, and thy wish shall be fulfilled."

He took poor Peter by the hand, and led him between some cliffs to a great cavern. When they entered it, everything was shining with gold, silver, and crystal, and in the midst of it twelve cradles were standing side by side. Then said the little angel, "Lie down in the first, and sleep a while, I will rock thee." Peter did so, and the angel sang to him and rocked him until he was asleep. And when he was asleep, the second brother came also, guided thither by his guardian angel, and he was rocked to sleep like the first, and thus came the others, one after the other, until all twelve lay there sleeping in the golden cradles. They slept, however, three hundred years, until the night when the Saviour of the world was born. Then they awoke, and were with him on earth, and were called the twelve apostles.

Faithful John

THERE WAS once an old King, who, having fallen sick, thought to himself, "This is very likely my death-bed on which I am lying."

Then he said, "Let Faithful John be sent for."

Faithful John was his best-beloved servant, and was so called because he had served the King faithfully all his life long. When he came near the bed, the King said to him, "Faithful John, I feel my end drawing near, and my only care is for my son; he is yet of tender years, and does not always know how to shape his conduct; and unless you promise me to instruct him in all his actions and be a true foster-father to him, I shall not be able to close my eyes in peace."

Then answered Faithful John, "I will never forsake him, and will serve him faithfully, even though it should cost me my life."

And the old King said, "Then I die, being of good cheer and at peace." And he went on to say, "After my death, you must lead him through the whole castle, into all the chambers, halls, and vaults, and show him the treasures that in them lie; but the last chamber in the long gallery, in which lies hidden the picture of the Princess of the Golden Palace, you must not show him. If he were to see that picture, he would directly fall into so great a love for her, that he would faint with the strength of it, and afterwards for her sake run into great dangers; so you must guard him well."

And as Faithful John gave him his hand upon it, the old King became still and silent, laid his head upon the pillow, and died.

When the old King was laid in the grave, Faithful John told the young King what he had promised to his father on his death-bed, and said, "And I will certainly hold to my promise and be faithful to you, as I was faithful to him, even though it should cost me my life."

When the days of mourning were at an end, Faithful John said to the Prince, "It is now time that you should see your inheritance; I will show you all the paternal castle."

Then he led him over all the place, upstairs and downstairs, and showed him all the treasures and the splendid chambers; one chamber only he did not open, that in which the perilous picture hung. Now the picture was so placed that when the door opened it was the first thing to be seen, and was so wonderfully painted that it seemed to breathe and move, and in the whole world was there nothing more lovely or more beautiful.

The young King noticed how Faithful John always passed by this one door, and asked, "Why do you not undo this door?" "There is something inside that would terrify you," answered he.

But the King answered, "I have seen the whole castle, and I will know what is in here also." And he went forward and tried to open the door by force.

Then Faithful John called him back, and said, "I promised your father on his death-bed that you should not see what is in that room; it might bring great misfortune on you and me were I to break my promise."

But the young King answered, "I shall be undone if I do not go inside that room; I shall have no peace day or night until I have seen it with these eyes; and I will not move from this place until you have unlocked it."

Then Faithful John saw there was no help for it, and he chose out the key from the big bunch with a heavy heart and many sighs. When the door was opened he walked in first, and thought that by standing in front of the King he might hide the picture from him, but that was no good, the King stood on tiptoe, and looked over his shoulder. And when he saw the image of the lady that was so wonderfully beautiful, and so glittering with gold and jewels, he fell on the ground powerless. Faithful John helped him up, took him to his bed, and thought with sorrow, "Ah me! the evil has come to pass; what will become of us?"

Then he strengthened the King with wine, until he came to himself. The first words that he said were, "Oh, the beautiful picture! Whose portrait is it?" "It is the portrait of the Princess of the Golden Palace," answered Faithful John.

Then the King said, "My love for her is so great that if all the leaves of the forest were tongues they could not utter it! I stake my life on the chance of obtaining her, and you, my Faithful John, must stand by me."

The faithful servant considered for a long time how the business should be begun; it seemed to him that it would be a difficult matter to come at just a sight of the Princess. At last he thought out a way, and said to the King,

"All that she has about her is of gold—tables, chairs, dishes, drinking-cups, bowls, and all the household furniture; in your treasury are five tons of gold, let the goldsmiths of your kingdom work it up into all kinds of vessels and implements, into all kinds of birds, and wild creatures, and wonderful beasts, such as may please her; then we will carry them off with us, and go and seek our fortune."

The King had all the goldsmiths fetched, and they worked day and night, until at last some splendid things were got ready. When a ship had been loaded with them, Faithful John put on the garb of a merchant, and so did the King, so as the more completely to disguise themselves. Then they journeyed over the sea, and went so far that at last they came to the city where the Princess of the Golden Palace dwelt.

Faithful John told the King to stay in the ship, and to wait for him. "Perhaps," said he, "I shall bring the Princess back with me, so take care that everything is in order; let the golden vessels be placed about, and the whole ship be adorned."

Then he gathered together in his apron some of the gold things, one of each kind, landed, and went up to the royal castle. And when he reached the courtyard of the castle there stood by the well a pretty maiden, who had two golden pails in her hand, and she was drawing water with them; and as she turned round to carry them away she saw the strange man, and asked him who he was.

He answered, "I am a merchant," and opened his apron, and let her look within it.

"Ah, what beautiful things!" cried she, and setting down her pails, she turned the golden toys over, and looked at them one after another.

Then she said, "The Princess must see these; she takes so much pleasure in gold things that she will buy them all from you." Then she took him by the hand and led him in, for she was the chamber-maid.

When the Princess saw the golden wares she was very pleased, and said, "All these are so finely worked that I should like to buy them of you."

But the Faithful John said, "I am only the servant of a rich merchant, and what I have here is nothing to what my master has in the ship—the cunningest and costliest things that ever were made of gold."

The Princess then wanted it all to be brought to her; but he said, "That would take up many days; so great is the number of them, and so much space would they occupy that there would not be enough room for them in your house."

But the Princess's curiosity and fancy grew so much that at last she said, "Lead me to the ship; I will go and see your master's treasures."

Then Faithful John led her to the ship joyfully, and the King' when he saw that her beauty was even greater than the picture had set forth, felt his heart leap at the sight. Then she climbed up into the ship, and the King received her. Faithful John stayed by the steersman, and gave orders for the ship to push off, saying, "Spread all sail, that she may fly like a bird in the air."

So the King showed her all the golden things, each separately— the dishes, the bowls, the birds, the wild creatures, and the wonderful beasts. Many hours were passed in looking at them all, and in her pleasure the Princess never noticed that the ship was moving onwards. When she had examined the last, she thanked the merchant, and prepared to return home; but when she came to the ship's side, she saw that they were on the high seas, far from land, and speeding on under full sail.

"Ah!" cried she, full of terror, "I am betrayed and carried off by this merchant. Oh that I had died rather than have fallen into his power!"

But the King took hold of her hand, and said, "No merchant am I, but a King, and no baser of birth than thyself; it is because of my over-mastering love for thee that I have carried thee off by cunning. The first time I saw thy picture I fell fainting to the earth."

When the Princess of the Golden Palace heard this she became more trustful, and her heart inclined favorably towards him, so that she willingly consented to become his wife.

It happened, however, as they were still journeying on the open sea, that Faithful John, as he sat in the forepart of the ship and made music, caught sight of three ravens in the air flying overhead. Then he stopped playing, and listened to what they said one to another, for he understood them quite well. The first one cried, "Ay, there goes the Princess of the Golden Palace."

"Yes," answered the second; "but he has not got her safe yet."

And the third said, "He has her, though; she sits beside him in the ship."

Then the first one spoke again, "What does that avail him? When they come on land a fox-red horse will spring towards them; then will the King try to mount him; and if he does, the horse will rise with him into the air, so that he will never see his bride again."

The second raven asked, "Is there no remedy?"

"Oh yes; if another man mounts quickly, and takes the pistol out of the holster and shoots the horse dead with it, he will save the young King. But who knows that? and he that knows it and does it will become stone from toe to knee."

Then said the second, "I know further, that if the horse should be killed, the young King will not even then be sure of his bride. When they arrive at the castle there will lie a wrought bride-shirt in a dish, and it will seem all woven of gold and silver, but it is really of sulphur and pitch, and if he puts it on it will burn him to the marrow of his bones."

The third raven said, "Is there no remedy?"

"Oh yes," answered the second; "if another man with gloves on picks up the shirt, and throws it into the fire, so that it is consumed, then is the young King delivered. But what avails that? He who knows it and does it will be turned into stone from his heart to his knee."

Then spoke the third, "I know yet more, that even when the bride-shirt is burnt up the King is not sure of his bride; when at the wedding the dance begins, and the young Queen dances, she will suddenly grow pale and fall to the earth as if she were dead, and unless some one lifts her up and takes three drops of blood from her right breast, she will die. But he that knows this and does this will become stone from the crown of his head to the sole of his foot."

When the ravens had spoken thus among themselves they flew away. Faithful John had understood it all, and from that time he remained quiet and sad, for he thought to himself that were he to conceal what he had heard from his master, misfortune would befall; and were he to reveal it his own life would be sacrificed. At last, however, he said within himself, "I will save my master, though I myself should perish!"

So when they came on land, it happened just as the ravens had foretold, there sprang forward a splendid fox-red horse.

"Come on!" said the King, "he shall carry me to the castle," and was going to mount, when Faithful John passed before him and mounted quickly, drew the pistol out of the holster, and shot the horse dead.

Then the other servants of the King cried out (for they did not wish well to Faithful John), "How shameful to kill that beautiful animal that was to have carried the King to his castle." But the King said, "Hold your tongues, and let him be, he is my Faithful John; he knows what is the good of it."

Then they went up to the castle, and there stood in the hall a dish, and the wrought bride-shirt that lay on it seemed as if of gold and silver. The young King went up to it and was going to put it on, but Faithful John pushed him away, picked it up with his gloved hands, threw it quickly on the fire, and there let it burn.

The other servants began grumbling again, and said, "Look, he is even burning up the King's bridal shirt!" But the young King said, "Who knows but that there may be a good reason for it? Let him be, he is my Faithful John."

Then the wedding feast was held; and the bride led the dance; Faithful John watched her carefully, and all at once she grew pale and fell down as if she were dead. Then he went quickly to her, and carried her into a chamber hard by, laid her down, and kneeling, took three drops of blood from her right breast. Immediately she drew breath again and raised herself up, but the young King witnessing all, and not knowing why Faithful John had done this, grew very angry, and cried out, "Throw him into prison!"

The next morning Faithful John was condemned to death and led to the gallows, and as he stood there ready to suffer, he said, "He who is about to die is permitted to speak once before his end; may I claim that right?"

"Yes," answered the King, "it is granted to you."

Then said Faithful John, "I have been condemned unjustly, for I have always been faithful," and he related how he had heard on the sea voyage the talk of the ravens, and how he had done everything in order to save his master.

Then cried the King, "O my Faithful John, pardon! pardon! Lead him down!" But Faithful John, as he spoke the last words, fell lifeless, and become stone.

The King and Queen had great grief because of this, and the King said, "Ah, how could I have evil-rewarded such faithfulness!" and he caused the stone image to be lifted up and put to stand in his sleeping-room by the side of his bed. And as often as he saw it he wept and said, "Would that I could bring thee back to life, my Faithful John!"

After some time the Queen bore twins—two little sons—that grew and thrived, and were the joy of their parents. One day, when the Queen was in church, the two children were sitting and playing with their father, and he gazed at the stone image full of sadness, sighed, and cried, "Oh that I could bring thee back to life, my Faithful John!"

Then the stone began to speak, and said, "Yes, thou canst bring me back to life again, if thou wilt bestow therefor thy best-beloved."

Then cried the King, "All that I have in the world will I give up for thee!"

The stone went on to say, "If thou wilt cut off the heads of thy two children with thy own hand, and besmear me with their blood, I shall receive life again."

The King was horror-struck at the thought that he must put his beloved children to death, but he remembered all John's faithfulness, and how he had died for him, and he drew his sword and cut off his children's heads with his own hand.

And when he had besmeared the stone with their blood, life returned to it, and Faithful John stood alive and well before him; and he said to the King, "Thy faithfulness shall not be unrewarded," and, taking up the heads of the children, he set them on again, and besmeared the wounds with their blood, upon which in a moment they were whole again, and jumped about, and went on playing as if nothing had happened to them.

Now was the King full of joy; and when he saw the Queen coming he put the Faithful John and the two children in a great chest. When she came in he said to her, "Hast thou prayed in church?"

"Yes," answered she, "but I was thinking all the while of Faithful John, and how he came to such great misfortune through us."

"Then," said he, "dear wife, we can give him life again, but it will cost us both our little sons, whom we must sacrifice."

The Queen grew pale and sick at heart, but said, "We owe it him, because of his great faithfulness."

Then the King rejoiced because she thought as he did, and he went and unlocked the chest and took out the children and Faithful John, and said, "God be praised, he is delivered, and our little sons are ours again"; and he related to her how it had come to pass.

After that they all lived together happily to the end of their lives.

The Six Swans

ONCE a King was hunting in a great wood, and he pursued a wild animal so eagerly that none of his people could follow him. When evening came he stood still, and looking round him he found that he had lost his way; and seeking a path, he found none. Then all at once he saw an old woman with a nodding head coming up to him; and it was a witch.

"My good woman," said he, "can you show me the way out of the wood?"

"Oh yes, my lord King," answered she, "certainly I can; but I must make a condition, and if you do not fulfill it, you will never get out of the wood again, but die there of hunger."

"What is the condition?" asked the King.

"I have a daughter," said the old woman, "who is as fair as any in the world, and if you will take her for your bride, and make her Queen, I will show you the way out of the wood."

The King consented, because of the difficulty he was in, and the old woman led him into her little house, and there her daughter was sitting by the fire.

She received the King just as if she had been expecting him, and though he saw that she was very beautiful, she did not please him, and he could not look at her without an inward shudder. Nevertheless, he took the maiden before him on his horse, and the old woman showed him the way, and soon he was in his royal castle again, where the wedding was held.

The King had been married before, and had his first wife had left seven children, six boys and one girl, whom he loved better than all the world, and as he was afraid the step-mother might not behave well to them, and perhaps would do them some mischief, he took them to a lonely castle standing in the middle of a wood. There they remained hidden, for the road to it was so hard to find that the King himself could not have found it, had it not been for a clew of yarn, possessing wonderful properties, that a wise woman had given him; when he threw it down before him, it unrolled itself and showed him the way.

And the King went so often to see his dear children, that the Queen was displeased at his absence; and she became curious and wanted to know what he went out into the wood for so often alone. She bribed his servants with much money, and they showed her the secret, and told her of the clew of yarn, which alone could point out the way; then she gave herself no rest until she had found out where the King kept the clew, and then she made some little white silk shirts, and sewed a charm in each, as she had learned witchcraft of her mother. And once when the King had ridden to the hunt, she took the little shirts and went into the wood, and the clew of yarn showed her the way. The children seeing some one in the distance, thought it was their dear father coming to see them, and came jumping for joy to meet him. Then the wicked Queen threw one of the little shirts over each, and as soon as the shirts touched their bodies, they were changed into swans, and flew away through the wood. So the Queen went home very pleased to think she had got rid of her step-children; but the maiden had not run out with her brothers, and so the Queen knew nothing about her.

The next day the King went to see his children, but he found nobody but his daughter. "Where are thy brothers?" asked the King.

"Ah, dear father," answered she, "they are gone away and have left me behind," and then she told him how she had seen from her window her brothers in the guise of swans fly away through the wood, and she showed him the feathers which they had let fall in the courtyard, and which she had picked up. The King was grieved, but he never dreamt that it was the Queen who had done this wicked deed, and as he feared lest the maiden also should be stolen away from him, he wished to take her away with him. But she was afraid of the step-mother, and begged the King to let her remain one more night in the castle in the wood.

Then she said to herself, "I must stay here no longer, but go and seek for my brothers."

And when the night came, she fled away and went straight into the wood. She went on all that night and the next day, until she could go no longer for weariness. At last she saw a rude hut, and she went in and found a room with six little beds in it; she did not dare to lie down in one, but she crept under one and lay on the hard boards and wished for night. When it was near the time of sun-setting she heard a rustling sound, and saw six swans come flying in at the window. They alighted on the ground, and blew at one another until they had blown all their feathers off, and then they stripped off their swan-skin as if it had been a shirt. And the maiden looked at them and knew them for her brothers, and was very glad, and crept from under the bed. The brothers were not less glad when their sister appeared, but their joy did not last long.

"You must not stay here," said they to her; "this is a robbers' haunt, and if they were to come and find you here, they would kill you."

"And cannot you defend me?" asked the little sister.

"No," answered they, "for we can only get rid of our swan-skins and keep our human shape every evening for a quarter of an hour, but after that we must be changed again into swans."

Their sister wept at hearing this, and said, "Can nothing be done to set you free?"

"Oh no," answered they, "the work would be too hard for you. For six whole years you would be obliged never to speak or laugh, and make during that time six little shirts out of aster-flowers. If you were to let fall a single word before the work was ended, all would be of no good."

And just as the brothers had finished telling her this, the quarter of an hour came to an end, and they changed into swans and flew out of the window.

But the maiden made up her mind to set her brothers free, even though it should cost her her life. She left the hut, and going into the middle of the wood, she climbed a tree, and there passed the night. The next morning she set to work and gathered asters and began sewing them together: as for speaking, there was no one to speak to, and as for laughing, she had no mind to it; so she sat on and looked at nothing but her work.

When she had been going on like this for a long time, it happened that the King of that country went a-hunting in the wood, and some of his huntsmen came up to the tree in which the maiden sat. They called out to her, saying, "Who art thou?" But she gave no answer. "Come down," cried they; "we will do thee no harm." But she only shook her head. And when they tormented her further with questions she threw down to them her gold necklace, hoping they could be content with that. But they would not leave off, so she threw down to them her girdle, and when that was no good, her garters, and one after another everything she had on and could possibly spare, until she had nothing left but her smock. But all was no good, the huntsmen would not be put off any longer, and they climbed the tree, carried the maiden off, and brought her to the King.

The King asked, "Who art thou? What wert thou doing in the tree?" But she answered nothing. He spoke to her in all the languages he knew, but she remained dumb: but, being very beautiful, the King inclined to her, and he felt a great love rise up in his heart towards her; and casting his mantle round her, he put her before him on his horse and brought her to his castle. Then he caused rich clothing to be put upon her, and her beauty shone as bright as the morning, but no word would she utter. He seated her by his side at table, and her modesty and gentle mien so pleased him, that he said, "This maiden I choose for wife, and no other in all the world," and accordingly after a few days they were married.

But the King had a wicked mother, who was displeased with the marriage, and spoke ill of the young Queen. "Who knows where the maid can have come from?" said she, "and not able to speak a word! She is not worthy of a king!"

After a year had passed, and the Queen brought her first child into the world, the old woman carried it away, and marked the Queen's mouth with blood as she lay sleeping. Then she went to the King and declared that his wife was an eater of human flesh. The King would not believe such a thing, and ordered that no one should do her any harm. And the Queen went on quietly sewing the shirts and caring for nothing else.

The next time that a fine boy was born, the wicked step-mother used the same deceit, but the King would give no credence to her words, for he said, "She is too tender and good to do any such thing, and if she were only not dumb, and would justify herself, then her innocence would be as clear as day."

When for the third time the old woman stole away the new-born child and accused the Queen, who was unable to say a word in her defense, the King could do no other but give her up to justice, and she was sentenced to suffer death by fire.

The day on which her sentence was to be carried out was the very last one of the sixth year of the years during which she had neither spoken nor laughed, to free her dear brothers from the evil spell. The six shirts were ready, all except one which wanted the left sleeve. And when she was led to the pile of wood, she carried the six shirts on her arm, and when she mounted the pile and the fire was about to be kindled, all at once she cried out aloud, for there were six swans coming flying through the air; and she saw that her deliverance was near, and her heart beat for joy. The swans came close up to her with rushing wings, and stooped round her, so that she could throw the shirts over them; and when that had been done the swan-skins fell off them, and her brothers stood before her in their own bodies quite safe and sound; but as one shirt wanted the left sleeve, so the youngest brother had a swan's wing instead of a left arm.

They embraced and kissed each other, and the Queen went up to the King, who looked on full of astonishment, and began to speak to him and to say, "Dearest husband, now I may dare to speak and tell you that I am innocent, and have been falsely accused," and she related to him the treachery of the step-mother, who had taken away the three children and hidden them. And she was reconciled to the King with great joy, and the wicked step-mother was bound to the stake on the pile of wood and burnt to ashes.

And the King and Queen lived many years with their six brothers in peace and joy.

The Seven Ravens

A MAN had seven sons, but not a single daughter. This made both him and his wife very unhappy. At last a daughter was born, to their great joy; but the child was very small and slight, and so weak that they feared it would die. So the father sent his sons to the spring to fetch water that he might baptize her.

Each of the boys ran in great haste to be the first to draw the water for their little sister's baptism, but in the struggle to be first they let the pitcher fall into the well.

Then they stood still and knew not what to do; not one of them dared to venture home without the water. As the time went on and they did not return, the father became very impatient, and said, "I suppose in the midst of their play they have forgotten what I sent them for, the careless children."

He was in such an agony lest the child should die unbaptized that he exclaimed thoughtlessly, "I wish the youngsters were all turned into ravens!"

The words were scarcely uttered when there was heard a rushing of wings in the air over his head, and presently seven coal-black ravens flew over the house.

The father could not recall the dreadful words, and both parents grieved terribly over the loss of their seven sons; their only consolation now was the little daughter, who every day grew stronger and more beautiful.

For a long time the maiden was not told that she had brothers; her parents were most careful to avoid all mention of them. But one day she overheard some persons talking, and they said that no doubt the young girl was very beautiful, but that there must have been some strange cause for the misfortune which had happened to her seven brothers.

Oh, how surprised and sad she felt when she heard this! She went at once to her father and mother and asked them if she really had

had any brothers, and what had become of them. Then her parents dared not any longer keep the secret from her. They told her, however, that it was the decree of Heaven, and that her birth was the innocent cause of all. As soon as she was alone she made a firm determination that she would try to break the enchantment in which her brothers were held.

She had neither rest nor peace till she had made up her mind to leave home and seek her brothers and set them free, cost what it might.

When at last she left home, she took nothing with her but a little ring, in memory of her parents, a loaf of bread, a jug of water, and a little stool, in case she felt tired.

So she went from her home, and traveled further and further, till she came to the end of the world, and there was the sun; but it was so hot and fierce that it scorched the little child, and she ran away in such a hurry that she ran into the moon. Here it was quite cold and dismal, and she heard a voice say, "I smell man's flesh," which made her escape from the moon as quickly as she could, and at last she reached the stars.

They were very kind and friendly to her. Each of the stars was seated on a wonderful chair, and the Morning Star stood up and said, "If you have not a key you will not be able to unlock the iceberg in which your brothers are shut up."

So the Morning Star gave the maiden the key, and told her to wrap it up carefully in her little handkerchief, and showed her the way to the iceberg. When she arrived the gate was closed; she opened her handkerchief to take out the key, but found it empty; she had forgotten the advice of the kind stars. What was she to do now? She wished to rescue her brothers and had no key to the iceberg.

At last the good little sister thought she would put her finger into the lock instead of a key. After twisting and turning it about, which hurt her very much, she happily succeeded in opening it, and immediately entered.

Presently a little dwarf came forward to meet her, and said, "My child, what are you seeking?" "I seek my brothers, the seven ravens," she said. "The seven ravens are not at home," replied the dwarf; "but if you would like to wait here till they return, pray step in."

Then the little dwarf took the maiden to the room where supper was prepared for the seven ravens, on seven little plates, by which stood seven little cups of water.

So the sister ate a few crumbs from each plate and drank a little draught from each cup, and into the last cup she let fall the ring that she brought from home.

Before she could get it out again she heard the rushing of wings in the air, and the little dwarf said, "Here come the seven Mr. Ravens flying home."

Then she hid herself behind the door to see and hear what they would do. They came in and were about to eat their supper, but as they caught sight of their little cups and plates, they said one to another: "Who has been eating from my little plate?" "Who has been drinking from my little cup?" "It has been touched by the mouth of a human being," cried one; "and, look here, what is this?" He took up his cup and turned it over, and out rolled the little ring, which they knew had once belonged to their father and mother.

Then said the eldest, "Oh, I remember that ring! Oh, if our sister would only come here, we should be free!" The maiden, who heard the wish from behind the door, came forth smiling, and stood before them.

In that same moment the seven ravens were freed from the enchantment, and became seven handsome young men. Oh, how joyfully they all kissed each other and their little sister, and started off at once in great happiness to their parents and their home!

The Twelve Brothers

ONCE UPON a time there lived a King and Queen very peacefully together; they had twelve children, all boys.

Now the King said to the Queen one day, "If our thirteenth child should be a girl the twelve boys shall die, so that her riches may be the greater, and the kingdom fall to her alone."

Then he caused twelve coffins to be made; and they were filled with shavings, and a little pillow laid in each, and they were brought and put in a locked-up room; and the King gave the key to the Queen, and told her to say nothing about it to any one.

But the mother sat the whole day sorrowing, so that her youngest son, who never left her, and to whom she had given the Bible name Benjamin, said to her, "Dear mother, why are you so sad?" "Dearest child," answered she, "I dare not tell you."

But he let her have no peace until she went and unlocked the room, and showed him the twelve coffins with the shavings and the little pillows.

Then she said, "My dear Benjamin, your father has caused these coffins to be made for you and your eleven brothers, and if I bring a little girl into the world you are all to be put to death together and buried therein." And she wept as she spoke, and her little son comforted her and said, "Weep not, dear mother, we will save ourselves and go far away."

Then she answered, "Yes, go with your eleven brothers out into the world, and let one of you always sit on the top of the highest tree that can be found, and keep watch upon the tower of this castle. If a little son is born I will put out a white flag, and then you may safely venture back again; but if it is a little daughter I will put out a red flag, and then flee away as fast as you can, and the dear God watch over you. Every night will I arise and pray for you—in winter that you may have a fire to warm yourselves by, and in summer that you may not languish in the heat."

After that, when she had given her sons her blessing, they went away out into the wood. One after another kept watch, sitting on the highest oak tree, looking towards the tower. When eleven days had passed, and Benjamin's turn came, he saw a flag put out, but it was not white, but blood red, to warn them that they were to die. When the brothers knew this they became angry, saying, "Shall we suffer death because of a girl! we swear to be revenged; wherever we find a girl we will shed her blood."

Then they went deeper into the wood; and in the middle, where it was darkest, they found a little enchanted house, standing empty. Then they said, "Here will we dwell; and you, Benjamin, the youngest and weakest, shall stay at home and keep house; we others will go abroad and purvey food."

Then they went into the wood and caught hares, wild roes, birds, and pigeons, and whatever else is good to eat, and brought them to Benjamin for him to cook and make ready to satisfy their hunger. So they lived together in the little house for ten years, and the time did not seem long.

By this time the Queen's little daughter was growing up; she had a kind heart and a beautiful face, and a golden star on her forehead.

Once when there was a great wash she saw among the clothes twelve shirts, and she asked her mother, "Whose are these twelve shirts? they are too small to be my father's." Then the mother answered with a sore heart, "Dear child, they belong to your twelve brothers." The little girl said, "Where are my twelve brothers? I have never heard of them." And her mother answered, "God only knows where they are wandering about in the world."

Then she led the little girl to the secret room and unlocked it, and showed her the twelve coffins with the shavings and the little pillows. "These coffins," said she, "were intended for your twelve brothers, but they went away far from home when you were born," and she related how everything had come to pass. Then said the little girl, "Dear mother, do not weep, I will go and seek my brothers."

So she took the twelve shirts and went far and wide in the great forest. The day sped on, and in the evening she came to the enchanted house. She went in and found a youth, who asked, "Whence do you come, and what do you want?" and he marveled at her beauty, her royal garments, and the star on her forehead.

Then she answered, "I am a King's daughter, and I seek my twelve brothers, and I will go everywhere under the blue sky until I find them." And she showed him the twelve shirts which belonged to them. Then Benjamin saw that it must be his sister, and said, "I am Benjamin, your youngest brother."

And she began weeping for joy, and Benjamin also, and they kissed and cheered each other with great love. After a while he said, "Dear sister, there is still a hindrance; we have sworn that any maiden that we meet must die, as it was because of a maiden that we had to leave our kingdom."

Then she said, "I will willingly die, if so I may benefit my twelve brothers." "No," answered he, "you shall not die; sit down under this tub until the eleven brothers come, and I agree with them about it." She did so; and as night came on they returned from hunting, and supper was ready.

And as they were sitting at table and eating, they asked, "What news?" And Benjamin said, "Don't you know any?" "No," answered they. So he said, "You have been in the wood, and I have stayed at home, and yet I know more than you." "Tell us!" cried they.

He answered, "Promise me that the first maiden we see shall not be put to death." "Yes, we promise," cried they all, "she shall have mercy; tell us now."

Then he said, "Our sister is here," and lifted up the tub, and the King's daughter came forth in her royal garments with her golden star on her forehead, and she seemed so beautiful, delicate, and sweet, that they all rejoiced, and fell on her neck and kissed her, and loved her with all their hearts.

After this she remained with Benjamin in the house and helped him with the work. The others went forth into the woods to catch wild animals, does, birds, and pigeons, for food for them all, and their sister and Benjamin took care that all was made ready for them. She fetched the wood for cooking, and the vegetables, and watched the pots on the fire, so that supper was always ready when the others came in. She kept also great order in the house, and the beds were always beautifully white and clean, and the brothers were contented, and lived in unity.

One day the two got ready a fine feast, and when they were all assembled they sat down and ate and drank, and were full of joy.

Now there was a little garden belonging to the enchanted house, in which grew twelve lilies; the maiden, thinking to please her brothers, went out to gather the twelve flowers, meaning to give one to each as they sat at meat. But as she broke off the flowers, in the same moment the brothers were changed into twelve ravens, and flew over the wood far away, and the house with the garden also disappeared. So the poor maiden stood alone in the wild wood, and as she was looking around her she saw an old woman standing by her, who said, "My child, what hast thou done! why couldst thou not leave the twelve flowers standing? They were thy twelve brothers, who are now changed to ravens forever."

The maiden said, weeping, "Is there no means of setting them free?"

"No," said the old woman, "there is in the whole world no way but one, and that is difficult; thou canst not release them but by being dumb for seven years: thou must neither speak nor laugh; and wert thou to speak one single word, and it wanted but one hour of the seven years, all would be in vain, and thy brothers would perish because of that one word."

Then the maiden said in her heart, "I am quite sure that I can set my brothers free," and went and sought a tall tree, climbed up, and sat there spinning, and never spoke or laughed. Now it happened that a King, who was hunting in the wood, had with him a large greyhound, who ran to the tree where the maiden was, sprang up at it, and barked loudly. Up came the King and saw the beautiful Princess with the golden star on her forehead, and he was so charmed with her beauty that he prayed her to become his wife. She gave no answer, only a little nod of her head. Then he himself climbed the tree and brought her down, set her on his horse and took her home. The wedding was held with great splendor and rejoicing, but the bride neither spoke nor laughed.

After they had lived pleasantly together for a few years, the King's mother, who was a wicked woman, began to slander the young Queen, and said to the King, "She is only a low beggar-maid that you have taken to yourself; who knows what mean tricks she is playing? Even if she is really dumb and cannot speak she might at least laugh; not to laugh is the sign of a bad conscience."

At first the King would believe nothing of it, but the old woman talked so long, and suggested so many bad things, that he at last let himself be persuaded, and condemned the Queen to death.

Now a great fire was kindled in the courtyard, and she was to be burned in it; and the King stood above at the window, and watched it all with weeping eyes, for he had held her very dear. And when she was already fast bound to the stake, and the fire was licking her garments with red tongues, the last moment of the seven years came to an end. Then a rushing sound was heard in the air, and twelve ravens came flying and sank downwards; and as they touched the earth they became her twelve brothers that she had lost. They rushed through the fire and quenched the flames, and set their dear sister free, kissing and consoling her. And now that her mouth was opened, and that she might venture to speak, she told the King the reason of her dumbness, and why she had never laughed. The King rejoiced when he heard of her innocence, and they all lived together in happiness until their death.

But the wicked mother-in-law was very unhappy, and died miserably.

Iron John

ONCE UPON a time there lived a King who had a great forest near his palace, full of all kinds of wild animals. One day he sent out a huntsman to shoot him a roe, but he did not come back. "Perhaps some accident has befallen him," said the King, and the next day he sent out two more huntsmen who were to search for him, but they too stayed away. Then on the third day, he sent for all his huntsmen, and said, "Scour the whole forest through, and do not give up until ye have found all three." But of these also, none came home again, and of the pack of hounds which they had taken with them, none were seen more. From that time forth, no one would any longer venture into the forest, and it lay there in deep stillness and solitude, and nothing was seen of it, but sometimes an eagle or a hawk flying over it.

This lasted for many years, when a strange huntsman announced himself to the King as seeking a situation, and offered to go into the dangerous forest. The King, however, would not give his consent, and said, "It is not safe in there; I fear it would fare with thee no better than with the others, and thou wouldst never come out again." The huntsman replied, "Lord, I will venture it at my own risk; I have no fear."

The huntsman therefore betook himself with his dog to the forest. It was not long before the dog fell in with some game on the way, and wanted to pursue it; but hardly had the dog run two steps when it stood before a deep pool, could go no farther, and a naked arm stretched itself out of the water, seized it, and drew it under. When the huntsman saw that, he went back and fetched three men to come with buckets and bail out the water. When they could see to the bottom there lay a wild man whose body was brown like rusty iron, and whose hair hung over his face down to his knees. They bound him with cords, and led him away to the castle. There was great astonishment over the wild man; the King, however, had him put in an iron cage in his court-yard, and forbade the door to be opened on pain of death, and the Queen herself was to take the key into her keeping. And from this time forth every one could again go into the forest with safety.

The King had a son eight years old, who was once playing in the court-yard, and while he was playing, his golden ball fell into the cage. The boy ran thither and said, "Give me my ball." "Not till thou hast opened the door for me," answered the man. "No," said the boy, "I will not do that; the King has forbidden it," and ran away. The next day he again went and asked for his ball; the wild man said, "Open my door," but the boy would not. On the third day the King had ridden out hunting, and the boy went once more and said, "I cannot open the door even if I wished, for I have not the key." Then the wild man said, "It lies under thy mother's pillow, thou canst get it there." The boy, who wanted to have his ball back, cast all thought to the winds, and brought the key. The door opened with difficulty, and the boy pinched his fingers. When it was open the wild man stepped out, gave him the golden ball, and hurried away. The boy had become afraid; he called and cried after him, "Oh, wild man, do not go away, or I shall be beaten!" The wild man turned back, took him up, set him on his shoulder, and went with hasty steps into the forest.

When the King came home, he observed the empty cage, and asked the Queen how that had happened. She knew nothing about it, and sought the key, but it was gone. She called the boy, but no one answered. The King sent out his people to seek for him in the fields, but they did not find him. Then he could easily guess what had happened, and much grief reigned in the royal court.

When the wild man had once more reached the dark forest, he took the boy down from his shoulder, and said to him, "Thou wilt never see thy father and mother again, but I will keep thee with me, for thou hast set me free, and I have compassion on thee. If thou dost all I bid thee, thou shalt fare well. Of treasure and gold I have enough, and more than any one in the world." He made a bed of moss for the boy on which he slept, and the next morning the man took him to a well, and said, "Behold, the gold well is as bright and clear as crystal; thou shalt sit beside it, and take care that nothing falls into it, or it will be polluted. I will come every evening to see if thou hast obeyed my order." The boy placed himself by the margin of the well, and often saw a golden fish or a golden snake show itself therein, and took care that nothing fell in. As he was thus sitting, his finger hurt him so violently that he involuntarily put it in the water. He drew it quickly out again, but saw that it was quite gilded, and whatsoever pains he took to wash the gold off again, all was to no purpose.

In the evening Iron John came back, looked at the boy, and said, "What has happened to the well?" "Nothing, nothing," he answered, and held his finger behind his back, that the man might not see it. But he said, "Thou hast dipped thy finger into the water; this time it may pass, but take care thou dost not let anything go in." By daybreak the boy was already sitting by the well and watching it. His finger hurt him again and he passed it over his head, and then unhappily a hair fell down into the well. He took it quickly out, but it was already quite gilded. Iron John came, and already knew what had happened. "Thou hast let a hair fall into the well," said he. "I will allow thee to watch by it once more, but if this happens for the third time then the well is polluted, and thou canst no longer remain with me."

On the third day, the boy sat by the well, and did not stir his finger, however much it hurt him. But the time was long to him, and he looked at the reflection of his face on the surface of the water. And as he still bent down more and more while he was doing so, and trying to look straight into the eyes, his long hair fell down from his shoulders into the water. He raised himself up and quickly, but the whole of the hair of his head was already golden and shone like the sun. You may imagine how terrified the poor boy was! He took his pocket-handkerchief and tied it round his head, in order that the man might not see it. When he came he already knew everything, and said, "Take the handkerchief off." Then the golden hair streamed forth, and let the boy excuse himself as he might, it was of no use. "Thou hast not stood the trial, and canst stay here no longer. Go forth into the world, there thou wilt learn what poverty is. But as thou hast not a bad heart, and as I mean well by thee, there is one thing I will grant thee; if thou fallest into any difficulty, come to the forest and cry, 'Iron John,' and then I will come and help thee. My power is great, greater than thou thinkest, and I have gold and silver in abundance."

Then the King's son left the forest, and walked by beaten and unbeaten paths ever onwards until at length he reached a great city. There he looked for work, but could find none, and he had learnt nothing by which he could help himself. At length he went to the palace, and asked if they would take him in. The people about court did not at all know what use they could make of him, but they liked him, and told him to stay. At length the cook took him into his service, and said he might carry food and water, and rake the cinders together. Once when it so happened that no one else was at hand, the cook ordered him to carry the food to the royal table, but as he did not like to let his golden hair be seen, he kept his little cap on.

Such a thing as that had never yet come under the King's notice, and he said, "When thou comest to the royal table thou must take thy hat off." He answered, "Ah, Lord, I cannot; I have a bad sore place on my head." Then the King had the cook called before him and scolded him, and asked how he could take such a boy as that into his service, and that he was to turn him off at once. The cook, however, had pity on him, and exchanged him for the gardener's boy.

Now the boy had to plant and water the garden, hoe and dig, and bear the wind and bad weather. Once in summer when he was working alone in the garden, the day was so warm he took his little cap off that the air might cool him. As the sun shone on his hair it glittered and flashed so that the rays fell into the bed-room of the King's daughter, and up she sprang to see what that could be. Then she saw the boy, and cried to him, "Boy, bring me a wreath of flowers." He put his cap on with all haste, and gathered wild field-flowers and bound them together. When he was ascending the stairs with them, the gardener met him, and said, "How canst thou take the King's daughter a garland of such common flowers? Go quickly, and get another, and seek out the prettiest and rarest." "Oh, no," replied the boy, "the wild ones have more scent, and will please her better."

When he got into the room, the King's daughter said, "Take thy cap off, it is not seemly to keep it on in my presence." He again said, "I may not, I have a sore head." She, however, caught at his cap and pulled it off, and then his golden hair rolled down on his shoulders, and it was splendid to behold. He wanted to run out, but she held him by the arm, and gave him a handful of ducats. With these he departed, but he cared nothing for the gold pieces. He took them to the gardener, and said, "I present them to thy children, they can play with them."

The following day the King's daughter again called to him that he was to bring her a wreath of field-flowers, and when he went in with it, she instantly snatched at his cap, and wanted to take it away from him, but he held it fast with both hands. She again gave him a handful of ducats, but he would not keep them, and gave them to the gardener for playthings for his children. On the third day things went just the same; she could not get his cap away from him, and he would not have her money.

Not long afterwards, the country was overrun by war. The King gathered together his people, and did not know whether or not he could offer any opposition to the enemy, who was superior in strength and had a mighty army. Then said the gardener's boy, "I am grown up, and will go to the wars also, only give me a horse." The others laughed, and said, "Seek one for thyself when we are gone, we will leave one behind us in the stable for thee." When they had gone forth, he went into the stable, and got the horse out; it was lame of one foot, and limped hobblety jig, hobblety jig; nevertheless he mounted it, and rode away to the dark forest. When he came to the outskirts, he called "Iron John" three times so loudly that it echoed through the trees. Thereupon the wild man appeared immediately, and said, "What dost thou desire?" "I want a strong steed, for I am going to the wars." "That thou shalt have, and still more than thou askest for."

Then the wild man went back into the forest, and it was not long before a stable-boy came out of it, who led a horse that snorted with its nostrils, and could hardly be restrained, and behind them followed a great troop of soldiers entirely equipped in iron, and their swords flashed in the sun. The youth made over his three-legged horse to the stable-boy, mounted the other, and rode at the head of the soldiers. When he got near the battle-field a great part of the King's had already fallen, and little was wanting to make the rest give way. Then the youth galloped thither with his iron soldiers, broke like a hurricane over the enemy, and beat down all who opposed him. They began to fly, but the youth pursued, and never stopped, until there was not a single man left. Instead, however, of returning to the King, he conducted his troop by bye-ways back to the forest, and called forth Iron John. "What dost thou desire?" asked the wild man. "Take back thy horse and thy troops, and give me my three-legged horse again." All that he asked was done, and soon he was riding on his three-legged horse.

When the King returned to his palace, his daughter went to meet him, and wished him joy of his victory. "I am not the one who carried away the victory," said he, "but a stranger knight who came to my assistance with his soldiers." The daughter wanted to hear who the strange knight was, but the King did not know, and said, "He followed the enemy, and I did not see him again." She inquired of the gardener where his boy was, but he smiled, and said, "He has just come home on his three-legged horse, and the others have been mocking him, and crying, 'Here comes our hobblety jig back again!' They asked, too, 'Under what hedge hast thou been lying sleeping all the time?' He, however, said, 'I did the best of all, and it would have gone badly without me.' And then he was still more ridiculed."

The King said to his daughter, "I will proclaim a great feast that shall last for three days, and thou shalt throw a golden apple. Perhaps the unknown will come to it." When the feast was announced, the youth went out to the forest, and called Iron John. "What dost thou desire?" asked he. "That I may catch the King's daughter's golden apple." "It is as safe as if thou hadst it already," said Iron John. "Thou shalt likewise have a suit of red armor for the occasion, and ride on a spirited chestnut horse." When the day came, the youth galloped to the spot, took his place amongst the knights, and was recognized by no one. The King's daughter came forward, and threw a golden apple to the knights, but none of them caught it but he, only as soon as he had it he galloped away.

On the second day Iron John equipped him as a white knight, and gave him a white horse. Again he was the only one who caught the apple, and he did not linger an instant, but galloped off with it. The King grew angry, and said, "That is not allowed; he must appear before me and tell his name." He gave the order that if the knight who caught the apple should go away again they should pursue him, and if he did not come back willingly, they were to cut him down and stab him.

On the third day, he received from Iron John a suit of black armor and a black horse, and again he caught the apple. But when he was riding off with it, the King's attendants pursued him, and one of them got so near him that he wounded the youth's leg with the point of his sword. The youth nevertheless escaped from them, but his horse leapt so violently that the helmet fell from the youth's head, and they could see that he had golden hair. They rode back and announced this to the King.

The following day the King's daughter asked the gardener about his boy. "He is at work in the garden; the queer creature has been at the festival too, and only came home yesterday evening; he has likewise shown my children three golden apples which he has won."

The King had him summoned into his presence, and he came and again had his little cap on his head. But the King's daughter went up to him and took it off, and then his golden hair fell down over his shoulders, and he was so handsome that all were amazed. "Art thou the knight who come every day to the festival, always in different colors, and who caught the three golden apples?" asked the King. "Yes," answered he, "and here the apples are," and he took them out of his pocket, and returned them to the King. "If thou desirest further proof, thou mayest see the wound which thy people gave me when they followed me. But I am likewise the knight who helped thee to thy victory over thine enemies." "If thou canst perform such deeds as that, thou art no gardener's boy; tell me, who is thy father?" "My father is a mighty King, and gold have I in plenty as great as I require." "I will see," said the King, "that I owe thanks to thee; can I do anything to please thee?" "Yes," answered he, "that indeed thou canst. Give me thy daughter to wife."

The maiden laughed, and said, "He does not stand much on ceremony, but I have already seen by his golden hair that he was no gardener's boy," and then she went and kissed him. His father and mother came to the wedding, and were in great delight, for they had given up all hope of ever seeing their dear son again. And as they were sitting at the marriage-feast, the music suddenly stopped, the doors opened, and a stately King came in with a great retinue. He went up to the youth, embraced him and said, "I am Iron John, and was by enchantment a wild man, but thou hast set me free; all the treasures which I possess, shall be thy property."

The King's Son Who Feared Nothing

ONCE THERE WAS a King's son who was no longer content to stay at home in his father's house. Since he had no fear of anything, he thought, "I will go forth into the wide world; there the time will not seem long to me, and I shall see wonders enough." So he took leave of his parents, and went forth, and on and on from morning till night, and whichever way his path led it was the same to him.

It came to pass that he got to the house of a giant, and as he was so tired he sat down by the door and rested. And as he let his eyes roam here and there, he saw the giant's playthings lying in the yard. These were a couple of enormous balls, and nine-pins as tall as a man. After a while he had a fancy to set the nine-pins up and then rolled the balls at them, and screamed and cried out when the nine-pins fell, and had a merry time of it.

The giant heard the noise, stretched his head out of the window, and saw a man who was not taller than other men, and yet played with his nine-pins. "Little worm," cried he, "why art thou playing with my balls? Who gave thee strength to do it?" The King's son looked up, saw the giant, and said, "Oh, thou blockhead, thou thinkest indeed that thou only hast strong arms. I can do everything I want to do."

The giant came down and watched the bowling with great admiration, and said, "Child of man, if thou art one of that kind, go and bring me an apple of the tree of life." "What dost thou want with it?" said the King's son. "I do not want the apple for myself," answered the giant, "but I have a betrothed bride who wishes for it. I have traveled far about the world and cannot find the tree." "I will soon find it," said the King's son, "and I do not know what is to prevent me from getting the apple down."

The giant said, "Thou really believest it to be so easy! The garden in which the tree stands is surrounded by an iron railing, and in front of the railing lie wild beasts, each close to the other, and they keep watch and let no man go in." "They will be sure to let me in," said the King's son. "Yes, but even if thou dost get into the garden, and seest the apple hanging to the tree, it is still not thine; a ring hangs in front of it, through which any one who wants to reach the apple and break it off, must put his hand, and no one has yet had the luck to do it." "That luck will be mine," said the King's son."

Then he took leave of the giant, and went forth over mountain and valley, and through plains and forests, until at length he came to the wondrous garden.

The beasts lay round about it, but they had put their heads down and were asleep. Moreover, they did not awake when he went up to them, so he stepped over them, climbed the fence, and got safely into the garden. There, in the very middle of it, stood the tree of life, and the red apples were shining upon the branches. He climbed up the trunk to the top, and as he was about to reach out for an apple, he saw a ring hanging before it; but he thrust his hand through that without any difficulty, and gathered the apple. The ring closed tightly on his arm, and all at once he felt a prodigious strength flowing through his veins.

When he had come down again from the tree with the apple, he would not climb over the fence, but grasped the great gate, and had no need to shake it more than once before it sprang open with a loud crash. Then he went out, and the lion, which had been lying down before, was awake and sprang after him, not in rage and fierceness, but following him humbly as its master.

The King's son took the giant the apple he had promised him, and said, "Seest thou, I have brought it without difficulty." The giant was glad that his desire had been so soon satisfied, hastened to his bride, and gave her the apple for which she had wished. She was a beautiful and wise maiden, and as she did not see the ring on his arm, she said, "I shall never believe that thou hast brought the apple, until I see the ring on thine arm."

The giant said, "I have nothing to do but go home and fetch it," and thought it would be easy to take away by force from the weak man what he would not give of his own free will. He therefore demanded the ring from him, but the King's son refused it. "Where the apple is, the ring must be also," said the giant; "if thou wilt not give it of thine own accord, thou must fight with me for it."

They wrestled with each other for a long time, but the giant could not get the better of the King's son, who was strengthened by the magical power of the ring. Then the giant thought of a stratagem, and said, "I have got warm with fighting, and so hast thou. We will bathe in the river, and cool ourselves before we begin again." The King's son, who knew nothing of falsehood, went with him to the water, and pulled off with his clothes the ring also from his arm, and sprang into the river. The giant instantly snatched the ring, and ran away with it, but the lion, which had observed the theft, pursued the giant, tore the ring out of his hand, and brought it back to its master. Then the giant placed himself behind an oak tree, and while the King's son was busy putting on his clothes again, surprised him, and put both his eyes out.

The unhappy King's son stood there, and was blind and knew not how to help himself. Then the giant came back to him, took him by the hand as if he were some one who wanted to guide him, and led him to the top of a high rock. There he left him standing, and thought, "Just two steps more, and he will fall down and kill himself, and I can take the ring from him." But the faithful lion had not deserted its master; it held him fast by the clothes, and drew him gradually back again.

When the giant came and wanted to rob the dead man, he saw that his cunning had been in vain. "Is there no way, then, of destroying a weak child of man like that?" said he angrily to himself, and seized the King's son and led him back again to the precipice by another way, but the lion, which saw his evil design, helped its master out of danger here also. When they had got close to the edge, the giant let the blind man's hand drop, and was going to leave him behind alone, but the lion pushed the giant so that he was thrown down and fell, dashed to pieces, on the ground.

The faithful animal again drew its master back from the precipice, and guided him to a tree by which flowed a clear brook. The King's son sat down there, but the lion lay down, and sprinkled the water in his face with its paws. Scarcely had a couple of drops wetted the sockets of his eyes, than he was once more able to see something, and remarked a little bird flying quite close by, which wounded itself against the trunk of a tree. On this it went down to the water and bathed itself therein, and then it soared upwards and swept between the trees without touching them, as if it had recovered its sight again. Then the King's son recognized a sign from God and stooped down to the water, and washed and bathed his face in it. And when he arose he had his eyes once more, brighter and clearer than they had ever been.

The King's son thanked God for his great mercy, and traveled with his lion onwards through the world. And it came to pass that he arrived before a castle which was enchanted. In the gateway stood a maiden of beautiful form and fine face, but she was quite black. She spoke to him and said, "Ah, if thou couldst but deliver me from the evil spell which is thrown over me." "What shall I do?" said the King's son. The maiden answered, "Thou must pass three nights in the great hall of this enchanted castle, but thou must let no fear enter thy heart. When they are doing their worst to torment thee, if thou bearest it without letting a sound escape thee, I shall be free. Thy life they dare not take." Then said the King's son, "I have no fear; with God's help I will try it."

So he went gaily into the castle, and when it grew dark he seated himself in the large hall and waited. Everything was quiet, however, till midnight, when all at once a great tumult began, and out of every hole and corner came little devils. They behaved as if they did not see him, seated themselves in the middle of the room, lighted a fire, and began to gamble. When one of them lost, he said, "It is not right; some one is here who does not belong to us; it is his fault that I am losing." "Wait, you fellow behind the stove, I am coming," said another. The screaming became still louder, so that no one could have heard it without terror. The King's son stayed sitting quite quietly, and was not afraid; but at last the devils jumped up from the ground, and fell on him, and there were so many of them that he could not defend himself from them. They dragged him about on the floor, pinched him, pricked him, beat him, and tormented him, but no sound escaped from him.

Towards morning they disappeared, and he was so exhausted that he could scarcely move his limbs, but when day dawned the black maiden came to him. She bore in her hand a little bottle wherein was the water of life wherewith she washed him, and he at once felt all pain depart and new strength flow through his veins. She said, "Thou hast held out successfully for one night, but two more lie before thee." Then she went away again, and as she was going, he observed that her feet had become white.

The next night the devils came and began their gambling anew. They fell on the King's son, and beat him much more severely than the night before, until his body was covered with wounds. But as he bore all quietly, they were forced to leave him, and when dawn appeared, the maiden came and healed him with the water of life. And when she went away, he saw with joy that she had already become white to the tips of her fingers.

Now he had only one night more to go through, but it was the worst. The hobgoblins came again: "Art thou there still?" cried they, "thou shalt be tormented till thy breath stops." They pricked him and beat him, and threw him here and there, and pulled him by the arms and legs as if they wanted to tear him to pieces, but he bore everything, and never uttered a cry. At last the devils vanished, but he lay fainting there, and did not stir, nor could he raise his eyes to look at the maiden who came in, and sprinkled and bathed him with the water of life. But suddenly he was freed from all pain, and felt fresh and healthy as if he had awakened from sleep, and when he opened his eyes he saw the maiden standing by him, snow-white, and fair as day. "Rise," said she, "and swing thy sword three times over the stairs, and then all will be delivered."

And when he had done that, the whole castle was released from enchantment, and the maiden was a rich King's daughter. The servants came and said that the table was already set in the great hall, and dinner served up. Then they sat down and ate and drank together, and in the evening the wedding was solemnized with great rejoicings.

The Drummer

A YOUNG DRUMMER went out alone one evening into the country, and came to a lake on the shore of which he perceived three pieces of white linen lying. "What fine linen," said he, and put one piece in his pocket. He returned home, thought no more of what he had found, and went to bed.

Just as he was going to sleep, it seemed to him as if some one was saying his name. He listened, and was aware of a soft voice which cried to him, "Drummer, drummer, wake up!" As it was a dark night he could see no one, but it appeared to him that a figure was hovering about his bed. "What do you want?" he asked. "Give me back my dress," answered the voice, "that you took away from me last evening by the lake." "You shall have it back again," said the drummer, "if you will tell me who you are." "Ah," replied the voice, "I am the daughter of a mighty King; but I have fallen into the power of a witch, and am shut up on the glass-mountain. I have to bathe in the lake every day with my two sisters, but I cannot fly back again without my dress. My sisters have gone away, but I have been forced to stay behind. I entreat you to give me my dress back." "Be easy, poor child," said the drummer. "I will willingly give it back to you."

He took it out of his pocket, and reached it to her in the dark. She snatched it in haste, and wanted to go away with it. "Stop a moment, perhaps I can help you." "You can only help me by ascending the glass-mountain, and freeing me from the power of the witch. But you cannot come to the glass-mountain, and indeed if you were quite close to it you could not ascend it." "When I want to do a thing I always can do it," said the drummer; "I am sorry for you, and have no fear of anything. But I do not know the way which leads to the glass-mountain." "The road goes through the great forest, in which the man-eaters live," she answered, "and more than that, I dare not tell you." And then he heard her wings quiver, and she flew away.

By daybreak the drummer arose, buckled on his drum, and went without fear straight into the forest. After he had walked for a while without seeing any giants, he thought to himself, "I must waken up the sluggards," and he hung his drum before him, and beat such a reveille that the birds flew out of the trees with loud cries. It was not long before a giant who had been lying sleeping among the grass, rose up, and was as tall as a fir tree.

"Wretch!" cried he; "what art thou drumming here for, and wakening me out of my best sleep?" "I am drumming," he replied, "because I want to show the way to many thousands who are following me." "What do they want in my forest?" demanded the giant. "They want to put an end to thee, and cleanse the forest of such a monster as thou art!" "Oho!" said the giant, "I will trample you all to death like so many ants." "Dost thou think thou canst do anything against us?" said the drummer; "if thou stoopest to take hold of one, he will jump away and hide himself; but when thou art lying down and sleeping, they will come forth from every thicket, and creep up to thee. Every one of them has a hammer of steel in his belt, and with that they will beat in thy skull."

The giant grew angry and thought, "If I meddle with the crafty folk, it might turn out badly for me. I can strangle wolves and bears, but I cannot protect myself from these earthworms." "Listen, little fellow," said he; "go back again, and I will promise thee that for the future I will leave thee and thy comrades in peace, and if there is anything else thou wishest for, tell me, for I am quite willing to do something to please thee."

"Thou hast long legs," said the drummer, "and canst run quicker than I; carry me to the glass-mountain, and I will give my followers

a signal to go back, and they shall leave thee in peace this time."
"Come here, worm," said the giant; "seat thyself on my shoulder, I
will carry thee where thou wishest to be." The giant lifted him up,
and the drummer began to beat his drum up aloft to his heart's
delight. The giant thought, "That is the signal for the other people
to turn back."

After a while, a second giant was standing in the road, who took
the drummer from the first, and stuck him in his own button-hole.
The drummer laid hold of the button, which was as large as a dish,
held on by it, and looked merrily around. Then they came to a
third giant, who took him out of the button-hole, and set him on
the rim of his hat. Then the drummer walked backwards and
forwards up above, and looked over the trees, and when he perceived a mountain in the blue distance, he thought, "That must be
the glass-mountain," and so it was. The giant only made two steps
more, and they reached the foot of the mountain, when the giant
put him down. The drummer demanded to be put on the summit
of the glass-mountain, but the giant shook his head, growled something in his beard, and went back into the forest.

And now the poor drummer was standing before the mountain,
which was as high as if three mountains were piled on each other,
and at the same time as smooth as a looking-glass, and did not know
how to get up it. He began to climb, but that was useless, for he
always slipped back again. "If one were a bird now," thought he;
but what was the good of wishing, no wings grew for him.

While he was standing thus, not knowing what to do, he saw, not
far from him, two men who were struggling fiercely together. He
went up to them and saw that they were disputing about a saddle
which was lying on the ground before them, and which both of
them wanted to have. "What fools you are," said he, "to quarrel
about a saddle, when you have not a horse for it!" "The saddle is
worth fighting about," answered one of the men; "whosoever sits
on it, and wishes himself in any place, even if it should be the very
end of the earth, gets there the instant he has uttered the wish. The
saddle belongs to us in common. It is my turn to ride on it, but that
other man will not let me do it." "I will soon decide the quarrel,"
said the drummer, and he went to a short distance and stuck a
white rod in the ground. Then he came back and said, "Now run to
the goal, and whoever gets there first, shall ride first." Both put
themselves into a trot; but hardly had they gone a couple of steps
before the drummer swung himself on the saddle, wished himself

on the glass-mountain, and before any one could turn round, he was there.

On the top of the mountain was a plain. There stood an old stone house, and in front of the house lay a great fish-pond, but behind it was a dark forest. He saw neither men nor animals, everything was quiet; only the wind rustled among the trees, and the clouds moved by quite close above his head. He went to the door and knocked. When he had knocked for the third time, an old woman with a brown face and red eyes opened the door. She had spectacles on her long nose, and looked sharply at him; then she asked what he wanted. "Entrance, food, and a bed for the night," replied the drummer. "That thou shalt have," said the old woman, "if thou wilt perform three services in return." "Why not?" he answered, "I am not afraid of any kind of work, however hard it may be."

The old woman let him go in, and gave him some food and a good bed at night. The next morning when he had had his sleep out, she took a thimble from her wrinkled finger, reached it to the drummer, and said, "Go to work now, and empty out the pond with this thimble; but thou must have it done before night, and must have sought out all the fishes which are in the water and laid them side by side, according to their kind and size." "That is strange work," said the drummer, but he went to the pond, and began to empty it. He bailed the whole morning; but what can any one do to a great lake with a thimble, even if he were to bail for a thousand years?

When it was noon, he thought, "It is all useless, and whether I work or not it will come to the same thing." So he gave it up and sat down. Then came a maiden out of the house who set a little basket with food before him, and said, "What ails thee, that thou sittest so sadly here?" He looked at her, and so that she was wondrously beautiful. "Ah," said he, "I cannot finish the first piece of work, how will it be with the others? I came forth to seek a King's daughter who is said to dwell here, but I have not found her, and I will go farther." "Stay here," said the maiden, "I will help thee out of thy difficulty. Thou art tired, lay thy head in my lap, and sleep. When thou awakest again, thy work will be done." The drummer did not need to be told that twice. As soon as his eyes were shut, she turned a wishing-ring and said, "Rise, water. Fishes, come out." Instantly the water rose on high like a white mist, and moved away with the other clouds, and the fishes sprang on the shore and laid themselves side by side each according to his size and kind.

When the drummer awoke, he saw with amazement that all was

done. But the maiden said, "One of the fish is not lying with those of its own kind, but quite alone; when the old woman comes to-night and sees that all she demanded has been done, she will ask thee, 'What is this fish lying alone for?' Then throw the fish in her face, and say, 'This one shall be for thee, old witch.'" In the evening the witch came, and when she had put this question, he threw the fish in her face. She behaved as if she did not remark it, and said nothing, but looked at him with malicious eyes.

Next morning she said, "Yesterday it was too easy for thee, I must give thee harder work. Today thou must hew down the whole of the forest, split the wood into logs, and pile them up, and everything must be finished by the evening." She gave him an axe, a mallet, and two wedges. But the axe was made of lead, and the mallet and wedges were of tin. When he began to cut, the edge of the axe turned back, and the mallet and wedges were beaten out of shape.

He did not know how to manage, but at mid-day the maiden came once more with his dinner and comforted him. "Lay thy head on my lap," said she, "and sleep; when thou awakest, thy work will be done." She turned her wishing-ring, and in an instant the whole forest fell down with a crash, the wood split, and arranged itself in heaps, and it seemed just as if unseen giants were finishing the work. When he awoke, the maiden said, "Dost thou see that the wood is piled up and arranged, one bough alone remains; but when the old woman comes this evening and asks thee about that bough, give her a blow with it, and say, 'That is for thee, thou witch.'"

The old woman came, "There! Thou seest how easy the work was!" said she; "but for whom hast thou left that bough which is lying there still?" "For thee, thou witch," he replied, and gave her a blow with it. But she pretended not to feel it, laughed scornfully, and said, "Early tomorrow morning thou shalt arrange all the wood in one heap, set fire to it, and burn it."

He rose at break of day, and began to pick up the wood, but how can a single man get a whole forest together? The work made no progress. The maiden, however, did not desert him in his need. She brought him his food at noon, and when he had eaten, he laid his head on her lap, and went to sleep. When he awoke, the entire pile of wood was burning in one enormous flame, which stretched its tongues out into the sky. "Listen to me," said the maiden, "when the witch comes, she will give thee all kinds of orders; do whatever she asks thee without fear, and then she will not be able to get the better of thee, but if thou art afraid, the fire will lay hold of thee, and consume thee. At last when thou hast done everything, seize her with both thy hands, and throw her into the midst of the fire."

The maiden departed, and the old woman came sneaking up to him. "Oh, I am cold," said she, "but that is a fire that burns; it warms my old bones for me, and does me good! But there is a log lying there which won't burn, bring it out for me. When thou hast done that, thou art free, and mayst go where thou likest; come, go in with a good will."

The drummer did not reflect long; he sprang into the midst of the flames, but they did not hurt him, and could not even singe a hair of his head. He carried the log out, and laid it down. Hardly, however, had the wood touched the earth than it was transformed, and the beautiful maiden who had helped him in his need stood before him, and by the silken and shining golden garments which she wore, he knew right well that she was the King's daughter. But the old woman laughed venomously, and said, "Thou thinkest thou hast her safe, but thou hast not got her yet!" Just as she was about to fall on the maiden and take her away, the youth seized the old woman with both his hands, raised her up on high, and threw her into the jaws of the fire, which closed over her as if it were delighted that the old witch was to be burnt.

Then the King's daughter looked at the drummer, and when she saw that he was a handsome youth and remembered how he had risked his life to deliver her, she gave him her hand, and said, "Thou hast ventured everything for my sake, but I also will do everything for thine. Promise to be true to me, and thou shalt be my husband. We shall not want for riches, we shall have enough with what the witch has gathered together here." She led him into the house, where there were chests and coffers crammed with the old woman's treasures. The maiden left the gold and silver where it was, and took only the precious stones. She would not stay any longer on the glass-mountain, so the drummer said to her, "Seat thyself by me on my saddle, and then we will fly down like birds." "I do not like the old saddle," said she, "I need only turn my wishing-ring and we shall be at home." "Very well, then," answered the drummer, "then wish us in front of the town-gate." In the twinkling of an eye they were there, but the drummer said, "I will just go to my parents and tell them the news, wait for me outside here, I shall soon be back." "Ah," said the King's daughter, "I beg thee to be careful. On thy arrival do not kiss thy parents on the right cheek, or else thou wilt forget everything, and I shall stay behind here outside, alone and deserted." "How can I forget thee?" said he, and promised her to come back very soon, and gave his hand upon it.

When he went into his father's house, he had changed so much that no one knew who he was, for the three days which he had passed on the glass-mountain had been three years. Then he made himself known, and his parents fell on his neck with joy, and his heart was so moved that he forgot what the maiden had said, and kissed them on both cheeks. But when he had given them the kiss on the right cheek, every thought of the King's daughter vanished from him. He emptied out his pockets, and laid handfuls of the largest jewels on the table. The parents had not the least idea what to do with the riches. Then the father built a magnificent castle all surrounded by gardens, woods, and meadows as if a Prince were going to live in it, and when it was ready, the mother said, "I have found a maiden for thee, and the wedding shall be in three days." The son was content to do as his parents desired.

The poor King's daughter had stood for a long time without the town waiting for the return of the young man. When evening came, she said, "He must certainly have kissed his parents on the right cheek, and has forgotten me." Her heart was full of sorrow, she wished herself into a solitary little hut in a forest, and would not return to her father's court. Every evening she went into the town and passed the young man's house; he often saw her, but he no longer knew her. At length she heard the people saying, "The wedding will take place tomorrow." Then she said, "I will try if I can win his heart back."

On the first day of the wedding ceremonies, she turned her wishing-ring, and said, "A dress as bright as the sun." Instantly the dress lay before her, and it was as bright as if it had been woven of real sunbeams. When all the guests were assembled, she entered the hall. Every one was amazed at the beautiful dress, and the bride most of all, and as pretty dresses were the things she had most delight in, she went to the stranger and asked if she would sell it to her. "Not for money," she answered, "but if I may pass the first night outside the door of the room where your betrothed sleeps, I will give it up to you." The bride could not overcome her desire and consented, but she mixed a sleeping-draught with the wine her betrothed took at night, which made him fall into a deep sleep. When all had become quiet, the King's daughter crouched down by the door of the bedroom, opened it just a little, and cried,

"Drummer, drummer, I pray thee hear!
Hast thou forgotten thou heldest me dear?
That on the glass-mountain we sat hour by hour?
That I rescued thy life from the witch's power?
Didst thou not plight thy troth to me?
Drummer, drummer, harken to me!"

But it was all in vain, the drummer did not awake, and when morning dawned, the King's daughter was forced to go back again as she came.

On the second evening she turned her wishing-ring and said, "A dress as silvery as the moon." When she appeared at the feast in the dress which was as soft as moonbeams, it again excited the desire of the bride, and the King's daughter gave it to her for permission to pass the second night also, outside the door of the bedroom. Then in the stillness of the night, she cried,

"Drummer, drummer, I pray thee hear!
Hast thou forgotten thou heldest me dear?
That on the glass-mountain we sat hour by hour?
That I rescued thy life from the witch's power?
Didst thou not plight thy troth to me?
Drummer, drummer, harken to me!"

But the drummer, who was stupefied with the sleeping-draught, could not be aroused. Sadly next morning she went back to her hut in the forest. But the people in the house had heard the lamentation of the stranger-maiden, and told the bridegroom about it. They told him also that it was impossible that he could hear anything of it, because the maiden he was going to marry had poured a sleeping-draught into his wine.

On the third evening, the King's daughter turned her wishing-ring, and said, "A dress glittering like the stars." When she showed herself therein at the feast, the bride was quite beside herself with the splendor of the dress, which far surpassed the others, and she said, "I must, and will have it." The maiden gave it as she had given the others for permission to spend the night outside the bridegroom's door. The bridegroom, however, did not drink the wine which was handed to him before he went to bed, but poured it behind the bed, and when everything was quiet, he heard a sweet voice which called to him,

"Drummer, drummer, I pray thee hear!
Hast thou forgotten thou heldest me dear?
That on the glass-mountain we sat hour by hour?

That I rescued thy life from the witch's power?
Didst thou not plight thy troth to me?
Drummer, drummer, harken to me!"

Suddenly, his memory returned to him. "Ah," cried he, "how can I have acted so unfaithfully; but the kiss which in the joy of my heart I gave my parents, on the right cheek, that is to blame for it all, that is what stupefied me!" He sprang up, took the King's daughter by the hand, and led her to his parents' bed. "This is my true bride," said he; "if I marry the other, I shall do a great wrong." The parents, when they heard how everything had happened, gave their consent. Then the lights in the hall were lighted again, drums and trumpets were brought, friends and relations were invited to come, and the real wedding was solemnized with great rejoicing. The first bride received the beautiful dresses as a compensation, and declared herself satisfied.

The Two Kings' Children

A KING had a little boy of whom it had been foretold that he should be killed by a stag when he was sixteen years of age. When he had reached that age the huntsmen once went hunting with him. In the forest, the King's son was separated from the others, and all at once he saw a great stag which he wanted to shoot but could not hit. At length he chased the stag so far that they were quite out of the forest, and then suddenly a great tall man was standing there instead of the stag, and said, "It is well that I have thee, I have already ruined six pairs of glass skates with running after thee, and have not been able to get thee."

Then he took the King's son with him, and dragged him through a great lake to a great palace, and then he had to sit down to table with him and eat something. When they had eaten something together the tall King said, "I have three daughters. Thou must keep watch over the eldest for one night, from nine in the evening till six in the morning, and every time the clock strikes, I will come myself and call, and if thou then givest me no answer, tomorrow morning thou shalt be put to death, but if thou always givest me an answer, thou shalt have her to wife."

When the young folks went to the bed-room there stood a stone image of St. Christopher, and the King's daughter said to it, "My father will come at nine o'clock, and every hour till it strikes six; when he calls, give him an answer instead of the King's son." Then the stone image of St. Christopher nodded its head quite quickly, and then more and more slowly till at last it stood still.

The next morning the King said to him, "Thou hast done the business well, but I cannot give my daughter away; thou must now watch a night by my second daughter, and then I will consider with myself whether thou canst have my eldest daughter to wife, but I shall come every hour myself, and when I call thee, answer me, and if I call thee and thou dost not reply, thy blood shall flow." Then the Prince and the Princess went into the sleeping-room, and there stood a still larger stone image of St. Christopher, and the King's daughter said to it, "If my father calls, do thou answer him." Then the great stone image of St. Christopher again nodded its head quite quickly and then more and more slowly, until at last it stood still again. And the King's son lay down on the threshold, put his hand under his head and slept.

The next morning the King said to him, "Thou hast done the business really well, but I cannot give my daughter away; thou must now watch a night by the youngest Princess, and then I will consider with myself whether thou canst have my second daughter to wife, but I shall come every hour myself, and when I call thee answer me, and if I call thee and thou answerest not, thy blood shall flow for me."

Then they once more went to the sleeping-room together, and there was a much greater and much taller image of St. Christopher than the two first had been. The King's daughter said to it, "When my father calls, do thou answer." Then the great tall stone image of St. Christopher nodded quite half an hour with its head, until at length the head stood still again. And the King's son laid himself down on the threshold of the door and slept.

The next morning the King said, "Thou hast indeed watched well, but I cannot give thee my daughter now; I have a great forest, if thou cuttest it down for me between six o'clock this morning and six at night, I will think about it." Then he gave him a glass axe, a glass wedge, and a glass mallet. When he got into the wood, he began at once to cut, but the axe broke in two, then he took the wedge, and struck it once with the mallet, and it became as short and as small as sand. Then he was much troubled and believed he would have to die, and sat down and wept.

Now when it was noon the King said, "One of you girls must take him something to eat." "No," said the two eldest, "we will not take it to him; the one by whom he last watched, can take him something." Then the youngest was forced to go and take him something to eat. When she got into the forest, she asked him how he was getting on. "Oh," said he, "I am getting on very badly." Then she said he was to come and just eat a little. "Nay," said he, "I cannot do that, I shall still have to die, so I will eat no more." Then she spoke so kindly to him and begged him just to try, that he came and ate something. When he had eaten something she said, "I will comb thy hair a while, and then thou wilt feel happier."

So she combed his hair, and he became weary and fell asleep, and then she took her handkerchief and made a knot in it, and struck it three times on the earth, and said, "Earth-workers, come forth." In a moment, numbers of little earth-men came forth, and asked what the King's daughter commanded. Then said she, "In three hours' time the great forest must be cut down, and the whole of the wood laid in heaps." So the little earth-men went about and got together the whole of their kindred to help them with the work. They began at once, and when the three hours were over, all was done, and they came back to the King's daughter and told her so. Then she took her white handkerchief again and said, "Earth-workers, go home." On this they all disappeared.

When the King's son awoke, he was delighted, and she said, "Come home when it has struck six o'clock." He did as she told him, and then the King asked, "Hast thou made away with the forest?" "Yes," said the King's son. When they were sitting at table, the King said, "I cannot yet give thee my daughter to wife, thou must still do something more for her sake." So he asked what it was to be, then. "I have a great fish-pond," said the King. "Thou must go to it tomorrow morning and clear it of all mud until it is as bright as a mirror, and fill it with every kind of fish." The next morning the King gave him a glass shovel and said, "The fish-pond must be done by six o'clock." So he went away, and when he came to the fish-pond he stuck his shovel in the mud and it broke in two, then he stuck his hoe in the mud, and broke it also. Then he was much troubled.

At noon the youngest daughter brought him something to eat, and asked him how he was getting on. So the King's son said everything was going very ill with him, and he would certainly have to lose his head. "My tools have broken to pieces again." "Oh," said she, "thou must just come and eat something, and then thou wilt be in another frame of mind." "No," said he, "I cannot

eat, I am far too unhappy for that!" Then she gave him many good
words until at last he came and ate something. Then she combed
his hair again, and he fell asleep, so once more she took her handkerchief, tied a knot in it, and struck the ground thrice with the
knot, and said, "Earth-workers, come forth." In a moment a great
many little earth-men came and asked what she desired, and she
told them that in three hours' time, they must have the fish-pond
entirely cleaned out, and it must be so clear that people could see
themselves reflected in it, and every kind of fish must be in it. The
little earth-men went away and summoned all their kindred to
help them, and in two hours it was done. Then they returned to her
and said, "We have done as thou hast commanded." The King's
daughter took the handkerchief and once more struck thrice on
the ground with it, and said, "Earth-workers, go home again."
Then they all went away.

When the King's son awoke the fish-pond was done. Then the
King's daughter went away also, and told him that when it was six
he was to come to the house. When he arrived at the house the
King asked, "Hast thou got the fish-pond done?" "Yes," said the
King's son. That was very good.

When they were again sitting at table the King said, "Thou hast
certainly done the fish-pond, but I cannot give thee my daughter
yet; thou must just do one thing more." "What is that, then?" asked
the King's son. The King said he had a great mountain on which
there was nothing but briars which must all be cut down, and at the
top of it the youth must build up a great castle, which must be as
strong as could be conceived, and all the furniture and fittings
belonging to a castle must be inside it. And when he arose next
morning the King gave him a glass axe and a glass gimlet with him,
and he was to have all done by six o'clock. As he was cutting down
the first briar with the axe, it broke off short, and so small that the
pieces flew all round about, and he could not use the gimlet either.
Then he was quite miserable, and waited for his dearest to see if
she would not come and help him in his need.

When it was mid-day she came and brought him something to
eat. He went to meet her and told her all, and ate something, and
let her comb his hair and fell asleep. Then she once more took the
knot and struck the earth with it, and said, "Earth-workers, come
forth!" Then came once again numbers of earth-men, and asked
what her desire was. Then said she, "In the space of three hours
you must cut down the whole of the briars, and a castle must be
built on the top of the mountain that must be as strong as any one

could conceive, and all the furniture that pertains to a castle must be inside it." They went away, and summoned their kindred to help them and when the time was come, all was ready. Then they came to the King's daughter and told her so, and the King's daughter took her handkerchief and struck thrice on the earth with it, and said, "Earth-workers, go home," on which they all disappeared. When therefore the King's son awoke and saw everything done, he was as happy as a bird in air.

When it had struck six, they went home together. Then said the King, "Is the castle ready?" "Yes," said the King's son. When they sat down to table, the King said, "I cannot give away my youngest daughter until the two eldest are married." Then the King's son and the King's daughter were quite troubled, and the King's son had no idea what to do. But he went by night to the King's daughter and ran away with her.

When they had got a little distance away, the King's daughter peeped round and saw her father behind her. "Oh," said she, "what are we to do? My father is behind us, and will take us back with him. I will at once change thee into a briar, and myself into a rose, and I will shelter myself in the midst of the bush." When the father reached the place, there stood a briar with one rose on it; then he was about to gather the rose, when the thorn came and pricked his finger so that he was forced to go home again. His wife asked why he had not brought their daughter back with him. So he said he had nearly got up to her, but that all at once he had lost sight of her, and a briar with one rose was growing on the spot.

Then said the Queen, "If thou hadst but gathered the rose, the briar would have been forced to come too." So he went back again to fetch the rose, but in the meantime the two were already far over the plain, and the King ran after them.

Then the daughter once more looked round and saw her father coming, and said, "Oh, what shall we do now? I will instantly change thee into a church and myself into a priest, and I will stand up in the pulpit, and preach." When the King got to the place, there stood a church, and in the pulpit was a priest preaching. So he listened to the sermon, and then went home again.

Then the Queen asked why he had not brought their daughter with him, and he said, "Nay, I ran a long time after her, and just as I thought I should soon overtake her, a church was standing there and a priest was in the pulpit preaching." "Thou shouldst just have brought the priest," said his wife, "and then the church would soon have come. It is no use to send thee, I must go there myself." When she had walked for some time, and could see the two in the distance, the King's daughter peeped round and saw her mother coming, and said, "Now we are undone, for my mother is coming herself. I will immediately change thee into a fish-pond and myself into a fish."

When the mother came to the place, there was a large fish-pond, and in the midst of it a fish was leaping about and peeping out of the water, and it was quite merry. She wanted to catch the fish, but she could not. Then she was very angry, and drank up the whole pond in order to catch the fish, but it made her so ill that she was forced to vomit, and vomited the whole pond out again. Then she cried, "I see very well that nothing can be done now," and said that now they might come back to her.

Then the King's daughter went back again, and the Queen gave her daughter three walnuts, and said, "With these thou canst help thyself when thou art in thy greatest need." So the young folks went once more away together. And when they had walked quite ten miles, they arrived at the castle from whence the King's son came, and close by it was a village. When they reached it, the King's son said, "Stay here, my dearest, I will just go to the castle, and then will I come with a carriage and with attendants to fetch thee."

When he got to the castle they all rejoiced greatly at having the King's son back again, and he told them he had a bride who was now in the village, and they must go with the carriage to fetch her. Then they harnessed the horses at once, and many attendants seated themselves outside the carriage. When the King's son was about to get in, his mother gave him a kiss, and he forgot everything which had happened, and also what he was about to do. On this his mother ordered the horses to be taken out of the carriage again, and every one went back into the house. But the maiden sat in the village and watched and watched, and thought he would come and fetch her, but no one came.

Then the King's daughter took service in the mill which belonged to the castle, and was obliged to sit by the pond every afternoon and clean the tubs. And the Queen came one day on foot from the castle, and went walking by the pond, and saw the well-grown maiden sitting there, and said, "What a fine strong girl that is! She pleases me well!" Then she and all with her looked at the maid, but no one knew her. So a long time passed by during which the maiden served the miller honorably and faithfully. In the meantime, the Queen had sought a wife for her son who came from quite a distant part of the world. When the bride came, they were at once to be married. And many people hurried together, all of whom wanted to see everything. Then the girl said to the miller that he might be so good as to give her leave to go also. So the miller said, "Yes, do go there."

When she was about to go, she opened one of the three walnuts, and a beautiful dress lay inside it. She put it on, and went into the church and stood by the altar. Suddenly came the bride and bride-groom, and seated themselves before the altar, and when the priest was just going to bless them, the bride peeped half round and saw the maiden standing there. Then she stood up again, and said she would not be given away until she also had as beautiful a dress as that lady there. So they went back to the house again, and sent to ask the lady if she would sell that dress. No, she would not sell it, but the bride might perhaps earn it. Then the bride asked her how she was to do this. Then the maiden said if she might sleep one night outside the King's son's door, the bride might have what she wanted. So the bride said, yes, she was to do that. But the servants were ordered to give the King's son a sleeping-drink, and then the maiden laid herself down on the threshold and lamented all night long. She had had the forest cut down for him, she had had the fish-pond cleaned out for him, she had had the castle built for him, she had changed him into a briar, and then into a church, and at last into a fish-pond, and yet he had forgotten her so quickly. The King's son did not hear one word of it, but the servants had been awakened, and had listened to it, and had not known what it could mean.

The next morning when they were all up, the bride put on the dress, and went away to the church with the bridegroom. In the meantime the maiden opened the second walnut, and a still more beautiful dress was inside it. She put it on, and went and stood by the altar in the church, and everything happened as it had hap-pened the time before. And the maiden again lay all night on the threshold which led to the chamber of the King's son, and the servant was once more to give him a sleeping-drink. The servant, however, went to him and gave him something to keep him awake, and then the King's son went to bed, and the miller's maiden bemoaned herself as before on the threshold of the door, and told of all that she had done. All this the King's son heard, and was sore troubled, and what was past came back to him. Then he wanted to go to her, but his mother had locked the door.

The next morning, however, he went at once to his beloved, and told her everything which had happened to him, and prayed her not to be angry with him for having forgotten her. Then the King's daughter opened the third walnut, and within it was a still more magnificent dress, which she put on, and went with her bridegroom to church, and numbers of children came who gave them flowers, and offered them gay ribbons to bind about their feet, and they were blessed by the priest, and had a merry wedding. But the false mother and the bride had to depart. And the mouth of the person who last told all this is still warm.

The Iron Stove

IN THE DAYS when wishing was still of some use, a King's son was bewitched by an old witch, and shut up in an iron stove in a forest. There he passed many years, and no one could deliver him. Then a King's daughter came into the forest, who had lost herself, and could not find her father's kingdom again. After she had wandered about for nine days, she at length came to the iron stove. Then a voice came forth from it, and asked her, "Whence comest thou, and whither goest thou?" She answered, "I have lost my father's kingdom, and cannot get home again." Then a voice inside the iron stove said, "I will help thee get home again, and that indeed most swiftly, if thou wilt promise to do what I desire of thee. I am the son of a far greater King than thy father, and I will marry thee."

Then was she afraid, and thought, "Good Heavens! What can I do with an iron stove?" But as she much wished to get home to her father, she promised to do as he desired. But he said, "Thou shalt return here, and bring a knife with thee, and scrape a hole in the iron." Then he gave her a companion who walked near her, but did not speak, but in two hours he took her home; there was great joy in the castle when the King's daughter came home, and the old King fell on her neck, and kissed her. She, however, was sorely troubled, and said, "Dear father, what I have suffered! I should never have got home again from the great wild forest, if I had not come to an iron stove, but I have been forced to give my word that I will go back to it, set it free, and marry it."

Then the old King was so terrified that he all but fainted, for he had but this one daughter. They therefore resolved they would send, in her place, the miller's daughter, who was very beautiful. They took her there, gave her a knife, and said she was to scrape at the iron stove. So she scraped at it for four-and-twenty hours, but could not bring off the least morsel of it. When day dawned, a voice in the stove said, "It seems to me it is day outside." Then she answered, "It seems to me too; I fancy I hear the noise of my father's mill."

"So thou art a miller's daughter! Then go thy way at once, and let the King's daughter come here." Then she went away at once, and told the old King that the man outside there, would have none of her—he wanted the King's daughter. They, however, still had a swine-herd's daughter, who was even prettier than the miller's daughter, and they determined to give her a piece of gold to go to the iron stove instead of the King's daughter. So she was taken thither, and she also had to scrape for four-and-twenty hours. She, however, made nothing of it. When day broke, a voice inside the stove cried, "It seems to me it is day outside!" Then answered she, "So it seems to me also; I fancy I hear my father's horn blowing."

"Then thou art a swine-herd's daughter! Go away at once, and tell the King's daughter to come, and tell her all must be done as was promised, and if she does not come, everything in the kingdom shall be ruined and destroyed, and not one stone be left standing on another." When the King's daughter heard that she began to weep, but now there was nothing for it but to keep her promise. So she took leave of her father, put a knife in her pocket, and went forth to the iron stove in the forest. When she got there, she began to scrape, and the iron gave way, and when two hours were over, she had already scraped a small hole. Then she peeped in, and saw a youth so handsome, and so brilliant with gold and with precious jewels, that her very soul was delighted. Now, therefore, she went on scraping, and made the hole so large that he was able to get out.

Then said he, "Thou art mine, and I am thine; thou art my bride, and hast released me." He wanted to take her away with him to his kingdom, but she entreated him to let her go once again to her father, and the King's son allowed her to do so, but she was not to say more to her father than three words, and then she was to come back again. So she went home, but she spoke more than three words, and instantly the iron stove disappeared, and was taken far away over glass-mountains and piercing swords; but the King's son was set free, and no longer shut up in it. After this she bade good-bye to her father, took some money with her, but not much, and went back to the great forest, and looked for the iron stove, but it was nowhere to be found. For nine days she sought it, and then her hunger grew so great that she did not know what to do, for she could no longer live.

When it was evening, she seated herself in a small tree, and made up her mind to spend the night there, as she was afraid of wild beasts. When midnight drew near she saw in the distance a small light, and thought, "Ah, there I should be saved!" She got down from the tree, and went towards the light, but on the way she prayed. Then she came to a little old house, and much grass had grown all about it, and a small heap of wood lay in front of it. She thought, "Ah, whither have I come," and peeped in through the window, but she saw nothing inside but toads, big and little, except a table well covered with wine and roast meat, and the plates and glasses were of silver. Then she took courage, and knocked at the door. The fat toad cried,

> *"Little green waiting-maid,*
> *Waiting-maid with the limping leg,*
> *Little dog of the limping leg,*
> *Hop hither and thither,*
> *And quickly see who is without."*

And a small toad came walking by and opened the door to her. When she entered, they all bade her welcome, and she was forced to sit down. They asked, "Where hast thou come from, and whither art thou going?" Then she related all that had befallen her, and how because she had transgressed the order which had been given her not to say more than three words, the stove, and the King's son also, had disappeared, and now she was about to seek him over hill and dale until she found him. Then the old fat one said,

> *"Little green waiting-maid,*
> *Waiting-maid with the limping leg,*
> *Little dog of the limping leg,*
> *Hop hither and thither,*
> *And bring me the great box."*

Then the little one went and brought the box. After this they gave her meat and drink, and took her to a well-made bed, which felt like silk and velvet, and she laid herself therein, in God's name, and slept. When morning came she arose, and the old toad gave her three needles out of the great box which she was to take with her; they would be needed by her, for she had to cross a high glass-mountain, and go over three piercing swords and a great lake. If she did all this she would get her lover back again. Then he gave her three things, which she was to take the greatest care of, namely, three large needles, a plough-wheel, and three nuts. With these she traveled onwards, and when she came to the glass-mountain which was so slippery, she stuck the three needles first behind her feet and then before them, and so got over it, and when she was over it, she hid them in a place which she marked carefully. After this she came to the three piercing swords, and then she seated herself on her plough-wheel, and rolled over them.

At last she arrived in front of a great lake, and when she had crossed it, she came to a large and beautiful castle. She went in and asked for a place; she was a poor girl, she said, and would like to be hired. She knew, however, that the King's son whom she had released from the iron stove in the great forest was in the castle. Then she was taken as a scullery-maid at low wages. But, already the King's son had another maiden by his side whom he wanted to marry, for he thought that she had long been dead.

In the evening, when she had washed up and was done, she felt in her pocket and found the three nuts which the old toad had given her. She cracked one with her teeth, and was going to eat the kernel when lo and behold there was a stately royal garment in it! But when the bride heard of this she came and asked for the dress, and wanted to buy it, and said, "It is not a dress for a servant-girl." But she said, no, she would not sell it, but if the bride would grant her one thing she should have it, and that was, leave to sleep one night in her bridegroom's chamber.

The bride gave her permission because the dress was so pretty, and she had never had one like it. When it was evening she said to her bridegroom, "That silly girl will sleep in thy room." "If thou art willing so am I," said he. She, however, gave him a glass of wine in which she had poured a sleeping-draught. So the bridegroom and the scullery-maid went to sleep in the room, and he slept so soundly that she could not waken him.

She wept the whole night and cried, "I set thee free when thou wert in an iron stove in the wild forest, I sought thee, and walked over a glass-mountain, and three sharp swords, and a great lake before I found thee, and yet thou wilt not hear me!"

The servants sat by the chamber-door, and heard how she thus wept the whole night through, and in the morning they told it to their lord. And the next evening when she had washed up, she opened the second nut, and a far more beautiful dress was within it, and when the bride beheld it, she wished to buy that also. But the girl would not take the money, and begged that she might once again sleep in the bridegroom's chamber. The bride, however, gave him a sleeping-drink, and he slept so soundly that he could hear nothing. But the scullery-maid wept the whole night long, and cried, "I set thee free when thou wert in an iron stove in the wild forest, I sought thee, and walked over a glass-mountain, and over three sharp swords and a great lake before I found thee, and yet thou wilt not hear me!"

The servants sat by the chamber-door and heard her weeping the whole night through, and in the morning informed their lord of it. And on the third evening, when she had washed up, she opened the third nut, and within it was a still more beautiful dress which was stiff with pure gold. When the bride saw that she wanted to have it, but the maiden only gave it up on condition that she might for the third time sleep in the bridegroom's apartment. The King's son was, however, on his guard, and threw the sleeping-draught away. Now, therefore, when she began to weep and to cry, "Dearest love, I set thee free when thou wert in the iron stove in the terrible wild forest," the King's son leapt up and said, "Thou art the true one, thou art mine, and I am thine." Thereupon, while it was still night, he got into a carriage with her, and they took away the false bride's clothes so that she could not get up.

When they came to the great lake, they sailed across it, and when they reached the three sharp-cutting swords they seated themselves on the plough-wheel, and when they got to the glass-mountain they thrust the three needles in it, and so at length they got to the little old house; but when they went inside that, it was a great castle, and the toads were all disenchanted, and were King's children, and full of happiness. Then the wedding was celebrated, and the King's son and the Princess remained in the castle, which was much larger than the castles of their fathers. As, however, the old King grieved at being left alone, they fetched him away, and brought him to live with them, and they had two kingdoms, and lived in happy wedlock.

> *Let the mouse run;*
> *My story's done.*

The Singing, Soaring Lark

THERE WAS once a man who was about to set out on a long journey, and on parting he asked his three daughters what he should bring back with him for them. The eldest wished for pearls, the second wished for diamonds, but the third said, "Dear father, I should like a singing, soaring lark." The father said, "Yes, if I can get it, you shall have it," kissed all three, and set out.

When the time had come for him to be on his way home again, he brought pearls and diamonds for the two eldest; but he had sought everywhere in vain for a singing, soaring lark for the youngest, and he was very unhappy about it, for she was his favorite child. His road lay through a forest, and in the midst of it was a splendid castle, and near the castle stood a tree, but quite on the top of the tree, he saw a singing, soaring lark. "Aha, you come just at the right moment!" he said, quite delighted, and called to his servant to climb up and catch the little creature.

But as he approached the tree, a lion leapt from beneath it, shook himself, and roared till the leaves on the tree trembled. "He who tries to steal my singing, soaring lark," he cried, "will I devour." Then the man said, "I did not know that the bird belonged to thee. I will make amends for the wrong I have done and ransom myself with a large sum of money, only spare my life." The lion said, "Nothing can save thee, unless thou wilt promise to give me for mine own what first meets thee on thy return home; but if thou wilt do that, I will grant thee thy life, and thou shalt have the bird for thy daughter, into the bargain."

But the man hesitated and said, "That might be my youngest daughter, she loves me best, and always runs to meet me on my return home." The servant, however, was terrified and said, "Why should your daughter be the very one to meet you, it might as easily be a cat, or dog?" Then the man allowed himself to be persuaded, took the singing, soaring lark, and promised to give the lion whatsoever should first meet him on his return home.

When he reached home and entered his house, the first who met him was no other than his youngest and dearest daughter, who came running up, kissed and embraced him, and when she saw that he had brought with him a singing, soaring lark, she was beside herself with joy. The father, however, could not rejoice, but began to weep, and said, "My dearest child, I have bought the little bird dear. In return for it, I have been obliged to promise thee to a savage lion, and when he has thee he will tear thee in pieces and devour thee," and he told her all, just as it had happened, and begged her not to go there, come what might. But she consoled him and said, "Dearest father, indeed your promise must be fulfilled. I will go thither and soften the lion, so that I may return to thee safely."

Next morning she had the road pointed out to her, took leave, and went fearlessly out into the forest. The lion, however, was an enchanted Prince and was by day a lion, and all his people were lions with him, but in the night they resumed their natural human shapes. On her arrival she was kindly received and led into the castle. When night came, the lion turned into a handsome man, and their wedding was celebrated with great magnificence. They lived happily together, remained awake at night, and slept in the daytime.

One day he came and said, "Tomorrow there is a feast in thy father's house, because thy eldest sister is to be married, and if thou art inclined to go there, my lions shall conduct thee." She said, "Yes, I should very much like to see my father again," and went thither, accompanied by the lions. There was great joy when she arrived, for they had all believed that she had been torn in pieces by the lion, and had long ceased to live. But she told them what a handsome husband she had, and how well off she was, remained with them while the wedding-feast lasted, and then went back again to the forest.

When the second daughter was about to be married, and she was again invited to the wedding, she said to the lion, "This time I will not be alone, thou must come with me." The lion, however, said that it was too dangerous for him, for if when there a ray from a burning candle fell on him, he would be changed into a dove, and for seven years long would have to fly about with the doves. She said, "Ah, but do come with me, I will take great care of thee, and guard thee from all light." So they went away together, and took with them their little child as well. She had a chamber built there, so strong and thick that no ray could pierce through it; in this he was to shut himself up when the candles were lit for the wedding-feast. But the door was made of green wood which warped and left a little crack which no one noticed.

The wedding was celebrated with magnificence, but when the procession with all its candles and torches came back from church, and passed by this apartment, a ray about the breadth of a hair fell on the King's son, and when this ray touched him, he was transformed in an instant, and when she came in and looked for him, she did not see him, but a white dove was sitting there. The dove said to her, "For seven years must I fly about the world, but at every seventh step that thou takest I will let fall a drop of red blood and a white feather, and these will show thee the way, and if thou followest the trace thou canst release me." Thereupon the dove flew out at the door, and she followed him, and at every seventh step a red drop of blood and a little white feather fell down and showed her the way.

So she went continually further and further in the wide world, never looking about her or resting, and the seven years were almost past; then she rejoiced and thought that they would soon be delivered; and yet they were so far from it! Once when they were thus moving onwards, no little feather and no drop of red blood fell, and when she raised her eyes the dove had disappeared. And as she thought to herself, "In this no man can help thee," she climbed up to the sun, and said to him, "Thou shinest into every crevice, and over every peak, hast not thou seen a white dove flying?" "No," said the sun, "I have seen none, but I present thee with a casket, open it when thou art in sorest need."

Then she thanked the sun, and went on until evening came and the moon appeared; she then asked her, "Thou shinest the whole night through, and on every field and forest, hast thou not seen a white dove flying?" "No," said the moon, "I have seen no dove, but here I give thee an egg, break it when thou art in great need." She thanked the moon, and went on until the night wind came up and blew on her, then she said to it, "Thou blowest over every tree and under every leaf, hast thou not seen a white dove flying?" "No," said the night wind, "I have seen none, but I will ask the three other winds, perhaps they have seen it."

The east wind and the west wind came, and had seen nothing, but the south wind said, "I have seen the white dove, it has flown to the Red Sea; there it has become a lion again, for the seven years are over, and the lion is there fighting with a dragon; the dragon, however, is an enchanted Princess." The night wind then said to her, "I will advise thee; go to the Red Sea, on the right bank are some tall reeds, count them, break off the eleventh, and strike the dragon with it, then the lion will be able to subdue it, and both then will regain their human form. After that, look round and thou wilt see the griffin which is by the Red Sea; swing thyself, with thy beloved, on to his back, and the bird will carry thee over the sea to thine own home. Here is a nut for thee, when thou art above the center of the sea, let the nut fall, it will immediately shoot up, and a tall nut tree will grow out of the water, on which the griffin may rest; for if he cannot rest, he will not be strong enough to carry thee across, and if thou forgettest to throw down the nut, he will let thee fall into the sea."

Then she went thither, and found everything as the night wind had said. She counted the reeds by the sea, and cut off the eleventh, struck the dragon therewith, whereupon the lion overcame it, and immediately both of them regained their human shapes. But when the Princess, who had before been the dragon, was delivered from enchantment, she took the youth by the arm, seated herself on the griffin, and carried him off with her.

There stood the poor maiden who had wandered so far and was again forsaken. She sat down and cried, but at last she took courage and said, "Still I will go as far as the wind blows and as long as the cock crows, until I find him," and she went forth by long, long roads, until at last she came to the castle where both of them were living together. There she heard that soon a feast was to be held, in which they would celebrate their wedding, but she said, "God still helps me," and opened the casket that the sun had given her. A dress lay therein as brilliant as the sun itself. So she took it out and put it on, and went up into the castle, and every one, even the bride herself, looked at her with astonishment.

The dress pleased the bride so well that she thought it might do for her wedding-dress, and asked if it was for sale. "Not for money or land," answered she, "but for flesh and blood." The bride asked her what she meant by that, then she said, "Let me sleep a night in the chamber where the bridegroom sleeps." The bride would not, yet wanted very much to have the dress; at last she consented, but the page was to give the Prince a sleeping-draught.

When it was night, therefore, and the youth was already asleep, she was led into the chamber; she seated herself on the bed and said, "I have followed after thee for seven years. I have been to the sun and the moon, and the four winds, and have inquired for thee, and have helped thee against the dragon; wilt thou, then, quite forget me?" But the Prince slept so soundly that it only seemed to him as if the wind were whistling outside in the fir trees.

When therefore day broke, she was led out again, and had to give up the golden dress. And as even that had been of no avail, she was sad, went out into a meadow, sat down there, and wept. While she was sitting there, she thought of the egg which the moon had given her; she opened it, and there came out a clucking hen with twelve chickens all of gold, and they ran about chirping, and crept again under the old hen's wings; nothing more beautiful was ever seen in the world! Then she arose, and drove them through the meadow before her, until the bride looked out of the window. The little chickens pleased her so much that she immediately came down and asked if they were for sale. "Not for money or land, but for flesh and blood; let me sleep another night in the chamber where the bridegroom sleeps." The bride said, "Yes," intending to cheat her as on the former evening. But when the Prince went to bed he asked the page what the murmuring and rustling in the night had been. On this the page told all; that he had been forced to give him a sleeping-draught, because a poor girl had slept secretly in the chamber, and that he was to give him another that night. The Prince said, "Pour out the draught by the bed-side."

At night, she was again led in, and when she began to relate how ill all had fared with her, he immediately recognized his beloved wife by her voice, sprang up and cried, "Now I really am released! I have been as it were in a dream, for the strange Princess has bewitched me so that I have been compelled to forget thee, but God has delivered me from the spell at the right time." Then they both left the castle secretly in the night, for they feared the father of the Princess, who was a sorcerer, and they seated themselves on the griffin, which bore them across the Red Sea, and when they were in the midst of it, she let fall the nut. Immediately a tall nut tree grew up, whereon the bird rested, and then carried them home, where they found their child, who had grown tall and beautiful, and they lived thenceforth happily until their death.

The Nixie of the Mill-Pond

ONCE UPON a time there was a miller who lived with his wife in great contentment. They had money and land, and their prosperity increased year by year more and more. But ill-luck comes like a thief in the night; as their wealth had increased so did it again decrease, year by year, and at last the miller could hardly call the mill in which he lived, his own. He was in great distress, and when he lay down after his day's work, found no rest, but tossed about in his bed, full of care.

One morning he rose before daybreak and went out into the open air, thinking that perhaps there his heart might become lighter. As he was stepping over the mill-dam the first sunbeam was just breaking forth, and he heard a rippling sound in the pond. He turned round and perceived a beautiful woman, rising slowly out of the water. Her long hair, which she was holding off her shoulders with her soft hands, fell down on both sides, and covered her white body. He soon saw that she was the Nixie of the Mill-pond, and in his fright did not know whether he should run away or stay where he was. But the nixie made her sweet voice heard, called him by his name, and asked him why he was so sad. The miller was at first struck dumb, but when he heard her speak so kindly, he took heart, and told her how he had formerly lived in wealth and happiness, but that now he was so poor that he did not know what to do. "Be easy," answered the nixie, "I will make thee richer and happier than thou hast ever been before, only thou must promise to give me the young thing which has just been born in thy house."

"What else can that be," thought the miller, "but a young puppy or kitten?" and he promised her what she desired. The nixie descended into the water again, and he hurried back to his mill, consoled and in good spirits. He had not yet reached it, when the maid-servant came out of the house, and cried to him to rejoice, for his wife had given birth to a little boy. The miller stood as if struck by lightning; he saw very well that the cunning nixie had been aware of it, and had cheated him. Hanging his head, he went up to his wife's bed-side and when she said, "Why dost thou not rejoice over the fine boy?" he told her what had befallen him, and what kind of a promise he had given to the nixie. "Of what use to me are riches and prosperity?" he added, "if I am to lose my child; but what can I do?" Even the relations, who had come thither to wish them joy, did not know what to say.

In the meantime prosperity again returned to the miller's house. All that he undertook succeeded, it was as if presses and coffers filled themselves of their own accord, and as if money multiplied nightly in the cupboards. It was not long before his wealth was greater than it had ever been before. But he could not rejoice over it untroubled, the bargain which he had made with the nixie tormented his soul. Whenever he passed the mill-pond, he feared she might ascend and remind him of his debt. He never let the boy

himself go near the water. "Beware," he said to him, "if thou dost
but touch the water, a hand will rise, seize thee, and draw thee
down." But as year after year went by and the nixie did not show
herself again, the miller began to feel at ease.

The boy grew up to be a youth and was apprenticed to a huntsman. When he had learnt everything, and had become an excellent huntsman, the lord of the village took him into his service. In
the village lived a beautiful and true-hearted maiden, who pleased
the huntsman, and when his master perceived that, he gave him a
little house, the two were married, lived peacefully and happily,
and loved each other with all their hearts.

One day the huntsman was chasing a roe; and when the animal
turned aside from the forest into the open country, he pursued it
and at last shot it. He did not notice that he was now in the
neighborhood of the dangerous mill-pond, and went, after he had
disembowelled the stag, to the water, in order to wash his blood-
stained hands. Scarcely, however, had he dipped them in than the
nixie ascended, smilingly wound her dripping arms around him,
and drew him quickly down under the waves, which closed over
him.

When it was evening, and the huntsman did not return home, his
wife became alarmed. She went out to seek him, and as he had
often told her that he had to be on his guard against the snares of
the nixie and dared not venture into the neighborhood of the mill-
pond, she already suspected what had happened. She hastened to
the water, and when she found his hunting-pouch lying on the
shore, she could no longer have any doubt of the misfortune. Lamenting her sorrow, and wringing her hands, she called on her
beloved by name, but in vain. She hurried across to the other side
of the pond, and called him anew; she reviled the nixie with harsh
words, but no answer followed. The surface of the water remained
calm, only the crescent moon stared steadily back at her. The poor
woman did not leave the pond. With hasty steps, she paced round
and round it, without resting a moment, sometimes in silence,
sometimes uttering a loud cry, sometimes softly sobbing. At last
her strength came to an end, she sank down to the ground and fell
into a heavy sleep.

Presently a dream took possession of her. She was anxiously
climbing upwards between great masses of rock; thorns and briars
caught her feet, the rain beat in her face, and the wind tossed her
long hair about. When she had reached the summit, quite a different sight presented itself to her; the sky was blue, the air soft, the

ground sloped gently downwards, and on a green meadow, gay with flowers of every color, stood a pretty cottage. She went up to it and opened the door; there sat an old woman with white hair, who beckoned to her kindly.

At that very moment, the poor woman awoke, day had already dawned, and she at once resolved to act in accordance with her dream. She laboriously climbed the mountain; everything was exactly as she had seen it in the night. The old woman received her kindly, and pointed out a chair on which she might sit. "Thou must have met with a misfortune," she said, "since thou hast sought out my lonely cottage." With tears, the woman related what had befallen her. "Be comforted," said the old woman, "I will help thee. Here is a golden comb for thee. Tarry till the full moon has risen, then go to the mill-pond, seat thyself on the shore, and comb thy long black hair with this comb. When thou hast done, lay it down on the bank, and thou wilt see what will happen."

The woman returned home, but the time till the full moon came, passed slowly. At last the shining disc appeared in the heavens, then she went out to the mill-pond, sat down and combed her long black hair with the golden comb, and when she had finished, she laid it down at the water's edge. It was not long before there was a movement in the depths, a wave rose, rolled to the shore, and bore the comb away with it. In not more than the time necessary for the comb to sink to the bottom, the surface of the water parted, and the head of the huntsman arose. He did not speak, but looked at his wife with sorrowful glances. At the same instant, a second wave came rushing up, and covered the man's head. All had vanished, the mill-pond lay peaceful as before, and nothing but the face of the full moon shone on it.

Full of sorrow, the woman went back, but again the dream showed her the cottage of the old woman. Next morning she again set out and complained of her woes to the wise woman. The old woman gave her a golden flute, and said, "Tarry till the full moon comes again, then take this flute; play a beautiful air on it, and when thou hast finished, lay it on the sand; then thou wilt see what will happen." The wife did as the old woman told her. No sooner was the flute lying on the sand than there was a stirring in the depths, and a wave rushed up and bore the flute away with it. Immediately afterwards the water parted, and not only the head of the man, but half of his body also arose. He stretched out his arms longingly towards her, but a second wave came up, covered him, and drew him down again. "Alas, what does it profit me?" said the unhappy woman, "that I should see my beloved, only to lose him again!"

Despair filled her heart anew, but the dream led her a third time to the house of the old woman. She set out, and the wise woman gave her a golden spinning-wheel, consoled her and said, "All is not yet fulfilled, tarry until the time of the full moon, then take the spinning-wheel, seat thyself on the shore, and spin the spool full, and when thou hast done that, place the spinning-wheel near the water, and thou wilt see what will happen." The woman obeyed all she said exactly; as soon as the full moon showed itself, she carried the golden spinning-wheel to the shore, and spun industriously until the flax came to an end, and the spool was quite filled with the threads. No sooner was the wheel standing on the shore than there was a more violent movement than before in the depths of the pond, and a mighty wave rushed up, and bore the wheel away with it. Immediately the head and the whole body of the man rose into the air, in a water-spout. He quickly sprang to the shore, caught his wife by the hand and fled. But they had scarcely gone a very little distance, when the whole pond rose with a frightful roar, and streamed out over the open country. The fugitives already saw death before their eyes, when the woman in her terror implored the help of the old woman, and in an instant they were transformed, she into a toad, he into a frog. The flood which had overtaken them could not destroy them, but it tore them apart and carried them far away.

When the water had dispersed and they both touched dry land again, they regained their human form, but neither knew where the other was; they found themselves among strange people, who did not know their native land. High mountains and deep valleys lay between them. In order to keep themselves alive, they were both obliged to tend sheep. For many long years they drove their flocks through field and forest and were full of sorrow and longing. When spring had once more broken forth on the earth, they both went out one day with their flocks, and as chance would have it, they drew near each other. They met in a valley, but did not recognize each other; yet they rejoiced that they were no longer so lonely. Henceforth they each day drove their flocks to the same place; they did not speak much, but they felt comforted.

One evening when the full moon was shining in the sky, and the sheep were already at rest, the shepherd pulled the flute out of his pocket, and played on it a beautiful but sorrowful air. When he had finished he saw that the shepherdess was weeping bitterly. "Why are thou weeping?" he asked. "Alas," answered she, "thus shone the full moon when I played this air on the flute for the last time, and the head of my beloved rose out of the water." He looked at her, and it seemed as if a veil fell from his eyes, and he recognized his dear wife, and when she looked at him, and the moon shone in his face she knew him also. They embraced and kissed each other, and no one need ask if they were happy.

The Raven

ONCE THERE was a Queen who had a little daughter who was still so young that she could not walk. One day the child was naughty. The mother might say what she liked, but the child would not be quiet. Then the Queen became impatient, and as the ravens were flying about the palace, she opened the window and said, "I wish you were a raven and would fly away, and then I should have some rest." Scarcely had she spoken the words, before the child was changed into a raven, and flew from her arms out of the window. It flew into a dark forest, and stayed in it a long time, and the parents heard nothing of their child.

One day a man was on his way through this forest and heard the raven crying, and followed the voice, and when he came nearer, the bird said, "I am a King's daughter by birth, and am bewitched, but thou canst set me free." "What am I to do?" asked he. She said, "Go further into the forest, and thou wilt find a house, wherein sits an aged woman, who will offer thee meat and drink, but thou must accept nothing; for if thou eatest or drinkest anything, thou wilt fall into a sleep, and then thou wilt not be able to deliver me. In the garden behind the house there is a great heap of tan, and on this thou shalt stand and wait for me. For three days I will come every afternoon at two o'clock in a carriage. On the first day four white horses will be harnessed to it, then four chestnut horses, and lastly four black ones; but if thou art not awake, but sleeping, I shall not be set free." The man promised to do everything that she desired, but the raven said, "Alas! I know already that thou wilt not deliver me; thou wilt accept something from the woman."

The man once more promised that he would certainly not touch anything either to eat or to drink. But when he entered the house the old woman came to him and said, "Poor man, how faint you are; come and refresh yourself; eat and drink." "No," said the man. "I will not eat or drink." She, however, let him have no peace, and said, "If you will not eat, take one drink out of the glass; one is nothing." Then he let himself be persuaded, and drank. Shortly before two o'clock in the afternoon he went into the garden to the tan heap to wait for the raven. As he was standing there, his weariness all at once became so great that he could not struggle against it, and lay down for a short time, but he was determined not to go to sleep. Hardly, however, had he lain down, than his eyes closed of their own accord, and he fell asleep and slept so soundly that nothing in the world could have aroused him.

At two o'clock the raven came driving up with four white horses, but she was already in deep grief and said "I know he is asleep." And when she came into the garden, he was indeed lying there asleep on the heap of tan. She alighted from the carriage, went to him, shook him, and called him, but he did not awake.

Next day about noon, the old woman came again and brought him food and drink, but he would not take any of it. But she let him have no rest and persuaded him until at length he again took one drink out of the glass. Towards two o'clock he went into the garden to the tan heap to wait for the raven, but all at once felt such a great weariness that his limbs would no longer support him. He could not stand upright, and was forced to lie down, and fell into a heavy sleep. When the raven drove up with four brown horses, she was already full of grief, and said, "I know he is asleep." She went to him, but there he lay sleeping, and there was no wakening him.

Next day the old woman asked what was the meaning of this? He was neither eating nor drinking anything; did he want to die? He replied, "I am not allowed to eat or drink, and will not do so." She, however, set a dish with meat, and a glass with wine before him, and when he smelt it he could not resist, and swallowed a deep draught. When the time came, he went out into the garden to the heap of tan, and waited for the King's daughter; but he became still more weary than on the day before, and lay down and slept as soundly as if he had been a stone.

At two o'clock the raven came with four black horses, and the coachman and everything else was black. She was was already in the deepest grief, and said, "I know that he is asleep and cannot deliver me." When she came to him, there he was lying fast asleep. She shook him and called him, but she could not waken him. Then she laid a loaf beside him, and after that a piece of meat, and thirdly a bottle of wine, and he might consume as much of all of them as he liked, but they would never grow less. After this she took a gold ring from her finger, and put it on his, and her name was graven on it. Lastly, she laid a letter beside him wherein was written what she had given him, and that none of the things would ever grow less; and in it was also written, "I see right well that thou wilt never be able to deliver me here, but if thou art still willing to deliver me, come to the golden castle of Stromberg; it lies in thy power, of that I am certain." And when she had given him all these things, she seated herself in her carriage, and drove to the golden castle of Stromberg.

When the man awoke and saw that he had slept, he was sad at heart, and said, "She has certainly driven by, and I have not set her free." Then he perceived the things which were lying beside him, and read the letter wherein was written how everything had happened. So he arose and went away, intending to go to the golden castle of Stromberg, but he did not know where it was. After he had walked about the world for a long time, he entered into a dark forest, and walked for fourteen days without stopping, and still could not find his way out. Then it was once more evening, and he was so tired that he lay down in a thicket and fell asleep.

Next day he went onwards, and in the evening, as he was again about to lie down beneath some bushes, he heard such a howling and crying that he could not go to sleep. And when the time came when people light the candles, he saw one glimmering, and arose and went towards it. Then he came to a house which seemed very small, for in front of it a great giant was standing. He thought to himself, "If I go in, and the giant sees me, it will very likely cost me my life."

At length he ventured it and went in. When the giant saw him, he said, "It is well that thou comest, for it is long since I have eaten; I will at once eat thee for my supper." "I'd rather thou wouldst leave that alone," said the man, "I do not like to be eaten; but if thou hast any desire to eat, I have quite enough here to satisfy thee." "If that be true," said the giant, "thou mayst be easy, I was only going to devour thee because I had nothing else." Then they went, and sat down to the table, and the man took out the bread, wine, and meat which would never come to an end. "This pleases me well," said the giant, and ate to his heart's content. Then the man said to him. "Canst thou tell me where the golden castle of Stromberg is?" The giant said, "I will look in my map; all the towns, and villages, and houses are to be found in it." He brought out the map which he had in the room and looked for the castle, but it was not to be found in it. "It's no matter!" said he, "I have some still larger maps in my cupboard upstairs, and we will look in them." But there, too, it was in vain.

The man now wanted to go onwards, but the giant begged him to wait a few days longer until his brother, who had gone out to bring some provisions, came home. When the brother came home they inquired about the golden castle of Stromberg. He replied, "When I have eaten and have had enough, I will look in the map." Then he went with them up to his chamber, and they searched in his map, but could not find it. Then he brought out still older maps, and they never rested until they found the golden castle of Stromberg, but it was many thousand miles away. "How am I to get there?" asked the man. The giant said, "I have two hours' time, during which I will carry thee into the neighborhood, but after that I must be at home to suckle the child that we have."

So the giant carried the man to about a hundred leagues from the castle, and said, "Thou canst very well walk the rest of the way alone." And he turned back, but the man went onwards day and night, until at length he came to the golden castle of Stromberg. It stood on a glass-mountain, and the bewitched maiden drove in her carriage round the castle, and then went inside it. He rejoiced when he saw her and wanted to climb up to her, but when he began to do so he always slipped down the glass again. And when he saw that he could not reach her, he was filled with trouble, and said to himself, "I will stay down here below, and wait for her."

So he built himself a hut and stayed in it for a whole year, and every day saw the King's daughter driving about above, but never could go to her. Then one day he saw from his hut three robbers who were beating each other, and cried to them, "God be with ye!" They stopped when they heard the cry, but as they saw no one, they once more began to beat each other, and that too most dangerously. So he again cried, "God be with ye." Again they stopped, looked round about, but as they saw no one they went on beating each other. Then he cried for the third time, "God be with ye," and thought, "I must see what these three are about," and went thither and asked why they were beating each other so furiously. One of them said that he had found a stick, and that when he struck a door with it, that door would spring open. The next said that he had found a mantle, and that whenever he put it on, he was invisible, but the third said he had found a horse on which a man could ride everywhere, even up the glass-mountain. And now they did not know whether they ought to have these things in common, or whether they ought to divide them.

Then the man said, "I will give you something in exchange for these three things. Money indeed have I not, but I have other things of more value; but first I must try yours to see if you have told the truth." They put him on the horse, threw the mantle round him, and gave him the stick in his hand, and when he had all these things they were no longer able to see him. So he gave them some vigorous blows and cried, "Now, vagabonds, you have got what you deserve; are you satisfied?"

He rode up the glass-mountain; but when he came in front of the castle at the top, it was shut. Then he struck the door with his stick, and it sprang open immediately. He went in and ascended the stairs until he came to the hall where the maiden was sitting with a golden cup full of wine before her. She, however, could not see him because he had the mantle on. And when he came up to her, he drew from his finger the ring which she had given him, and threw it into the cup so that it rang. Then she cried, "That is my ring, so the man who is to deliver me must be here." They searched the whole castle and did not find him, but he had gone out, and had seated himself on the horse and thrown off the mantle. When they came to the door, she saw him and cried aloud in her delight. Then he alighted and took the King's daughter in his arms, but she kissed him and said, "Now hast thou set me free, and tomorrow we will celebrate our wedding."

The Crystal Ball

THERE WAS once an enchantress who had three sons who loved each other as brothers, but the old woman did not trust them, and thought they wanted to steal her power from her. So she changed the eldest into an eagle, which was forced to dwell in the rocky mountains, and was often seen sweeping in great circles in the sky. The second, she changed into a whale, which lived in the deep sea, and all that was seen of it was that it sometimes spouted up a great jet of water in the air. Each of them only bore his human form for two hours daily. The third son, who was afraid she might change him into a raging wild beast—a bear perhaps, or a wolf—went secretly away."

He had heard that a King's daughter who was bewitched, was imprisoned in the Castle of the Golden Sun, and was waiting for deliverance. Those, however, who had tried to free her risked their lives; three-and-twenty youths had already died a miserable death, and now only one other might make the attempt, after which no more must come. And as his heart was without fear, he caught at the idea of seeking out the Castle of the Golden Sun. He had already traveled about for a long time without being able to find it, when he came by chance into a great forest, and did not know the way out of it.

All at once he saw in the distance two giants, who made a sign to him with their hands, and when he came to them they said, "We are quarreling about a cap, and which of us it is to belong to, and as we are equally strong, neither of us can get the better of the other. The small men are cleverer than we are, so we will leave the decision to thee." "How can you dispute about an old cap?" said the youth. "Thou dost not know what properties it has! It is a wishing-cap; whosoever puts it on, can wish himself away wherever he likes, and in an instant he will be there." "Give me the cap," said the youth, "I will go a short distance off, and when I call you, you must run a race, and the cap shall belong to the one who gets first to me." He put it on and went away, and thought of the King's daughter, forgot the giants, and walked continually onward. At length he sighed from the very bottom of his heart, and cried, "Ah, if I were but at the Castle of the Golden Sun," and hardly had the words passed his lips than he was standing on a high mountain before the gate of the castle.

He entered and went through all the rooms, until in the last he found the King's daughter. But how shocked he was when he saw her. She had an ashen-grey face full of wrinkles, blear eyes, and red hair. "Art thou the King's daughter, whose beauty the whole world praises?" cried he. "Ah," she answered, "this is not my form; human eyes can only see me in this state of ugliness, but that thou mayst know what I am like, look in the mirror—it does not let itself be misled—it will show thee my image as it is in truth." She gave him the mirror in his hand, and he saw therein the likeness of the most beautiful maiden on earth, and saw, too, how the tears were rolling down her cheeks with grief.

Then said he, "How canst thou be set free? I fear no danger." She said, "He who gets the crystal ball, and holds it before the enchanter, will destroy his power with it, and I shall resume my true shape. Ah," she added, "so many have already gone to meet death for this, and thou art so young; I grieve that thou shouldst encounter such great danger." "Nothing can keep me from doing it," said he, "but tell me what I must do." "Thou shalt know everything," said the King's daughter; "when thou descendest the mountain on which the castle stands, a wild bull will stand below by a spring, and thou must fight with it, and if thou hast the luck to kill it, a fiery bird will spring out of it, which bears in its body a burning egg, and in the egg the crystal ball lies like a yolk. The bird will not, however, let the egg fall until forced to do so, and if it fall on the ground, it will flame up and burn everything that is near, and melt even ice itself, and with it the crystal ball, and then all thy trouble will have been in vain."

The youth went down to the spring, where the bull snorted and bellowed at him. After a long struggle he plunged his sword in the animal's body, and it fell down. Instantly a fiery bird arose from it, and was about to fly away, but the young man's brother, the eagle, who was passing between the clouds, swooped down, hunted it away to the sea, and struck it with his beak until, in its extremity, it let the egg fall. The egg did not, however, fall into the sea, but on a fisherman's hut which stood on the shore and the hut began at once to smoke and was about to break out in flames.

Then arose in the sea waves as high as a house, they streamed over the hut, and subdued the fire. The other brother, the whale, had come swimming to them, and had driven the water up on high. When the fire was extinguished, the youth sought for the egg and happily found it; it was not yet melted, but the shell was broken by being so suddenly cooled with the water, and he could take out the crystal ball unhurt.

When the youth went to the enchanter and held it before him, the latter said, "My power is destroyed, and from this time forth thou art the King of the Castle of the Golden Sun. With this canst thou likewise give back to thy brothers their human form." Then the youth hastened to the King's daughter, and when he entered the room, she was standing there in the full splendor of her beauty, and joyfully they exchanged rings with each other.

The Donkey

ONCE UPON a time there lived a King and a Queen, who were rich, and had everything they wanted except one thing: they had no children. The Queen lamented over this day and night, and said, "I am like a field on which nothing grows." At last God gave her her wish, but when the child came into the world, it did not look like a human child, but was a little donkey. When the mother saw that, her lamentations and outcries began in real earnest; she said she would far rather have had no child at all than have a donkey, and that they were to throw it into the water that the fishes might devour it. But the King said, "No, since God has sent him he shall be my son and heir, and after my death sit on the royal throne, and wear the kingly crown."

The donkey, therefore, was brought up and grew bigger, and his ears grew up beautifully high and straight. He was, however, of a merry disposition, jumped about, played and had especial pleasure in music, so that he went to a celebrated musician and said, "Teach me thine art, that I may play the lute as well as thou dost." "Ah, dear little master," answered the musician, "that would come very hard to you, your fingers are certainly not suited to it, and are far too big. I am afraid the strings would not last."

No excuses were of any use. The donkey was determined to play the lute; he was persevering and industrious, and at last learnt to do it as well as the master himself. The young lordling once went out walking full of thought and came to a well; he looked into it and in the mirror-clear water saw his donkey's form. He was so distressed about it, that he went out into the wide world and only took with him one faithful companion. They traveled up and down, and at last they came into a kingdom where an old King reigned who had an only but wonderfully beautiful daughter. The donkey said, "Here we will stay," knocked at the gate, and cried, "A guest is without—open, that he may enter." As, however, the gate was not opened, he sat down, took his lute and played it in the most delightful manner with his two fore-feet. Then the door-keeper opened his eyes most wonderfully wide, and ran to the King and said, "Outside by the gate sits a young donkey which plays the lute as well as an experienced master!" "Then let the musician come to me," said the King.

When, however, a donkey came in, every one began to laugh at the lute-player. And now the donkey was to sit down and eat with the servants. He, however, was unwilling, and said, "I am no common stable-ass, I am a noble one." Then they said, "If that is what thou art, seat thyself with the men of war." "No," said he, "I will sit by the King." The King smiled, and said good-humoredly, "Yes, it shall be as thou wilt, little ass, come here to me." Then he asked, "Little ass, how does my daughter please thee?" The donkey turned his head towards her, looked at her, nodded and said, "I like her above measure, I have never yet seen any one so beautiful as she is." "Well, then, thou shalt sit next to her too," said the King. "That is exactly what I wish," said the donkey, and he placed himself by her side, ate and drank, and knew how to behave himself daintily and cleanly.

When the noble beast had stayed a long time at the King's court, he thought, "What good does all this do me, I shall still have to go home again," let his head hang sadly, and went to the King and asked for his dismissal. But the King had grown fond of him, and said, "Little ass, what ails thee? Thou lookest as sour as a jug of vinegar; I will give thee what thou wantest. Dost thou want gold?" "No," said the donkey, and shook his head. "Dost thou want jewels and rich dress?" "No." "Dost thou wish for half my kingdom?" "Indeed, no." Then said the King, "If I did but know what would make thee content. Wilt thou have my pretty daughter to wife?" "Ah, yes," said the ass, "I should indeed like her," and all at once he became quite merry and full of happiness, for that was exactly what he was wishing for.

So a great and splendid wedding was held. In the evening, when the bride and bridegroom were led into their bed-room, the King wanted to know if the ass would behave well, and ordered a servant to hide himself there. When they were both within, the bridegroom bolted the door, looked around, and as he believed that they were quite alone, he suddenly threw off his ass's skin, and stood there in the form of a handsome royal youth. "Now," said he, "thou seest who I am, and seest also that I am not unworthy of thee." Then the bride was glad, and kissed him, and loved him dearly.

When morning came, he jumped up, put his animal's skin on again, and no one could have guessed what kind of a form was hidden beneath it. Soon came the old King, "Ah," cried he, "is the little ass merry? But surely thou art sad," said he to his daughter, "that thou hast not got a proper man for thy husband?" "Oh, no, dear father, I love him as well as if he were the handsomest in the world, and I will keep him as long as I live." The King was surprised, but the servant who had concealed himself came and revealed everything to him. The King said, "That cannot be true." "Then watch yourself the next night, and you will see it with your own eyes; and hark you, lord King, if you were to take his skin away and throw it in the fire, he would be forced to show himself in his true shape." "Thy advice is good," said the King, and at night when they were asleep, he stole in, and when he got to the bed he saw by the light of the moon a noble-looking youth lying there, and the skin lay stretched on the ground.

So he took it away, and had a great fire lighted outside, and threw the skin into it, and remained by it himself until it was all burnt to ashes. As, however, he was anxious to know how the robbed man would behave himself, he stayed awake the whole night and watched. When the youth had slept his sleep out, he got up by the first light of morning, and wanted to put on the ass's skin, but it was not to be found. On this he was alarmed, and, full of grief and anxiety, said, "Now I shall have to contrive to escape." But when he went out, there stood the King, who said, "My son, whither away in such haste? what hast thou in thy mind? Stay here, thou art such a handsome man, thou shalt not go away from me. I will now give thee half my kingdom, and after my death thou shalt have the whole of it." "Then I hope that what begins so well may end well, and I will stay with you," said the youth.

And the old man gave him half the kingdom, and in a year's time, when he died, the youth had the whole, and after the death of his father he had another kingdom as well, and lived in all magnificence.

Hans the Hedgehog

THERE ONCE was a countryman who had money and land in plenty, but no matter how rich he was, one thing was still wanting to complete his happiness—he had no children. Often when he went into the town with the other peasants they mocked him and asked why he had no children. At last he became angry, and when he got home he said, "I will have a child, even if it be a hedgehog." Then his wife had a child, that was a hedgehog in the upper part of his body, and a boy in the lower, and when she saw the child, she was terrified, and said, "See, there thou hast brought ill-luck on us." Then said the man, "What can be done now? The boy must be christened, but we shall not be able to get a godfather for him." The woman said, "And we cannot call him anything else but Hans the Hedgehog."

When he was christened, the parson said, "He cannot go into any ordinary bed because of his spikes." So a little straw was put behind the stove, and Hans the Hedgehog was laid on it. His mother could not suckle him, for he would have pricked her with his quills. So he lay there behind the stove for eight years, and his father was tired of him and thought, "If he would but die!" He did not die, however, but remained lying there.

Now it happened that there was a fair in the town, and the peasant was about to go to it, and asked his wife what he should bring back with him for her. "A little meat and a couple of white rolls which are wanted for the house," said she. Then he asked the servant, and she wanted a pair of slippers and some stockings with clocks. At last he said also, "And what wilt thou have, Hans my Hedgehog?" "Dear father," he said, "do bring me bagpipes."

When, therefore, the father came home again, he gave his wife what he had bought for her—meat and white rolls, and then he gave the maid the slippers, and the stockings with clocks; and lastly, he went behind the stove, and gave Hans the Hedgehog the bagpipes. And when Hans the Hedgehog had the bagpipes, he said, "Dear father, do go to the forge and get the cock shod, and then I will ride away, and never come back again." On this, the father was delighted to think that he was going to get rid of him, and had the cock shod for him, and when it was done, Hans the Hedgehog got on it, and rode away, but took swine and asses with him which he intended to keep in the forest.

When they got there he made the cock fly on to a high tree with him, and there he sat for many a long year, and watched his asses and swine until the herd was quite large, and his father knew nothing about him. While he was sitting in the tree, however, he played his bagpipes, and made music which was very beautiful. Once a King came traveling by who had lost his way and heard the music. He was astonished at it, and sent his servant forth to look all round and see from whence this music came. He spied about, but saw nothing but a little animal sitting up aloft on the tree, which looked like a cock with a hedgehog on it which made this music.

Then the King told the servant he was to ask why he sat there, and if he knew the road which led to his kingdom.

So Hans the Hedgehog descended from the tree, and said he would show the way if the King would write a bond and promise him whatever he first met in the royal courtyard as soon as he arrived at home. Then the King thought, "I can easily do that, Hans the Hedgehog understands nothing, and I can write what I like." So the King took pen and ink and wrote something, and when he had done it, Hans the Hedgehog showed him the way, and he got safely home. But his daughter, when she saw him from afar, was so overjoyed that she ran to meet him, and kissed him. Then he remembered Hans the Hedgehog, and told her what had happened, and that he had been forced to promise whatsoever first met him when he got home, to a very strange animal which sat on a cock as if it were a horse, and made beautiful music, but that instead of writing that he should have what he wanted, he had written that he should not have it. Thereupon the Princess was glad, and said he had done well, for she never would have gone away with the Hedgehog.

Hans the Hedgehog, however, looked after his asses and pigs, and was always merry and sat on the tree and played his bagpipes.

Now it came to pass that another King came journeying by with his attendants and runners, and he also had lost his way, and did not know how to get home again because the forest was so large. He likewise heard the beautiful music from a distance, and asked his runner what that could be, and told him to go and see. Then the runner went under the tree, and saw the cock sitting at the top of it, and Hans the Hedgehog on the cock. The runner asked him what he was about up there. "I am keeping my asses and my pigs; but what is your desire?" The messenger said that they had lost their way, and could not get back into their own kingdom, and asked if he would not show them the way. Then Hans the Hedgehog got down the tree with the cock, and told the aged King that he would show him the way, if he would give him for his own whatsoever first met him in front of his royal palace. The King said, "Yes," and wrote a promise to Hans the Hedgehog that he should have this. That done, Hans rode on before him on the cock, and pointed out the way, and the King reached his kingdom again in safety.

When he got to the courtyard, there were great rejoicings. The King had an only daughter who was very beautiful; she ran to meet him, threw her arms round his neck, and was delighted to have her old father back again. She asked him where in the world he had been so long. So he told her how he had lost his way, and had very nearly not come back at all, but that as he was traveling through a great forest, a creature, half hedgehog, half man, who was sitting astride a cock in a high tree, and making music, had shown him the way and helped him to get out; but that in return he had promised him whatsoever first met him in the royal courtyard, and how that was she herself, which made him unhappy now. But on this she promised that, for love of her father, she would willingly go with this Hans if he came.

Hans the Hedgehog, however, took care of his pigs, and the pigs multiplied until they became so many in number that the whole forest was filled with them. Then Hans the Hedgehog resolved not to live in the forest any longer, and sent word to his father to have every sty in the village emptied, for he was coming with such a great herd that all might kill who wished to do so. When his father heard that he was troubled, for he thought Hans the Hedgehog had died long ago. Hans the Hedgehog, however, seated himself on the cock, and drove the pigs before him into the village, and ordered the slaughter to begin. Ha!—but there was a killing and a chopping that might have been heard two miles off! After this Hans the Hedgehog said, "Father, let me have the cock shod once more at the forge, and then I will ride away and never come back as long as I live." Then the father had the cock shod once more, and was pleased that Hans the Hedgehog would never return again.

Hans the Hedgehog rode away to the first kingdom. There the King had commanded that whosoever came mounted on a cock and had bagpipes with him should be shot at, cut down, or stabbed by every one, so that he might not enter the palace. When, therefore, Hans the Hedgehog came riding thither, they all pressed forward against him with their pikes, but he spurred the cock and it flew up over the gate in front of the King's window and lighted there, and Hans cried that the King must give him what he had promised, or he would take both his life and his daughter's.

Then the King began to speak softly to his daughter and beg her to go away with Hans in order to save her own life and her father's. So she dressed herself in white, and her father gave her a carriage with six horses and magnificent attendants together with gold and possessions. She seated herself in the carriage, and placed Hans the Hedgehog beside her with the cock and the bagpipes, and then they took leave and drove away, and the King thought he should never see her again. He was, however, deceived in his expectation, for when they were at a short distance from the town, Hans the Hedgehog took her pretty clothes off, and pierced her with his hedgehog's skin until she bled all over. "That is the reward of your falseness," said he, "go your way, I will not have you!" and on that he chased her home again, and she was disgraced for the rest of her life.

Hans the Hedgehog, however, rode on further on the cock, with his bagpipes, to the dominions of the second King to whom he had shown the way. This one, however, had arranged that if any one resembling Hans the Hedgehog should come, they were to present arms, give him safe conduct, cry long life to him, and lead him to the royal palace.

But when the King's daughter saw him she was terrified, for he looked quite too strange. She remembered, however, that she could not change her mind, for she had given her promise to her father. So Hans the Hedgehog was welcomed by her, and married to her, and had to go with her to the royal table, and she seated herself by his side, and they ate and drank. When the evening came and they wanted to go to sleep, she was afraid of his quills, but he told her she was not to fear, for no harm would befall her, and he told the old King that he was to appoint four men to watch by the door of the chamber, and light a great fire, and when he entered the room and was about to get into bed, he would creep out of his hedgehog's skin and leave it lying there by the bed-side, and that the men were to run nimbly to it, throw it in the fire, and stay by it until it was consumed.

When the clock struck eleven, he went into the chamber, stripped off the hedgehog's skin, and left it lying by the bed. Then came the men and fetched it swiftly, and threw it in the fire; and when the fire had consumed it, he was delivered, and lay there in bed in human form, but he was coal-black as if he had been burnt. The King sent for his physician who washed him with precious salves, and anointed him, and he became white, and was a handsome young man. When the King's daughter saw that she was glad, and the next morning they arose joyfully, ate and drank, and then the marriage was properly solemnized, and Hans the Hedgehog received the kingdom from the aged King.

When several years had passed he went with his wife to his father, and said that he was his son. The father, however, declared he had no son—he had never had but one, and he had been born like a hedgehog with spikes, and had gone forth into the world. Then Hans made himself known, and the old father rejoiced and went with him to his kingdom.

The King of the Golden Mountain

A CERTAIN MERCHANT had two children, a boy and a girl; they were both young, too young to walk. And two richly-laden ships of his sailed forth to sea with all his property on board, and just as he was expecting to win much money by them, news came that they had gone to the bottom, and now instead of being a rich man he was a poor one, and had nothing left but one field outside the town.

In order to drive his misfortune a little out of his thoughts, he went out to this field, and as he was walking backwards and forwards in it, a little black mannikin stood suddenly by his side, and asked why he was so sad, and what he was taking so much to heart.

Then said the merchant, "If thou couldst help me I would willingly tell thee." "Who knows?" replied the black dwarf. "Perhaps I can help thee." Then the merchant told him that all he possessed had gone to the bottom of the sea, and that he had nothing left but this field. "Do not trouble thyself," said the dwarf. "If thou wilt promise to give me the first thing that rubs itself against thy leg when thou art at home again, and to bring it here to this place in twelve years' time, thou shalt have as much money as thou wilt." The merchant thought, "What can that be but my dog?" and did not remember his little boy, so he said yes, gave the black man a written and sealed promise, and went home.

When he reached home, his little boy was so delighted that he held by a bench, tottered up to him and seized him fast by the legs. The father was shocked, for he remembered his promise, and now knew what he had pledged himself to do; as, however, he still found no money in his chest, he thought the dwarf had only been jesting. A month afterwards he went up to the garret, intending to gather together some old tin and to sell it, and saw a great heap of money lying. Then he was happy again, made purchases, became a greater merchant than before, and felt that this world was well governed.

In the meantime the boy grew tall, and at the same time sharp and clever. But the nearer the twelfth year approached the more anxious grew the merchant, so that his distress might be seen in his face. One day his son asked what ailed him, but the father would not say. The boy, however, persisted so long, that at last he told him that without being aware of what he was doing, he had promised him to a black dwarf, and had received much money for doing so. He said likewise that he had set his hand and seal to this, and that now when twelve years had gone by he would have to give him up.

Then said the son, "Oh, father, do not be uneasy, all will go well. The black man has no power over me." The son had himself blessed by the priest, and when the time came, father and son went together to the field, and the son made a circle and placed himself inside it with his father. Then came the black dwarf and said to the old man, "Hast thou brought with thee that which thou hast promised me?" He was silent, but the son asked, "What dost thou want here?" Then said the black dwarf, "I have to speak with thy father, and not with thee." The son replied, "Thou hast betrayed and misled my father; give back the writing." "No," said the black dwarf, "I will not give up my rights."

They spoke together for a long time after this, but at last they agreed that the son, as he did not belong to the enemy of mankind, nor yet to his father, should seat himself in a small boat, which should lie on water which was flowing away from them, and that the father should push it off with his own foot, and then the son should remain given up to the water. So he took leave of his father, placed himself in a little boat, and the father had to push it off with his own foot. The boat capsized so that the keel was uppermost, and the father believed his son was lost, and went home and mourned for him.

The boat, however, did not sink, but floated quietly away, and the boy sat safely inside it, and it floated thus for a long time, until at last it stopped by an unknown shore. Then he landed and saw a beautiful castle before him, and set out to go to it.

When he entered it, however, he found that it was bewitched. He went through every room, but all were empty until he reached the last, where a snake lay coiled in a ring. The snake, however, was an enchanted maiden, who rejoiced to see him, and said, "Hast thou come, oh, my deliverer? I have already waited twelve years for thee; this kingdom is bewitched, and thou must set it free." "How can I do that?" he inquired. "Tonight come twelve black men, covered with chains, who will ask what thou art doing here; keep silence, however; give them no answer, and let them do what they will with thee; they will torment thee, beat thee, stab thee; let everything pass, only do not speak; at twelve o'clock, they must go away again.

"On the second night twelve others will come; on the third, four-and-twenty, who will cut off thy head, but at twelve o'clock their power will be over, and then if thou hast endured all, and hast not spoken the slightest word, I shall be released. I will come to thee, and will have, in a bottle, some of the water of life. I will rub thee with that, and then thou wilt come to life again, and be as healthy as before." Then said he, "I will gladly set thee free."

Everything happened just as she had said. The black men could not force a single word from him, and on the third night the snake became a beautiful princess who came with the water of life and brought him back to life again. So she threw herself into his arms and kissed him, and there was joy and gladness in the whole castle. After this their marriage was celebrated, and he was King of the Golden Mountain.

They lived very happily together, and the Queen bore a fine boy. Eight years had already gone by, when the King bethought him of his father; his heart was moved, and he wished to visit him. The Queen, however, would not let him go away, and said, "I know beforehand that it will cause my unhappiness"; but he suffered her to have no rest until she consented. At their parting she gave him a wishing-ring, and said, "Take this ring and put it on thy finger, and then thou wilt immediately be transported whithersoever thou wouldst be, only thou must promise me not to use it in wishing me away from this place and with thy father." That he promised her, put the ring on his finger, and wished himself at home, just outside the town where his father lived.

Instantly he found himself there, and made for the town, but when he came to the gate, the sentries would not let him go in, because he wore such strange and yet such rich and magnificent clothing. Then he went to a hill where a shepherd was watching his sheep, changed clothes with him, put on his old shepherd's-coat, and then entered the town without hindrance. When he came to his father, he made himself known to him, but he did not at all believe that the shepherd was his son, and said he certainly had had a son, but that he was dead long ago; however, as he saw he was a poor, needy shepherd, he would give him something to eat.

Then the shepherd said to his parents, "I am verily your son. Do you know of no mark on my body by which you could recognize me?" "Yes," said his mother, "our son had a raspberry mark under

his right arm." He slipped back his shirt, and they saw the raspberry under his right arm, and no longer doubted that he was their
son. Then he told them that he was King of the Golden Mountain,
and a King's daughter was his wife, and that they had a fine son of
seven years old. Then said the father, "That is certainly not true; it
is a fine kind of King who goes about in a ragged shepherd's-coat."
At these words the son flew into a passion, and without thinking of
his promise, turned his ring round, and wished both his wife and
child with him. They were there in a second, but the Queen wept,
and reproached him, and said that he had broken his word, and
had brought misfortune upon her. He said, "I have done it thoughtlessly, and not with evil intention," and tried to calm her, and she
pretended to believe this; but she had mischief in her mind.

Then he led her out of the town into the field, and showed her
the stream where the little boat had been pushed off, and then he
said, "I am tired; sit down, I will sleep awhile on thy lap." And he
laid his head on her lap, and fell asleep. When he was asleep, she
first drew the ring from his finger, then she drew away the foot
which was under him, leaving only the slipper behind her, and she
took her child in her arms, and wished herself back in her own
kingdom.

When he awoke, there he lay quite deserted, and his wife and
child were gone, and so was the ring from his finger; the slipper
only was still there as a token. "Home to thy parents thou canst not
return," thought he, "they would say that thou wast a wizard; thou
must be off, and walk on until thou arrivest in thine own kingdom."
So he went away and came at length to a hill by which three giants
were standing, disputing with each other because they did not
know how to divide their father's property. When they saw him
passing by, they called to him and said little men had quick wits,
and that he was to divide their inheritance for them.

The inheritance, however, consisted of a sword, which had this
property that if any one took it in his hand, and said, "All heads off
but mine," every head would lie on the ground; secondly, of a cloak
which made any one who put it on invisible; thirdly, of a pair of
boots which could transport the wearer to any place he wished in a
moment. He said, "Give me the three things that I may see if they
are still in good condition." They gave him the cloak, and when he
had put it on, he was invisible and changed into a fly. Then he
resumed his own form and said, "The cloak is a good one, now give
me the sword." They said, "No, we will not give thee that; if thou
wert to say, 'All heads off but mine,' all our heads would be off, and

thou alone wouldst be left with thine." Nevertheless they gave it to him with the condition that he was only to try it against a tree. This he did, and the sword cut in two the trunk of a tree as if it had been a blade of straw. Then he wanted to have the boots likewise, but they said, "No, we will not give them; if thou hadst them on thy feet and wert to wish thyself at the top of the hill, we should be left down here with nothing." "Oh, no," said he, "I will not do that." So they gave him the boots as well.

And now when he had got all these things, he thought of nothing but his wife and his child, and said just as it were to himself, "Oh, if I were but on the Golden Mountain," and at the same moment he vanished from the sight of the giants, and thus their inheritance was divided.

When he was near his palace, he heard sounds of joy, and fiddles, and flutes, and the people told him that his wife was celebrating her wedding with another. He fell into a rage, and said, "False woman, she betrayed and deserted me while I was asleep!" So he put on his cloak, and unseen by all went into the palace. When he entered the dining-hall a great table was spread with delicious food, and the guests were eating and drinking, and laughing and jesting. She sat on a royal seat in the midst of them in splendid apparel, with a crown on her head. He placed himself behind her, and no one saw him. When she put a piece of meat on a plate for herself, he took it away and ate it, and when she poured out a glass of wine for herself, he took it away and drank it. She was always helping herself to something, and yet she never got anything, for plate and glass disappeared immediately. Then dismayed and ashamed, she arose and went to her chamber and wept, but he followed her there. She said, "Has the devil power over me, or did my deliverer never come?" Then he struck her in the face, and said, "Did thy deliverer never come? It is he who has thee in his power, thou traitress. Have I deserved this from thee?" Then he made himself visible, went into the hall, and cried, "The wedding is at an end, the true King has returned."

The Kings, Princes and councillors who were assembled there, ridiculed and mocked him, but he did not trouble to answer them, and said, "Will you go away, or not?" On this they tried to seize him and pressed upon him, but he drew his sword and said, "All heads off but mine," and all the heads rolled on the ground. And he alone was master, once more King of the Golden Mountain.

The Golden Bird

IN TIMES GONE BY there was a King who had at the back of his castle a beautiful pleasure-garden, in which stood a tree that bore golden apples. As the apples ripened they were counted, but one morning one was missing. Then the King was angry, and he ordered that watch should be kept about the tree every night. Now the King had three sons, and he sent the eldest to spend the whole night in the garden: so he watched till midnight, and then he could keep off sleep no longer, and in the morning another apple was missing. The second son had to watch the following night; but it fared no better, for when twelve o'clock had struck he went to sleep, and in the morning another apple was missing. Now came the turn of the third son to watch, and he was ready to do so; but the King had less trust in him, and believed he would acquit himself still worse than his brothers, but in the end he consented to let him try. So the young man lay down under the tree to watch, and resolved that sleep should not be master. When it struck twelve something came rushing through the air, and he saw in the moonlight a bird flying towards him, whose feathers glittered like gold. The bird perched upon the tree, and had already pecked off an apple, when the young man let fly an arrow at it. The bird flew away, but the arrow had struck its target, and one of its golden feathers fell to the ground. The young man picked it up, and taking it next morning to the King, told him what had happened in the night.

The King called his council together, and all declared that such a feather was worth more than the whole kingdom. "Since the feather is so valuable," said the King, "one is not enough for me; I must and will have the whole bird."

So the eldest son set off, and relying on his own cleverness he thought he should soon find the golden bird. When he had gone some distance he saw a fox sitting at the edge of a wood, and he pointed his gun at him.

The fox cried out, "Do not shoot me, and I will give you good counsel. You are on your way to find the golden bird, and this evening you will come to a village, in which two taverns stand facing each other. One will be brightly lighted up, and there will be plenty of merriment going on inside; do not mind about that, but go into the other one, although it will look to you very uninviting."

"How can a silly beast give one any rational advice?" thought the King's son, and let fly at the fox, but missed him, and he stretched out his tail and ran quickly into the wood. Then the young man went on his way, and towards evening he came to the village, and there stood the two taverns; in one singing and dancing was going on, the other looked quite dull and wretched. "I should be a fool," said he, "to go into that dismal place, while there is anything so good close by." So he went into the merry inn, and there lived in clover, quite forgetting the bird and his father, and all good counsel.

As time went on, and the eldest son never came home, the second son set out to seek the golden bird. He met with the fox, just as the eldest did, and received good advice from him without attending to it. And when he came to the two taverns, his brother was standing and calling to him at the window of one of them, out of which came sounds of merriment; so he could not resist, but went in and reveled to his heart's content.

And then, as time went on, the youngest son wished to go forth, and to try his luck, but his father would not consent. "It would be useless," said he; "he is much less likely to find the bird than his brothers, and if any misfortune were to happen to him he would not know how to help himself; his wits are none of the best."

But at last, as there was no peace to be had, he let him go. By the side of the wood sat the fox, begged him to spare his life, and gave him good counsel. The young man was kind, and said, "Be easy, little fox, I will do you no harm."

"You shall not repent of it," answered the fox, "and that you may get there all the sooner, get up and sit on my tail."

And no sooner had he done so than the fox began to run, and off they went over stock and stone, so that the wind whistled in their hair. When they reached the village the young man got down, and, following the fox's advice, went into the mean-looking tavern, without hesitating, and there he passed a quiet night.

The next morning, when he went out into the field, the fox, who was sitting there already, said, "I will tell you further what you have to do. Go straight on until you come to a castle, before which a great band of soldiers lie, but do not trouble yourself about them, for they will be all asleep and snoring; pass through them and forward into the castle, and go through all the rooms, until you come to one where there is a golden bird hanging in a wooden cage. Near at hand will stand, empty, a golden cage of state, but you must beware of taking the bird out of his ugly cage and putting him into the fine one; if you do so you will come to harm."

After he had finished saying this the fox stretched out his tail again, and the King's son sat him down upon it; then away they went over stock and stone, so that the wind whistled through their hair. And when the King's son reached the castle he found everything as the fox had said, and he at last entered the room where the golden bird was hanging in a wooden cage, while a golden one was standing by; the three golden apples too were in the room. Then, thinking it foolish to let the beautiful bird stay in that mean and ugly cage, he opened the door of it, took hold of it, and put it in the golden one. In the same moment the bird uttered a piercing cry. The soldiers awaked, rushed in, seized the King's son and put him in prison. The next morning he was brought before a judge, and, as he confessed everything, condemned to death. But the King said he would spare his life on one condition, that he should bring him the golden horse whose paces were swifter than the wind, and that then he should also receive the golden bird as a reward.

So the King's son set off to find the golden horse, but he sighed, and was very sad, for how should it be accomplished? And then he saw his old friend the fox sitting by the roadside.

"Now, you see," said the fox, "all this has happened because you would not listen to me. But be of good courage, I will bring you through, and will tell you how you are to get the golden horse. You must go straight on until you come to a castle, where the horse stands in his stable; before the stable-door the grooms will be lying, but they will all be asleep and snoring; and you can go and quietly lead out the horse. But one thing you must mind—take care to put upon him the plain saddle of wood and leather, and not the golden one, which will hang close by; otherwise it will go badly with you."

Then the fox stretched out his tail, and the King's son seated himself upon it, and away they went over stock and stone until the wind whistled through their hair. And everything happened just as the fox had said, and he came to the stall where the golden horse was, and as he was about to put on him the plain saddle, he thought to himself, "Such a beautiful animal would be disgraced were I not to put on him the good saddle, which becomes him so well."

However, no sooner did the horse feel the golden saddle touch him than he began to neigh. And the grooms all awoke, seized the King's son and threw him into prison. The next morning he was delivered up to justice and condemned to death, but the King promised him his life, and also to bestow upon him the golden horse, if he could convey thither the beautiful Princess of the golden castle.

With a heavy heart the King's son set out, but by great good luck he soon met with the faithful fox.

"I ought now to leave you to your own ill-luck," said the fox, "but I am sorry for you, and will once more help you in your need. Your way lies straight up to the golden castle. You will arrive there in the evening, and at night when all is quiet, the beautiful Princess goes to the bath. And as she is entering the bathing-house, go up to her and give her a kiss, then she will follow you, and you can lead her away; but do not suffer her first to go and take leave of her parents, or it will go ill with you."

Then the fox stretched out his tail, the King's son seated himself upon it, and away they went over stock and stone, so that the wind whistled through their hair. And when he came to the golden castle all was as the fox had said. He waited until midnight, when all lay in deep sleep, and then as the beautiful Princess went to the bathing-house he went up to her and gave her a kiss, and she willingly promised to go with him, but she begged him earnestly, and with tears, that he would let her first go and take leave of her parents. At first he denied her prayer, but as she wept so much the more, and fell at his feet, he gave in at last. And no sooner had the Princess reached her father's bedside than he, and all who were in the castle, waked up, and the young man was seized and thrown into prison.

The next morning the King said to him, "Thy life is forfeit, but thou shalt find grace if thou canst level that mountain that lies before my windows, and over which I am not able to see; and if this is done within eight days thou shalt have my daughter for a reward."

So the King's son set to work, and dug and shoveled away without ceasing, but when, on the seventh day, he saw how little he had accomplished, and that all his work was as nothing, he fell into great sadness, and gave up all hope. But on the evening of the seventh day the fox appeared, and said, "You do not deserve that I should help you, but go now and lie down to sleep, and I will do the work for you."

The next morning when he awoke, and looked out of the window, the mountain had disappeared. The young man hastened full of joy to the King, and told him that his behest was fulfilled, and, whether the King liked it or not, he had to keep to his word, and let his daughter go.

So they both went away together, and it was not long before the faithful fox came up to them.

"Well, you have got the best first," said he; "but you must know the golden horse belongs to the Princess of the golden castle."

"But how shall I get it?" asked the young man.

"I am going to tell you," answered the fox. "First, go to the King who sent you to the golden castle, and take to him the beautiful Princess. There will then be very great rejoicing; he will willingly give you the golden horse, and they will lead him out to you; then mount him without delay, and stretch out to your hand to each of them to take leave, and last of all to the Princess, and when you have her by the hand swing her up on the horse behind you, and off you go! nobody will be able to overtake you, for that horse goes swifter than the wind."

And so it was all happily done, and the King's son carried off the beautiful Princess on the golden horse. The fox did not stay behind, and he said to the young man, "Now, I will help you to get the golden bird. When you draw near the castle where the bird is, let the lady alight, and I will take her under my care; then you must ride the golden horse into the castle-yard, and there will be great rejoicing to see it, and they will bring out to you the golden bird. As soon as you have the cage in your hand, you must start off back to us, and then you shall carry the lady away."

The plan was successfully carried out; and when the young man returned with the treasure, the fox said, "Now, what will you give me for my reward?"

"What would you like?" asked the young man.

"When we are passing through the wood, I desire that you should slay me, and cut my head and feet off."

"That were a strange sign of gratitude," said the King's son, "and I could not possibly do such a thing."

Then said the fox, "If you will not do it, I must leave you; but before I go let me give you some good advice. Beware of two things: buy no gallows-meat, and sit at no brook-side." With that the fox ran off into the wood.

The young man thought to himself, "That is a wonderful animal, with most singular ideas. How should any one buy gallows-meat? and I am sure I have no particular fancy for sitting by a brook-side."

So he rode on with the beautiful Princess, and their way led them through the village where his two brothers had stayed. There they heard great outcry and noise, and when he asked what it was all about, they told him that two people were going to be hanged. And when he drew near he saw that it was his two brothers, who had done all sorts of evil tricks, and had wasted all their goods. He asked if there were no means of setting them free.

"Oh yes! if you will buy them off," answered the people; "but why should you spend your money in redeeming such worthless men?"

But he persisted in doing so; and when they were let go they all went on their journey together.

After a while they came to the wood where the fox had met them first, and there it seemed so cool and sheltered from the sun's burning rays that the two brothers said, "Let us rest here for a little by the brook, and eat and drink to refresh ourselves."

The young man consented, quite forgetting the fox's warning, and he seated himself by the brook-side, suspecting no evil. But the two brothers thrust him backwards into the brook, seized the Princess, the horse, and the bird, and went home to their father.

"Is not this the golden bird that we bring?" said they; "and we have also the golden horse, and the Princess of the golden castle."

Then there was great rejoicing in the royal castle, but the horse did not feed, the bird did not chirp, and the Princess sat still and wept.

The youngest brother, however, had not perished. The brook was, by good fortune, dry, and he fell on soft moss without receiving any hurt, but he could not get up again. But in his need the faithful fox was not lacking; he came up running, and reproached him for having forgotten his advice.

"But I cannot forsake you all the same," said he; "I will help you back again into daylight." So he told the young man to grasp his tail, and hold on to it fast, and so he drew him up again.

"Still you are not quite out of all danger," said the fox; "your brothers, not being certain of your death, have surrounded the wood with sentinels, who are to put you to death if you let yourself be seen."

A poor beggar-man was sitting by the path, and the young man changed clothes with him, and went in that disguise into the King's courtyard. Nobody knew him, but the bird began to chirp, and the horse began to feed, and the beautiful Princess ceased weeping.

"What does this mean?" said the King, astonished.

The Princess answered, "I cannot tell, except that I was sad, and now I am joyful; it is to me as if my rightful bridegroom had returned."

Then she told him all that happened, although the two brothers had threatened to put her to death if she let out anything. The King then ordered every person who was in the castle to be brought before him, and with the rest came the young man like a beggar in his wretched garments; but the Princess knew him, and greeted him well, falling on his neck and kissing him. The wicked brothers were seized and put to death, and the youngest brother was married to the Princess, and succeeded to the inheritance of his father.

But what became of the poor fox? Long afterwards the King's son was going through the wood, and the fox met him and said, "Now, you have everything that you can wish for, but my misfortunes never come to an end, and it lies in your power to free me from them." And once more he prayed the King's son earnestly to slay him, and cut off his head and feet. So, at last, he consented, and no sooner was it done than the fox was changed into a man, and was no other than the brother of the beautiful Princess; and thus he was set free from a spell that had bound him for a long, long time.

And now, indeed, there lacked nothing to their happiness as long as they lived.

Strong Hans

THERE WERE once a man and a woman who had an only child, and lived quite alone in a solitary valley. It came to pass that the mother once went into the wood to gather branches of fir, and took with her little Hans, who was just two years old. As it was springtime, and the child took pleasure in the many-colored flowers, she went still further onwards with him into the forest. Suddenly two robbers sprang out of the thicket, seized the mother and child, and carried them far away into the black forest, where no one ever came from one year's end to another. The poor woman urgently begged the robbers to set her and her child free, but their hearts were made of stone, they would not listen to her prayers and entreaties, and drove her on farther by force.

After they had worked their way through bushes and briars for about two miles, they came to a rock where there was a door, at which the robbers knocked and it opened at once. They had to go through a long dark passage, and at last came into a great cavern, which was lighted by a fire which burnt on the hearth. On the wall hung swords, sabers, and other deadly weapons which gleamed in the light, and in the midst stood a black table at which four other robbers were sitting gambling, and the captain sat at the head of it. As soon as he saw the woman he came and spoke to her, and told her to be at ease and have no fear, they would do nothing to hurt her, but she must look after the housekeeping, and if she kept everything in order, she should not fare ill with them. Thereupon they gave her something to eat, and showed her a bed where she might sleep with her child.

The woman stayed many years with the robbers, and Hans grew tall and strong. His mother told him stories, and taught him to read an old book of tales about knights which she found in the cave. When Hans was nine years old, he made himself a strong club out of a branch of fir, hid it behind the bed, and then went to his mother and said, "Dear mother, pray tell me who is my father; I must and will know." His mother was silent and would not tell him, that he might not become home-sick; moreover she knew that the godless robbers would not let him go away, but it almost broke her heart that Hans should not go to his father. In the night, when the robbers came home from their robbing expedition, Hans brought out his club, stood before the captain, and said, "I now wish to know who is my father, and if thou dost not at once tell me I will strike thee down." Then the captain laughed, and gave Hans such a box on the ear that he rolled under the table. Hans got up again, held his tongue, and thought, "I will wait another year and then try again, perhaps I shall do better then." When the year was over, he brought out his club again, rubbed the dust off it, looked at it well, and said, "It is a stout strong club."

At night the robbers came home, drank one jug of wine after another, and their heads began to be heavy. Then Hans brought out his club, placed himself before the captain, and asked him who was his father. But the captain again gave him such a vigorous box on the ear that Hans rolled under the table, but it was not long before he was up again, and beat the captain and the robbers so with his club, that they could no longer move either their arms or their legs. His mother stood in a corner full of admiration of his bravery and strength. When Hans had done his work, he went to his mother, and said, "Now I have shown myself to be in earnest, but now I must also know who is my father." "Dear Hans," answered the mother, "come, we will go and seek him until we find him."

She took from the captain the key to the entrance-door, and Hans fetched a great meal-sack and packed into it gold and silver, and whatsoever else he could find that was beautiful, until it was full, and then he took it on his back. They left the cave, but how Hans did open his eyes when he came out of the darkness into daylight, and saw the green forest, and the flowers, and the birds, and the morning sun in the sky. He stood there and wondered at everything just as if he had not been very wise. His mother looked for the way home, and when they had walked for a couple of hours, they got safely into their lonely valley and to their little house.

The father was sitting in the doorway. He wept for joy when he recognized his wife and heard that Hans was his son, for he had long regarded them both as dead. But Hans, although he was not twelve years old, was a head taller than his father. They went into the little room together, but Hans had scarcely put his sack on the bench by the stove, than the whole house began to crack—the bench broke down and then the floor, and the heavy sack fell through into the cellar. "God save us!" cried the father, "what's that? Now you have broken our little house to pieces!" "Don't grow any gray hairs about that, dear father," answered Hans; "there, in that sack, is more than is wanting for a new house." The father and Hans at once began to build a new house; to buy cattle and land, and to keep a farm. Hans ploughed the fields, and when he followed the plough and pushed it into the ground, the bullocks had scarcely any need to draw.

Next spring Hans said, "Keep all the money and get a walking-stick that weighs a hundred-weight made for me that I may go a-traveling." When the wished-for stick was ready, he left his father's house, went forth, and came to a deep, dark forest. There he heard something crunching and crackling, looked around, and saw a fir tree which was wound round like a rope from the bottom to the top, and when he looked upwards he saw a great fellow who had laid hold of the tree and was twisting it like a willow-wand. "Hollo!" cried Hans, "What are you doing up there?" The fellow replied, "I got some faggots together yesterday and am twisting a rope for them." "That is what I like," thought Hans, "he has some strength," and he called to him, "Leave that alone, and come with me." The fellow came down, and he was taller by a whole head than Hans, and Hans was not little. "Your name is now Fir-twister," said Hans to him.

Thereupon they went further and heard something knocking and hammering with such force that the ground shook at every stroke. Shortly afterwards they came to a mighty rock, before which a giant was standing and striking great pieces of it away with his fist. When Hans asked what he was about, he answered, "At night, when I want to sleep, bears, wolves, and other vermin of that kind come, which sniff and snuffle about me and won't let me rest; so I want to build myself a house and lay myself inside it, so that I may have some peace." "Oh, indeed," thought Hans, "I can make use of this one also"; and said to him, "Leave your house-building alone, and go with me; you shall be called Rock-splitter." The man consented, and they all three roamed through the forest, and wherever they went the wild beasts were terrified, and ran away from them.

In the evening they came to an old deserted castle, went up into it, and laid themselves down in the hall to sleep. The next morning Hans went into the garden. It had run quite wild, and was full of thorns and bushes. And as he was thus walking round about, a wild boar rushed at him; he, however, gave it such a blow with his club that it fell directly. He took it on his shoulders and carried it in, and they put it on a spit, roasted it, and enjoyed themselves. Then they arranged that each day, in turn, they should go out hunting, and one should stay at home, and cook nine pounds of meat for each of them. Fir-twister stayed at home the first, and Hans and Rock-splitter went out hunting.

When Fir-twister was busy cooking, a little shriveled-up old mannikin came to him in the castle, and asked for some meat. "Be off, sly hypocrite," he answered, "you need no meat." But how astonished Fir-twister was when the little insignificant dwarf sprang up at him, and belabored him so with his fists that he could not defend himself, but fell on the ground and gasped for breath! The dwarf did not go away until he had thoroughly vented his anger on him. When the two others came home from hunting, Fir-twister said nothing to them of the old mannikin and of the blows which he himself had received, and thought, "When they stay at home, they may just try their chance with the little scrubbing-brush"; and the mere thought of that gave him pleasure already.

The next day Rock-splitter stayed at home, and he fared just as Fir-twister had done, he was very ill-treated by the dwarf because he was not willing to give him any meat. When the others came home in the evening, Fir-twister easily saw what he had suffered, but both kept silence, and thought, "Hans also must taste some of that soup."

Hans, who had to stay at home the next day, did his work in the kitchen as it had to be done, and as he was standing skimming the pan, the dwarf came and without more ado demanded a bit of meat. Then Hans thought, "He is a poor wretch, I will give him some of my share, that the others may not run short," and handed him a bit. When the dwarf had devoured it, he again asked for some meat, and good-natured Hans gave it to him, and told him it was a handsome piece, and that he was to be content with it. But the dwarf begged again for the third time. "You are shameless!" said Hans, and gave him none. Then the malicious dwarf wanted to spring on him and treat him as he had treated Fir-twister and Rock-splitter, but he had got to the wrong man. Hans, without exerting himself much, gave him a couple of blows which made him jump down the castle steps. Hans was about to run after him, but fell right over him, for he was so tall. When he rose up again, the dwarf had got the start of him. Hans hurried after him as far as the forest, and saw him slip into a hole in the rock. Hans now went home, but he had marked the spot.

When the two others came back, they were surprised that Hans was so well. He told them what had happened, and then they no longer concealed how it had fared with them. Hans laughed and said, "It served you quite right; why were you so greedy with your meat? It is a disgrace that you who are so big should have let yourselves be beaten by the dwarf." Thereupon they took a basket and a rope, and all three went to the hole in the rock into which the dwarf had slipped, and let Hans and his club down in the basket.

When Hans had reached the bottom, he found a door, and when he opened it a maiden was sitting there who was lovely as any picture, nay, so beautiful that no words can express it, and by her side sat the dwarf and grinned at Hans like a sea-cat! She, however, was bound with chains, and looked so mournfully at him that Hans felt great pity for her, and thought to himself, "You must deliver her out of the power of the wicked dwarf," and gave him such a blow with his club that he fell down dead. Immediately the chains fell from the maiden, and Hans was enraptured with her beauty.

She told him she was a King's daughter whom a savage count had stolen away from her home, and imprisoned there among the rocks, because she would have nothing to say to him. The count had, however, set the dwarf as a watchman, and he had made her bear misery and vexation enough. And now Hans placed the maiden in the basket and had her drawn up; the basket came down again, but Hans did not trust his two companions, and thought, "They have already shown themselves to be false, and told me nothing about the dwarf; who knows what design they may have against me?" So he put his club in the basket, and it was lucky he did; for when the basket was half-way up, they let it fall again, and if Hans had really been sitting in it he would have been killed. But now he did not know how he was to work his way out of the depths, and when he turned it over and over in his mind he found no counsel. "It is indeed sad," said he to himself, "that I have to waste away down here," and as he was thus walking backwards and forwards, he once more came to the little chamber where the maiden had been sitting, and saw that the dwarf had a ring on his finger which shone and sparkled.

Then he drew it off and put it on, and when he turned it round on his finger, he suddenly heard something rustle over his head. He looked up and saw spirits of the air hovering above, who told him he was their master, and asked what his desire might be. Hans was at first struck dumb, but afterwards he said that they were to carry him above again. They obeyed instantly, and it was just as if he had flown up himself. When, however, he was above again, he found no one in sight. Fir-twister and Rock-splitter had hurried away, and had taken the beautiful maiden with them. But Hans turned the ring, and the spirits of the air came and told him that the two were on the sea.

Hans ran and ran without stopping, until he came to the sea-shore, and there far, far out on the water, he perceived a little boat in which his faithless comrades were sitting; and in fierce anger he leapt, without thinking what he was doing, club in hand, into the water, and began to swim, but the club, which weighed a hundred-weight, dragged him deep down until he was all but drowned. Then in the very nick of time he turned his ring, and immediately the spirits of the air came and bore him as swift as lightning into the boat. He swung his club and gave his wicked comrades the reward they merited and threw them into the water, and then he sailed with the beautiful maiden, who had been in the greatest alarm, and whom he delivered for the second time, home to her father and mother, and married her, and all rejoiced exceedingly.

The Blue Light

A SOLDIER had served the King faithfully for many years, but when
the war came to an end could serve no longer because of the many
wounds he had received. The King said to him, "You may return to
your home, I need you no longer, and you will not receive any
more money, for he only receives wages who renders me service
for them." Then the soldier did not know how to earn a living,
went away greatly troubled, and walked the whole day, until in the
evening he entered a forest.

When darkness came on, he saw a light, which he went up to,
and came to a house wherein lived a witch. "Do give me one
night's lodging, and a little to eat and drink," said he to her, "or I
shall starve." "Oho!" she answered, "who gives anything to a run-
away soldier? Yet will I be compassionate, and take you in, if you
will do what I wish." "What do you wish?" said the soldier. "That
you should dig all round my garden for me, tomorrow." The soldier
consented, and next day labored with all his strength, but could not
finish it by the evening. "I see well enough," said the witch, "that
you can do no more today, but I will keep you yet another night, in
payment for which you must tomorrow chop me a load of wood,
and make it small." The soldier spent the whole day in doing it, and
in the evening the witch proposed that he should stay one night
more. "Tomorrow, you shall only do me a very trifling piece of
work. Behind my house, there is an old dry well, into which my
light has fallen; it burns blue, and never goes out, and you shall
bring it up again for me."

Next day the old woman took him to the well, and let him down
in a basket. He found the blue light, and made her a signal to draw
him up again. She did draw him up, but when he came near the
edge, she stretched down her hand and wanted to take the blue
light away from him. "No," said he, perceiving her evil intention,
"I will not give you the light until I am standing with both feet
upon the ground." The witch fell into a passion, let him down again
into the well, and went away.

The poor soldier fell without injury on the moist ground, and the
blue light went on burning, but of what use was that to him? He
saw very well that he could not escape death. He sat for a while
very sorrowfully, then suddenly he felt in his pocket and found his

tobacco pipe, which was still half full. "This shall be my last pleasure," thought he, pulled it out, lit it at the blue light and began to
smoke. When the smoke had circled about the cavern, suddenly a
little black dwarf stood before him, and said, "Lord, what are your
commands?" "What commands have I to give you?" replied the
soldier, quite astonished. "I must do everything you bid me," said
the little man. "Good," said the soldier; "then in the first place help
me out of this well."

The little man took him by the hand, and led him through an
underground passage, but he did not forget to take the blue light
with him. On the way the dwarf showed him the treasures which
the witch had collected and hidden there, and the soldier took as
much gold as he could carry. When he was above, he said to the
little man, "Now go and bind the old witch, and carry her before
the judge." In a short time she, with frightful cries, came riding by,
as swift as the wind on a wild tom-cat, nor was it long after that
before the little man reappeared. "It is all done," said he, "and the
witch is already hanging on the gallows. What further commands
has my lord?" inquired the dwarf. "At this moment, none," answered the soldier; "you can return home, only be at hand immediately, if I summon you." "Nothing more is needed than that you
should light your pipe at the blue light, and I will appear before
you at once." Thereupon he vanished from his sight.

The soldier returned to the town from which he had come. He
went to the best inn, ordered himself handsome clothes, and then
bade the landlord furnish him a room as handsomely as possible.
When it was ready and the soldier had taken possession of it, he
summoned the little black mannikin and said, "I have served the
King faithfully, but he has dismissed me, and left me to hunger,
and now I want to take my revenge." "What am I to do?" asked the
little man. "Late at night, when the King's daughter is in bed,
bring her here in her sleep, she shall do servant's work for me."
The mannikin said, "That is an easy thing for me to do, but a very
dangerous thing for you, for if it is discovered, you will fare ill."
When twelve o'clock had struck, the door sprang open, and the
mannikin carried in the Princess. "Aha! are you there?" cried the
soldier, "get to your work at once! Fetch the broom and sweep
the chamber." When she had done this, he ordered her to come to
his chair, and then he stretched out his feet and said, "Pull off my
boots for me," and then he threw them in her face, and made her
pick them up again, and clean and brighten them. She, however,
did everything he bade her, without opposition, silently and with

half-shut eyes. When the first cock crowed, the mannikin carried her back to the royal palace, and laid her in her bed.

Next morning when the Princess arose, she went to her father, and told him that she had had a very strange dream. "I was carried through the streets with the rapidity of lightning," said she, "and taken into a soldier's room, and I had to wait upon him like a servant, sweep his room, clean his boots, and do all kinds of menial work. It was only a dream, and yet I am just as tired as if I really had done everything." "The dream may have been true," said the King, "I will give you a piece of advice. Fill your pocket full of peas, and make a small hole in it, and then if you are carried away again, they will fall out and leave a track in the streets." But unseen by the King, the mannikin was standing beside him when he said that, and heard all. At night when the sleeping Princess was again carried through the streets, some peas certainly did fall out of her pocket, but they made no track, for the crafty mannikin had just before scattered peas in every street there was. And again the Princess was compelled to do servant's work until cock-crow.

Next morning the King sent his people out to seek the track, but it was all in vain, for in every street poor children were sitting, picking up peas, and saying, "It must have rained peas, last night." "We must think of something else," said the King; "keep your shoes on when you go to bed, and before you come back from the place where you are taken, hide one of them there; I will soon contrive to find it." The black mannikin heard this plot, and at night when the soldier again ordered him to bring the Princess, revealed it to him, and told him that he knew of no expedient to counteract this stratagem, and that if the shoe were found in the soldier's house it would go badly with him. "Do what I bid you," replied the soldier, and again this third night the Princess was obliged to work like a servant, but before she went away, she hid her shoe under the bed.

Next morning the King had the entire town searched for his daughter's shoe. It was found at the soldier's, and the soldier himself, who at the entreaty of the dwarf had gone outside the gate, was soon brought back, and thrown into prison. In his flight he had forgotten the most valuable things he had, the blue light and the gold, and had only one ducat in his pocket. And now, loaded with chains, he was standing at the window of his dungeon, when he chanced to see one of his comrades passing by. The soldier tapped at the pane of glass, and when this man came up, said to him, "Be so kind as to fetch me the small bundle I have left lying in the inn, and I will give you a ducat for doing it. "His comrade ran thither and brought him what he wanted. As soon as the soldier was alone again, he lighted his pipe and summoned the black mannikin. "Have no fear," said the latter to his master, "Go wheresoever they take you, and let them do what they will, only take the blue light with you."

Next day the soldier was tried, and though he had done nothing wicked, the judge condemned him to death. When he was led forth to die, he begged a last favor of the King. "What is it?" asked the King. "That I may smoke one more pipe on my way." "You may smoke three," answered the King, "but do not imagine that I will spare your life." Then the soldier pulled out his pipe and lighted it at the blue light, and as soon as a few wreaths of smoke had ascended, the mannikin was there with a small cudgel in his hand, and said, "What does my lord command?" "Strike down to earth that false judge there, and his constable, and spare not the King who has treated me so ill." Then the mannikin fell on them like lightning, darting this way and that way, and whosoever was so much as touched by his cudgel fell to earth, and did not venture to stir again. The King was terrified. He threw himself on the soldier's mercy, and merely to be allowed to live at all, gave him his kingdom for his own, and the Princess to wife.

The Fisherman and His Wife

THERE WAS once a fisherman and his wife who lived together in a hovel by the sea-shore, and the fisherman went out every day with his hook and line to catch fish, and he angled and angled.

One day he was sitting with his rod and looking into the clear water, and he sat and sat.

At last down went the line to the bottom of the water, and when he drew it up he found a great flounder on the hook. And the flounder said to him, "Fisherman, listen to me; let me go. I am not a real fish but an enchanted Prince. What good shall I be to you if you land me? I shall not taste well; so put me back into the water again, and let me swim away."

"Well," said the fisherman, "no need of so many words about the matter; as you can speak I had much rather let you swim away."

Then he put him back into the clear water, and the flounder sank to the bottom, leaving a long streak of blood behind him. Then the fisherman got up and went home to his wife in their hovel.

"Well, husband," said the wife, "have you caught nothing to-day?" "No," said the man—"that is, I did catch a flounder, but as he said he was an enchanted Prince, I let him go again." "Then, did you wish for nothing?" said the wife. "No," said the man; "what should I wish for?"

"Oh dear!" said the wife; "and it is so dreadful always to live in this evil-smelling hovel; you might as well have wished for a little cottage. Go again and call him; tell him we want a little cottage, I daresay he will give it us; go, and be quick."

And when he went back, the sea was green and yellow, and not nearly so clear. So he stood and said,

> "O man, O man!—if man you be,
> Or flounder, flounder, in the sea—
> Such a tiresome wife I've got,
> For she wants what I do not."

Then the flounder came swimming up, and said, "Now then, what does she want?"

"Oh," said the man, "you know when I caught you my wife says I ought to have wished for something. She does not want to live any longer in the hovel, and would rather have a cottage." "Go home with you," said the flounder, "she has it already."

So the man went home, and found, instead of the hovel, a little cottage, and his wife was sitting on a bench before the door. And she took him by the hand, and said to him, "Come in and see if this is not a great improvement."

So they went in, and there was a little house-place and a beautiful little bed-room, a kitchen and larder, with all sorts of furniture, and iron and brass ware of the very best. And at the back was a little yard with fowls and ducks, and a little garden full of green vegetables and fruit.

"Look," said the wife, "is not that nice?" "Yes," said the man, "if this can only last we shall be very well contented." "We will see about that," said the wife. And after a meal they went to bed.

So all went well for a week or fortnight, when the wife said, "Look here, husband, the cottage is really too confined, and the yard and garden are so small; I think the flounder had better get us a larger house; I should like very much to live in a large stone castle; so go to your fish and he will send us a castle."

"Oh my dear wife," said the man, "the cottage is good enough;

what do we want a castle for?" "We want one," said the wife; "go along with you; the flounder can give us one."

"Now, wife," said the man, "the flounder gave us the cottage; I do not like to go to him again, he may be angry." "Go along," said the wife, "he might just as well give us it as not; do as I say!"

The man felt very reluctant and unwilling; and he said to himself, "It is not the right thing to do"; nevertheless he went.

So when he came to the sea-side, the water was purple and dark blue and gray and thick, and not green and yellow as before. And he stood and said,

> *"O man, O man!—if man you be,*
> *Or flounder, flounder, in the sea—*
> *Such a tiresome wife I've got,*
> *For she wants what I do not."*

"Now then, what does she want?" said the flounder.

"Oh," said the man, half frightened, "she wants to live in a large stone castle." "Go home with you, she is already standing before the door," said the flounder.

Then the man went home, as he supposed, but when he got there, there stood in the place of the cottage a great castle of stone, and his wife was standing on the steps, about to go in; so she took him by the hand, and said, "Let us enter."

With that he went in with her, and in the castle was a great hall with a marble pavement, and there were a great many servants, who led them through large doors, and the passages were decked with tapestry, and the rooms with golden chairs and tables, and crystal chandeliers hanging from the ceiling; and all the rooms had carpets. And the tables were covered with eatables and the best wine for any one who wanted them. And at the back of the house was a great stable-yard for horses and cattle, and carriages of the finest; besides, there was a splendid large garden, with the most beautiful flowers and fine fruit trees, and a pleasance full half a mile long, with deer and oxen and sheep, and everything that heart could wish for.

"There!" said the wife, "is not this beautiful?" "Oh yes," said the man, "if it will only last we can live in this fine castle and be very well contented." "We will see about that," said the wife, "in the meanwhile we will sleep upon it." With that they went to bed.

The next morning the wife was awake first, just at the break of day, and she looked out and saw from her bed the beautiful country lying all round. The man took no notice of it, so she poked him in the side with her elbow, and said, "Husband, get up and just look out of the window. Look, just think if we could be King over all this country! Just go to your fish and tell him we should like to be King."

"Now, wife," said the man, "what should we be Kings for? I don't want to be King." "Well," said the wife, "if you don't want to be King, I will be King."

"Now, wife," said the man, "what do you want to be King for? I could not ask him such a thing." "Why not?" said the wife, "you must go directly all the same; I must be King."

So the man went, very much put out that his wife should want to be King.

"It is not the right thing to do—not at all the right thing," thought the man. He did not at all want to go, and yet he went all the same.

And when he came to the sea the water was quite dark gray, and rushed far inland, and had an ill smell. And he stood and said,

> *"O man, O man!—if man you be,*
> *Or flounder, flounder, in the sea—*
> *Such a tiresome wife I've got,*
> *For she wants what I do not."*

"Now then, what does she want?" said the fish. "Oh dear!" said the man, "she wants to be King." "Go home with you, she is King already," said the fish.

So the man went back, and as he came to the palace he saw it was very much larger, and had great towers and splendid gateways; the herald stood before the door, and a number of soldiers with kettle-drums and trumpets.

And when he came inside everything was of marble and gold, and there were many curtains with great golden tassels. Then he went through the doors of the saloon to where the great throne-room was, and there was his wife sitting upon a throne of gold and diamonds, and she had a great golden crown on, and the scepter in her hand was of pure gold and jewels, and on each side stood six pages in a row, each one a head shorter than the other. So the man went up to her and said, "Well, wife, so now you are King!" "Yes," said the wife, "now I am King."

So then he stood and looked at her, and when he had gazed at her for some time he said, "Well, wife, this is fine for you to be King! Now there is nothing more to wish for." "Oh husband!" said the wife, seeming quite restless, "I am tired of this already. Go to your fish and tell him that now I am King I must be Emperor."

"Now, wife," said the man, "what do you want to be Emperor for?" "Husband," said she, "go and tell the fish I want to be Emperor."

"Oh dear!" said the man, "he could not do it—I cannot ask him such a thing. There is but one Emperor at a time; the fish can't possibly make any one Emperor—indeed he can't."

"Now, look here," said the wife, "I am King, and you are only my husband, so will you go at once? Go along! for if he was able to make me King he is able to make me Emperor; and I will and must be Emperor, so go along!"

So he was obliged to go; and as he went he felt very uncomfortable about it, and he thought to himself, "It is not at all the right thing to do; to want to be Emperor is really going too far; the flounder will soon be beginning to get tired of this."

With that he came to the sea, and the water was quite black and thick, and the foam flew, and the wind blew, and the man was terrified. But he stood and said,

> *"O man, O man!—if man you be,*
> *Or flounder, flounder, in the sea—*
> *Such a tiresome wife I've got,*
> *For she wants what I do not."*

"What is it now?" said the fish. "Oh dear!" said the man, "my wife wants to be Emperor." "Go home with you," said the fish, "she is Emperor already."

So the man went home, and found the castle adorned with polished marble and alabaster figures, and golden gates. The troops were being marshaled before the door, and they were blowing trumpets and beating drums and cymbals; and when he entered he saw barons and earls and dukes waiting about like servants; and the doors were of bright gold. And he saw his wife sitting upon a throne made of one entire piece of gold, and it was about two miles high; and she had a great golden crown on, which was about three yards high, set with brilliants and carbuncles; and in one hand she held the scepter, and in the other the globe; and on both sides of her stood pages in two rows, all arranged according to their size, from the most enormous giant of two miles high to the tiniest dwarf of the size of my little finger; and before her stood earls and dukes in crowds.

So the man went up to her and said, "Well, wife, so now you are Emperor." "Yes," said she, "now I am Emperor."

Then he went and sat down and had a good look at her, and then he said, "Well now, wife, there is nothing left to be, now you are Emperor." "What are you talking about, husband?" said she; "I am Emperor, and next I will be Pope! so go and tell the fish so."

"Oh dear!" said the man, "what is it that you don't want? You can never become Pope; there is but one Pope in Christendom, and the fish can't possibly do it." "Husband," said she, "no more words about it; I must and will be Pope; so go along to the fish."

"Now, wife," said the man, "how can I ask him such a thing? It is too bad—it is asking a little too much; and, besides, he could not do it." "What rubbish!" said the wife; "if he could make me Emperor he can make me Pope. Go along and ask him; I am Emperor, and you are only my husband, so go you must."

So he went, feeling very frightened, and he shivered and shook, and his knees trembled; and there arose a great wind, and the clouds flew by, and it grew very dark, and the sea rose mountains high, and the ships were tossed about, and the sky was partly blue in the middle, but at the sides very dark and red, as in a great tempest. And he felt very despondent, and stood trembling and said,

> *"O man, O man!—if man you be,*
> *Or flounder, flounder, in the sea—*
> *Such a tiresome wife I've got,*
> *For she wants what I do not."*

"Well, what now?" said the fish. "Oh dear!" said the man, "she wants to be Pope." "Go home with you, she is Pope already," said the fish.

So he went home, and he found himself before a great church, with palaces all round. He had to make his way through a crowd of people; and when he got inside he found the place lighted up with thousands and thousands of lights; and his wife was clothed in a golden garment, and sat upon a very high throne, and had three golden crowns on, all in the greatest priestly pomp; and on both sides of her there stood two rows of lights of all sizes—from the size of the longest tower to the smallest rushlight, and all the Emperors and Kings were kneeling before her and kissing her foot.

"Well, wife," said the man, and sat and stared at her, "so you are Pope." "Yes," said she, "now I am Pope!"

And he went on gazing at her till he felt dazzled, as if he were sitting in the sun. And after a little time he said, "Well, now, wife, what is there left to be, now you are Pope?" And she sat up very stiff and straight, and said nothing.

And he said again, "Well, wife, I hope you are contented at last with being Pope; you can be nothing more."

"We will see about that," said the wife. With that they both went to bed; but she was as far as ever from being contented, and she could not get to sleep for thinking of what she should like to be next.

The husband, however, slept as fast as a top after his busy day; but the wife tossed and turned from side to side the whole night through, thinking all the while what she could be next, but nothing would occur to her; and when she saw the red dawn she slipped off the bed, and sat before the window to see the sun rise, and as it came up she said, "Ah, I have it! Cannot I make the sun and moon to rise? Husband!" she cried, and stuck her elbow in his ribs, "wake up, and go to your fish, and tell him I want to be God."

The man was so fast asleep that when he started up he fell out of bed. Then he shook himself together, and opened his eyes and said, "Oh wife, what did you say?"

"Husband," said she, "if I cannot get the power of making the sun and moon rise when I want them, I shall never have another quiet hour. Go to the fish and tell him so."

"Oh wife!" said the man, and fell on his knees to her, "the fish can really not do that for you. I grant you he could make you Emperor and Pope. Do be contented with that, I beg of you."

And she became wild with impatience, and screamed out, "I can wait no longer, go at once! I want to be God!"

And so off he went as well as he could for fright. And a dreadful storm arose, so that he could hardly keep his feet; and the houses and trees were blown down, and the mountains trembled, and rocks fell in the sea; the sky was quite black, and it thundered and lightninged; and the waves, crowned with foam, ran mountains high. So he cried out, without being able to hear his own words,

> *"O man, O man!—if man you be,*
> *Or flounder, flounder, in the sea—*
> *Such a tiresome wife I've got,*
> *For she wants what I do not."*

"Well, what now?" said the flounder.

"Oh dear!" said the man, "she wants to be God!" "Go home with you!" said the flounder, "you will find her the way she was—in the old hovel."

And there they are sitting to this very day.

The Good Bargain

A PEASANT had led his cow to the market and sold her for seven dollars. On his way home he had to pass a pond, but long before he reached it he could hear the frogs crying "Akt! akt! akt! akt!"*

"Yes, I hear you," he said, "screaming out in your snug quarters; but it's seven I have received, not eight" As soon as he reached the water he exclaimed: "Stupid creatures that you are, don't you know better? Seven dollars are not eight dollars."

The frogs, taking no heed, continued to cry "Akt! akt! akt!"

"Now," said the peasant, "if you do not believe me, I can count it out to you"; and he took the money out of his pocket and counted out his seven dollars in groschen.

The frogs cared nothing for the peasant's reckoning, but went on croaking "Akt! akt! akt! akt!"

"Oh!" cried the peasant in a rage, "do you know better how to count than I do?" and he threw the money into the water right in the midst of them. Then he stood and waited till they were ready to return his property to him, but the frogs were constant to their first opinion and screamed out still louder, "Akt! akt! akt! akt!" and did not attempt to throw the money back again to him.

He waited for a good while till evening came on, and he knew he must go home. Then he abused the frogs, and cried, "You water plashers! you thick heads! you blind eyes! With your great jaws, you can scream enough to split one's ears, but you cannot count seven dollars; and do you think I am going to stay here and wait till you are ready? "Then he walked away very fast, but he heard the frogs still croaking "Akt! akt!" for a long distance, and he arrived home quite out of humor.

After a time he bought another cow, which he slaughtered, and while reckoning how much he should get by the sale of the flesh, as well as the skin, he hoped to make a good bargain with profits, even with the loss caused by the obstinacy of the frogs.

So he started off to the town to sell his dead cow, but on arriving at the butcher's stall he saw a pack of hounds, who all surrounded him, barking and smelling at the meat. "Was! was!"* they cried.

* The word "acht" is German for eight.
* The German "was" is translated "what." It is used instead of "bow-wow" for the bark of a dog.

"Ah, yes!" said the peasant, "it is all very well to say, 'What? what?' as if you wanted to know what I have got here, and you know it is meat all the while."

There was no one to watch the butcher's shop but a large house dog, and the countryman had often heard his master say how true and faithful he was. So he said to him, "If I leave this meat here, will you answer for these friends of yours that it shan't be touched?" "Was! was!" cried the dog; while the others barked "Was! was!" and sprang at the meat.

"Oh, well!" said the peasant to the butcher's dog, "as you have promised, I will leave the meat for your master to sell; but, remember, I must have the money in three days, and if he doesn't send it, I shall come for it." Thereupon he laid the meat down on the counter, and turned to go. The dogs all ran round it barking "Was! was!" and the peasant heard them for a long distance. "Ah!" he said, "they are all longing for a piece; but it's all right, the big one is answerable for them."

Three days passed, and the countryman made himself quite comfortable in the thought of what he was to receive. "I shall have plenty of money in my pocket by tomorrow evening," he said in a contented tone.

But the morrow came, and no money. He waited two days and then said, "I can't stand this; I must go and demand my money." The butcher at first thought he was talking about a sparrow.

"Sparrow, indeed!" replied the peasant. "I want my money for the meat I left under the care of your great dog three days ago—the flesh of a whole cow."

At this the butcher flew in a rage, and seizing a broom, laid it over the peasant's shoulders and drove him out of the shop.

"Just wait," cried the peasant; "there is some justice after all left in the world." And away he went to the castle, where, as it happened on that day, the King himself sat as chief magistrate, with his daughter by his side.

"What is your trouble?" asked the King. "Alas! Your Majesty," he replied, "the frogs and the dogs have taken all I possess, and when I asked the butcher for my money, he beat me with a broomstick." And then he related in a confused manner all that had occurred.

On hearing the countryman's story, the King's daughter burst into a fit of laughter, and laughed so loudly that for some minutes the King could not speak. At length he said, "I cannot restore to you the money you have lost, but I can give you my daughter in marriage. She has never during her whole life laughed till now. I long ago promised her as a wife to the first man who could make her laugh, and you are that man, so you may thank Heaven for your good fortune."

"Ah, my lord King!" replied the peasant, "I cannot marry the Princess; I have one wife at home already, and she is quite too much for me to manage; there is no room for another in our chimney corner."

Then was the King angry, and said, "You are a rude clown!" "Ah, my lord King!" he replied, "what can you expect from a pig but a grunt?" and he turned to go.

"Stay!" cried the King, calling him back; "I mean you to have some reward after all. Five hundred times as much as you have lost shall be ready for you if you come here again in three days."

The peasant looked so joyful as he passed out after hearing this that the sentinel asked him the cause. "You have made the Princess laugh, I hear. What reward are you to have?" "Five hundred dollars," he replied.

"Why, what will you do with all that money?" asked the sentinel. "You may as well give me some." "I will, if you like," he said; "and if you will go with me to the King in three days, he shall pay you two hundred dollars instead of me"; and away he went.

A Jew, who was standing near, overheard this promise, and running after the peasant, pulled him by the sleeve, and said, "You are a lucky fellow, friend, to have all that money promised you, but you must wait three days for it; would you not like to receive it at once, cash down?" "I should, indeed," replied the peasant. "How can it be managed?" "Oh, very easily! You shall give me an order to receive the three hundred dollars, and I will pay you the amount in silver and small coin."

So the bill of exchange was drawn, and the money paid; but the Jew charged such enormous interest, and some of the coins were so bad, that the peasant did not get much, after all.

At the end of three days the peasant went to the King, according to his command. "You must open your pockets very wide to receive all these dollars," said the King.

"Ah, no!" cried the peasant, "they do not belong to me. Two hundred I have promised to the sentinel, and I have given a Jew a bill to receive three hundred, as he gave me cash for it, so that I have justly nothing to receive." While he spoke in came the soldier and the Jew, who demanded what they had obtained from the peasant, and persisted that the money was justly theirs.

At first the King could not help laughing at the countryman's folly, and then he became angry at the conduct of the Jew and the soldier. "So," he said to the peasant, "as you have been so foolish as to give up your money, before it even belonged to you, to strangers, I suppose I must make you some compensation. Go into that room opposite, and help yourself to as much money as your pockets will hold." The countryman did not require to be told twice; he went, as he was told, and filled his wide pockets to overflowing.

Away he started to the inn to count his money, and the Jew sneaked after him and heard him talking to himself. "Now, if I had been a knave and hidden all this from the King, he would never have allowed me to take this money. I wish I knew how much I had. Oh, if the King had only told me what amount I was to take. I'm so afraid I may have taken more than I ought."

"Ah! ah!" muttered the Jew, "he is grumbling even now, and speaking disrespectfully of my lord the King. Catch me quarreling with such a sum of money because I couldn't count it."

The Jew had spoken loud enough for the King to hear, and he called him, and desired him to fetch the ungrateful man again before His Majesty. "You must appear before the King immediately!" cried the Jew. "There must be no excuse."

"Indeed, I cannot," he replied. "Whoever heard of a man with such a heap of gold in his pockets as I have, going before the King in such a ragged coat as this?"

The Jew, seeing that the peasant was determined, and fearing that the wrath of the King would cool, promised to lend him a coat, which was very good and nearly new. "I lend it you for true friendship's sake," he said; "and that is seldom done in the world."

So the peasant put it on and went into the King's presence. But when the King repeated what he had been told by the Jew, the peasant exclaimed, "Your Majesty, it is all false; there is never a true word out of that Jew's mouth. I dare say he will affirm that the coat I have on belongs to him."

"What do you mean?" screamed the Jew. "You know it is my coat! I lent it you out of pure friendship, that you might appear before the King!"

"Yes, of course, to hear your lies about me, and get punished by having the money taken from me," replied the peasant. Then he repeated what he had really said at the inn; and the King dismissed them both, saying that the Jew's word was evidently not to be taken, and therefore the countryman might keep the coat as his own as some recompense for the Jew's false accusation.

The peasant went home joyfully to count the gold in his pockets, and said to himself, "This time, at least, I have made a good bargain."

Prudent Hans

ONE DAY, Hans's mother said, "Where are you going, Hans?" Hans answered, "To Gretel's, mother."

"Manage well, Hans."

"All right! Good-bye, mother."

"Good-bye, Hans."

Then Hans came to Gretel's.

"Good morning, Gretel."

"Good morning, Hans. What have you brought me today?"

"I have brought nothing, but I want something."

So Gretel gave Hans a needle; and then he said, "Good-bye, Gretel," and she said, "Good-bye, Hans."

Hans carried the needle away with him, and stuck it in a hay-cart that was going along, and he followed it home.

"Good evening, mother."

"Good evening, Hans. Where have you been?"

"To Gretel's, mother."

"What did you take her?"

"I took nothing, but I brought away something."

"What did Gretel give you?"

"A needle, mother."

"What did you do with it, Hans?"

"Stuck it in the hay-cart."

"That was very stupid of you, Hans. You should have stuck it in your sleeve."

"All right, mother! I'll do better next time."

When next time came, Hans's mother said, "Where are you going, Hans?"

"To Gretel's, mother."

"Manage well, Hans."

"All right. Good-bye, mother."

"Good-bye, Hans."

Then Hans came to Gretel.

"Good morning, Gretel."

"Good morning, Hans. What have you brought me today?"

"I've brought nothing, but I want something."

So Gretel gave Hans a knife, and then he said, "Good-bye, Gretel," and she said, "Good-bye, Hans."

Hans took the knife away with him, and stuck it in his sleeve, and went home.

"Good evening, mother."

"Good evening, Hans. Where have you been?"

"To Gretel's."

"What did you take her?"

"I took nothing, but I brought away something."

"What did Gretel give you, Hans?"

"A knife, mother."

"What did you do with it, Hans?"

"Stuck it in my sleeve, mother."

"That was very stupid of you, Hans. You should have put it in your pocket."

"All right, mother! I'll do better next time."

When next time came, Hans's mother said, "Where to, Hans?"

"To Gretel's, mother."

"Manage well, Hans."

"All right! Good-bye, mother."

"Good-bye, Hans."

So Hans came to Gretel's.

"Good morning, Gretel."

"Good morning, Hans. What have you brought me today?"

"I've brought nothing, but I want to take away something."

So Gretel gave Hans a young goat; then he said, "Good-bye, Gretel," and she said, "Good-bye, Hans."

So Hans carried off the goat, and tied its legs together, and put it in his pocket, and by the time he got home it was suffocated.

"Good evening, mother."

"Good evening, Hans. Where have you been?"

"To Gretel's mother."

"What did you take her, Hans?"

"I took nothing, but I brought away something."

"What did Gretel give you, Hans?"

"A goat, mother."

"What did you do with it, Hans?"

"Put it in my pocket, mother."

"That was very stupid of you, Hans. You should have tied a cord round its neck, and led it home."

"All right, mother! I'll do better next time."

Then when next time came, "Where to, Hans?"

"To Gretel's, mother."

"Manage well, Hans."

"All right! Good-bye, mother."

"Good-bye, Hans."

Then Hans came to Gretel's.

"Good morning, Gretel."

"Good morning, Hans. What have you brought me today?"

"I've brought nothing, but I want to take away something."

So Gretel gave Hans a piece of bacon; then he said, "Good-bye, Gretel."

She said, "Good-bye, Hans."

Hans took the bacon, and tied a string round it, and dragged it after him on his way home, and the dogs came and ate it up, so that when he got home he had the string in his hand, and nothing at the other end of it.

"Good evening, mother."

"Good evening, Hans. Where have you been?"

"To Gretel's, mother."

"What did you take her, Hans?"

"I took her nothing, but I brought away something."

"What did Gretel give you, Hans?"

"A piece of bacon, mother."

"What did you do with it, Hans?"

"I tied a piece of string to it, and led it home, but the dogs ate it, mother."

"That was very stupid of you, Hans. You ought to have carried it on your head."

"All right! I'll do better next time, mother."

When next time came, "Where to, Hans?"

"To Gretel's, mother."

"Manage well, Hans."

"All right! Good-bye, mother."

"Good-bye, Hans."

Then Hans came to Gretel's."

"Good morning, Gretel."

"Good morning, Hans. What have you brought me?"

"I have brought nothing, but I want to take away something."

So Gretel gave Hans a calf.

"Good-bye, Gretel."

"Good-bye, Hans."

Hans took the calf, and set it on his head, and carried it home, and the calf scratched his face.

"Good evening, mother."

"Good evening, Hans. Where have you been?"

"To Gretel's, mother."

"What did you take her?"

"I took nothing, but I brought away something."

"What did Gretel give you, Hans?"

"A calf, mother."

"What did you do with the calf, Hans?"

"I carried it home on my head, but it scratched my face."

"That was very stupid of you, Hans. You ought to have led home the calf, and tied it to the manger."

"All right! I'll do better next time, mother."

"When next time came, "Where to, Hans?"

"To Gretel's, mother."

"Manage well, Hans."

"All right, mother! Good-bye."

"Good-bye, Hans."

Then Hans came to Gretel's.

"Good morning, Gretel."

"Good morning, Hans. What have you brought me today?"

"I have brought nothing, but I want to take away something."

"Then Gretel said to Hans, "You shall take away me."

Then Hans took Gretel, and tied a rope round her neck, and led her home, and fastened her up to the manger, and went to his mother.

"Good evening, mother."

"Good evening, Hans. Where have you been?"

"To Gretel's, mother."

"What did you take her, Hans?"

"Nothing, mother."

"What did Gretel give you, Hans?"

"Nothing but herself, mother."

"Where have you left Gretel, Hans?"

"I led her home with a rope, and tied her up to the manger to eat hay, mother."

"That was very stupid of you, Hans. You should have cast sheep's eyes at her."

"All right, mother! I'll do better next time."

Then Hans went into the stable, and taking all the eyes out of the sheep, he threw them in Gretel's face. Then Gretel was angry, and getting loose, she ran away and became the bride of another.

Hans in Luck

HANS HAD SERVED his master seven years, and at the end of the seventh year he said, "Master, my time is up; I want to go home and see my mother, so give me my wages."

"You have served me truly and faithfully," said the master; "as the service is, so must the wages be," and he gave him a lump of gold as big as his head. Hans pulled his handkerchief out of his pocket and tied up the lump of gold in it, hoisted it on his shoulder, and set off on his way home. And as he was trudging along, there came in sight a man riding on a spirited horse, and looking very gay and lively. "Oh!" cried Hans aloud, "how splendid riding must be! Sitting as much at one's ease as in an arm-chair, stumbling over no stones, saving one's shoes, and getting on one hardly knows how!"

The horseman heard Hans say this, and called out to him, "Well Hans, what are you doing on foot?" "I can't help myself," said Hans, "I have this great lump to carry; to be sure, it is gold, but then I can't hold my head straight for it, and it hurts my shoulder." "I'll tell you what," said the horseman, "we will change; I will give you my horse, and you shall give me your lump of gold." "With all my heart," said Hans; "but I warn you, you will find it heavy." And the horseman got down, took the gold, and, helping Hans up, he gave the reins into his hand. "When you want to go fast," said he, "you must click your tongue and cry 'Gee-up!'"

And Hans, as he sat upon his horse, was glad at heart, and rode off with merry cheer. After a while he thought he should like to go quicker, so he began to click with his tongue and to cry "Gee-up!" And the horse began to trot, and Hans was thrown before he knew what was going to happen, and there he lay in the ditch by the side of the road. The horse would have got away but that he was caught by a peasant who was passing that way and driving a cow before him. And Hans pulled himself together and got upon his feet, feeling very vexed. "Poor work, riding," said he, "especially on a jade like this, who starts off and throws you before you know where you are, going near to break your neck; never shall I try that game again; now, your cow is something worth having, one can jog on comfortably after her and have her milk, butter, and cheese every day, into the bargain. What would I not give to have such a cow!"

"Well now," said the peasant, "since it will be doing you such a favor, I don't mind exchanging my cow for your horse."

Hans agreed most joyfully, and the peasant, swinging himself into the saddle, was soon out of sight.

And Hans went along driving his cow quietly before him, and thinking all the while of the fine bargain he had made.

"With only a piece of bread I shall have everything I can possibly want, for I shall always be able to have butter and cheese to it, and if I am thirsty I have nothing to do but to milk my cow; and what more is there for heart to wish!"

And when he came to an inn he made a halt, and in the joy of his heart ate up all the food he had brought with him, dinner and supper and all, and bought half a glass of beer with his last two pennies. Then on he went again driving his cow, until he should come to the village where his mother lived. It was now near the middle of the day, and the sun grew hotter and hotter, and Hans found himself on a heath which it would be an hour's journey to cross. And he began to feel very hot, and so thirsty that his tongue clove to the roof of his mouth.

"Never mind," said Hans; "I can find a remedy. I will milk my cow at once." And tying her to a dry tree, and taking off his leather cap to serve for a pail, he began to milk, but not a drop came. And as he set to work rather awkwardly, the impatient beast gave him such a kick on the head with his hind foot that he fell to the ground, and for some time could not think where he was; when luckily there came by a butcher who was wheeling along a young pig in a wheelbarrow.

"Here's a fine piece of work!" cried he, helping poor Hans on his legs again. Then Hans related to him all that had happened; and the butcher handed him his pocket flask, saying, "Here, take a drink, and be a man again; of course the cow would give no milk; she is old and only fit to draw burdens, or to be slaughtered."

"Well, to be sure," said Hans, scratching his head. "Who would have thought it? Of course it is a very handy way of getting meat when a man has a beast of his own to kill; but for my part I do not care much about cow beef, it is rather tasteless. Now, if I had but a young pig, that is much better meat, and then the sausages!"

"Look here, Hans," said the butcher, "just for love of you I will exchange, and will give you my pig instead of your cow." "Heaven reward such kindness!" cried Hans, and handing over the cow, received in exchange the pig, who was turned out of his wheelbarrow and was to be led by a string.

So on went Hans, thinking how everything turned out according to his wishes, and how, if trouble overtook him, all was sure to be set right directly. After a while he fell in with a peasant, who was carrying a fine white goose under his arm. They bid each other good-day, and Hans began to tell about his luck, and how he had made so many good exchanges. And the peasant told how he was taking the goose to a christening feast.

"Just feel how heavy it is," said he, taking it up by the wings; "it has been fattening for the last eight weeks; and when it is roasted, won't the fat run down!" "Yes, indeed," said Hans, weighing it in his hand, "very fine to be sure; but my pig is not to be despised."

Upon which the peasant glanced cautiously on all sides, and shook his head. "I am afraid," said he, "that there is something not quite right about your pig. In the village I have just left one had actually been stolen from the bailiff's yard. I fear—I fear you have it in your hand; they have sent after the thief, and it would be a bad look-out for you if it were found upon you; the least that could happen would be to be thrown into a dark hole."

Poor Hans grew pale with fright. "For heaven's sake," said he, "help me out of this scrape; I am a stranger in these parts; take my pig and give me your goose." "It will be running some risk," answered the man, "but I will do it sooner than that you should come to grief."

And so, taking the cord in his hand, he drove the pig quickly along a by-path, and lucky Hans went on his way home with the goose under his arm. "The more I think of it," said he to himself, "the better the bargain seems; first I get the roast goose, then the fat; that will last a whole year for bread and dripping; and lastly the beautiful white feathers which I can stuff my pillow with; how comfortably I shall sleep upon it, and how pleased my mother will be!"

And when he reached the last village, he saw a knife-grinder with his barrow; and his wheel went whirring round, and he sang,

"My scissors I grind, and my wheel I turn;
And all good fellows my trade should learn,
For all that I meet with just serves my turn."

And Hans stood and looked at him; and at last he spoke to him and said, "You seem very well off, and merry with your grinding."

"Yes," answered the knife-grinder, "my handiwork pays very well. I call a man a good grinder who every time he puts his hand in his pocket finds money there. But where did you buy that fine goose?" "I did not buy it, but I exchanged it for my pig," said Hans. "And the pig?" "That I exchange for a cow." "And the cow?" "That I exchanged for a horse." "And the horse?" "I gave for the horse a lump of gold as big as my head." "And the gold?" "Oh, that was my wage for seven years' service."

"You seem to have fended for yourself very well," said the knife-grinder. "Now, if you could but manage to have money in your pocket every time you put your hand in, your fortune is made." "How shall I manage that?" said Hans.

"You must be a knife-grinder like me," said the man. "All you want is a grindstone, the rest comes of itself. I have one here; to be sure it is a little damaged, but I don't mind letting you have it in exchange for your goose; what say you?"

"How can you ask?" answered Hans. "I shall be the luckiest fellow in the world, for if I find money whenever I put my hand in my pocket, there is nothing more left to want."

And so he handed over the goose to the peddler and received the grindstone in exchange.

"Now," said the knife-grinder, taking up a heavy common stone that lay near him, "here is another proper sort of stone that will stand a good deal of wear and that you can hammer out your old nails upon. Take it with you, and carry it carefully."

Hans lifted up the stone and carried it off with a contented mind. "I must have been born under a lucky star!" cried he, while his eyes sparkled for joy. "I have only to wish for a thing and it is mine."

After a while he began to feel rather tired, as indeed he had been on his legs since daybreak; he also began to feel rather hungry, as in the fullness of his joy at getting the cow, he had eaten up all he had. At last he could scarcely go on at all, and had to make a halt every moment, for the stones weighed him down most unmercifully, and he could not help wishing that he did not feel obliged to drag them along. And on he went at a snail's pace until he came to a well; then he thought he would rest and take a drink of the fresh water. And he placed the stones carefully by his side at the edge of the well; then he sat down, and as he stopped to drink, he happened to give the stones a little push, and they both fell into the water with a splash. And then Hans, having watched them disappear, jumped for joy, and thanked his stars that he had been so lucky as to get rid of the stones that had weighed upon him so long without any effort of his own.

"I really think," cried he, "I am the luckiest man under the sun." So on he went, void of care, until he reached his mother's house.

Clever Else

THERE WAS once a man who had a daughter who was called "Clever Else," and when she was grown up, her father said she must be married, and her mother said, "Yes, if we could only find some one that she would consent to have."

At last one came from a distance, and his name was Hans, and when he proposed to her, he made it a condition that Clever Else should be very careful as well.

"Oh," said the father, "she does not want for brains."

"No, indeed," said the mother, "she can see the wind coming up the street and hear the flies cough."

"Well," said Hans, "if she does not turn out to be careful too, I will not have her."

Now when they were all seated at table, and had well eaten, the mother said, "Else, go into the cellar and draw some beer."

Then Clever Else took down the jug from the hook in the wall, and as she was on her way to the cellar she rattled the lid up and down so as to pass away the time. When she got there, she took a stool and stood it in front of the cask, so that she need not stoop and make her back ache with needless trouble. Then she put the jug under the tap and turned it, and while the beer was running, in order that her eyes should not be idle, she glanced hither and thither, and finally caught sight of a pickaxe that the workmen had left sticking in the ceiling just above her head.

Then Clever Else began to cry, for she thought, "If I marry Hans, and we have a child, and it grows big, and we send it into the cellar to draw beer, that pickaxe might fall on his head and kill him." So there she sat and cried with all her might, lamenting the anticipated misfortune.

All the while they were waiting upstairs for something to drink, and they waited in vain. At last the mistress said to the maid, "Go down to the cellar and see why Else does not come."

So the maid went, and found her sitting in front of the cask crying with all her might. "What are you crying for?" said the maid.

"Oh dear me," answered she, "how can I help crying? If I marry Hans, and we have a child, and it grows big, and we send it here to draw beer, perhaps the pickaxe may fall on its head and kill it." "Our Else is clever indeed!" said the maid, and directly sat down to bewail the anticipated misfortune.

After a while, when the people upstairs found that the maid did not return, and they were becoming more and more thirsty, the master said to the boy, "You go down into the cellar, and see what Else and the maid are doing."

The boy did so, and there he found both Clever Else and the maid sitting crying together. Then he asked what was the matter. "Oh dear me," said Else, "how can we help crying? If I marry Hans, and we have a child, and it grows big, and we send it here to draw beer, the pickaxe might fall on its head and kill it." "Our Else is clever indeed!" said the boy, and sitting down beside her, he began howling with a good will.

Upstairs they were all waiting for him to come back, but as he did not come, the master said to the mistress, "You go down to the cellar and see what Else is doing."

So the mistress went down and found all three in great lamentations, and when she asked the cause, then Else told her how the future possible child might be killed as soon as it was big enough to be sent to draw beer, by the pickaxe falling on it. Then the mother at once exclaimed, "Our Else is clever indeed!" and, sitting down, she wept with the rest.

Upstairs the husband waited a little while, but as his wife did not return, and as his thirst constantly increased, he said, "I must go down to the cellar myself, and see what has become of Else."

And when he came into the cellar, and found them all sitting and weeping together, he was told that it was all owing to the child that Else might possibly have, and the possibility of its being killed by the pickaxe so happening to fall just at the time the child might be sitting underneath it drawing beer; and when he heard all this, he cried, "How clever is our Else!" and sitting down, he joined his tears to theirs.

The intended bridegroom stayed upstairs by himself a long time, but as nobody came back to him, he thought he would go himself

and see what they were all about. And there he found all five
lamenting and crying most pitifully, each one louder than the
other. "What misfortune has happened?" cried he.

"O my dear Hans," said Else, "if we marry and have a child, and
it grows big, and we send it down here to draw beer, perhaps that
pickaxe which has been left sticking up there might fall down on
the child's head and kill it; and how can we help crying at that!"

"Now," said Hans, "I cannot think that greater sense than that
could be wanted in my household; so as you are so clever, Else, I
will have you for my wife," and taking her by the hand he led her
upstairs, and they had the wedding at once.

A little while after they were married, Hans said to his wife, "I
am going out to work, in order to get money; you go into the field
and cut the corn, so that we may have bread." "Very well, I will do
so, dear Hans," said she.

And after Hans was gone she cooked herself some nice stew, and
took it with her into the field. And when she got there, she said to
herself, "Now, what shall I do? Shall I reap first, or eat first? All
right, I will eat first." Then she ate her fill of stew, and when she
could eat no more, she said to herself, "Now, what shall I do? Shall I
reap first, or sleep first? All right, I will sleep first." Then she lay
down in the corn and went to sleep.

And Hans got home, and waited there a long while, and Else did
not come, so he said to himself, "My Clever Else is so industrious
that she never thinks of coming home and eating."

But when evening drew near and still she did not come, Hans set
out to see how much corn she had cut; but she had cut no corn at
all, but there she was lying in it asleep. Then Hans made haste
home, and fetched a bird-net with little bells and threw it over her;
and still she went on sleeping. And he ran home again and locked
himself in, and sat him down on his bench to work.

At last, when it was beginning to grow dark, Clever Else woke,
and when she got up and shook herself, the bells jingled at each
movement that she made. Then she grew frightened, and began to
doubt whether she were really Clever Else or not, and said to
herself, "Am I, or am I not?" And, not knowing what answer
to make, she stood for a long while considering; at last she thought,
"I will go home to Hans and ask him if I am or not; he is sure to
know."

So she ran up to the door of her house, but it was locked; then she
knocked at the window, and cried, "Hans, is Else within?" "Yes,"
answered Hans, "she is in."

Then she was in a greater fright than ever, and crying, "Oh dear, then I am not I," she went to inquire at another door, but the people hearing the jingling of the bells would not open to her, and she could get in nowhere. So she ran beyond the village, and since then no one has seen her.

Hans Married

THERE WAS once a young country chap called Hans, whose Uncle wanted very much to marry him to a rich wife, so he set him beside the oven and let a good fire be lighted. Then he fetched a jug of milk and a large piece of white bread, and gave Hans a shining newly-coined penny, saying, "Hans, keep this penny safely, and break your white bread into this milk; and mind you stop here, and do not stir from your stool till I return."

"Yes," said Hans, "I will faithfully do all you require."

Then the Uncle went and drew on a pair of old spotted breeches, and, walking to the next village, called on a rich farmer's daughter, and asked her whether she would marry his nephew Hans, assuring her that he was a prudent and clever young man, who could not fail to please her. The girl's covetous father, however, asked, "How is he situated with regard to property? Has he the wherewithal to live?"

"My dear friend," said the Uncle, "my nephew is a warm youth, and has not only a nice penny in hand, but plenty to eat and drink. He can count too, quite as many specks" (meaning money) "as I"; and as he spoke, he slapped his hand upon his spotted breeches. "Will you," he continued, "take the trouble to go with me, and in an hour's time you shall see everything as I have said?"

The offer appeared so advantageous to the covetous farmer that he would not let it slip, and therefore said, "If it is so, I have nothing more to say against the wedding."

So the ceremony was performed on an appointed day, and afterwards the young wife wished to go into the fields and view the property of her husband. Hans drew his spotted smock first over his Sunday clothes, saying to his bride, "I do not wish to spoil my best things!" This done, they went together into the fields, and wherever a vine-stock was planted on the road, or the meadows and fields divided, Hans pointed with his finger there, and then laid it on one great spot or another on his smock, and said, "This spot is mine and thine too, my dear! Do just look at it." Hans meant by this, not that his wife should gaze at the broad fields, but that she should look at his smock, which was really his own!

"Did you then go to the wedding?" "Yes! I was there in full toggery. My head-piece was of snow, and there came the sun and melted it; my clothes were of worsted, and I walked through thorns, so that they were torn off; my shoes were of glass, and I stepped upon a stone, and they cracked and fell to pieces."

The Youth Who Could Not Shiver and Shake

A FATHER had two sons. The elder was smart and could do anything. But the younger was so stupid that he could neither learn nor understand a thing, and people would say, "What a burden that stupid boy must be to his father."

Whatever the father wanted done, Jack, the elder boy, was obliged to do, even to take messages, for his brother was too stupid to understand or remember. But Jack was a terrible coward, and if his father wished him to go anywhere late in the evening, and the road led through the churchyard, he would say, "Oh, no, father, I can't go there, it makes me tremble and shake so."

Sometimes when they sat round the fire in the evening, while someone told stories that frightened him, he would say, "Please don't go on, it makes me shake all over."

The younger boy, seated in his corner among the listeners, would open his eyes quite wide and say, "I can't think what he means by saying it makes him shiver and shake. It must be something very wonderful that could make me shiver and shake."

At last one day the father spoke to his younger son very plainly and said, "Listen, you there in the corner; you are growing tall and strong, you must learn very soon to earn your own living. See how your brother works, while you do nothing but run and jump about all day."

"Well, father," he replied, "I am quite ready to earn my own living when you like, if I may only learn to shiver and shake, for I don't know how to do that at all."

His brother laughed at this speech, and said to himself, "What a simpleton my brother is! He will have to sweep the streets by and by or else starve."

His father sighed and said, "You will never get your living by that, boy, but you will soon learn to shiver and shake, no doubt."

Just at this moment the sexton of the church came in, and the father related the trouble he was in about his younger son who was so silly and unable to learn. "What do you think he said to me when I told him he must learn to earn his own living?" asked the father. "Something silly, I suppose," answered the sexton. "Silly, indeed! he said he wished he could learn to shiver and shake." "Oh!" cried the sexton, "let him come to me, I'll soon manage that for him; he won't be long learning to shiver and shake if I have him with me."

The father was delighted with this proposal; it was really a good beginning for his stupid son. So the sexton took the youth in hand at once, led him to the church tower, and made him help ring the bells. For the first two days he liked it very well, but on the third at midnight the sexton roused him out of his sleep to toll the passing bell; he had to mount to the highest part of the church tower. "You will soon learn what it is to shiver and shake now, young man," thought the sexton, but he did not go home, as we shall hear later on.

The youth walked through the churchyard and mounted the steps to the belfry without feeling the least fear, but just as he reached the bell rope, he saw a figure in white standing on the steps. "Who's there?" he cried. But the figure neither moved nor spoke. "Answer me," he said, "or take yourself off; you have no business here."

But the sexton, who had disguised himself to frighten the boy, remained immovable, for he wished to be taken for a ghost, but Hans was not to be frightened. He exclaimed, for the second time, "What do you want here? Speak, if you are an honest man, or I will throw you down the steps."

The sexton, thinking he could not intend to do anything so dreadful, answered not a word, but stood still, as if he were made of stone. "Once more, I ask you what you want," said Hans; and as there was still no answer, he sprung upon the sham ghost, and giving him a push, he rolled down ten steps, and falling into a corner, there remained.

Thereupon Hans went back to the bell, tolled it for the proper number of minutes, then went home, laid himself down without saying a word, and went fast asleep.

The sexton's wife waited a long time for her husband, and finding he did not come home she became alarmed, and going to Hans, woke him and said, "Do you know why my husband is staying out so late—he was with you in the tower I suppose?"

"There was someone dressed in white standing on the top of the steps when I went into the belfry, and as he would not answer a word when I spoke to him, I took him for a thief and kicked him downstairs. We will go and see who it is; if it should be your husband I shall be sorry, but of course I did not know."

The wife ran out to the tower and found her husband lying in a corner groaning, for he had broken his leg. Then she went to the father of Hans with a loud outcry against the boy. "Your son," cried she, "has brought bad luck to the house; he has thrown my husband down the steps and broken his leg; he shan't stay with us any longer, send for him home."

Then the father was terribly vexed, sent for his son, and scolded him. "What do you mean, you wretched boy," he said, "by these wicked tricks?" "Father," answered the boy, "hear what I have to say. I never meant to do wrong, but when I saw a white figure standing there in the night, of course I thought it was there for some bad purpose. I did not know it was the sexton, and I warned him three times what I would do, if he did not answer."

"Ah! yes, you are the plague of my life," said his father. "Now get out of my sight, and never let me see you again." "Yes, father, I will go right willingly tomorrow, and then if I learn to shiver and shake, I shall acquire knowledge that will enable me to earn my living at all events."

"Learn what you like," said his father, "it's all the same to me. There are fifty dollars, take them and go out into the world when you please; but don't tell any one where you come from, or who is your father, for I am ashamed to own you." "Father," said Hans, "I will do just as you tell me; your orders are very easy to perform."

At daybreak the next morning, the youth put the fifty dollars into his pocket, and went out into the highroad, saying to himself as he walked on, "When shall I learn to shiver and shake—when shall I learn to be afraid?"

Presently a man met him on the road, overheard what he said, and saw at once that the young man was fearless. He quickly joined him, and they walked a little way together till they came to a spot where they could see a gallows.

"Look," he said, "there is a tree where seven men have been married with the ropemaker's daughter, and have learned how to swing; if you only sit down here and watch them till night comes on, I'll answer for it you will shiver and shake before morning." "I never had a better opportunity," answered the youth. "That is very easily done. You come to me again early tomorrow morning, and if it teaches me to shiver and shake, you shall have my fifty dollars."

Then the young man went and seated himself under the gallows and waited till the evening, and feeling cold he lighted a fire; but at midnight the wind rose and blew so fiercely and chill, that even a large fire could not warm him.

The high cold wind made the bodies of the murderers swing to and fro, and he thought to himself, if I am so cold down here by the fire, they must be frozen up there; and after pitying them for some time he climbed up, untied the ropes and brought down all the seven bodies, stirred the fire into a blaze, and seated them round it so close, that their clothes caught fire. Finding they did not move, he said to them, "Sit farther back, will you, or I will hang you up again." But the dead could not hear him, they only sat silent and let their rags burn.

Then Hans became angry, and said, "If you will not move, there is no help for it; I must not let you burn, I must hang you up." So he hung the seven bodies up again all in a row, then laid himself down by the fire and fell fast asleep.

In the morning the man came, according to his promise, hoping to get the fifty dollars. "Well, I suppose you know now what it is to shiver and shake?" he said.

"No, indeed," he replied. "Why should I? Those men up there have not opened their mouths once; and when I seated them round the fire, they allowed their old rags to burn without moving, and if I had not hung the bodies up again, they would have been burned also." The man looked quite scared when he heard this, and went away without attempting to ask for the fifty dollars.

Then Hans continued his journey, and again said aloud to himself, "I wonder what this shivering and shaking can be."

A wagoner walking along the road by his horses overtook him, and asked who he was. "I don't know," he replied. The wagoner asked again, "Why are you here?" "I can't tell," said Hans. "Who is your father?" "I dare not say." "What were you grumbling about just now, when I came up with you?" "I want to learn to shiver and shake," said Hans.

"Don't talk nonsense," said the wagoner. "Come with me, I will show you a little of the world, and find you something to do better than that."

So the young man went with the wagoner, and about evening they arrived at an inn, where they put up for the night. No sooner, however, did Hans enter the room than he muttered to himself, "Oh! if I could only learn to shiver and shake." The landlord heard him, and said with a laugh, "If that is all you wish to learn, I can tell you of a splendid opportunity in this part of the world."

"Ah! be silent now," said the landlady. "You know how many people have already lost their lives through their curiosity. It would be a pity for a nice young man like this, with such fine blue eyes, never to see daylight again."

But Hans spoke for himself at once. "If it is so bad as you say," he cried, "I should like to try as soon as possible; all I want is to learn how to shiver and shake, so tell me what I am to do." And the youth gave the landlord no rest till he had explained the matter to him.

"Well," he said at last, "not far from here stands an enchanted castle, where you could easily learn to shiver and shake, if you remain in it. The King of the country has promised to give his daughter in marriage to any one who will venture to sleep in the castle for three nights, and she is as beautiful a young lady as the sun ever shone upon. Rich and valuable treasures in the castle are watched over by wicked spirits, and any one who could destroy these goblins and demons, and set free the treasures which are rotting in the castle, would be made a rich and lucky man. Lots of people have gone into the castle full of hope that they should succeed, but they have not been heard of since."

Hans was not in the least alarmed by this account, and the next morning he started off early to visit the King.

When he was admitted to the palace the King looked at him earnestly, and seemed much pleased with his appearance; then he said, "Do you really wish to be allowed to remain for three nights in the enchanted castle?" "Yes," replied Hans, "I do request it."

"You can take no living creature with you," said the King; "what else will you have?" "I only ask for a fire, a turning lathe, a cutting board, and a knife," he replied.

To this the King readily agreed, and these articles Hans was permitted to take into the castle during the day. When night came, he took up his abode in one of the rooms, lighted a fire which soon burned brightly, placed the turning lathe and the cutting board near it, and sat down on the cutting board, determined to make

himself comfortable. Presently he exclaimed, "Oh, when shall I
learn to shiver and shake? Not here, I am certain, for I am feeling
too comfortable."

But at midnight, just as he had stirred the fire into a blaze, he
suddenly heard in a corner the cry of a cat: "Miou, miou; how cold
it is!" "What a fool you must be, then," cried Hans, "to stay out
there in the cold; come and seat yourself by the fire, and get warm
if you will."

As he spoke, two very large black cats sprang forward furiously,
seated themselves on each side of the fire, and stared at him with
wild, fiery eyes. After a while, when the cats became thoroughly
warm, they spoke, and said, "Comrade, will you have a game of
cards?" "With all my heart," answered Hans; "but first stretch out
your feet, and let me examine your claws."

The cats stretched out their paws. "Ah!" said he, "what long nails
you have, and now that I have seen your fingers, I would rather be
excused from playing cards with you."

Then he killed them both, and threw them out of the window
into the moat. As soon as he had settled these two intruders, he
seated himself again by the fire, hoping to have a little rest; but in a
few moments there rushed out from every corner of the room
black cats and black dogs with fiery chains one after another, till
there seemed no end to them. They mewed, and barked, and
growled, and at length jumped on his fire and scattered it about the
room, as if they wished to put it out.

For a while he watched them in silence, till at last he got angry,
and seizing his cutting board, exclaimed, "Be off! you horrid creatures!" and then rushing after them, he chased them round the
room. Some few escaped in the clamor, but the rest he killed with
his cutting-knife, and threw into the moat.

As soon as he had cleared the room, he rekindled his fire, by
gathering the sparks together, and sat down to warm himself in the
blaze. After a time he began to feel so sleepy that his eyes would
not keep open any longer; so he looked round the room, and espied
in a corner a large bed. "That is the very place for me," he said,
rising, and laying himself upon it; but just as he was closing his eyes
to sleep, the bed began to move about the room, and at last increased its speed, and went off at a gallop through the castle.

"All right," cried Hans, "now, go on again." At this the bed
started off, as if six horses were harnessed to it, through the doorway, down the steps, to the great gates of the castle, against which
it came with a great bump, and tumbled, legs uppermost, throwing

all the pillows and blankets on Hans, who lay underneath, as if a mountain were upon him. He struggled out from the load, and said, "Anyone may travel in that fashion who likes, but I don't." So he laid himself down again by the fire, and slept till the daybreak.

In the morning the King came to the castle, and, as he caught sight of Hans lying by the fire asleep, he thought the evil spirits had killed him, and that he was dead. "Alas!" said the King, "I am very sorry; it is a great pity that such a fine youth should lose his life in this manner."

But Hans, who heard, sprang up in a moment and exclaimed, "No, King, I am not dead yet." The King, quite astonished and joyful at finding him unhurt, asked him how he had passed the night. "Oh, very pleasantly indeed," replied Hans; and then he related to the King all that had passed, which amused him very much.

On returning to the inn, the landlord stared at him with wide open eyes: "I never expected to see you again alive; but I suppose you have learned to shiver and shake by this time." "Not I," he replied; "I believe it is useless for me to try, for I never shall learn to be afraid."

The second night came, and he again went up to the old castle, and seated himself by the fire, singing the burden of his old song, "When shall I learn to shiver and shake?"

At midnight he heard a noise, as of something falling. It came nearer; then for a little while all was quiet; at last, with a tremendous scream, half the body of a man came tumbling down the chimney, and fell right in front of Hans.

"Holloa!" he cried, "all that noise, and only half a man; where's the other half?" At this, the noise and tumult began again, and, amid yellings and howlings, the other half of the man fell on the hearth.

"Wait," said Hans, rising; "I will stir the fire into a blaze first." But when he turned to sit down again, he found that the two halves of the man had joined, and there sat an ugly-looking object in his place. "Stay," cried the young man. "I did not bargain for this; that seat is mine."

The ugly man tried to push Hans away; but he was too quick for him, and putting out all his strength, he dislodged the creature from his seat, and placed himself again upon it.

Immediately there came tumbling down the chimney nine more of these horrid men, one after the other; each of them held a human thigh-bone in his hand, and the first who appeared brought

out two skulls, and presently they set up the nine bones like skittles, and began to play, with the skulls for balls.

"Shall I play with you?" asked Hans, after he had looked on for
some time. "Yes, willingly," they replied, "if you have any money."
"Plenty," he said. "But your balls are not quite round." So he took
the skulls and turned them on his lathe. "Now they will roll better;
come on, let us set to work."

The strange men played with great spirit, and won a few of his
dollars; but all at once the cock crowed, and they vanished from his
eyes. After they were gone he laid himself down and slept peacefully till the King arrived, and asked him what had happened, and
how it had fared with him during the night.

"Well," said Hans, "I played a game of skittles with some horrid-
looking fellows who had bones and skulls for skittles and balls. I
won sometimes, and I lost a couple of dollars." "Did you not shiver
and shake?" asked the King, in surprise. "Not I, indeed! I wish I
could! Oh, if I only knew how to shiver and shake."

The third night came, and found our hero once more seated on
his bench by the fire, and saying quite mournfully, "When shall I
ever learn to shiver and shake?"

As he spoke there came into the room six tall men, bearing a
coffin containing a dead man. "Ah!" said Hans, "I know what you
have there, it is the body of my cousin. He has been dead two
days." Then he beckoned with his finger and said, "Come here,
little cousin, I should like to see you!"

The men placed the coffin on the ground before him, and took
off the lid. Hans touched the face, and it felt as cold as ice. "Wait,"
he said, "I will soon warm it!" so he went to the fire, and warming
his hand, laid it on the face of the dead man, which remained as
cold as ever.

At last he took him out of the coffin, carried him to the fire, and
placed him on his lap, while he rubbed the hands and chest that he
might cause the blood to circulate, but all to no purpose; the body
remained as cold as before. Presently he remembered that when
two lie in bed together they warm each other, so he placed the
dead man in bed, covered him over, and lay down beside him.
After a while this seemed to produce warmth in the body, the
blood began to circulate, and at last the dead man moved and
spoke.

"There, now, dear cousin," said Hans, "see, I have warmed you
into life again, as I said I could." But the dead man sprang up and
cried, "Yes, and now I will strangle you."

"What!" cried Hans, "is that your gratitude? You may as well go back into your coffin again." He leaped out of bed as he spoke, and, seizing the body, he threw it into the coffin and shut the lid down closely upon it. Then the six tall men walked in, lifted up the coffin and carried it away.

"That's over," said Hans. "Oh! I am sure nothing will ever teach me to shiver and shake."

As he spoke a man walked in who was taller and larger than any of the others, and the look of his eyes was frightful; he was old, and wore a long white beard.

"You wretched creature," cried the man, "I will soon teach you what it is to shiver and shake, for you shall die." "Not so fast, friend," answered Hans. "You cannot kill me without my own consent." "I will soon have you on the ground," replied the monster. "Softly, softly, do not boast; you may be strong, but you will find that I am stronger than you." "That is to be proved," said the old man. "If you are stronger than I am, I will let you go. Come, we will try."

The old man, followed by Hans, led the way through long dark passages and cellars, till they saw the reflection of a smith's fire, and presently came to a forge. Then the old man took an axe, and with one blow cut through the anvil right down to the ground.

"I can do better than that," said Hans, taking up the axe and going towards another anvil. The monster was so surprised at this daring on the part of Hans that he followed him closely, and as he leaned over to watch what the youth was going to do, his long white beard fell on the anvil.

Hans raised his axe, split the anvil at one blow, wedging the old man's beard in the opening at the same time.

"Now I have got you, old fellow," cried Hans, "prepare for the death you deserve." Then he took up an iron bar and beat the old man till he cried for mercy, and promised to give him all the riches that were hidden in the castle.

At this Hans drew out the axe from the anvil, and set the old man's beard free, while he watched him closely. He kept his word, however, and leading the young man back to the castle, pointed out to him a cellar in which were three immense chests full of gold. "There is one for the poor," said he; "another for the King, and the third for yourself."

Hans was about to thank him, when the cock crowed, and the old man vanished, leaving the youth standing in the dark.

"I must find my way out of this place," he said, after groping about for some time, but at last daylight penetrated into the vaults, and he succeeded in reaching his old room, and lying down by the fire, slept soundly till he was aroused by the King's arrival.

"Well," he said, in a glad voice when he saw the young man alive, "have you learned to shiver and shake yet?" "No!" replied Hans, "what was there to make me fear? My dead cousin came to see me, and a bearded old man tried to conquer me, but I managed him, and he has shown me where to find hidden treasures of gold, and how could I shiver and shake at these visitors?"

"Then," said the King, "you have released the castle from enchantment. I will give you, as I promised, my daughter in marriage."

"That is good news," cried Hans. "But I have not learned to shiver and shake after all."

The gold was soon after brought away from the castle, and the marriage celebrated with great pomp. Young Prince Hans, as he was now called, did not seem quite happy after all. Not even the love of his bride could satisfy him. He was always saying: "When shall I learn to shiver and shake?"

This troubled the Princess very much, till her lady's-maid said, "I will help you in this matter; I will show you how to make the Prince shiver and shake, that you may depend upon." So the Princess agreed to do what the lady's-maid advised.

First she went out to a brook that flowed through the gardens of the palace, and brought in a whole pailful of water, containing tiny fish, which she placed in the room.

"Remember," said the lady's-maid, "when the Prince is asleep in bed, you must throw this pail of water over him; that will make him shiver and shake, I am quite certain, and then he will be contented and happy."

So that night while Hans was in bed and asleep, the Princess drew down the bedclothes gently, and threw the cold water with the gudgeons all over him. The little fish wriggled about as they fell on the bed, and the Prince, waking suddenly, exclaimed, "Oh! dear, how I do shiver and shake, what can it be?" Then seeing the Princess standing by his bed, he guessed what she had done.

"Dear wife," he said, "now I am satisfied, you have taught me to shiver and shake at last," and from that hour he lived happily and contented with his wife, for he had learned to shiver and shake—but not to fear.

Fred and Kate

THERE WERE once a young husband and wife, and their names were Fred and Kate. One day said Fred, "I must go now to my work in the fields, Kate, and when I come back you must have on the table some roast meat to satisfy my hunger, and some cool drink to quench my thirst." "All right, Fred," answered Kate; "be off with you, I will see to it."

When dinner-time began to draw near, she took down a sausage from the chimney, put it in a frying-pan with some butter, and stood it over the fire. The sausage began to frizzle and fry, and Kate stood holding the handle of the pan, and fell into deep thought. At last she said to herself, "While the sausage is cooking I might as well be drawing the beer in the cellar."

So she saw that the frying-pan was standing firmly, and then took a can and went down into the cellar to draw the beer. Now, while Kate was watching the beer run into the can, a sudden thought came into her mind.

"Holloa! the dog is not fastened up; he may perhaps get at the sausage," and in a trice she was up the cellar steps: but already the dog had it in his mouth, and was making off with it. Then Kate, with all haste, followed after him and chased him a good way into the fields, but the dog was quicker than Kate, and, never letting slip the sausage, was soon at a great distance. "Well, it can't be helped!" said Kate turning back, and as she had tired herself with running, she took her time about going home, and walked slowly to cool herself.

All this time the beer was running out of the cask, for Kate had not turned off the tap, and as the can was soon full, it began to run over on the cellar floor, and ran, and ran, until the cask was empty. Kate stood on the steps and saw the misfortune. "Dear me!" cried she, "what am I to do to prevent Fred from noticing it!"

She considered for a while, and then remembered that there was remaining in the loft from the last fair time a sack of fine wheat-flour; she determined to bring it down, and strew it over the beer. "To be sure," said she, "those who know how to save have somewhat in time of necessity."

And going up to the loft, she dragged the sack down and threw it right upon the can full of beer, so that Fred's drink ran about the cellar with the rest. "It is all right," said Kate; "where some goes the rest must follow," and she strewed the meal all over the cellar. When all was done, she was highly pleased, and thought how clean and neat it looked.

At dinner-time home came Fred. "Now, wife, what have you got for me?" said he.

"O Fred," answered she, "I was going to cook a sausage for you, but while I was drawing the beer the dog got it out of the pan, and while I was running after the dog the beer all ran away, and as I was going to stop up the beer with the wheat-meal I knocked over the can: but it is all right now; the cellar is quite dry again."

But said Fred, "O Kate, Kate! what have you been about, letting the sausage be carried off, and the beer run out of the cask, and then to waste all our good meal into the bargain?" "Well, Fred, I did not know; you should have told me," said Kate.

So the husband thought to himself, "If my wife is like this, I must look after things a little better."

Now he had saved a very pretty sum of money, and he changed it all to gold, and said to Kate, "Do you see these yellow counters? I am going to make a hole in the stable underneath the cows' manger and bury them; see that you do not meddle with them, or it will be the worse for you." And she said, "Oh no, Fred, certainly I won't."

Now, one day when Fred was away, there came some peddlers to the village, with earthen pots and basins to sell, and they asked the young wife if she had nothing to give in exchange for them.

"O my good men," said Kate, "I have no money to buy anything with, but if you had any use for yellow counters, I might do some business with you." "Yellow counters! why not? We might as well see them," said they. "Then go into the stable and dig under the cows' manger, and you will find them; but I dare not go near the place."

So those rogues went and dug, and found the gold accordingly. And they seized it quickly, and ran off with it, leaving the pots and pans behind them in the house. Kate thought she must make some use of her new possession, so, as she had no need of them in the kitchen, she spread them out on the ground, and then stuck them, one after another, for ornament, on the fence which ran round the house.

When Fred came home and saw the new decorations, he said, "Kate, what have you been doing?" "I bought them every one, Fred, with those yellow counters that were buried under the man-

ger, and I did not go there myself; the peddlers had to dig them up
for themselves."

"O wife!" cried Fred, "what have you done? They were not
counters, but pure gold, and all our capital; you should not have
done so." "Well, Fred, I did not know; you should have told me that
before," answered Kate.

Then Kate stood still a little while to consider, and at last she said,
"Listen, Fred, we may be able to get the gold back again. Let us
run after the thieves." "Very well," said Fred, "we will try; only let
us take some bread and cheese with us, that we may have something to eat on the way." "All right," she answered.

So they set out, and as Fred was a better walker than Kate, she
was soon left behind. "All the better for me," said she, "for when
we turn back I shall have so much the less distance to go."

And they came to a mountain where on both sides of the road
there were deep cart-ruts. And Kate said to herself, "How sad to
see the poor earth torn, and vexed, and oppressed in this way! It
will never be healed again in all its life."

And with a compassionate heart, she took out her butter and
smeared the cart-ruts right and left, so that they might not be so
cut by the wheels; and as she was stooping to perform this merciful
act a cheese fell out of her pocket and rolled down the mountain.

And Kate said, "I have walked over the ground once, and I am
not going to do it again, but another shall run after the cheese, and
bring it back." So saying, she took another cheese, and rolled it
after the first one; and as it did not seem to be coming back again,
she sent a third racing after them, thinking, "Perhaps they are
waiting for company, and are not used to traveling alone."

But when they all three delayed coming, she said, "I can't think
what this means! Perhaps it is that the third one has lost his way, so
I will send a fourth that he may call out to him as he goes by." But it
went no better with the fourth than with the third. And Kate lost
all patience and threw down the fifth and sixth, and that was all.

A long while she stood and waited for them to come up, but as
still they did not come, she said, "Oh, it's like sending good money
after bad; there is no getting you back again. If you suppose I am
going to wait for you any longer, you are very much mistaken: I
shall go on my way and you may overtake me; your legs are
younger than mine." Kate then went on until she overtook Fred,
who was standing still and waiting, as he wanted something to eat.

"Now, be quick," he said, "and hand over what you have

brought." And she handed him the dry bread. "Now for the butter and the cheese," said the man.

"O Fred," said Kate, "I anointed the cart-ruts with the butter, and the cheeses will soon be here, they are upon the road; one of them ran away, and I sent the others to fetch it back."

Then said Fred, "It was very wrong of you, Kate, to waste the butter, and roll the cheeses down the hill." And Kate answered, "Well then, you should have told me so."

As they were eating the dry bread together, Fred said "Kate, did you lock up the house before leaving?" "No, Fred; you ought to have told me that before."

And her husband answered, "Well, you must go home at once and lock up the house before we go any farther, and you might as well bring something more to eat with you, and I will wait for you here."

So Kate went, and she thought to herself, "As Fred wants something more to eat, and he does not care much about butter and cheese, I will bring some dried apples and a jug of vinegar back with me."

Then she bolted the front door, but the back door she took off its hinges, and lifted it on her shoulders, thinking that if she had the door all safe no harm could come to the house. And she took her time on the way back, and thought to herself, "Fred will have so much the longer to rest." So when she got back to him, she called out, "Fred, if the house-door is safe, no harm can come to the house!"

"Oh dear!" cried he, "what a prudent wife have I! To carry away the back-door, so that any one may get in, and to bolt the front door! It is too late now to go home, but as you have brought the door so far, you may carry it on farther."

"All right, I will carry the door, Fred," said she, "but the dried apples and the vinegar will be too heavy for me; I will hang them on the door and make it carry them."

Now they went into the wood to look for the thieves, but they could not find them. When it grew dark they got up into a tree to pass the night there. No sooner had they settled down when up came the peddlers, some of those fellows who carry away what should not go with them, and who find things before they are lost. They laid themselves down directly under the tree where Fred and Kate were, and they made a fire, and began to divide their spoil.

Then Fred got down on the farther side of the tree and gathered together some stones, and then got up again, intending to stone the robbers to death with them. The stones, however, did not hit them, and they said, "It will soon be morning; the wind is rising and shaking down the fir-cones."

Now all the time Kate had the door on her shoulder, and as it weighed upon her heavily, she thought it must be the dried apples, and she said, "Fred, I must throw down the dried apples." "No, Kate, not now," answered he; "we might be discovered." "Oh dear, Fred, but I must! They weigh me down so!" said she. "Well then, do it, if you must, in the name of all that's tormenting!" cried he.

And down rolled the apples between the boughs; and the robbers cried, "There are birds in this tree!"

After a while, as the door still weighed her down heavily, Kate said, "O Fred, I must pour away the vinegar"; and he answered, "No, Kate, you must not do that; we might be discovered." "Oh dear me, Fred, but I must! it weighs me down so!" "Then do it, if you must, in the name of all that's tormenting!"

And she poured out the vinegar, so that the men were all besprinkled. And they said one to another, "The morning dew is beginning to fall already."

At last Kate began to think that it must really be the door that weighed so heavy, and she said, "Fred, I must throw down the door"; and he answered, "No, Kate, not now; we might be discovered." "Oh dear me, Fred, but I must! It weighs me down so." "No, Kate, you must hold it fast." "O Fred, it's slipping, it's falling!" "Well then, let it fall in the name of torment!" cried Fred in a passion.

And so it fell with a great crash, and the thieves below cried, "There is something wrong about this tree!" and they got up in a great hurry and ran off, leaving their spoil behind them. And early in the morning when Fred and Kate came down from the tree they got all their gold again and carried it home.

And when they reached their house again Fred said, "Now, Kate, you must fall to and be very industrious and work hard." "All right, Fred, I will go into the field and cut corn," said she.

And when she came into the field she said to herself, "Shall I eat before I cut, or shall I sleep before I cut? Well, I will eat first." And so she ate, and after that she felt sleepy, but she began to cut and went on half asleep cutting her own clothes, skirts, gown, and all, and when she at last woke up and found herself in rags, she said to herself, "Is this really I or not? Oh dear, it is not I!"

After a while night came on, and Kate ran into the village and knocked at her husband's door calling out, "Fred!" "What is it?" said he. "I want to know if Kate is at home," said she. "Oh yes," he answered, "she is lying here fast asleep."

So she said to herself, "All right then, I am certainly at home," and she ran on farther.

Soon she came upon some thieves who were looking about for something to steal, and she went up to them and offered to help them, and the thieves thought she knew of a good place and opportunity, and were glad of her offer. But Kate walked in front of the houses calling out, "Good people, what have you for us to steal?"

So the thieves thought to themselves, "This will never do," and wished themselves quit of her. At last they said to her, "Just at the end of the village there are some turnips in the parson's field; go and fetch us some."

So Kate went into the field and began to pull some up, but very lazily, and never raised herself. Presently came by a man who saw her, and thought she was some evil thing grubbing for the turnips. So he ran quickly into the village and said to the parson, "O parson, some evil creature is grubbing in your turnip-field!"

"Oh dear!" answered the parson, "I have a lame foot, I cannot go to drive it away." And the man at once offered to take him on his back, and he did so.

Just as they reached the field Kate got up and stood upright.

"Oh, the devil!" cried the parson, and both took to their heels, and the parson was able, out of his great fear, to run faster with his lame foot than the man who had carried him on his back with both legs sound.

Wise Folks

ONE DAY a peasant took his good hazel-stick out of the corner and said to his wife, "Trina, I am going across country, and shall not return for three days. If during that time the cattle-dealer should happen to call and want to buy our three cows, you may strike a bargain at once, but not unless you can get two hundred thalers for them; nothing less, do you hear?" "For heaven's sake just go in peace," answered the woman, "I will manage that." "You, indeed," said the man. "You once fell on your head when you were a little child, and that affects you even now; but let me tell you this, if you do anything foolish, I will make your back black and blue, and not with paint, I assure you, but with the stick which I have in my hand, and the coloring shall last a whole year, you may rely on that." And having said that, the man went on his way.

Next morning the cattle-dealer came, and the woman had no need to say many words to him. When he had seen the cows and heard the price, he said, "I am quite willing to give that; honestly speaking, they are worth it. I will take the beasts away with me at once." He unfastened their chains and drove them out of the byre, but just as he was going out of the yard-door, the woman clutched him by the sleeve and said, "You must give me the two hundred thalers now, or I cannot let the cows go." "True," answered the man, "but I have forgotten to buckle on my money-belt. Have no fear, however, you shall have security for my paying. I will take two cows with me and leave one, and then you will have a good pledge." The woman saw the force of this, and let the man go away with the cows, and thought to herself, "How pleased Hans will be when he finds how cleverly I have managed it!"

The peasant came home on the third day as he had said he would, and at once inquired if the cows were sold. "Yes, indeed, dear Hans," answered the woman, "and as you said, for two hundred thalers. They are scarcely worth so much, but the man took them without making any objection." "Where is the money?" asked the peasant. "Oh, I have not got the money," replied the woman; "he had happened to forget his money-belt, but he will soon bring it, and he left good security behind him." "What kind of security?" asked the man. "One of the three cows, which he shall not have until he has paid for the other two. I have managed very cunningly, for I have kept the smallest, which eats the least." The man was enraged and lifted up his stick, and was just going to give her the beating he had promised her. Suddenly he let the stick fall and said, "You are the stupidest goose that ever waddled on God's earth, but I am sorry for you. I will go out into the highways and wait for three days to see if I find any one who is still stupider than you. If I succeed in doing so, you shall go scot-free, but if I do not find him, you shall receive your well-deserved reward without any discount."

He went out into the great highways, sat down on a stone, and waited for what would happen. Then he saw a peasant's wagon coming towards him, and a woman was standing upright in the middle of it, instead of sitting on the bundle of straw which was lying beside her, or walking near the oxen and leading them. The man thought to himself, "That is certainly one of the kind I am in search of," and jumped up and ran backwards and forwards in front of the wagon like one who is not very wise. "What do you want, my friend?" said the woman to him; "I don't know you, where do you come from?" "I have fallen down from Heaven," replied the man, "and don't know how to get back again; couldn't you drive me up?" "No," said the woman, "I don't know the way, but if you come from Heaven you can surely tell me how my husband, who has been there these three years, is. You must have seen him?" "Oh, yes, I have seen him, but all men can't get on well. He keeps sheep, and the sheep give him a great deal to do. They run up the mountains and lose their way in the wilderness, and he has to run after them and drive them together again. His clothes are all torn to pieces too, and will soon fall off his body. There is no tailor there, for Saint Peter won't let any of them in, as you know by the story." "Who would have thought it?" cried the woman. "I tell you what, I will fetch his Sunday coat which is still hanging at home in the cupboard; he can wear that and look respectable. You will be so kind as to take it with you." "That won't do very well," answered the peasant; "people are not allowed to take clothes into Heaven, they are taken away from one at the gate."

"Then listen," said the woman, "I sold my fine wheat yesterday and got a good lot of money for it; I will send that to him. If you hide the purse in your pocket, no one will know that you have it." "If you can't manage it any other way," said the peasant, "I will do you that favor." "Just sit still where you are," said she, "and I will drive home and fetch the purse, I shall soon be back again. I do not sit down on the bundle of straw, but stand up in the wagon, because it makes it lighter for the cattle." She drove her oxen away, and the peasant thought, "That woman has a perfect talent for folly, if she really brings the money, my wife may think herself fortunate, for she will get no beating." It was not long before she came in a great hurry with the money, and with her own hands put it in his pocket. Before she went away, she thanked him again a thousand times for his courtesy.

When the woman got home again, she found her son who had come in from the field. She told him what unlooked-for things had befallen her, and then added, "I am truly delighted at having found an opportunity of sending something to my poor husband.

Who would ever have imagined that he could be suffering for want
of anything up in Heaven?"

The son was full of astonishment. "Mother," said he, "it is not
every day that a man comes from Heaven in this way, I will go out
immediately, and see if he is still to be found; he must tell me what
it is like up there, and how the work is done." He saddled the horse
and rode off with all speed. He found the peasant who was sitting
under a willow tree, and was just going to count the money in the
purse. "Have you seen the man who has fallen down from
Heaven?" cried the youth to him. "Yes," answered the peasant, "he
has set out on his way back there, and has gone up that hill, from
whence it will be rather nearer; you could still catch him if you
were to ride fast." "Alas," said the youth, "I have been doing tiring
work all day, and the ride here has completely worn me out; you
know the man, be so kind as to get on my horse, and go and
persuade him to come here." "Aha!" thought the peasant, "here is
another who has no wick in his lamp!" "Why should I not do you
this favor?" said he, and mounted the horse and rode off in a quick
trot.

The youth remained sitting there till night fell, but the peasant
never came back. "The man from Heaven must certainly have
been in a great hurry, and would not turn back," thought he, "and
the peasant has no doubt given him the horse to take to my father."
He went home and told his mother what had happened, and that
he had sent his father the horse so that he might not have to be
always running about. "You have done well," answered she, "your
legs are younger than his, and you can go on foot."

When the peasant got home, he put the horse in the stable
beside the cow which he had as a pledge, and then went to his wife
and said, "Trina, as your luck would have it, I have found two who
are still sillier fools than you; this time you escape without a beating; I will store it up for another occasion." Then he lighted his
pipe, sat down in his grandfather's chair, and said, "It was a good
stroke of business to get a sleek horse and a great purse full of
money into the bargain, for two lean cows. If stupidity always
brought in as much as that I would be quite willing to hold it in
honor." So thought the peasant, but you no doubt prefer the simple
folks.

The Lazy Spinner

IN A CERTAIN VILLAGE there once lived a man and his wife. The wife was so idle that she would never work at anything; whatever her husband gave her to spin, she did not get done, and what she did spin she did not wind, but let it all remain entangled in a heap. If the man scolded her, she was always ready with her tongue, and said, "Well, how should I wind it, when I have no reel? Just you go into the forest and get me one." "If that is all," said the man, "then I will go into the forest, and get some wood for making reels." Then the woman was afraid that if he had the wood he would make her a reel of it, and she would have to wind her yarn off, and then begin to spin again. She bethought herself a little, and then a lucky idea occurred to her, and she secretly followed the man into the forest, and when he had climbed into a tree to choose and cut the wood, she crept into the thicket below where he could not see her, and cried,

> *"He who cuts wood for reels shall die,*
> *And he who winds, shall perish."*

The man listened, laid down his axe for a moment, and began to consider what that could mean. "Hollo," he said at last, "what can that have been; my ears must have been singing; I won't alarm myself for nothing." So he again seized the axe, and began to hew; then again there came a cry from below:

> *"He who cuts wood for reels shall die,*
> *And he who winds, shall perish."*

He stopped, and felt afraid and alarmed, and pondered over the circumstance. But when a few moments had passed, he took heart again, and a third time he stretched out his hand for the axe, and began to cut. But some one called out a third time, and said loudly,

> *"He who cuts wood for reels shall die,*
> *And he who winds, shall perish."*

That was enough for him, and all inclination had departed from him, so he hastily descended the tree, and set out on his way home. The woman ran as fast as she could by byways so as to get home first. So when he entered the parlor, she put on an innocent look as if nothing had happened, and said, "Well, have you brought a nice piece of wood for reels?" "No," said he, "I see you very well that winding won't do," and told her what had happened to him in the forest, and from that time forth left her in peace about it.

Nevertheless, after some time, the man again began to complain of the disorder in the house. "Wife," said he, "it is really a shame that the spun yarn should lie there all entangled!" "I'll tell you what," said she, "as we still don't come by any reel, go you up into the loft, and I will stand down below, and will throw the yarn up to you, and you will throw it down to me, and so we shall get a skein after all." "Yes, that will do," said the man. So they did that, and when it was done, he said, "The yarn is in skeins, now it must be boiled." The woman was again distressed; she said certainly, "Yes, we will boil it tomorrow morning early," but she was secretly contriving another trick.

Early in the morning she got up, lighted a fire, and put the kettle on, only instead of the yarn, she put in a lump of tow, and let it boil. After that she went to the man, who was still lying in bed, and said to him, "I must just go out, you must get up and look after the yarn which is in the kettle on the fire, but you must be at hand at once; mind that, for if the cock should happen to crow, and you are not attending to the yarn, it will become tow."

The man was willing and took good care not to loiter. He got up as quickly as he could, and went into the kitchen. But when he reached the kettle and peeped in, he saw, to his horror, nothing but a lump of tow. Then the poor man was as still as a mouse, thinking he had neglected it, and was to blame, and in future said no more about yarn and spinning. But you yourself must own she was an odious woman!

The Three Sluggards

A CERTAIN King had three sons who were all equally dear to him, and he did not know which of them to appoint as his successor after his own death. When the time came when he was about to die, he summoned them to his bedside and said, "Dear children, I have been thinking of something which I will declare unto you; whichsoever of you is the laziest shall have the kingdom."

The eldest said, "Then, father, the kingdom is mine, for I am so idle that if I lie down to rest, and a drop falls in my eye, I will not open it that I may sleep."

The second said, "Father, the kingdom belongs to me, for I am so idle that when I am sitting by the fire warming myself, I would rather let my heel be burnt off than draw back my leg."

The third said, "Father, the kingdom is mine, for I am so idle that if I were going to be hanged, and had the rope already round my neck, and any one put a sharp knife into my hand with which I might cut the rope, I would rather let myself be hanged than arise my hand to the rope."

When the father heard that, he said, "You have carried it the farthest, and shall be King."

The Twelve Idle Servants

TWELVE SERVANTS who had done nothing during the day would not exert themselves at night either, but laid themselves on the grass and boasted of their idleness. The first said, "What is your laziness to me, I have to concern myself about mine own? The care of my body is my principal work; I eat not a little and drink still more. When I have had four meals, I fast a short time until I feel hunger again, and that suits me best. To rise betimes is not for me; when it is getting near midday, I already seek out a resting-place for myself. If the master call, I do exactly as if I had not heard him, and if he call for the second time, I wait a while before I get up, and go to him very slowly. In this way life is endurable."

The second said, "I have a horse to look after, but I leave the bit in his mouth, and if I do not want to do it, I give him no food, and I say he has had it already. I, however, lay myself in the oat-chest and sleep for four hours. After this I stretch out one foot and move it a couple of times over the horse's body, and then he is combed and cleaned. Who is going to make a great business of that? Nevertheless service is too toilsome for me."

The third said, "Why plague oneself with work? Nothing comes of it! I laid myself in the sun, and fell asleep. It began to rain a little, but why should I get up? I let it rain on in God's name. At last came a splashing shower, so heavy indeed, that it pulled the hair out of my head and washed it away, and I got a hole in the skull; I put a plaster on it, and then it was all right. I have already had several injuries of that kind."

The fourth said, "If I am to undertake a piece of work, I first loiter about for an hour that I may save up my strength. After that I begin quite slowly, and ask if no one is there who could help me. Then I let him do the chief of the work, and in reality only look on; but that also is still too much for me."

The fifth said, "What does that matter? Just think, I am to take away the manure from the horse's stable, and load the cart with it. I let it go on slowly, and if I have taken anything on the fork, I only half-raise it up, and then I rest just a quarter of an hour until I quite throw it in. It is enough and to spare if I take out a cartful in the day. I have no fancy for killing myself with work."

The sixth said, "Shame on you. I am afraid of no work, but I lie down for three weeks, and never once take my clothes off. What is the use of buckling your shoes on? For aught I care they may fall off my feet, it is no matter. If I am going up some steps, I drag one foot slowly after the other on to the first step, and then I count the rest of them that I may know where I must rest."

The seventh said, "That will not do with me. My master looks after my work, only he is not at home the whole day. But I neglect nothing, I run as fast as it is possible to do when one crawls. If I am to get on, four sturdy men must push me with all their might. I came where six men were lying sleeping on a bed beside each other. I lay down by them and slept too. There was no wakening me again, and when they wanted to have me home, they had to carry me."

The eighth said, "I see plainly that I am the only active fellow; if a stone lie before me, I do not give myself the trouble to raise my legs and step over it. I lay myself down on the ground, and if I am wet and covered with mud and dirt, I stay lying until the sun has dried me again. At the very most, I only turn myself so that it can shine on me."

The ninth said, "That is the right way! Today the bread was before me, but I was too idle to take it, and nearly died of hunger! Moreover a jug stood by it, but it was so big and heavy that I did not like to lift it up, and preferred bearing thirst. Just to turn myself round was too much for me! I remained lying like a log the whole day."

The tenth said, "Laziness has brought misfortune on me, a broken leg and swollen calf. Three of us were lying in the road, and I had my legs stretched out. Some one came with a cart, and the wheels went over me. I might indeed have drawn my legs back, but I did not hear the cart coming, for the midges were humming about my ears, and creeping in at my nose and out again at my mouth; who can take the trouble to drive the vermin away?"

The eleventh said, "I gave up my place yesterday. I had no fancy for carrying the heavy books to my master any longer or fetching them away again. There was no end of it all day long. But to tell the truth, he gave me my dismissal, and would not keep me any longer, for his clothes, which I had left lying in the dust, were all moth-eaten, and I am very glad of it."

The twelfth said, "Today I had to drive the cart into the country, and made myself a bed of straw on it, and had a good sleep. The reins slipped out of my hand, and when I awoke, the horse had nearly torn itself loose; the harness was gone, the strap which fastened the horse to the shafts was gone, and so were the collar, the bridle and bit. Some one had come by, who had carried all off. Besides this, the cart had got into a quagmire and stuck fast. I left it standing, and stretched myself on the straw again. At last the master came himself, and pushed the cart out, and if he had not come I should not be lying here but there, and sleeping tranquilly."

Lazy Harry

HARRY WAS lazy, and although he had nothing else to do but drive his goat daily to pasture, he nevertheless groaned when he went home after his day's work was done. "It is a heavy burden," said he, "and a wearisome employment to drive a goat into the field this way year after year, till late into the autumn! If one could but lie down and sleep, but no, one must have one's eyes open lest it hurts the young trees, or squeezes itself through the hedge into a garden, or runs away altogether. How can one have any rest, or peace of one's life?" He seated himself, collected his thoughts, and considered how he could set his shoulders free from this burden.

For a long time all thinking was to no purpose, but suddenly it was as if scales fell from his eyes. "I know what I will do," he cried,

"I will marry fat Trina who has also a goat, and can take mine out with hers, and then I shall have no more need to trouble myself."

So Harry got up, set his weary legs in motion, and went right across the street, for it was no farther, to where the parents of fat Trina lived, and asked for their industrious and virtuous daughter in marriage. The parents did not reflect long. "Birds of a feather, flock together," they thought, and consented.

So fat Trina became Harry's wife and led out both the goats. Harry had a good time and had no work to rest from but his own idleness. He went out with her only now and then, and said, "I merely do it that I may afterwards enjoy rest more; otherwise one loses all feeling for it."

Fat Trina was no less idle. "Dear Harry," said she one day, "why should we make our lives so toilsome when there is no need for it, and thus ruin the best days of our youth? Would it not be better for us to give the two goats which disturb us in our sweetest sleep with their bleating, to our neighbor, and will give us a beehive for them? We will put the beehive in a sunny place behind the house, and trouble ourselves no more about it. Bees do not require to be taken care of, or driven to the field; they fly out and find the way home again for themselves, and collect honey without giving the very least trouble." "You have spoken like a sensible woman," replied Harry. "We will carry out your proposal without delay; and besides all that, honey tastes better and nourishes one better than goat's milk, and it can be kept longer, too."

The neighbor willingly gave a beehive for the two goats. The bees flew in and out from early morning till late evening without ever tiring, and filled the hive with the most beautiful honey, so that in autumn Harry was able to take a whole pitcherful out of it.

They placed the jug on a board which was fixed to the wall of their bed-room, and as they were afraid that it might be stolen from them, or that the mice might find it, Trina brought in a stout hazel-stick and put it beside her bed, so that without unnecessary getting up she might reach it with her hand, and drive away the uninvited guests.

Lazy Harry did not like to leave his bed before noon. "He who rises early," said he, "wastes his substance."

One morning when he was lying among the feathers in broad daylight, resting after his long sleep, he said to his wife, "Women are fond of sweet things, and you are always tasting the honey in private; it will be better for us to exchange it for a goose with a young gosling, before you eat up the whole of it." "But," answered

Trina, "not before we have a child to take care of them! Am I to worry myself with the little geese, and spend all my strength on them to no purpose?" "Do you think," said Harry, "that the youngster will look after geese? Nowadays children no longer obey; they do according to their own fancy, because they consider themselves cleverer than their parents, just like that lad who was sent to seek the cow and chased three blackbirds." "Oh," replied Trina, "this one shall fare badly if he does not do what I say! I will take a stick and belabor his skin for him with more blows than I can count. Look, Harry," cried she in her zeal, and seized the stick which she had to drive the mice away with, "Look, this is the way I will fall on him!"

She reached her arm out to strike, but unhappily, hit the honey pitcher above the bed. The pitcher struck against the wall and fell down in fragments, and the fine honey streamed down on the ground. "There lie the goose and the young gosling," said Harry, "and want no looking after. But it is lucky that the pitcher did not fall on my head. We have all reason to be satisfied with our lot." And then as he saw that there was still some honey in one of the fragments he stretched out his hand for it, and said quite gaily, "The remains, my wife, we will still eat with a relish, and we will rest a little after the fright we have had. What matters if we do get up a little later—the day is always long enough." "Yes," answered Trina, "we shall always get to the end of it at the proper time. Do you know that the snail was once asked to a wedding and set out to go? Instead, it arrived at the christening. In front of the house it fell over the fence, and said, 'Speed does no good.'"

Odds and Ends

THERE WAS once on a time a maiden who was pretty, but idle and negligent. When she had to spin she was so out of temper that if there was a little knot in the flax, she at once pulled out a whole heap of it, and strewed it about on the ground beside her. Now she had a servant who was industrious, and gathered together the bits of flax which were thrown away, cleaned them, span them fine, and had a beautiful gown made out of them for herself.

A young man had wooed the lazy girl, and the wedding was to

take place. On the eve of the wedding, the industrious one was dancing merrily about in her pretty dress, and the bride said, "Ah, how that girl does jump about, dressed in my odds and ends."

The bridegroom heard that, and asked the bride what she meant by it. Then she told him that the girl was wearing a dress made of the flax which she had thrown away. When the bridegroom heard that and saw how idle she was, and how industrious the poor girl was, he gave the lazy girl up, went to the other, and chose her as his wife.

Brides on Trial

THERE WAS once a young shepherd who wished much to marry, and was acquainted with three sisters who were all equally pretty, so that it was difficult to him to make a choice, and he could not decide to give the preference to any one of them.

Then he asked his mother for advice, and she said, "Invite all three, and set some cheese before them, and watch how they eat it." The youth did so. The first, however, swallowed the cheese with the rind on; the second hastily cut the rind off the cheese, but she cut it so quickly that she left much good cheese with it, and threw that away also; the third peeled the rind off carefully, and cut neither too much nor too little.

The shepherd told all this to his mother, who said, "Take the third for your wife." This he did, and lived contentedly and happily with her.

The Spindle, the Shuttle, and the Needle

THERE WAS once a girl whose father and mother died while she was still a little child. All alone, in a small house at the end of the village, dwelt her godmother, who supported herself by spinning, weaving, and sewing. The old woman took the forlorn child to live with her, kept her to her work, and educated her in all that is good.

When the girl was fifteen years old, the old woman became ill, called the child to her bedside, and said, "Dear daughter, I feel my end drawing near. I leave you the little house, which will protect you from wind and weather; and my spindle, shuttle, and needle, with which you can earn your bread." Then she laid her hands on the girl's head, blessed her, and said, "Only preserve the love of God in your heart, and all will go well with you." Thereupon she closed her eyes, and when she was laid in the earth, the maiden followed the coffin, weeping bitterly, and paid her the last mark of respect.

And now the maiden lived quite alone in the little house, and was industrious, and span, wove, and sewed, and the blessing of the good old woman was on all that she did. It seemed as if the flax in the room increased of its own accord, and whenever she wove a piece of cloth or carpet, or had made a shirt, she at once found a buyer who paid her amply for it, so that she was in want of nothing, and even had something to share with others.

About this time, the son of the King was traveling about the country looking for a bride. He was not to choose a poor one, and did not want to have a rich one. So he said, "She shall be my wife who is the poorest, and at the same time the richest." When he came to the village where the maiden dwelt, he inquired, as he did wherever he went, who was the richest and also the poorest girl in the place. They first named the richest; the poorest, they said, was the girl who lived in the small house quite at the end of the village.

The rich girl was sitting in all her splendor before the door of her house, and when the Prince approached her, she got up, went to meet him, and made him a low curtsey. He looked at her, said nothing, and rode on. When he came to the house of the poor girl, she was not standing at the door, but sitting in her little room. He stopped his horse, and saw through the window, on which the bright sun was shining, the girl sitting at her spinning-wheel, busily spinning. She looked up, and when she saw that the Prince was looking in, she blushed all over her face, let her eyes fall, and went on spinning. I do not know whether, just at that moment, the thread was quite even; but she went on spinning until the King's son had ridden away again. Then she went to the window, opened it, and said, "It is so warm in this room!" But she still looked after him as long as she could distinguish the white feathers in his hat.

Then she sat down to work again in her own room and went on with her spinning, and a saying which the old woman had often repeated when she was sitting at her work, came into her mind, and she sang these words to herself:

> *"Spindle, my spindle, haste, haste thee away,*
> *And here to my house bring the wooer, I pray."*

And what do you think happened? The spindle sprang out of her hand in an instant, and out of the door, and when, in her astonishment, she got up and looked after it, she saw that it was dancing out merrily into the open country, and drawing a shining golden thread after it. Before long, it had entirely vanished from her sight. As she had now no spindle, the girl took the weaver's shuttle in her hand, sat down to her loom, and began to weave.

The spindle, however, danced continually onwards, and just as the thread came to an end, reached the Prince. "What do I see?" he cried; "the spindle certainly wants to show me the way!" He turned his horse about, and rode back with the golden thread. The girl was, however, sitting at her work singing,

> *"Shuttle, my shuttle, weave well this day,*
> *And guide the wooer to me, I pray."*

Immediately the shuttle sprang out of her hand and out by the door. Before the threshold, however, it began to weave a carpet which was more beautiful than the eyes of man had ever yet beheld. Lilies and roses blossomed on both sides of it, and on a golden ground in the center green branches ascended, under which bounded hares and rabbits; stags and deer stretched their heads in between them, brightly colored birds were sitting in the branches above; they lacked nothing but the gift of song. The shuttle leapt hither and thither, and everything seemed to grow of its own accord.

As the shuttle had run away, the girl sat down to sew. She held the needle in her hand and sang,

> *"Needle, my needle, sharp-pointed and fine,*
> *Prepare for a wooer this house of mine."*

Then the needle leapt out of her fingers, and flew everywhere about the room as quick as lightning. It was just as if invisible spirits were working; they covered tables and benches with green cloth in an instant, and the chairs with velvet, and hung the windows with silken curtains. Hardly had the needle put in the last stitch than the maiden saw through the window the white feathers of the Prince, whom the spindle had brought thither by the golden thread. He alighted, stepped over the carpet into the house, and when he entered the room, there stood the maiden in her poor garments, but she shone out from within them like a rose surrounded by leaves. "You are the poorest and also the richest," said he to her. "Come with me; you shall be my bride." She did not speak, but she gave him her hand. Then he gave her a kiss, led her forth, lifted her on to his horse, and took her to the royal castle, where the wedding was solemnized with great rejoicings. The spindle, shuttle, and needle were preserved in the treasure-chamber, and held in great honor.

The Peasant's Wise Daughter

A POOR PEASANT had no land but only a small house and one daughter. Then said the daughter, "We ought to ask our lord the King for a bit of newly cleared land." When the King heard of their poverty, he presented them with a bit of land, which she and her father dug up, and intended to sow with a little corn and grain of that kind. When they had dug nearly the whole of the field, they found in the earth a mortar made of pure gold. "Listen," said the father to the girl, "as our lord the King has been so gracious and presented us with the field, we ought to give him this mortar in return for it." The daughter, however, would not consent to this, and said, "Father, if we have the mortar without having the pestle as well, we shall have to get the pestle, so you had much better say nothing about it." He would, however, not obey her, but took the mortar and carried it to the King, said that he had found it in the cleared land, and asked if he would accept it as a present.

The King took the mortar, and asked if he had found nothing besides that. "No," answered the countryman. Then the King said that he must now bring him the pestle. The peasant said they had not found that, but he might just as well have spoken to the wind; he was put in prison, and was to stay there until he produced the pestle. The servants had daily to carry him bread and water, which is what people get in prison, and they heard how the man cried out continually, "Ah! if I had but listened to my daughter! Alas, alas, if I had but listened to my daughter!"

Then the servants went to the King and told him how the prisoner was always crying, "Ah! if I had but listened to my daughter!" and would neither eat nor drink. So he commanded the servants to bring the prisoner before him, and then the King asked the peasant why he was always crying, "Ah! if I had but listened to my daughter!" and what it was that his daughter had said. "She told me that I ought not to take the mortar to you, for I should have to produce the pestle as well." "If you have a daughter who is as wise as that, let her come here." She was therefore obliged to appear before the King, who asked her if she really was so wise, and said he would set her a riddle, and if she could guess that, he would marry her. She at once said yes, she would guess it. Then said the King, "Come to me not clothed, not naked, not riding, not walking, not in the road, and not out of the road, and if thou canst do that I will marry thee."

So she went away, put off everything she had on, and then she was not clothed, and took a great fishing net, and seated herself in it and wrapped it entirely round and round her, and then she was not naked; and she hired an ass, and tied the fisherman's net to its tail, so that it was forced to drag her along, and that was neither riding nor walking. The ass had also to drag her in the ruts, so that she only touched the ground with her great toe, and that was neither being in the road nor out of the road. And when she arrived in that fashion, the King said she had guessed the riddle and fulfilled all the conditions. Then he ordered her father to be released from the prison, took her to wife, and gave into her care all the royal possessions.

Now when some years had passed, the King was once drawing up his troops on parade, when it happened that some peasants who had been selling wood stopped with their wagons before the palace; some of them had oxen yoked to them, and some horses. There was one peasant who had three horses, one of which was delivered of a young foal, and it ran away and lay down between two oxen which were in front of the wagon. When the peasants came together, they began to dispute, to beat each other and make a disturbance, and the peasant with the oxen wanted to keep the foal, and said one of the oxen had given birth to it, and the other said his horse had had it, and that it was his.

The quarrel came before the King, and he gave the verdict that the foal should stay where it had been found, and so the peasant with the oxen, to whom it did not belong, got it. Then the other went away, and wept and lamented over his foal. Now he had heard how gracious his lady the Queen was because she herself had sprung from poor peasant folks, so he went to her and begged her to see if she could not help him to get his foal back again. Said she, "Yes, I will tell you what to do, if you will promise me not to betray me. Early tomorrow morning, when the King parades the guard, place yourself there in the middle of the road by which he must pass, take a great fishing-net and pretend to be fishing; go on fishing too, and empty out the net as if you had got it full"—and then she told him also what he was to say if he was questioned by the King. The next day, therefore, the peasant stood there, and fished on dry ground.

When the King passed by, and saw that, he sent his messenger to ask what the stupid man was about. He answered, "I am fishing." The messenger asked how he could fish when there was no water whatever there. The peasant said, "It is as easy for me to fish on dry land as it is for an ox to have a foal." The messenger went back and took the answer to the King, who ordered the peasant to be brought to him. The peasant told him that this was not his own idea, and the King wanted to know whose it was. The peasant must confess that at once. The peasant, however, would not do so, and said always, God forbid he should!—the idea was his own. They laid him, however, on a heap of straw, and beat him and tormented him so long that at last he admitted that he had got the idea from the Queen.

When the King reached home again, he said to his wife, "Why hast thou behaved so falsely to me? I will not have thee any longer for a wife; thy time is up, go back to the place from whence thou camest—to thy peasant's hut." One favor, however, he granted her; she might take with her the one thing that was dearest and best in her eyes; and thus was she dismissed. She said, "Yes, my dear husband, if thou commandest this, I will do it," and she embraced him and kissed him, and said she would take leave of him. Then she ordered a powerful sleeping draught to be brought, to drink farewell to him; the King took a long draught, but she took only a little. He soon fell into a deep sleep, and when she perceived that, she called a servant and took a fair white linen cloth and wrapped the King in it, and the servant was forced to carry him into a carriage that stood before the door, and she drove with him to her own little house. She laid him in her own little bed, and he slept one day and one night without awakening, and when he awoke he looked round and said, "Good God! where am I?" He called his attendants, but none of them were there.

At length his wife came to his bedside and said, "My dear lord and King, thou toldest me I might bring away with me from the palace that which was dearest and most precious in my eyes—I have nothing more precious and dear than thyself, so I have brought thee with me." Tears rose to the King's eyes and he said, "Dear wife, thou shalt be mine and I will be thine," and he took her back with him to the royal palace and was married again to her, and at the present time they are very likely still living.

The Shepherd Boy

ONCE UPON a time there was a shepherd boy whose fame spread far and wide because of the wise answers which he gave to every question. The King of the country heard of it likewise, but did not believe it, and sent for the boy. Then he said to him, "If you can give me an answer to three questions which I will ask you, I will look on you as my own child, and you shall dwell with me in my royal palace." The boy said, "What are the three questions?"

The King said, "The first is, how many drops of water are there in the ocean?" The shepherd boy answered, "Lord King, if you will have all the rivers on earth dammed up so that not a single drop runs from them into the sea until I have counted it, I will tell you how many drops there are in the sea."

The King said, "The next question is, how many stars are there in the sky?" The shepherd boy said, "Give me a great sheet of white paper," and then he made so many fine points on it with a pen that they could scarcely be seen, and it was all but impossible to count them; any one who looked at them would have lost his sight. Then he said, "There are as many stars in the sky as there are points on the paper; just count them." But not one was able to do it."

The King said, "The third question is, how many seconds of time are there in eternity?" Then said the shepherd boy, "In Lower Pomerania is the Diamond Mountain, which is two miles and a half high, two miles and a half wide, and two miles and a half in depth; every hundred years a little bird comes and sharpens its beak on it, and when the whole mountain is worn away by this, then the first second of eternity will be over."

The King said, "You have answered the three questions like a wise man, and you shall henceforth dwell with me in my royal palace, and I will regard you as my own child."

The Master-Thief

ONE DAY an old man and his wife were sitting in front of a dilapidated house resting a while from their work. Suddenly a splendid carriage with four black horses came driving up, and a richly-dressed man descended from it. The peasant stood up, went to the great man, and asked what he wanted, and in what way he could be useful to him. The stranger stretched out his hand to the old man, and said, "I want nothing but to enjoy for once a country dish. Cook me some potatoes, in the way you always have them, and then I will sit down at your table and eat them with pleasure." The peasant smiled and said, "You are a count or a Prince, or perhaps even a duke; noble gentlemen often have such fancies, but you shall have your wish." The wife went into the kitchen, and began to wash and rub the potatoes, and to make them into balls, as they are eaten by the country-folks.

While she was busy with this work, the peasant said to the stranger, "Come into my garden with me for a while, I have still something to do there." He had dug some holes in the garden, and now wanted to plant some trees in them. "Have you no children," asked the stranger, "who could help you with your work?" "No," answered the peasant, "I had a son, it is true, but it is long since he went out into the world. He was a ne'er-do-well; sharp, and knowing, but he would learn nothing and was full of bad tricks; at last he ran away from me, and since then I have heard nothing of him."

The old man took a young tree, put it in a hole, drove in a post beside it, and when he had shoveled in some earth and had trampled it firmly down, he tied the stem of the tree above, below, and in the middle, fast to the post by a rope of straw. "But tell me," said the stranger, "why you don't tie that crooked knotted tree, which is lying in the corner there, bent down almost to the ground, to a post also that it may grow straight, as well as these?" The old man smiled and said, "Sir, you speak according to your knowledge, it is easy to see that you are not familiar with gardening. That tree there is old, and misshapen, no one can make it straight now. Trees must be trained while they are young."

"That is how it was with your son," said the stranger, "if you had trained him while he was still young, he would not have run away; now he too must have grown hard and misshapen." "Truly it is a long time since he went away," replied the old man, "he must have changed." "Would you know him again if he were to come to you?" asked the stranger. "Hardly by his face," replied the peasant, "but he has a mark about him, a birth-mark on his shoulder, that looks like a bean." When he had said that the stranger pulled off his coat, bared his shoulder, and showed the peasant the bean. "Good God!" cried the old man, "you are really my son!" and love for his child stirred in his heart. "But," he added, "how can you be my son? You have become a great lord and live in wealth and luxury. How have you contrived to do that?" "Ah, father," answered the son, "the young tree was bound to no post and has grown crooked; now it is too old, it will never be straight again. How have I got all that? I have become a thief, but do not be alarmed, I am a master-thief. For me there are neither locks nor bolts, whatsoever I desire is mine. Do not imagine that I steal like a common thief! I only take some of the superfluity of the rich. Poor people are safe! I would rather give to them than take anything from them. It is the same with anything which I can have without trouble, cunning and dexterity—I never touch it." "Alas, my son," said the father, "it still does not please me, a thief is still a thief, I tell you it will end badly." He took him to his mother, and when she heard that was her son, she wept for joy, but when he told her that he had become a master-thief, two streams flowed down over her face. At length she said, "Even if he has become a thief, he is still my son, and my eyes have beheld him once more." They sat down to table, and once again he ate with his parents the wretched food which he had not eaten for so long. The father said, "If our Lord, the count up there in the castle, learns who you are and what trade you follow, he will not take you in his arms and cradle you in them as he did when he held you at the font, but will cause you to swing from a halter." "Be easy, father, he will do me no harm, for I understand my trade. I will go to him myself this very day."

When evening drew near, the master-thief seated himself in his carriage, and drove to the castle. The count received him civilly, for he took him for a distinguished man. When, however, the stranger made himself known, the count turned pale and was quite silent for some time. At length he said, "You are my godson, and on

that account mercy shall take the place of justice, and I will deal
leniently with you. Since you pride yourself on being a master-
thief, I will put your art to the proof, but if you do not stand the test,
you must marry the rope-maker's daughter, and the croaking of
the raven must be your music on the occasion." "Lord count,"
answered the master-thief, "Think of three things as difficult as you
like, and if I do not perform your tasks, do with me what you will."
The count reflected for some minutes, and then said, "Well, then,
in the first place, you shall steal the horse I keep for my own riding,
out of the stable; in the next, you shall steal the sheet from beneath
the bodies of my wife and myself when we are asleep, without our
observing it, and the wedding-ring of my wife as well; thirdly and
lastly, you shall steal away out of the church, the parson and clerk.
Mark what I am saying, for your life depends on it."

The master-thief went to the nearest town; there he bought the
clothes of an old peasant woman, and put them on. Then he stained
his face brown, and painted wrinkles on it as well, so that no one
could have recognized him. Then he filled a small cask with old
hungary wine in which was mixed a powerful sleeping-drink. He
put the cask in a basket, which he took on his back, and walked
with slow and tottering steps to the count's castle. It was already
dark when he arrived. He sat down on a stone in the court-yard
and began to cough, like an asthmatic old woman, and to rub his
hands as if he were cold.

In front of the door of the stable some soldiers were lying round a
fire; one of them observed the woman, and called out to her,
"Come nearer, old mother, and warm yourself beside us. After all,
you have no bed for the night, and must take one where you can
find it." The old woman tottered up to them, begged them to lift
the basket from her back, and sat down beside them at the fire.
"What have you got in the little cask, old lady?" asked one. "A good
mouthful of wine," she answered. "I live by trade; for money and
fair words I am quite ready to let you have a glass." "Let us have it
here, then," said the soldier, and when he had tasted one glass he
said, "When wine is good, I like another glass," and had another
poured out for himself, and the rest followed his example. "Hallo,
comrades," cried one of them to those who were in the stable,
"here is an old goody who has wine that is as old as herself; take a
draught, it will warm your stomachs far better than our fire." The
old woman carried her cask into the stable. One of the soldiers had
seated himself on the saddled riding-horse, another held its bridle

in his hand, a third had laid hold of its tail. She poured out as much as they wanted until the spring ran dry.

It was not long before the bridle fell from the hand of the one, and he fell down and began to snore, the other left hold of the tail, lay down and snored still louder. The one who was sitting in the saddle, did remain sitting, but bent his head almost down to the horse's neck, and slept and blew with his mouth like the bellows of a forge. The soldiers outside had already been asleep for a long time, and were lying on the ground motionless, as if dead. When the master-thief saw that he had succeeded, he gave the first a rope in his hand instead of the bridle, and the other who had been holding the tail, a wisp of straw, but what was he to do with the one who was sitting on the horse's back? He did not want to throw him down, for he might have awakened and have uttered a cry. He had a good idea; he unbuckled the girths of the saddle, tied a couple of ropes which were hanging to a ring on the wall fast to the saddle, and drew the sleeping rider up into the air on it, then he twisted the rope round the posts, and made it fast. He soon unloosed the horse from the chain, but if he had ridden over the stony pavement of the yard they would have heard the noise in the castle. So he wrapped the horse's hoofs in old rags, led him carefully out, leapt upon him, and galloped off.

When day broke, the master galloped to the castle on the stolen horse. The count had just got up, and was looking out of the window. "Good morning, Sir Count," he cried to him, "here is the horse, which I have got safely out of the stable! Just look, how beautifully your soldiers are lying there sleeping; and if you will but go into the stable, you will see how comfortable your watchers have made it for themselves." The count could not help laughing, then he said, "For once you have succeeded, but things won't go so well the second time, and I warn you that if you come before me as a thief, I will handle you as I would a thief."

When the countess went to bed that night, she closed her hand with the wedding-ring tightly together, and the count said, "All the doors are locked and bolted, I will keep awake and wait for the thief, but if he gets in by the window, I will shoot him." The master-thief, however, went in the dark to the gallows, cut a poor sinner who was hanging there down from the halter, and carried him on his back to the castle. Then he set a ladder up to the bedroom, put the dead body on his shoulders, and began to climb up. When he had got so high that the head of the dead man showed at the window, the count, who was watching in his bed, fired a pistol at him, and immediately the master let the poor sinner fall down, and hid himself in one corner. The night was sufficiently lighted by the moon, for the master to see distinctly how the count got out of the window on to the ladder, came down, carried the dead body into the garden, and began to dig a hole in which to lay it.

"Now," thought the thief, "the favorable moment has come," stole nimbly out of his corner, and climbed up the ladder straight into the countess's bedroom. "Dear wife," he began in the count's voice, "the thief is dead, but, after all, he is my godson, and has been more of a scapegrace than a villain. I will not put him to open shame. Besides, I am sorry for the parents. I will bury him myself before daybreak, in the garden that the thing may not be known, so give me the sheet, I will wrap up the body in it, and bury him as a dog buries things by scratching." The countess gave him the sheet. "I tell you what," continued the thief, "I have a fit of magnanimity on me; give me the ring too—the unhappy man risked his life for it, so he may take it with him into his grave." She would not gainsay the count, and although she did it unwillingly she drew the ring from her finger, and gave it to him. The thief made off with both these things, and reached home safely before the count in the garden had finished his work of burying.

What a long face the count did pull when the master came next morning, and brought him the sheet and the ring. "Are you a wizard?" said he, "who has fetched you out of the grave in which I myself laid you, and brought you to life again?" "You did not bury me," said the thief, "but the poor sinner on the gallows." And he told him exactly how everything had happened, and the count was forced to own to him that he was a clever, crafty thief. "But you have not reached the end yet," he added. "You still have to perform the third task, and if you do not succeed in that, all is of no use." The master smiled and returned no answer.

When night had fallen he went with a long sack on his back, a bundle under his arms, and a lantern in his hand to the village-church. In the sack he had some crabs, and in the bundle short wax-candles. He sat down in the churchyard, took out a crab, and stuck a wax-candle on his back. Then he lighted the little light, put the crab on the ground, and let it creep about. He took a second out of the sack, and treated it in the same way, and so on until the last was out of the sack. Hereupon he put on a long black garment that looked like a monk's cowl, and stuck a gray beard on his chin. When at last he was quite unrecognizable, he took the sack in which the crabs had been, went into the church, and ascended the pulpit. The clock in the tower was just striking twelve; when the last stroke had sounded, he cried with a loud and piercing voice, "Hearken, sinful men, the end of all things has come! The last day is at hand! Hearken! Hearken! Whosoever wishes to go to heaven with me must creep into the sack. I am Peter, who opens and shuts the gate of heaven. Behold how the dead outside there in the churchyard, are wandering about collecting their bones. Come, come, and creep into the sack; the world is about to be destroyed!"

The cry echoed through the whole village. The parson and clerk who lived nearest to the church, heard it first, and when they saw the lights which were moving about the churchyard, they observed that something unusual was going on, and went into the church. They listened to the sermon for a while, and then the clerk nudged the parson and said, "It would not be amiss if we were to use the opportunity together, and before the dawning of the last day, find an easy way of getting to heaven." "To tell the truth," answered the parson, "that is what I myself have been thinking, so if you are inclined, we will set out on our way." "Yes," answered the clerk, "but you, the pastor, have the precedence, I will follow." So the parson went first, and ascended the pulpit where the master opened his sack. The parson crept in first, and then the clerk.

The master immediately tied up the sack tightly, seized it by the middle, and dragged it down the pulpit-steps, and whenever the heads of the two fools bumped against the steps, he cried, "We are going over the mountains." Then he drew them through the village in the same way, and when they were passing through puddles, he cried, "Now we are going through wet clouds," and when at last he was dragging them up the steps of the castle, he cried, "Now we are on the steps of heaven, and will soon be in the outer court." When he had got to the top, he pushed the sack into the pigeon-house, and when the pigeons fluttered about, he said, "Hark how glad the angels are, and how they are flapping their wings!" Then he bolted the door upon them, and went away.

Next morning he went to the count, and told him that he had performed the third task also, and had carried the parson and clerk out of the church. "Where have you left them?" asked the lord. "They are lying upstairs in a sack in the pigeon-house, and imagine that they are in heaven." The count went up himself, and convinced himself that the master had told the truth. When he had delivered the parson and clerk from their captivity, he said, "You are an arch-thief, and you have won the wager. For once you escape with a whole skin, but leave my land; for if you ever set foot on it again, you may count on your elevation to the gallows." The arch-thief took leave of his parents, once more went forth into the wide world, and no one has ever heard of him since.

The Three Brothers

THERE WAS once a man who had three sons, and nothing else in the world but the house in which he lived. Now each of the sons wished to have the house after his father's death; but the father loved them all alike, and did not know what to do; he did not wish to sell the house, because it had belonged to his forefathers, else he might have divided the money among them. At last a plan came into his head, and he said to his sons, "Go into the world, and try each of you to learn a trade, and, when you all come back, he who makes the best masterpiece shall have the house."

The sons were satisfied with this; and the eldest determined to be a blacksmith, the second a barber, and the third a fencing-master. They fixed a time when they should all come home again, and then each went his way.

It chanced that they all found skilful masters, who taught them their trades well. The blacksmith had to shoe the King's horses, and he thought to himself, "The house is mine, without doubt." The barber only shaved great people, and he too already looked upon the house as his own. The fencing-master got many a blow, but he only bit his lip, and let nothing vex him; "for," said he to himself, "if you are afraid of a blow, you'll never win the house."

When the appointed time had gone by, the three brothers came back home to their father; but they did not know how to find the best opportunity for showing their skill, so they sat down and consulted together. As they were sitting thus, all at once a hare came running across the field. "Ah, ha, just in time!" said the barber. So he took his basin and soap, and lathered away until the hare came up; then he soaped and shaved off the hare's whiskers while he was running at the top of his speed, and did not even cut his skin or injure a hair on his body. "Well done!" said the old man, "your brothers will have to exert themselves wonderfully, or the house will be yours."

Soon after, up came a nobleman in his coach, dashing along at full speed. "Now you shall see what I can do, father," said the blacksmith; so away he ran after the coach, took all four shoes off the feet of one of the horses while he was galloping, and put on him four new shoes without stopping him. "You are a fine fellow, and as clever as your brother," said his father; "I do not know to which I ought to give the house."

Then the third son said, "Father, let me have my turn, if you please"; and, as it was beginning to rain, he drew his sword, and flourished it backwards and forwards about his head so fast that not a drop fell upon him. It rained still harder and harder, till at last it came down in torrents; but he only flourished his sword faster and faster, and remained as dry as if he were sitting in a house. When his father saw this he was amazed, and said, "This is the masterpiece, the house is yours!"

His brothers were satisfied with this, as was agreed beforehand; and, as they loved one another very much, they all three stayed together in the house, followed their trades, and, as they had learnt them so well and were so clever, they earned a great deal of money. Thus they lived together happily until they grew old; and at last, when one of them fell sick and died, the two others grieved so sorely about it that they also fell ill, and soon after died. And because they had been so clever, and had loved one another so much, they were all laid in the same grave.

The Four Skilful Brothers

THERE WAS once a poor man who had four sons, and when they were grown up, he said to them, "My dear children, you must now go out into the world, for I have nothing to give you, so set out, and go to some distance and learn a trade, and see how you can make your way." So the four brothers took their sticks, bade their father farewell, and went through the town-gate together. When they had traveled about for some time, they came to a cross-way which branched off in four different directions. Then said the eldest, "Here we must separate, but on this day in four years, we will meet each other again at this spot, and in the meantime we will seek our fortunes."

Then each of them went his way, and the eldest met a man who asked him where he was going, and what he was intending to do. "I want to learn a trade," he replied. Then the other said, "Come with me, and be a thief." "No," he answered, "that is no longer regarded as a reputable trade, and the end of it is that one has to swing on the gallows." "Oh," said the man, "you need not be afraid of the gallows; I will only teach you to get such things as no other man could ever lay hold of, and no one will ever detect you." So he allowed himself to be talked into it, and while with the man became an accomplished thief, and so dexterous that nothing was safe from him if he once desired to have it.

The second brother met a man who put the same question to him—what he wanted to learn in the world. "I don't know yet," he replied. "Then come with me, and be an astronomer; there is nothing better than that, for nothing is hid from you." He liked the idea, and became such a skilful astronomer that when he had learnt everything, and was about to travel onwards, his master gave him a telescope and said to him, "With that you can see whatsoever takes place either on earth or in heaven, and nothing can remain concealed from you."

A huntsman took the third brother into training, and gave him such excellent instruction in everything which related to huntsmanship, that he became an experienced hunter. When he went away, his master gave him a gun and said, "It will never fail you; whatsoever you aim at, you are certain to hit."

The youngest brother also met a man who spoke to him, and inquired what his intentions were. "Would you not like to be a tailor?" said he. "Not that I know of," said the youth; "sitting doubled up from morning till night, driving the needle and the goose backwards and forwards, is not to my taste." "Oh, but you are speaking in ignorance," answered the man; "with me you would learn a very different kind of tailoring, which is respectable and proper, and for the most part very honorable." So he let himself be persuaded, and went with the man, and learnt his art from the very beginning. When they parted, the man gave the youth a needle, and said, "With this you can sew together whatever is given you, whether it is as soft as an egg or as hard as steel; and it will all become one piece of stuff, so that no seam will be visible."

When the appointed four years were over, the four brothers arrived at the same time at the cross-roads, embraced and kissed each other, and returned home to their father. "So now," said he, quite delighted, "the wind has blown you back again to me." They told him of all that had happened to them, and that each had learnt his own trade. Now they were sitting just in front of the house under a large tree, and the father said, "I will put you all to the test, and see what you can do."

Then he looked up and said to his second son, "Between two branches up at the top of this tree, there is a chaffinch's nest, tell me how many eggs there are in it." The astronomer took his glass, looked up, and said, "There are five." Then the father said to the eldest, "Fetch the eggs down without disturbing the bird which is sitting hatching them." The skilful thief climbed up and took the five eggs from beneath the bird, which never observed what he was doing, and remained quietly sitting where she was, and brought them down to his father. The father took them, and put one of them on each corner of the table, and the fifth in the middle, and said to the huntsman, "With one shot you shall shoot me the five eggs in two, through the middle." The huntsman aimed, and shot the eggs, all five as the father had desired, and that at one shot. He certainly must have had some of the powder for shooting round corners. "Now it's your turn," said the father to the fourth son; "you shall sew the eggs together again, and the young birds that are inside them as well, and you must do it so that they are not hurt by the shot." The tailor brought his needle, and sewed them as his father wished. When he had done this the thief had to climb up the tree again, and carry them to the nest, and put them back again under the bird without her being aware of it. The bird sat her full time, and after a few days the young ones crept out, and they had a red line round their necks where they had been sewn together by the tailor.

"Well," said the old man to his sons, "I begin to think you are worth more than green clover; you have used your time well, and learnt something good. I can't say which of you deserves the most praise. That will be proved if you have but an early opportunity of using your talents."

Not long after this, there was a great uproar in the country, for the King's daughter was carried off by a dragon. The King was full of trouble about it, both by day and night, and caused it to be proclaimed that whosoever brought her back should have her to wife. The four brothers said to each other, "This would be a fine opportunity for us to show what we can do!" and resolved to go forth together and liberate the King's daughter. "I will soon know where she is," said the astronomer, and looked through his telescope and said, "I see her already, she is far away from here on a rock in the sea, and the dragon is beside her watching her."

Then he went to the King, and asked for a ship for himself and his brothers, and sailed with them over the sea until they came to the rock. There the King's daughter was sitting and the dragon was lying asleep on her lap. The huntsman said, "I dare not fire, I should kill the beautiful maiden at the same time." "Then I will try my art," said the thief, and he crept thither and stole her away from under the dragon, so quietly and dexterously, that the monster never remarked it, but went on snoring. Full of joy, they hurried off with her on board ship, and steered out into the open sea; but the dragon, who when he awoke had found no Princess there, followed them, and came snorting angrily through the air. Just as he was circling above the ship, and about to descend on it, the huntsman shouldered his gun, and shot him to the heart. The monster fell down dead, but was so large and powerful that his fall shattered the whole ship. Fortunately, however, they laid hold of a couple of planks, and swam about the wide sea. Then again they were in great peril, but the tailor, who was not idle, took his wondrous needle, and with a few stitches sewed the planks together, and they seated themselves upon them, and collected together all the fragments of the vessel. Then he sewed these so skilfully together, that in a very short time the ship was once more seaworthy, and they could go home again in safety.

When the King once more saw his daughter, there were great rejoicings. He said to the four brothers, "One of you shall have her to wife, but which of you it is to be you must settle among yourselves." Then a warm contest arose among them, for each of them preferred his own claim. The astronomer said, "If I had not seen the Princess, all your arts would have been useless, so she is mine." The thief said, "What would have been the use of your seeing, if I had not got her away from the dragon? So she is mine." The huntsman said, "You and the Princess, and all of you, would have been torn to pieces by the dragon if my ball had not hit him, so she is mine." The tailor said, "And if I, by my art, had not sewn the ship together again, you would all of you have been miserably drowned, so she is mine." Then the King uttered this saying, "Each of you has an equal right, and as all of you cannot have the maiden, none of you shall have her, but I will give to each of you, as a reward, half a kingdom." The brothers were pleased with this decision, and said, "It is better thus than that we should be at variance with each other." Then each of them received half a kingdom, and they lived with their father in the greatest happiness as long as it pleased God.

Tales of Snakes

i

THERE WAS once a little child whose mother gave her every afternoon a small bowl of milk and bread, and the child seated herself in the yard with it. When she began to eat, however, a snake came creeping out of a crevice in the wall, dipped its little head in the dish, and ate with her. The child had pleasure in this, and when she was sitting there with her little dish and the snake did not come at once, she cried,

> *"Snake, snake, come swiftly,*
> *Hither come, thou tiny thing,*
> *Thou shalt have thy crumbs of bread,*
> *Thou shalt refresh thyself with milk."*

Then the snake came in haste, and enjoyed its food. Moreover it showed gratitude, for it brought the child all kinds of pretty things from its hidden treasures, bright stones, pearls, and gold playthings. The snake, however, only drank the milk, and left the bread-crumbs alone. Then one day the child took its little spoon and struck the snake gently on its head with it, and said, "Eat the bread-crumbs as well, little thing." The mother, who was standing in the kitchen, heard the child talking to some one, and when she saw that she was striking a snake with her spoon, ran out with a log of wood, and killed the good little creature.

From that time forth, a change came over the child. As long as the snake had eaten with her, she had grown tall and strong, but now she lost her pretty rosy cheeks and wasted away. It was not long before the funeral bird began to cry in the night, and the redbreast to collect little branches and leaves for a funeral garland, and soon afterwards the child lay on her bier.

ii

A SNAKE cries "Huhu, huhu." A child says, "Come out." The snake comes out, then the child inquires about her little sister: "Hast thou not seen little Red-stockings?" The snake says, "No." "Neither have I." "Then I am like you. Huhu, huhu, huhu."

iii

AN ORPHAN child was sitting on the town walls spinning, when she saw a snake coming out of a hole low down in the wall. Swiftly she spread out beside this one of the blue silk handkerchiefs which snakes have such a strong liking for, and which are the only things they will creep on. As soon as the snake saw it, it went back, then returned, bringing with it a small golden crown, laid it on the handkerchief, and then went away again. The girl took up the crown; it glittered and was of delicate golden filagree work. It was not long before the snake came back for the second time, but when it no longer saw the crown, it crept up to the wall, and in its grief smote its little head against it as long as it had strength to do so, until at last it lay there dead. If the girl had but left the crown where it was, the snake would certainly have brought still more of its treasures out of the hole.

The Turnip

THERE WERE once two brothers who both served as soldiers; one of them was rich, and the other poor. The poor one, to escape from his poverty, put off his soldier's coat and turned farmer. He dug and hoed his bit of land, and sowed it with turnip-seed. The seed came up, and one turnip grew there which became large and vigorous, and visibly grew bigger and bigger, and seemed as if it would never stop growing, so that it might have been called the princess of turnips, for never was such an one seen before, and never will such an one be seen again.

It finally became so enormous that it filled a whole cart, and two oxen were required to draw it, and the farmer had not the least idea what he was to do with the turnip, or whether it would be a fortune to him or a misfortune. At last he thought, "If I sell it, what will I get for it; and if I eat it myself, why the small turnips would taste just as good. It would be better to take it to the King, and make him a present of it."

So he placed it on a cart, harnessed two oxen, took it to the palace, and presented it to the King. "What strange thing is this?" said the King. "Many wonderful things have come before my eyes, but never such a monster as this! From what seed can this have sprung, or are you a luck-child and have met with it by chance?" "Ah, no!" said the farmer, "no luck-child am I. I am a poor soldier, who because he could no longer support himself hung his soldier's coat on a nail and took to farming land. I have a brother who is rich and well known to you, Lord King, but I, because I have nothing, am forgotten by every one."

Then the King felt compassion for him, and said, "You shall be raised from poverty, and shall have such gifts from me that you shall be equal to your rich brother." Then he bestowed on him much gold, and lands, and meadows, and herds, and made him immensely rich, so that the wealth of the other brother could not be compared with his. When the rich brother heard what the poor one had gained for himself with one single turnip, he envied him, and thought in every way how he also could get hold of a similar piece of luck. He would, however, set about it in a much wiser way, and took gold and horses and carried them to the King, and made certain the King would give him a much larger present in return. If his brother had got so much for one turnip, what would he not carry away with him in return for such beautiful things as these? The King accepted his present, and said he had nothing to give him in return that was more rare and excellent than the great turnip.

So the rich man was obliged to put his brother's turnip in a cart and have it taken to his home. When there he did not know on whom to vent his rage and anger, until bad thoughts came to him, and he resolved to kill his brother. He hired murderers, who were to lie in ambush, and then he went to his brother and said, "Dear brother, I know of a hidden treasure, we will dig it up together, and divide it between us." The other agreed to this, and accompanied him without suspicion. While they were on their way, however, the murderers fell on him, bound him, and would have hanged him to a tree. But just as they were doing this, loud singing and the sound of a horse's feet were heard in the distance. On this their hearts were filled with terror, and they pushed their prisoner head first into the sack, hung it on a branch, and took to flight. He, however, worked up there until he had made a hole in the sack through which he could put his head.

The man who was coming by was no other than a traveling student, a young fellow who rode on his way through the wood joyously singing his song. When he who was aloft saw that some one was passing below him, he cried, "Good day! You have come at a lucky time." The student looked round on every side, but did not know whence the voice came. At last he said, "Who calls me?" Then an answer came from the top of the tree, "Raise your eyes; here I sit aloft in the Sack of Wisdom. In a short time have I learnt great things. Compared with this all schools are a jest; in a very short time I shall have learnt everything, and shall descend wiser than all other men. I understand the stars, and the signs of the zodiac, and the tracks of the winds, the sand of the sea, the healing of illness, and the virtues of all herbs, birds, and stones. If you were once within it you would feel what noble things issue forth from the Sack of Knowledge."

The student, when he heard all this, was astonished, and said, "Blessed be the hour in which I have found you! May not I also enter the sack for a while?" He who was above replied as if unwillingly, "For a short time I will let you get into it, if you reward me and give me good words; but you must wait an hour longer, for one thing remains which I must learn before I do it." When the student had waited a while he became impatient, and begged to be allowed to get in at once, his thirst for knowledge was so very great. So he who was above pretended at last to yield, and said, "In order that I may come forth from the house of knowledge you must let it down by the rope, and then you shall enter it."

So the student let the sack down, untied it, and set him free, and then cried, "Now draw me up at once," and was about to get into the sack. "Halt!" said the other, "that won't do," and took him by the head and put him upside down into the sack, fastened it, and drew the disciple of wisdom up the tree by the rope. Then he swung him in the air and said, "How goes it with you, my dear fellow? Behold, already you feel wisdom coming, and are gaining valuable experience. Keep perfectly quiet until you become wiser." Thereupon he mounted the student's horse and rode away, but in an hour's time sent some one to let the student out again.

The Twelve Huntsmen

THERE WAS once a King's son who was betrothed to a maiden, and he loved his bride very much. One day, as they were sitting very happily together, there came information that his father lay ill and dying, and wished to see him for the last time before his death. "I must go and leave you, darling," said the King's son, "and directly too, for I have a long journey to take; but I will give you this ring as a memory token, and when I am King I will come and fetch you home."

Then he rode away, and when he reached the castle he found his father dying and his end very near. But he was able to speak, and said, "Dearest son, I have sent for you because I want you to promise to do as I wish about your marriage."

And then he named to him a King's daughter who was well known, and asked him to take her as his wife. The son was so sad at these words that he hardly knew at first what to say; still, he could not refuse his dying father, so he replied, "Dear father, whatever your will is shall be done."

Then the King closed his eyes and died. As soon as the son became King, and the mourning was over, he remembered that he must keep the promise which he had given to his father. He sent, therefore, to the King's daughter, and as she was willing to be his bride they were betrothed to each other.

The first bride very soon heard of what he had done, and she grieved so bitterly over her lover's unfaithfulness that her life seemed passing away. At last her father, who was also a King, said to her, "Dearest child, why are you so sad? If anything you wish can be done, I will do it for you."

She roused herself in a moment, and said, "Dear father, I should so like to have as companions eleven maidens exactly like myself in countenance, shape, and size."

Her father replied: "As soon as possible your wish shall be fulfilled."

He sent messengers all over the kingdom, who were ordered to find eleven maidens who should resemble his daughter in face, figure, and size; and after a long time they succeeded, and brought them to the King's daughter.

As soon as they arrived she ordered twelve hunting dresses to be made exactly alike, and when they were finished, each of the eleven maidens put one on, and she did the same. Then she bade her father farewell and rode away to the castle of her former bridegroom, whom she still loved. On arriving she sent a message to the King, saying she was the chief of twelve young huntsmen who wished to be taken into the King's service.

He came out to see them, but in the huntsmen's dress he did not recognize his former bride; but he was so pleased with their appearance that he said he should like them to serve him very much, and so they all became the King's huntsmen.

But the King had a lion who was a wonderful animal, for he found out every concealment or secret.

So it happened one evening that he said to the King, "You think that you have engaged twelve young huntsmen to serve you." "Yes," said the King, "I have engaged twelve huntsmen." "You are mistaken," replied the lion; "they are maidens, not huntsmen." "Well," said the King, "that cannot be true; or, if it is, how can you prove it?" "Oh, easily," said the lion; "strew peas in the antechamber, and you will soon see. A man has a firm step; he will either crush the peas or pass over them without moving them; but maidens will come tripping or shuffling along, and set the peas rolling."

The King was very much pleased with this advice, and ordered the room to be strewn with peas.

But one of the King's own servants was kind-hearted, and as he overheard the lion's advice, he went at once and told the young huntsmen how they were to be put to the proof, and said also, "The lion wants the King to believe that you are women."

The King's daughter thanked him, and when she spoke afterward to the maidens about it, she said, "Remember to step strongly and with a firm foot on the peas."

The next morning the King sent for the twelve huntsmen, and met them in the antechamber; but as they passed through where the peas lay they stepped upon them so heavily, and had such a firm, strong walk, that not a single pea rolled or even moved.

After they were gone the King said to the lion, "You have spoken falsely to me; they walk like men." "Yes," answered the lion; "they knew that the peas were put there to prove them, so they exerted all their strength; but now give them another trial; have twelve spinning-wheels placed in the anteroom, and when they see them they will look quite delighted, whereas no man would notice them."

The King was pleased with this advice also, and gave orders for twelve spinning-wheels to be placed in the anteroom.

The servant, however, who really believed in the truthfulness of the young huntsmen, disclosed the plan to them. When they were alone the King's daughter cautioned them not even to glance at the spinning-wheels, and to walk firmly.

The next morning the King sent for his twelve huntsmen; but as they passed through the anteroom with a firm step not one of them took the slightest notice of the spinning-wheels.

"Wrong again, lion," said the King; "they must be men, for they did not even see the spinning-wheels." "Because," answered the lion, "they knew that you were trying them with another test."

But after this the King would not believe the lion.

The twelve huntsmen generally followed or accompanied the King when he went hunting, and the more he knew of them the more he liked them.

It happened one day while they were out hunting that information was brought of the approach of the King's bride. As soon as the chief huntsmen—who really was the King's first bride, and rode near him—heard the news, such a pang of grief came upon her that her heart seemed to stop, and she fell off her horse to the ground insensible. The King, who supposed that his favorite huntsman had met with an accident, ran to help him; and raising him up, his glove fell off. Then the King saw with surprise that he wore on his finger a ring which he had given to his first bride, and looking earnestly in the face, he recognized her. Then was his heart so completely at rest that he kissed her, and as she opened her eyes he exclaimed, "You are mine, and I am yours, and no one in the world shall separate us again."

To his other bride he sent a messenger to say that he had a wife already whom he had chosen before he knew her, and that he prayed her to return to her own country.

Soon after the marriage was celebrated, and the lion taken into favor; for, after all, he had spoken the truth.

The Maid of Brakel

A GIRL from Brakel once went to St. Anne's Chapel at the foot of the Hinnenberg, and as she wanted to have a husband, and thought there was no one else in the chapel, she sang,

> *"Oh, holy Saint Anne!*
> *Help me soon to a man.*
> *Thou know'st him right well,*
> *By Suttmer gate does he dwell.*
> *His hair it is golden,*
> *Thou know'st him right well."*

The clerk, however, was standing behind the altar and heard that, so he cried in a very gruff voice, "Thou shalt not have him! Thou shalt not have him!"

The girl thought that the child Mary who stood by her mother, Anne, had called out that to her. She became angry and cried, "Hush, you conceited thing. Hold your tongue, and let your mother speak!"

Going Traveling

THERE WAS once a poor woman who had a son, who much wished to travel, but his mother said, "How canst thou travel? We have no money for thee to take away with thee." Then said the son, "I will manage very well for myself. I will always say, Not much, not much, not much."

So he walked for a long time and always said, "Not much, not much, not much." Then he passed by a company of fishermen and said, "God speed you! not much, not much, not much." "What sayst thou, churl, 'not much?' " And when the net was drawn out they had not caught much fish. So one of them fell on the youth with a stick and said, "Hast thou never seen me threshing?" "What ought I to say, then?" asked the youth. "Thou must say, 'Get it full, get it full.' "

After this he again walked a long time, and said, "Get it full, get it full," until he came to the gallows, where they had got a poor sinner whom they were about to hang. Then said he, "Good morning; get it full, get it full." "What sayst thou, knave, 'get it full'? Dost thou want to make out that there are still more wicked people in the world—is not this enough?" And he again got some blows on his back. "What am I to say, then?" said he. "Thou must say, 'may God have pity on the poor soul.' "

Again the youth walked on for a long while and said, "May God have pity on the poor soul!" Then he came to a pit by which stood a knacker who was cutting up a horse. The youth said, "Good morning; God have pity on the poor soul!" "What dost thou say, thou ill-tempered knave?" And the knacker gave him such a box on the ear, that he could not see out of his eyes. "What am I to say, then?" "Thou must say, 'There lies the carrion in the pit!' "

So he walked on, and always said, "There lies the carrion in the pit, there lies the carrion in the pit." And he came to a cart full of people, so he said, "Good morning, there lies the carrion in the pit!" Then the cart pushed him into a hole, and the driver took his whip and cracked it upon the youth, till he was forced to crawl back to his mother, and as long as he lived he never went traveling again.

Knoist and His Three Sons

BETWEEN Werrel and Soist there lived a man whose name was Knoist, and he had three sons. One was blind, the other lame, and the third stark-naked. Once on a time they went into a field, and there they saw a hare. The blind one shot it, the lame one caught it, the naked one put it in his pocket. Then they came to a mighty big lake, on which there were three boats; one sailed, one sank, the third had no bottom to it. They all three got into the one with no bottom to it. Then they came to a mighty big forest in which there was a mighty big tree; in the tree was a mighty big chapel; in the chapel was a sexton made of beech-wood and a box-wood parson, who dealt out holy-water with cudgels.

> *"How truly happy is that one*
> *Who can from holy water run!"*

The Story of Schlauraffen Land

IN THE TIME of Schlauraffen* I went there, and saw Rome and the Lateran hanging by a small silken thread, and a man without feet who outran a swift horse, and a keen sharp sword that cut through a bridge. There I saw a young ass with a silver nose which pursued two fleet hares, and a lime tree that was very large, on which hot cakes were growing. There I saw a lean old goat which carried about a hundred cart-loads of fat on his body, and sixty loads of salt. Have I not told enough lies?

There I saw a plough ploughing without horse or cow; and a child of one year threw four millstones from Ratisbon to Treves, and from Treves to Strasburg; and a hawk swam over the Rhine, which he had a perfect right to do. There I heard some fishes begin to make such a disturbance with each other, that it resounded as far as Heaven; and sweet honey flowed like water from a deep valley at the top of a high mountain, and these were strange things. There were two crows which were mowing a meadow; and I saw two gnats building a bridge, and two doves tore a wolf to pieces; two children brought forth two kids; and two frogs threshed corn together. There I saw two mice consecrating a bishop, and two cats scratching out a bear's tongue. Then a snail came running up and killed two furious lions. There stood a barber and shaved a woman's beard off; and two sucking-children bade their mother hold her tongue. There I saw two greyhounds which brought a mill out of the water; and a sorry old horse was beside it, and said it was right. And four horses were standing in the yard threshing corn with all their might, and two goats were heating the stove, and a red cow shot the bread into the oven.

Then a cock crowed, Cock-a-doodle-doo! The story is all told—Cock-a-doodle-doo!

* A legendary fantastic region, similar to the fabulous Cockaigne, land of luxury and idleness.

The Ditmarsch Tale of Wonders

I WILL TELL you something. I saw two roasted fowls flying; they flew quickly and had their breasts turned to Heaven and their backs to Hell; and an anvil and a mill-stone swam across the Rhine prettily, slowly, and gently; and a frog sat on the ice at Whitsuntide and ate a ploughshare.

Four fellows who wanted to catch a hare, went on crutches and stilts; one of them was deaf, the second blind, the third dumb, and the fourth could not stir a step. Do you want to know how it was done? First, the blind man saw the hare running across the field, the dumb one called to the deaf one, and the lame one seized it by the neck.

There were certain men who wished to sail on dry land, and they set their sails in the wind, and sailed away over great fields. Then they sailed over a high mountain, and there they were miserably drowned.

A crab was chasing a hare which was running away at full speed; and high up on the roof lay a cow which had climbed up there. In that country the flies are as big as the goats are here.

Open the window that the lies may fly out.

Domestic Servants

"WHITHER GOEST thou?" "To Walpe." "I to Walpe, thou to Walpe; so, so, together we'll go."

"Hast thou a man? What is his name?" "Cham." "My man Cham, thy man Cham; I to Walpe, thou to Walpe; so, so, together we'll go."

"Hast thou a child; how is he styled?" "Wild." "My child Wild, thy child Wild; my man Cham, thy man Cham; I to Walpe, thou to Walpe; so, so, together we'll go."

"Hast thou a cradle? How callest thou thy cradle?" "Hippodadle." "My cradle Hippodadle, thy cradle Hippodadle; my child Wild, thy child Wild; my man Cham, thy man Cham; I to Walpe, thou to Walpe; so, so, together we'll go."

"Hast thou also a drudge? What name has thy drudge?" "From-thy-work-do-not-budge." "My drudge, From-thy-work-do-not-budge, thy drudge, From-thy-work-do-not-budge; my cradle Hippodadle, thy cradle Hippodadle; my child Wild, thy child Wild; my man Cham, thy man Cham; I to Walpe, thou to Walpe; so, so, together we'll go."

The Rogue and His Master

A MAN NAMED John greatly desired that his son should learn some trade, and he went into the church to ask the priest's opinion what would be most desirable. Just then the clerk was standing near the altar, and he cried out, "The rogue, the rogue!" At these words the man went away, and told his son he must learn to be a rouge, for so the priest had said. So they set out, and asked one man after another whether he was a rogue, till, at the end of the day, they entered a large forest, and there found a little hut with an old woman in it.

John asked the old woman, "Do you know any man who can teach roguery?" "Here," said the old woman, "here you may learn, for my son is a master of the art." Then John asked the son whether he could teach it perfectly, and the rogue replied, "I will teach your son well; return in four years, and if you know your son then I will not ask any recompense; but if you do not, then you must give me two hundred dollars."

John now went home, and left his son to learn roguery and witchcraft. When the time was up, the father set out to see his son, considering as he went along by what he should know him. On his way he met a little man, who stopped him, and asked, "Why are you grieving and looking so mournful?" "Oh," replied John, "four years ago I left my son to learn roguery, and the master said if I returned in that time and knew my son, I should have nothing to pay; but if I did not know him, I must give him two hundred dollars; and, since I have no means of recognizing him, I am troubled where to procure the money."

Then the little man told him to take a basket of bread with him, and when he came to the rogue's house to put the basket under a hollow tree which stood there, and the little bird which should peep out would be his son.

John went and did as he was told, and out came a little bird to peck at the bread. "Holloa, my son! Are you here?" said John. The son was very glad to hear his father's voice, and said, "Father, let us go!" But first the rogue-master called out, "The Evil One must have told you where to find your son!"

So the father and son returned home, and on their way they met a coach, and the son said to his father, "I will change myself into a fine greyhound, and then you can earn some money by me."

The lord who was riding in the coach called out, "Man, will you sell your dog?" "Yes," replied the father. "How much do you want for him?" "Thirty dollars," was the reply. "That is too much, my man," said the lord, "but on account of his very beautiful skin I will buy him of you."

The bargain concluded, the dog was put inside the coach; but when they had traveled a mile or two the greyhound jumped right out through the glass, and rejoined his father.

After this adventure they went home together, and the following day they went to the next village to market. On their way the son said, "Father, I will change myself into a horse, and then you can sell me; but first untie my bridle, and then I can change myself into the form of a man."

The father drove his horse to market, and thither came the rogue-master and bought him for a hundred dollars, but the father forgot to untie the bridle.

The rogue rode his horse home, and put him in the stable, and, when the maid came with the corn, the horse said to her, "Undo my bridle, undo my bridle!" "Ah, can you speak?" said she, terrified, and untied the horse directly. The horse thereupon became a sparrow, and flew away out at the door, pursued by the rogue, who changed himself also into a bird. When they came up with each other, the rogue changed himself into water, and the other into a fish. But the rogue could not catch him so, and he changed himself into a cock, but the other instantly became a fox, and bit his master's head off, so that he died.

And he lies there to this very day.

The Wise Servant

HOW FORTUNATE is the master, and how well all goes in his house, when he has a wise servant who listens to his orders and does not obey them, but prefers following his own wisdom.

A clever John of this kind was once sent out by his master to seek a lost cow. He stayed away a long time, and the master thought, "Faithful John does not spare any pains over his work!" As, however, he did not come back at all, the master was afraid lest some misfortune had befallen him, and set out himself to look for him. He had to search a long time, but at last he perceived the boy who was running up and down a large field. "Now, dear John," said the master when he had got up to him, "have you found the cow which I sent you to seek?" "No, master," he answered, "I have not found the cow, but then I have not looked for it." "Then what have you looked for, John?" "Something better, and that luckily I have found." "What is that, John?" "Three blackbirds," answered the boy. "And where are they?" asked the master. "I see one of them, I hear the other, and I am running after the third," answered the wise boy.

Take example by this; do not trouble yourselves about your masters or their orders, but rather do what comes into your head and pleases you, and then you will act just as wisely so prudent John!

The Seven Swabians

SEVEN Swabians once held a meeting. The first was Master Schulz; the second, Jackli; the third, Marli; the fourth, Jergli; the fifth, Michal; the sixth, Hans; the seventh, Veitli. All seven had made up their minds to travel about the world to seek adventures, and perform great deeds. But in order that they might go in security and with arms in their hands, they thought it would be advisable that they should have one very strong and very long spear made for them. This spear all seven of them took in their hands at once.

In front walked the boldest and bravest, and that was Master Schulz; all the others followed in a row, and Veitli was the last.

It came to pass one day in the hay-making month, when they had walked a long distance, and still had a long way to go before they reached the village where they were to pass the night, that as they were in a meadow in the twilight a great beetle or hornet flew by them from behind a bush, and hummed in a menacing manner. Master Schulz was so terrified that he all but dropped the spear, and a cold perspiration broke out over his whole body. "Hark! hark!" cried he to his comrades, "good heavens! I hear a drum." Jackli, who was behind him holding the spear, and who perceived some kind of a smell, said, "Something is most certainly going on, for I taste powder and matches."

At these words Master Schulz began to take to flight, and in a trice jumped over a hedge, but as he just happened to jump on to the teeth of a rake which had been left lying there after the hay-making, the handle of it struck against his face and gave him a tremendous blow." "Oh dear!" Oh dear!" screamed Master Schulz. "Take me prisoner; I surrender! I surrender!" The other six all leapt over, one on the top of the other, crying, "If you surrender, I surrender too!" If you surrender, I surrender too!" At length, as no enemy was there to bind and take them away, they saw that they had been mistaken, and in order that the story might not be known, and they be treated as fools and ridiculed, they all swore to each other to hold their peace about it until one of them accidentally spoke of it.

Then they journeyed onwards. The second danger which they survived cannot be compared with the first. Some days afterwards, their path led them through a fallow-field where a hare was sitting sleeping in the sun. Her ears were standing straight up, and her great glassy eyes were wide open. All of them were alarmed at the sight of the horrible wild beast, and they consulted together as to what would be the least dangerous thing to do. For if they were to run, they knew that the monster would pursue and swallow them whole. So they said, "We must go through a great and dangerous struggle. Boldly ventured, is half won," and all seven grasped the spear, Master Schulz in front, and Veitli behind. Master Schulz was always trying to keep the spear back, but Veitli had become quite brave while behind, and wanted to dash forward and cried,

> "Strike home, in every Swabian's name,
> Or else I wish ye may be lame."

But Hans knew how to meet this, and said,

> *"Thunder and lightning, it's fine to prate,*
> *But for dragon-hunting thou'rt aye too late."*

Michal cried,

> *"Nothing is wanting, not even a hair,*
> *Be sure the Devil himself is there."*

Then it was Jergli's turn to speak,

> *"If it be not, it's at least his mother,*
> *Or else it's the Devil's own step-brother."*

And now Marli had a bright thought, and said to Veitli,

> *"Advance, Veitli, advance, advance,*
> *And I behind will hold the lance."*

Veitli, however, did not attend to that, and Jackli said,

> *" 'Tis Schulz's place the first to be,*
> *No one deserves that honor but he."*

Then Master Schulz plucked up his courage, and said, gravely,

> *"Then let us boldly advance to the fight,*
> *And thus we shall show our valor and might."*

Hereupon they all together set on the dragon. Master Schulz crossed himself and prayed for God's assistance, but as all this was of no avail, and he was getting nearer and nearer to the enemy, he screamed, "Oho! Oho! ho! ho! ho!" in the greatest anguish. This awakened the hare, which in great alarm darted swiftly away. When Master Schulz saw her thus flying from the field of battle, he cried in his joy,

> *"Quick, Veitli, quick, look there, look there,*
> *The monster's nothing but a hare!"*

But the Swabian allies went in search of further adventures, and came to the Moselle, a mossy, quiet, deep river, over which there are few bridges, and which in many places people have to cross in boats. As the seven Swabians did not know this, they called to a man who was working on the opposite side of the river, to know how people contrived to get across. The distance and their way of speaking made the man unable to understand what they wanted, and he said, "What? what?" in the way people speak in the neighborhood of Treves. Master Schulz thought he was saying, "Wade,

wade through the water," and as he was the first, began to set out and went into the Moselle.

It was not long before he sank in the mud and the deep waves which drove against him, but his hat was blown on the opposite shore by the wind, and a frog sat down beside it, and croaked "Wat, wat, wat." The other six on the opposite side heard that, and said, "Oho, comrades, Master Schulz is calling us; if he can wade across, why cannot we?" So they all jumped into the water together in a great hurry, and were drowned, and thus one frog took the lives of all six of them, and not one of the Swabian allies ever reached home again.

Lean Lisa

LEAN LISA was of a very different way of thinking from lazy Harry and fat Trina, who never let anything disturb their peace. She scoured everything with ashes, from morning till evening, and burdened her husband, Long Laurence, with so much work that he had heavier weights to carry than an ass with three sacks. It was, however, all to no purpose; they had nothing and came to nothing.

One night as she lay in bed, and could hardly move one limb for weariness, she still did not allow her thoughts to go to sleep. She thrust her elbows into her husband's side, and said, "Listen Lenz, to what I have been thinking: if I were to find one florin and one was given to me, I would borrow another to put to them, and you too should give me another, and then as soon as I had got the four florins together, I would buy a young cow."

This pleased the husband right well. "It is true," said he, "that I do not know where I am to get the florin which you want as a gift from me; but, if you can get the money together, and can buy a cow with it, you will do well to carry out your project. I shall be glad," he added, "if the cow has a calf, and then I shall often get a drink of milk to refresh me." "The milk is not for you," said the woman; "we must let the calf suck that it may become big and fat, and we may be able to sell it well." "Certainly," replied the man, "but still we will take a little milk; that will do no harm." "Who has taught you to manage cows?" said the woman; "whether it does harm or not, I will not allow it, and even if you were to stand on your head for it, you should not have a drop of the milk! Do you think, because there is no satisfying you, Long Laurence, that you are to eat up what I earn with so much difficulty?" "Wife," said the man, "be quiet, or I will give you a blow on your mouth!" "What!" cried she, "you threaten me, you glutton, you rascal, you lazy Harry!" She was just laying hold of his hair, but Long Laurence got up, seized both Lean Lisa's withered arms in one hand, and with the other he pressed down her head into the pillow, let her scold, and held her until she fell asleep for very weariness.

Whether she continued to wrangle when she awoke next morning, or whether she went out to look for the florin which she wanted to find, that I know not.

Godfather Death

A POOR MAN had twelve children and was forced to work night and day to give them even bread. When therefore the thirteenth came into the world, he knew not what to do in his trouble, but ran out into the great highway, and resolved to ask the first person whom he met to be godfather.

The first to meet him was the good God who already knew what filled his heart, and said to him, "Poor man, I pity you. I will hold your child at its christening, and will take charge of it and make it happy on earth." The man said, "Who are you?" "I am God." "Then I do not desire to have you for a godfather," said the man; "you give to the rich, and leave the poor to hunger."

Thus spoke the man, for he did not know how wisely God apportions riches and poverty. He turned therefore away from the Lord, and went farther.

Then the Devil came to him and said, "What do you seek? If you will take me as a godfather for your child, I will give him gold in plenty and all the joys of the world as well." The man asked, "Who are you?" "I am the Devil." "Then I do not desire to have you for godfather," said the man; "you deceive men and lead them astray."

He went onward, and then came Death striding up to him with withered legs, and said, "Take me as godfather." The man asked, "Who are you?" "I am Death, and I make all equal." Then said the man, "You are the right one, you take the rich as well as the poor, without distinction; you shall be godfather." Death answered, "I will make your child rich and famous, for he who has me for a friend can lack nothing." The man said, "Next Sunday is the christening; be there at the right time." Death appeared as he had promised, and stood godfather quite in the usual way.

When the boy had grown up, his godfather one day appeared and bade him go with him. He led him forth into a forest, and showed him a herb which grew there, and said, "Now shall you receive your godfather's present. I make you a celebrated physician. When you are called to a patient, I will always appear to you. If I stand by the head of the sick man, you may say with confidence that you will make him well again, and if you give him of this herb he will recover; but if I stand by the patient's feet, he is mine, and you must say that all remedies are in vain, and that no physician in the world could save him. But beware of using the herb against my will, or it might fare ill with you."

It was not long before the youth was the most famous physician in the whole world. He had only to look at the patient and he knew his condition at once, and if he would recover, or must needs die. From far and wide people came to him, sent for him when they had anyone ill, and gave him so much money that he soon became a rich man.

Now it befell that the King became ill, and the physician was summoned, and was to say if recovery were possible. But when he came to the bed, Death was standing by the feet of the sick man, and the herb did not grow which could save him.

"If I could but cheat Death for once," thought the physician, "he is sure to take it ill if I do, but, as I am his godson, he will shut one eye; I will risk it." He therefore took up the sick man, and laid him the other way, so that now Death was standing by his head. Then he gave the King some of the herb, and he recovered and grew healthy again. But Death came to the physician, looking very black and angry, threatened him with his finger, and said, "You have overreached me. This time I will pardon it, as you are my godson; but if you venture it again, it will cost you your neck, for I will take you yourself away with me."

Soon afterwards the King's daughter fell into a severe illness. She was his only child, and he wept day and night, so that he began to lose the sight of his eyes, and he caused it to be made known that whosoever rescued her from death should be her husband and inherit the crown. When the physician came to the sick girl's bed, he saw Death by her feet. He ought to have remembered the warning given by his godfather, but he was so infatuated by the great beauty of the King's daughter, and the happiness of becoming her husband, that he flung all thought to the winds. He did not see that Death was casting angry glances on him, that he was raising his hand in the air, and threatening him with his withered fist. He raised up the sick girl, and placed her head where her feet had lain. Then he gave her some of the herb, and instantly her cheeks flushed red, and life stirred afresh in her.

When Death saw that for a second time he was defrauded of his own property, he walked up to the physician with long strides, and said, "All is over with you, and now the lot falls on you," and seized him so firmly with his ice-cold hand, that he could not resist, and led him into a cave below the earth. There he saw how thousands and thousands of candles were burning in countless rows, some large, others half-sized, others small. Every instant some were extinguished, and others again burned up, so that the flames seemed to leap hither and thither in perpetual change.

"See," said Death, "these are the lights of men's lives. The large ones belong to children, the half-sized ones to married people in their prime; the little ones belong to old people; but children and young folks likewise have often only a tiny candle."

"Show me the light of my life," said the physician, and he thought that it would be still very tall. Death pointed to a little end which was just threatening to go out, and said, "Behold, it is there."

"Ah, dear godfather," said the horrified physician, "light a new one for me, do it for love of me, that I may enjoy my life, be King, and the husband of the King's beautiful daughter."

"I cannot," answered Death, "one must go out before a new one is lighted." "Then place the old one on a new one, that will go on burning at once when the old one has come to an end," pleaded the physician. Death behaved as if he were going to fulfill his wish, and took hold of a tall new candle; but as he desired to revenge himself, he purposely made a mistake in fixing it, and the little piece fell down and was extinguished. Immediately the physician fell on the ground. And now he himself was in the hands of Death.

Death's Messengers

IN ANCIENT TIMES a giant was once traveling on a great highway, when suddenly an unknown man sprang up before him, and said, "Halt, not one step farther!" "What!" cried the giant, "a creature whom I can crush between my fingers, wants to block my way? Who art thou that darest to speak so boldly?" "I am Death," answered the other. "No one resists me, and thou also must obey my commands." But the giant refused, and began to struggle with Death. It was a long, violent battle. At last the giant got the upper hand, and struck Death down with his fist, so that he dropped by a stone. The giant went his way, and Death lay there conquered, and so weak that he could not get up again. "What will be done now," said he, "if I stay lying here in a corner? No one will die now in the world, and it will get so full of people that they won't have room to stand beside each other."

In the meantime a young man came along the road, who was strong and healthy, singing a song, and glancing around on every side. When he saw the half-fainting one, he went compassionately to him, raised him up, poured a strengthening draught out of his flask for him, and waited till he came round. "Dost thou know," said the stranger, while he was getting up, "who I am, and who it is whom thou hast helped on his legs again?" "No," answered the youth, "I do not know thee." "I am Death," said he. "I spare no one, and can make no exception with thee—but that thou mayst see that I am grateful, I promise thee that I will not fall on thee unexpectedly, but will send my messengers to thee before I come and take thee away." "Well," said the youth, "it is something gained that I shall know when thou comest, and at any rate be safe from thee for so long." Then he went on his way, and was light-hearted, and enjoyed himself, and lived without thought. But youth and health did not last long; soon came sicknesses and sorrows, which tormented him by day, and took away his rest by night. "Die, I shall not," said he to himself, "for Death will send his messengers before that, but I do wish these wretched days of sickness were over."

As soon as he felt himself well again he began once more to live merrily. Then one day some one tapped him on the shoulder. He looked round, and Death stood behind him, and said, "Follow me, the hour of thy departure from this world has come." "What," replied the man, "wilt thou break thy word? Didst thou not promise me that thou wouldst send thy messengers to me before coming thyself? I have seen none!" "Silence!" answered Death. "Have I not sent one messenger to thee after another? Did not fever come and smite thee, and shake thee, and cast thee down? Has dizziness not bewildered thy head? Has not gout twitched thee in all thy limbs? Did not thine ears sing? Did not tooth-ache bite into thy cheeks? Was it not dark before thine eyes? And besides all that, has not my own brother, Sleep, reminded thee every night of me? Didst thou not lie by night as if thou wert already dead?" The man could make no answer; he yielded to his fate, and went away with Death.

The Wonderful Glass

A MAN once had so many children that all his friends had been asked to become sponsors, so when another child was born he had no one to ask, and knew not what to do.

One night when he had laid himself down to sleep in great trouble, he had a wonderful dream. He dreamed that a voice said to him, "Go out early tomorrow morning, and the first person you meet, ask him to be godfather." On awaking, he determined to follow the advice given in his dream, and, dressing himself quickly, he went out. Near his door he met a man, and immediately asked him to be sponsor for his child.

The stranger, before giving his consent, presented the man with a glass, and said, "This is a most wonderful glass. The water with which you fill it has the power of curing sick persons; you have only to observe where Death stands. If he stands by the head of the sick person then give him the water, and he will be soon well; but if he stands by the feet all your trouble will be useless, the sick person must die."

So the stranger became sponsor for his child, and gave to the father the wonderful goblet, which endowed the water he put into it with such healing qualities. Besides this, he could always tell whether the sick person would recover or not, and could therefore speak confidently about curing him. By this he made a great deal of money, and his fame spread far and wide.

Even the King sent for him, when one of his children was ill but as the wonderful doctor entered, he saw Death standing at the head of the bed, and knew that the child would recover after drinking the water in the magic glass; and so he did. The second time he was sent for the same occurred; but on his third visit the doctor saw Death seated at the foot of the bed, and he told the parents that the child must die.

After a while this doctor became curious, and thought he should like to see where his child's godfather, who had given him such a valuable present, lived, and tell him how he was getting on. But when he reached the house the household quite startled him. On the first step a mop and a broom were quarreling together and fighting furiously. "Where shall I find the master of this house?" he asked. "A step higher," answered the broom.

But when he arrived on the second step, he saw a number of dead fingers lying together, and he inquired again, "Where is the master?" "A step higher," replied one of the fingers."

On the third step lay a heap of human heads, who directed him to go a step higher. On the fourth step he saw a fish frizzling in the pan, and cooking himself. He spoke to the man and told him to go a step higher. On he went, and at last, on the fifth step he came upon the door of a room, and peeping through the keyhole, saw the godfather, and to his surprise, he had large horns; but as soon as he opened the door and went in, the strange man with the horns rushed away suddenly, laid himself on the bed, and drew the clothes over him.

Then said the man, "What is the meaning of this strange household, good sir? On the steps I met with all sorts of strange things, and was told to go up higher; and when I came to the door of this room, I peeped through the keyhole and saw you with a pair of horns on your head."

"That is not true," cried the pretended godfather, in such a terrible voice that the man, in a fright, turned to run away; but no one knows what has become of him, for he has never been heard of since.

The Old Witch

THERE WAS once a little girl who was very obstinate and wilful, and who never obeyed when her elders spoke to her; and so how could she be happy? One day she said to her parents, "I have heard so much of the old Witch, that I will go and see her. People say she is a wonderful old woman, and has many marvelous things in her house; and I am very curious to see them."

Her parents, however, forbade her going, saying, "The Witch is a wicked old woman, who performs many godless deeds; and if you go near her, you are no longer a child of ours."

The girl, however, would not turn back at her parents' command, but went to the Witch's house. When she arrived there the woman asked her, "Why are you so pale?"

"Ah," replied she, trembling all over, "I have frightened myself so with what I have just seen."

"And what did you see?" inquired the old Witch.

"I saw a black man on your steps."

"That was a collier," replied she.

"Then I saw a gray man."

"That was a sportsman," said the old woman.

"After him I saw a blood-red man."

"That was a butcher," replied the woman.

"But oh, I was most terrified," continued the girl, "when I peeped through your window, and saw not you, but a creature with a fiery head."

"Then you have seen the Witch in her proper dress," said the old woman. "For you I have long waited, and now you shall give me light." So saying, she changed the girl into a block of wood, and then threw it into the fire; and when it was fully alight she sat down on the hearth, warmed herself, and said, "Ah, now for once it burns brightly!"

The Devil's Sooty Brother

A DISCHARGED SOLDIER had no money left and did not know how to get on. So he went out into the forest, and when he had walked for a short time, he met a little man who was, however, the Devil. The little man said to him, "What ails you, you seem so very sorrowful?" Then the soldier said, "I am hungry, but have no money." The Devil said, "If you will hire yourself to me, and be my serving-man, you shall have enough for all your life. You shall serve me for seven years, and after that you shall again be free. But one thing I must tell you, and that is, you must not wash, comb, or trim yourself, or cut your hair or nails, or wipe the water from your eyes." The soldier said, "All right, if there is no help for it," and went off with the little man, who straightway led him down into hell.

Then he told him what he had to do: he was to poke the fire under the kettles wherein the hell-broth was stewing, keep the house clean, drive all the sweepings behind the doors, and see that everything is in order; but if he once peeped into the kettles, it would go ill with him. The soldier said, "Good, I will take care." And then the old Devil went out again on his wanderings, and the soldier entered upon his new duties, made the fire, and swept the dirt well behind the doors, just as he had been bidden. When the old Devil came back again, he looked to see if all had been done, appeared satisfied, and went forth a second time.

The soldier now took a good look on every side; the kettles were standing all round hell with a mighty fire below them, and inside they were boiling and sputtering. He would have given anything to look inside them, if the Devil had not so particularly forbidden him. At last, he could no longer restrain himself, slightly raised the lid of the first kettle, and peeped in, and there he saw his former corporal shut in. "Aha, old bird!" said he. "Do I meet you here? You once had me in your power, now I have you," and he quickly let the lid fall, poked the fire, and added a fresh log. After that, he went to the second kettle, raised its lid also a little, and peeped in; his former ensign was inside that. "Aha, old bird, so I find you here! You once had me in your power, now I have you." He closed the lid again, and fetched yet another log to make it really hot. Then he wanted to see who might be shut up in the third kettle—it was actually a general. "Aha, old bird, do I meet you here? Once you had me in your power, now I have you," and he fetched the bellows and made hell-fire flare well up under him.

So he did his work seven years in hell, did not wash, comb, or trim himself, or cut his hair or nails, or wash the water out of his eyes, and the seven years seemed so short to him that he thought he had only been half a year. Now when the time had fully gone by, the Devil came and said, "Well, Hans, what have you done?" "I have poked the fire under the kettles, and I have swept all the dirt well behind the doors."

"But you have peeped into the kettles as well; it is lucky for you that you added fresh logs to them, or else your life would have been forfeited. Now that your time is up, will you go home again?" "Yes," said the soldier, "I should very much like to see what my father is doing at home." The Devil said, "In order that you may receive the wages you have earned, go and fill your knapsack full of the sweepings, and take it home with you. You must also go unwashed and uncombed, with long hair on your head and beard, and with uncut nails and dim eyes; and when you are asked whence you come, you must say, 'From hell,' and when you are asked who you are, you are to say, 'The Devil's sooty brother, and my king as well.'" The soldier held his peace, and did as the Devil bade him, but he was not at all satisfied with his wages.

As soon as he was in the forest again, he took his knapsack from his back to empty it, but on opening it, the sweepings had become pure gold. "I should never have expected that," said he, and was well pleased, and entered the town. The landlord was standing in front of the inn, and when he saw the soldier approaching, he was terrified, because Hans looked so horrible—worse than a scarecrow. He called to him and asked, "Whence comest thou?" "From hell." "Who art thou?" "The Devil's sooty brother, and my King as well." Then the host would not let him enter, but when Hans showed him the gold, he came and unlatched the door himself. Hans then ordered the best room and attendance, ate and drank his fill, but neither washed nor combed himself as the Devil had bidden him, and at last lay down to sleep. But the knapsack full of gold remained before the eyes of the landlord, and left him no peace, and during the night he crept in and stole it away.

Next morning, however, when Hans got up and wanted to pay the landlord and travel further, behold, his knapsack was gone! But he soon composed himself and thought, "Thou hast been unfortunate from no fault of thine own," and straightway went back again

to hell, complained of his misfortune to the old Devil, and begged
for his help. The Devil said, "Seat yourself, I will wash, comb, and
trim you, cut your hair and nails, and wash your eyes for you." And
when he had done with him, he gave him the knapsack back again
full of sweepings, and said, "Go and tell the landlord that he must
return you your money, or else I will come and fetch him, and he
shall poke the fire in your place." Hans went up and said to the
landlord, "Thou hast stolen my money; if thou dost not return it,
thou shalt go down to hell in my place, and wilt look as horrible as
I." Then the landlord gave him the money, and more besides, only
begging him to keep it secret, and Hans was now a rich man.

He set out on his way home to his father, bought himself a shabby
smock-frock to wear, and strolled about making music, for he had
learned to do that while he was with the Devil in hell. There was,
however, an old King in that country, before whom he had to play,
and the King was so delighted with his playing, that he promised
him his eldest daughter in marriage. But when she heard that she
was to be married to a common fellow in a smock-frock, she said,
"Rather than do it, I would go into the deepest water." And then
the King gave him the youngest, who was quite willing to do it to
please her father, and thus the Devil's sooty brother got the King's
daughter, and when the aged King died, the whole kingdom likewise.

Bearskin

A YOUNG FELLOW enlisted as a soldier and conducted himself so
bravely that he was always the foremost when it rained bullets. As
long as the war lasted, all went well, but when peace was made, he
received his dismissal, and the captain said he might go where he
liked. His parents were dead, and he had no longer a home, so
he went to his brothers and begged them to take him in, and keep
him until war broke out again. The brothers, however, were hard-
hearted and said, "What can we do with thee? Thou art of no use to
us; go and make a living for thyself." The soldier had nothing left
but his gun; he took that on his shoulder, and went forth into the
world.

He came to a wide heath, on which nothing was to be seen but a circle of trees; under these he sat sorrowfully down, and began to think over his fate. "I have no money," thought he, "I have learnt no trade but that of fighting, and now that they have made peace they don't want me any longer; so I see beforehand that I shall have to starve." All at once he heard a rustling, and when he looked round, a strange man stood before him, who wore a green coat and looked right stately, but had a hideous cloven foot. "I know already what thou art in need of," said the man; "gold and possessions shalt thou have, as much as thou canst make away with, do what thou wilt, but first I must know if thou art fearless, that I may not bestow my money in vain." "A soldier and fear—how can those two things go together?" he answered; "thou canst put me to the proof." "Very well, then," answered the man, "look behind thee."

The soldier turned round, and saw a large bear, which came growling towards him. "Oho!" cried the soldier, "I will tickle thy nose for thee, so that thou shalt soon lose thy fancy for growling," and he aimed at the bear and shot it through the muzzle; it fell down and never stirred again. "I see quite well," said the stranger, "that thou art not wanting in courage, but there is still another condition which thou wilt have to fulfill." "If it does not endanger my salvation," replied the soldier, who knew very well who was standing by him. "If it does, I'll have nothing to do with it." "Thou wilt look to that for thyself," answered Greencoat; "thou shalt for the next seven years neither wash thyself, nor comb thy beard, nor thy hair, nor cut thy nails, nor say one paternoster. I will give thee a coat and a cloak, which during this time thou must wear. If thou diest during these seven years, thou art mine; if thou remainest alive, thou art free, and rich to boot, for all the rest of thy life."

The soldier thought of the great extremity in which he now found himself, and as he so often had gone to meet death, he resolved to risk it now also, and agreed to the terms. The Devil took off his green coat, gave it to the soldier, and said, "If thou hast this coat on thy back and puttest thy hand into the pocket, thou wilt always find it full of money." Then he pulled the skin off the bear and said, "This shall be thy cloak, and thy bed also, for thereon shalt thou sleep, and in no other bed shalt thou lie, and because of this apparel shalt thou be called Bearskin." After this the Devil vanished.

The soldier put the coat on, felt at once in the pocket, and found that the thing was really true. Then he put on the bearskin and went forth into the world, and enjoyed himself, refraining from nothing that did him good and his money harm. During the first year his appearance was passable, but during the second he began to look like a monster. His hair covered nearly the whole of his face, his beard was like a piece of coarse felt, his fingers had claws, and his face was so covered with dirt that if cress had been sown on it, it would have come up. Whosoever saw him, ran away, but as he everywhere gave the poor money to pray that he might not die during the seven years, and as he paid well for everything, he still always found shelter. In the fourth year, he entered an inn where the landlord would not receive him, and he would not even let him have a place in the stable, because he was afraid the horses would be scared. But as Bearskin thrust his hand into his pocket and pulled out a handful of ducats, the host let himself be persuaded and gave him a room in an outhouse. Bearskin was, however, obliged to promise not to let himself be seen, lest the inn should get a bad name.

As Bearskin was sitting alone in the evening, and wishing from the bottom of his heart that the seven years were over, he heard a loud lamenting in a neighboring room. He had a compassionate heart, so he opened the door, and saw an old man weeping bitterly, and wringing his hands. Bearskin went nearer, but the man sprang to his feet and tried to escape from him. At last when the man perceived that Bearskin's voice was human he let himself be prevailed on, and by kind words Bearskin succeeded so far that the old man revealed the cause of his grief. His property had dwindled away by degrees, he and his daughters would have to starve, and he was so poor that he could not pay the innkeeper, and was to be put in prison. "If that is thy only trouble," said Bearskin, "I have plenty of money." He caused the innkeeper to be brought thither, paid him and put a purse full of gold into the poor man's pocket besides.

When the old man saw himself set free from all his troubles he did not know how to be grateful enough. "Come with me," said he to Bearskin; "my daughters are all miracles of beauty; choose one of them for thyself as a wife. When she hears what thou hast done for me, she will not refuse thee. Thou dost in truth look a little strange, but she will soon put thee to rights again." This pleased Bearskin well, and he went. When the eldest saw him she was so terribly alarmed at his face that she screamed and ran away. The second stood still and looked at him from head to foot, but then she said, "How can I accept a husband who no longer has a human form? The shaven bear that once was here and passed itself off for a man pleased me far better, for at any rate it wore a hussar's dress and white gloves. If it were nothing but ugliness, I might get used to that." The youngest, however said, "Dear father, that must be a good man to have helped you out of your trouble, so if you have promised him a bride for doing it, your promise must be kept."

It was a pity that Bearskin's face was covered with dirt and with hair, for if not they might have seen how delighted he was when he heard these words. He took a ring from his finger, broke it in two, and gave her one half, the other he kept for himself. He wrote his name, however, on her half, and hers on his, and begged her to keep her piece carefully, and then he took his leave and said, "I must still wander about for three years, and if I do not return then, thou art free, for I shall be dead. But pray to God to preserve my life."

The poor betrothed bride dressed herself entirely in black, and when she thought of her future bridegroom tears came into her eyes. Nothing but contempt and mockery fell to her lot from her sisters. "Take care," said the eldest, "if thou givest him thy hand, he will strike his claws into it." "Beware!" said the second. "Bears like sweet things, and if he takes a fancy to thee, he will eat thee up." "Thou must always do as he likes," began the eldest again, "or else he will growl." And the second continued, "but the wedding will be a merry one, for bears dance well." The bride was silent, and did not let them vex her. Bearskin, however, traveled about the world from one place to another, did good where he was able, and gave generously to the poor that they might pray for him.

At length, as the last day of the seven years dawned, he went once more out on the heath, and seated himself beneath the circle of trees. It was not long before the wind whistled, and the Devil stood before him and looked angrily at him; then he threw Bearskin his old coat, and asked for his own green one back. "We have not got so far as that yet," answered Bearskin, "thou must first make me clean." Whether the Devil liked it or not, he was forced to fetch water, and wash Bearskin, comb his hair, and cut his nails. After this, he looked like a brave soldier, and was much handsomer than he had ever been before.

When the Devil had gone away, Bearskin was quite light-hearted. He went into the town, put on a magnificent velvet coat, seated himself in a carriage drawn by four white horses, and drove to his bride's house. No one recognized him, the father took him for a distinguished general, and led him into the room where his daughters were sitting. He was forced to place himself between the two elder ones; they helped him to wine, gave him the best pieces of meat, and thought that in all the world they had never seen a handsomer man. The bride, however, sat opposite to him in her black dress, and never raised her eyes, nor spoke a word.

When at length he asked the father if he would give him one of his daughters to wife, the two eldest jumped up, ran into their bedrooms to put on splendid dresses, for each of them fancied she was the chosen one. The stranger, as soon as he was alone with his bride, brought out his half of the ring, and threw it in a glass of wine which he reached across the table to her. She took the wine, but when she had drunk it, and found the half ring lying at the bottom, her heart began to beat. She got the other half, which she wore on a ribbon round her neck, joined them, and saw that the two pieces fitted exactly together. Then said he, "I am thy betrothed bridegroom, whom thou sawest as Bearskin, but through God's grace I have again received my human form, and have once more become clean." He went up to her, embraced her, and gave her a kiss.

In the meantime the two sisters came back in full dress, and when they saw that the handsome man had fallen to the share of the youngest, and heard that he was Bearskin, they ran out full of anger and rage. One of them drowned herself in the well, the other hanged herself on a tree. In the evening, some one knocked at the door, and when the bridegroom opened it, it was the Devil in his green coat, who said, "Seest thou, I have now got two souls in the place of thy one!"

The Devil and His Grandmother

THERE WAS a great war in which the King had many soldiers. But he gave them small pay, so small that they could not live upon it. Three of them agreed among themselves to desert. One of them said to the others, "If we are caught we shall be hanged on the gallows; how shall we manage it?" Another said, "Look at that great cornfield, if we were to hide ourselves there, no one could find us; the troops are not allowed to enter it, and tomorrow they are to march away." They crept into the corn, but the troops did not march away, but remained lying all round about it. They stayed in the corn for two days and two nights, and were so hungry that they all but died, but if they had come out, their death would have been certain. Then said they, "What is the use of our deserting if we have to perish miserably here?"

But now a fiery dragon came flying through the air and it came down to them and asked why they had concealed themselves there. They answered, "We are three soldiers who have deserted because the pay was so bad, and now we shall have to die of hunger if we stay here, or to dangle on the gallows if we go out." "If you will serve me for seven years," said the dragon, "I will convey you through the army so that no one shall seize you." "We have no choice and are compelled to accept," they replied. Then the dragon caught hold of them with his claws, and carried them away through the air over the army, and put them down again on the earth far from it; but the dragon was no other than the Devil. He gave them a small whip and said, "Whip with it and crack it, and then as much gold will spring up round about as you can wish for; then you can live like great lords, keep horses, and drive your carriages, but when the seven years have come to an end, you are my property." Then he put before them a book which they were all three forced to sign. "I will, however, then set you a riddle," said he, "and if you can guess that, you shall be free, and released from my power."

Then the dragon flew away from them, and they went away with their whip, had gold in plenty, ordered themselves rich apparel, and traveled about the world. Wherever they were they lived in pleasure and magnificence, rode on horseback, drove in carriages, ate and drank, but did nothing wicked. The time slipped quickly away, and when the seven years were coming to an end, two of them were terribly anxious and alarmed; but the third took the affair easily, and said, "Brothers, fear nothing, my head is sharp enough, I shall guess the riddle." They went out into the open country and sat down, and the two pulled sorrowful faces.

Then an aged woman came up to them who inquired why they were so sad. "Alas!" said they, "how can that concern you? After all, you cannot help us." "Who knows?" said she, "confide your trouble to me." So they told her that they had been the Devil's servants for nearly seven years, and that he had provided them with gold as plentifully as if it had been blackberries, but that they had sold themselves to him, and were forfeited to him, if at the end of the seven years they could not guess a riddle. The old woman said, "If you are to be saved, one of you must go into the forest; there he will come to a fallen rock which looks like a little house; he must enter that, and then he will obtain help." The two melancholy ones thought to themselves, "That will still not save us," and stayed where they were, but the third, the merry one, got up and walked on in the forest until he found the rock-house.

In the little house, however, a very aged woman was sitting, who was the Devil's grandmother, and she asked the soldier where he came from, and what he wanted there. He told her everything that had happened, and as he pleased her well, she had pity on him, and said she would help him. She lifted up a great stone which lay above a cellar, and said, "Conceal yourself there, you can hear everything that is said here; only sit still, and do not stir. When the dragon comes, I will question him about the riddle. He tells everything to me, so listen carefully to his answer."

At twelve o'clock at night, the dragon came flying thither, and asked for his dinner. The grandmother laid the table, and served up food and drink, so that he was pleased, and they ate and drank together. In the course of conversation, she asked him what kind of a day he had, and how many souls he had got. "Nothing went very well today," he answered, "but I have laid hold of three soldiers—I have them safe." "Indeed! Three soldiers! That's something like, but they may escape you yet." The Devil said mockingly, "They are mine! I will set them a riddle, which they will never in this world be able to guess!" "What riddle is that?" she inquired. "I will tell you. In the great North Sea lies a dead dog-fish; that shall be your roast meat, and the rib of a whale shall be your silver spoon, and a hollow old horse's hoof shall be your wine-glass."

When the Devil had gone to bed, the old grandmother raised up the stone, and let out the soldier. "Have you paid particular attention to everything?" "Yes," said he, "I know enough, and will contrive to save myself." Then he had to go back another way, through the window, secretly and with all speed, to his companions. He told them how the Devil had been overreached by the old grandmother, and how he had learned the answer to the riddle from him. Then they were all joyous, and of good cheer, and took the whip and whipped so much gold for themselves that it ran all over the ground.

When the seven years had fully gone by, the Devil came with a book, showed the signatures, and said, "I will take you with me to hell. There you shall have a meal! If you can guess what kind of roast meat you will have to eat, you shall be free and released from your bargain, and may keep the whip as well." Then the first soldier began and said, "In the great North Sea lies a dead dog-fish, that no doubt is the roast meat." The Devil was angry, and began to mutter "Hm! hm! hm!" and asked the second, "But what will your spoon be?" "The rib of a whale, that is to be our silver spoon." The Devil made a wry face, again growled "Hm! hm! hm!" and said to the third, "And do you also know what your wine-glass is to be?" "An old horse's hoof is to be our wine-glass."

Then the Devil flew away with a loud cry, and had no more power over them, but the three kept the whip, whipped as much money for themselves with it as they wanted, and lived happily to their end.

The Grave Mound

A RICH FARMER was one day standing in his yard inspecting his fields and gardens. The corn was growing up vigorously and the fruit trees were heavily laden with fruit. The grain of the year before still lay in such immense heaps on the floors that the rafters could hardly bear it. Then he went into the stable, where were well-fed oxen, fat cows, and horses bright as looking-glass. At length he went back into his sitting-room, and cast a glance at the iron chest in which his money lay.

While he was thus standing surveying his riches, all at once there was a loud knock close by him. The knock was not at the door of his room, but at the door of his heart. It opened, and he heard a voice which said to him, "Hast thou done good to thy family with it? Hast thou considered the necessities of the poor? Hast thou shared thy bread with the hungry? Hast thou been contented with what thou hast, or didst thou always desire to have more?" The heart was not slow in answering, "I have been hard and pitiless, and have never shown any kindness to my own family. If a beggar came, I turned away my eyes from him. I have not troubled myself about God, but have thought only of increasing my wealth. If everything which the sky covers had been mine own, I should still not have had enough."

When he was aware of this answer he was greatly alarmed, his knees began to tremble, and he was forced to sit down.

Then there was another knock, but the knock was at the door of his room. It was his neighbor, a poor man who had a number of children whom he could no longer satisfy with food. "I know," thought the poor man, "that my neighbor is rich, but he is as hard as he is rich. I don't believe he will help me, but my children are crying for bread, so I will venture it." He said to the rich man, "Thou dost not readily give away anything that is thine, but I stand here like one who feels the water rising above his head. My children are starving; lend me four measures of corn."

The rich man looked at him long, and then the first sunbeam of mercy began to melt away a drop of the ice of greediness. "I will not lend thee four measures," he answered, "but I will make thee a present of eight, but thou must fulfill one condition." "What am I to do?" said the poor man. "When I am dead, thou shalt watch for three nights by my grave." The peasant was disturbed in his mind at this request, but in the need in which he was, he would have consented to anything; he accepted, therefore, and carried the corn home with him.

It seemed as if the rich man had foreseen what was about to happen, for when three days were gone by, he suddenly dropped down dead. No one knew exactly how it came to pass, but no one grieved for him. When he was buried, the poor man remembered his promise. He would willingly have been released from it, but he thought, "After all, he acted kindly by me. I have fed my hungry children with his corn, and even if that were not the case, where I have once given my promise I must keep it." At nightfall he went into the churchyard, and seated himself on the grave mound. Everything was quiet; only the moon appeared above the grave, and frequently an owl flew past and uttered her melancholy cry. When the sun rose, the poor man betook himself in safety to his home, and in the same manner the second night passed quietly by. On the evening of the third day he felt a strange uneasiness; it seemed to him that something was about to happen. When he went out he saw, by the churchyard-wall, a man whom he had never seen before. He was no longer young, had scars on his face, and his eyes looked sharply and eagerly round. He was entirely covered with an old cloak, and nothing was visible but his great riding-boots. "What art thou looking for here?" the peasant asked. "Art thou not afraid of the lonely churchyard?"

"I am looking for nothing," he answered, "and I am afraid of nothing! I am like the youngster who went forth to learn how to shiver, and had his labor for his pains, but got the King's daughter to wife and great wealth with her, only I have remained poor. I am nothing but a paid-off soldier, and I mean to pass the night here, because I have no other shelter." "If thou art without fear," said the peasant, "stay with me, and help me to watch that grave there."

"To keep watch is a soldier's business," he replied, "whatever we fall in with here, whether it be good or bad, we will share it between us." The peasant agreed to this, and they seated themselves on the grave together.

All was quiet until midnight, when suddenly a shrill whistling was heard in the air, and the two watchers perceived the Evil One standing bodily before them. "Be off, you ragamuffins!" cried he to them, "the man who lies in that grave belongs to me; I want to take him, and if you don't go away I will wring your necks!" "Sir with the red feather," said the soldier, "you are not my captain, I have no need to obey you, and I have not yet learned how to fear. Go away, we shall stay sitting here."

The Devil thought to himself, "Money is the best thing with which to get hold of these two vagabonds." So he began to play a softer tune, and asked quite kindly, if they would not accept a bag of money, and go home with it. "That is worth listening to," answered the soldier, "but one bag of gold won't serve us. If you will give as much as will go into one of my boots, we will quit the field for you and go away."

"I have not so much as that about me," said the Devil, "but I will fetch it. In the neighboring town lives a money-changer who is a good friend of mine, and will readily advance it to me." When the Devil had vanished the soldier took his left boot off, and said, "We will soon pull the charcoal-burner's nose for him; just give me your knife, comrade." He cut the sole off the boot, and put it in the high grass near the grave on the edge of a hole that was half overgrown. "That will do," said he; "now the chimney-sweep may come."

They both sat down and waited, and it was not long before the Devil returned with a small bag of gold in his hand. "Just pour it in," said the soldier, raising up the boot a little, "but that won't be enough." The Black One shook out all that was in the bag; the gold fell through, and the boot remained empty. "Stupid Devil," cried the soldier, "it won't do! Didn't I say so at once? Go back again, and bring more."

The Devil shook his head, went, and in an hour's time came with a much larger bag under his arm. "Now pour it in," cried the soldier, "but I doubt the boot will be full." The gold clinked as it fell, but the boot remained empty. The Devil looked in himself with his burning eyes, and convinced himself of the truth. "You have shamefully big calves to your legs!" cried he, and made a wry face. "Did you think," replied the soldier, "that I had a cloven foot like you? Since when have you been so stingy? See that you get more gold together, or our bargain will come to nothing!"

The Wicked One went off again. This time he stayed away longer, and when at length he appeared he was panting under the weight of a sack which lay on his shoulders. He emptied it into the boot, which was just as far from being filled as before. He became furious, and was just going to tear the boot out of the soldier's hands, but at that moment the first ray of the rising sun broke forth from the sky, and the Evil Spirit fled away with loud shrieks. The poor soul was saved.

The peasant wished to divide the gold, but the soldier said, "Give what falls to my lot to the poor. I will come with thee to thy cottage, and together we will live in rest and peace on what remains, as long as God is pleased to permit."

The Peasant and the Devil

THERE WAS once on a time a far-sighted, crafty peasant whose tricks were much talked about. The best story is, however, how he once got hold of the Devil and made a fool of him.

The peasant had one day been working in his field, and as twilight had set in, was making ready for the journey home, when he saw a heap of burning coals in the middle of his field, and when, full of astonishment, he went up to it, a little black devil was sitting on the live coals. "Thou dost indeed sit upon a treasure!" said the peasant. "Yes, in truth"; replied the Devil, "on a treasure which contains more gold and silver than thou hast ever seen in thy life!" "The treasure lies in my field and belongs to me," said the peasant. "It is thine," answered the Devil, "if thou wilt for two years give me the half of everything thy field produces. Money I have enough of, but I have a desire for the fruits of the earth." "The peasant agreed to the bargain. "In order, however, that no dispute may arise about the division," said he, "everything that is above ground shall belong to thee, and what is under the earth to me." The Devil was quite satisfied with that, but the cunning peasant had sown turnips.

Now when the time for harvest came, the Devil appeared and wanted to take away his crop; but he found nothing but the yellow withered leaves, while the peasant, full of delight, was digging up his turnips. "Thou hast had the best of it for once," said the Devil, "but the next time that won't do. What grows above ground shall be thine, and what is under it, mine." "I am willing," replied the peasant; but when the time came to sow, he did not again sow turnips, but wheat. The grain became ripe, and the peasant went into the field and cut the full stalks down to the ground. When the Devil came, he found nothing but the stubble, and went away in a fury down into a cleft in the rocks. "That is the way to cheat the Devil," said the peasant, and went and fetched away the treasure.

The Three Apprentices

THERE WERE once three apprentices who had agreed to keep always together while traveling, and always to work in the same town. At one time, however, their masters had no more work to give them, so that at last they were in rags, and had nothing to live on. Then one of them said, "What shall we do? We cannot stay here any longer, we will travel once more, and if we do not find any work in the town we go to, we will arrange with the innkeeper there, that we are to write and tell him where we are staying, so that we can always have news of each other, and then we will separate." And that seemed best to the others also.

They went forth, and met on the way a richly dressed man who asked who they were. "We are apprentices looking for work; up to this time we have kept together, but if we cannot find anything to do we are going to separate." "There is no need for that," said the man, "if you will do what I tell you, you shall not want for gold or for work—nay, you shall become great lords, and drive in your carriages!" One of them said, "If our souls and salvation be not endangered, we will certainly do it." "They will not," replied the man, "I have no claim on you."

One of the others had, however, looked at his feet, and when he saw a horse's foot and a man's foot, he did not want to have anything to do with him. The Devil, however, said, "Be easy, I have no designs on you, but on another soul, which is half my own already, and whose measure shall but run full." As they were now secure, they consented, and the Devil told them what he wanted. The first was to answer, "All three of us," to every question; the second was to say, "For money," and the third, "And quite right too!" They were always to say this, one after the other, but they were not to say one word more, and if they disobeyed this order, all their money would disappear at once, but so long as they observed it, their pockets would always be full.

As a beginning, he at once gave them as much as they could carry, and told them to go to such and such an inn when they got to the town. They went to it, and the innkeeper came to meet them, and asked if they wished for anything to eat. The first replied, "All three of us." "Yes," said the host, "that is what I mean." The second said, "For money." "Of course," said the host. The third said, "And quite right too!" "Certainly it is right," said the host.

Good meat and drink were now brought to them, and they were well waited on. After the dinner came the payment, and the innkeeper gave the bill to the one who said, "All three of us," the second said, "For money," and the third, "And quite right too!" "Indeed it is right," said the host, "all three pay, and without money I can give nothing." They, however, paid still more than he had asked. The lodgers, who were looking on, said, "These people must be mad." "Yes, indeed they are," said the host, "they are not very wise." So they stayed some time in the inn, and said nothing else but "All three of us," "For money," and "And quite right too!" But they saw and knew all that was going on.

It so happened that a great merchant came with a large sum of money, and said, "Sir host, take care of my money for me; here are three crazy apprentices who might steal it from me." The host did as he was asked. As he was carrying the trunk into his room, he felt that it was heavy with gold. Thereupon he gave the three apprentices a lodging below, but the merchant came upstairs into a separate apartment. When it was midnight, and the host thought that all were asleep, he came with his wife, and they had an axe and struck the rich merchant dead; and after they had murdered him they went to bed again.

When it was day there was a great outcry; the merchant lay dead in bed bathed in blood. All the guests ran at once, but the host said, "The three crazy apprentices have done this"; the lodgers confirmed it, and said, "It can have been no one else." The innkeeper, however, had them called, and said to them, "Have you killed the merchant?" "All three of us," said the first; "For money," said the second; and the third added, "And quite right too!" "There now, you hear," said the host, "they confess it themselves." They were taken to prison, therefore, and were to be tried. When they saw that things were going so seriously, they were after all afraid, but at night the Devil came and said, "Bear it just one day longer, and do not play away your luck; not one hair of your head shall be hurt."

The next morning they were led to the bar, and the judge said, "Are you the murderers?" "All three of us." "Why did you kill the merchant?" "For money." "You wicked wretches, you have no horror of your sins?" "And quite right too!" "They have confessed, and are still stubborn," said the judge, "lead them to death instantly." So they were taken out, and the host had to go with them into the circle. When they were taken hold of by the executioner's men, and were just going to be led up to the scaffold where the headsman was standing with naked sword, a coach drawn by four blood-red chestnut horses came up suddenly, driving so fast that fire flashed from the stones, and some one made signs from the window with a white handkerchief.

Then said the headsman, "It is a pardon coming," and "Pardon! pardon!" was called from the carriage also. The Devil stepped out as a very noble gentleman, beautifully dressed, and said, "You three are innocent; you may now speak, make known what you have seen and heard." Then said the eldest, "We did not kill the merchant; the murderer is standing there in the circle," and he pointed to the innkeeper. "In proof of this, go into his cellar, where many others whom he has killed are still hanging."

The judge sent the executioner's men thither, and they found it was as the apprentices said, and when they had informed the judge of this, he caused the innkeeper to be led up, and his head was cut off. Then said the Devil to the three, "Now I have got the soul which I wanted to have, and you are free, and have money for the rest of your lives."

Doctor Knowall

THERE WAS once on a time a poor peasant called Crabb, who drove with two oxen a load of wood to the town, and sold it to a doctor for two thalers. When the money was being counted out to him, it so happened that the doctor was sitting at table, and when the peasant saw how daintily he ate and drank, his heart desired what he saw, and he would willingly have been a doctor too. So he remained standing a while, and at length inquired if he too could not be a doctor. "Oh, yes," said the doctor, "that is soon managed." "What must I do?" asked the peasant. "In the first place, buy thyself an A B C book of the kind which has a cock on the frontispiece; in the second, turn thy cart and thy two oxen into money, and get thyself some clothes, and whatsoever else pertains to medicine; thirdly, have a sign painted for thyself with the words, 'I am Doctor Knowall,' and have that nailed above thy house-door." The peasant did everything that he had been told to do.

When he had doctored people awhile, but not long, a rich and great lord had some money stolen. Then he was told about Doctor Knowall who lived in such and such a village, and must know what had become of the money. So the lord had the horses put in his carriage, drove out to the village, and asked Crabb if he were Doctor Knowall. Yes, he was, he said. Then he was to go with him and bring back the stolen money. "Oh, yes, but Grethe, my wife, must go too." The lord was willing, and let both of them have a seat in the carriage, and they all drove away together.

When they came to the nobleman's castle, the table was spread, and Crabb was told to sit down and eat. "Yes, but my wife, Grethe, too," said he, and he seated himself with her at the table. And when the first servant came with a dish of delicate fare, the peasant nudged his wife, and said, "Grethe, that was the first," meaning that was the servant who brought the first dish. The servant, however, thought he intended by that to say, "That is the first thief," and as he actually was so, he was terrified, and said to his comrade outside, "The doctor knows all: we shall fare ill, he said I was the first."

The second did not want to go in at all, but was forced. So when he went in with his dish, the peasant nudged his wife, and said, "Grethe, that is the second." This servant was just as much alarmed, and he got out. The third did not fare better, for the peasant again said, "Grethe, that is the third."

The fourth had to carry in a dish that was covered, and the lord told the doctor that he was to show his skill, and guess what was beneath the cover. The doctor looked at the dish, had no idea what to say, and cried, "Ah, poor Crabb." When the lord heard that, he cried, "There! He knows who has the money!"

On this the servants looked terribly uneasy, and made a sign to the doctor that they wished him to go out for a moment. When therefore he went out, all four of them confessed to him that they had stolen the money, and said that they would willingly restore it and give him a heavy sum into the bargain, if he would not denounce them, for if he did they would be hanged. They led him to the spot where the money was concealed.

With this the doctor was satisfied, and returned to the hall, sat down to the table, and said, "My lord, now will I search in my book where the gold is hidden." The fifth servant, however, crept into the stove to hear if the doctor knew still more. The doctor, however, sat still and opened his A B C book, turned the pages backwards and forwards, and looked for the cock. As he could not find it immediately he said, "I know you are there, so you had better show yourself." Then the fellow in the stove thought that the doctor meant him, and full of terror, sprang out crying, "That man knows everything!" Then Doctor Knowall showed the count where the money was, but did not say who had stolen it, and received from both sides much money in reward, and became a renowned man.

The Three Army Surgeons

THREE ARMY SURGEONS who thought they knew their art perfectly and were traveling about the world, came to an inn where they wanted to pass the night. The host asked whence they came, and whither they were going. "We are roaming about the world and practicing our art." "Just show me for once in a way what you can do," said the host. Then the first said he would cut off his hand, and put it on again early next morning; the second said he would tear out his heart. and replace it next morning; the third said he would cut out his eyes and heal them again next morning. "If you can do that," said the innkeeper, "you have learnt everything." They, however, had a salve, with which they rubbed themselves, which joined parts together, and they carried the little bottle in which it was, constantly with them. Then they cut the hand, heart and eyes from their bodies as they had said they would, and laid them all together on a plate, and gave it to the innkeeper. The innkeeper gave it to a servant who was to set it in the cupboard, and take good care of it.

The girl, however, had a lover in secret, who was a soldier. When the innkeeper, the three army surgeons, and every one else in the house were asleep, the soldier came and wanted something to eat. The girl opened the cupboard and brought him some food, and forgot to shut the cupboard-door again; she seated herself at the table by her lover, and they chattered away together. While she sat so contentedly there thinking of no ill luck, the cat came creeping in, found the cupboard open, took the hand and heart and eyes of the three army surgeons, and ran off with them.

When the soldier had done eating, and the girl was taking away the things and going to shut the cupboard, she saw that the plate which the innkeeper had given her to take care of, was empty. Then she said in a fright to her lover, "Ah, what shall I do? The hand is gone, the heart and the eyes are gone too, what will become of me in the morning?" "Be easy," said he, "I will help you out of your trouble—there is a thief hanging outside on the gallows, I will cut off his hand. Which hand was it?" "The right one." Then the girl gave him a sharp knife, and he went and cut the poor sinner's right hand off, and brought it to her. After this he caught the cat and cut its eyes out, and now nothing but the heart was wanting. "Have you not been slaughtering? And are not the dead pigs in the cellar?" said he. "Yes," said the girl. "That's well," said the soldier, and he went down and fetched a pig's heart. The girl placed all together on the plate, and put it in the cupboard, and when after her lover took leave of her, she went quietly to bed.

In the morning when the three army surgeons got up, they told the girl she was to bring them the plate on which the hand, heart, and eyes were lying. Then she brought it out of the cupboard, and the first fixed the thief's hand on and smeared it with salve, and it grew to his arm directly. The second took the cat's eyes and put them in his own head. The third fixed the pig's heart firm in the place where his own had been, and the innkeeper stood by, admired their skill, and said he had never yet seen such a thing as that done, and would sing their praises and recommend them to every one. Then they paid their bill, and traveled farther.

As they were on their way, the one with the pig's heart did not stay with them at all, but wherever there was a corner he ran to it, and rooted about in it with his nose as pigs do. The others wanted to hold him back by the tail of his coat, but that did no good; he tore himself loose, and ran wherever the dirt was thickest. The second also behaved very strangely; he rubbed his eyes, and said to the others, "Comrades, what is the matter? I don't see at all. Will one of you lead me, so that I do not fall." Then with difficulty they traveled on till evening, when they reached another inn.

They went into the bar together, and there at a table in the corner sat a rich man counting money. The one with the thief's hand walked round about him, made a sudden movement twice with his arm, and at last when the stranger turned away, he snatched at the pile of money, and took a handful from it. One of them saw this and said, "Comrade, what are you about? You must not steal—shame on you!" "Eh," said he, "but how can I stop myself? My hand twitches, and I am forced to snatch things whether I will or not."

After this, they lay down to sleep, and while they were lying there it was so dark that no one could see his own hand. All at once the one with the cat's eyes awoke, aroused the others, and said, "Brothers, just look up, do you see the white mice running about there?" The two sat up, but could see nothing. Then said he, "Things are not right with us, we have not got back again what is ours. We must return to the innkeeper, he has deceived us."

They went back, therefore, the next morning, and told the host they had not got what was their own again; that the first had a thief's hand, the second cat's eyes, and the third a pig's heart. The innkeeper said that the girl must be to blame for that, and was going to call her, but when she had seen the three coming, she had run out by the back door, and not come back. Then the three said he must give them a great deal of money, or they would set his house on fire. He gave them what he had, and whatever he could get together, and the three went away with it. It was enough for the rest of their lives, but they would rather have had their own proper organs.

The Spirit in the Bottle

THERE WAS once a poor woodcutter who toiled from early morning till late night. When at last he had laid by some money he said to his boy, "Thou art my only child, I will spend the money which I have earned with the sweat of my brow on thy education; if thou learnest some honest trade thou canst support me in my old age, when my limbs have grown stiff and I am obliged to stay at home."

Then the boy went to a High School and learned diligently so that his masters praised him, and he remained there a long time. When he had worked through two classes, but was still not yet perfect in everything, the little pittance which the father had earned was all spent, and the boy was obliged to return home to him. "Ah," said the father, sorrowfully, "I can give thee no more, and in these hard times I cannot earn a farthing more than will suffice for our daily bread."

"Dear father," answered the son, "do not trouble thyself about it, if it is God's will, it will turn to my advantage. I shall soon accustom myself to it." When the father wanted to go into the forest to earn money by helping to pile and stack wood and also to chop it, the son said, "I will go with thee and help thee." "Nay, my son," said the father, "that would be hard for thee; thou art not accustomed to rough work, and wilt not be able to bear it, besides I have only one axe and no money left wherewith to buy another." "Just go to the neighbor," answered the son, "he will lend thee his axe until I have earned one for myself."

The father then borrowed an axe of the neighbor, and next morning at break of day they went out into the forest together. The son helped his father and was quite merry and brisk about it. But when the sun was right over their heads, the father said, "We will rest, and have our dinner, and then we shall work as well again." The son took his bread in his hands, and said, "Rest thou, father, I am not tired; I will walk up and down a little in the forest, and look for birds' nests." "Oh, thou fool," said the father, "why shouldst thou want to run about there? Afterwards thou wilt be tired, and no longer able to raise thy arm; stay here, and sit down beside me." The son, however, went into the forest, ate his bread, was very merry and peered in among the green branches to see if he could discover a bird's nest anywhere.

So he went up and down to see if he could find a bird's nest, until at last he came to a great dangerous-looking oak, which certainly was already many hundred years old, and which five men could not have spanned. He stood still and looked at it, and thought, "Many a bird must have built its nest in that." Then all at once it seemed to him that he heard a voice. He listened and became aware that some one was crying in a very smothered voice, "Let me out, let me out!" He looked around, but could discover nothing; nevertheless, he fancied that the voice came out of the ground. Then he cried, "Where art thou?" The voice answered, "I am here down among the roots of the oak tree. Let me out! Let me out!"

The scholar began to loosen the earth under the tree, and search among the roots, until at last he found a glass bottle in a little hollow. He lifted it up and held it against the light, and then saw a creature shaped like a frog springing up and down in it. "Let me out! Let me out!" it cried anew, and the scholar, thinking no evil, drew the cork out of the bottle. Immediately a spirit ascended from it, and began to grow, and grew so fast that in a very few moments he stood before the scholar, a terrible fellow as big as half the tree by which he was standing.

"Knowest thou," he cried in an awful voice, "what thy wages are for having let me out?" "No," replied the scholar fearlessly, "how should I know that?" "Then I will tell thee," cried the spirit; "I must strangle thee for it." "Thou shouldst have told me that sooner," said the scholar, "for I should then have left thee shut up, but my head shall stand fast for all thou canst do; more persons than one must be consulted about that." "More persons here, more persons there," said the spirit. "Thou shalt have the wages thou hast earned. Dost thou think that I was shut up there for such a long time as a favor? No, it was a punishment for me. I am the mighty Mercurius. Whoso releases me, him must I strangle." "Softly," answered the scholar, "not so fast. I must first know that thou wert shut up in that little bottle, and that thou art the right spirit. If, indeed, thou canst get in again, I will believe, and then thou mayst do as thou wilt with me." The spirit said haughtily, "That is a very trifling feat," drew himself together, and made himself as small and slender as he had been at first, so that he crept through the same opening, and right through the neck of the bottle in again. Scarcely was he within than the scholar thrust the cork he had drawn back into the bottle, and threw it among the roots of the oak into its old place, and the spirit was betrayed.

And now the scholar was about to return to his father, but the spirit cried very piteously, "Ah, do let me out! ah, do let me out!" "No," answered the scholar, "not a second time! He who has once tried to take my life shall not be set free by me, now that I have caught him again." "If thou wilt set me free," said the spirit, "I will give thee so much that thou wilt have plenty all the days of thy life." "No," answered the scholar, "thou wouldst cheat me as thou didst the first time." "Thou art playing away thy own good luck," said the spirit; "I will do thee no harm, but will reward thee richly." The scholar thought, "I will venture it, perhaps he will keep his word, and anyhow he shall not get the better of me."

Then he took out the cork, and the spirit rose up from the bottle as he had done before, stretched himself out and became as big as a giant. "Now thou shalt have thy reward," said he, and handed the scholar a little bag just like a plaster, and said, "If thou spreadest one end of this over a wound it will heal, and if thou rubbest steel or iron with the other end it will be changed into silver." "I must just try that," said the scholar, and went to a tree, tore off the bark with his axe, and rubbed it with one end of the plaster. It immediately closed together and was healed. "Now, it is all right," he said to the spirit, "and we can part." The spirit thanked him for his release, and the scholar thanked the spirit for his present, and went back to his father.

"Where hast thou been racing about?" said the father; "why hast thou forgotten thy work? I said at once that thou wouldst never get on with anything." "Be easy, father, I will make it up." "Make it up indeed," said the father angrily, "there's no art in that." "Take care, father, I will soon hew that tree there, so that it will split." Then he took his plaster, rubbed the axe with it, and dealt a mighty blow, but as the iron had changed into silver, the edge turned. "Hollo, father, just look what a bad axe thou hast given me, it has become quite crooked." The father was shocked and said, "Ah, what hast thou done? Now I shall have to pay for that, and have not the wherewithal, and that is all the good I have got by thy work." "Don't get angry," said the son, "I will soon pay for the axe." "Oh, thou blockhead," cried the father, "wherewith wilt thou pay for it? Thou hast nothing but what I give thee. These are students' tricks that are sticking in thy head, but thou hast no idea of woodcutting." After a while the scholar said, "Father, I can really work no more, we had better take a holiday." "Eh, what!" answered he. "Dost thou think I will sit with my hands lying in my lap like thee? I must go on working, but thou mayst take thyself home." "Father, I am here in this wood for the first time, I don't know my way alone. Do go with me."

As his anger had now abated, the father at last let himself be persuaded and went home with him. Then he said to the son, "Go and sell thy damaged axe, and see what thou canst get for it, and I must earn the difference, in order to pay the neighbor." The son took the axe, and carried it into town to a goldsmith, who tested it, laid it in the scales, and said, "It is worth four hundred thalers; I have not so much as that by me." The son said, "Give me what you have, I will lend you the rest." The goldsmith gave him three hundred thalers, and remained a hundred in his debt. The son thereupon went home and said, "Father, I have got the money, go and ask the neighbor what he wants for the axe." "I know that already," answered the old man, "one thaler six groschen." "Then give him two thalers, twelve groschen, that is double and enough; see, I have money in plenty," and he gave the father a hundred thalers, and said, "You shall never know want; live as comfortably as you like." "Good heavens!" said the father, "how hast thou come by these riches?"

The scholar then told how all had come to pass, and how he, trusting in his luck, had made such a good hit. But with the money that was left, he went back to the High School and went on learning more, and as he could heal all wounds with his plaster, he became the most famous doctor in the whole world.

The Three Children of Fortune

ONCE UPON a time a father sent for his three sons. He gave to the eldest a cock, to the second a scythe, and to the third a cat.

"I am now old," said he, "my end is approaching, and I would like to provide for you before I die. Money I have none, and what I now give you seems of but little worth. Yet it rests with yourselves to turn my gifts to good account. Go to a country where what you have is as yet unknown, and your fortune is made."

After the death of the father, the eldest set out with his cock. But wherever he went, in every town he saw from afar off a cock sitting upon the church steeple, and turning round with the wind. In the villages he always heard plenty of them crowing, and his bird was therefore nothing new; so there did not seem much chance of his making his fortune. At length it happened that he came to an island where the people who lived there had never heard of a cock, and knew not even how to reckon the time. They knew, indeed, if it were morning or evening; but at night, if they lay awake, they had no means of knowing how time went.

"Behold," said he to them, "what a noble animal this is! How like a knight he is! He carries a bright red crest upon his head, and spurs upon his heels; he crows three times every night, at stated hours, and at the third time the sun is about to rise. But this is not all. Sometimes he screams in broad daylight, and then you must take warning, for the weather is surely about to change."

This pleased the natives mightily. They kept awake one whole night, and heard to their great joy how gloriously the cock called the hour, at two, four, and six o'clock. Then they asked him whether the bird was to be sold, and how much he would sell it for. "About as much gold as an ass can carry," said he. "A very fair price for such an animal," they cried with one voice, and agreed to give him what he asked.

When he returned home with his wealth, his brothers wondered greatly; and the second said, "I will now set forth likewise, and see if I can turn my scythe to as good an account." There did not seem, however, much likelihood of this; for go where he would, he was met by peasants who had as good a scythe on their shoulders as he had. At last, as good luck would have it, he came to an island where the people had never heard of a scythe. There, as soon as the corn was ripe, they went into the fields and pulled it up with their hands, but this was very hard work, and a great deal of it was lost. The man then set to work with his scythe, and mowed down their whole crop so quickly that the people stood staring open-mouthed with wonder. They were willing to give him what he asked for such a marvelous thing; but he only took a horse laden with as much gold as it could carry.

Now the third brother had a great longing to go and see what he could make of his cat. So he set out. At first it happened to him as it had to the others; so long as he kept upon the main land, he met with no success. There were plenty of cats everywhere, indeed too many, so that the young ones were for the most part, as soon as they came into the world, drowned in the water. At last he passed over to an island, where, as it chanced most luckily for him, nobody had ever seen a cat, and they were overrun with mice to such a degree, that the little wretches danced upon the tables and chairs, whether the master of the house were at home or not. The people complained loudly of this grievance; the King himself knew not how to rid himself of them in his palace. In every corner mice were squeaking, and they gnawed everything that their teeth could lay hold of. Here was a fine field for Puss. She soon began her chase, and had cleared two rooms in the twinkling of an eye. Then the people besought their King to buy the wonderful animal for the good of the public, at any price. The King willingly gave what was asked—a mule laden with gold and jewels. And thus the third brother returned home with a richer prize than either of the others.

Meantime the cat feasted away upon the mice in the royal palace, and devoured so many that they were no longer in any great numbers. At length, quite spent and tired with her work, she became extremely thirsty; so she stood still, drew up her head, and cried, "Miau, Miau!"

The King gathered together all his subjects when they heard this strange cry, and many ran shrieking in a great fright out of the palace. But the King held a council below as to what was best to be done; and it was at length fixed to send a herald to the cat, to warn her to leave the castle forthwith, or that force would be used to remove her. "For," said the counsellors, "we would far more willingly put up with the mice (since we are used to that evil), than get rid of them at the risk of our lives." A page accordingly went, and asked the cat, whether she were willing to quit the castle. But Puss, whose thirst became every moment more and more pressing, answered nothing but "Miau! Miau!" which the page interpreted to mean "No! No!" and therefore carried this answer to the King.

"Well," said the counsellors, "then we must try what force will do." So the guns were planted, and the palace was fired upon from all sides. When the fire reached the room where the cat was, she sprang out of the window and ran away. But the besiegers did not see her, and went on firing until the whole palace was burnt to the ground.

The Cunning Little Tailor

ONCE UPON a time there was a Princess who was extremely proud. If a wooer came she gave him some riddle to guess, and if he could not find it out, he was sent contemptuously away. She let it be made known also that whosoever solved her riddle should marry her, no matter who he might be.

At length three tailors fell in with each other. The two eldest thought they had done so many dexterous bits of work successfully that they could not fail to succeed in this also; the third did not even know his trade, but thought he must have some luck in this venture, for where else was it to come from? Then the two others said to him, "Just stay at home; thou canst not do much with thy little bit of understanding." The little tailor, however, did not let himself be discouraged, and said he had set his head to work about this for once, and he would manage well enough, and he went forth as if the whole world were his.

All three announced themselves to the Princess, and said she was to propound her riddle to them, and that the right persons were now come who had understandings so fine that they could be threaded in a needle. Then said the Princess, "I have two kinds of hair on my head, of what color is it?" "If that be all," said the first, "it must be black and white, like the cloth which is called 'pepper and salt.'" The Princess said, "Wrongly guessed; let the second answer." Then said the second, "If it be not black and white, then it is brown and red, like my father's company coat." "Wrongly guessed," said the Princess, "let the third give the answer, for I see very well he knows it for certain." Then the little tailor stepped boldly forth and said, "The Princess has a silver and a golden hair on her head, and those are the two different colors."

When the Princess heard that, she turned pale and nearly fell down with terror, for the little tailor had guessed her riddle, and she had firmly believed that no man on earth could discover it. When her courage returned she said, "Thou hast not won me yet by that; there is still something else that thou must do. Below, in the stable, is a bear with which thou shalt pass the night, and when I get up in the morning if thou art still alive, thou shalt marry me." She expected, however, she should thus get rid of the tailor, for the bear had never yet left any one alive who had fallen into his clutches. The little tailor did not let himself be frightened away, but was quite delighted, and said, "Boldly ventured is half won."

When, therefore, the evening came, our little tailor was taken down to the bear. The bear was about to set at the little fellow at once, and give him a hearty welcome with his paws. "Softly, softly," said the little tailor, "I will soon make thee quiet." Then quite composedly, and as if he had not an anxiety in the world, he took some nuts out of his pocket, cracked them, and ate the kernels. When the bear saw that, he was seized with a desire to have some nuts too. The tailor felt in his pockets, and reached him a handful; they were, however, not nuts, but pebbles. The bear put them in his mouth, but could get nothing out of them, let him bite as he would. "Eh!" thought he, "what a stupid blockhead I am! I cannot even crack a nut!" and then he said to the tailor, "Here, crack me the nuts." "There, see what a stupid fellow thou art!" said the little tailor, "to have such a great mouth, and not be able to crack a small nut!" Then he took the pebble and nimbly put a nut in his mouth in the place of it, and crack, it was in two! "I must try the thing again," said the bear; "when I watch thee, I then think I ought to be able to do it too." So the tailor once more gave him a pebble, and the bear tried and tried to bite into it with all the strength of his body. But no one will imagine that he accomplished it.

When that was over, the tailor took out a violin from beneath his coat, and played a piece on it to himself. When the bear heard the music, he could not help beginning to dance, and when he had danced a while, the thing pleased him so well that he said to the little tailor, "Hark you, is the fiddle heavy?" "Light enough for a child. Look, with the left hand I lay fingers on it, and with the right I stroke it with the bow, and then it goes merrily, hop sa sa vivallalera!" "So," said the bear; "fiddling is a thing I should like to understand too, that I might dance whenever I had a fancy. What dost thou think of that? Wilt thou give me lessons?" "With all my heart," said the tailor, "if thou hast a talent for it. But just let me see thy claws, they are terribly long, I must cut thy nails a little." Then a vise was brought, and the bear put his claws in it, and the little tailor screwed it tight, and said, "Now wait until I come with the scissors," and he left the bear growl as he liked, and lay down in the corner on a bundle of straw, and fell asleep.

When the Princess heard the bear growling so fiercely during the night, she believed nothing else but that he was growling for joy, and had made an end of the tailor. In the morning she arose careless and happy, but when she peeped into the stable, the tailor stood gaily before her, and was as healthy as a fish in the water. Now she could not say another word against the wedding because she had given a promise before every one, and the King ordered a carriage to be brought in which she was to drive to church with the tailor, and there she was to be married. When they had got into the carriage, the two other tailors, who had false hearts and envied him his good fortune, went into the stable and unscrewed the bear again. The bear in great fury ran after the carriage. The Princess heard him snorting and growling; she was terrified, and she cried, "Ah, the bear is behind us and wants to get thee!" The tailor was quick and stood on his head, stuck his legs out of the window, and cried, "Dost thou see the vise? If thou dost not be off thou shalt be put into it again." When the bear saw that, he turned round and ran away. The tailor drove quietly to church, and the Princess was married to him at once, and he lived with her as happy as a woodlark. . . . And whoever does not believe this, must pay a thaler.

The Riddle

A KING'S SON once had a great desire to travel through the world, so he started off, taking no one with him but one trusty servant. One day he came to a great forest, and as evening drew on and he could find no shelter he could not think where to spend the night. All of a sudden he saw a girl going toward a little house, and as he drew near he saw that she was both young and pretty. He spoke to her, and said, "Dear child, could I spend the night in this house?"

"Oh, yes," said the girl in a sad tone, "you can if you like, but I should not advise you to do so. Better not go in."

"Why not?" asked the King's son.

The girl sighed, and answered, "My stepmother deals in black magic, and she is not friendly to strangers."

The Prince guessed easily he had come to a witch's house, but it was now dark and he could go no farther. Moreover, he was not afraid, and he stepped in with his groom.

An old woman sat in an armchair near the fire, and as they entered, she turned her red eyes on them. "Good evening," she muttered, pretending to be friendly. "Won't you sit down?"

She blew up the fire on which she was cooking something in a little pot. But her daughter had warned the travelers to be careful not to eat or drink anything, as the old woman's brews were likely to be dangerous.

They went to bed and slept soundly till morning. When they were ready to start, and the King's son had already mounted his horse, the old woman said, "Wait a minute, I must give you a stirrup cup." While she went to fetch it the King's son rode off, and the groom who had waited to tighten his saddle girths was alone when the witch returned.

"Take that to your master," she said. But as she spoke the glass cracked and the poison spurted over the horse. It was so powerful the poor creature sank down dead. The servant ran after his master and told him what had happened, and then, not wishing to lose the saddle as well as the horse, he went back to fetch it. When he reached the spot he saw a raven had perched on the carcass and was pecking at it.

"Who knows whether we shall get anything better to eat today!" said the man, and he shot the raven and carried it off.

Then they rode on all day through the forest without coming to the end. At nightfall they reached an inn. The servant made the landlord a present of the raven. Now, as it happened, this inn was the resort of a band of robbers, and the old witch, too, was in the habit of frequenting it.

As soon as it was dark twelve thieves arrived, with the full intention of killing and robbing the strangers. However, they sat down first to table, where the landlord and the old witch joined them, and they all ate some broth in which the flesh of the raven had been boiled. They had hardly taken a couple of spoonfuls when they all fell down dead, for the poison had passed from the horse to the raven and so into the broth. There was no one left belonging to the house but the landlord's daughter, who was a good, well-meaning girl and had taken no part in all the evil doings.

She opened all the doors and showed the strangers the treasures the robbers had gathered together. The Prince bade her keep them all for herself, as he wanted none of them, and so he rode on with his servant.

After traveling about for some time they reached a town where lived a lovely but arrogant Princess. She had announced that anyone who asked her a riddle which she was unable to guess should be her husband, but should she guess it he must forfeit his head. She claimed three days in which to think over the riddles, but she was so clever she invariably guessed them in much shorter time. Nine suitors had already lost their lives when the King's son arrived, and, dazzled by her beauty, determined to risk his life. He came before her and propounded his riddle.

"What is this?" he asked. "One slew none and yet killed twelve."

She could not think what it was! She thought and thought and looked through all her books of riddles and puzzles. She found nothing to help her and could not guess. In fact, she was at her wits' end. As she could think of no way to guess the riddle, she ordered her maid to steal at night into the Prince's bedroom and listen. She thought he might talk aloud in his dreams and so betray the secret. But the clever servant had taken his master's place, and when the maid came, he tore off the cloak she had wrapped about herself and chased her off.

On the second night the Princess sent her lady-in-waiting, hoping she might succeed better. But the servant took away her mantle and chased her away also.

On the third night the King's son thought he really might feel safe, so he went to bed. But in the middle of the night the Princess came herself, wrapped in a misty gray mantle, and sat down near him. When she thought he was fast asleep, she spoke to him, hoping he would answer in the midst of his dreams as many people do. But he was wide awake all the time and heard and understood everything very well.

Then she asked, "One slew none—what is that?" And he answered, "A raven which fed on the carcass of a poisoned horse."

She went on, "And yet killed twelve—what is that?" "Those are twelve robbers who ate the raven and died of it."

As soon as she knew the riddle she tried to slip away, but he held her mantle so tightly she was obliged to leave it behind.

Next morning the Princess announced she had guessed the riddle and sent for the twelve judges, before whom she declared it. But the young man begged to be heard. Then he said, "She came by night to question me; otherwise she never could have guessed it."

The judges said, "Bring us some proof." So the servant brought out the three cloaks. When the judges saw the gray one, which the Princess was in the habit of wearing, they said, "Let it be embroidered with gold and silver. It shall be your wedding mantle."

A Riddling Tale

THREE WOMEN were changed into flowers which grew in the field, but one of them was allowed to be in her own home at night. Then once when day was drawing near, and she was forced to go back to her companions in the field and become a flower again, she said to her husband, "If you will come this afternoon and gather me, I shall be set free and henceforth stay with you." And he did so.

Now the question is, how did her husband know her, for the flowers were exactly alike, and without any difference?

Answer: Since she was at her home during the night and not in the field, no dew fell on her as it did on the others, and by this her husband knew her.

The Beam

THERE WAS once a magician who was standing in the midst of a great crowd of people performing his wonders. He had a cock brought in, which lifted a heavy beam and carried it as if it were as light as a feather. But a girl was present who had just found a bit of four-leaved clover, and had thus become so wise that no deception could stand out against her, and she saw that the beam was nothing but a straw. So she cried, "You people, do you not see that it is a straw that the cock is carrying, and no beam?" Immediately the enchantment vanished, and the people saw what it was, and drove the magician away in shame and disgrace. He, however, full of inward anger, said, "I will soon revenge myself."

After some time the girl's wedding-day came, and she was decked out, and went in a great procession over the fields to the place where the church was. All at once she came to a stream which was very much swollen, and there was no bridge and no plank to cross it. Then the bride nimbly took her clothes up, and wanted to wade through it. And just as she was thus standing in the water a man—and it was the enchanter—cried mockingly close beside her, "Aha! Where are thine eyes that thou takest that for water?" Then her eyes were opened, and she saw that she was standing with her clothes lifted up in the middle of a field that was blue with flowers of blue flax. Then all the people saw it likewise, and chased her away with ridicule and laughter.

Index of Fairy Tales